STRANGELY BEAUTIFUL

TWO NOVELS IN ONE VOLUME!
·······
AUTHOR'S PREFERRED EDITION

D0048575

LEANNA RENEE HIEBER

Praise for Leanna Renee Hieber

"A many-layered tale gorgeously told. *The Strangely Beautiful Tale of Miss Percy Parker* is *Bulfinch's Mythology* and *Harry Potter* and *Wuthering Heights* mashed in a blender. It is a historical, dark, fantasy mystery. I am happy to have been as impressed by this book as I was by its author."
> —*USA Today* bestselling author Alethea Kontis in
> *Orson Scott Card's InterGalactic Medicine Show*

"Tender, poignant, exquisitely written."
> —*New York Times* bestselling author C. L. Wilson on
> *The Strangely Beautiful Tale of Miss Percy Parker*

"A strangely beautiful tale indeed! An ethereal, lyrical story that combines myth, spiritualism, and the gothic in lush prose and sweeping passion."
> —*USA Today* bestselling author Kathryn Smith on
> *The Strangely Beautiful Tale of Miss Percy Parker*

"A delightfully lush and richly imagined tale. The characters are realistic and have depth, and the plot builds to a stunning conclusion. This novel is a transcendent example of the genre."
> —*Fresh Fiction* on *The Strangely Beautiful Tale of Miss Percy Parker*

"I cannot recommend this book, this series, or this author enough."
> —*True-Blood.net* on *The Darkly Luminous Fight for Persephone Parker*

"Enthralling. Hieber skillfully creates a lush, sensual spirit world with tactile imagery while at the same time imbuing her human London with a Victorian sensibility. Crafting an engrossing historical urban fantasy novel with intriguing characters, the author provides a highly satisfying reading experience with a wide appeal."
> —*Bitten by Books* on *The Strangely Beautiful Tale of Miss Percy Parker*

"Hieber gives us plenty of her lovely, delicate prose, and a few moments that are riotously funny. If anything, I wanted more!"
> —*Fantasy Literature* on *The Darkly Luminous Fight for Persephone Parker*

"Hieber has created a secretive, gothic, paranormal world as well as a character who will resonate with anyone who has found the beauty in being different."
> —*Booklist* on *The Strangely Beautiful Tale of Miss Percy Parker*

"A fantastic tale that combines myth, religion, and the paranormal. Perfect for fans of the paranormal who enjoy a gothic setting."
> —*ParaNormalRomance* on *The Strangely Beautiful Tale of Miss Percy Parker*

TOR BOOKS BY
LEANNA RENEE HIEBER

The Eterna Files
Strangely Beautiful

STRANGELY BEAUTIFUL

Which is comprised of

THE STRANGELY BEAUTIFUL TALE OF MISS PERCY PARKER

&

THE DARKLY LUMINOUS FIGHT FOR PERSEPHONE PARKER

&

diverse smaller works

AUTHOR'S PREFERRED EDITION

LEANNA RENEE HIEBER

TOR

A Tom Doherty Associates Book
New York

STRANGELY BEAUTIFUL

Copyright © 2016 by Leanna Renee Hieber

A Tor Book
Published by Tom Doherty Associates, LLC
175 Fifth Avenue
New York, NY 10010

www.tor-forge.com

Tor® is a registered trademark of Tom Doherty Associates, LLC.

The Library of Congress Cataloging-in-Publication Data
is available upon request.

ISBN 978-0-7653-7743-2 (trade paperback)
ISBN 978-1-4668-5587-8 (e-book)

Our books may be purchased in bulk for promotional, educational, or business use. Please contact your local bookseller or the Macmillan Corporate and Premium Sales Department at 1-800-221-7945, extension 5442, or by e-mail at MacmillanSpecialMarkets@macmillan.com.

This novel was originally published in substantially different form in two separate volumes, *The Strangely Beautiful Tale of Miss Percy Parker*, which was published by Leisure Books in 2009, and *The Darkly Luminous Fight for Persephone Parker*, which was published by Leisure Books in 2010.

First Edition: April 2016

Printed in the United States of America

0 9 8 7 6 5 4 3 2 1

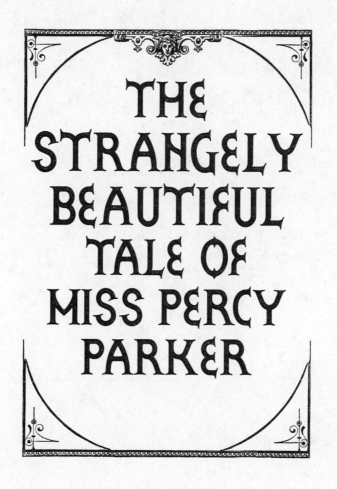

THE STRANGELY BEAUTIFUL TALE OF MISS PERCY PARKER

PROLOGUE

London, England, 1867

THE AIR IN LONDON WAS GRAY. THIS WAS NO SURPRISE; BUT THE COMMON eye could not see the particular heaviness of the atmosphere or the unusual weight of this special day's charcoal clouds: The sky roiled with a potent wind, for the Guard was searching for new hosts.

To London they came, and that wind full of spirits began to course through the streets of the city; merciless, searching. Around corners, elbowing aside London's commoners and high society alike, nudging through market crowds and tearing down dirty alleys, they sought their intended. A candle burst into flame in the window of a marquess's house. The tiny cry of a young boy summoned his mother into the drawing room. Similar sounds went up in other parts of the city, confused gasps growing into amazed giggles before being subdued into solemnity. One by one the intended targets were seized.

Six. Five . . .

Where is four? Ah . . . Four.

Now, three.

Alone and unaccompanied, the children left their respective houses and began to walk.

And two.

Searching for the final piece, the greatest of the possessors paused, a hesitating hunter. Deliberate. And, finally . . . the brightest, boldest, most promising catch of the day.

One.

Complete. A sigh of relief. The city's infamous fog thinned.

Only a bird above espied the six drawing toward London's center; weaving through a maze of clattering carriages, stepping cautiously over putrid puddles, a sextet of children looked about the cluttered merchant lanes and sober business avenues with new eyes and saw strange sights. There were ghosts everywhere: Floating through walls and windows, they rose up through streets and strolled beside quiet couples. One by one, each transparent form turned to the children, who stared in wonder and apprehension. In ethereal rags, spirits of every century bowed in deference, as if they were passing royalty.

Drawn from all corners of London, five children gathered in a knot at the crest of Westminster Bridge. Nodding a silent greeting to one another, or curtseying, the youths found each other's faces unsettlingly mature. Excitement tempered by confusion crept into their expressions as they evaluated their new peers, in garb ranging from fine clothing to simple frocks, their social statuses clearly as varied as their looks.

A spindly girl whose brown hair was pinned tightly to her head kept turning, looking for something, clutching the folds of her linen frock and shifting on the heels of her buttoned boots. It was her tentative voice that at last broke the silence: "Hello. I'm Rebecca. Where is our leader, then?"

A sturdy, ruddy-cheeked boy in a vest and cap, cuffs rolled to his elbows, gestured to the end of the street. "Hello, Rebecca, I'm Michael. Is that him?"

Approaching the cluster was a tall, well-dressed, unmistakable young man. A mop of dark hair held parley with the wind, blowing about the sharp features of his face, while timeless, even darker eyes burned in their sockets. His fine black suit gave the impression of a boy already a man. He reached the group and bowed, his presence magnetic, confident . . . and somewhat foreboding. In a rich, velvet voice deep as the water of the Thames, he spoke. "Good day. My name is Alexi Rychman, and this has turned into the strangest day of my life." He glanced at the spindly brunette next to him, who blushed.

"Hello, Alexi, I'm Rebecca, and I feel the same."

Alexi firmly met every child's gaze in turn, prompting introductions.

"Elijah," a thin blond boy said, his features sharp and his eyes a startling blue. He was garbed in striped satin finery that seemed rakish if not foppish on such a young man, and he was clearly the wealthiest of the lot.

"Josephine," a beautiful olive-skinned brunette added in a soft French accent. She sported the latest fashions; two shocks of white hair framed her face.

"Michael," chimed in the sturdy boy with a brilliant, contagious smile.

"Lucretia Marie O'Shannon Connor," replied the last in an Irish accent. The speaker stared shyly at the cobblestones, dark blond hair falling to veil her frightened face. Her plain calico dress bespoke modest means.

"Pardon?" Elijah's drawn and angular face became even more pinched.

"I suppose you could call me Jane if that's easier," the girl murmured with a shrug, still staring at the street.

"I'll say." Elijah laughed.

Alexi's eyes flashed with a sudden unfocused anger. "And here I thought all my life I'd be a scientist. It seems forces at large have other plans. I don't suppose any of you has the slightest idea what we're supposed to do?"

Everyone shook their heads, as surprised with their new destinies as he.

"Then let me ask a mad question." Alexi's tone was cautious. "Does anyone, all of a sudden . . . see ghosts?"

"Yes!" the others chorused, relieved that if this were madness, they weren't alone in it.

"Can you hear them speak?" he asked.

"No," was the universal reply.

"Neither can I, thank God, or we'd never have another moment's peace." Alexi sighed. "Well, I suppose we'd better get to the bottom of this. I . . . saw a chapel. But I've never been there and don't know where it is."

Rebecca, still blushing, pointed. "I . . . I think that raven can show us."

Above, a hovering black bird was waiting for them. The new Guard looked up and nodded, then followed the bird through the bustling heart of the city.

The raven stopped at an impressive edifice labeled ATHENS ACADEMY. The red sandstone building had appeared all of a sudden, nestled impossibly among several less interesting lots. The multistoried construction was shuttered, clearly unoccupied by staff or students. It was the summer holiday, after all. Yet it was occupied by ghosts. And, as the wide wooden doors opened for the six children, these ghosts pointed the way toward an interior chapel.

While the others walked ahead, Alexi lingered, studying what seemed to be a normal school, with typical halls and stately foyers, hoping to find further clues. When he at last reached the chapel doors, the candles upon the altar burst into flame. The ladies in the group gasped.

Alex lifted his palm—and the candles extinguished. He furrowed his brow. A young man of methods and proofs he was; such happenings defied his knowledge of a more definite world.

The bright white chapel possessed simple decor, with a painted dove high above a plain altar. A hole formed in the air before the six young people, first as a black point then growing into a rectangle. This dark portal, which opened with a sound like a piece of paper being torn, surely led to a place more foreign than the children had ever seen. They approached it in silence.

"This must be a sacred space for us alone," Michael quietly surmised, peering into the void, seeing a staircase that led to a beckoning light below.

Alexi set his jaw, strode forward and descended the stair. The others followed.

The room below was circular, lined with Corinthian pillars but blurred in the shadows, as if this were a place at the edge of time. A different bird was depicted in stained glass overhead, not a dove but something great and fiery. A feather was engraved in the stone below the glass, with an inscription. Alexi read it aloud: "'In darkness, a door. In bound souls, a circle of fire. Immortal force in mortal hearts. Six to calm the restless dead. Six to shield the restless living.'"

Immediately, a circle of blue-colored fire leaped up. Everyone gasped except Alexi, who looked curiously at the cerulean flame, wondering how on earth such a thing was possible: The fire described a perfect circle around them, rose to a height of a few inches and no farther, and gave off no heat.

"Alexi, look!" Rebecca cried, pointing to his hands. He'd been contemplating the possible chemical compounds inherent to the fire, not noticing the licking tendrils of that same blue conflagration emanating from his palms and trickling down to the circle. Another ripping sound tore through the room, this one far greater, and at the threshold of a new portal there suddenly stood an unfathomable woman.

Alexi forgot the fire and the fact that it was coming from his hands. He forgot his troubled, logical concerns. He could only stare, overtaken. His mind, body, and heart exploded with new sensations.

The woman was tall and lithe, glowing with a light of power and love, with features as perfect as a statue and hair that was golden. No; it was lustrous brown. No, rich red . . . She shifted from one hue to the next, maintaining her breathtaking beauty but seeming to radiate all colors at once. Diaphanous material wrapped her perfect body, sweeping layers and transitioning hues like the rest. Her eyes were crystalline lamps, sparkling and magnetic. There was no other possibility but that she was a divine creature.

She spoke. Her voice held echoes of every element; an orchestra of stars.

"My beloveds. I've not much time, but I must inaugurate you, as I have done since your circle began the Grand Work in ancient times. You won't remember those who came before. Nor has what's inside over-taken you. It heightens you. You are heroes of your age. The Guard picked you six because your mortal hearts are bold and strong.

"There has never been a more crucial time than this century, this city. Your world is filled with new ideas, new science, new ideas on God and the body . . . and most importantly, spirits. There's never been such talk of spirits. You are the ones who must respond."

She turned to Alexi, and he felt himself stop breathing. Her gemlike eyes filled with tears that became rubies, then emeralds, then sapphires as they coursed down her perfect cheeks and tinkled to the stone floor before vanishing. Unconsciously, Alexi reached out a hand to touch those tears, though the woman remained beyond his reach within her portal.

"Alexi, you are the leader here. Inside of you alone lives what's left of my true love, a winged being of power and light—the first phoenix of ancient times. Murdered by jealous Darkness, he was burned alive. His great power was splintered but not destroyed. The fire from your hands is your tool. It was the weapon used against you long ago, but now you control the element and are born again within it. My love lives on in you, worthy Alexi, and you will fight Darkness by bearing the eternal flame of our vendetta." She turned to the others, and breath stole back into Alexi's lungs.

"The power that inhabits the rest of you comes from great beings in those days—Muses, forces of Beauty that chose to follow our broken phoenix as votaries, to keep chaotic Darkness from infiltrating this world. Together you are the new Guard, and this task is yours."

"The Guard?" Rebecca piped up, confused.

"That is what you will do: guard the living from the dead that wander the earth, whom you now see but cannot hear. Your Grand Work is to maintain the balance between this world and the one beyond, beside. Darkness would run rampant over your great city and more—and will, unless you silence his emissaries. Hold fast, for the struggle will worsen. Darkness will seek to destroy the barrier pins between worlds. To fight this, a prophecy must be fulfilled. A seventh member will join you. She will come as your peer to create a new dawn."

Suddenly, their oracle winced as if struck. Alexi rushed forward—to protect or comfort, he did not know—but the divine apparition put out a hand that stopped him dead. "You must understand that once the seventh joins you, it will mean war."

The group couldn't help but shiver, even if they didn't fully understand.

"Who are you?" Alexi asked, unable to hide the yearning in his voice.

She smiled sadly but did not answer his question. "I hope you will know her when she comes, Alexi, my love. And I hope she will know you, too. Await her, but beware. She will not come with answers but be lost, confused. I have put protections in place, but she will be threatened and seeking refuge. There shall be tricks, betrayals, and many second guesses. Caution, beloved. Mortal hearts make mistakes. Choose your seventh carefully, for if you choose the false prophet, the end of your world shall follow."

"A sign, then—surely there will be a sign!" The boy named Michael couldn't hold back a string of desperate questions. "When will she come? And how will we know how, and what, to fight against?"

"You'll be led to fight the machinations of Darkness by instincts within you. But you shall not always be fighting. You are also as you were—your mortal lives and thoughts remain unchanged, though they are augmented by the spirits inside you. Each of you has a specific strength."

She looked to Josephine, then, naming her the Artist; turned to Jane, the Healer; then to Rebecca, the Intuition. Michael she named the Heart, and Elijah, the Memory. Then, finally, Alexi: the Power.

"As for a sign when she has come, your seventh, look for a door. A door like this"—the woman gestured to the portal in which she stood—"should be your gauge. But don't go in," she cautioned, glancing around herself woefully. "You wouldn't want to come here.

"You'll see this threshold together, all of you, I'm sure, when it is time. As for when your seventh will come . . . I cannot say. I'm powerful, but only the great Cosmos is omnipotent. Time is different where I am and we are in uncharted waters. But she will be placed in your path. And once she is, you won't have much time. Then, a terrible storm."

There was a disturbing sound from the darkness behind her. The woman glanced back, looking fearful.

"What is your name?" Alexi insisted, desperate to know more.

The woman smiled sadly, and her glimmering eyes changed hue. "It hardly matters. We've had so many names over the years—all of us." She surveyed the group before her eyes rested once more on Alexi. "Especially you, my love: Please be careful. Listen to your instincts and stay together. A war is coming, and it isn't what you think. Hell isn't down, it's around us, pressing inward. And it will come. But your seventh will be there when it does, or she will have died in vain."

"Died?" Alexi cried. It seemed some new horror appeared at every turn.

The woman smiled again: wisely, sadly. "One must die to live again." Then, blowing a kiss to Alexi, she disappeared.

The sacred space faded, returning the dazed group to the empty chapel. In overwhelmed silence they filed out the back doors into a quiet London alley. The group looked at one another in alarm and wonder.

Alexi stalked off. Something bitter in the air indicated unity was wise, but he was wracked with emotions he could not decipher and unable to face his new friends for the shame of his confusion. Rebecca started after him, even called his name, but his head throbbed and he took no heed. He wished to lock himself away, to go back to simpler days of pillaging the secrets of science.

And yet, that oracle—that goddess—had given him a task. He was meant to be a leader.

The new power coursing through him could not calm his inner tumult. Head spinning and heart pounding, transformed in one afternoon from boy to a man craving an otherworldly woman, he retreated to his family estate.

There he found chaos, as if an angry hand had swept down and smote the entrance foyer and staircase. At the foot of the stair lay his elder sister, Alexandra, crumpled in a heap of taffeta, her body unnaturally twisted. Alexi's grandmother, clutching her heart, all fine lace and severe looks, was bent over her.

"Alexandra!" he cried as he rushed forward, scared to touch his sister's body lest he somehow break it further. The girl was whimpering, staring from their grandmother to him alternately, obviously paralyzed from the waist down. "What happened?"

"Something terrible," their grandmother wheezed in her heavy Russian accent. "A force . . . Oh, I cannot describe. Evil swept through." Suddenly the woman's eyes grew bright. Always had she demonstrated a frightening knowledge. "There's something different about you," she said to Alexi, then began speaking in Russian: "The firebird—that's it. There is a darkness coming, my boy. And you must light the darkness with your fire."

Taking a shuddering breath, she eased back against the wall. She did not breathe again. The Rychman family thus was dealt a double blow in a single day.

Alexi felt the blood drain from his face. Could he, with his new power, have prevented this? Did failure mark his very start? He'd meant to be a man of science, not . . . whatever he now was. How could he lead when he couldn't even believe what he'd seen and heard? Clearly he was a mortal, as were the others in his charge. The coming battles would not be easy. But that powerful stranger, that strange seventh . . . Maybe his goddess would return.

CHAPTER
ONE

London, England, 1888

A YOUNG WOMAN, THE LIKES OF WHICH LONDON HAD NEVER SEEN, alighted from a carriage near Bloomsbury and gazed at the grand façade before her. Breathless at the sight of the Romanesque fortress of red sandstone that was to be her new home, she ascended the front steps beneath the portico, with carpetbag in tow. One slender, gloved hand heaved open the great arched door; Miss Percy Parker paused, then stepped inside.

The foyer of Athens Academy held a few milling young men, papers and books in hand. Their jaws fell as each caught sight of the newcomer. In the diffuse light cast by a single chandelier they saw a petite, unmistakable apparition. Dark blue glasses kept eerie, ice blue eyes from unsettling those whose stares she nervously returned. Much of her snow-white skin was hidden from view by a scarf draped around her head and bosom, but only a mask could have hidden the ghostly pallor of her fine-featured face.

The sudden tinkling of a chandelier crystal broke the thick silence. Percy's gaze flickered up to behold a young man, pale as herself, floating amid the gas flames. The transparent spirit wafted down to meet her. It was clear from the stares of the young men of solid mass, rudely focused on Percy, that they were oblivious to the phantasm. She acknowledged the ghost only subtly, lest she be thought distracted as well as deformed.

The spectral schoolboy spoke in a soft Scots brogue. "You'd best give up your pretensions, miss. You'll never be one of them. And you're certainly not one of us. What the devil are you?"

Percy met the spirit's hollow gaze. Behind her glasses, her opalescent eyes flared with defiance as she asked the room, her voice sweet and timid, "Could someone be so kind as to direct me to the headmistress's office?" A gaping, living individual pointed to a hallway on her left, so she offered him a "Thank you, sir," and fled, eager to escape all curiosity. The only sounds that followed were the rustling layers of her sky-blue taffeta skirts and the echo of her booted footfalls down the hall.

HEADMISTRESS THOMPSON was scribed boldly across a large wooden door. Percy took a moment to catch her breath before knocking.

She soon found herself in an office filled to overflowing with books. A sharp voice bade her sit, and she was promptly engulfed in a leather armchair. Across the desk sat a severe woman dressed primly in gray wool. Middle-aged and thin, she had a pinched nose and high cheekbones that gave her a birdlike quality; her tight lips were twisted in a half frown. Brown hair was piled atop her head, save one misbehaving lock at her temple.

Blue-gray eyes pierced Percy's obscuring glasses. "Miss Parker, we've received word that you're an uncommonly bright girl. I'm sure you're well aware that your previous governance, unsure what to do with you, supposed you'd best be sent somewhere else. Becoming a sister did not suit you?"

Percy had no time to wonder if this was sardonic or understanding, for the headmistress continued: "Your reverend mother made many inquiries before stumbling across our quiet little bastion. Considering your particular circumstances, I accepted you despite your age of eighteen. You're older than many who attend here. I'm sure I needn't tell you, Miss Parker, that at your age most women do not think it advantageous to remain . . . *academic.* I hope you know enough of the world outside convent walls to understand." Headmistress Thompson's sharp eyes suddenly softened and something mysterious twinkled there. "We must acknowledge the limitations of our world, Miss Parker. I, as you can see, chose to run an institution rather than a household."

Percy couldn't help but smile, drawn in by the headmistress's conspiratorial turn, as if the woman considered herself unique by lifestyle inasmuch as Percy was unique by fate.

Miss Thompson's amiability abruptly vanished. "We expect academic excellence in all subjects, Miss Parker. Your reverend mother proclaimed you proficient in several languages, with particularly keen knowledge of Latin, Hebrew, and Greek. Would you consider yourself proficient?"

"I have no wish to flatter myself—"

"Honesty will suffice."

"I'm f-fluent in several tongues," Percy stammered. "I'm fondest of Greek. I know French, German, Spanish, and Italian well. I dabble in Russian, Arabic, Gaelic . . . as well as a few ancient and obscure dialects."

"Interesting." The headmistress absently tapped the desk with her pen. "Do you attribute your affinity for foreign tongues to mere interest and diligence?"

Percy thought a moment. "This may sound very strange . . ."

"It may shock you how little I find strange, Miss Parker," the headmistress replied. "Go on."

Percy was emboldened. "Since childhood, certain things were innate. The moment I could read, I read in several languages as if they were native to me." She bit her lip. "I suppose that sounds rather mad."

There was a pause, yet to Percy's relief the headmistress appeared unmoved. "Should you indeed prove such a linguist, and a well-rounded student, Athens may have ongoing work for you next year as an apprentice, Miss Parker."

"Oh!" Percy's face lit like a sunbeam. "I'd relish the opportunity! Thank you for your generous consideration, Headmistress."

"You were raised in the abbey?"

"Yes, Headmistress."

"No immediate family?"

"None, Headmistress."

"Do you know anything of them? Is there a reason . . . ?"

Percy knew it was her skin that gave the woman pause. "I wish I could offer you an answer regarding my color, Headmistress. It's always been a mystery. I know nothing of my father. I was told my mother was Irish."

"That is all you know?"

Percy shifted in her seat. "She died within the hour she brought me to the sisters. Perhaps I was a traumatic birth. She told Reverend Mother that she brought me to the Institute of the Blessed Virgin Mary because the Blessed Virgin herself had come proclaiming the child she bore must be an educated woman. And so she left them with that dying wish . . ." Percy looked away, pained. "My mother said her purpose had been fulfilled, and, as if she were simply used up, she died."

"I see." Miss Thompson made a few notes. It was well that Percy did not expect pity or sentiment, for she was given neither. "Miss Parker, Athens is unique in that we recognize all qualities in our students. We've a Quaker model here at Athens. We champion the equality of the sexes and I happen to believe that learning is not bound in books alone. It is my personal practice to ask our students if they believe they possess a gift. Other than your multiple languages, do you have any other particular talents?"

Percy swallowed hard. She was unprepared for this question. For anyone else it might have been a perfectly normal inquiry, but Percy knew she was far from average. "I have a rather strange manner of dreams."

The headmistress blinked. "We all dream, Miss Parker. That is nothing extraordinary."

"No. Of course not, Headmistress."

"Unless these dreams come more in the manner of visions?"

Percy hoped the flash of panic in her eyes remained hidden behind her tinted glasses. Years ago, when Reverend Mother had found out about the visions and ghosts, she'd put aside her shock to caution Percy about speaking of such things. Neither was something the science-mad, rational world would celebrate. It was lonely to look—and be—so strange, and Percy wanted to confess everything she felt was wrong with her and have the headmistress accept her. But she also recalled the horrible day when unburdening her soul had caused a priest to try to exorcise her best friend, a ghost named Gregory, from the convent courtyard. She knew she'd never find anyone who could truly understand. Thus, she would not associate herself with the word "vision," and she would never again admit to seeing ghosts.

She cleared her throat. "Those who claim to have visions are either holy or madmen."

The headmistress was clearly taken aback, as much as her patrician façade might indicate: She arched an eyebrow. "As a girl raised in a convent, do you not consider yourself a woman of religion?"

Percy shifted again. Miss Thompson had unwittingly touched upon a troubling topic. Percy could not help but wonder about her faith. Those in her abbey's order, the oldest of its kind in England, had withstood innumerable trials. Every novice and sister took fierce pride in her resilience and that of their elders. But Percy, a girl who kept and was left to herself, felt out of place. The colorless curiosity of her skin notwith-standing, her restless disposition had difficulty acquiescing to the rigors of the cloth. Only the presence of a spirit out of its time—such as her Elizabethan-era Gregory—had made her feel at home. No, doctrine could not explain the world as Percy knew it. An unsettling sense of fate made her ache in ways prayer could not wholly relieve.

But none of this was appropriate to discuss in present circumstances. "I am a woman of . . . *spirit*, Headmistress. By no means would I com-mend myself holy. And I'd like to think I'm not mad."

The raucous shriek of a bird outside Miss Thompson's window made Percy jump. A raven settled on the ledge beyond the glass. Percy couldn't help but notice an odd-colored patch on the large black bird's breast. Percy didn't stare further, lest she seem easily distracted. She waited for Headmistress Thompson's gaze to pin her again, which it soon did.

"Dreams then, Miss Parker?"

"Yes, Headmistress. Just dreams."

The headmistress scribbled a note and frowned curiously at an un-opened envelope in Percy's file before placing it carefully at the back of the folder. Before Percy could wonder, the headmistress continued. "We have no dream study, Miss Parker. It seems fitting your focus should be languages; however you must maintain high marks in all courses in order to continue at the academy. Do you have other interests, Miss Parker?"

"Art has always been a great love of mine," Percy stated. "I used to paint watercolors for the parish. I also adore Shakespeare."

A scrawl into the file. "Dislikes?"

"I'm afraid the sciences and mathematics are beyond me. Neither were subjects the convent felt necessary for young ladies."

The headmistress loosed a dry chuckle that made Percy uneasy. "There is no escaping at least one mathematics or science sequence. I am placing you in our Mathematics and Alchemical Study."

Percy held back a grimace. "Certainly, Headmistress."

Miss Thompson cleared her throat and leveled a stern gaze at her. "And now, Miss Parker, I must warn you of the dangers of our unique, coeducational institution. There is to be no—I repeat, *no*—contact between members of the opposite sex. Not of your peer group, and most certainly not with your teachers. The least infraction, however innocent it may seem—the holding of a hand, a kiss on a cheek—requires immediate dismissal. You must understand our position: Any word of fraternization or scandal will doom our revolutionary program. And while I hardly think any of this will be an issue for you in particular, Miss Parker, I must say it nonetheless."

Percy nodded, at first proud the headmistress should think so highly of her virtue; then came the sting as she realized the headmistress meant her looks would garner no such furtive conduct. Worse, Percy felt sure she was right.

"Classes begin Monday. Here is a schedule and key for your quarters: Athene Hall, room seven."

As Percy took the papers and key, she was gripped by a thrill. "Thank you so very much, Miss Thompson! I cannot thank you enough for the opportunity to be here."

The headmistress maintained a blank, severe stare. "Do not thank me. Do not fail."

"I promise to do my best, Headmistress!"

"If it be of any interest to you, a meditative Quaker service is held Sundays. You'll find none of your Catholic frills here. But indeed, Miss Parker, the school keeps quiet about all of that, as I am sure you may well do yourself, living in intolerant times."

"Yes, Headmistress."

"Good day, Miss Parker—and welcome to Athens."

"Thank you, Headmistress. Good day!" Percy beamed and darted out the door to explore her new home.

REBECCA THOMPSON STARED AT THE DOOR AFTER MISS PARKER LEFT, feeling the strange murmur in her veins that was part of her intuitive gift. Her instincts were never clarion, but they alerted her to things of import. Miss Parker, her gentle nature evident in the sweet timbre of her voice, had set off a signal.

Rebecca considered the envelope in the girl's file. *Please open upon Miss Parker's graduation—or when she has been provided for*, it read. "I daresay she won't find herself 'provided for,'" Rebecca muttered.

Turning to the window, she opened the casement. The raven hopped in and strutted over the wooden file cabinets, occasionally stopping to preen the bright blue breast feather that indicated his service to the Guard.

"It's odd, Frederic," Rebecca remarked, "I can't imagine that awkward, unfortunate girl has anything to do with us; it doesn't follow. It *shouldn't* follow."

Growing up, as the Guard chose their mortal professions, it was agreed that a few of them should remain near the chapel and portal of the Grand Work, on the fortresslike grounds of Athens. Rebecca and Alexi were the perfect candidates for academia, and for twenty years now had followed that path. At Athens, Alexi and Rebecca were known as nothing other than upstanding Victorian citizens, providing for the intellectual improvement of the young. The two had agreed to never bring the Grand Work upon their students. The school was the one place where it seemed they controlled destiny rather than destiny controlling them—and they had fought to keep it that way.

Yes, the secrets of the Grand Work were matters for the world beyond the school walls. Their prophetic seventh had been named a *peer,* and thus students were not subjects of scrutiny. No, while Miss Parker did not appear a "normal" girl, and though she happened to spark interest, she was likely nothing more than a child deserving a solid education.

Rebecca sighed, easing into her chair as Frederic hopped onto her shoulder. She considered inviting Alexi to tea, then allowed he would prefer to be steeped as usual in solitude. As predicted, their personalities and desires had not changed when the six great spirits entered them. Still, Rebecca and her friends' lives revolved around duty, a reality that Rebecca resented more with each passing year. Privately she wished those spirits *had* taken her heart when they arrived, for it was a terribly lonely destiny, and even the Grand Work couldn't change that.

CHAPTER
TWO

PERCY ENTERED ATHENS'S COURTYARD, A LARGE RECTANGULAR SPACE
surrounded by archways. Covered corridors with sparkling, diamond-
shaped panels of Bavarian glass linked each building, and every façade
sported identical Romanesque features hewn from red sandstone. The
dormitories rose at the narrow ends, while the academic halls constituted the tall, clerestoried length of the rectangle. Athens was sealed
entirely by walls from the bustle of London beyond, a sanctuary where
only the ambient sound of a throbbing city washed over the stones like
the lap of waves.

The centerpiece of the cobblestone courtyard immediately took
Percy's interest. An angel towered over a fountain of deep bronze, a book
in her upraised hand. Lilies at her feet spewed water from their widening
buds.

Next, the ladies' student quarters caught her eye, and she saw they
were smaller than those of the gentlemen. As she was surely to be an out-
numbered female in her classes, Percy began to realize the differences
of this world—a world that held infinite possibility. Percy had long
dreamed of romance. Aided by dear Gregory, that genial middle-aged
spirit, she'd played every Shakespearean heroine in the privacy of her
convent room. However, interactions between Percy and living men, who
of course didn't speak in pentameter, were uncommon. Should occasion
call for masculine contact, the abbey specimens were dour men of the
cloth who barely acknowledged Percy as human let alone female. Recalling the well-assembled, handsome young men who'd gaped rudely
upon her arrival here, Percy recalled Miss Thompson's pointed remarks
on her age and state . . . and resigned herself to scorning rather than
soliciting romantic prospects.

Years ago she'd fallen in love with Mr. Darcy, as she supposed every young woman had while reading Austen and first discovering her femininity. Romance and imagination were elemental to Percy's heart. She'd never been in love with a *real* man, of course, for her skin and convent shelter kept her from ever being noticed or appreciated by any suitable candidates—and she supposed it was safer to relegate love to the realm of fantasy, anyway. But though she might never feel the reality of love, the ache of its absence she understood well.

Perhaps, she rallied, she might follow the headmistress's independent example and someday run a school of her own, full of unfortunates like herself.

Gazing at her surroundings, she reminded herself she was here solely to learn. Recalling the headmistress's mention of possible employment, she reminded herself to be grateful: An unfortunate such as herself was lucky to get anything at all.

Strolling along the courtyard, Percy found she could easily keep her delicate skin safely beneath the shadows of an arched walkway; the sun would do her no damage here. Realizing that each hall branching off the yard had a variant name of a Greek god or goddess etched above its wooden entryway, Percy smiled.

Stepping onto the small landing of Athene Hall, she threw her slight weight against the thick door to open it and entered into a paneled foyer. Below narrow stairs beyond, a sour-faced woman sat surrounded by lists, notices, and unopened post.

The woman started at the sight of Percy. "My, my. Good afternoon, miss, are you a student here?"

"Yes, madame, I only just arrived," Percy replied. "My name is Percy Parker." When the woman at the desk blinked dull eyes, Percy's fingers nervously intertwined. "Room seven?" she added.

The matron broke from a disapproving stare to skim a list of names. "Ah, yes. P. Parker. I'm Miss Jennings. You'll find me here should you dream of slipping out after hours, no matter your appearance. Your room is just upstairs." Done with Percy, Miss Jennings returned to her lists.

Above, the dark doors were numbered in gold paint. Room seven was small but far airier than the brick of Percy's quarters at the abbey. A window inset with Tudor roses faced the door. A still life hung above the iron-framed bed: wildflowers beside a pomegranate, the fruit's red-dish skin parted to reveal glistening ruby seeds so ripe they appeared bloody. This innocuous image made Percy shudder, and she turned to unpack her meager belongings.

Opening a velvet box, she took out a silver necklace. Near the door was a long mirror, and Percy donned the necklace and stared: A silver bird with outstretched wings and a tail of flame now flew over the fabric around her neck. She unwound layers of scarves and lace, freeing her pearlescent hair to tumble around her shoulders and down her side. In the mirror, a barely corporeal reflection stared back.

She touched her face and sighed, confirming that she was indeed flesh and blood, then tucked the phoenix pendant below the folds of her dress, out of sight and close to her heart. An ancient pagan symbol, she could not wear it visibly at the convent, so had developed the habit of keeping it close but unseen. It was the only thing her mother had left her.

A movement near the window caught her eye as a spirit in a mess of a Regency gown stuck her head through the panes. When Percy met the girl's transparent eyes, the invader made a face and withdrew as quickly as she had appeared. Percy shook her head. London had an incredible number of ghosts, and she felt like she'd seen every single one on her journey from York.

She'd wished to take the train, but Father Harris had insisted upon a carriage. Percy suspected he dared not be seen at the York station platform in the company of such an odd charge. The city had grown slowly before her eyes as they rode: an intricate, messy, living creature. Country pastures speckled with cottages had given way to stout brick houses that narrowed and nestled closer and closer together. Houses compressed into apartments, gardens were traded for window boxes; flowers kissed from one wooden trough to the next before there ceased to be flowers at all; and living quarters were stacked haphazardly amid pubs, banks, shops and city halls. All surfaces had grown progressively darker, choked by the im-mense soot of the city, which added a grim weight to the fog.

In the heart of London, stately façades were followed by dark lanes increasingly peopled by spirits. Shadowed doorways containing desper-ate, shivering figures opened onto malls where hansom cabs trotted in conspicuous display, grit coupling with grandeur. Down every cluttered lane, wraiths of every station represented the vast spread of life that had built the city over the centuries. Percy's sight was full of ghosts walking next to unsuspecting humans, floating through wooden pub walls and up from the sewers, turning eerie heads as she passed, acknowledging her.

One disheveled bricklayer floated near a window on Tottenham Court Road, his laboring spirit using a transparent trowel to edge mortar that had long since hardened. A society lady in a grand gown passed down the same avenue, vanished, then repeated her journey, perhaps awaiting deferential hails or an escort that never came. Percy could never have imagined the veritable crowds of London specters. Smiling, she entertained the thought that they welcomed her.

London was a tangled mess of streets rebuilt after the Great Fire and according to ancient maps. Roads twisted, took full-corner turns and vanished completely, began and changed names at strange places and disorienting angles, wound around masses of cramped architecture. From the Thames one gained one's bearings, but up just one cluttered lane from the bank there was no hope to see anything but perhaps a fresh, stately spire of Parliament. She noticed only one Catholic chapel, its Gothic windows nestled between a cobbler and a butcher. Finally, a fortress the color of a sooty autumn maple leaf revealed itself, tucked within the district of Bloomsbury on a road that remained nameless. It had seemed that her destination, Athens, a place the reverend mother had referred to as "London's best-kept secret," was perhaps a good place to keep one's own secrets. Percy certainly hoped so.

Allowing a sudden exhaustion, she sank onto her new bed in her new room. Her eyes felt strange, as if a curtain were drawn across them, and a vision followed: Tendrils of mist emanated from a dim opening and a white glimmer appeared at the bottom of the widening black portal. A skeletal hand crept to the edge of the hole. Another hand appeared at the opposite corner. Another, and another . . . The bony host of hands clicked as they reached upon one another, and there came murmuring whispers of a thousand years. From the shadowy center of the door, something shifted into view—the huge head of a ghoulish dog. Wide canine eyes glistened and shone with an alien, crimson light. A dripping, gruesome snout sniffed as if the beast were on the hunt, preparing to race off and consume its prey . . .

Percy shrank back, the vision fading. She had no idea what the creature might have to do with her—and she didn't want to know.

From the eternally dim shadows of the Whisper-world a voice resonated like a deep, angry bell tolling three o'clock: "Where. Is. She?"

"I've no idea, dear," replied a softer, feminine voice. "Was I supposed to do something about her? I thought you'd been looking all this time. While you've only just noticed, it's been eighteen of their years. She could be anywhere. She's not my responsibility, you know."

The deep voice grunted. "Do. Something."

The woman sighed, her fair skin glowing in the moonlight. Placing her hands to the coiled tresses atop her head, she found something sharp. With a hiss, she brought her thumbs back into view; their pricked pads sprouted thick, dark jewels, garnets that began to overflow and weep. Lifting up her hands, she watched in fascination as the crimson trail spread from her thumbs onto her palms. She turned her hands one direction, then the other.

"Hmm," she said after a long moment.

"Well?" pressed the voice in the shadows.

"London," she replied.

"Something wicked, then?" the voice gurgled.

The woman turned and smiled, nonchalant. "By all means, let the dog loose."

There was a grinding of stone. A ferocious growl erupted from the deep, before a barking, snarling, ugly cloud leaped into the sky. It vanished into the shimmering portal opposite the shadows where the woman's master stood brooding, a portal where now rose the Tower of London.

The voice tolled again from the shadows. "There will be hell to pay."

CHAPTER
THREE

London's fashionable dead populated Highgate Cemetery, near the suitably Gothic moorland of Hampstead Heath. It was fitting that the estate of Professor Alexi Rychman was as striking, dark, and brooding as its master had grown up to be, a building nestled at an equidistant point from those two eerily beautiful expanses of rugged flora and carved stone.

All in black, greatcoat billowing about him, a wide-brimmed hat low over his noble brow, Alexi strode toward the carriage at the end of his drive.

"Evening, Professor," called the driver from up top, bushy sideburns peppered with gray and a handlebar mustache framing a familiar, jolly grin.

"Evening, Vicar Carroll."

"Evening, Alexi," Rebecca Thompson echoed from within.

"Evening, Headmistress." Alexi nodded as he climbed into the carriage, removing his hat, dark eyes flashing with banked fires. He loosened the signature red cravat about his throat as moonlight fell through the carriage windows onto those striking features his friends hardly ever saw fixed in anything but unbreakable concentration.

"*Bonsoir*," said a soft French voice from the opposite bench.

Alexi nodded to Josephine. "Do you have your piece?"

She held up a small canvas wrapped in paper.

Josephine Belledoux was an artist whose impressive credits included a painting in nearly every major English museum and countless private residences. However, no one seemed to remember her name. Her shimmering, calming pictures produced such a profound effect that they were immediately forgotten . . . and thus never removed. It wasn't only the living who were touched by Josephine's talents; a few of her paintings hung in the British Museum, keeping the treasure of the empire free from spectral disturbance.

In the years since the six had first met, Josephine had grown into the sort of beauty who could prompt a war. Tonight, her shocks of prematurely white hair were wound into the elaborate coiffure atop her head. If she'd borne those marks since before the day on the bridge, she never said, and out of respect, no one asked.

Alexi closed his eyes and felt within himself for the Pull. The Guard all knew that unmistakable alarm of spectral disturbance. His mind coursed the streets of London, as if tracing a specific drop of his own blood; the massive arteries of London were superimposed upon his own, and wherever there was a spasm, there was his destination.

Rebecca watched Alexi's brow furrow in mild strain. Alexi's inner cartography was keen, but her own was unmatched.

"South of Holborn . . . north of Embankment this evening. Am I right?" He eyed her.

She smirked. "Indeed you are. Impressive." Each of the six tried to outdo the others in pinpointing their subjects, not only to an address but often giving a specific floor and room. Once, Rebecca had even identified the victim's attire.

The carriage cleared the countryside and was soon rattling through the dark, bustling streets of London, in and out of gaslit avenues both wide and narrow before slowing on Fleet Street.

"Prepare ye!" Michael's merry voice sounded from above.

Screams usually alerted the Guard that they had reached their destination. So it was this time: Strangled cries and intermittent bestial growls came from a shattered window a few stories above. A crowd had gathered, murmuring low and excited. The Guard's carriage stopped nearby, and Vicar Michael Carroll descended from the driver's seat to help the ladies disembark. He took particular care with Rebecca. His hand lingered on her arm for a bit longer than mere friendship would require, but Rebecca didn't notice; her attention was on Alexi, as usual. A raven was hopping on the roof of the carriage and making noise.

Elijah Jay, Lord Withersby, stood not far away along the dim, cobbled street, pretending to be a bystander, but his fine, rich clothes screamed that he didn't belong. At his side was a hearty, dark blond Irishwoman wearing a modest dress and a distant smile.

Once assembled, the Guard formed a line and took hands, and Frederic the raven flew to the window. Something magical was undoubtedly present. A wary cry came from above.

Alexi's commanding voice pierced the evening, a single word plucked on the lyre of an ancient language known only to the Guard. The foreign declaration reverberated down the street, and the eyes of the six gleamed brightly as they turned to gaze upon the bystanders. One by one, as if tired or bored, the crowd wandered off. Wiped from their memories was the incident, as if nothing odd had occurred at all. England's populace at large was not involved with the Grand Work. Neither were the denizens of London to know about it.

The raven returned to Rebecca's shoulder, biting her ear fondly. He pecked at her shoulder rhythmically, and she passed along his information:

"Frederic reports one priest, two parents, and a little girl—inhabitant volatile."

Alexi nodded. "'Once more into the breach, dear friends, once more.'"

The company stepped to the landing. Alexi summoned Michael forward with a command: "Come, the gentle heart opens many doors."

The vicar stepped ahead, placed bent fingers in front of his chest, and the locked front door swung open with a strange, metallic sound. The Guard swept inward, and the six tore up the stairs to the flat on the second floor, where Michael's fingers rose again and the flat's door opened with the same odd noise. Passing through the parlor and dining room toward an unnatural light spilling from the bedroom, Alexi flung the unlocked door wide.

Inside, an eight-year-old girl lay rigid upon her bed, her skin glowing.

"Luminous!" Alexi declared her state as a matter of protocol—of course all could see that the girl was possessed. Planting his imposing presence at the foot of her bed, he looked at the parents, then at the priest, and smiled broadly. "Good evening! It would appear you have an intruder!"

Before the horrified parents or the priest, mid-Scripture, could react to this invasion, Elijah fixed them each with an intent stare. The three relaxed at once and their gazes misted contentedly over. Elijah patted each on the head, satisfied with their submission.

Michael placed a hand on the priest's shoulder and indicated his own Anglican vestments. "Bless you, Father—and not to worry," he added to the fellow clergyman, who would remember nothing. "You're doing a lovely job. We're just helping." He always felt the need to explain himself.

Alexi, his expression fierce, tossed off his black greatcoat and suit jacket and began rolling up his charcoal-colored shirtsleeves. He lifted his hands, conjuring the usual inexplicable blue flame before him. As he turned his palms outward, more fire issued forth, and he began to weave the hovering wisps into a graceful dance. A circle of flickering blue now framed the little girl's body, but a sick gray light pulsed like a heartbeat within, illuminating her skeleton and shuddering organs.

Rebecca and Michael took positions across the room. Josephine ripped paper away from a shimmering painting and hung the dynamic portrait of a winged, airborne angel in the center of the wall opposite the bed.

"Name of victim?" Rebecca asked with crisp efficiency, taking notes on a small pad.

Elijah bent over the girl and pressed his hand to hers. He gasped, pictures searing his mind with their psychometric power. "Emily. A quiet child. Inhabitant came upon her during evening prayers. Inhabitant is angry and dangerous—responsible for a death half a century ago. It won't show me how."

Rebecca nodded. "That shall suffice, Elijah. Thank you for your talents."

"It's cruel. But it isn't our Ripper," Elijah went on, shuddering, wiping away the sweat that had burst forth upon his brow.

"Damn," Alexi muttered.

Remaining unobtrusive, Michael moved to Elijah's side and gave his friend a serene smile. He gently pressed Elijah's hands in his, calming him with the effects of his enormous heart. Indeed, an endlessly kind soul could achieve almost anything.

"Thank you, Vicar," Elijah breathed, and returned to maintaining control over the girl's family and priest.

"Emily," whispered Josephine, standing at the foot of the girl's bed. The child's eyes, squeezed shut in great pain, opened to stare at her and plead for help. Josephine directed the child's gaze to the painting of the angel. "Stare long and hard, mademoiselle. This is your guardian, Emily. Look here, he will ease your pain."

Moving to the parents, who were staring dreamily at the ceiling, Josephine placed a hand above them and turned her palms. Like marionettes, their heads followed her movements toward the picture on the wall. "That is never to be removed," she commanded.

The little girl began to choke. Michael breathed in a steady rhythm, guiding everyone's breath by example, and Jane moved opposite Alexi, standing on the other side of the bed. The Irishwoman placed two suddenly glowing hands upon the circle of azure flame that Alexi had summoned to contain the inhabitant, and the rigidity of Emily's limbs eased.

There came an indignant rumble. Emily's back arched unnaturally. Blood dribbled from her chapped lips. Jane's fingers bent as if playing the keys of a piano, and the blood vanished.

"Name of inhabitant?" Rebecca asked, having concluded a page of notes on the conditions of the evening: weather, locale, persons present, services rendered.

Elijah bent again, this time touching Emily's shoulder, where the spirit inside strained against her little limbs. "Muezzin," he gasped painfully. Michael placed a hand upon Elijah's collar and began to laugh quietly. Elijah's face twisted but, after a moment, a sigh escaped and he was able to nod and smile.

"Muezzin is a title, not a name, but I suppose it will do," Rebecca replied. She began to recite a text that the spirit would recognize and heed. Such literary knowledge was particular to Rebecca, and not strictly a required part of the ritual, but she had found it useful in commanding spirits' attention and respect. "'Alike for those who for Today prepare, and those that after some Tomorrow stare, A Muezzin from the Tower of Darkness cries, *Fools! Your Reward is neither Here nor There.*'"

The transparent, skeletal form jolted in response.

"Nicely done, Rebecca, what was that? And what did you mean, a title, not a name?" Elijah was flipping through the Bible he'd taken from the priest's hands.

"In life, this spirit was a muezzin, calling men of Muslim faith to prayer," Rebecca clarified. "But I sense it began to denounce Allah for his mercy and peace, turning away from faith and from him. No, it will *not* disperse quietly. I don't know that anything will—" Rebecca suddenly whimpered, overwhelmed by the helplessness the spirit hoped to foist upon them.

Michael stepped forward to dispel the dread, kissing her gently upon the forehead. Her face relaxing, she gave him thanks.

Rebecca then repeated the verse pulled from *The Rubaiyat*, recently translated by an Englishman and perfect for the occasion. The muezzin's spirit moved in Emily, as if trying to respond: A few gurgling sounds emerged from the numb lips of the child. The sounds resembled words in a distant tongue. Then, sensing it could not use the child's mouth as it wished, the specter shifted out of her face and strained a ghastly head away from Emily's body. Its unnatural mouth contorted in spasms.

"It speaks," Jane noted ruefully.

It was a particular nuisance of the Grand Work that the Guard was granted a modicum of control over troubled spirits, but no direct communication. They could hear the occasional murmur, but could not always understand.

"Regardless of it knowing my translation of *The Rubaiyat*, I cannot speak its language," Rebecca stated, then sighed in frustration. "Why is one of us not a translator, Alexi, for the tiny bits we can hear? Though for that matter, why should we need one? Alexi, why are we mediating spirits from the East? Since when do we traffic in international trade?"

"Yes, Alexi," Jane piped up. "Nonnative spirits have increased dramatically. Eight within recent months have traversed the whole of the Atlantic and more to rattle our isle. That damned American war alone will have us reeling until we die. And every year it grows worse."

"I suppose it could be a sign," Alexi replied. His voice was quiet.

Rebecca stopped and stared. "You mean, a *sign*?"

Emily began mumbling. The spirit was contracting and wrestling more fiercely against her face, desperate to win the child's mouth.

"Sh . . . she . . . she's coming," Emily said. "She's coming!" Then suddenly: *"She is coming!"*

Everyone gasped. Jane held Emily down as the child shook, and Alexi bound the spirit tighter with violent swipes of his hand and flame.

"You don't suppose Emily means Prophecy is coming . . . does she?" Michael asked, surprised.

The group stared, apprehensive. They'd begun to think it just a dream, a hallucination they'd all shared. It had been so many years since that incredible woman had told them such improbable tales in their chapel, and they weren't quite sure what to believe anymore.

Alexi set his jaw. "I will believe nothing until I see the foretold signs, and I urge you to do the same. Until then, words are just words. Remember to beware of false prophets." From his tone, the matter was clearly closed to further discussion.

"Bind with us, Alexi. It gathers vehemence," Michael warned, reaching out his hand.

Elijah whispered to the parents and priest, and those three continued to stare blankly at Josephine's painting. The Guard joined hands in a circle around the bed.

Emily's arms flew out, rigid. There came a horrible crunching noise from her hands—bones breaking—and the child screamed. Jane set her jaw and disengaged from the circle, taking the child's damaged flesh in hers, bestowing a misty sphere of glowing light upon each fingertip; then she again joined the circle.

"Hold on, Emily, dear heart, this will be over soon."

"Cantus of the Eviscerate," Alexi proclaimed, and magnificence coursed through him, making him a brilliant, powerful conduit. The Guard began to chant something low and lovely that formed in the air like particles of heaven. It was full of music, as if accompanied by an orchestra of a thousand, yet barely rang louder than a whisper. They were the simple words of their private, ancient order, words that Emily's possessor hated.

The blue flames wound tighter and tighter, sinews binding the spirit. The specter opened its jaws as if howling. Emily manifested the nightmarish sound, making it twice as horrible.

The child's skin became brittle. Hairline fissures, like the cracking of a porcelain doll, began to spread across her arms and legs. Blood, thickened by possession and steeped in a glowing gray light, slowly dribbled up through her splitting flesh. Jane tried to counteract this without success.

Intense beams of gray light shot from the cracks in Emily's skin and a strange mist began to pour from all orifices in her face. The vapor clung outside the girl's body, growing into a shuddering human form that curled into the fetal position, cowering as she lay sobbing.

"Emily, look to the wall, to your angel, sweet child," Josephine urged.

The parasitic vapors wrapped around the child's neck, cursing her for the accessible soul that drew the spirit in, then imprisoned it with the righteous fear that was ultimately the body's savior: Emily's unspoiled heart would rather let the beast destroy her than turn violence upon others. The Guard wasn't always so fortunate. Weaker subjects could always be found and driven to unspeakable things. London's mysterious Ripper was likely evidence of such horror.

The cantus reached its climax, an unyielding "Shhhh." The Guard released their clasped hands; each placed a finger to their lips in a gesture that called for silence and stillness. The intruder burst apart like ashes in a gust of wind, leaving behind only a tendril of mist.

Emily lay silent. Her bloodshot eyes were fixed to the painting across the room, and she looked as ghastly as ever.

Jane sat by the child's side and began to sing a lullaby, brushing hair from the girl's face with a glowing hand. She placed illuminated fingertips on each of Emily's hands, and the glow spread. The blood that had risen to the surface retreated and the child's flesh regained the smooth perfection of youth. The tiny spheres of ivory light that had been left floating above Emily's mending fingers merged into a larger ball of light that returned to Jane's abdomen. A shiver worked up the Irishwoman's spine as the power reentered her.

Michael scooped Jane into a warm embrace, softly murmuring what an amazing job she'd done. Josephine bent, whispering a French benediction upon Emily's forehead. The child responded by falling into a comatose slumber. Alexi's shoulders fell and he moved to lean against the wall, rubbing his temples.

Michael next gathered Rebecca in his arms; with a contented giggle, he gave her a smacking kiss on the cheek. Rebecca made a face and batted her hand at him. Michael's giggle turned into his very special laugh—a necessary part of the night. The laugh was contagious. All six now laughed loudly and openly, and the dark energy that had permeated the room was banished. The room, and each soul within it, was cleansed.

The mesmerized priest's fingers closed around his Bible, his eyes vacant as Elijah sent him out the bedroom door with a pat on the back. Elijah then patted the parents, who drifted off to their bedchambers. In the morning, the trio would remember nothing, as hazily blank as the onlookers Elijah had dismissed on the street.

Rebecca finished her notes before moving toward Alexi. She carefully smoothed a lock of black hair on his damp forehead and kissed his cheek, then forced herself to retreat. Alexi's lips twisted into a weary smile as his eyes flickered across her, but the expression faded as he looked out the window with a melancholy stare. Tears rolled down Josephine's smooth cheeks, and she made no effort to stop them. Such extraordinary circumstances never failed to stir up emotion.

Alexi straightened into his typical, formidable presence. "Well done, my compatriots."

"Time for a drink!" Elijah declared, his fist high in the air. "To Café La Belle et La Bête!"

Everyone filed out of the building and into the night.

Alexi, exhausted, took one final moment to contemplate an alternate history where he might have become a renowned scientist instead of an academic who chased ghosts. But the Grand Work had its own agenda, and his mortal desires were in no way considered. Prophecy suggested, of course, that someday his empty heart would be warmed and refreshed, but until he could be sure, until *she* came forward and his divine goddess could again speak to him, everything, including Alexi, was holding its breath—and choking on it. A little girl on Fleet Street might be safe for the moment, but the rest of London was not.

Still . . . she was coming, wasn't she? She'd best show herself before the last of his hope died and he didn't recognize her at all.

CHAPTER
FOUR

PERCY WOKE WITH A START, ROUSED BY NIGHTMARES OF HER FIRST DAY of class. The dreams had climaxed with a hundred eyes that bored so deeply into her that her skin peeled away piece by piece, leaving only bones sitting at a classroom table.

A single bell struck softly somewhere above: It was only Sunday.

She dressed and left her chambers, entered Promethe Hall, following a small stream of people—and an equal number of spirits—to the school chapel. Thankfully, the gray shadows of morning, together with the cover of her soft blue shawl, kept her from attracting attention; living or deceased, no Sunday morning penitent whispered, pointed, or even stared at her.

Percy would not have thought to find such a unique chapel within a Quaker school. The place seemed . . . alive. Rows of amber stained-glass angels burned with inner light. White pillars supported smooth, arched rafters and made the tiny building appear larger than possible, as if it annexed a portion of heaven itself. An elegant fresco of a white dove of peace covered the dome above a modest altar dressed in white linen. To Percy's delight, the shape of the bird's outstretched wings, and the generous spread of light about its feathers, reminded her of the pendant she wore against her skin.

The service was sprinkled with long, reflective silences for the benefit of meditation. It was peaceful, vastly different than the elaborate Catholic rituals she was familiar with. Yet, oddly, something here felt like home.

Leaving the chapel in a daze, Percy wandered back to her hall and sat in the shade of the front stairs. Listening to the splash of the fountain in the courtyard, she eventually found herself roused from her reverie by the anxious sound of a young lady struggling to say an English word. Behind her stood a pair, one of whom was attempting to overcome a thick German accent. The other, a plump brunette, stared blankly.

"I'm sorry, miss, but I don't understand you," snapped the brunette at last, and walked away.

The German girl watched the other girl depart. Clad in an elegant, russet-colored traveling dress, she put her pretty face into her hands. Her blond hair, set in elaborate braids atop her head, shuddered as she began to cry.

Percy rose with a hesitant smile. *"Guten tag, Fräulein."*

The young lady looked up with a priceless expression and turned to see who spoke. Percy expected the girl to gape, and was surprised when there was no reaction to her odd appearance.

Instead, "Oh!" the girl exclaimed happily before flying into a torrent of German. She'd lost her room key, wasn't sure of her hall assignment, didn't know what to do about it or with whom to speak.

Percy pledged her assistance and began leading the way toward the headmistress's office.

"Danke! Danke!"

"Bitte." Percy smiled. "I'm Percy Parker."

"Marianna Farelei. Forgive me, I try English. I need speak as much as I can to be better student, yet some words I always . . . *vergesse.* I'm especially bad when others are impatient."

"Well, I'm happy to assist, Marianna."

"Thank you so much . . . Percy. How happy I was to hear *Deutsch*!" The girl's pleasure was obvious.

"It must be overwhelming for you here in England," Percy pointed out.

"Ja. Do you have . . . relatives who speak my language?"

"No, I have none. But I love all languages." Percy smiled warmly. "I suppose you could say I collect them, and have since long before I came here."

"How interesting," Marianna said. "Your previous place of study must have been very nice."

Percy paused. "I am an orphan. Raised and taught in a convent."

"Ah."

Marianna had finally taken the time to consider Percy's face. This prompted Percy to explain, "I was born with this terrible pallor. Forgive me if I frighten you."

"Frighten? No, I think it is lovely, your face. You are like a doll—I do not know the name . . . one of those that break if you drop them. I used to have one. She was my favorite."

However awkward, Marianna had chosen the perfect words. Percy smiled at the girl's kindness. "What happened to your doll?"

"She broke. I dropped her." Marianna bit her lip. "I am sometimes very clumsy."

Percy giggled. Marianna stole a glance at her, then started to giggle, too.

With one quick trip to the headmistress's office, the two solved Marianna's problem, facilitated by Percy's translation. The girls then strolled back across the courtyard toward their dormitory.

"What are the words on each building?" Marianna asked.

"They are odd variants of Greek names. I've never seen them written quite like this."

"Greek names?"

"Yes, tributes to Greek gods—like my name is."

"Yours? I do not remember a 'Percy' goddess."

Percy smiled. "It's a pet name of sorts."

"Are you the same age as me?" Marianna asked, peering at her. "I cannot tell. You could be young, or much older, with that face."

"I am eighteen, older than most here. I was matriculated due to my . . . circumstances."

"Ah, I see. I am . . ." Marianna fought for an English number. "Fifteen."

"And how did you find Athens?" Percy doubted the German girl had been sent away due to any oddness.

Marianna shrugged. "I desire school, my parents did not and hoped I would change my mind if they applied far away, somewhere quiet like this. But I would have done *anything* to continue." She smiled suddenly. "Of course, if they truly know what I wish to do . . ."

"And what is that?" Percy prompted.

"I would give my heart to be . . . an *actress*." She sighed. "But my father would run me through with a sword!"

Percy laughed. "The only plays I have ever seen were Nativities at the

abbey. I loved them, of course. They were magical. But I have read all of
Shakespeare, and—"

"*Ich liebe* Shakespeare!"

"Good, then we'll have much to quote each other, you and I!" Percy
felt a rush of pleasure at having found a possible friend—a *living* friend—
to share her time here.

From behind her glasses, she squinted at the blue-gray sky and added,
"I never knew my parents. I wonder about them, though, and imagine
how it would be to look like everyone else. To consider dreams, and fu-
tures, like they do. Of course, were I to dream of the stage, I'd only be fit
to play Hamlet's ghost." Percy sighed.

Marianna's eyes lit, and she exclaimed excitedly, "Or Ariel or
Titania!"

Percy grinned as she realized this was perfectly true.

Inside, they reached their respective chamber doors, and Marianna
said, "I must . . . settle in and write letters now. Percy, will you sit with
me at first meal?"

"I'd be delighted," Percy replied. A sliver of desperation edged her
words as she added, "I would like to consider you a friend. May I?"

"Of course you are a friend! Why do you ask?" The German girl
seemed surprised.

Percy stared at the cobblestones. "I look strange, Marianna. I'm
nothing like the others. If things are the same here . . . well, people will
whisper and scoff, repulsed by the look of me. I don't want to make you
uncomfortable, and—"

"I speak different. You do not . . . look at me strange when I talk.
You help. And you think you look *frightening*?"

Percy shrugged. "My skin, my eyes, my hair . . . No single aspect of
me is normal."

"Your hair is white? Your eyes, too?" Marianna asked, peering closer.

Percy nodded, wondering if she should take off her glasses.

Marianna shrugged. "You are . . . pretty as a sculpture is pretty. Do
not be ashamed," she ordered.

"I am grateful for your kindness."

"And I for yours," Marianna replied.

"Indeed. I shall see you soon."

"Yes, my friend. Good afternoon!"

Percy returned to her room, spirit uplifted. She listened to greetings spoken loudly in the hallways, friends returning and catching up, and decided she was not yet brave enough to make any other forays toward interaction. She would leave such bravery for another day.

ON THE EDGE OF THE WHISPER-WORLD, THE SHADOWS RANG WITH the voice of Darkness. "What has the dog found in London?"

His female servant sank onto the eternally cold stones, stretching out languidly, attempting to look inviting. The shadows didn't move and the woman scowled. "Only East End whores. Fitting, don't you think? Isn't that what she is—a whore?"

The shadows grunted. There was a slow, methodical sound: footfalls, back and forth. "Whatever is left of that bird . . . I'll burn him all over again."

The woman waved her hand. "Yes, yes, I'm sure you will. And her? When it finds her, will you tell the dog to bring her back alive? Or shredded into pieces?"

The shadows roared, and the woman realized she'd misspoken. Still, there was no going back. "Why, you truly *miss* that troublesome wench, don't you?"

CHAPTER
FIVE

BLOOD WAS EVERYWHERE, DRENCHING THE DIRTY STONES OF HANBURY Street, flooding the gutter below a wooden gate. A bleary-eyed crowd, growing despite the ungodly hour of the morning, gazed down in horror at the mangled corpse. Constables and a haggard investigator crawled the scene like insects; actual flies buzzed alongside. Rumors and shrieks filled the air, and the word "Ripper" was on everyone's lips.

A lean, severe woman stood just beyond the horrified East End crowd. Her brown hair pinned tightly beneath a simple touring hat, save for one renegade lock, Rebecca Thompson folded her arms and gazed down at the scene from the steps of an adjacent tenement. At her elbow, a tall, formidable man in a long black greatcoat, tipped his top hat and squinted upward, his mop of dark hair rustling in the breeze.

"My God, Alexi," Rebecca murmured, brushing her gloved hand across his forearm before resting it again upon the buttons of her sleeve. "Darkly Luminous work this must have been, to have produced such an effect." She shuddered. "Is this a sign of something new?"

A distracted hum was the only reply.

"Alexi, are you listening?"

"There are gargoyles atop this shabby roof," Alexi mused, "yet they neglected their sole duty—to deter whatever demon struck here. Poor girl. Poor dead girl."

"You're *not* listening to me."

"I always listen, Rebecca." He turned dark eyes to hers and his sculpted lips softened into a slight smile; a rare occurrence. "It indeed may be a sign. But we cannot know for sure until this"—he gestured grimly toward the body—"is added to something more substantial. Until we see all that was foretold."

"I confess, I'm shocked we've had so long to wait for Prophecy."

Alexi's jaw hardened. "As am I."

"May she actually help us," Rebecca muttered, squinting at a flock of ravens sweeping around a nearby spire. As Frederic, that unique bird with a patch on his breast, hopped down from a rafter to squawk at them, she waved a mollifying finger. "Forgive me for asking, Alexi, but could you . . . could you have neglected her along the way? Could we have missed her? We're not growing any younger. If—"

His stern gaze halted her speech. "'Placed in my path,' it was said. No one has been placed in my path that we have not considered and discounted. Please don't distrust my sensibilities, Rebecca."

She hurried to say, "Of course, I was never suggesting—"

"Please trust that I'm well aware of my age, and that I will remain all the more alert for it!"

Rebecca sighed. "Why do you dislike talking about Prophecy so?"

"Why? Because it's private."

"Private? What's private about a public prophecy?" Rebecca scoffed. "There's nothing private about the fact that our number of six will become seven."

"The . . . fate of the seventh and myself is private."

Rebecca groaned and clenched her fists. "You're still going on about that? About the two of you? Alexi, in what part of her speech did your goddess say you were supposed to love the seventh? Those words were never spoken; love has nothing to do with it!"

He turned and pinned her with his eyes. "I've always believed it, Rebecca. You alone know this. Unless . . ."

Rebecca held up a hand. "I've never said a word."

"And you must not until the time is right. I can only imagine the dreadful gossip." He grimaced, pained. "Elijah wagering on my intimate thoughts . . . The years have proven that my fellow foes of Darkness are drawn to melodrama and rumor." He ground his teeth. "A bond of love *is* implicit in Prophecy, Rebecca, though you claim otherwise. I've made my life choices accordingly, difficult as that has been."

"No, no. *Convenient* as that has been," Rebecca muttered.

Alexi folded his arms and eyed her. "Pardon?"

"It's very convenient for a man as stoic as yourself to decide you'll simply wait for Prophecy like some arranged marriage. None of that dreary mortal pining; none of that average, human mess of emotions for you. No, you'll just wait for something divine, and when 'all the appropriate criteria have been met,' like one of your algebraic equations . . . huzzah, you have a bride!" She turned away, hands clenching the folds of her skirts.

After a moment, she whirled on him again, as if she could keep silent no longer. "Should you be right, would you even know what to do with her? No, Alexi, I daresay you wouldn't. And as you persist in thinking of Prophecy as some sacred love affair rather than an order of business, you're making it more complicated for yourself—and more dangerous for us. Mortal hearts make mistakes. They are cruel, unpredictable things." There was a tense silence as Rebecca caught her breath.

Alexi's jaw worked slowly as he stared down at her. "Is that all?"

Rebecca's eyes flashed. "Hardly. But I'll stop there."

"Why are you so adamant that I am mistaken?"

Rebecca simply stared at him. She opened her mouth and closed it, then shook her head, defeated.

The crowd shifted, and she and Alexi caught sight of the dead body again, now being placed gingerly on a board and hauled away. "Enough to give one nightmares for months, that," Rebecca murmured.

Alexi tilted his head. "Of course. But we've seen such horrors before."

"When?"

"One lifetime or another," he replied, absently holding out his arm. Rebecca took it, and he continued speaking as they stepped down to the pavement. "And this tragedy may be only the cry of poor Whitechapel, nothing more. We've no concern with human crimes, no matter how ghastly. If it becomes our Work—if the supernatural becomes evident— we will act."

"Patience, eh? It never fails to surprise me when that is your counsel, Professor."

A brief spark passed through his eyes. "Was that not what we just discussed, my dear? If I had no patience, I'd have gone mad long ago."

Entering the dank shadow of a nearby alley, Rebecca sighed. "Fifty Berkeley Square is causing trouble again," she remarked. As was often the case, she was the first to feel the burning in her veins.

"The usual? Noises?"

"Yes, and moving lights. Books ejected from second-story windows, blood dripping from their bindings. It will be rather a mess."

Alexi sighed. "Shall we clean it up, then?"

She shook her head. "Let me handle it."

"Rebecca, Bloody Bones is a trial. It's not a task for you alone."

"Alexi, please. You've enough to worry about," she assured him. When he raised an eyebrow, she asked, "You truly think I cannot arraign the subject myself?"

Alexi was silent.

"Shall we bet on the matter?"

Alexi's lips curved. "Why, Headmistress, you surprise me. I didn't think you a wagering woman."

"You press me to strange deeds, Professor."

"Indeed. Well, then: a bottle of my favorite sherry. It shall await me at La Belle et La Bête upon your failure. I do believe Josephine keeps several in stock—perhaps for just such an occasion."

Rebecca grimaced. "While I have every faith in my success, I do wish your tastes were less expensive. But a bottle of sherry it is. And now we'd best get back to Athens."

"Should we?" he asked.

"It *is* the first day of class, Professor, and you have students to terrify."

"Ah yes, so I do."

THE SMALL STUDENT BODY OF THE ACADEMY BUSTLED NOISILY through the halls. Percy, however, prepared in quiet.

Her linen gown of her favorite light blue color was simple yet elegant. She tucked her silver phoenix pendant between her chemise and dress, for the familiar comfort of its chain around her neck and its solid form below her breast. Of ritual necessity, Percy shrouded herself further. She draped a blue scarf about her head, circling her neck with the soft fabric and folding its edges into the neckline of her bodice. She buttoned satin gloves that hid her deathly pale hands. Donning her tinted glasses as her final barrier, she was seized by a fit of nerves—despite a hint of rouge upon her cheeks and lips, there remained no cure for her unmistakable pallor.

Glancing once more at her first class assignment, she gathered her books and opened the door into the busy hall, hoping to remain as inconspicuous as possible. But the instant she appeared, it began. And while the reverend mother had warned her, Percy couldn't have known the ongoing shock of being stared at so intently and by so many. Whispers and curious peering created a cacophony of sound and sensation; Percy felt riddled by pinpricks. The journey down the hall and through the foyer was a gauntlet filled with snickers and gasped comments, students poking one another and pointing.

Overhearing one young lady ask a friend when Athens had begun to admit carnival attractions, Percy had had quite enough. She threw her slight weight against the front door, grateful to slip into the outside breeze. The welcome sight of Marianna, smiling at her and waiting on the steps, lessened the weight of her circus novelty.

The girls walked toward Promethe Hall, where they had a literature class together. "I see now, Percy," the German girl offered quietly, "how people look at you."

"I must admit, Marianna, I was not prepared for the extent of it."

"You are, how do I say . . . ? *Attractive,* Percy. You 'attract' many looks."

Percy smiled wearily. "I suppose you could say that."

"In time you will no longer be a surprise," her friend stated with confidence.

"I hope. Have you met other girls in our hall? I've remained solitary."

"A few ladies came by and introduced themselves. They were polite."

Entering a book-filled room lined with tables, the two girls took to the corner. A few students nodded at Marianna as they passed, and one civil young man deigned to smile at Percy as well.

Marianna poked Percy's arm. "That one looks nice."

"Hmm?"

"The boy who just smiled. He is . . . handsome." Marianna peered for a bit at the student in question.

"You may look, Marianna, but I beg you to recall the headmistress's speech. She gave it to you as well, did she not? We are to have not the least bit of contact with men, however handsome."

Her friend just shrugged and, as roll call was read by the instructor—a round woman named Mrs. Henrick, who spoke in a shrill tone—she paid particular attention to the name of the young man she had noticed: Edward Page.

Mrs. Henrick went about the room and asked students to name their favorite author. Marianna named Goethe, while Percy said, "Shakespeare." Percy felt the teacher's eyes upon her, as well as those of the other students, and was grateful for her glasses, meager protection that they were.

Mrs. Henrick pried further. "Favorite play?"

"*Hamlet*," Percy replied, and immediately felt a pang for her dear ghostly friend Gregory, to whom she had played Horatio a hundred times, holding his dying—already dead—body.

Mrs. Henrick prated on, and Percy became confident the class would pose no trouble. She also pledged to help if Marianna got behind in her reading.

After class, the girls headed in separate directions as Marianna strolled off to a composition class. Percy headed for Mathematical and Alchemical Studies. The words sounded both exotic and threatening, a true barrier to what she imagined would otherwise be effortless study.

It was hard to ignore the murmurs of the living, let alone those of the dead who sprinkled the school grounds. Percy heard everything, despite her numerous accoutrements. Living and dead alike wondered if she was a ghost haunting the academy. She prayed to someday grow accustomed to this trial.

Alongside her, nineteen other students shuffled into a chamber that looked more like the nave of a Gothic church than a classroom. The room was filled with long tables, lined with stone beams, and bordered by stained-glass windows of mythical creatures.

Sitting near the back, Percy tried to become invisible. However, pale as she was, transparency was impossible. Around her, the dead floated through the walls. Some spirits paid avid attention to the assembling class; some simply hung in a wandering breeze; while others chattered softly about the woes that tethered them to this world.

Percy mentally denounced the gift that alienated her from both the living and the dead; cursing her ability to see and hear those she so closely resembled as well as her kinship to those of flesh and blood, who would never understand the strange sights that her eyes found commonplace. It was as if she watched members of her family through windows that precluded her from joining them. Yet she could not ignore them; there was always noise to keep them in mind.

A door burst open, and the assembled company, ghosts included, started. Out from an office at the front of the room strode a tall figure in black, and the ensuing silence was deafening.

The professor turned to face his students. Percy's breath caught. Here stood the most striking man she had ever seen. Lustrous dark hair hung loosely to broad shoulders. A few locks turned out in an unkempt manner contrary to the rest of his restrained appearance; his noble, chiseled countenance featured a long nose, high cheekbones, defined lips like a Grecian sculpture, and impossibly dark eyes. He was dressed in a long professorial robe that hung open over a smartly buttoned velvet vest. A crimson cravat at the throat was the only spot of color on his distinguished figure.

Percy gaped a moment before coming to her senses and shutting her mouth, her face growing hot. The professor's hair was not graying, yet a few creases upon his regal forehead betrayed years of deep thought. Percy guessed that he might be twice her own eighteen years. There was something in his personality, in his commanding presence, that was beyond the limits of mortality.

She felt a pang of recognition, and that bothered her greatly. She would never have forgotten seeing such a man.

As the two other females in the room appeared wholly unaffected, Percy ordered her heart to stop racing; its intoxicated pace was alarming, and she chided herself for such a foolish, hasty spark. Nonetheless, her distaste for science suddenly seemed an extraordinary misfortune, as she hated the thought of doing poorly in a class taught by someone so breathtaking.

The newcomer wrote upon the board in scrawling script. His captivating voice was a richly resonant baritone. "I am Professor Rychman. Welcome to my class." He swept the room with his eyes, coolly evaluating his new students. When his gaze found Percy, it lingered. Caught in that stare, she shrank into her chair.

Though his eyes widened, she could see him make an effort to remain polite. After a moment, Percy realized his expression wasn't one of disgust, mockery, or even surprise; it was confusion. Odd.

He began a roll call, managing to steal one more glance in her direction. Then he arrived at her name. "Miss P. Parker?"

"H-here, sir." Percy raised her hand.

The professor looked up from his roster. All eyes were upon her. Percy squirmed. The professor nodded slowly, as if he were trying to decipher a riddle. Then he moved on to the next name and Percy could breathe again.

Class began. Professor Rychman was ruthless with his subject matter, and he flew through what he clearly considered background material and began scribbling unending sequences of letters and symbols in all manner of baffling arrangements. Percy attempted to take notes but was soon lost. Hypnotized by the stern yet melodic sound of his voice, she found herself swept away by the cadence of his speech. Every movement and sentence held impossible confidence. Even when his back was turned, his presence gripped the room. By the end of the session, Percy had a page full of numbers, dashes, and circles, but no clue as to their meaning.

OVER THE COURSE OF HIS SECOND CLASS OF THE DAY, ALEXI repeatedly found himself staring past the spirits that floated through his classroom, focusing instead on a living girl who looked like a ghost herself. He would never admit to his students that he saw spirits; it was not something a man of science or sanity admitted. Still, he could not help but think *Luminous* as he stared at Miss P. Parker, imagining her a body possessed, like little Emily. But she seemed in no distress and none of his internal alarms were raised.

He wondered at the age of this unmistakable Miss Parker, for while it was clear her smooth cheek was young, there was something that distinguished her from youth. A timelessness.

It did not signify. The true Grand Work would not involve his students.

PERCY AND MARIANNA MET AGAIN IN THE DINING HALL, A ROOM WITH wooden rafters and low chandeliers; portraits of dour men and women paraded the paneled walls. Cliques of other young ladies sat chattering.

Percy and Marianna sat near a bay window that looked out onto the courtyard, sharing their thoughts on various teachers and what they foresaw as potential strengths and difficulties. Marianna was particularly worried about a speech barrier in her last class, while Percy couldn't forget Professor Rychman.

"I'm afraid I'll be made a fool in mathematics, I'm dreadful at the subject. But, oh, the professor! He's magnificent!" she breathed.

"Yes?"

"Oh, yes, Professor Rychman. I can't say I've ever . . ."

"Ever what?"

Percy had to turn away and butter another piece of bread to hide her blush. "Seen anyone like him," she finished, attempting to sound nonchalant.

Marianna leaned forward with a smile. "I would think he has never seen anyone like you, either."

Percy bit her lip. Though she'd been tortured over Mr. Darcy as a girl, she was terribly unprepared for being smitten with a living man. A blazing bonfire deep inside sent lightning flashes to wake dormant dragons all over her body whenever she thought of him or spoke his name. She knew better than to relay this to her new friend.

That evening, as Percy readied for bed, she was struck by a vision: a floating feather, something on fire, the flapping of great wings; herself running barefoot down a long and misty corridor . . . She could ignore it no longer. The visions were coming more rapidly than ever before, once a week now rather than every few months. She thanked heaven that the images usually waited until she was alone.

Suddenly she was overcome by the first vision she remembered ever having, and as it presented itself once again, Percy groaned. It *hurt*. There were . . . spirits in the sky. Hungry and searching for something. These spirits, smoky tendrils on the wind, were part angel. Beautiful yet dizzying, they darted helter-skelter under a bloodred canopy. They descended rapaciously, careening about the streets of London. One by one, they found new homes. A jolt shook her, a deafening thunder both outside Percy and within. Something was about to merge; immortal force seeking out mortal bodies for grand and magnificent purpose . . .

The vision faded and Percy collapsed onto her bed, gulping for air and drowning in yearning. It was times such as these when she needed to believe there was a God of love and comfort, a Being of peace and beauty who could one day offer meaning. Her body shook until sleep won out . . . but even in sleep there was no rest. Someone kept screaming her name, over and over, matching the rhythm of her heartbeat, and the person screaming was very, very angry. Just as Percy was looking for answers, someone was looking for her. She prayed she found her truths before her pursuer found her.

CHAPTER
SIX

HEADMISTRESS REBECCA THOMPSON OWED PROFESSOR ALEXI RYCHMAN a very expensive bottle of sherry. Luckily, spirits—alcoholic as well as ghostly—were in ample supply at Café La Belle et La Bête.

The specters came and went as they pleased, now and then troubling to adjust the glassware, to owner Josephine's unending irritation. A pair of Restoration wraiths kept to a corner, eternally interested in gossip divined from the living. A former army general never left his post at the end of the bar. Countless others came and went.

Everyone inside, living and dead, turned as the door opened and the scowling Rebecca entered.

"Good afternoon, my dear Miss Thompson!" hailed her jovial, rosy-cheeked friend who wore a modest suit, rising from a table by the window to press her hand. The other gentleman at the table, more finely dressed, waved a limp hand and resumed gazing out the window.

"Hello, Michael . . . Elijah," Rebecca murmured with a curt nod.

Vicar Michael Carroll, maintaining his affable grin, pulled out a chair. "And what has you so flustered?"

"Alexi, of course," she spat, taking a seat between them, removing her hat and gloves to replace stubborn locks of hair falling from her coiffure. She failed to notice Elijah roll his eyes.

"What now?" Michael asked, twirling his gray-peppered mustache.

Rebecca sighed, adjusting the gathered folds of her navy skirt with a pronounced rustle. "Do you recall the trouble at fifty Berkeley Square?"

"What of it?"

"Alexi seemed to think I was outmatched. But as we often perform alone, I never dreamed—"

"Old Bloody Bones got the better of you, eh?" Michael grinned.

"Yes," Rebecca muttered. "What a horrid sight. And stench. It wouldn't stay *still* long enough to bind properly! I'm afraid I made a mess of it."

"Alexi's been hard on you, then? Did he come to your aid?"

"Yes, yes. He was right. It took the two of us to dispel the bloody devil." Rebecca glowered. "So, as was our wager, I owe him a bottle of sherry. His absurdly expensive label, of course."

"Ah! A bet against Alexi?" Michael shook his head. "While I admire your pluck, my dear, I must say I'd have foregone that temptation. Now he will be gloating and unbearable."

Elijah sniggered against the window.

Rebecca turned. "Good afternoon to you, too, Lord Withersby. Your impeccable manners are always a balm."

Elijah turned, as if he hadn't yet noticed Rebecca or heard her previous greeting, and inclined his head in an exaggerated bow. "Miss Thompson. Delighted."

"You know, Elijah," Michael began, "you match the consumptive artwork Josephine has on these walls. You really should sit for Rosetti. Or . . . I suppose we could simply leave you in your seat and hand you a gold frame to hold over your face."

Elijah pursed his thin lips in annoyance.

"Oh, is that a new one of Josephine's?" Rebecca pointed to the opposite wall, then rose to examine the canvas. Michael followed, always eager to be near her side. Elijah remained seated . . . and took advantage of his friends' departure to hold a peppermill over Michael's tea.

A clatter of glasses above the polished oak bar brought the lovely, olive-skinned Josephine, cursing in French, out from a back room. Brandishing a wet towel, she waved it in the air with a few words that were not French but instead The Guard's strange and ancient tongue. The towel passed straight through the portly body of that spirit in military uniform who was trying unsuccessfully to help himself to a glass of wine. Glumly, the general heard the odd words, felt the tickle of the towel, and went to sulk in his usual place.

It was good the four friends were the sole living occupants of the bar, Rebecca mused; the afternoon was shaping up to be a bit of a production unfit for outsiders. Improper familiarity across class lines was one thing, but blatant interaction with the dead was another.

"Ah, Rebecca!" Josephine, tucking one thin lock of silver hair behind her ear, moved to kiss her friend on both cheeks. She drew back, noticing Rebecca's sour look, and her French accent made her words all the more provocative. "What, what is that face you give me?"

Rebecca grimaced as she drew a stack of notes from her reticule. "Josie, would you fetch me a bottle of sherry—your best, if you please? And tie a ribbon or something around it."

"Ooh! And what might the occasion be?"

"Alexi," Rebecca muttered. "We wagered on a spiritual matter, and I lost."

Josephine clicked her tongue and shook her head, rolling back the sleeves of her blouse. "Someday we'll find something he can't master, and we'll drink sherry on his remittance for a change." She refilled Elijah's cabernet, then set off to procure the prize.

"Where's Jane?" Rebecca asked.

Michael shrugged. "Off on her own, as usual."

"Never trust the Irish. Never know what they're up to," Elijah muttered.

Michael cleared his throat. "Rebecca, forgive my cold heart that I haven't yet inquired. Did you and Alexi discover anything at that last Ripper site? Can we help?"

"I'd have preferred a waltz with Bloody Bones than to have seen that poor wretch . . ." Rebecca shuddered. "But no. There's nothing to do but wait and listen. London is terrified and so am I. Such gruesome evil is usually within our control—part of our Grand Work. But these murders on Buck's Row and Hanbury Street . . . we had no warning, no feel of the supernatural. I'm worried about our school. What if one of our girls wanders out? They're all so innocent—and my responsibility."

"How was the start of term?" Michael asked, trying to access happier fare. He inched his hand toward Rebecca's but at the last moment lost courage and withdrew.

"Only a few new students," Rebecca replied, oblivious. She shifted uncomfortably, thinking of Miss Parker. "One girl is startlingly unique. Must have some sort of condition, poor thing. Deathly pale skin, the whole of her white as snow. Glasses shaded her pale eyes, which, through their glass, appeared almost violet."

"You're certain she's mortal and not Luminous?" Michael asked, again twirling his mustache.

"You think I can't tell the difference? Still, it is eerie to see a living girl so similar. And the spirits gaze at her so. Perhaps they are just as curious."

"What do they call people without color?" Michael scratched his head, ruffling a patch of gray-peppered hair and not bothering to comb it back into place.

"Albinos," supplied Elijah.

Rebecca nodded and continued her musing. "Eerie, indeed. A timid girl, orphaned, raised in a Catholic convent. When asked if she considered herself gifted in any way, she replied that she had a strange manner of dreams. I tried to clarify whether these were dreams or visions, but she didn't know or want to admit."

Elijah snorted. "Damn Catholics. Don't they all think they see things—Christ in a spoon or the Virgin in a crumpet? Delusional fanatics. God bless Mr. Darwin for setting us straight."

Michael waggled his mustache. "Please, Elijah, your compassion is leaking onto the tablecloth, and it's making an awful mess."

Elijah's hand hovered over a butter knife.

"No silverware duels today, gentlemen. Please," Rebecca implored.

Michael leaned over the table, not to be dissuaded. "Mr. Darwin, Lord Withersby, was a man of God. As a scientist, he believed in the sacred process of life designed by an omnipotent Creator. Men who lack imagination will say he's not of God for their own purposes." He turned away. "Now, what of this girl's dreams, Rebecca?"

"I wasn't at liberty to press her. Timid as she was, I doubt she'd have shared."

"You are rather intimidating on the job, *Headmistress* Thompson." Elijah snickered. "You and Alexi both—our resident gargoyles."

Rebecca offered Elijah a cold, cautionary smile.

"Did Alexi think anything of the girl?" Michael asked.

Rebecca shook her head. "I've no idea. The students are simply our employment, and bless them for that. We decided long ago that we should bring none near our madness, and that has served us well. I therefore leave Alexi to his own impressions regarding her. The girl was nothing to bring to account, merely interesting, that's all."

There was a long period of silence as the three friends picked like birds at the dry biscuits before them.

"We're overdue for a meeting. The air is sick with forces. There may yet be more murders," Michael finally said. "Supernatural or no."

"Two fewer harlots on the streets," Elijah offered, his bony fingers toying with his fork.

"Sunshine, you are," Michael replied. "A joy to all mankind."

"I do my best." Elijah punctuated his words by threading his dessert fork into the lace of Rebecca's cuffs. She responded by tossing a piece of biscuit at his head. It bounced and hit the window, and a voice scolded suddenly in a thick French accent.

"*Mon Dieu!* No refinement! Even you, Rebecca, whom I hold to a higher standard than these heathens at your side. You let them goad you into misbehaving?" Josephine strode toward them, cradling a bottle of fine sherry.

"Josie, now, don't curse your kin," Rebecca replied, blowing the other a kiss.

Josephine glared, but the men at the table gasped. "Did you see, Josie?" Elijah exclaimed. "Her Arctic Highness just sent you a token of affection floating on an icy breeze! Come, a smile is due at least for such a novelty."

"You give me no credit!" Rebecca cried. "I'm never as frigid as you all make me out to be."

Michael clapped his hands to his arms and rubbed them furiously. "Elijah, what on earth could be causing that draft?"

Rebecca folded her arms and scowled.

"She awaits a man's embrace," Elijah blurted. "That alone will remedy her chill."

Michael choked first on his biscuit, then, taking a drink of tea, choked once more—this time due to Elijah's work with the pepper-mill.

Rebecca's hand flew to her snug collar, her heart seizing. She masked her sudden wound with bluster. "If I wasn't bound to you by damnable fate, if you were *proper* gentlemen, you might consider etiquette, for such talk surpasses scandal!" She rose from her chair, throwing down her napkin, trying to deter further scrutiny. "I'll never know why you tease Alexi and me so, Elijah, when *you* are the impossible one!"

Elijah grinned, unrepentant. He looked innocently at his fellows. "Me? *I* do not stalk about like one of those gothic *vampir* onstage at the Royal. Nor do I brood with dramatic zeal, nor daily dress as if in mourning, nor can I start fires of my own accord. Nor do the first bars of Beethoven's Fifth seem to burst forth each time I enter a room!"

"Shameful! All of you!" Josephine scolded, though she fought back a smile. Removing her apron, she dusted the bottle in her hand briefly before depositing the white linen garment on the bar. It passed through the head of the general whose transparent body was folded over, asleep.

"Poor Alexi," Rebecca huffed, collapsing into a chair. "If he only knew how he was abused. To think that the serious boy of so many years ago—"

"If we didn't know and love him, this would be cruel," Elijah interrupted. "But as all of us adore his brilliance—insufferable though he is—and though he appears a dark thespian rather than a chemist, we gladly admit we'd fall apart without him."

"Alexi Rychman, melancholy prince of Denmark!" Michael proclaimed, pounding his fist on the table in delight and raising his teacup in a toast. The others followed suit.

Through their laughter, they failed to hear the door open and shut. A tall, cloaked figure dressed all in black approached. His stoic features were offset only by his blazing eyes. Alexi stared down at his friends with a frown.

"Something amusing?" he asked.

At the sound of his low, rich voice, the group looked up and shrieked, delighted. Elijah cried out the first notes of Beethoven's Fifth, unable to help himself. This did nothing for the others' composure. In fact, Michael, head thrown back in a wail of laughter, lost his balance and fell from his chair.

"You really should have your own personal orchestra, Alexi!" Elijah gasped for breath.

"'To be or not to be . . . !'" Michael wailed from the floor, waving an arm grandly.

"An appropriate theme for you, you must admit!" Elijah continued, offering Alexi a sharp-toothed grin.

Rebecca, flushed, stood with an uneven breath and handed Alexi the sherry bottle, with a ribbon tied lopsidedly around the neck. "Professor, your prize. I acquiesce to your eminence and superiority—sir," she stated with a curtsey. There was a hint of a smile as she did so, however, and Josephine masked a sputtering giggle with a cough.

Alexi snatched the sherry from Rebecca's hand. "Whenever you heathens can regain a modicum of sense, it's time for a meeting," he stated coldly. This quieted the group enough for him to continue. "There now. Sanity has returned to La Belle et La Bête, but I'd best speak quickly as I fear its presence is fleeting. But before we begin . . . could someone go and remind our gray friend down the street not to push the actors into their places quite so hard? Since the discovery of his dead body during the renovations, his ghost has become increasingly meddlesome, causing many complaints."

He waited a moment for one of his companions to volunteer for the routine policing of Drury Lane's most infamous specter, but none did. Then: "Fine, you lazy fools, I'll go. Considering your present behavior, I'd not trust one of you to admonish this spiritual hooligan. But I warn you: Sharpen yourselves." He turned and exited, his long black cloak billowing behind him. A few more bars of the Fifth Symphony were hummed in his wake.

CHAPTER
SEVEN

THE THIRD FLOOR OF PROMETHE HALL, NOT OFTEN USED AS ANYTHING other than a passage between the north and south wings, was an open foyer with wide windows looking onto the school courtyard. The whole was draped in white fabric, making the room softly but generously lit by the dawn. Two weeks into classes, Headmistress Thompson was ascending to this level when she stopped abruptly at the top of the stairs. The sight that greeted her was unlike any she had ever seen before.

Shimmering and flickering like a candle, a large, transparent feather made of glittering wisps of blue flame floated two feet above the seal of Athens Academy, which was engraved on the floor. Rebecca approached in awe. As she moved close, the feather brightened and seemed to dance, almost as if it were happy to see her.

The usual trickle of morning students began to walk through the arched entryways of the foyer, on their way to classes. A rush of nerves caused Rebecca's skin to moisten, but she took care to mask her amazement and maintain her composure. The students passed by with a nod of deference and nothing more. As their headmistress hoped, they could not see the feather.

Rebecca exhaled slowly. "Things like this are supposed to stay relegated to our sacred circle and the chapel, thank you very much," she muttered, scolding the phenomenon.

She glanced down at the seal of the academy, a golden eagle bearing a lit torch in its great claws. The school's motto was inscribed below, first in Greek, then English:

**As the Promethean fire which banished darkness,
so knowledge bears the power and the light.**

The feather, ephemeral as smoke and delicate as spider's thread, gave off no heat or sound, but its blue flame was instantly familiar. Slowly moving down the stairs, Rebecca eyed the feather to the last, then scurried to her office. She had often wondered if there was more to the building than it cared to tell. Urgently, she sent Frederic to fetch Alexi.

"YOUR ENGLISH HAS IMPROVED GREATLY, MARIANNA." PERCY SAT AT the feet of the courtyard's statuary angel, twirling the water in the fountain's basin with distracted fingertips.

Marianna reclined beside her, finishing her picnic breakfast. "I am trying. I wish we spent more than one class together, but I have made a few friends."

"Wonderful," Percy replied in earnest, before glancing away. "You remain my only friend. At times I see that Edward boy. Every now and then he nods a greeting. Everyone else is afraid. I can't blame them. I *do* look like a ghost—"

"No, Percy. Do not make excuses," Marianna said. When her friend stayed silent, gazing at the angel above, she declared, like an elder sister, "I accept melancholy for one moment, Percy, but that moment has passed. So. Are language classes still your favorite?"

Percy smiled. "I wish they were more challenging, but they do provide a lovely escape to different worlds. It makes me forget myself, if only for a moment."

"Ah! Doth I hear melancholy again, my dear Hamlet?" Marianna chided. Percy laughed. "There. Much better. Is that alchemic—what is it called?—class still giving you trouble, despite your 'magnificent professor'?"

Percy groaned. "Oh, that class remains my bane! I pay attention, take countless notes, but all I remember is the sound of Professor Rychman's voice. Every syllable he speaks is like a hypnotic delicacy, like dark velvet. I try to grasp his explanations, but all I can see is how his robe sweeps as he moves, how his presence commands the room, how his brow furrows in thought, how his eyes blaze, how he calmly brushes a lock of dark hair from his noble face . . ." She trailed off, horrified by the vividness of her descriptions. With a fearful glance at Marianna, she folded her hands in her lap.

Marianna's eyes gleamed as she whispered in Percy's ear, "Someone is most certainly smitten!"

Percy swallowed. "Marianna, you mustn't say such a thing—even a suggestion could get me expelled! This institution, in its unique position, cannot be too careful with the men and women under its protection. While I admit I may be . . . *intrigued* by him, this man is my professor, Marianna, and nothing more. You must realize that! Perhaps one day"—it was Percy's turn to take a sage tone—"you'll realize that there is a supreme delicacy to such matters."

There was a long pause, and Marianna bit back a grin. "Does he wear a ring?"

"No," Percy replied.

Marianna smiled. "I see. Who *is* this dashing hero? Have I met him?"

"You'd know if you had, I assure you. Wait! Oh, why, speak of the devil!" As if on cue, from Apollo Hall strode an impressive figure. Engrossed in his thoughts and ignoring the students sure to dive clear of his path, he strode briskly toward Promethe Hall. His academic's robe and dark locks billowed about him, giving him the appearance of a great swooping bird. He looked up as if sensing Percy. His dark eyes pierced her to the core and all breath flew from her lips. "There," she whispered.

The two held each other's stares for a moment, student and teacher. Percy was paralyzed, unable to break from his gaze until he snapped his head to the side and moved across the courtyard.

Marianna shuddered slightly. "Goodness, Percy!"

"What?"

"Well, he is striking indeed—but grim!"

"Distinguished, regal, elegant, fascinating . . ."

"*Eerie*," Marianna argued.

Percy turned suddenly, removed her glasses and pinned her friend with a stare. "Eerie, you say? 'Eerie' should daunt me, should it? What am I, then?"

Though the light hurt her eyes, the desired effect occurred. Percy's irises flashed in the sunlight, the tiny blue and white slivers of color glowing. Marianna gasped. Percy replaced her glasses and closed the lids of her eyes, favoring them from the pain to which she'd just subjected herself.

After a moment, Marianna spoke. "Well, Percy, I will give you this. There is certainly *something* about the man."

"Yes. But I cannot know more of him."

Marianna sighed. "My dearest Percy, welcome to the ranks of the unrequited."

Percy turned, grave. "You *must* refrain from such statements. Such talk is scandal. The only reason he affects me so is that I feel . . . strange around him. I sense he knows something that I need to know. I've had such an odd sense of things my entire life, Marianna, such dreams while awake, such beautiful and haunting images! It must lead to something."

"And you think your professor of science may have answers?"

"That's just it: The thought is absurd! *Of course* this could just be a fascination, which I dare not foster, but nonetheless I wonder . . . Please, Marianna, never one word of this."

Her friend held up a hand, her obligation to duty clear.

Professor Rychman continued walking and the two girls continued watching. Just outside the arch into Promethe Hall, Headmistress Thompson waited. Percy and Marianna observed as the professor held out his arm. She took it, and they fell into immediate, intense discussion.

"They know each other well," Marianna stated, watching closely.

Something the headmistress said must have irked him, for Rychman glared at her as they turned to go inside. She patted his hand, to which the professor responded by lifting his head high.

"Very well indeed," Marianna continued, giving Percy a grimace. "By the look of them, they deserve each other."

Percy found she could not argue. She watched the professor's great robed arm open one of the tall doors of Apollo Hall. He motioned his equally severe companion inside with a familiarity that surely only great intimacy could create. Percy yearned for his intoxicating stare one more time, but she wasn't so lucky. Indeed, she felt oddly abandoned.

Marianna gave a gentle inquiry. "Are you all right?"

"Of course I'm all right. Why wouldn't I be?" Percy retorted.

"Indeed. Come, my dear girl, let us bemoan your fate over tea and crumpets." Marianna giggled. "Loneliness should never be faced on an empty stomach."

Percy whimpered. "Marianna, look at me, then remind yourself not to joke in such a manner. A lonely fate is all too probable, thank you very much."

"Somehow I do not think so. I think fate will provide."

"I can only hope." Percy chose to adopt her friend's optimism. "Come, then, tea. Then, on to our mountain of studies."

ALEXI AND REBECCA STARED AT THE FEATHER OF BLUE FIRE FLOATING at the center of the foyer.

"Incredible," Alexi stated, approaching. "What an omen."

"Indeed," Rebecca murmured, following.

"And here we were worried about signs being too subtle to detect."

Alexi drew close. The transparent feather responded to his proximity, its fire leaping higher. The image danced and shimmered, inviting Alexi to reach out a hand. Rebecca steadied him, cautious, but he shirked her warning and allowed his fingers to tickle the edges, to pass through the phantom image.

Rebecca clamped her hands across her mouth to hold in a cry of surprise. Though she knew her students could not see what she saw, she would not take chances; she had cordoned off the entire floor, claiming repairs. But . . . Alexi had turned into an angel. Huge phantom wings burst from his back, made of that same bluish, wispy flame, and he was snapped into place atop the school seal by a force unseen, the feather emblazoning his torso. He stared, wide-eyed, at the gossamer wings and robe whipping about his ankles with great force.

"My God," he declared. "Perhaps that myth of ours is true after all . . ."

IT WAS PAST TIME FOR THEIR MEETING. FIVE OF THE SIX GUARD entered the chapel at intervals, filing past the amber stained-glass seraphim in the windows, whispering devotions and phrases in a tongue long unheard and long forgotten. A warm blue glow grew in the air, beginning as tendrils of mist upon the marble floor before lifting like a breeze to the rafters above and hanging there like a cloud.

The five figures soon stood silently at the altar beneath the white bird of peace and closed their eyes in meditation. The stained-glass guardian angels glowed. The blue cloud of power trembled.

The door of the chapel was thrown open and the formidable Professor

Rychman swept in, his black garments accented by a flourish of burgundy at his throat. Six candles upon the altar immediately burst into flame. Alexi's voice broke the silence. "Good evening, friends. To our sacred depths," he commanded, "where I'll tell you of our omen. And perhaps the goddess will return to tell us more!"

With a slight rending sound, the altar became their large black door, bluish light dancing around it, a corridor and staircase beyond. The Guard filed past and down, into their sacred space. A strange music, a low chant of mysterious vintage, floated up through the air.

Closing, the door once again gave way to a plain altar, and the chapel was left empty.

From the far reaches of the Whisper-world, there came a pounding sound of organic matter against stone. The woman in the silver moonlight winced as the shadows rumbled in anger.

"What to do, then, if she cannot be found?" asked the tolling voice of Darkness.

"Give us time, dear," the woman answered. "You've been without her for many mortal years. You could do with a bit of patience."

"They. Are. *Protecting*. Her."

"I rather think she's protecting herself," was the woman's muttered reply.

"Then we must shake the city. The world. Until we find her. Undo it. Take down the barrier, rip it open."

"Really?" The woman brightened, her lips suddenly wet. "Loosening the pins? Why, Master, that's quite bold of you after all these years."

"Desperate. Times."

"So it would seem!" the woman breathed, excited. "I'll tell the Groundskeeper to attempt the Undoing. Chaos, heed the cries of waking war!"

CHAPTER
EIGHT

A DOORWAY SURROUNDED BY LIGHT. A WISPY RING OF FEATHERS FLOAT-
ing at the center of a portal before shifting into flame. There were
glyphs, like those in Egypt . . . Behind the door, music—

Percy's mind returned to class.

She had been soaring through all her courses except one. She had
endless pages of notes in Mathematical and Alchemical Studies, but
nothing to show for them save a loss of breath whenever she beheld
her professor. She was certain she was failing the class. Failing and
falling . . .

Her eyes narrowed on Professor Rychman, who had momentarily
paused at the chalkboard mid-script, an equation in progress. Subtly he
cocked his head, as if sensing something or catching a note of faraway
music, then resumed his lecture.

Percy realized she had no idea where in the lesson she had left off or
where she might pick back up. Looking hopelessly at her notebook, she
wanted to cry. Worse, the vision refused to leave her mind. Seizing a
piece of paper and a bit of hardened charcoal that she kept in her pencil
box, she began to purge the image by transcribing it onto paper.

She ought to have waited until her drawing class for such a flurry of
creation, she knew. But even then, all she was allowed to do in Professor
Bryan's class was sit with a tedious still life while the woman moved
about the room with her thumb in the air measuring perspective. This
searing image could not wait.

Class ended and students began to file from the room, but Percy
remained oblivious even to her professor's unmistakable presence.

"Miss Parker?"

That stern, rich voice was so sudden and startling that Percy jumped, staring up in horror. How long had he been watching her scribble? "Oh! Yes, Professor?"

"Meet me in my office at six, Miss Parker. Room sixty-one, upstairs."

"Y-yes, Professor."

Professor Rychman stared at her, expressionless, for a moment longer, then strode out of the room, robe billowing behind him.

Percy fought off anxious tears, chided herself and left the classroom. She stepped into the lavatory to adjust her shawl, apply a bit of rouge, and attempt to stop trembling, but it was no use. She went back to her bedroom, where she paced and shook until it was time.

Rychman was carved in bold, golden script across the large wooden door, above the number sixty-one. Percy knocked hesitantly. "Come." The resonant voice emanating from the other side was impossibly both monotone and melodious. Percy opened the door.

The professor's office was large, filled with tall bookshelves and decorated with paintings and relics. He sat across the room at a marble-topped desk, a fire blazing behind his throne of a leather chair. Twilight shone through a narrow stained-glass window that stretched nearly floor to ceiling on the left wall, and faint slivers of light fell upon the charcoal-colored frock coat he now wore instead of his robe. Two candelabras bearing flickering ivory tapers sat at either end of the desk. The room was filled with a warm, antique light.

An inscrutable yet pervasive power emanated from Professor Rychman's person like a scent, something heady and alluring. Percy stared at him in wonder for a very long time until at last he looked up.

Her face colored; Percy could feel mottling rosy patches burst forth upon her cheeks in a patchwork blush. She stared, mortified, at the floor, knowing that her skin's deformity was now further evidenced. Out of the corner of her downcast eye she noticed a spirit hovering by the window, staring at nothing in particular, and she wished that she, too, could vanish through the wall.

The professor removed thin wire reading glasses and beckoned Percy to sit across from him at the desk. She sat, but did not dare remove her glasses in turn. Instead, she chose to examine the art on the walls. There were angels, figures in robes—some looking heavenly, others dark—and a few ancient religious icons. Percy stared at a stately bird against a bloodred sunset for a long moment, feeling transported away from this time and place. A spirit entered through one of the professor's bookcases just as another wafted in, then immediately out, the window. They said nothing and their expressions indicated neither interest nor pity. They were merely passing through.

"I see you fancy art, Miss Parker," Professor Rychman scolded quietly.

Percy fixed her eyes on the patterns in the marble desk before her. "I-I am so terribly sorry for drawing in your class, Professor. It will never happen again."

There was a long pause. Too timid to glance up past her tinted glasses, she could feel his intense scrutiny. She shrank into her chair and began to count the tiny specks of tea leaves scattered about the desk.

"You fancy art. You do not, it would seem, fancy the sciences?" His tone was snide, and Percy bit her lip. "Please, Miss Parker, do be honest," he continued. "You won't be graded—yet."

"It isn't that I dislike the sciences, Professor. It is more that I don't have the mind for them."

The professor frowned, looking disappointed. "Well, Miss Parker, it is true that you are doing rather poorly in my class. Am I, perhaps, unclear in my lectures . . . ?"

She dared glance up. "Oh, *no*, Professor, it isn't you. It most certainly isn't you!"

"Then what, Miss Parker, happens to be the trouble?"

Her cheeks burned hotter. "Me, sir. I-I cannot make a bit of sense of the subject," she fumbled, and a tear escaped her cheek to splash on the marble desk. She tried to wipe it away before he noticed, but she was certain nothing escaped him. "I want so badly to learn. I'm just—"

"Preoccupied?"

Percy cleared her throat. "Perhaps. I—"

A flash of pain shot through her. She saw herself in the middle of a stone hallway, immersed in a shaft of bright light. The light transfixed her core, as if she were a butterfly on a pin. She heard anxious voices far away, and something very angry, growling.

"Miss Parker?"

As quickly as it came, the intense vision vanished. Percy's head snapped back as she focused again on her professor, whose angular features sharpened as he stared at her.

"Oh, goodness—forgive me, Professor!" Percy panicked. "Heaven knows what comes over me, these little flashes. I'm terribly sorry, pay me no mind, please don't think me rude! It's never before happened when someone was near, speaking to me. I don't know what's wrong, but—"

"Slow your tongue, Miss Parker. Flashes, you say?"

"It's nothing, Professor, please forgive me."

"Miss Parker, you seemed in pain for a moment. Please explain."

"I'm . . . I'm fine, sir. There are moments—tiny dreams, no, I mean to say a splitting headache, and then gone."

"Visions?" he posed quietly as Percy wrung her hands. "Do you have the gift of visions, Miss Parker?"

She shook her head. "I'm not mad, Professor. I dream. Headmistress Thompson said dreams are not 'gifts.' Gifts mean academic excellence or one keen particular talent—"

"I know what gifts are, Miss Parker, for heaven's sake."

Percy shrank back in her chair.

The professor drew a measured breath and leveled his tone. "Miss Parker, I'd rather not remove you from my class for your poor grades. However, I demand that you pay better heed to my words. No drawing! I am, in addition, forced to begin a private tutorial so that I may more directly monitor your progress. If I see no improvement, I will have to remove you from my class and the headmistress must determine what is to be done with you. Such are our rules."

"Yes, sir." Percy nodded, commanding her tears to remain at bay.

"Look at me please, Miss Parker."

Percy looked up, sure her glasses only half hid her fear. Neither the professor's rigid expression nor his dark eyes—as inscrutable to her as her own dark lenses must be to him—softened.

"A series of tutorials will commence, dependent on your progress. We will begin tomorrow at six in the evening. Do I make myself clear?"

"Yes, Professor."

"You are dismissed."

"Yes, Professor. Thank you, sir, for your gracious patience with my inability."

"Try not to test that patience, Miss Parker, for it does not run in ample supply," her instructor offered blandly, returning to his paperwork.

Percy rose, attempting to be as unobtrusive as possible on her way to the door, but Rychman's voice halted her. "Trying to make yourself invisible is to no avail, Miss Parker, no matter how hard you try," he declared. She did not turn around, for she was at the exit. Then he added, "You have to know the correct spell."

Percy raised her eyebrows and spun, expecting to see that he was joking, but his face was stoic as ever.

"Tomorrow at six," he reminded her.

"Yes, sir!" Percy opened the door and felt a cool draft tickle the hem of her dress.

"Miss Parker," Professor Rychman called, just before she fled. "One more question, if I may." His voice was careful.

"Of course, sir." Percy faced him.

"What was that door you were drawing?"

Percy wrung gloved fingers together. "I do not know, sir. I saw it in a . . . dream." There was a long pause. The weight of the professor's stare was heavy. "If you don't mind, Professor, why do you ask?"

Rychman leaned back in his chair, tapping his fingers upon his desk. "It reminded me of something."

Percy smiled timidly. "Well, if you could decipher the meaning, Professor, I'd be much obliged."

"Indeed." He held her with his stare a moment longer. Percy hoped she had calmed her blush, but she couldn't be sure. The professor returned his attention to his paperwork. "Good day, Miss Parker."

"Good day, sir." She curtseyed and left the room.

ALEXI WATCHED THE DOOR CLOSE SLOWLY BEHIND HIS STUDENT AND listened to her darting footfalls recede, then unlocked a drawer in his desk and pulled out a notebook. As usual, he ignored the spirits wafting in and out of his office, even when they tried to speak to him. He wished he could hear them for just a moment, enough to determine if they knew about Prophecy or had a message from his long silent goddess. But, to his infinite chagrin, since that first day in the chapel she'd never again been seen. Still . . . this girl had drawn a door. That was the sign.

And yet, this wasn't an actual portal; it was just a picture. He couldn't base the fate of his world on a *sketch*. Prophecy decreed the seventh would be his peer. This girl, however unique, was his student, not his peer, and there were rules. It was his job to teach here, not to look for his destiny; he had to set aside foolish notions.

Opening a leather-bound volume, Alexi hummed a melancholy little tune as he thumbed the pages. Finally arriving at a blank sheet, he scrawled a few hasty sentences into the book before closing it. He stared at its cover, black and plain save for a tiny circle of feathers, and demanded his heart slow its uncharacteristically brisk pace.

A MAN IN A DUSTY COAT BENT OVER A PARTICULAR PIECE OF ROCK ON A distant coast. A remote and once sacred place, it was now unguarded. The Groundskeeper hummed, brushing stray locks of multicolored hair from his weather-beaten face which was both old and young. The only unchanging thing about him was his caste; his voice shifted and melded into every servile accent of the ancient and New World, with a few conquered dialects between.

"So much work to do. Loosening the Sepulchral Seals!" he said as he wielded his hammer and chisel. "My sweet, milky white lady . . . I work for *you* now that Majesty's gone! Loosening, loosening, to slit the seal!"

He threw his weight against the stone and it turned like a screw in a piece of wood. A wet exhalation sounded and vapor lifted from the rock like a puff of tobacco smoke from an ancient pipe. A sound of glee gurgled in the man's throat. "Only a few more, my dear!"

The Groundskeeper pressed his head to the stone. A sound rattled from behind it. A skeletal finger shot from the crevice, but the Groundskeeper swatted at the protruding digit. "Patience, you'll have your time! But give me leave. So much work to do for my lady, and so many seals yet to break!"

CHAPTER
NINE

PERCY COULD NOT CALM DOWN. SHE AND MARIANNA HAD BEEN studying in her room when the bell tolled half past five, and now she jumped to her feet with a distracted whimper.

"And where are you off to?" her friend asked, looking up from her books.

She had been too embarrassed to tell Marianna prior to the engagement. "Since I'm a disaster at mathematics, I'm required to attend evening tutorials with Professor Rychman."

The German girl raised an eyebrow, grinning. "Tutorials with *him*? In private? Is that even allowed? Well . . . I suppose you are a bit of an exception here to begin with."

Percy collapsed upon her bed with a groan. "Oh, how he intimidates me! He speaks the one language I can't understand. Yet, there's so much to commend him. Art and books fill his office. He writes by candlelight, not gas lamp. So melancholy, a philosopher of the world whose heart is cool, but deep within . . . in the moments when he almost smiles, those eyes . . ."

"Listen to yourself, Percy!" Marianna fought back a laugh.

Percy winced. "I know. I know, God help me. I'm utterly hopeless, and this talk will be my undoing." She picked up her books, adjusted her glasses, drew her shawl tighter around herself as if it were armor, and set off.

Hurried, nervous steps carried her toward Apollo Hall, where her quaking, gloved hand knocked clumsily on door sixty-one.

"Come," said the voice within.

Percy mused that if she heard a voice from Olympus, her professor's might sound similar. She pressed her hand to her collarbone and the pendant hidden under her dress. The weight of the phoenix against her flesh bolstered her, as it always had.

She slipped into the office and stood quietly at the door. The warm firelight was inviting, at odds with the professor's cool demeanor. He stood before one of his massive bookcases; long fingers plucked a volume free, then he moved to his desk and nodded her to a seat. They both sat and took a long moment to evaluate each other.

"Miss Parker." The professor finally broke the silence.

"Yes, Professor?"

He fixed her with a measured stare and folded his hands upon his desk. "After some reflection, what seems to give you the most trouble?"

"The actual mathematics, Professor. I have no problem with remembering terminology. That is simply language. I'm actually very good at languages—"

"Numbers are no different, Miss Parker. They are a language in and of themselves."

"I wish my mind could consider them as such, sir."

"You are the verbal type, I see."

Percy offered a tiny smile. "Well, actually, sir, I'm rather quiet."

"Your mind prefers words to numbers," the professor clarified, unamused.

"Yes, Professor."

"I see. This book covers basic mathematics I've not thought to review in class, as they should already be commonly known." He handed her the book, open to a specific chapter. "Read this chapter for our next meeting."

Percy nodded, feeling very small. "I am sorry, Professor."

"Do not apologize. Not all of us can be mathematicians or master chemists," he replied with a lofty air.

"I suppose not," Percy agreed, setting her jaw.

"Return with this book next session, and with any questions that you may have. I will do my best to translate."

"Thank you, sir."

"Not at all," the professor replied. After a moment: "You are quite proficient in language, then, Miss Parker?"

"So it would seem, sir," she replied.

"What tongues are known to you?"

"Latin, Greek, Hebrew, German, French, Swedish, some Spanish, Portuguese, Italian, Gaelic . . ."

"Rather studious of you, Miss Parker. Convent education alone?"

"Yes, sir."

"You learned all these in your time there?"

"Mostly, sir. They came to me . . . easily, as if I had heard them before. But I suppose that sounds terribly strange."

"It would surprise you how little I find strange, Miss Parker," the professor said, tapping his fingertips upon the marble desk.

"How odd," Percy mused. "Headmistress Thompson expressed a similar sentiment. In exactly the same fashion."

"Did she now?" Professor Rychman smiled slightly, as if Percy had referenced some private amusement. There was an awkward pause; then the professor rose from his chair, towering above her, and Percy looked up, unable to hide her awe. "Miss Parker, I don't suppose you might hazard a guess as to the only question you answered correctly on your last exam?"

"'What symbol crowns the alchemical pyramid?'" Percy replied instantly, then gave the answer. "The phoenix."

Something flashed across the professor's face. "Transformative power. Rebirth," he said, narrowing his eyes. "What do *you* think of the symbol, Miss Parker?"

Baffled, Percy considered her reply, unconsciously pressing her hidden pendant to her flesh. "I . . . I think him beautiful, and comforting."

The professor seized on her words. "*Him?* How so?"

"The phoenix myth has always captivated me—the idea that, if something lovely perishes, it might have the chance to rise again."

The professor's eyes were fixed upon her with an intensity she found thrilling. Percy shyly took folds of her dress into her hands; the fabric rustled in the silence that followed.

"Indeed," he muttered with an odd sharpness, breaking contact with her and turning away. "Good evening, Miss Parker."

"Good evening, Professor." Percy rose awkwardly and moved to the door.

"Dream well," the professor added.

Percy stopped in her tracks but did not turn around. She nodded slowly, allowing his words to sink in, then opened the door and disappeared into the hall.

* * *

INTO ALEXI'S NOTEBOOK WENT THE RECORD OF HIS CONVERSATION about the phoenix, another possible clue. But if he was gathering data from Miss Parker, which he shouldn't, he needed also to be looking elsewhere. Prophecy would never come so young, so meek, so unlike the goddess he had long expected. She'd come in a blaze of light, glory, and beauty. Not quietly. And yet, something was keeping him rooted to Athens, keeping him looking for the next moment he'd talk with this ghost of a girl . . .

BEFORE SHE KNEW IT, THERE WERE THE BELLS AGAIN, LURING HER TO the professor. Alarmingly, it seemed to Percy as if no time had passed. Had she daydreamed the minutes into oblivion? There had been two full days of classes between tutorials, two days she did not actively remember, though, oddly, she recalled the growling and barking of a dog.

At room sixty-one, Percy knocked. The idea that she might be living solely for the moments spent in the professor's private company concerned her; her entire body had thrilled in class today when he'd asked her to visit.

"Come," the unmistakable voice called from within.

Percy entered the office and waited for an invitation to sit. The professor, writing at his desk, did not glance up. He had replaced his professorial robe with a long black frock coat and a cravat in a distinct shade of crimson. He waved a hand to the chair opposite. Percy slowly took that seat, silent.

The professor set his papers aside. Percy could see him parceling her by pieces: her snow-white face with the length of scarf about her head, her high-collared dress, her gloves and tinted glasses. Percy watched him watch her and was prepared for more questions.

"Before we begin today, may I ask, Miss Parker—?"

"About my appearance, sir?"

The professor tried to smooth the pause that followed with a strained, unsuccessful smile. He said nothing.

"Ask anything you wish, Professor. You may stare in wonder. Gape, even. I've grown accustomed to it all."

"I hope you would not consider me so rude," her instructor retorted.

Percy offered a conciliatory smile and was appalled by the subsequent spots she felt bloom upon her cheeks like fiery carnations. "Of course not, Professor. I did not . . . I mean, you have never gazed at me in a way . . . in *that* way . . . I mean, in a rude manner. I—" Her gloved hand flew to her lips to stop the hemorrhage. Terrified that her private fascination could be seen through her awkwardness of speech and the transparency of her skin, Percy prayed she would not be sent away immediately. Humiliated, she took a long breath and tried to begin anew. "I was born with this skin, Professor. I'm well in health; my pallor has never been indicative of my constitution. Except, of course, that while I do enjoy sunlight, it isn't very kind to me."

"I see. And the glasses?" Professor Rychman asked.

"I have quite sensitive eyes as well, sir."

"Ah. I hope you find yourself comfortable here? In my office?"

"Yes, thank you. I've always been most comfortable by candlelight."

The professor nodded. "It's always more of dusk than daylight in here, as I tend toward the nocturnal." He plucked a book from behind his desk and leafed through the pages, not glancing at her.

"As do I, sir. The night is full of mystery and magic—though sometimes the magic may tend toward nightmare. My stars of birth are governed by the moon."

"Ah, we have a romantic in our midst. And an astrologer as well?" Percy could not tell if the professor's tone was cordial or disdainful. His expression, however, was stern. "Before we continue, Miss Parker, I must find a more basic guide than the one I previously gave you—your work in class over the past few days has shown several new deficiencies. If you have any interest, you may peruse my library while I look for something suitable."

Percy winced. Never before had she been the handicapped student; she'd always excelled. Nevertheless, she rose and glided across the room while the professor hunted for what she felt sure would be a grade-school primer.

As she expected, many shelves were devoted to mathematics and the sciences, natural and arcane. She was delighted to discover various books of drama as well, including a *Compleat Works of Shakespeare*, and the collected works of other great poets. But what engaged her most was a particular shelf bookended by Pythagoras and Leibniz. In the middle of these treatises by academia's gods of logic sat books on ghosts, possession, exorcism, mesmerism, witchcraft, demons, angels, and all manner of unexplained phenomena.

"Fascinating," Percy couldn't help but murmur.

"Hmm?"

"Oh!" Percy started, whirling around to find the professor standing close. "I didn't mean to disturb you, sir."

"What are you—?" The professor looked up briefly from the book through which he was flipping. "Ah. I see you have found my particular collection on the occult." He returned to the contents of his tome as he walked back toward his desk.

"Yes," Percy breathed in wonder. "I assumed that, as a man of science, you would discount such things."

"There are many types of science, Miss Parker," was the professor's sharp reply.

"Quite right," Percy agreed. "Quite right indeed." She glanced at the shelf below, which was filled with books on the mythologies of manifold cultures. "Ah." She smiled, spotting a popular modern volume, which she retrieved. "Dear Bulfinch. I rather say he had me inventing my own myths at an early age. I'll never forget when Reverend Mother brought a copy from the city. I must have read it a hundred times." Percy felt a glow of pleasure, her passionate nature sneaking past her timidity. When she stole a glance at Professor Rychman, he was staring at her with impatience.

She looked away. "I'm sorry, Professor, I do not mean to prattle on—"

"Bring the volume with you if you must, Miss Parker, but take your seat. We're well into our time."

"Yes, sir." Percy hurried to her chair, the book still in her grasp.

The professor glanced at the copy of *The Age of Fable* clutched in her hands and admitted, "I always found the ancient religions far more entertaining than England's sober Christianity."

Percy raised an eyebrow, surprised by such a personal comment. "Do you not consider yourself a Christian, Professor?"

He regarded her for a moment. "Forgive me, Miss Parker. I forget I speak to one who was convent educated. Worry not for my soul. I am . . . a man of spirit."

"Of course, Professor." Percy nodded, compelled by the fact she had similarly described herself to the headmistress.

Her teacher continued to stare at her. "Perhaps you consider your faith of stronger mettle, Miss Parker, having been raised as you were?"

Percy had not expected to be asked further questions on the topic, especially not such a private one, having just been reminded it was past time for their lesson. "Well, to be quite honest," she began awkwardly, "and I hope the Lord will forgive me for saying so, but I have seen so many strange things that I do not know exactly what to believe. Raised as I was, sir, aspects of the Christian faith fascinate me, but I feel so much is left unexplained . . ."

"Indeed," the professor replied. He opened his mouth as if to continue along this course of discussion, then seemed to think better of it. "No matter. We stray from the subject at hand. You are here for a mathematical tutorial."

"My apologies, Professor."

"No need for apologies," he replied. "I was the one asking the questions."

"Thank you, sir."

"And there's no need to thank me!" the professor snapped.

"I'm sorry—Oh dear!" Percy murmured, biting her lip and yearning to retreat into her corset. Two ghosts at either end of the room had stopped swaying and turned to evaluate her. It would seem they were laughing.

Professor Rychman chuckled, himself. However, though the noise indicated amusement, no such sentiment was reflected upon his face. "Miss Parker, you'll never learn from me if you fear speaking incorrectly, out of turn, or, dare I say, against popular opinion. I am perfectly capable of commandeering a conversation should it be necessary. I speak when I please. I suppose I cannot begrudge anyone else the same."

"Even if I am a woman?" Percy asked. When the professor raised an eyebrow she added, "Miss Jennings said that, even if I could speak every language known to man, no matter, it remains far better to be seen than heard."

The professor put his book down. "And who is this sage Jennings?"

"Our dormitory chaperone."

"Ah," replied Rychman. "I should hesitate to regard your dormitory chaperone's words as gospel, Miss Parker. In my presence you will speak, ask questions, and answer mine whenever I pose them. As for my thoughts on circumstances when men and women should best be silent . . . they are not covered in today's lesson."

Percy, at a loss, said nothing, but allowed a slight smile to grace her lips. The professor seemed satisfied that he had been understood.

He opened her class book to several previously assigned pages and gestured. "These basic mathematics, Miss Parker. What did you make of them?"

"The geometry I understood more than all the rest, Professor." She produced the corresponding homework, a piece of paper with a few numbers and scribbles a lesser mathematician might construe as equations.

The professor peered at the paper, grimaced and hastily penned over the entire page. "It would seem that the geometric problem was the single thing you managed to answer correctly, Miss Parker. As for the rest of your answers, they might as well be one of your foreign tongues." He furrowed his brow over a particular notation. "I assure you, I speak all forms of mathematics but the one you've created here."

"I was afraid you might say as much, sir."

The professor spent the next half hour attempting to explain where Percy had gone wrong in her figures, and to discern at which step she had lost her way. At long last he sat back in his chair, put his fingers to the bridge of his nose and gave a sigh. Percy drew her scarf about her cheeks, trying to hide from both his regard and her own shame.

"Miss Parker, now it is I who cannot understand." The professor spoke in an even tone. "You are quite adept with language. Mathematics is a language. Look at these rules, and think of them as if they were the same as conjugating a verb. Think of these symbols as if they are simply a foreign alphabet!"

"I've tried, sir," she cried. "I understand how to read the formula, and I can translate, partially, but it's in the wrong tense. I could list every element in the pyramid chart on the wall behind you, but if you were to ask me how to configure a compound, I'd be at a loss."

Professor Rychman sighed and rose from his chair. He turned to the fire behind him and muttered irritably in what seemed to be an archaic tongue. What was it? All Percy knew was that, after a moment, the words became clear: *"None shall weave of my teaching who cannot first grasp a thread. And why am I wasting my time when there's so much else to be done?"*

In response, Percy raised her eyebrows and replied in the same long-dead language, *"One must* wish *to weave if she is to excel at the loom. But if you've more important work, Professor, is there a way I may be of assistance?"*

The professor faced her, amazed. His expression quickly returned to its usual cold and careless façade, but not before Percy's heart missed a beat. "You are a linguist indeed, Miss Parker. Aramaic. Impressive. I spoke hastily, in a language I assumed you would not know, and I have been proven a fool."

Delighted with herself, Percy fought back a smile. "My apologies, Professor—and I'd never call you a fool. But," she added sheepishly, "if you wish to mutter something secret, I suggest sticking to a Chinese dialect. I'm quite insufficient in Mandarin, for example."

The professor smiled. "I'll bear that in mind, Miss Parker. Tell me again how you learned so many languages while behind convent walls."

Percy shrugged. "I wish I could explain, sir. But they just come to me, like the melodies of long-forgotten songs."

"Interesting, indeed." He gestured to her assignment. "I can only hope the meaning of mathematics is similarly long forgotten, yet waiting to be discovered. *¿Comprende?*"

"Sí, señor."

"Versteht?"

"Ja, Herr Rychman."

The professor set his jaw. "I suppose I could continue to ask, and you'd continue to understand, wouldn't you?"

"Oui, monsieur."

"Every tongue except mathematics."

"I'm afraid not, sir. Forgive me."

"I expect all those problems finished to the best of your ability," he commanded abruptly, pointing to a new page in her text.

"Of course, Professor. Thank you."

"You're very welcome. Good evening, Miss Parker."

"Do svidaniya," Percy replied.

The professor's ears perked up and a smile toyed at the corner of his mouth. "My grandmother was a Russian immigrant," he admitted, looking as if he had found something long misplaced. "I've not heard a word of that language in many, many years. It is a beautiful sound, and I thank you for it. Good night, lady of all lands."

Feeling a little silly but nonetheless pleased, Percy blushed, gave a tiny wave and scurried out the door.

UNABLE TO SLEEP FOR NERVES, PERCY TOOK TO THE LIBRARY TO DIVE into the company of her dearest friends: books. She shouldn't have been in the library at Apollo Hall at such an hour, it was against the rules, but Miss Jennings was frankly scared of her and let her come and go as she pleased. As if she were a ghost. And, Percy confessed to herself with a little thrill, the idea that she was in the same building as Professor Rychman, whose candelabras she'd seen lit from the courtyard window, produced a titillating effect. She wondered what he was reading, thinking, doing . . .

A book about Newton's deterministic universe lay open at her fingertips. She'd been hoping a grand theory might crack open the mysteries of mathematics. The theory was fascinating, the calculations daunting.

The librarian, an elegantly featured, black-skinned woman, was shutting down and trimming the lights at her desk. From the corner of her eye, Percy saw the woman—Percy hadn't had the courage to introduce herself and so did not know the other's name—take note of her presence at a back table. The librarian abruptly straightened up and gasped. Percy flushed. She'd removed her accoutrements due to the lateness of the hour, but now hastily put on her glasses. Perhaps she was less frightening that way?

"I'm sorry, Madame Librarian, I'm sure I'm well past a reasonable time . . . I . . . couldn't sleep." Percy stood. "I'm Percy Parker, I'm fairly new here."

The librarian was dressed in a modest, freshly pressed dress, her black hair pinned tightly beneath a sensible dark bonnet. She smiled, her brown cheeks dimpling.

"No, miss, it is I who should apologize. I thought you were . . ."

"A ghost," Percy finished. She'd heard that phrase so often. "It's understandable."

The librarian came closer. "Of all the things," she said softly, her tone rueful. "Of all the things a woman like me ought never do is react to a person's skin color as if it were shocking."

Percy blinked. Then she smiled. Perhaps there *were* oases in Athens, places where she could be on some level understood. Certainly a woman such as this had withstood plenty.

"I am Miss Mina Wilberforce," the woman offered. "Pleasure to meet you, Miss Parker."

"Wilberforce?" Percy breathed. Such a famous name, that: the man who had ended English slavery.

Mina grinned. "No relation. But I decided I'd take the name of an emancipator rather than any from a master."

Percy grinned back. "Brilliant."

"Shall I leave you to your studies? I can't get enough of these books. I think a woman should read every one that's ever been written. So you've got a deal of work to do, Miss Parker. Just drop the latch on your way out."

"Thank you, Miss Wilberforce."

"Mina, please. And if you ever get tired of the harsh stares, come sit with me, we'll stare at each other, unflinching, for a good long while."

Percy laughed. Mina turned and shut the door behind her.

Buoyant, Percy went back to her studies and didn't notice the sudden chill on the air, nor the pale hovering figure beside her, until it spoke. "Ah, Newton . . ." cooed a wispy, feminine voice.

Percy jumped slightly. She looked up to find a young woman much like herself in both pallor and age, but with the distinct difference that this young woman was transparent and floating. The female spirit glided backward, obviously startled to see Percy's eyes meet hers.

"Yes, I can see and hear you," Percy clarified, familiar with the reaction. Many spirits spoke to mortals. Few received a reply.

"Indeed! Most exciting!" exclaimed the specter. Tightly spiraled curls floated about a face cherubic save for dark, sunken circles around the eyes. The frayed dress was dated; the open neck of the gown hung loose on a frail frame. "My name is Constance."

"Hello, Constance. I'm Percy."

The two girls nodded, knowing they could not take hands.

"Percy? That's a woman's name, is it?" the spirit asked.

Percy smiled. "It stands for something ancient."

"You do not look a bit ancient."

"Well, I'm not," Percy admitted.

"But you do look like one of us. How did you learn to see my kind?"

"I've always had the ability," Percy explained. "But I've dared not speak of it, else I'd be thought mad."

Constance batted Percy's stack of books with a hand that passed right through. "Mortals know nothing," she scoffed. "I thought I knew everything when I sat at that table. On the other side, you realize how little you really know."

"Really?" Percy breathed.

"Indeed. I now know the most important lesson: Not everything can be explained. When I was alive, I thought I understood the whole of science, life, God . . . Went quite mad because of it."

"Is that why you travel this hall?" Percy asked.

"My body lies in a tiny plot behind. I come into this room looking for something"—Constance made one floating turn around the table—"but I cannot, for the death of me, recall what I seek. Here I drift, looking for a once-insignificant item that now means peace."

"And you think you'll find it in this hall?"

"I spent inordinate amounts of time here when the academy first opened, years ago," the ghost explained. "It was the first in the area to let young women attend a full curriculum. My family disowned me when I told them I wished to become a scientist. No daughter of theirs would become educated beyond eligibility, doomed to a field meant only for men! I was a revolutionary, here by the grace of the founder . . ." Constance trailed off. "Ah, well. I shall keep looking. I don't have much choice." Her hollow face took on a hopeless expression and she glanced around, her ethereal curls quivering in a nonexistent breeze. "Perhaps it's over there," she murmured, beginning to fade.

"I hope you find whatever you seek, Constance."

The spirit looked Percy in the eyes. "Same to you, Percy of the spirit flesh." The ghost brightened, as if an afterthought increased her link to the world of the living. "And do be careful. London is going absolutely mad."

Percy shivered. "How so?"

Constance failed to answer; she simply disappeared. The lamp grew brighter and the air warmer.

Percy gave a yawn, closed Newton, and turned down the lamp.

Moonlight fell in great pearly slabs against the bookshelves as she made her way to the library door, which clicked softly shut behind her. Percy slipped through the darkened corridors of Apollo Hall and back to her bed. Despite all that she'd learned, she knew exactly what would occupy her dreams until morning. It wouldn't be ghosts or mathematics or Newton's deterministic universe, but something—some*one*—infinitely more corporeal.

"The Groundskeeper reports destabilization. Shall I go and see for myself? I've an idea where to find them," the servant of shadow stated, her toe on the threshold between the eternal and the mundane, listening from a portal she'd made by the pricking of her thumbs. Her blood made a map upon her hand, directing her. "Do let me go!"

The Darkness shook and roared. "Go! For the love of the Unholy, go already!"

"You don't have to be such a brute about it." The woman made a fierce face and turned in a huff toward the portal. "You'd be wise to respect my powers."

With her bloody finger, she smeared droplets onto her collarbone, then dragged a clean hand across the gray, ashy grit of the Whisper-world interior and pressed it to her bosom. A hissing, rattling sound echoed about her head as she breathed life into the blood and grime. When she lifted her hand again, a silver pendant with a bloodred ruby hung at the swell of her breasts. She raised her arms, fingertips still dripping blood, and the mists of the Whisper-world responded to her bidding. With another hissing rattle and a swirl of death's miasma, her garb transformed from Whisper-world winding-sheets into a tailored satin bodice and elaborate skirts of the latest human style.

Swishing through the portal into a cobblestone alley, the mouth of which opened onto a promenade over the Thames, Darkness's best asset turned to his shadowed form. "You know, you'd best be nice to me. Or I'll switch sides and join *their* fight instead!"

The shadows grunted. "You wouldn't dare."

The woman narrowed emerald eyes. "Are you threatening me? I'd advise against that. You'd best consider a promotion, too. Minor Arcana status? I'm far too talented not to be better recognized. If you knew what was best for you, you'd replace her with me."

Darkness roared, but the servant expected it and did not flinch.

"Treat me better, or I *will* turn on you. It's high time I was important to someone." She turned to the cityscape before her. "Hello, London, what a pleasure it is to descend upon you as the herald of your dark age to come."

CHAPTER
TEN

JOSEPHINE ARRIVED AT THE TABLE WITH SEVERAL GLASSES OF RED wine. She tousled Elijah's hair and mimed a kiss—but only when her friends weren't looking.

It wasn't that fraternization within the Guard was prohibited, of course. There were several miserable triangles of unrequited affection, at the very least. Elijah and Josephine had simply decided to love each other in private.

Just as Elijah was about to reach around and give Josephine a surreptitious but deliciously inappropriate pat, Alexi whisked in through the door of the café, his black robes swirling, and halted the frivolous chatter of his friends with one quiet question. "I don't suppose any of you has seen a door?"

The group blinked up at him.

"You mean a portal?" Michael clarified.

"Of course I mean a portal," Alexi snapped.

"No. Why? Whom have you met?" Rebecca asked. Everyone looked at her, unable to mistake her sharp tone.

Alexi held up a hand. "Don't be hasty, Rebecca. It's nothing. I'm simply on guard," he explained. "As we all should be." He seated himself, then fidgeted. "At our last meeting in the chapel I assumed we'd get some sort of help or direction, but . . ."

Michael laughed. "I gave up hope of ever seeing that goddess again years ago." Only Rebecca noticed the flash of profound sorrow that passed over Alexi's face.

Elijah leaned forward, pulling a gold-plated notebook from his vest pocket. "Now that you mention it, *I'm* adding a name to our list."

Alexi raised an eyebrow. "You think you've met a candidate?"

Lord Withersby smiled. "My dear professor, I just saw the incomparable Ellen Terry play Lady Macbeth." He placed a dramatic hand over the sumptuous silk of his breast pocket. "She brought the Lyceum to its knees. She channeled raw power. The spirits trembled. *I* trembled. I'm sure she could do wonders with us. Even if not, we'd get a hell of a performance."

Alexi grimaced as he stared at the list before him on the table, the notebook of candidates with nothing to recommend them but either beauty, prominence, or sham spiritualist credentials; every one had been a failure, at least to his mind. "Come now, Elijah, we considered and crossed Queen Victoria off our list. You truly think an actress, however talented, will prove to be our seventh?"

Getting a private audience with Her Royal Highness had been a feat Lord Elijah Withersby had been able to manage only because the poor woman was hysterical, desperate to see her dear Albert on the other side. Alexi had apologized, explaining that it wasn't their job to reunite the living and the dead, even for royalty. As with everyone else they interviewed, the Guard had been forced to wipe Her Royal Highness's memory clean, and they had departed a bit more worried about the Crown than ever before.

"I daresay, Terry is a visionary," Elijah promised, penning the name in bold strokes at the bottom of the list. "I'll try to obtain a private audience with her soon."

Josephine eyed him, then turned to the Guard's leader. "You must admit it's thrilling to consider, Alexi. Why *shouldn't* Prophecy be famous?"

Alexi simply shook his head. "It's not *that*. But . . . one would think none of you sees any excitement of your own. Chasing celebrities and actresses—"

"We can't, the lot of us, be above everything like you, Alexi. We must take our pleasures when they're thrown at us . . . or must try to get in their way," remarked Elijah.

"Above everything?" Rebecca scoffed. "Please. Don't encourage him. He already thinks himself omniscient. Omnipotent. Tortured."

Alexi rose from the table, long folds of black fabric rustling. He offered his companions both an expression of pity and the comment, "How little you all understand."

"Of course we don't," Elijah mocked. "Only you do. Only you ever have." The others laughed, albeit nervously.

"If you're all so brilliant, discern Prophecy," Alexi snapped. "Oh, but *do* be looking for a door while you're out chasing actresses. Don't forget that. Remember, a door's the one sign we were given. I doubt it'll be a stage door." With those words, he made a grand, sweeping exit—while Elijah hummed a bit of Beethoven in his wake.

"He couldn't have been *truly* offended," Josephine tittered once the door shut behind him.

"If he didn't maintain such an absurd stoicism, we'd have nothing to tease him about. And then how would he know we care?" Rebecca smiled suddenly, thinking of something else, something from long ago. "You know, our dear professor wasn't always as omniscient and omnipotent as he now pretends. There was a time when he was just learning. Michael, would you like to tell this, or shall I?"

Grinning, the vicar gestured for her to continue.

"We weren't yet fifteen when Alexi started first experimenting with alchemy, thinking his powers granted him insights beyond the texts and treatises he'd already devoured. So there he was, hovering over an array of powders, books, and bottles when Michael and I came to escort him to a meeting. Flowers were bound by metal clamps at the center of the room. He was muttering things, swirling fingers in the powder. He gestured to the flowers . . . and the stone wall opposite him burst into flame. Poor Michael nearly lost what little mustache he was trying to cultivate!"

The company chuckled as Rebecca continued. "Alexi cursed and the fire extinguished itself, leaving a charred wall. Best of all, though, bits of exploded flower landed on his head and he didn't notice. Alexi said—in that voice of his, mind you, while wearing a crown of daisy petals—'Bloody hell, I'll never be able to explain *that* to the help.'"

The table rang with laughter—a sound that bound the group together through happiness and strife. Michael's hand, shaking with his guffaws, found Rebecca's, and the shared amusement made all the Guard feel for just a moment as if they were once again young.

OUT ON THE STREET, ALEXI PAUSED WHEN HE HEARD LAUGHTER from inside La Belle et La Bête. As was often the case these days, he was not included, and he couldn't help but fear that he had nothing to look forward to but an empty life of spectral policing until his body or mind gave out. Perhaps Prophecy was all a lie, a carrot to keep the Guard trotting along in a life of service with no reward. He felt like a failing actor who no longer believed his own lines.

One of the neighborhood spirits was acting up, but Alexi had no desire to give chase. He was contemplating ignoring it altogether when he bumped shoulders with a cloaked figure moving quickly in the opposite direction.

"Oh!" the figure exclaimed, with a feminine gasp. The hood of her cloak fell back to reveal the most beautiful woman he had ever seen. The woman and Alexi both stopped and stared at each other. After a moment Alexi recovered himself, bowed and tipped his hat.

"Don't I know you?" the woman breathed. Her perfectly coiffed, raven black hair glinted blue in the falling twilight and her green eyes sparkled with mystery. A fine gemstone glittered, a focal point, against smooth decolletage.

Alexi's heart faltered, for he remembered the words of his goddess. She had hoped they would know each other instantly. But . . . there was nothing here beyond recognition of someone of note. "Pardon me, miss. I don't believe we've met. I am Professor Alexi Rychman."

The woman blinked and seemed to recover herself. "Of course. Do forgive me, Professor. You merely reminded me . . ." She shook her head. "Ah, I grow distracted. My name is Miss Linden, and I've only just arrived unaccompanied in the city. I know how that must seem to a gentleman, a man of letters such as you. Please forgive my desperate air, but do you have any idea where I might find shelter? I . . ." Her voice broke. "I'm sorry, but I . . . I am escaping something terrible." There was a pause. The woman's emerald green eyes shimmered with tears.

Alexi ruminated. His goddess had said the prophesied seventh would need refuge. He needed to entertain that idea.

"I am aggrieved to hear it, Miss Linden. Might I recommend this very café before you?" He gestured to La Belle. "I know the owner and clientele well. Though you are in trouble, I know it to be a place of safety."

Miss Linden looked immediately relieved. "Thank you, kind Professor. But, were you just leaving?"

"Yes, I . . . I have work I must attend to."

"Of course. And thank you." She smiled demurely. "Perhaps we shall cross paths again."

Alexi chose not to respond to that, no matter the temptation. "You are welcome. Good evening, Miss Linden." He bowed and stalked off, fighting the urge to glance back. He was used to ignoring such urges. He didn't like what had begun wrestling within him, the breathless anticipation that Prophecy was surely drawing nigh, mixed with the deep discomfort of the unknown.

His racing blood calmed after he'd walked the whole of Covent Garden and circled Bloomsbury. Until there was a critical mass of prophetic evidence, he could not allow his thoughts or sentiments to run ahead. There was no margin for error, not when one was blessed or cursed with his fate. Mortal hearts were known to make mistakes, but he would make none.

The door of the café opened, and a woman entered whom none of the Guard would ever forget. She pulled back the hood of her cloak with shaking hands, revealing a beautiful face creased with worry. She looked up, met Josephine's welcoming gaze, and offered a strained smile. Elijah and Michael both stood, bowing slightly. She nodded to each in turn, and took a few steps inside.

Josephine, as hostess, attended the new guest. "Mademoiselle, welcome to La Belle et La Bête! I am Mademoiselle Belledoux, proprietor." She collected the newcomer's cloak and placed it in an alcove nearby.

With raven black curls piled delicately atop her head, she was truly a vision, a beauty clad in a mixture of deep crimson velvet and satin brocade. A slender gloved hand flew to the gem at her bosom. Her emerald eyes glowed, warm and hopeful.

"Greetings, mademoiselle. Forgive my intrusion, but I, seeking refuge, was sent here by the kind professor I just met outside."

"*Kind?*" Elijah snorted. Rebecca elbowed him.

"We are honored that you take refuge here," Josephine was swift in welcome. "Please, have a seat. What may I procure for you this early evening, mademoiselle? Tea, perhaps? Or"—Josephine leaned in—"we have been known to tempt royalty with our special cabernet."

The woman smiled. "How can I refuse?"

"Compliments of the house, mademoiselle!" Elijah stated, rising from the table. Josephine flashed him a glare, but he simply beamed at her in response.

The newcomer's lips curved into a wide smile. "Why, thank you, sir! What a relief to find a haven in such an out-of-the-way place."

Elijah hurried to settle her at a table. "Please allow me to introduce myself. Lord Elijah Withersby, miss, at your service." When the woman offered it, Elijah took and gave her satin-gloved hand a kiss.

"Miss Lucille Linden. A pleasure to make your acquaintance, Lord Withersby."

"And may I introduce my esteemed colleagues? Miss Rebecca Thompson, Mr. Michael Carroll, and that French tart fetching your wine is—"

"My mutually esteemed colleague, Lord Withersby, curb your heathen tongue or I'll not hesitate to remove it," Josephine called from the cellar stair.

Rebecca also scowled at Elijah before she turned to address the newcomer. "Please forgive Lord Withersby. He ought not be allowed out in polite society, for reasons which should be clearly evident to a lady such as yourself."

"Terribly sorry, Miss Linden. I *am* a cad," Elijah admitted. He paused a moment before grinning wickedly. Rebecca and Josephine both shook their heads.

Miss Linden brimmed with amusement. "So it would seem, Lord Withersby. A scandal to your class."

"Thank heavens I'm a second son and my family's all abroad, else I believe I'd have been shipped off to some tedious war somewhere rather than slumming about in this tedious city," Elijah said with a casual wave.

Josephine set one glass of wine before her guest, kept a glass for herself and raised it. "To new acquaintances! Not many fresh faces find us here, but when they do, they are always welcome."

"I too shall raise a glass!" Elijah cried.

"Pity you don't have one, Lord Withersby," his secret mistress replied; and she and the newcomer shared an innately feminine smile as they toasted and sipped the bloodred liquid.

"I offer you my sincerest appreciation, my new friends!" Miss Linden exclaimed. But then her hand rose to her throat again, and she leaned forward, her beautiful face clouded with worry. "May I call you friends? To be honest, I am in most desperate need of them. I realize this is a great imposition after so short an acquaintance, but . . . I need to hide."

"From the law?" Vicar Carroll asked. He was determined to be careful. They couldn't have the law snooping about, not if they intended to continue their Grand Work unhindered.

"No. From a . . . beast of a man," she said at last.

"Your husband?"

"Of sorts. My Lord . . . He's—oh, I do not wish to bore you with my unfortunate, improbable details. I've lived a strange life. You'd not believe me were I to explain."

"You might be surprised," Elijah suggested. Rebecca gave him a warning glance.

Miss Linden raised an eyebrow. "I need shelter," she explained after a moment. "I cannot go to my family; he'll know where to find me. I have to throw myself upon others' kindness and wait out this terrible storm. Any suggestions you may have I would deeply appreciate."

Josephine looked at Elijah, Michael, and Rebecca before returning her gaze to Lucille. She seemed to come to a decision. "There is a room two floors above. You may call it your own, so long as you don't bring the law or your master's wrath down upon us. We are a secretive group but kind. You need pay only what you can afford—if that is anything at all."

Tears filled the newcomer's eyes. "Bless you. Bless all of you! My new life begins," she murmured. She unclasped the silver chain and passed the deep red ruby to Josephine. "Take this, please, as I don't know how long I shall stay and I cannot impose upon you without offering something in return."

Josephine held the gem in her palm, the silver chain dripping from between her fingers. The others leaned toward the stone as if seeing something in a scrying glass. The breathless moment of anticipation faded as Josephine closed her hand and dreamily replied, "Indeed, this shall be safeguarded."

Miss Linden smiled. "Wonderful. But now, you must forgive me again. This may seem frightfully forward, but as my life has come undone at the very seams I have little to lose. Tell me more about your professor." As Elijah began to chuckle, Miss Linden's face flushed. She hurried to add, "Perhaps I spoke too hastily. I—"

"Professor Alexi Rychman," Elijah interrupted. "Our master of ceremonies, minister of revels, our melancholy Prince of Denmark."

Michael failed to contain a chuckle. Miss Linden appeared confused.

Rebecca stepped forward. "I am truly sorry, Miss Linden. Our ill breeding again rears its ugly head. We can beg only the excuse of weariness and the trying fact that we've spent far, far too long with one another. Please forgive us."

"I think you're charming," Miss Linden assured them, as if their particular quirks were nothing out of the ordinary. "Clearly, this Professor Rychman is a friend of yours."

"Like it or not, he's stuck with us," Elijah agreed.

Miss Linden smiled. "Well, forgive my boldness, but I am glad. I hope to see him again. There are few into whose path I would rather again be cast."

"Indeed?" Rebecca said.

"Indeed." Miss Linden's eyes glittered warmly as she took another sip of cabernet.

Elijah turned to Rebecca, clearly surprised, mouthing the words, "Placed in our path?"

Rebecca's lips became a grim line. The blood in her veins murmured, churning up her instincts at the introduction of this new and beautiful face. Miss Linden had indeed been placed in their path, seeking refuge.

CHAPTER
ELEVEN

PERCY'S LATEST RECURRENT VISION WAS A HAZY ONE WHERE SHE WAS standing in the middle of a circle, surrounded by shafts of light. Music—inhuman, beautiful, incomprehensible—was everywhere, inside her and out, and lingered on in faint strains throughout the day.

Once Percy roused from the vision to find Professor Rychman snapping his fingers in front of her face. She started, fumbled an apology, wrung her hands. "Oh, Professor! I've no d-doubt that your patience for me is at an end," she stammered. "But I swear on my life that I listen to your every word and—"

The professor sighed. "Miss Parker, I wish you felt more at ease here. If you did, you might take to things with more surety."

"I am, sir. At ease, I mean. Well, I . . . Oh, dear." Feeling a fool, she looked away.

"At ease. Indeed?"

Percy folded her hands upon the desk. "I suppose not. Forgive my timidity. It undermines any hope I have for collected composure."

"Your composure, Miss Parker, is nearly regal," he replied. "That is, it would be if you stopped hiding."

Percy blinked through her glasses at him. "Hiding?"

"With your shrouds and your shields I cannot tell when you comprehend what I say. It is common knowledge that the eyes are the window to the soul, but your windows are shuttered. What they have to say has been muted."

"But sir, the sun, the light—"

"Does the sun shine here, Miss Parker? You told me you were comfortable."

"Well, I am, sir. This room is perfect but, outside, people stare and—"

The professor interrupted without pity or pause. "Do you include me in that number, Miss Parker? I would hope you realize that I have more important things to do than gawk as if you were a museum piece." He leveled his gaze at her.

"Of course, sir," Percy replied. "Of course I realize that."

"I call it hiding," the professor repeated.

Percy let out a brief sigh, knowing she had no choice but to muster a bit of courage. She feared his reaction more than she could say, but he left no other option. "Very well, sir," she remarked with quiet resolution. She rose from her chair, turned her back to him, and began to remove her barriers.

She had not realized the entirety of the feeling of security they gave until she was confronted with their removal. After her careful hands removed glasses, gloves, and long scarf, Percy felt naked. Vulnerable. *Indecent.* Yet, she reminded herself, it had not been her idea to lower her defenses. If the professor was to be disgusted—which was her greatest fear—it was through no fault of her own.

The thought brought no comfort.

TRESSES OF LUSTROUS, SNOW-WHITE HAIR TUMBLED FROM THEIR CLOTH-bound imprisonment, streaming like snowfall down the girl's back. In an effort to make his student more at ease, Alexi did his best to appear wholly disinterested as she carefully removed her protections with delicate, private ceremony. Then she turned to face him, clutching those items that had held her unusual features in mystery.

"As you would have it so, Professor, here is your pupil in all her ghastliness." Though Miss Parker's hands clearly trembled, her voice did not.

His furrowed, generally disapproving brow rose slightly as he leaned back in his chair and took her in. Luminous crystal eyes held streaks of pale blue shooting from tiny black pupils. A face youthful but devoid of color, smooth and unblemished like porcelain, was as graceful, well defined, and proportioned as a marble statue. Her long, blanched locks shimmered in the candlelight like spider silk. Upon high cheekbones lay hints of rouge—any more would have appeared garish against her blindingly white skin, but she had been artful in her application. Her rosebud lips were tinted in the same manner.

She was attuned to even the most minuscule response. Her merci-less, hypnotic gaze found his and she frowned. "You see, Professor, even you, so stern and stoic, cannot hide your shock, surprise, distaste—"

"Distaste?" he interrupted quietly. "Is that what you see?"

IF PERCY HAD TAKEN THE TIME TO TRULY CONSIDER HIS RESPONSE, she would have noticed that his tone was far from distasteful; it was, in fact, flattering. But she plowed on, choosing hurt. "What else can one feel when they behold living flesh that looks dead?"

"You assume ghost and not angel?"

Those words, uttered in regard to herself, made Percy's heart con-vulse. Surely he could not have intended a compliment? "I . . . I would never presume to liken myself to anything heavenly, Professor."

"Indeed? Then it would seem that you, Miss Parker, are more modest than I." If there had been an admiring look in his eye, it was quickly gone. The professor blandly donned his glasses. "Now, come take your seat. No more hiding, not in this office. Never again."

"That is still your wish?" Percy asked.

"It is."

Percy put down her things with a sigh. But as the lesson continued, she began to relax, seeing that he looked at her with no other quality but the expectation of fastidious attention. Once his lecture was com-plete, she was excused with an assignment and a curt nod. Percy donned her scarf, her gloves, and her glasses with delicate deliberation, prepar-ing to walk out again into the world. But halfway to the door after bidding the professor a quiet farewell, books in hand, she stopped and turned around.

The professor, busying himself at his desk, could evidently feel the weight of her stare; he looked up after a moment. "Yes, Miss Parker?"

"Thank you, Professor."

"For what?"

"You are . . . the only man who has not made me feel as if I were on display."

The professor blinked, his face expressionless. "You are a student and not an exhibit, Miss Parker. Good day."

Percy curtseyed in response. Exiting the office, she wasn't sure she'd ever been so happy.

* * *

As soon as the door closed behind Miss Parker, Alexi opened a drawer, withdrew his notebook, and hurled it onto his desk. His pen flew. He did not allow himself to think of the implications of what he wrote or the previously unknown anxiety that was building inside.

"Miss Parker," he said aloud as he wrote. "A ghost? Not my goddess in colors, but in fact the mirror opposite. Colorless. And yet, uniquely beautiful. Could her ghostly yet angelic appearance be a warning? Is she to be trusted or avoided? Why am I not dismissing her entirely, as I ought? She is a *student*! Why dare I even consider her?

"More the goddess is that ineffable Miss Linden, with her own clues, all those familiar words . . . And yet I sense in Miss Parker a gentleness similar to my goddess of two decades past. Which of them is the true seventh—if either? Neither gentleness nor beauty, no matter how unusual, fulfills Prophecy!"

He slammed the book closed, knowing the fate of the world rested on his shoulders.

"I've found them. I'm Lucille Linden now. Isn't that a lovely name?" the servant of shadow said proudly, having crossed the threshold back home. She spun, appreciating the rustle of her fine, blood-colored dress, the exotic sculpting of her body beneath her corset, the absurdity of her bustle, the useless but fashionable layers of doubled skirts.

Darkness growled. "Why. Do. They. Live?"

"Come now!" Lucille smiled broadly. "Let me have a bit of fun. One of them in particular I want to toy with. How I've missed mortal games. I gave them my pendant, which binds them to me. In the stone is a breath of their future, for it comes from this place, into which all must pass when it comes their time . . . I've charmed the place where they offered me rooms, and while they are no fools and I must weave my wiles with careful subtlety, I am confident of my success in wooing them."

"Is she *with* them?"

"No. I've not seen her. Or anything like her. Perhaps she's abandoned them, too—just like she did you." She couldn't help pointing this out, and shrugged when Darkness growled. "Oh, *stop*. I'm sure she'll be along soon; she can never stay away. She's so pathetically predictable."

"Don't be long," Darkness commanded.

Lucille waved a languid hand. "Remember my warning. I want to be important. For that reason, I shall take the time I please, enjoy my games and make my own choices, thank you very much. I don't see that you have much alternative, my *lord*."

CHAPTER

TWELVE

REACHING INTO ONE OF HIS OFFICE'S MYRIAD HIDING PLACES, ALEXI withdrew a small wooden container and handed it to Josephine. Opening the lid, she saw sealed vials of colored powder that shimmered in the fading light. Her slender fingers closed protectively around the box. Alexi's alchemical study hadn't been for naught. He'd found a way to transfer blue fire directly into paint pigment, which the Guard's artist employed upon her ethereal canvases.

"Use it sparingly," he cautioned. "It's a powerful mixture this time. I eagerly await your creation, Josie. I expect it to be ravishing."

There was a knock upon the door.

"Come."

A slender figure entered the room, shawl draped around her bowed head as if she were votaress for a goddess. Per the professor's request, she threw back her wrap and removed her dark glasses.

"Ah, Miss Parker!" Alexi boomed.

The figure jumped, smiling nervously at the professor before her gaze riveted upon his lovely companion in her impeccable gown. Josephine was taken aback by the appearance of this unparalleled girl, and she gasped at the sight of those unearthly, crystalline eyes.

The girl shoved her tinted glasses back onto her face, tossed her shawl over her head, and turned to the professor with a strained expression, as if he had betrayed her. "Forgive me, Professor, I did not mean to interrupt—" She choked, stealing another furtive glance at his ravishing companion before moving toward the door.

"No, no," Alexi assured her. "I'm completing a matter of business. Miss Parker, this is Mademoiselle Josephine Belledoux, an esteemed colleague of mine. Josephine, this is Miss . . ." He hesitated, realizing he did not know how to continue. He did not know her first name.

"Percy," she supplied.

"Thank you. Miss *Percy* Parker, one of my students."

"*Enchantée, mademoiselle.*" Josephine bowed her head.

"*Moi aussi, enchantée, mademoiselle.*"

"*Ah, français!*" Josephine beamed, basking in the warmth of her native language.

"Miss Parker is adept at many tongues," Alexi explained.

Percy gazed ruefully at the floor. "Unfortunately my talent doesn't apply to mathematics." Contemplating the presence of this other woman in Professor Rychman's office, her heart faltered.

"That's quite all right, Miss Parker," Josephine said softly. "Personally, I detest mathematics and all sciences. So I paint."

"Oh?" Percy looked at this woman who was surely years older than she, yet showed no sign of age apart from the two white streaks of hair that framed her face. The rest of her dark, shining locks were swept into an elaborate knot.

"It would seem, Miss Belledoux, that you two are of like minds. Miss Parker would rather sketch her dreams than pay attention in class."

Percy cringed.

"Can you blame the young lady?" the Frenchwoman replied.

The professor ignored his friend's smile, gesturing broadly to the south wall and speaking for Percy's edification. "My paintings are Miss Belledoux's own, and I am in the process of commissioning a new piece."

"Your work is captivating, mademoiselle," Percy breathed, looking around.

"*Je vous remercie.*"

"Miss Belledoux, I must now uphold my duty as Prometheus, bearing the torch of education to darkened minds," the professor declared.

Josephine raised an eyebrow. "Well, aren't we grand?" She bowed and moved to the door, giving Percy a knowing grin. "Don't let him fool you into thinking he bears any such light," she whispered. "It's been nothing but darkness for ages."

Percy couldn't help but respond to the other's warmth and the two women shared a smile.

"Excuse me!" The professor shook his head and glowered. "There will be no slander in this shrine of knowledge!"

"All right, he's brilliant," Josephine offered, but she winked as she opened the door to the hall. "But his social graces leave something to be desired."

"Out, I say!"

"*Au revoir!*" And with a carefree laugh, the Frenchwoman disappeared.

"Infidels, every one of them," the professor muttered, gesturing for Percy to sit.

"Who?"

The professor sighed, irritated, searching for his pen. "My colleagues. Social graces? Ha! I hope you're ready to learn something."

"Certainly."

"You've forgotten," the professor remarked, gesturing.

"Oh." Percy removed her shawl again. Sliding her glasses from her face, she steeled herself for the brief flash of distaste she was so accustomed to seeing. But the professor launched directly into his lesson without a moment's pause, never once shying away from the sight of her. He hadn't changed, and the fact filled her with joy.

Though she attempted to pay attention as Professor Rychman began his lecture, when Percy glimpsed an open book at the corner of his desk, she could not resist leaning over to see what her teacher had been reading. It was a volume of Shakespeare; the margins bore the professor's notes and scribbles.

"Miss Parker, what now . . . ?" the professor said, obviously noticing that she had lost focus. "Oh. *Hamlet?*"

"I promise I was listening, sir. It's just that this play is my favorite."

"I acquiesce," he muttered to himself. "The grip of this mathematical theory is not to be regained. And so, if nothing else, I'll commend your theatrical taste. Have you heard of the recent production in town where Hamlet marries Ophelia at the end?"

Percy's jaw dropped. "*What?!*"

"I suppose this day and age cannot be trusted with a good tragedy. So you do not approve?"

"Of course not, Professor! I hope you'd give me that much credit!"

"As a professed Romantic, I wasn't entirely sure."

Percy rallied a meek rebuttal. "I have standards, Professor."

"Indeed? Well, get out of my office before I raise your standard of attention. I may have even had you for fifteen minutes before you wandered off."

"Professor, I assure you that I always listen—"

He shrugged. "Never mind, I have work to do. I must go home and gather my wits for a whole night of study. I have a ride ahead of me." But as the professor shooed her from his desk, his face seized with a flash of discomfort. His hand flew to his temple.

"Professor, are you all right, sir?"

"As my 'social graces leave something to be desired,' will you be so kind as to see yourself out? Good evening, Miss Parker," he replied, clutching his forehead.

Realizing he wanted her companionship no longer, Percy rushed out. "Good evening, Professor, do feel better." She tried to shake him from her mind but it was a matter as difficult as grasping mathematics.

THE FEMALE CALLING HERSELF LUCILLE LINDEN LEANED OUT THE window of the tiny room she'd graciously accepted above La Belle et La Bête. Her new friends were dining below, in a room decorated by bouquets of flowers marked with her preternatural scent. She'd spent midnight hours at labor, creating the subtle perfume she hoped would became their favorite odor, further binding them to her. They would regard her as a staple of their community without much question.

Feigning illness, she had declined the group's generous invitation to join them for the meal. Instead, she stared out over London's sooty, dirty rooftops; her body thrilled at the game to come.

A growl sounded, and she turned to see a cloud of horror awaiting direction. "Go ahead," she said.

The cloud turned tail and dove through the roof. There came a cry from below, and then the voices of Lord Withersby, Miss Thompson, Mr. Carroll, and Miss Connor. The foursome sounded afraid but determined. There were the continued noises of a fracas.

Lucille grinned, her mouth watering. "Listen to them play!" she crowed.

A knock on her door interrupted her pleasure. "Miss Linden," a strained voice called out, "it's Josephine. There's an intruder down below so you must lock yourself in. The gentlemen are taking care of him, all right?"

"Yes, yes, of course," Lucille replied, ducking inside and feigning innocence.

She appreciated the illusion they were trying to maintain. They assumed, of course, that she had no idea of their true nature. They also assumed that she was a harmless, powerless young woman. It suited her to have them remain ignorant for the moment.

An infernal thing the likes of which the Guard had never seen descended upon their table. Snarling, horrific, snapping teeth in their faces and shredding tablecloths, the abomination was a huge cloud of black smog that became one dog and then one hundred, a chimerical, shifting creature that was at one instant incorporeal, at the next something deadly with claws, jaws, and horrible, red eyes, and then a cloud again, impossible to catch.

"What in God's name is this?" Rebecca shrieked, scooping up her wool skirts as she spun and dashed to the door, her companions following. "Josie, Miss Linden's upstairs. We'll not test her with a thing such as this. Have her lock herself in!"

Josephine raced upstairs.

Elijah backed down the alley outside, staring at the demon cloud with horrified fascination as it followed, floating at the level of their heads and taking up nearly the entire width of the alley with its bulky canine body and flickering profusion of heads. It hunched forward, ready to attack.

Michael took Rebecca's hand on one side, and Jane took the other. A powerful wind whipped around them. Josephine, having bade Miss Linden stay within, swiftly joined their ranks. She took Michael's left hand.

"Elijah, come," Rebecca commanded.

The beast lunged, but Withersby ducked out of the way. "Please tell me this is just the Black Dog of Newgate," he exclaimed, joining his friends in their circle of clasped hands. London's most gruesome tale of spectral revenge was much less horrifying than entertaining thoughts of a whole new breed.

Rebecca shook her head. "No," she replied. "We've never seen this."

The dog whipped around to face them, snarling. But as it prepared its next attack, Rebecca shouted a command in the ancient language of the Guard. The hellish thing cocked its head, opened its many maws wide and jumped—only to disperse at the last moment into a gray mist and pass through them.

At the other end of the alley the creature coalesced and hurtled away. The Guard gave chase. Elijah trailed after, cleaning up any mess that might reveal their battle. They all gave thanks that none of London's passersby could see ghosts, as their spectral quarry would have caused a riot. They simply had to deal with being considered lunatics.

As they ran, Josephine sought to pinpoint Elijah's reference. "Wait. The Black Dog . . . Was that the sorcerer?"

"Yes," Rebecca answered, panting as they turned a corner. "The scholar imprisoned in Newgate centuries ago for sorcery."

"The one where the starving inmates ate his body and then a huge, avenging black dog tore them limb from limb?"

"That would be the one. But this is not that dog."

Michael seemed just as eager to make this beast something they knew. "What about the stench of decay that follows the Newgate dog? You smell it now, don't you?" There was comfort in the familiar, even one of London's most macabre specters. More importantly, the Newgate dog was something they could best. They already had.

"No," Rebecca replied, breathless. "I smell brimstone. This is not that beast! Do you feel anything in your blood? Any of you? I feel nothing. We can't track this, we can't sense it . . ." She stumbled, losing her footing on a cobblestone. Michael was quick to catch her arm. "Damnable heels," Rebecca muttered, righting herself. "Why don't they make a boot a woman can run in?"

A fierce form on a black steed appeared at the opposite end of the street. Staring up at the floating, shifting beast, Alexi cried, "What the hell is this?"

A snarl and a swipe knocked his hat off his head. Alexi growled right back, jumping off his horse and shrieking a curse in the ancient language of the Guard. Blue flame leaped from his hands and singed the spectral dog's many noses. The blue flame streamed a circle around the shifting cur, which hunkered down opposite Alexi and seemed to be tensing its haunches. However, instead of attacking, the beast turned and swarmed back the way it had come, tearing off down the street in a gruesome splintering of canine forms—and through Elijah. Lord Withersby groaned and collapsed in a heap.

"Coward, face me!" Alexi cried, mounting his horse after glancing down worriedly at his unconscious friend. Elijah had been swept into Jane's arms, her healing powers at the ready—if she was not already too late.

Rebecca ran toward Alexi's horse. "Alexi, don't you dare—" But he was already after it, yelling curses and chasing the monster down the next avenue with bolts of blue fire.

While he knew he couldn't destroy the hellish thing on his own, Alexi felt the least he could do was reverse the game, be the fox tracking the hound. For that reason he gave chase, spurring his stallion, Prospero, into areas of London he preferred to forget, the city's dark and dirty underbelly. Urchins, beggars, and streetwalkers beckoned, unaware of the terror that had just flashed past. He hissed at their advances, stricken into anger at their desperation.

One particular young woman, barely more than a child, called up to him, asking if he wanted company for the evening. Alexi gritted his teeth and cried, "Find shelter, for God's sake! Don't you know something terrible is on the loose?" He flung coins into the street as he passed.

"I know, sir," the consumptive waif called back, darting to pick up his offerings. "Where lurks the Ripper? But we've nowhere to hide. We've got no choice. Bless ye for the shilling!"

It was too much. Alexi reined in his horse, suddenly turning back toward the form silhouetted in dim gaslight, locks of hair piled haphazardly beneath a moth-eaten bonnet. She, thinking perhaps that she had procured a client after all, gave him a practiced, inviting look far more desperate than attractive.

He shook his head and emptied the entirety of his cash into her hands. "Find as many of your lot as you can and take them to spend the night in safe shelter."

The young woman gazed up in awe. "Are ye trackin' 'im, then, good sir? Are you the detective?"

"Of sorts, dear girl," Alexi replied.

She reached up to stroke his horse's black neck. "Then you're our guardian angel."

Reins in hand, Alexi could neither acknowledge the sentiment nor look the waif in the eye, knowing he must fail at guarding all the poor wretches society cast onto the street. "Don't take long, and don't part company," he commanded gruffly, and set off.

"I won't, sir!" she cried. "Bless you, sir. I was a friend of Annie Chapman, may she rest in peace! By God, she's lookin' out for me by sendin' you this night!"

These wards were the poorest, the most hopeless. Their inhabitants were the dregs, hapless souls who had come to London seeking fortune and found none.

Though there were no street lamps beyond Commercial Street and Whitechapel Road, this was usually no problem for Alexi—on all his previous visits, ethereal light had shown him the way. Tonight, the sector was black. Even the ghosts were hiding.

Heaven must have felt a bit of pity, for the clouds above thinned to allow a dim gray moonlight to filter down. It was just enough for navigation at a slow plod. Prospero stamped impatiently, messily splashing through muddy puddles and then clacking forward across the cobblestones.

Past a wide corner just inside the dim, sooty haze of Duffield's Yard, just off a set of train tracks, Alexi drew the horse to a halt; he'd caught sight of something amorphous rustling in a space between two miserable brick buildings. He gave a cry, shouted a command, a verse in an ancient rite of which he was the master. The shadows shifted. Two bloodred eyes fixed on him. Then ten. Then came a swish of air and a muffled cry, changing suddenly into an ungodly gurgling noise. There came the smell of blood.

Prospero reared. The cloud of evil rose, a flickering mass of violence and vermin, shifting, doglike shapes floating up into the night sky. Alexi's heart exploded with hopeless fury at the lifeless heap he dimly saw crumpled below.

He dismounted and ran, his hand flying to his mouth upon closer inspection: the woman's throat had been slashed open and there were cuts on her cheeks. The victim's eyes suddenly shot open—or so it seemed. Alexi retreated a step, watching as a ghost lifted from the woman's body, creating a double image: the lit, monochromatic, unmarred form of the spirit, superimposed upon the still-bleeding corpse. The specter rose to a standing position where both Alexi and she could evaluate her bodily remains, which had been spared the more severe mutilation of the Ripper's other subjects. But the beast hadn't finished. Would it therefore strike again?

He turned to offer the victim's ghost what paltry benediction he could, but her defiant face stared back at him. Her arm lifted and she pointed west, toward the black cloud roiling with horror, toward that bestial form floating above the crumbling tenement roofs near Aldgate. There was hatred in her eyes and her transparent lips mouthed the word "Go." Alexi hurried back to his horse.

His journey now consisted of sharp turns down bleary alleys and dank gutters clogged with refuse and the occasional corpse of an animal. Alexi and Prospero took care not to trample any huddled, sleeping children, the saddest of all the ward's forgotten horde, tucked into the endless shadows. The Guard's leader looked frequently at the malevolent mass, passing low in the sky ahead, ensuring that he stayed on track. When it suddenly plunged below the rooftops, Alexi loosed a string of curses and spurred his horse down another dark street.

As he rounded the corner of Mitre Square, an incantation died on his lips at the sight of the beast's next victim. A wispy ghost, a weary-looking, wide-eyed young woman, peeled upward and into the night sky. There was no sign of her killer.

Alexi murmured a benediction in the spirit's direction, watching her ascend. He prayed that she would continue upward into what was now a calm haze of silver moonlight, rather than return and be tethered to the unspeakable reality of her mortal remains below. Ruffled skirts and pooling blood from a torn abdomen and something that was hardly a face lay before him and Alexi wondered if the sight would ever leave his mind. He choked back a wail and darted out of the walled space, well aware that there were officers on patrol who would soon find her. Everyone was vigilant these nights, but no one was of any use. Not even him.

Still, Alexi no longer doubted that he had found the source of Whitechapel's recent woe.

His Pale eyes flew open and he gasped, and Elijah found himself in Michael Carroll's modest sitting room.

"Elijah, thank God," Jane murmured in her soft brogue, returning glowing hands to her sides.

"Where are the others? Are they safe?" he asked.

Another voice answered: Josephine. "We're here. Michael's home was the closest to where you fell." She placed a gloved hand upon Jane's broad shoulder. "Nicely done."

"Thank you, Josie," the Irishwoman replied. Seeing that her hands were no longer glowing, she brushed damp hair from Elijah's face.

He grinned. "Jane, darling, Irish or no, please know we're nothing without you. You can place those healing hands on me at any turn."

Jane frowned. "Lord Withersby, that was a rather frightenin' display, and by the Holy Saints don't *ever* repeat it." Anxiety and exhaustion had heightened her accent.

"You think I planned it, do you? It passed through me with no warning—"

"We know. We saw," stated a new voice. Another figure stepped into the light.

"Why, my dear Miss Thompson, you look dourer than usual."

"Hush, you reckless infidel!" Rebecca retorted. Her expression softened into a fatigued smile but a moment later her tone was again sharp. "Elijah—truly, we thought we lost you."

Glancing around, he frowned. "Where is our fearless leader?"

There was a tense silence. "On his way," Rebecca replied.

Elijah shook his head. "Don't tell me he *pursued* it?"

None of them wanted to answer. "Yes," Rebecca finally murmured.

"Why aren't you following him?" Elijah cried, struggling to get out of bed. "He needs our help!"

"I don't, but London does." The door of Michael's sitting room flew open, and Alexi entered in a storm of dark robes, his face ashen. "Two!" he cried, pacing the room and pounding his fist against a window frame. "It shredded two women tonight! There was nothing I could do! I don't understand what it could want with those poor wretches! What is it, and what does it gain?" He collapsed on the settee only to stand again and continue pacing. "It isn't a ghost. We deal in spiritual disturbances, when spirits and humans mix poorly. This is a *demonic* force. I . . ." He trailed off, stalking over to peer down at Elijah. "Are you all right?"

"Yes, thanks for asking," his friend replied. "Jane pulled me back from the brink, apparently, though it has taken her since you left."

Moving to the window, Alexi looked across London toward Athens, to where the first light of dawn was licking the horizon. He pounded a fist against the sill. "Damn it all! Those poor girls. It was my fault. I should have stopped it somehow."

"Alexi, it was *our* fault," Rebecca corrected, taking a step closer. "*We* should have stopped it. You cannot take it upon yourself—"

"What good are we if there are things beyond our power?" he cried. "In the end, are we just useless mortals?" After a long, tense moment, he turned to Rebecca. "Headmistress . . ." he began.

She anticipated him. "Yes, Professor. We'll inform the students. And we must place guards there. For our peace of mind, we must implement whatever protections we can."

"What do *we* do?" Michael asked, for the benefit of those who were not involved in the school. He moved to place a hand on Rebecca's shoulder, which was trembling ever so slightly.

"We attend to whatever work we can manage. And pray Prophecy becomes clear," Alexi replied.

"How cowardly," Michael murmured. "This creature preys only on single, unaccompanied women. We must pray most heartily for their peace."

The Guard nodded, sitting in uncomfortable, dangerously unresolved silence.

Alexi gazed out the window. "I need you now," he murmured against the glass, yearning for his goddess. "Proclaim yourself before more innocents die." But then a sudden thought occurred to him. "Miss Linden. Where was she during all of this?"

Josephine replied. "I told her to remain at La Belle, locked in her room. She knows nothing of what transpired. Should we mention it to her?"

Alexi breathed a sigh of relief. "Heavens, no. I'll not let a stranger in on our business until they give me good cause." He scowled. "No matter how intriguing she may be."

Yet, it was time to consider Miss Linden. It was time to see if she was more than just compelling beauty and a few leading clues. War was coming, just like his goddess had foretold. Or maybe he and his friends had missed the beginning and were running late to the front lines.

CHAPTER
THIRTEEN

ATHENS'S STUDENTS STUMBLED INTO THE AUDITORIUM, HAVING BEEN
abruptly roused by their house wardens at the break of dawn. In the front
of the room, near the raised lip of the stage, several professors milled about,
their arms folded as if in effort to contain themselves. Rumor among the
students was that the murderer, the Ripper, must have come close, was
perhaps in their midst, or had perhaps struck down one of their own in
the night.

The chamber where they assembled was a mix of function and form,
with a vaulted, frescoed ceiling depicting birds on wing. The center of
the stage's crimson curtain parted as Headmistress Thompson stepped
forward, dressed in her usual prim, conservative layers of gray. The
ambient yellow glow of the gas lamps, set in golden sconces at intervals
across the scalloped walls, created warmth in sharp contrast to her cold
expression. The assembled faculty took their seats. Mina Wilberforce
scanned the crowd, found Percy, and the two shared a nervous smile
before Mina turned back to the headmistress.

Percy felt her pulse quicken as Professor Rychman entered from a
dark wing, stage left. He squinted against the glare of the wide gas
lamps that focused on the stage, peering into the dimmer house beyond.
Bowing to the headmistress, he descended the stair to the floor, and
stood like a sentry, head swiveling, eyes searching the crowd. Unable to
change her focus, Percy waited, praying for him to find her where she sat
in a shadowed seat to the side, Marianna fidgeting nearby. When their
intent gazes at last met, his eyes actually lingered a moment as he gave a
subtle nod. Percy thrilled. Had he truly been assuring himself she was
safe?

Only an astute observer could have noticed the drawn looks, the hard weariness in the eyes of both Professor Rychman and the head-mistress, but Percy had made a habit of studying them—especially together—and so was deeply concerned. He did not take a seat beside the other faculty. Perhaps his instinct to guard the academy to which he seemed so bonded was too great to allow him to relax. His entire frame seemed ready to bound into action at any moment.

"Ladies and gentlemen, esteemed students and faculty of Athens," the headmistress began. "I regret many things this morning. I regret the necessity of having to gather you. I regret that there must be a change in school policy. And I regret most deeply to report that there were two additional murders last night."

The auditorium burst into hushed murmurs and a few soft cries. The headmistress took a step forward and the sound quieted to a hiss. "In response, there will be guards posted at every doorway, entrance, or egress of Athens."

The room buzzed.

"Quiet," Professor Rychman boomed from his sentry post beside the stage and there fell immediate silence. The ferocity of his expression would still a screaming infant, and his voice resounded throughout the chamber. A collective shudder went through the crowd. The Head-mistress continued:

"I am sure the sensationalistic rags of this city will address every question you may have, and relate every heinous, disgusting detail of the murders," she remarked bitterly. "But let me come straight to the point. The murders fit the Ripper's profile; he continues to attack the defense-less. For that reason, though the violence remains so far centered in White-chapel, we shall take every precaution." Miss Thompson cast a pointed glance at a few known pranksters among the crowd, those most likely to sneak out late at night. These few students had the good sense to stay silent or nod. "Our buildings are not fortresses. But until this violence is no longer a threat, our *grounds* shall be. I expect full cooperation," she continued. "For now classes will remain on their regular schedule, and there are no substantive changes to protocol or events. I wish I could of-fer a message of comfort and inspiration this morning, but until we hear more from the authorities, any such statement would be a contrivance. You are dismissed."

Percy and Professor Rychman caught each other's eyes once more before she filed out of the auditorium. There was something in the lines of his face that was new and infinitely more complex, as if something in this great tragedy struck a personal chord. Percy didn't know why this instinct fluttered in her mind, other than that studying him so intently perhaps gave her strange ideas. Her imagination was simply too vivid.

Marianna looked ashen. She took Percy's hand as they exited into Promethe Hall, and Percy heard her utter a few Lutheran prayers. In the courtyard, many students were glancing up at the sky and doing the same. Percy noticed the dawn sparkled oddly.

There were already guards posted at the doors. Percy recognized some of them as janitors, some as teaching assistants, and a few were faculty themselves. This gave Athens a new air, as if preparing for a siege. Before her first class Percy took out the small pearl-beaded rosary that Reverend Mother had entrusted to her and prayed it several times. It had been too long since she had said even a word of the elaborate liturgies that she knew by rote, and she resolved to be better about her personal rituals of faith. She had a sense London could use every prayer it could muster.

A SOFT MODERN MELODY CRACKLED FROM A WONDER OF MODERN technology, the phonograph sitting in the corner of Professor Rychman's office. The cylinder that bore the tune was a gift from Josephine from Paris, some breezy, impressionistic French melody. The two clinked aperitif glasses, choosing to offer a toast to mankind's finer sensibilities.

"I've noticed the guards. I hope they leave everyone with some small comfort."

Alexi nodded. "We must be careful. Still, I'll be damned if our Grand Work will affect the operations of this school. It's the only thing Rebecca and I have to remind us that we're really human and not merely freakish hosts to guardian angels," he remarked mordantly, sipping his liqueur. Turning to survey the covered canvas she'd brought, he added, "So, you're finished? Such expediency with this painting, Josie. I'm impressed—especially after the work we've been forced to do . . . and after your rude exit last time you were here. At least my *students* still respect me."

"Fear you, appreciate you," Josephine corrected with a meaningful smile. "Indeed, that ivory girl with the amazing eyes seems to appreciate you a good deal. Bless her gentle heart, I think she was rather put out by my presence in your office."

Alexi scoffed. "What? Miss Parker?"

"Eyes like that can't conceal the way they look at you," Josephine replied.

"Don't be ridiculous."

"A beautiful girl. She's an inspiration."

"If only she could hear you say that, Josie." Alexi looked thoughtful. "The poor woman considers herself repulsive. I think that's hardly the case . . ." Josephine blinked at him as he trailed off, so he shifted and grumbled, "Of course, who am I to say, seeing as my 'social graces leave something to be desired.' I *do* say, Josephine, it is one thing to taunt me to my face, another entirely to undermine me in front of a student."

"Ah, is the impenetrable professor actually concerned with what that young lady thinks?"

"That is uncalled for," Alexi warned. "And dangerous to make any such impli—"

"There is something about that girl, Alexi," Josephine cut him off. "In fact . . . I've worked so fervently on this piece, I've hardly slept." Her saffron gown kissed the floor as she swept over to her covered canvas. Draining the last of her liqueur with dramatic flourish, she drew the curtain aside. Beneath was a sunlit seascape. Upon a jagged shore, two robed figures stood against the growing shadow of a dark cave entrance: A pale, regal young woman was being led into the increasing darkness by a man with luminous skin and unkempt auburn hair that fell about naked, muscular shoulders. The woman's pale hair blew before her, as if the locks were desperately reaching out, seeking purchase in the wind. A third figure stood near a rock, cloaked and hooded, raising a clenched fist. The clouds on the horizon were ominously black.

"Well?" Josie asked.

"Oh, my," Alexi breathed. But the painting, while gorgeous, left a bitter taste in his mouth.

"Your student will like it, I trust. She was the muse, heaven alone knows why. As always, I chase inspiration." Josephine sighed, pressing her hands to her eyes and taking a seat. "Also, Alexi . . . I must confess there is another reason I have worked night and day. I am frightened. Ever since that attack by *la bête* . . . I cannot sleep for the nightmares."

"Change is upon us," Alexi agreed.

Josephine noted the edge to his tone as he moved to hang her new work by the door. "You are scared, too."

"It isn't that I mind the idea of change. It's the possibility we might react improperly." He clenched his jaw and changed the subject. "So, you think there's something to Miss Parker, do you?"

Josephine shrugged. "*Oui*. Miss Linden, too, but I do not know what."

"Hmm." Alexi's eyes lingered on the painting, contemplating the shadows into which the slender woman was being led. Then the clock chimed and his brisk manner heightened. "It is six, my dear. Time for the arrival of the very girl in question."

"Ah," Josephine murmured. She had just risen from her chair when there was a knock upon the door.

"Come!" Alexi called out. "Now, good day, Josie, and thank you for the painting."

THROUGH THE PROFESSOR'S DOOR, PERCY HEARD MUSIC. SHE HEARD also her cue to enter but nonetheless hovered outside, drinking in the delightful sound.

A call from behind the wood made her jump. "Miss Parker, we cannot conduct a tutorial with a door between us, can we?"

She hurried into the room with a murmured apology. As she did, Percy noticed Josephine, and drew back for fear of interrupting. But the Frenchwoman beckoned her forward before amiably waving farewell and slipping out. Percy's gaze did not follow Josephine out the door, and so she did not witness the knowing wink, nor Alexi's glare in return. Instead, Percy glided to the desk and began removing her protections.

The lesson passed as usual and without event. The professor spoke, and she listened. But Percy's mind was far from the mathematical lecture. While integers and equations might prove an impassable gulf, she sensed their time together was of grave import aside from education; but she had no idea how to say so.

The professor handed over an assignment with a sigh and leaned back, pressing thumb and forefinger to his nose in characteristic thought. Percy bit her lip and read this as her cue to leave. With the same unconscious ceremony as accompanied her disrobing, she reversed the process.

Wrapping her length of blue muslin about her head and neck, donning gloves and glasses, she rose from her chair and lifted books into her slender arms.

She didn't know how to bring up the subject of the Ripper, yet she felt she must before walking out the door. Quietly she said: "It is good that the school has taken precautions, considering the recent state of affairs. It's such a frightful thing—and it troubles you greatly, doesn't it, Professor?"

"Yes, Miss Parker, it does," Professor Rychman replied. She wanted to ask his further opinion, but the gravity of his expression stilled her inquiry.

He glanced past her, a smile flickering across his face. "On your way in, Miss Parker, did you notice the new addition?" he asked.

"Oh, no, Professor, I didn't," Percy replied, seeing Josephine's newest painting. Her books fell from her arms. Papers scattered. Choking, she sank to her knees, glasses falling from her face and into the folds of her dress.

"Miss Parker?" Professor Rychman called out.

Dimly, Percy saw him rise from his desk and rush to her side. But compelled by the force that had overtaken her, she spoke in a voice that was not quite her own: *"No, I'll yearn for the sea,"* she insisted, speaking in Greek and seeing not the professor's study but another place altogether, glancing fearfully at the cave entrance before turning back to the shore. *"I hear crying. Who's crying?"*

"You are."

An overwhelming smell accosted her nostrils; a very specific fruit. A beautiful, unearthly man touched her arm and she chilled. Light bounced off the sea before her. Darkness was behind. In the sunlight ahead, out on the rocks, a figure reached toward her in anguish.

"No." She shook her head. *"Don't take me just yet; give me one more hour . . ."*

"Your time has come, love," said the eerie man, and his cold hand seized her shoulder to lead her into the darkness.

She reached out to the figure who wept in the light. The sweet smell of fruit turned her stomach. *"Shall I never see them again? Him?"*

"Perhaps someday, in some other era. But never the bird again. Never that bird." And the luminous man pressed something into her hand.

* * *

"Miss Parker!" Alexi said, kneeling before her. The girl's eyes looked unseeing into the distance. He took her outstretched hand and squeezed it, hoping to bring her gently back from her sudden transportation. A soft breath escaped her lips, but she remained far away.

Staring at her with fascination, he tightened his grip about her fingers. A breeze rustled through the room, and he felt his powers rise. What was happening in that moment was unparalleled. He'd never encountered anything like it. And while there was no visible door to indicate Prophecy was occurring, this was unmistakably a sign. Perhaps his goddess was trying to speak through Percy Parker.

"Yes, come to me," he breathed.

A sound came across the waves, a whisper to rouse a dreamer. Percy felt something in her hand and so she opened her palm.

Seeds. Juicy, ruby red seeds.

She stifled a cry. How could she be parted from her angel? There was a sensation upon her outstretched fingertips, feathery like wings which she heard rustling. And a murmur so like the waves called to her again and spoke a name that sounded vaguely familiar. She wanted to go to that voice. It was calling her.

"Miss Parker," Alexi said again, patiently.

He felt her fingers stir in his palm and draw away. He murmured an ancient benediction known only to the Guard, then pressed his fingertip first to her forehead and then to her collarbone. She was still lost. He couldn't help but notice her resonant beauty, captured in the passionate throes of this faraway vision.

Finally, clutching her by the arms: "Percy." A gentle yet firm command.

"He'll come for me, I swear it. Please don't let the dark take me again!" the girl cried, in English this time. Her eyes were full of horror as they snapped into focus. The spell was broken.

Percy stared up at her dear professor, who now knelt before her, firmly holding her arms in his hands. Terror overwhelmed her and she scrambled to her feet. The professor rose and, with swift control, seized her.

She stared deeply into his eyes, blushing, and shook her head. "Please, Professor, don't send me to an asylum! I'm not mad, I swear to you. Forgive me, I had no warning, I don't know what that w—"

"Miss Parker, shhh." He forced her to meet his gaze. "No one is going to commit you."

"Oh, Professor, good God, what you must think of me." She fought back tears.

"Calm yourself, Miss Parker. All is well. Whatever held you for a moment is gone. No one will take you anywhere."

Percy had never been so close to him and her senses reeled. Her blush could grow no more fiery, yet she had no choice but to believe her stern professor. She took a long breath.

He released her. She looked at him shyly as she bent to collect her books and papers, trying desperately to think of something redeeming to say, but her tongue was shackled. Her shaking hands placed her small, dark glasses back upon her face.

The professor calmly watched her fumble for her things. "You have no idea what had you just then, Miss Parker? Were you aware you were speaking Greek?"

Percy picked up the last of her papers and stood. She shook her head. "I have no idea, Professor. No idea at all!" she murmured helplessly. "But I owe you so much. My life is in your debt. If you had not brought me back . . . I wonder if I might ever have returned!"

Scurrying to the door, she gave no further explanation but was careful not to give the painting a second glance. The door half open, she turned again, murmured another thank-you brimming with emotion, and disappeared into the hall.

ALEXI SAT AT HIS DESK, MAKING NOTES. HIS HEAD SWAM.

Miss Parker had not been his goddess speaking to him. She hadn't come with answers; she was as lost as he in this place of waiting and wondering. She didn't seem to know what she was, or what she might be; so he couldn't be sure she was Prophecy. Not yet. And there was too much at stake to guess.

But she had, in a way, dealt with a door. It was a portal that only she had entered. Could Prophecy be interpreted broadly?

"One step at a time, or everything will be ruined," he muttered. "The goddess warned caution. It could all be a trap. Everything could be a ruse, and you dare not fail." But his stomach tightened when he thought of how it had felt to grasp Miss Parker's delicate hands in his own, and he burned with an exotic shame.

No. Students were not involved in the Grand Work. He and Rebecca had long ago pledged this. The school was a boundary, both wall and link—a bridge between an average human life and the strange fate foisted upon him; fate that made him an outcast in the very society he was sworn to protect. An outcast like Miss Parker. Maybe she would understand . . .

"You are her teacher," he reminded himself. "She is not a peer, so you cannot be more." But a foreign sensation was waking inside of him, burning with emotion locked tightly away.

On the opposite side of the academy, Percy burst into Marianna's room and collapsed upon the bed. Her friend sat at her desk with a book. Starting with surprise, she shook her head. "What is it now, my dear?"

"I had a vision tonight, a vision that pulled me in and would not let go!" Percy wailed into a pillow. "When I came to, I was kneeling in the professor's office. I must have appeared absolutely raving!"

"What? A vision . . . took you in?"

"It was as if I was suddenly in a dream, and I collapsed—Oh, dear Lord! He was there before me, trying to bring me back. Oh, Marianna, it was humiliating!"

"I'm sure it was."

"And I was speaking Greek." Percy loosed a sickly laugh. "The professor asked how I liked his new painting, and when I looked at it, it was as if I went *into* the painting! My vision was the painting come to life. I had no power to resist; it was as if it had all happened before."

"This is so strange, Percy," Marianna said. "What shall you do?"

Percy shrugged, helpless. There was a long silence. "Could he have something to do with it?" she murmured at last.

"Your professor?"

Percy shook her head, feeling ill. "I must clear my mind of this. I must find some distraction."

"Well, I'm having a frightful time with *The Odyssey*," Marianna admitted. "You might assist me."

"Wonderful!" Percy cried. She spent the rest of the evening helping Marianna grapple with Homer. It was much easier than dealing with the fact that her inscrutable professor was unquestionably part of her destiny.

CHAPTER
FOURTEEN

PERCY'S HEART FALTERED AS PROFESSOR RYCHMAN OPENED THE DOOR to his classroom. Today she feared not only what he must think of her, but the repetition of an uncontrolled vision. There was the additional terror of the day's alchemy and mathematics exam.

He stalked quietly into the room, glancing at each student in turn as he discussed the usual manner of his examinations. She heard the rustling of his robe behind her but couldn't bring herself to look up when he passed her table. He paused nearby. Percy's pulse quickened.

"... And I do, ladies and gentlemen, expect your answers to be in English and no other language." The professor then offered Percy a soft aside, in Greek. *Do I make myself clear, Miss Parker?*

Her eyes shot up and she gave him an expression of helpless apology. He rewarded her with a fleeting half-smile. Relief flooded her body and she beamed at him: He wasn't wholly put off by last night's inexplicable encounter. He nodded briefly to indicate the subject a closed matter, then the classroom echoed with the remainder of his exam particulars.

After taking the test, Percy spent the entire afternoon bemoaning it . . . and dwelling upon the professor's little smirk and gracious understanding. Before she knew it, it was nearly six and she was rushing off to see him.

On his office door a tack held a folded piece of paper marked "Miss Parker." The note inside read:

> *I shall likely be otherwise engaged at the time of your arrival,*
> *Miss Parker. The door is open; you may enter and await me*
> *inside.*
>
> *—Rychman*

Percy folded the note with care and tucked it into her corset, placing the lovely spiral script next to her heart. Dreaming it a note of a more personal bent, she suddenly flushed, appalled at how easily her fancy took flight.

Glancing furtively about the room, she couldn't help but make a bold dash to the professor's phonograph, a luxury of which she was sure her convent would never have approved. Her skirts fluttering as she knelt, Percy examined the various wax cylinders stored on a shelf beneath the machine. Her gaze fell upon a red velvet box labeled in gilt letters: "Lacrimosa," from Mozart's *Requiem*. Her choice was made.

Inserting the cylinder, she turned the crank and a needle made contact. The melody began as a simple, ascending line of strings, mournful and glorious, and it halted Percy's breath. She stepped away, beaming, relishing every note.

The choir began to sing, their voices ebbing and flowing. Within the first few bars, as if summoned, spirits began to pour through the walls, windows, and ceiling of Professor Rychman's magnificent office. Each note drew a new soul from the fabric of the air, as if all the spirits of Athens Academy had been beckoned to fill the room in rapture.

Percy stood amazed and delighted at the influx ot spirits of all times, cultures, and classes. They twirled around her, dancing and reveling to the gorgeous death mass, singing in unison with the choir. Like a butterfly shedding its chrysalis, Percy tossed her shawl, eyeglasses, and gloves upon the desk and abandoned herself, as the spirits did, to the music, sharing a bond with them that went beyond coloration. Her skirts spun out around her.

Constance, haunt of the science library, wafted near. Her spiral curls bounced weightlessly. "Hello, Miss Percy! This one is our favorite! However did you know?" Percy just giggled and spun beside her ghostly friend, closing her eyes in a moment of ecstasy.

The entire lot, human and spirits, failed to notice as the office door quietly opened and shut.

Alexi stood just inside the threshold and raised an eyebrow at the spectral bedlam. Setting his jaw, he stared at the veritable army of spirits that had collected in his office uninvited. As he folded his arms and shook his head, a veritable column of black fabric, the haunts began to notice. He shooed each off with a wave of his hand, and they knew enough not to disobey.

Miss Percy Parker. What a curious one she was. He wished the mortal young woman could see what kind of chaos she had stirred up, but surely she couldn't.

One spirit remained unaware of his presence, staring at Miss Parker with such longing that he reluctantly decided to let it stay. The spirit, a hollow-eyed girl with ringlets and clothing from long past, reached toward Percy, wishing to touch her. Alexi understood. When left to her own devices, Miss Parker was neither shy nor awkward; she was radiant.

The spirit turned and caught Alexi's gaze. He nodded a slight greeting. The ghost's eyes widened and a hand flew to her lips, suddenly delighted, though he wasn't exactly sure why. He shook his head and stalked to his desk.

Hearing sudden, firm footfalls against the wooden floor, Percy opened her eyes and cried out, embarrassment surging. Fervently blurting apologies, she ran to the phonograph to stop the music. Professor Rychman halted her.

"Let it play, Miss Parker. Perhaps you will better absorb your studies when they are underscored by Mozart."

"Th-thank you, Professor, for yet another instance of your kind patience. I am—"

The professor narrowed his eyes, clearly wishing to hear no more. Percy scurried to her seat as he gracefully took his.

Constance floated to her side. Percy glanced up and tried to nod the ghost toward the door. Constance just grinned and shook her head, refusing. Percy pursed her lips.

The entirety of the lesson passed with Constance hovering just behind and to the side of Percy's chair in what appeared to be an attempt to distract her. Dread that the professor might finally snap under the strain of her odd behavior and send her packing made Percy's hands shake, but she certainly could not explain to him that she was having difficulty concentrating because a dead girl was breathing down her neck.

Once the professor had finished his complex little lecture, he sat back in his chair and folded his hands in his lap. Constance, who had attended the lesson as if she, too, were his pupil, leaned in, her translucent face just above Percy's head. Feeling the cold draft in the ghost's wake, Percy batted at her hair in irritation.

"That will be all for today, Miss Parker," the professor declared, promptly picking up a book and burying himself in it.

Percy gathered her shrouds in haste. Constance took this opportunity. She whirled to Percy's side and whispered, "You realize, Percy, that he can see me, too."

"What?" Percy breathed.

The professor glanced up from his book. Percy stared at him, wide-eyed, then at the ghost, and then back at the professor. Professor Rychman furrowed his brow, looked at the ghost, then back at Percy.

"You can see Constance?" Percy squeaked.

Professor Rychman frowned. "Constance?" He nodded slowly. "I did not know the two of you were . . . acquainted."

"But you can see her?"

"If you mean this transparent woman with curled hair and dated fashion, yes, Miss Parker, I can."

Percy nearly wept with joy.

"You, strange one, who never cease to surprise me, how do you know that she is Constance?"

"She told me, sir."

"Told you?"

"He cannot hear me, Percy. That is the difference between the two of you," Constance clarified.

"Yes, sir, she told me."

"You can see *and* speak with them?" the professor clarified.

"Yes, sir."

"My, my, Miss Parker. How very useful," he mused.

Percy narrowed her eyes. "I beg your pardon, sir?"

"Never mind. When did this ability of yours begin?"

She could not answer at first; only his nodding encouragement convinced her to continue.

"It has been with me since I can remember, Professor," Percy admitted. "My earliest memories are of Gregory, an Elizabethan spirit. In life, his daughter was trampled by a horse and I became a surrogate child to his restless soul. I never thought anything amiss until I unwittingly told Reverend Mother. She, of course, was quite shocked . . ." Percy chuckled as memories washed over her. "Dear Gregory, I do hope he has found peace!" She suddenly remembered herself. "Oh, but forgive my prattling on, Professor!"

"It's fascinating," he replied in earnest.

"Could *you* always see them, Professor?"

"No," he replied simply, and seemed taken by sudden memories himself.

"When did it happen that you could, sir?"

"I'm afraid, Miss Parker, that would take more time to explain than I have to give. Did anyone other than your mother superior know of your ability?"

"No. She did not want anyone to declare me mad. Of course, there was the day she sent a priest to exorcise Gregory. I made a terrible fuss, screaming that they didn't dare take my friend away. Can't say I endeared myself to the priesthood, and Reverend Mother made it clear to keep my sight a secret ever after. But Professor, how happy this makes me! To know I'm not the only one, and that perhaps you may know why—"

"Do not expect answers from me, Miss Parker," he said, stemming Percy's excitement.

"Forgive me. It's just that I've prayed desperately for someone who knows something—"

"We are all looking for something, Miss Parker," was his reply. When Percy glanced at Constance, she nodded in agreement. "And on that note, *I* happen to need to look for something, so I bid you *adieu*."

Percy rose, dazed. "Thank you, Professor. Have a lovely evening."

"Same to you, Miss Parker," he replied, furiously scribbling down several notes.

Percy once again gathered her things, gestured for Constance and left the office. "He could see you! I am amazed!" she exclaimed to the ghost as they entered the hall.

Constance was gliding at her side. "There is something to all of this, Percy. I can feel it." A fellow student was walking up the stairwell, so the conversation paused while the two women descended the steps. Constance resumed speech as soon as Percy was free to respond. "I saw the way you gazed at him when he wasn't looking . . ."

Percy experienced an odd ache and said nothing. She shook a finger at her noncorporeal companion, a firm warning not to speak of such things again. "Until next haunting," she said.

The two friends waved good-bye. But as Constance vanished through a nearby wall, Percy could hardly contain herself. Surely fate was beginning to find her.

ALEXI WAS BROODING MORE THAN USUAL.

"Why did you come to my office for tea?" Rebecca asked wearily. "So I could watch you scowl? I assure you, I've seen quite enough of that through the years."

"A prophecy. How ridiculous! What respectable man of science lives his life in accordance with some mad vision?"

"Only you, I'm sure. It isn't like anyone else has our lot in life."

"Waiting for a promise I can't prove and a woman I can't see, blindly trusting that someone is going to waltz in and change everything."

"Well. Has she?" Rebecca asked.

Alexi pinned her with a cool stare. "What?"

Rebecca sighed. "Has someone waltzed in and changed everything, rearranged the order of your world? You normally aren't so forthcoming in your laments."

Alexi lapsed into silence. After a while, he voiced the true reason for his visit and pinned her with a stare. "Do you know one unmistakable Miss Parker?"

Rebecca shifted uncomfortably in her chair, but her face remained neutral. "Yes, what about her?"

"She sees ghosts."

Rebecca raised an eyebrow. "Does she now? And how did you find that out?"

"The girl's wretched at mathematics. I'm giving her tutorials. Our sessions have led to several interesting revelations."

This was the first Rebecca had heard of it. "Private lessons? You have a chaperone, I hope." She leveled her gaze upon Alexi, shaking her head. "Although with you I've nothing to worry about. You've never been one for an affair, much less taking liberties with an oddity. Still, perhaps just for propriety we should send someone—"

"She can also *speak* with ghosts," Alexi continued angrily. "She draws strange symbols that relate to our work, and recently was transported by a painting, crying out in Greek. If those aren't signs, I don't know what are."

"And was there a portal?" Rebecca asked.

"No." Alexi sighed. "And she's not our peer. Yet, I cannot help but wonder. Do you think we are looking for a literal portal, or might we accept the suggestion of one? Is Prophecy flexible? Miss Parker *is* extraordinary." His eyes flashed as he processed his friend's previous statement. "Honestly, Rebecca. To call her an oddity? I'd expect more kindness, considering our fate makes us no less—"

"What of Miss Linden?" Rebecca interrupted. "She has most certainly been 'placed in our path.' All of us except Jane, who isn't impressed by anything, find her charming. Miss Linden speaks cryptically, as if she's scared to admit her powers, just as we are. Remember the part of Prophecy that said she would be escaping something? Well, Miss Linden is now our guest, and we suspect she's—"

"Please don't say it."

A long silence passed as they stared at each other. Rebecca finally reached and placed her hand on his. "Your goddess isn't coming back, Alexi. Not in the way you think. That's what you're struggling with, I know. You want *her*, the former lover of whatever possesses you. But that isn't to be, and it isn't what was foretold. You are here, a mortal. With us, other mortals. There's work to be done and choices to be made. So come and be present with your friends rather than hiding in your office."

Alexi furrowed his brow. "I'm supposed to love her, Rebecca."

His friend's eyes flashed. "For the last time, Alexi, love has nothing to do with the prophecy!"

"Goodness, Rebecca, it's nothing to be upset about."

"Of course it's something to be upset about! The fate of many lives hangs in the balance! Love will only complicate matters, don't you see?" She rose from her chair and went to the window. After a long moment she turned, her expression pinched. "Don't tell me you've fallen in love. If you're avoiding Miss Linden . . . Don't tell me *Miss Parker* has your interest. That simply cannot be—"

"I'm not in love with anyone, Rebecca," Alexi replied. "Other than the goddess—"

"Your goddess isn't coming, Alexi! And she didn't love you. She loved what was taking up residence inside you."

Alexi froze, his friend's words like a flash of lightning. He hadn't really thought of that. He'd never wanted to think that his goddess never loved *him*; but, truly, what did his goddess know of Alexi Rychman? What could she know? He was just a vessel, after all.

Slowly he rose from his chair and turned to the door. He wanted nothing to do with this, any of this, anymore. "To hell with Prophecy, Rebecca. Let the war come. I'll just teach mathematics and we'll all die alone."

As he flung the door open and exited, Rebecca cried out, "Alexi, no! Don't take it like that! Come back . . ."

The door shut.

Pounding her fist on her desk, Rebecca collapsed into her chair with a string of curses.

ALEXI WENT HOME TO HIS COLD, EMPTY ESTATE, WHERE HE SOUGHT to divert himself with brandy and volumes of scientific journals, listening to crackling wax recordings of Chopin. This, his usual pastime, had once sufficed, but now his desire for something richer out of life stirred an irrepressible anger.

"If you won't help me, Goddess, if you've no care for me, then you can't ask me to suffer your cryptic riddles," he hissed. "No more. Prophecy be damned."

It wasn't until he caught a whiff of smoke that he realized with surprise that his anger had set the room on fire. He had sway over candles and the occasional gas lamp but inadvertent arson hadn't previously been in his repertoire. He raised his hands and the flames went out, and then he sank deeper into his thronelike leather chair and fell into a wretched sleep.

HAVING TRANSPORTED HIMSELF A FULL CONTINENT SOUTH OF HIS previous travails, the Groundskeeper grunted, wiping sweat from his furrowed brow with the sleeve of his long gray coat. The ash caked on his cuff smeared dark lines across his forehead.

"So much work, my lady! If you've gone before to help, seems your work's been undone. The seals hold fast. Damn those mortals!"

He brought his chisel down hard, its metal singing against the glassy base of a lava flow. The surrounding rock seemed to shudder, almost to belch, and a fresh, thin layer of dust began to settle over his skin and begrimed clothes.

"Ah . . ." He pressed thin lips into a smirk. "Loosening, loosening, for chaos to come." His song was like the voice of a strangled bird.

CHAPTER
FIFTEEN

THERE WAS A KNOCK AT ALEXI'S DOOR. HE DIDN'T WANT TO SEE OR speak with anyone, but it was time for Miss Parker's tutorial, and of all the people in his life, she was the one he least minded. "Come!"

She entered with her usual deference, but Alexi noticed a lightness to Miss Parker's step. As she took her seat, he held out an expectant hand and she produced her assignment, though the fingers of her left hand danced busily out of sight.

To Percy it seemed as if Professor Rychman would rather be anywhere else. It troubled her that she should be so attuned to his energy, to the key changes in the music of his presence. As the lesson came to a close, she leaned forward to gather her things.

"Are you well, sir?" she asked, daring to look directly at him. He waved a dismissive hand. "Truly?" she pressed.

The professor raised an eyebrow. "You know, for a meek young lady, you can be dreadfully persistent. My life outside of this campus, Miss Parker, is trying. Not that it's any of your business. Also, someone close to me is not well."

"Ah. Miss Thompson," Percy guessed.

"What? No. Why her?" The professor narrowed his eyes.

Percy shrugged, staring into her lap. "Well, sir, I thought perhaps you and she—"

"She and I? Nonsense, whatever it is you're insinuating," he barked. "My sister is ill."

Percy wished she had remained silent, yet felt overjoyed. Was her professor actually free after all? It seemed that neither the Frenchwoman named Josephine nor Headmistress Thompson laid claim to him. "My prayers shall be for your sister," she murmured, rising to her feet. "And for your life here and outside."

"Are *you* well, Miss Parker?" the professor asked. "You've been fiddling with something all evening that has nearly driven me to distraction." He looked pointedly at her left hand.

"My apologies, Professor. I haven't been able to part with it all day. I just received it," she confessed, holding up an ornate little cross, "for my birthday, along with my favorite book of fairy tales. Reverend Mother is so thoughtful."

"Fairy tales?" When Percy cringed, the professor spoke with less disdain. "Which is your favorite?"

It never failed to surprise her when he asked questions that bred familiarity. "Well . . ." She hesitated, looking away. "'Beauty and the Beast,'" she said finally. "I identify with the characters."

"Because you think yourself the beast."

Percy bit her lip and tried to stare through the floor.

"Foolish girl," the professor said, and Percy could not tell if his intent was gentle, condescending or both.

Feeling ugly and childish, she began donning her defenses, drawing her scarf tight about her head. At the same time, she reassured herself that his words were meant as an encouragement.

"Have I rattled you so very much?" he pressed, his voice like faraway thunder.

She paused. Then, in a moment of fleeting bravery, she removed her glasses and stared deep into his eyes. "Always."

The professor almost smiled. "Finally, you are honest with me."

"I've never been dishonest."

"Be of good cheer, faint heart, you are too easily hurt," he chided.

"My heart is fortified with passions, Professor; it is my confidence that is too easily undone."

The professor pursed his lips. Percy lingered a moment in the power of his stoicism. She reminded herself she'd been treated no differently than any other here, beast or no, and she would be forever grateful to him for that.

"Until next time," he stated, releasing her from the bondage of his stare with the wave of a finger. As Percy opened the door, feeling she would breathe easier once she reached the hallway, he called, "Miss Parker?"

"Yes, Professor?" She turned, a hitch in her breath.

"Happy birthday. Which is it?"

"Nineteen," she replied.

"Nineteen," he repeated, evaluating the number with a slight grimace. "Well, Miss Parker, may your birthday wish come true."

Percy felt a bright smile cross her face and she curtseyed. "Thank you, Professor!" Recalling the particulars of her birthday wish, she disappeared out the door before Professor Rychman could note her guilty blush.

As she exited Apollo Hall, dreaming what her professor's birthday embrace might feel like, a dozen pink roses suddenly appeared from behind a courtyard pillar. Percy leaped back. Edward, who was in her literature class, peered around the pillar, his eyes aglow. Percy blushed and put gloved hands over her cheeks to hide.

"*Alles Gute zum Geburtstag!*" Marianna cried, jumping into view. "Happy birthday!"

"Marianna, Edward—thank you both! How sweet you are!" Percy giggled. Edward mimed taking her hand and kissing it chivalrously, not willing to incur the wrath of the school by actually touching her.

"Merry natal day!" he cried, bowing with an exaggerated and endearing flourish. The walking stick he carried made him look the youthful dandy.

The three strolled to the fountain, where Edward begged leave to attend his studies. He leaned in to mime kissing Marianna's hand. The German girl's face turned pink, but her eyes were bright and gay.

As Edward backed away, he stumbled. He spun upon the culpable stone with mock fury, trouncing it soundly with his walking stick while the girls laughed. Marianna's cheeks grew increasingly flushed, and Percy wondered if her friend might swoon right then and there.

"How was your lesson today, alone in that room with your dear professor?" the German girl said airily, abruptly turning the tables.

Percy replied calmly, refusing to betray herself with giggles. "It was professional and uneventful. He said he hoped my birthday wish came true."

"If only he knew," Marianna murmured.

Percy turned and clapped a hand over her friend's mouth. The German girl squealed with muffled glee.

"You will be my undoing, Marianna. I swear, that talk of yours will get me expelled!"

"No, I promise, Percy, your fascination remains our secret alone!"

Marianna's friendship with Edward could not have come at a better time. At dinner in the ladies' dining hall, as Percy and her friend sat sipping a bland soup, a few chattering girls posted a banner above the dining room doorway.

> If you will patiently dance in our round and see
> our moonlight revels, go with us!
> Autumnal gala of 1888
> Saturday, 8 p.m.

A girlish cheer went up about the room. Anxieties over Jack the Ripper, whose name had been ceaseless in its flow through the dining hall for the past month, especially with all the newspaper coverage, vanished in the excitement. For the first time all year, the girls of Athens would actually be able to touch the opposite sex without reprimand. For how else could they dance?

"*Oh!* Percy, I must send home for my gowns!"

"'If not, shun me, and I will spare your haunts,'" Percy murmured.

"What?"

"Titania's next line is more appropriate for me."

Marianna sighed. "Is that your poetic way of declining the invitation?"

"Why attend? I was never taught to dance." Percy's attempt at disinterest failed, however, for fantasy had got the better of her and she imagined elegant couples aglow with cheer, chandeliers, music . . .

"You must attend," Marianna said gently. "For such nights are the stuff dreams are made of."

"What could I expect other than cruel whispers and derision? No, I cannot go," Percy replied. She tried to return to her soup, but a sudden vision of a dog's bloody muzzle appeared and ruined her appetite.

THE GUARD SAT BY THEIR USUAL WINDOW AT LA BELLE ET LA BÊTE. The circle was not complete, for Alexi and Jane were again missing, but their party included a beautiful new face. As had quickly become custom, a vase of flowers sat upon the table.

Alexi hadn't visited the café for several days, and Rebecca was quieter than usual, her shoulders tight and her words clipped. Jane had visited earlier for a cup of tea, but upon hearing of Miss Linden's arrival had excused herself, stating that she didn't have a use for new friends. From what Lucille gathered, Jane kept to herself and was wary of anyone but her Guard cohorts. She couldn't win them all, she supposed.

A candle at the center of the table dripped onto the tablecloth. Elijah absently gathered some of the still-soft wax into a ball. Josephine hovered nearby, pouring tea.

"What a shame, Miss Linden, that you've come to London during a spate of such horror," Michael remarked.

Lucille agreed softly. "But it would always be daunting, to be a lone woman in London, would it not, no matter the circumstances? When Fate draws you to a place, to important people, how can we not rejoice?" She paused, then asked, "Why haven't I seen that professor of yours?"

Rebecca replied through clenched teeth. "I cannot answer for him, Miss Linden." Then, struck by an idea, she exclaimed, "The gala! That would be the perfect opportunity. Our academy is about to have its annual soiree. It will be so good for the poor dears, as our students are not accustomed to guards at their doors; they must feel like they're imprisoned. Professor Rychman thinks the festivity stuff and nonsense . . . so I'll arrange the chaperone list to include his name." Rebecca smirked. "Elijah, if Miss Linden cares to attend, would you escort her?"

"I'd be honored," Elijah replied—a bit too eagerly for Josephine, who surreptitiously picked up her dinner knife and held it near his fingertips. Below the table, he placed a tiny object atop the many folds of fabric over her thigh; Josephine glanced down to see he had fashioned his little ball of wax into a tiny heart. Her immaculate olive cheek gained a hint of color.

"You once told us you hail from Bath, Miss Linden," Elijah remarked. "You must be no stranger to a fine soiree."

"Belle of the ball, I'm sure," Michael declared, raising his glass.

Miss Linden's eyes sparkled. "You flatter me, Mr. Carroll. Lord Withersby, indeed you are correct—I'm no stranger to a ball. There were so many, you'd think Bath had nothing else to do. All the faces, eager eyes, the flitting fans of young ladies in tense clusters or tucked on a divan, vying so desperately for a glance or a dance . . ."

Rebecca snickered. "Well, then, you'll love gala night at Athens. It's the only time students are allowed even the slightest fraternization, and it's the very picture of ineptitude."

"I most heartily look forward to it," Lucille exclaimed. Her eyes grew misty. "A dance where no one would find me. I might finally feel free, be part of society once again." She glanced away as her voice faltered. The Guard, embarrassed for her, found fascination in their steaming teacups. They did not dare pry further into her past; such questions were simply improper. They had long been a refuge for one another, joined in their understanding of strange fates, so it seemed only natural to extend that comfort to the newcomer.

After a moment Josephine nearly whispered, "Do you think the Ripper is finally finished? There has been no recent . . . violence in the paper." Elijah placed his hand on her leg; the gentle pressure through the fabric of her dress was a tiny comfort.

"Something is searching for an answer," Lucille remarked. "And I pray it has something to do with us." When everyone stared at her, surprised, she smiled graciously and explained, "I personally comfort myself with the idea that truly terrible things are only omens of better days to come."

The Guard glanced at one another and looked around for more signs of prophecy.

CHAPTER
SIXTEEN

A SHIMMERING GRAY FORM BURST THROUGH THE WALL AS PERCY made her way toward the professor's office. "Oh, Percy, the gala!"

"Goodness, Constance, don't startle me so!" Percy laughed softly, careful to make sure they were alone.

"Do forgive me, but each year I forget how delightful it is."

"I'm sure the gala is lovely," Percy muttered. "If I could float invisibly, as you do, I would gladly attend."

"But, Miss Percy, the dancing—"

"I never learned. Now, please, Constance, I mustn't be late."

"You ought to have the professor teach you."

"Constance, I beg you—"

"There's nothing scandalous about a *dance lesson*, Percy. He's a teacher. He'd be teaching you."

"I . . . wouldn't dare hope," Percy replied.

A strange look came over the ghost's face. "Hope? Just remember. Alive or dead, we are all looking for something."

A flurry of students appeared, and Percy was unable to reply. Constance pinned her with a stare before vanishing into the paneling.

Percy knocked upon the professor's door. Above the din, she barely heard his reply. She scurried into the office and closed the door on the cacophony of excited students outside. The professor was pacing behind his desk, seemingly angry and tired. Percy wondered at his mood; surely he couldn't be anxious about mathematics alone.

"Damnable gala," he muttered, making a face. "Sends the entire school into a juvenile tizzy."

"Yes, it's all the girls can speak of," Percy admitted. She took her seat, watching him. "Do faculty attend?" Constance's suggestion nagged at her thoughts.

"Many serve as chaperones. We take turns year to year. I suppose you're looking forward to it, Miss Parker?"

"No," Percy replied, removing her accoutrements. "I shan't attend."

The professor raised an eyebrow. "Why not?"

"Look at me," she stated, glaring. When he stared back, undaunted, she explained, "I'm abnormal, and I don't know how to dance. The sight of a ball gown with one of my scarves draped about it . . . They'd wonder what nervous phantasm plagued their fete."

"Nonsense. You're no ghost, Miss Parker."

"Thank you, Professor. And while you're someone who would know, I wish I could share your optimism."

"I'm sure it's not been easy for you, Miss Parker, but not everyone thinks you frightening."

She allowed herself to smile. His unfaltering acceptance was the dearest thing she could imagine.

"Is it the world that scares you so, Miss Parker? Or the strange things that you see? What exactly *is* it that you see?" the professor asked. Percy was lost for a moment, intoxicated by his concern, enjoying how every rich syllable he spoke lingered in her ears.

"Many things," she finally said. "Some . . . nightmarish visions."

"You admit to visions at last, Miss Parker?" the professor asked. When she glanced up in panic, he held out a hand. "Miss Parker. Did I call you mad when you transported yourself to Greece? When you spoke to spirits? You ought to think better of me. And you might be surprised what people other than yourself see . . ." There was a strange light in his eyes.

Percy's melancholy vanished. She gasped, "You have visions, too, Professor?" Startled into brazen action, she leaned forward and reached across the desk.

Professor Rychman's demeanor shifted abruptly and he pulled back. Still, there was a thoughtful look on his face as he added, "No, Miss Parker, I do not. And we have strayed long enough from our lesson."

Excitement and disappointment churned through Percy as she handed over her assignment. The professor scrawled notes upon the page and slid it back. "The left column is correct; the right, incorrect. You have an amazing capacity to learn what I teach—in halves." As he began to elaborate upon where she'd gone wrong, Percy sighed. Her heart raced and she prayed he could not hear it pound. Suddenly her eyes blurred and she was watching a new scene—another vision. People, fire, color . . .

And then it was gone. Percy jumped as her eyes focused again on the professor, who was waiting for her to re-inhabit herself. "If you're going to leave your corporeal form when I am midsentence, Miss Parker, at least have the courtesy to tell me where you travel," he declared.

Furrowing her brow, she took a hesitant breath. "There was music"— she bit her lip—"and people in a ring, and there seemed to be some sort of strange fire . . ."

The professor's jaw clenched. "How familiar," he murmured softly.

Percy fought back shock. "You know more than you've shared, Professor!"

He gave a curt nod. "I know far more than I've shared—or that I'm willing to share."

Percy could not help herself. "Why do I have these visions, Professor?" she asked. *And why are they even more frequent around you?*

The professor shook his head. "I assure you, I do not know. Now, review these conversions from class. And get this from the library." He handed her a note with a filing number. "Perhaps you'll understand general theorems better in Italian."

Percy took the paper and stood, understanding that she was being dismissed.

As she shrouded herself in her scarf, a knock sounded at the door. "Come," was Rychman's response. Headmistress Thompson entered, her presence in the office nearly as commanding as the professor's. She evaluated Percy, eyes narrowed, and Percy held her breath. Finally the woman nodded and turned to address the professor.

There was a terrible awkwardness between the two that Percy could not help but notice, and it made her uncomfortable. There was surely something between these two, no matter what the professor said. Percy chided herself for jealousy, but it would not be quieted.

Miss Thompson smiled, most uncharacteristically, and said, her amusement clear, "We are rotating the gala's chaperone list this year, Professor. You have been voted in. I told the committee I would relay the information to you in person."

"Thank you for the message, Miss Thompson," he grumbled. "You're a dear." Percy giggled in spite of herself and the professor turned a stony glare in her direction. With one finger he pointed, saying, "Silence. You are dismissed, Miss Parker. May your next *vision* include some correct answers for tomorrow's lesson."

Percy bit her lip, bowed to both the professor and the headmistress, and fled.

When the door slid shut, Rebecca said, "What a strange girl."

Alexi nodded. "New elements have come to light regarding her."

"Really? What?" Rebecca sat straighter in her chair.

Alexi chewed on his lip, thoughtful. "Miss Parker has visions. I believe they relate to our work. I think she might even have seen our chapel. But I still have a hard time believing we would be sent a student when we were told our seventh would be a peer. And to pursue it further, to involve her—"

"I wholeheartedly agree," the headmistress interrupted. "Be careful what you ask her to do. I shouldn't want to be forced to expel the girl."

Alexi made a face. "You needn't worry; I'm through searching. This nonsense is driving me mad. Let Prophecy come and hit me over the head if she's going to come at all. I'm sick of the whole preposterous game. As I said last time we spoke—"

"Ah, yes. You're giving up after all these years. How noble," Rebecca scoffed. "Remember, ten years ago, when Elijah decided he'd had enough? How he stopped coming to meetings? Do you remember how the papers were filled with ghost stories, how we had to run around in cloaks and conceal our faces since he wasn't there to wipe scenes clean? A child died—"

"I remember it well," Alexi growled. He'd been the one to fetch Elijah and give him a ferocious set-down.

"Then stop posturing. You're no more done with Prophecy than it's done with us. Alexi, you *must* come to La Belle and talk with Miss Linden. You must determine her importance to us, if she has one. You sent her there in the first place—as we do, you must have felt something powerful about the woman."

Alexi gritted his teeth. Usually patience was not so hard for him to muster. "If I have been avoiding our haunt, it was not a conscious choice. My life need not revolve solely around this institution and that pub,

Rebecca. How tedious has been our routine. May I not have leave to go about my life without question? I've never abandoned a Pull or any of our Work, I've no need to be *social*. That's for calling hours and ladies who have nothing better to do than gossip."

His friend shook her head. "Goodness, listen to you complain! You should know more of Miss Linden, that's all. She spoke last night as if everything happening in London was meant to bring us together," Rebecca explained. "If she's our seventh . . . Well, to be perfectly honest, I thought that seemed possible."

Alexi's expression clouded. "Indeed."

"*Indeed*," the headmistress snapped when the mathematics professor said nothing further. Bristling, she rose and went to the door. "Do recall the task we've all been set, no matter your frustration or . . . interest in a student. If anyone should be interesting, it should be Miss Linden! As for the ball, are you so melancholy that your duties take—?"

"I'll attend the blasted ball!" Alexi muttered, exasperated and more than a bit confused. "And for you to make insinuations and then push me toward Miss Linden makes me wonder what's possessed you."

Rebecca slowed, suddenly contrite. Turning, she said, "Forgive me, Alexi. I've been inappropriate. You would not dare impropriety. I do know that, I've spoken in error—"

He shook his head. "I value your opinion and cautions, as always, but do take care." While his words were forgiving, his tone was cold. He recognized that something personal drove his dear friend to agitation about Prophecy, but what it was, he couldn't begin to imagine. While others might pry, he would not. "Assign some kind of useful research to Lord Withersby—he causes trouble if he's not busy."

Alexi returned to his work then, and Rebecca nodded, fumbled with uncharacteristic nervousness at a filigree broach worn over her heart, and silently took her leave.

MARIANNA CHASED HER FRIEND INTO HER BEDROOM IN ATHENE Hall. "You *must* attend, Percy."

"I told you, I cannot."

"But our dear little Edward will so be unhappy if you are not there. If you fear he will fill my dance card and not yours, I am certain—"

"Marianna." Percy placed a pale hand on her friend's anxious face.

"You dear, dear girl. I know that you fancy him, and that he fancies you. Please, do not trouble yourself over me. I'm very happy for you both, and all I want is—"

"I want you to have someone, too."

Percy smiled sadly, patting Marianna's hand and staring out her window.

For the second time that day, Constance startled her by bursting through the wall. "Forgive my intrusion, Miss Percy, but you simply must come to the Apollo lot!" The ghost's transparent eyes were sparkling. "If you don't, you surely will regret—"

Percy motioned the specter to silence. She wasn't sure how Marianna would feel about Constance and had not yet brought up any of her abilities regarding the dead. She had no idea how to begin.

"Percy?" the German girl said, seeing her friend's shift in focus.

"Marianna, my dear," Percy replied, deciding to take a chance. "Would you like a little adventure?"

"Always."

"Come on then." Gesturing for the ghost to lead the way, Percy dragged Marianna to her feet and out the door.

"What are we—?"

"The night is beautiful," Percy explained. "Out for a bit of fresh air, Miss Jennings!" she called as they rushed past the front desk.

"You won't get beyond the courtyard!" the woman shrieked.

"Don't worry, we're not trying!"

"Where *are* we going?" Marianna breathed.

"There." Percy pointed to the little graveyard behind Apollo Hall.

"Are we allowed? Is there a guard?"

"Don't worry," Percy promised. "We're still within school grounds."

"Who lies buried there?" Marianna asked.

"I was told it's for students and professors who have no other family. Oh! I suppose *I* might be buried here someday . . ."

Constance hovered nearby. "Once a year, Miss Percy, near my headstone, the ghosts of two professors celebrate their wedding anniversary. I thought you might appreciate it."

Through an open arch in the courtyard, behind Apollo Hall, the two living girls and the spectral one approached a heavy, spiked gate bordered by a rough stone wall. Marianna remained at the entrance, shaking her head.

Respecting her friend's limits but unwilling to turn back, Percy opened the hefty gate enough to wedge herself through. Gliding up a stone path that led to an inlaid circle, she took in the sight before her: two transparent figures in midcentury clothes, a man and a woman, waltzing. Their weightless feet spun gracefully above the ground and their feather-light forms held each other with confidence and care.

"Oh, to dance . . . To merely be *touched*," Percy whispered, dropping to her knees. Constance hovered silently nearby.

"What is it you see?" Marianna called.

Percy gave an aching sigh, which was caught by the breeze. "A waltz."

The sound of voices in the courtyard below drew Alexi away from the book he was reading by candlelight. The ghost that Miss Parker knew as Constance appeared, pointing emphatically below.

"What do you want?" he asked, irritated.

The ghost pointed again.

Gazing down from his window, he saw an incredible sight: two glowing, floating figures twirling above the tiny collection of graves. A third figure knelt nearby, long white hair billowing in the breeze, and Alexi recognized Percy, arms outstretched as if to embrace the dancers. He sighed, feeling a strange and tearing discomfort. Constance gestured with great detail, emphatic.

"All right, I'll do it. I'll teach her tomorrow." Alexi paused. "Stop staring at me, I said I'd do it. You've never bothered me before. Is the sole purpose of your afterlife to meddle in my affairs? Or is it Miss Parker to whom you're so drawn?"

Constance simply gave an enormous smile.

"You shouldn't, you know," Alexi grumbled. "Meddle. It's dangerous." No one knew better than he.

A stone gave way, and from a gaping hole in the Southern Hemisphere, spirits floated free, amazed and gleeful, hell-bent on trouble. The Groundskeeper giggled as each emerged. "Come on, come on!" He gestured them onward. "We're about to undo the wall between! If we can't find her, we'll shake the world till she tumbles out!"

Watching from across a portal, Lucille turned to the impatient Darkness, who rumbled, "I want you to kill them."

"What would be the point? They'll just inhabit new bodies. They always do. Don't you understand? This will never end. This vendetta of yours will never be settled until an all-out war is waged. You realize that, don't you?"

"But. Where. Is. She?"

Lucille took a deep breath. "I do not know."

Thunder crashed. "Break all the seals! Shred them! War!"

Lucille's eyes burned with emotion. "Not yet, my lord. Listen to me. It will all come together. We will find her. When I have them in my hands, she will follow."

The thunder turned to a hopeful whisper. "She will?"

Lucille reached out a hand. The long, thin fingers of Darkness reached back.

"There now. At last. Trust me, for once, would you? They've no idea the surprises that await."

CHAPTER
SEVENTEEN

ALONE IN THE SCIENTIFIC LIBRARY, HER BONE-WHITE FINGERS ABSENTLY tapping the table, Percy bent over a tome of Italian mathematics. She could not concentrate. Out of the corner of her eye she noticed a man enter the room and meander halfheartedly to a shelf. After a few moments he procured an armful of books. Evaluating his cargo with great disdain, he moved to sit opposite her.

Percy looked up in her usual meek manner. The finely dressed gentleman, incredibly lean and sharp-featured, bowed his head in acknowledgment. His eyes went wide as he took in her coils of snow-white hair and spectral appearance. Percy returned to her work. The gentleman, casting one last sideways glance, did the same.

It was not long before he rose from his seat and moved past Percy to return the volumes, one by one. On the fourth pass, his last book fell from his hands and an irritated sigh escaped his lips.

"Here, sir," Percy offered, bending to pick up the volume.

"Thank you, m'lady," the man replied.

As he took the book, their fingers brushed. Percy felt something overwhelming sweep through her, as if a thunderstorm broke open her veins. The two gasped in unison, and the gentleman's eyes clouded and his face contorted as if he'd seen something horrible.

It was best that the kind yet protective Miss Wilberforce had gone, lest she imagine an impropriety was taking place. Percy removed her glasses. The man seemed to be reeling from the odd moment, and reeled again from the vision of her irises. "Oh, my," he exclaimed. "Allow me to offer an apology, Miss . . ."

"Parker," Percy supplied.

"You are . . . quite unique."

"So I've been told," Percy remarked. "Now, if I may ask: Who are you, sir, and what did you just do to me?"

The man blinked, confused. "Well, my name is Withersby. Lord Withersby. I was sent here to do a bit of research. And I . . . touched you, Miss Parker. Accidentally."

"Lord Withersby, accidental brushes do not cause such . . . palpable shock."

"Ah. Yes. Well. That *was* rather odd, wasn't it?" He seemed at a loss.

"Indeed. So I must ask: Was it you or was it me?"

"I'm afraid it must have been my doing. Unless, Miss Parker, you are in the habit of such exchanges . . . ?" The man's eyes narrowed.

"No."

The two considered each other for a long moment. Withersby finally said, "The incident was entirely my fault. Do forgive me." With a bow, he turned to depart.

"But Lord Withersby," Percy called, "what *happened*?"

He halted and turned. "Have you, Miss Parker, ever witnessed someone burn to death?"

Percy recoiled, horrified. "N-no. Not that I recall!"

"No, no. Of course not. My mistake."

"Is that what you saw?" Percy pressed. "You touched me and saw *that*? A vision?"

"No, no," he said. "Nothing to trouble yourself about. Now, if I may . . . ?" He held up a hand, intending to take his leave.

"Wait, please," Percy begged.

He huffed. "Yes?"

"I have dreamed of fire, Lord Withersby. You see, the strangest things have happened all my life. Things like this. I yearn to find others who might be able to explain. I believe one professor here at Athens—Professor Rychman—might be just such a man. Do you know of him?"

An odd look crossed Withersby's face. "As a matter of fact, Miss Parker, I *have* heard of him, the mean old codger." The nobleman scoffed. "Sending a lord to a *library*."

Percy laughed. "Oh, the professor can be quite severe, it's true." Percy found herself all too eager to praise her professor. "But he's brilliant. He's been so tolerant of me and . . . I owe him much. May I speak to him of you?"

The man gave her an inscrutable smirk. "If you like, Miss Parker. If you like."

"I shall, Lord Withersby, thank you. What do you call what you just did?"

"Well . . ." The nobleman shrugged. "It is somewhat of a 'cognitive touch.'"

"And this happens whenever you have contact with another person?" she marveled.

"Person or thing," the man admitted, squirming. "But really, Miss Parker, we should not be having this conversation. It's improper. In *many* ways." Languidly, he waved a hand across Percy's face and seemed to be waiting for something to occur. After a moment, he furrowed his brow. Percy blinked at him, equally baffled.

"Well, damn!" Without another word, he turned and vacated the premises.

Bewildered, Percy wandered along the shelves, wondering what to make of the encounter. Passing a case wedged between the wall and a staircase, she felt the air around her grow cold. The chill seemed to be emanating from a moldy book, which Percy took down. The volume, an old biology text, fell open to a page that bore a note in the margin:

> *Constant is my care for you, sweet girl, my Constancy. All I ask*
> *is that you, for one blissful moment, put aside your obsession*
> *long enough to look into my eyes.—P.*

Percy gasped and turned to the front of the book, where she found a faded name: Constance Peterson. She flipped through the pages, quickly spotting another inscription written next to a diagram of the human heart:

> *Can science explain everything, my Constancy, when my heart*
> *beats only for you?*

On the opposite margin, there was a shaky reply:

> *Dear P., though you share my library table, I cannot commit*
> *any part of my heart, for I fear I do not have one to divide. The*
> *course of my blood flows toward science alone.—C.*

"Oh, Constance," Percy breathed. "Have I found your lost treasure at last?"

THE DOORBELL ECHOED HOLLOWLY THROUGH HIS DARK ESTATE. Grumbling, Alexi rose from his study chair to answer. He was not expecting visitors.

"Well, well," he remarked blandly, staring down at Elijah Withersby, who stood on his front stoop, smirking. "What do you want?"

"Aren't you going to invite me in?"

Alexi turned and walked away, knowing Withersby would follow. "Would you like something to drink?" he asked, leading his friend to the library. It was one of the few rooms in the sprawling estate that he maintained.

Elijah smiled. "Some rare and exceedingly expensive sherry, perhaps?"

Alexi went to a cabinet and returned with a little glass filled with the precious liquid. "Here." He handed it to Elijah, trying not to look as begrudging as he felt. "Enjoy."

"Such a host."

"You weren't invited," Alexi reminded him.

"I know." Elijah sighed.

"Tell me you did something useful today."

"I did that research you wanted on ghostly dogs." He dropped some parchment onto a nearby table. "While I was in the library, I met a student of yours. Ghastly pale girl."

"Ah." Alexi clenched his jaw and folded his hands. "Miss Parker. Why didn't you tell me you met her—"

"I'm telling you now, Lord and Master."

"Don't call me that," Alexi snapped, evoking Withersby's grin.

"Your Royal Eeriness? Melancholy Minister of the Constant Sneer?"

"I do not sneer."

Elijah snorted. "I beg to differ, Your Eeriness, but perhaps I alone see your disdainful glances."

"Lord Withersby, I'd sneer at the devil to halt your endless flow of drivel."

Elijah bowed, delighted. "That student of yours," he continued. "She seemed awfully fond of you. I cannot, upon my life, understand why."

Alexi shook his head. "Is that why you've come? Josephine suggested something similar, but I think you both daft. I don't want to hear another word about it."

Elijah looked taken aback. "Josephine? How did she meet Miss Parker?"

"In my office," Alexi replied.

"Indeed? In your office. Beguiling your students in the evening hours? Alexi, I'm—"

"Elijah!"

The nobleman wouldn't be silenced. Adopting a contemplative mien, he mused, "She'd be a fitting match for you, Alexi. Really, she's suitably haunting. You'd make a pair indeed; dark and light, quiet and bombastic."

"You fool, inviting *unwarranted* scandal!"

"Oh, but Alexi, you're all riled up! We've been waiting years for any sort of fancy to sprout up in your cold and dreary life, and now this? What fun!" Elijah stopped smiling and looked closely at Alexi.

"There's one awkward thing, which is why I've come. I touched the girl by accident and, well, she sensed my power. I tried to wipe her clean of the memory but it did not take." He braced himself for a reprimand.

Oddly, Alexi just smirked. "Miss Parker has talents unlike anyone I've ever met. She is a unique young lady."

Elijah rose with a chuckle, drained the rest of his sherry, and slipped toward the door. As an afterthought he added, "Oh, because I'm sure you're yearning to know, when I touched the girl, I saw a figure in flames. I'll be damned if I know what that means."

"A figure in flames?" Alexi leaned forward. "Did it resemble a phoenix? Was there a door?"

Elijah furrowed his brow. "Oh. Are you thinking . . . ?" He shrugged. "While I admit she's intriguing, she's hardly a likely candidate for Prophecy. Our seventh is most certainly Miss Linden. We're just waiting for the right sign. To that end, since you have neglected to visit us, I have been directed to bring her round to see you at the academy ball. So . . . dress pretty!"

Alexi's expression was grave. "Please, Elijah. Tell the group. No jumping to conclusions until we see all the facts."

"Yes, well, we're sure." Elijah grinned suddenly. "But why not? If you think our seventh is Miss Parker, why don't *you* touch her and see what you find out?"

As the clock struck six, a familiar form burst through Alexi's office wall. She fixed her gaze upon him until he gave her some acknowledgment: "I know! For God's sake, I'll teach her. Now leave me be." He batted his hand at the spirit. Constance smiled, satisfied, and vanished as there came a knock at the door.

"Come."

Miss Parker hurried in. She removed her scarf, causing her white hair to tumble around her shoulders, and removed her glasses. It occurred to Alexi that he had never seen her without her accoutrements outside of this room, and found himself pondering whether she was ever without them or if this ritualistic disrobing was alone for him and her bedroom mirror.

Perhaps she was conscious of being examined, for color flooded her cheeks and she blurted, "A fascinating few days I've had."

Alexi lifted an eyebrow. "Oh?"

"I met a man who brushed my hand and had a vision. Have you ever heard of such a thing?"

"Once," he replied, suppressing a weary chuckle.

"Really? Please tell me about it!"

"Sadly, I don't know any more, Miss Parker. I only *heard* of it. Now, your lesson, if you please."

The young woman sighed, riffled through her books and produced a paper. Each corner had a symbol scribbled upon it absentmindedly, a habit from having so many visions.

He examined her work. "On the last five, your mind evidently was more preoccupied with decorating your pages." He peered at the symbols as if they formed their own equation.

"Professor, I promise it's no fault of yours." Her shoulders rose and fell helplessly. "I'm past hope, I suppose."

Alexi shook his head. "You know, Miss Parker, you are too intelligent to be so melancholy."

Her eyes slowly rose to meet his. They glittered, pinning him with an unintentionally merciless stare. "Your contemporaries might say the same of you." Her bold moment then faded. "B-but you flatter me, sir. You have seen nothing of my intelligence, only my ineptitude."

"There are as many types of intelligence as there are sciences. That's the reason I continue these sessions, as I've given up on you ever truly mastering mathematics." Alexi paused as she gasped, having expected it. "Come now—don't look mortified, little specter."

Her hands clenched. "Please, sir, I ask you never to call me such a thing. Never!"

"There, finally! *Spine*, Miss Parker. Thank you," Alexi replied, smiling. Then he turned his attention to the book he had been underlining when she arrived, flung it down and launched into a lecture, ignoring that her mouth was still agape.

"Now. Here the Y value is manipulated. You will graph these. The lines follow a certain pattern, but you must follow the equation, not merely sketch a line. You might catch hold of this, merging as it is geometry with algebra."

Percy struggled to catch up. "It is?"

"Well, not exactly—but think of it as such and you'll like it better. That will be all."

Miss Parker shook her head and gathered her scarf. "Yes, of course. Good evening, sir." With a curtsey, she scurried to the door.

"Did I say you were dismissed?" he called.

She whirled. "You said, 'That will be all . . .'"

"For the *first* lesson." Alexi rose and went to a shelf. "Turn the phonograph handle," he instructed.

Miss Parker's pale face lit up and she rushed to do so, then turned back to face him. Soon the glorious sound of strings lifted sinuously into the air.

"The pleasant surprise about music and mathematics, Miss Parker, is that it's all numbers," Alexi began casually, striding to the center of the floor and holding out a hand. "And so is a dance."

The music became a lilting waltz. Miss Parker's eyes widened and a hand flew to her mouth. Joy radiated from her like a sunbeam, and for a brief moment, Alexi forgot what he was about to say.

"Don't make me regret taking the time to do this. Come here, silly girl."

Percy darted forward, but when she stood before him, looking up, she became so frightened that the professor might read her mind that she shrank back, embarrassed and awkward.

His own composure remained cool as he offered a noble bow. "That is your cue to curtsey, Miss Parker."

"Oh, yes, of course." She curtseyed, and the professor closed the distance between them to a decorous familiarity. She stared up at him. Her pounding heart made her mind swim. The professor placed a hand around her waist and took her right hand. When they made physical contact, Percy thought she might faint. Actual, voluntary human contact from a man she so admired . . . Tears rolled down Percy's white cheeks.

"My goodness, Miss Parker, if I thought this would upset you . . ." Alarmed, Professor Rychman withdrew. "Of course there is an academy rule of no contact, but a dance lesson is most certainly an exception, and if you fear—"

"Oh, no, my dear professor! You must understand. In the convent, the only man I ever could call a friend was a ghost. We could never so much as take hands . . ."

There was a moment, as they stared at each other, where Percy thought they shared a keen understanding. Two lone souls for whom touch was uncommon. The professor's dark eyes softened. He held out his hand, patiently allowing her to approach when ready.

Percy wiped her eyes and stepped forward. His hand rested at her waist. Her fingers touched upon his other palm, and he coaxed her hand into his, squeezing gently.

"Your fear of me simply must cease," he commanded.

"It . . . it isn't that I'm *afraid*, Professor."

"If I'm not mistaken, Miss Parker, you quake."

"Not out of fear, I assure you!" After this declaration, more mottled patches burst upon Percy's porcelain cheeks. She was terrified anew that he'd expel her on the spot.

The professor cleared his throat and simply said, "The rhythm guides us, Miss Parker. One-two-three, one-two-three." He tapped time upon her finger. "Your feet must do the same. Place your other hand on my shoulder."

Percy complied. She was far too nervous to look at him. Instead, she stared at the ornate silver button that clasped his robe about his neck and held his signature scarlet cravat in place.

"I will lead with my right foot. Step back with your left." The professor moved forward. As Percy faltered he said, "No, the other—"

"I'm so sorry!"

"Stop apologizing, Miss Parker, and *move*."

Percy stepped back, obedient if rigid. The professor added, "Repeat this, following my lead, stepping back when I step forward, interchanging." As he did so, Percy followed with hesitation but precision. She felt a giddy rush.

"I see!" She dared to look up at him, and grinned.

"It's rather simple once you know the steps," he stated, and began again. "Can you feel the pulse?"

Their steps remained small and controlled. "Yes," she breathed, shocked at her voice, which was a good deal more sensual than she intended. Their eyes locked, Percy stumbled and broke away. "I am sorry, Professor, but—"

He stepped forward and grabbed her hand, firmly turning her to face him again. Percy gasped as he clamped his other hand upon her waist, putting an abrupt halt to her cringing retreat. He stepped forward. She stepped back. They moved around the open spaces of the office, each turn imparting confidence. Finally, Percy could not hold back a delighted laugh. Constance was watching, hovering above the professor's desk, smiling proudly.

"I'm dancing!" Percy whispered with glee.

The professor smiled, his eyes sparkling for the moment. "Indeed you are," he replied, and Percy felt a tug upon her right hand. She allowed his pull—and twirled beneath his arm. As she spun to face him again, his hand returned to her waist. It took everything she had not to swoon.

The professor lowered his head in approval. "Not a bad start, Miss Parker. You see, if you pay attention to your partner, you can react without even being warned." He smirked, displaying a mischievousness Percy had never seen—or perhaps it was merely wishful thinking on her part.

The music ended in a crackle. The professor released Percy and stepped back, bowed, holding her gaze. Percy curtseyed in return, wishing the music had gone on indefinitely.

"Now . . . no more moping about that damnable gala!" he commanded, moving to the phonograph and lifting the needle.

"Oh, Professor, how can I ever thank you?" She ran forward, then stopped, realizing with sudden horror that she had meant to embrace him.

"Good night, Miss Parker," he said.

"Yes, of course. Good night, Professor Rychman. Thank you!" She hurriedly gathered her things to cover her dangerous intention. "I shall see you on Saturday?"

"Perhaps you will find me in a dark corner, hiding," he admitted, grimacing as he took to the chair behind his desk and busied himself with a cup of spiced tea.

"Well. Good night, then." She hurried to the door, wondering if the blush upon her cheeks would ever fade. However, her gaze fell upon the painting that earlier had done her such an ill turn, and she couldn't help but comment. "Do you know why that painting is so ironic to me, Professor?" She stared at the woman being led down into the darkness.

"Do tell, Miss Parker."

Percy removed her glasses again and turned to face him. "Percy is my *nick*name." Then she quit his chamber.

Outside, in the hall, she swooned. Constance bobbed at her side. "You looked so beautiful together," the ghost breathed.

"Oh, no, none of that, Constance, I've warned you against insinuation," Percy snapped. But then, suddenly: "Oh, my! I nearly forgot!" She fumbled among her books and drew one out. "This was in the library, and I believe it's yours. The writing in the margins . . . do you recall it?" She flipped to the appropriate page.

Constance stared, a translucent hand at her lips. "That's it," she choked, reading. A drop of water splashed the floor: a tear, made manifest. "My greatest folly," the ghost admitted, "was to deny a lovely soul who asked nothing more than to remain by my side." She looked desperately at Percy. "You and I seek such similar comfort, do we not? Shall I now find mine?"

"Perhaps your 'P.' wanders nearby, seeking you. Or perhaps . . . perhaps you are simply free to be at peace."

"Yes, yes! I feel peace, Percy, no longer any sickness in my hollow head. It's why I was pushing you toward your professor—because no matter what may stand between, love is the highest power on earth and our one true purpose. You realize that now, don't you, Percy?"

"Of course," Percy murmured, looking at the ground.

The spirit continued blithely. "Now that *I* know, and now that I've helped you, I can rest."

Percy waved the ghost onward, smiling. "Go! Go and find rest, my friend."

Constance nodded and grew blindingly bright. "At last. I shall see you on the other side," she said. And with a loving wave of her hand, at last the specter dissipated, leaving behind only the hint of a word: *"Paul . . ."*

Percy wiped her watering eyes and darted back to her residence hall, ignoring the guard she passed along the way; she couldn't be troubled by murderers or fear when there was so much beauty in the world. Bursting through Marianna's door, she wailed, "He taught me how to waltz!" then clapped her hands over her mouth.

Marianna looked up from her bed, a smile creeping over her face. "Who?"

"You'll never guess!"

Her friend leaned forward, clearly titillated.

Percy clasped her hands and whispered, "I can't begin to describe how incredible it felt to be touched on the waist, held by the hand . . . Oh, this is silly and dangerous!"

"Waltzing?"

Percy looked around as if the walls had ears. "We should not speak of it."

"Because Miss Thompson might dismiss you out of jealousy?"

Percy squealed. "It was a *lesson*, Marianna. There was nothing untoward—truly! This was utterly innocent! I am his student!"

"Are not some people drawn to each other, no matter their professions, age, or circumstances? Does fate mean nothing? Are you not nineteen, no longer a girl but a woman? Back in my homeland—"

Percy shook her head, crushing all hope. "We cannot pose such questions, Marianna, no matter where we are. I shan't risk my future at this academy. Whatever exists between him and the headmistress, so be it. And . . . there's been nothing remotely inappropriate. He's only trying to help."

Marianna shrugged, thoughtful. "Well, no matter. We must find you a dress."

"A dress?"

"For the ball, silly. You do not mean to tell me after that rousing lesson you plan to miss it?"

"Oh. Well. Perhaps I'll go—but I'll still look a fright, and no one will want to dance with me."

"You will not look a fright, Percy," her friend promised, moving to her wardrobe. "Love's bloom becomes you."

Percy hissed. "Never say that, Marianna."

Marianna withdrew a gorgeous satin mass from the wardrobe. "I was sent three gowns, Percy, you must have one!" When Percy laughed, overcome, and nearly knocked her to the floor in an exuberant hug, Marianna added, "Come, *meine Liebe,* there are errands to run, flowers to gather and dreams yet to be planned!"

THE GROUNDSKEEPER STOOD LOOKING THROUGH THE PORTAL, HIS GAZE sweeping the river Thames up to the Tower of London. He was finally home, and he stood with callused feet planted firmly on his natural soil, his arms folded.

"Oh, my darling Lucy-loo!" he cried, not knowing where she was but certain that she would soon make the Whisper-world proud. "With you *and* the Guard on the loose, my dear, nothing will stop you. Not this time. Nothing between you and the last pin. Pry, pry, my lovey, it's up to you," he chortled, the pitch of his singsong voice rising. "We've loosened, we've loosened, and everything's ready. Now . . . shatter the seal!"

CHAPTER
EIGHTEEN

THE CORRIDORS OF ATHENE HALL WERE FILLED WITH THE SOFT MUR-
murs of women, the rustle of expensive fabrics, and the occasional giggle.
Excitement had transformed Marianna into a force of nature. Only once
she and Percy had donned their finery and done up all their buttons and
clasps did she let either of them pause to breathe—and breathing was
difficult given the tight press of their undergarments. With grand ceremony, both girls turned to look in the mirror.

Percy did not recognize herself. Pale lavender satin enveloped her.
Paired with a snug corset, Percy's flowing skirt swept out into a bell,
with a gathered layer drawn up on either side and cinched into a bustle
at the back. A high-backed dress with buttons all down the spine, its
neckline was elegantly sloped to allow generous amounts of flesh to be
shown without scandal, the bust accented by flowers embroidered in silver thread and seed pearls. The glitter of her necklace chain matched the
sparkle of Percy's eyes and her phoenix charm lay reassuringly tucked
into her bodice. A perfect braid swept her hair into a circlet and sprigs of
heather crowned her a veritable fairy queen. Marianna had rubbed the
oil of the flowers behind Percy's ears and around her wrists, and the
smell filled Percy's nostrils with calm delight.

Marianna, elegant in burgundy taffeta with fitted sleeves and a slender V-line waist, spun about slowly. She presented a pair of pale lavender
lace gloves to her friend. "You are an incredible sight, Percy. You *are*
Titania. This gala is yours."

"I . . . I do look all right, don't I?" Percy breathed. For the first time
in her life, she was nearly pretty. She could not stop staring at her reflection. But there was one hesitation: She had never once left her room

without a scarf. "Marianna, I can't, I'm frightened." Overwhelmed, she reached for the muslin.

"Percy, I tell you, you look amazing. *Schöne!*"

"But you're accustomed to me." Percy paused. "Well, you and the professor. He's seen me, too. He demanded I be brave and not hide beneath shrouds while I'm in his office." She was surprised she'd never before admitted this to her friend.

Marianna seemed pleased. "Tonight, Percy, you'll be braver than ever before."

A second-floor chamber long locked away, the ballroom of Promethe Hall was a dreamily glittering sight to behold. This gala was the academy's one grand indulgence, and Percy and Marianna hesitated at the threshold.

The ballroom was long, one side lined with high windows that made a dark, starry night visible above the rim of the courtyard. At the center, French doors opened onto little balconies. Past filmy white curtains rustling in the wake of a crisp fall breeze, the silhouettes of coupled men and women stood staring contemplatively at each other's faces or the evening sky. The opposite wall was golden and colonnaded, with wide doors at both ends. Alcoves exhibited gaggles of murmuring young ladies who reclined upon benches lined with crimson velvet. Busts of philosophers and literary figures stood silent sentry amid the frivolity.

After drinking in the sights, the two girls crept beyond the threshold. Marianna caught Percy's eye and nodded across the long hall. Like a guardian statue, there stood an unmistakable figure swathed in black. Percy let out a choking sigh.

Marianna shook her head. "You are hopeless, my friend. Why is it you have set your sights on the forbidden? Is it because you feel no one else will court you?"

The evening had made her friend bold, but Percy did not mind. In this atmosphere, it seemed as if almost anything could happen. "No. He just . . ." Percy found she had no words.

Marianna's friend Edward approached, cutting a dashing figure in a navy coat that fit him like a glove, a gray silk cravat tucked neatly into his vest. His tousled chestnut hair hanging adorably down over his eyebrows, he stared at Marianna with unabashed rapture. "Miss Farelei," he murmured, clearly relishing the opportunity to kiss her gloved hand. Their bodies shivered simultaneously.

He turned to Percy with a wide and welcoming smile and kissed her lace-covered hand in turn. "Miss Parker, I am delighted you're here!" He squeezed her hand in his. "You are unlike anyone I have ever seen— and I mean that kindly. Come into the light, Miss Parker, I'll not allow you to slink in the shadows. To do so would be to eclipse the moon."

Percy beamed. "Your kind words, Mr. Page, are a gift. A professor of mine recently expressed similar sentiments. Perhaps I ought to listen." Her eyes flicked to the opposite corner of the room, where Professor Rychman conversed with a history teacher, looking thoroughly bored.

"Perhaps," Marianna supplied with a smirk.

The three students amused themselves with punch and confections, listening to the string quartet, watching and appreciating the gala's attendees. Everyone boasted breathtaking finery, the very latest fashions in sleeves, bustles, and buttons.

Edward held out an arm for Marianna. "Miss Parker," he said, "would you mind if I escorted your friend about the room? I promised I'd introduce her to a fellow recently returned from her homeland."

Percy nodded graciously, seeing how Marianna's eyes lit up. "By all means," she said, waving them off. Her friend replied with a look of gratitude, and Percy smiled again, happy until she was assailed by a tinge of jealousy, jealousy for the way Edward looked at the other girl's normal, beautiful face.

Moving to sit alone in a chair by the wall, she noted some unwanted attention—murmurs and the occasional titter—but ignored them as best she could, determinedly studying her peers in turn.

Batted eyelashes, soft words exchanged by inviting lips, giggles, smiles, butterfly kisses upon palms, scarlet flushes, fans held at precise angles to indicate unspoken signals, a world unfolded around Percy in a language she knew painfully that she didn't understand, a world in which she had no place and was not welcome.

After a bit, the living dancers failed to amuse and Percy instead watched the dead, who hovered beyond the ballroom windows, hesitant to join the party. Her gaze crossed with that of one she recognized from her residence hall; he lifted a transparent hand in greeting. Percy waved back with a smile—and then realized she ought not be seen waving to thin air. Quickly she changed the motion to adjusting a bud of heather in her hair. The subtle pointing and whispers of her peers increased, and Percy blushed, knowing she was on display.

MRS. RATHBINE WAS DRONING ON ABOUT ROMAN POTTERY WHEN Alexi first noticed the goddess across the ballroom: Miss Parker had come, and admirably without her shields. A goddess indeed, for he had guessed her full name after her hint about the painting in his office. She had the name of *his* goddess, though that long-ago oracle had never given it. Prophecy had come, surely, and in the surprising form of a student. He knew she could not know that truth for herself, troublesome as her ignorance was. They would both have to await the final revelation.

Miss Parker's elegant dress and elaborate coif were stunning. Her fine features had been painted with the softest rose blush and her pale eyes flashed like diamonds. She was by far the most captivating thing ever seen at this silly event.

Over the course of several minutes, as dancing continued, he noted her talking to a couple of young ladies who drifted past. She was gracious and returned their trivial, polite conversation, but when she glanced away, he read her struggle and isolation. She alone, he was sure, understood why he dreaded this event every year. Such recognition was profound.

An enraptured young couple twirled past Percy and waved. She returned the gesture happily but her warm smile faded quickly. Something seized deep inside Alexi. Perhaps she felt the weight of his stare, for she looked up. Eyes like snowcaps finally met his, and the rest of the world was muted.

"There you are—my favorite gargoyle!" came a taunting voice.

Alexi turned to see Elijah Withersby leading a woman through one of the arched entrances to the ballroom. Miss Linden. Having only seen her briefly, in the moonlight, Alexi was unprepared for her beauty. Her sensual ruby lips twisted in a smile, and her green eyes glittered with pleased recognition. Her red satin dress was simple yet tremendously flattering.

"Here's the man of the hour at last," Elijah said. "Professor Rychman, our dear Miss Lucille Linden."

Alexi kissed the woman's gloved hand with solemn courtesy. Rosy-cheeked, with black hair curled immaculately in place, she was indeed breathtaking. "A pleasure to see you, Miss Linden. I am sorry it has taken so long for our paths to again cross."

"The pleasure is entirely mine, Professor Rychman, and I forgive you your absence, sorrowful though it has been. Lord Withersby has been kind, as has Miss Belledoux. If you hadn't pointed me there, I'd have been without recourse! I am forever in your debt. Fate brought me to you, I am sure of it."

Alexi could see Elijah nodding eagerly.

"Of your little coterie, Professor, you're the only one I haven't gotten to know, though Lord Withersby has told me much about you."

"Has he now?" Alexi eyed his friend.

Miss Linden sighed. "It is difficult to be a stranger in such a large place, and to feel safe when the world is coming apart at the seams . . ."

She possessed a magnetic intensity Alexi had never encountered, and her regard surpassed custom. Just over the woman's perfect, bare shoulder, Alexi caught the opal eyes of Miss Parker, looking on in stricken sorrow. Her pale, heather-framed face quickly rallied into a hollow smile, and she tried to pretend she hadn't been staring. But eyes like hers could truly hide nothing; when the music slowed and the couples parted and no one approached her, Percy rose from her chair and fled the room. Alexi's instinct was to follow.

"Professor Rychman?" chimed a musical voice, jarring him from his reverie. "Are you all right?"

Alexi faced Miss Linden. "My apologies. Something caught my eye."

"Ah, we interrupt his chaperoning, Miss Linden," Elijah taunted. "The good professor handles every task with the utmost gravity. He takes great care with his *students*."

Alexi looked sharply at his friend, but Miss Linden smiled and he felt her smooth gloved hand graze his. "I admire gravity in a man." Her eyes were precious emeralds, sparkling at him. Yet they could not keep his mind from wandering.

"If you wouldn't mind, Miss Linden . . . I am terribly sorry. It was a true pleasure to see you, but I must beg your leave. I believe someone requires my assistance. A *student*," he added, staring at Withersby.

"I shall miss you," Miss Linden replied. "But I leave you to your duty."

Elijah was quick to take the hand she waved in languid dismissal. Giving Alexi a vicious, scornful look, he led her away.

Percy clutched the folds of her fine skirts as she swept up the stairs to the third floor, far from the ballroom. "This must end," she commanded herself in a mournful whisper. "Your heart is dangerously out of hand! You're here to be a student, not a romantic. And if no one asks you to dance and you're jealous of a beautiful woman whose hair looks coiffed with serpents, so be it—but you cannot let it destroy you!"

The stairs opened onto a foyer, red granite columns rising like stone tree trunks in a forest clearing. The walls were plain and stately. White drapes at each window appeared silver in the moonlight. The solitude of the place let Percy breathe again. She felt far more at home here than she had under the chandeliers. Music wafted from below in a spectral waltz.

The click of her dainty shoes echoed softly upon the marble. She made her way to the center of the open space and stopped inside a mosaic circle—Athens's seal, a golden eagle. "'As the Promethean fire which banished darkness, so Knowledge bears the Power and the Light,'" Percy murmured, reading the motto.

Whirling slowly in time to the music, she released the tension in her arms, let her head loll, and loosed a sigh. Percy felt the strings play as if they were kisses across her face, light touches of the feathers of birds. She was monarch of this moonlit hall: the air, light and shadows obeyed her command. Of course her mind placed her dear professor in her grasp, one hand holding hers and the other firmly upon her waist. And rather than fighting the image or letting it embarrass her, she gave in fully and welcomed Professor Rychman into her dream.

Suddenly, Percy felt something cold graze her hand. Her eyes opened in a flash and she saw a worn, smiling old man in tattered Elizabethan garb—an old friend she never thought she'd see again. "Gregory!"

"Hello, dear girl," said the faint, raspy voice.

"How in heaven—? How did you come here?"

"I've only a moment before my weary wisp be finally laid to rest. But ye shan't take me, said I to the heavens, before my girl's first dance!" The wizened face widened in a smile.

Percy laughed. "Indeed, my dearest Gregory, how dare *you* not be my first?"

Cold air found Percy's left side and touched Percy's outstretched right palm, and with a nod she led the spirit in the waltz rising from below—a dance an Elizabethan would not know, but as there were no corporeal feet for her to trip on, it proceeded without flaw.

"Hast thou found happiness, my child?"

"Sometimes," Percy replied, as she and the ghost glided across the marble floor.

"Dost a brave young lad own your heart? Thou wert lost in reverie when I found thee, and—"

"Hush! None of that. Your hopeless romantic of a girl has merely grown older, not wiser, I'm afraid. My desired match is . . . unlikely."

"Foolish girl! Thou art mad, to fix thy heart on what cannot be, when thou hast so much to give!"

"Don't chide, dear Gregory. My fate is my own to choose . . ."

"But who shall care for my little swan?"

"God shall provide," Percy replied—the words Reverend Mother always used to assure her. She hoped they were true.

The waltz drifted to its dainty end. Gregory reached out a translucent hand, and Percy felt a cold trickle of air down her cheek. "Percy, my time hath run its compass." The ghost's voice was thin; he was beginning to fade. "My little one is now a lady. Dost thou relinquish me?"

"With all my heart. Good night, sweet prince, I wish you peace!" Percy blew her friend's diminishing figure a kiss. In moments Gregory was nothing but a lingering sound and a cool patch of air. "'Flights of angels sing thee to thy rest,'" Percy added, her voice breaking, hoping their familiar, final benediction would carry him home.

Tears sprang forth at the loss of her greatest friend and Percy let them come.

"Now, now, Miss Parker, what's this?" a voice scolded from behind.

Percy whirled at the familiar, stern sound. A figure broke from shadow, clad in an elegantly tailored frock coat trimmed with ornate embroidery. His cravat was snowy white tonight and his black hair was combed neatly, framing that noble, stoic face which Percy spent countless hours contemplating. Percy's heart throbbed in her throat.

"Oh, Professor! Good evening!" All grace drained away, cut to the quick by his unexpected appearance. She tried to bat away her tears but his firm hand caught her pale, lace-covered fingers. He took her hand, their entwined fingers bridging the cold chasm between their bodies.

"May I have this dance, Miss Parker?"

"Oh . . . of course, sir." A blush bloomed ferociously in her cheeks but she was helpless to stop it.

As his hand grasped hers, she examined his full lips, which had just enough curve to make his expression inviting. There was just enough light in those dark eyes to make Percy wholly forget about breathing, and without words or even a nod he drew her hand to his side. He slid his opposite hand around layers of smooth lavender satin and placed the fullness of his palm assuredly upon her waist.

Percy's hand flew to his shoulder, alighting like a lark on a branch. She saw his nostrils flare, as if he took in the intoxicating scent of the heather she wore. They began to waltz—slowly at first, their circles precise and narrow, their gazes locked. Percy, who had already memorized the professor's features, now savored each pore, crease, and eyelash. The study of his sculpted lips forced her to close her eyes or else, truly, her knees would have buckled. In turn she knew she was being parceled out; but from *him,* she welcomed the scrutiny.

Their bodies were one with the music and Percy found she didn't have to think about the correct steps any longer. In and out of the moonlight they floated, silent save for the deft clicks of their heels, the whispers of the music rising from below, and the occasional sigh escaping Percy's lips.

Professor Rychman spun her, and Percy swept fully against him, lingering for a moment. She took a deep breath: He smelled faintly of clove tea and leather-bound books. She did not want to remove her cheek from the thick black lapel of his jacket; she could have nestled in that warm darkness indefinitely. This was surely a glorious dream . . .

Had they not been interrupted, they might have danced till dawn, time slowing as they stared into each other's eyes and dreamed volumes neither could voice. But their magical moment was fleeting. A raucous squawk sounded. The professor's brow furrowed and his eyes clouded. He broke away, and a hand went to his temple as if he had been pierced by a sharp pain.

They both turned to the window, staring at the large black bird upon the branch outside. "Professor?" Percy said.

He turned, focusing on her, then sighed as if heavily burdened. "Pardon me, sweet girl. I must go."

Percy blinked, enraptured by his endearment and at the same moment distraught at his retreat. "My apologies, Professor. I did not mean to keep you—"

"It was I who asked you to dance, Miss Parker, but I'm afraid it may have been in error," he explained, raking his hand through his hair.

"Oh." Percy looked at the floor, her blush reignited. Was he sorrowful that they had broken the school rules of conduct?

Perhaps he sensed her fear, for he reassured her with weary gentleness, "You've done nothing wrong, Miss Parker, only provided a welcome distraction. But work calls."

The raven squawked impatiently. Percy glanced over. There was something strange about the bird; a tiny patch of blue glistened upon its black breast. Was it the same raven that had perched outside the headmistress's office?

Percy shuddered. What strange omens were these? What exactly did her professor hide?

A CRISP EVENING WIND BLEW THROUGH THE OPEN WINDOW NEAR Lucretia Marie O'Shannon Connor, known commonly as Jane. Her fellows in the Guard were never sure if her name was the one she'd been given at birth or a romanticized invention, but they enjoyed her eccentricities where her actual family did not. Such as her fondness for solitude: She was not a social creature, and certain secrets increased her proclivity for isolation.

A white cat padded around the fireplace as if looking for something misplaced. The wind whipped more strongly through the open window, blowing the damask curtains and rattling the pages of Jane's open book. She saw the cat stop pacing and stare past her toward the door, ears erect and tail pointed.

"What is it, Marlowe?" The cat looked up with flashing, intelligent golden eyes, and wrapped a long tail around her ankle. "Ah, something's here, is it?" Jane said. She closed her book and stood. "Well, Marlowe, we'll just have to encourage it to leave, won't we?" She turned to face the open doorway. "Holy Mother of—"

* * *

"I'VE WORK TO DO," ALEXI REPEATED HASTILY, BACKING TO THE STAIRS. "And you have a ball to attend. You must return." As Miss Parker moved forward, unconsciously maintaining their proximity, he held up a hand. "*Good night,* Miss Parker."

"Good night, Professor Rychman." A hand rose to her lips but the girl caught herself, never actually blowing him the kiss. Exchanging such a token of affection would have been wholly inappropriate on any night, but Alexi allowed a flickering smile to nonetheless toy at the corner of his mouth. Then he bowed slightly and turned to hurry down the stairs.

"Professor?" she called. He turned back. "Thank you. Thank you so much."

"What else was I to do?" he replied, letting her interpret as she would. Then he turned and was off again.

There was no choice but to abandon her. Alexi's temple throbbed, his chest tightened and his stomach churned, and he knew some evil had come to one of his companions. He was being punished for his foolish indulgence. Taunting Prophecy came with consequences. He was moving too fast, not waiting for the appropriate sign.

Rushing out the door into the cool evening air, past giddy partygoers and whispering couples, Alexi's anxiety was only heightened by thoughts of Miss Parker, who had stood unabashedly enraptured by the touch of his hand. Percy's laughter, the radiance of her sweet, innocent soul— every aspect of her had been aphrodisiac, gently alleviating years of weight upon his soul. Her eyes had betrayed both of them: They shouted her feelings and stirred up his own, unfamiliar and unsettling as they were.

Rebecca was awaiting him on the steps of the academy, tapping her foot in supreme irritation. "Where have you been?" she snapped as a carriage sped around the corner and shrieked to a halt.

Alexi shrugged as he climbed inside, following her. "Waltzing." The carriage set off.

"Waltzing? Are you ill?" Rebecca asked.

"Fevered, perhaps. Do we know what we're in for?"

"Marlowe came to my window."

"Really? You ought to have asked him to dinner. I have a question about Faustus—"

"Shut up." Rebecca scowled. "Marlowe, Jane's familiar. She's in trouble."

"She'll stave it off, whatever it is. I have complete faith in—"

"Remember the dog?"

Alexi blanched. "I assume the others are on their way and will meet us there. Elijah was attending Miss Linden," Alexi recalled, seized with sudden guilt. "I assume he'll offer her some grand excuse and find us?"

"You mean, you weren't waltzing with her? Who, then?"

Alexi rolled his eyes. "What does it matter?"

Rebecca clenched her fists but said nothing.

Alexi stared at her. "I know you all think she's our seventh, but nothing's yet proven. If—"

Josephine's cry outside the carriage and the pounding of horse hooves beside them alerted him that their time was short. They were almost at Aldgate, and Alexi prayed they weren't too late.

"'WORK CALLS . . .'" PERCY REPEATED THE PROFESSOR'S WORDS, STANDing alone once more in the moonlit foyer. She wanted to laugh and cry, but mostly she wished to scream. Had there indeed been a spark between them? Could she trust her memory and senses? She shook her head, feeling faint. Surely it had been imagination.

Darting down the stairs, she was out the front door before her mind caught up. "What sort of work at Saturday midnight?" she asked herself. "And what am I doing?"

A guard called out, asking why she was running, but she was inside Apollo Hall before she could answer, darting up the stairs and knocking on Professor Rychman's door with no idea of what she was going to say if he answered. Her heart thundered. She had no right to inquire of him, yet here she was, compelled to question. She knocked again. There was no response.

The door was unlocked. Boldly she opened it. The room was dark and uninhabited.

"What work has he to do?" she asked the empty chamber. "Please tell me your mysteries, Professor Rychman. Perhaps they shall illuminate mine . . ."

* * *

"My God. Not you again . . ."

Jane was not a weak woman. She trekked down the Minories to the Tower of London on a regular basis to face the local specters. While none of her illustrious group could ever completely confine or expel the tower's many spirits, with a gentle Celtic admonition she policed its boundaries, keeping the antics of centuries of ghosts inside the ancient, worn stone walls. She bade poor Margaret Pole and her brutal, ax-wielding executioner remain within Tower Green lest they disrupt the whole of Tower Hill with the gruesome repetition of her death. But the black cloud floating before her was more terrifying than any of the tower's offerings. This blackness was terror itself. It hovered at the threshold, taking up her entire doorway. When last Jane had seen it, she'd had the aid of her companions. Even then, it had almost taken Elijah's life.

The cloud congealed into the form of a single-headed canine. That head then multiplied, and the beast stalked forward and began to circle her chair. From its feet, which hovered a good six inches from the ground, blood appeared to drip. Blood culled from Whitechapel.

The monster opened a hellacious maw and growled: the whispers of a thousand damnations. It sniffed her then struck. Jane screamed as blood poured from a deep rent across her forearm, and a shriek flew from her lips as she pressed back hard against her chair. The incantation worked, if only for a moment; the abomination jumped back as if scalded.

"What do you want?" Jane demanded, as the infuriated beast slashed her curtains. "Damned Ripper. What are ye looking for?"

The monster lashed out. Shallow wounds grew in Jane's cheeks, stinging and creating tearlike trails of blood. Like the Ripper's other victims, Jane would die ignominiously, cloven and torn. She prepared herself, knowing that wars always had casualties. She had just expected to remain safe, a healer—

Her front door suddenly burst open and the back of her library exploded in flame. The beast turned, startled. Alexi Rychman, chanting in an ancient tongue rich and beautiful, entered the room. A whirlwind surrounded him; his dark eyes were blazing and, with a wave of his hand, he extinguished the fire.

"Impeccable timing, my friends," Jane murmured—and promptly fainted.

"*Non, non!* None of us have your hands to heal, *chérie*." Josephine rushed forward. Ripping fabric from her dress and winding it around her friend's injured arm, she massaged Jane's temple.

"Hello again, you filthy creature of hell!" Alexi growled, staring unflinchingly at the beast.

A keening note rose from Rebecca's throat, a call for the Guard to unite in their attack. It was a noise sweet and ancient, as if the wind were singing. The room filled with whispers, the beating of a thousand wings. Forked blue lightning crackled above their heads.

Alexi's arms rose, his hands deftly flicking forward as if conducting violinists to lift their bows for a symphony's seminal note. Ringlets of blue flame danced across his fingertips. Threads of lightning arced forward to bind their foe. The abomination writhed, groaning like a sinking ship and spitting like a rainstorm.

Josephine, tending to Jane, was suddenly knocked to the ground. She rose up, hand to her forehead, and stared deeply into the center of the vaporous beast, transfixed by the spear of madness itself. Elijah called out her name, and Josephine felt something warm wash over her, as if her veins were caressed from the inside out, and her mind was released from the void. She stepped back and into her lover's arms. "*Merci* . . ."

Jane's head lolled to the side. "Ah, ah, none of that!" Josie snapped, calling, "Lucretia Marie O'Shannon Connor!" Jane's eyes shot open. "Good. Now, *look*." Josephine pulled a golden locket from around her neck, opened it and held out the shimmering image of an angel. The rest would take care of itself.

"Rebecca, dear, could you enlighten us a bit?" Alexi asked with mild strain. He did not want his companions to worry, but this creature was like nothing he'd ever contained.

Rebecca cried out, "'How you have fallen from Heaven, bright morning star, felled to the Earth, sprawling helpless across the nations! You thought in your own mind, I will scale the heavens . . . Yet shall you be brought down to Sheol, to the depths of the Abyss!'" When in doubt, the King James Bible often sufficed.

Alexi applauded as the creature snapped its many jaws and howled. "Well said, Rebecca! This puppy does not care for the Word of God. Now, my friends, I think it goes without saying that all shows must eventually let down their curtains. Cantus of Extinction!" Clearing his throat as if preparing a lecture, he peered into the contracting form of their enemy and confided, "You should feel privileged, we've never had to sing this one."

Music rose in the room, an overture from the night sky, every star an instrument. However, just as the cantus swelled, their foe writhed from the grasp of Alexi's blue flame and burst out the window. *"No!"* Alexi shrieked. Jagged shards of glass rained down on the Guard.

Once again the creature was gone but not destroyed.

CHAPTER
NINETEEN

PERCY STOOD AT THE CENTER OF HER ROOM, WEARING A LONG NIGHT-gown of filmy white fabric. It swished around her as she rocked from side to side, humming softly. Absently fingering the contours of the phoenix pendant between her breasts, she hardly noticed how warm it felt. One sensation obliterated all else: the firm press of Professor Rychman's hand upon her waist. That memory was euphoria.

The obsession was silly, of course. Percy hated it. She had prayed the rosary repeatedly to try to derail her fixation, but she remained trapped in abject adoration.

She lay back on her bed. The more she tried to fight her daydreams, the more scorching they became. She imagined him bent over her, eas-ing her onto her pillow as carnality consumed them. Her back arched upward, and as she pressed herself into his covetous, illicit, imaginary embrace, the phoenix pendant shifted and came to rest upon her ster-num.

"WE DEMAND PROPHECY NOW!"

In their chapel, the voices of the Guard rose like the blowing sands of a thousand years. A hazy door burst through the air, swinging open at the altar. The Guard descended, formed a circle, hands clasped and heads held high, responding in otherworldly liturgy as instinctive as their breath.

"In darkness, a door. In bound souls, a circle of fire. Immortal force in mortal hearts. Six to calm the restless dead. Six to shield the restless living."

A ring of blue flame leaped into being, harmlessly licking their ankles.

"Great spirit of the Grand Work, we are here because we're weak!" Alexi cried. "Since childhood we've looked for you, beautiful creature, to return and guide us. Be silent no longer! Give us the friend you promised. *Seven* to calm the restless dead. *Seven* to shield the restless living."

He lifted his head to the image topping the altar. "Great One, let your feathers unfurl. Your wisdom!" A disembodied burst of music sounded. "Your power!" The music grew louder. "Your light!" A shaft of ruby-orange fire leaped from the center of the floor to illuminate a burning heart in the white stained-glass bird above.

"We demand Prophecy! We cannot wait! Where *is* she?"

SOMEONE WAS SCREAMING, BURNING, HIS BODY ENCASED IN BLOODRED flames. A divine force was splintering before her eyes. Lying on her bed, Percy cried out in empathy, the terrible vision like hot oil upon her eyes.

There was a piercing, burning pain just below her throat. She looked down in horror at her glowing red pendant. Her ivory skin was sizzling. Percy quickly unclasped the necklace and hurled it to the floor, where it lay, inert. Upon her skin, just above her breasts, she could see the perfect imprint of a phoenix. Blood welled at its edges.

Breath hissed through her teeth as she rushed to the lavatory, where she stared into the large mirror at the blood-lined stamp of symbolic rebirth. She dipped a cloth into a basin of cool water and pressed it to her chest, moaning.

"Such strange things! Mother, why did you leave me this bird? Why won't you guide me now? I see so many spirits; why are you not among them? Why am I left in the dark? Please, tell me something."

Her stinging skin was her only response.

"PLEASE, TELL US SOMETHING," ALEXI BEGGED.

Warm, vibrating power coursed through the Guard, but the only sound was a lingering note of music and no goddess appeared to help them.

His shoulders fell slightly but Alexi steeled himself; he would not show the others his defeat. While they had not received an answer, the ring of blue fire still surrounded them. Hazy, shimmering beams of light connected the Guard, heart to heart and giving them a sense of hope.

"Silence. Still," Alexi said.

"Yet we are renewed," Jane murmured, placing her hands on her wounded cheeks and healing them. "We are recharged, and that has ever been the purpose of this sacred space."

The circle of flame died and the beams between the hearts of the Guard dissipated. The shaft of light illuminating the stained-glass dove slowly faded.

"'Once more unto the breach, dear friends, once more'?" Michael asked.

Alexi nodded, fearing to say more. He had always grieved when his goddess declined to appear at their meetings, but tonight he had begged and still she was silent. Perhaps—his heart quickened—it was because she could no longer come to him in such a vision . . . because she now wore skin of snow and had forgotten her lineage. If this was so, his hand was still checked, awaiting a sign only she could give. If she even knew how.

The Guard broke into conversation as they ascended to the nave of the chapel. Michael related a pun he'd heard in the pub earlier that day. Elijah denounced it as the stupidest thing he had ever heard, then took a moment to assure his friends that he'd hired a carriage to return Miss Linden safely from the ball . . . and wouldn't it be nice to see her lovely face again after all this turmoil. Jane, still a bit weak, discussed with Josephine whether the scars on her cheeks gave her character.

Alexi's mind wandered to a moonlit foyer that had doubled as a ball-room. He placed a hand absently on the small of Rebecca's back, guiding her up the stairs. This sent a tangible shiver up her spine, which brought him back to himself, and he retrieved his hand.

All he could think of was waltzing.

CHAPTER
TWENTY

When Percy crept into the professor's office for her usual tutorial on Monday evening, he was standing by the stained-glass window. Shafts of colored light fell in patches upon his distinguished face. His expression was blank but Percy felt his pull upon her blood. He had said nothing about the gala night during class today—and no wonder; a dimly lit dance without a chaperone was the stuff of paramours, not professors.

"Good evening, Miss Parker," he murmured without looking at her. A thrill raced up her spine.

"Good evening, Professor," Percy replied, unwrapping her scarf, then removing her glasses and placing them on the table. She swept a few locks of pearlescent hair forward to cover the burn visible above the bustline of her dress.

"How are you this evening?" Professor Rychman asked.

"Well, thank you." She took a long breath. "And you?"

"There is a strange feeling in the air, Miss Parker. Forces are at work."

Percy gasped. "You've noticed it, too?"

The professor turned, raising an eyebrow. "You are a curious one, Miss Parker."

"Am I?" she asked, only afterward realizing the coy manner in which she replied. She bit her lip and looked at him, hoping he would not be disgusted.

He was not. The sparkle in his eye did not go unnoticed as he moved to take his seat. "You have work for me?"

"Indeed," Percy said, sliding a paper across the desk. Her fingertips brushed his and her temperature rose. She wondered at the volatile nature of her blood—or at the preternatural effect of his presence upon her.

He spoke, breaking the tense silence. "What think you of the new geometrics in the last chapter?"

"Well, to be perfectly honest . . . I would rather it were a waltz," she replied. When he eyed her, she hastily added, "Sir."

The professor's half-smile ignited fires all across her body. "Indeed. Our sessions would be less painful if I were your professor of dance." Then he stared down at her paper and said, "Actually, Miss Parker . . . you may be improving. A few of these are correct. Or perhaps my standards are lowering."

Percy grimaced, wishing he could see her excel at *something*.

He rose and walked to a crystal bowl near the phonograph, saying, "I've a test of a different sort today, Miss Parker. May I offer you a piece of fruit?" He picked up something and kept it cupped behind his back as he returned.

"I . . . suppose so," Percy replied, confused.

"For you." The professor held out a half-peeled, waxen-skinned, orange-red fruit with seeds like rubies. A pomegranate. The smell overcame her. Percy leaped from her chair and began to choke, reeling backward.

The professor, clearly unprepared for such a reaction, cast the fruit aside and rushed forward. "Miss Parker, my apologies! I had no idea you would react so violently. Please—"

"That horrid smell! Those horrid seeds!" Percy cried, struggling against his grip, gagging. "It's like that vision!"

He held her safe in his arms. "Forgive me my little game! I had to test my theory . . . *Persephone*."

She stared at him, startled, so he continued: "Am I wrong? You bade me guess your name. It's true I could have taken a moment to pull your file from the headmistress's office to verify my supposition, but you've become such an intriguing puzzle. . . . Is it not strange that a mere namesake should have had such a vision in this office—and such a reaction to that fruit? Persephone, Greek goddess, bound to the underworld after consuming pomegranate seeds offered her by Hades . . . Why, Miss Persephone Parker, there *must* be more to your story than you know yourself."

She had quieted, hearing her full name spoken in his delectably sonorous voice. When she could once more breathe, she became aware of the protective nature of his embrace—and that again made her gasp. A violent cough racked her, and she lurched forward, her hair falling aside.

"My God, what is happening to me?" she wheezed.

The professor's gaze was fixed upon her bosom where it pressed against his arm, smooth and white against the black fabric of his sleeve. "What is this mark upon you?"

Suddenly and keenly aware of his fixation upon a rather personal part of her anatomy, every inch of her flushed. "Oh! That— Well, it is a burn. From my pendant." Embarrassed, she again covered the mark with her hair. "I . . . I cannot explain it, Professor."

"Try."

"I've always worn this against my skin," she remarked, pulling the chain from inside her dress and showing him her pendant, which glittered in the candlelight. "It has grown warm before, periodically. I thought nothing of it, and it is the only thing my mother left me, so I did not want to remove it. But as I lay dreaming . . . it burned me." She looked up at him helplessly as his brow furrowed, and wrung her hands. "And now you think I'm raving at last. Oh, Professor, why do you ask such questions when my answers will only appear mad?"

"*When* did it scald you?" he asked.

"After the gala . . . I suppose it was after midnight. I did not hear bells, for there was singing in my mind. Don't you see? Madness!"

"Singing?" The professor's eyes were wide.

Percy sighed. "In one voice, there were two. One spoke an ancient language I've never heard, and one our native tongue."

"What were the words?"

"Why do you ask? Surely you do not care what—"

"I care very much!"

Baffled and rattled by his urgency, Percy began to recite what she remembered. Her eyes closed in a moment of exquisite pain. "'In darkness, a door. In bound souls . . . a circle of fire. Immortal force in mortal hearts. Six to calm the restless dead. Six to shield the restless living.' Angelic voices sang. It was how I always dreamed a mother's lullaby would sound: the most beautiful music . . ."

Opening her eyes, she saw incredulity upon the professor's face—and hope. As if in a trance, he took her by the arms and lifted her to her feet. "Our seventh—surely it is you! You'll do so much for us, Persephone, especially for me. With things they way they are . . . I can't wait any longer. I asked for you to be revealed, and you come to answer my prayers!"

Percy was overcome by his words, by the lurid intensity rising between them. "Your *seventh*, Professor? What will I do for you?"

The fire in his hearth flickered, and it was as if he suddenly realized where he was. *Who* he was. Flustered, he took a moment to recover. Stepping back, breathing shallowly, he stared at her with confusion and wonder. "Forgive me, Miss Parker. Perhaps now it is *you* who thinks *me* mad."

"Professor, please, you must explain—" But she was not allowed to finish; a vision came in a wave of heat: She was seized and cradled in the professor's arms. His eyes were a raging inferno, and his face moved closer. A strong yet gentle hand drove into her hair, tenderly grasped her neck. Professor Rychman was bending as if to kiss her, a lock of his lustrous black hair brushing her forehead . . .

The vision faded as abruptly as it began. Percy's eyes unclouded once more to see him staring at her. A furious flush broke out across her skin, and her heart leaped in sickening waves.

"And what had you in its clutches *this* time, Miss Parker?"

You, she thought, trying to mask her panic. She was desperate to flee, afraid he could read her mind. But oh, how she yearned for that vision to become truth. Light-headed, she placed her hands upon her cheeks in an attempt to cool them.

"Percy, what did you see?"

She shook her head, backing around the desk. "It was nothing. I'm terrible!"

"Was it an unpleasant vision?"

"Oh, no, it most certainly was not," Percy breathed, a voluptuous murmur. Then she clapped her hand to her mouth and cursed herself, biting her fingers.

He kept stride as she retreated. "Why do you flee me, Percy? What has you so rattled? Was I in this vision?"

Percy's blushing silence was her admission. Suddenly he was upon her, his hands at her shoulders, and he bent, whispering, low and rich, "Tell me, Persephone, *goddess* . . ." The tip of his nose brushed her earlobe, his breath lingering there, and Percy swooned against him.

She jerked herself away, facing him with a mixture of fear and desire. Dimly she realized that his pursuit had backed her up to his desk. He was luminous, his gaze intoxicating. His noble features and suddenly otherworldly presence made Percy think she was witnessing the coming of an angel.

He reached out to cup her cheek in his palm. "Persephone Parker, you *must* tell me what you see. I need to know everything."

Percy buckled again at the sound of his voice speaking achingly her name and the feel of his hand on her face. His eyes were raging fire as a strong yet gentle hand drove into her hair. He was bending as if to kiss her, a lock of his lustrous black hair brushed her forehead—

Persephone cried out.

He gazed down at her. "My dear Miss Parker . . ."

"Professor! The moment you took hold of me was my vision coming true! This has never happened before! It must mean something . . ."

Their eyes locked and his grasp about her tightened. "It must," he murmured.

He pressed his lips to hers.

His arms locked around her waist, and in a rustling of fabric and soft breath he lifted her off her feet and made her captive against a bookshelf. He was thirsty yet gentle. His lips hungrily devoured hers, and she returned the kiss with eagerness. The reality of what she had so achingly dreamed was pure heaven.

When his mouth broke from hers, he moaned, raking a hand down her body. Percy gasped and threw her arms about his neck, clinging to him as tears leaked from her eyes. He lowered her to the floor.

"I am sorry, Persephone, I could not help myself," he gasped. "Forgive me."

Percy laughed, delirious. "What's to forgive? I'm so tired of caution."

Releasing her, he murmured hoarsely, cryptically, "Caution? Without a door, a portal . . . What am I doing?"

Professor Rychman rushed to the window as if seeking refuge. "You must think me a monster to behave in such an inexcusable way. I, your superior! I, who must be strong and just! I beg you not to think I have taken advantage of my station . . ." He shook his head. "Such actions are uncalled for, and are certainly not my fashion. You must forgive me, Miss Parker. I don't know what came over me."

"Please, do not apologize!" Percy gasped, feeling as if she'd been doused in cold water. "I cannot help being your student. But I'm older, and unlike every other student here. Many girls are married by my age, to men of your age and station. There's surely something pushing us toward each other, no matter where we stand."

Rychman clenched his fists. "I cannot deny that, Persephone."

Seeing he would say no more, she shook her head, recalling how they had broken apart. "A door, a portal? You speak in riddles. Help me understand."

He stepped back, raking a hand through his hair. "I can't."

"Well, I can't help what I feel," Percy replied.

"What you feel, Miss Parker?" he murmured.

"Would you like me to tell you exactly?"

The professor cleared his throat. "I fear that would be extremely difficult for me at the moment. But . . . you must call me Alexi from now on, Persephone. I believe you have earned my familiarity."

"Very well then . . . *Alexi*," she murmured.

A sinking feeling suddenly seized Percy, a fear of the worst. Her own attachment was strong, but she had heard that men often punished women for their own loss of control. Her fingers fluttered at her sides and she whispered, "Please, Professor—Alexi—I know the rules of contact. Please don't have me expelled."

He looked horrified, retreated behind the familiar boundary of his marble desk. "I would not dream of it, Miss Parker. I'd never punish you for my mistake."

"'Mistake,'" Percy repeated.

The look he turned on her was pained, but his voice was hard. "I dare not allow myself any other such indulgence . . ." His tone softened. "Thrilling as it was, I dare not cross such a line again. Not until I can be certain."

"Certain of what, Professor?" Percy asked. When he opened his mouth and closed it without reply, she pressed, "Certain of *what*? You owe me some insight, Professor. You spoke of a number, a prophecy. What do you mean? Where did you go after the ball?"

Rychman stared deep into her eyes as if willing her to understand. "I . . . I beg your patience."

Percy touched her lips. "And what of this?"

"I suppose you'll have to keep quiet, my dear—out of respect for both of our places here," he snapped.

Percy's happiness vanished.

Alexi's shoulders fell, and he sighed. "Blessed creature with such a gentle heart . . ." He skirted his desk and took her arms in his hands. "Miss Parker, Persephone, my dear goddess of a girl—however I am to address you—look at me, please." She did as requested. A tear fell from her eye and Alexi drew his fingertips across her cheek. "Please listen. There are forces at work upon my life that are beyond my control. I know you, of all people, can empathize. Have you strength enough to bear with me until I see the signs I need?"

Percy blinked. "I don't understand, but I'm in your hands." She gave him a radiant smile, praying he understood the faith she was putting in him. He released her and turned away.

"There is much to make us cautious, Miss Parker. I have a duty toward you; that much is clear. But do not ask too much of me or think too much of me—not yet. Those beautiful eyes of yours say so much, and I simply cannot . . . This is all rather sudden, untoward, and more than a little upsetting."

"For us both," Percy agreed, noticing how labored his breath had become, how white his knuckles on his chair. She took a step closer. "However, I—"

"Get out," he demanded. "Get out of this office before you drive me mad. Have mercy upon me, Persephone. I do not trust myself."

"I trust you," she said.

He smiled, and there, in the weariness of his smile, she saw years of loneliness and the toll they had taken. He said, "You trust the man who just set upon you? You are as foolish as I." Gently he turned her away and gave her a slight push. "Go, beautiful creature. Until next time."

"Alexi," she insisted, reaching for his hand.

He placed a finger upon her lips, hushing her. A thrill took her, and the bones of her corset were a sudden prison. He commanded, "Elsewhere you must call me 'Professor.' And—as I am still your professor, here and everywhere on these grounds—do as I say: Get out of my office. And keep your silence or all is lost. More than you can possibly know."

"But—"

"I shall silence you by any method necessary," he finished, staring wistfully at her lips.

"Is that a threat?"

He smiled sadly at her breathy, hopeful reply. "Out. Mercy, I say. I'll call for you soon." Stepping out the door, she turned, but he waved her on and she could see the battle in his eyes. "Sweet dreams, sweet Persephone. Sweet dreams."

A TALL, DARK FIGURE BURST INTO THE HEADMISTRESS'S OFFICE, muttering to himself, and Rebecca jumped, her pen scrawling across her paper. "Alexi—dear God, knock, will you? Your presence is startling enough as is."

Her friend crossed to the window, brooding.

"What is it, Alexi?"

"Prophecy," he breathed.

Rebecca rose anxiously from her chair. "Did you see the sign? Was there a door?"

"Not exactly," Alexi admitted. "I . . . I need to clear my mind. But there's an answer here, timid as she is, *unexpected* as she is. But must I not wait? This admission is just between us for the moment, Rebecca. Until I have more proof, until I have—"

"You've been speaking with Miss Linden?"

Alexi turned. "No."

Rebecca raised an eyebrow. "No? After everything I've alerted you to, in more than one infuriating conversation? Who do you think it is, if not her? The rest of us are sure she's the one! Placed in our path as she was . . . Didn't you sense it? Why else would you send her into the tavern? What in the world are you on about?"

Alexi scowled, dropping into the seat opposite.

Rebecca sighed. "Alexi, come now. Elijah spoke of how Miss Linden looked at you at the gala—as if she'd come home. I knew from the first that there was something powerful and fateful about her, but you've been nothing but rude. When you disappeared she was crestfallen. She said you seemed distracted. Where *did* you wander the night of the ball?"

Alexi warmed at the thought of Miss Parker's face by moonlight. "I was waltzing."

Rebecca snorted. "With whom?"

"A girl far too unique to feel comfortable in that gaudy, flighty crowd. A girl who forsook the frivolous sparkle of chandeliers for the simple moonlight of the upper foyer."

Though Alexi attempted to remove the poetry from his voice, Rebecca was not fooled. "How popular you've become, Alexi. Who could have imagined?" She took a long breath and spoke through clenched teeth. "And so you yet place your bets upon Miss Parker."

"You should have told me about her the moment she stepped through our doors, rather than leaving me alone to think we'd enrolled a ghost," Alexi reproached. "We should have used all our gifts to glean her information. Did your instincts not cry out when you met her?"

Rebecca shrugged, unable to look at him. "A bit."

"A bit?" Alexi cried. "And you didn't tell me? Rebecca, can I not trust you?"

"For the love of God, did we not set boundaries?" she defended herself. "Need I remind you once again that she is a student? I don't like this, Alexi; it is surely a trap as your goddess warned. And how am I to keep this school running if you fail to obey the rules of propriety? I ought to fire you and expel her!"

"Rebecca—"

"You're threatening everything we've worked so hard to create!"

"I'm doing nothing but trying to determine Prophecy. There are forces that press our boundaries, however carefully and sensibly we might have placed them. Do you know Miss Parker's full name, Rebecca?"

"I do not recall. Shall I go peruse her file?" the headmistress asked, exasperated. "So you may send a bouquet?"

"Persephone," Alexi replied. "*Persephone* Parker."

"Persephone," Rebecca repeated blankly.

"Yes. Don't you find that interesting?"

"What, are we now looking for the bride of the underworld?"

"Yes, since she was the one who appeared to us all those years ago."

Rebecca looked dubious. "You believe this because of all the references to the spirit world? You believe that is the reason we are here at *Athens* Academy, because a Greek goddess has entwined us in her mythology?"

His friend was trying to make it sound absurd, but Alexi would have none of it. "Yes! She bears our clue in her very name. That, and the phoenix pendant she wears about her neck."

Rebecca leaned back. "A phoenix?"

"A pendant that burned her at the very moment I cried out for a sign the other night," Alexi explained.

Rebecca bit her lip. "It burned her? Couldn't that be a sign of the opposite, warning us against her? And these coincidences, Alexi, however uncanny, are nothing. Not if there isn't a door—the *one* definite we were given in a host of damnable ambiguities. Aren't you the one always counseling patience? I tell you, Alexi, we need more than a myth, a pale face and a pendant. And . . . the others are sure it's Miss Linden."

"It isn't up to the others."

"Alexi, we're all in this—"

"She's mine to find!"

"And ours to agree on!" Rebecca cried in response, her face reddening and her pitch rising. "Does Miss Parker know about any of this? About our work, about the danger?"

Alexi shook his head, glowering. "I'm more cautious than that. You of all people should know my code." He rose and hovered over her. "But, Rebecca . . . she knew our incantation. She *sang* it to me. It came to her in her mind. She's the one—our seventh. You'll see that I'm right!"

Rebecca shook her head and said, "Alexi, the hour grows late. We've no time for games."

He sighed and, in a splay of dark fabric, collapsed into a chair. "Am I to have no support or encouragement from you? My oldest and dearest confidante?"

His friend shook her head, an ache in her voice that almost matched the uncharacteristic pleading in his. "Alexi, I do not mean to be difficult. I am simply frightened of mistaking Prophecy. Please, do not entangle your heart," she added. "It only will make matters worse. You need to give Miss Linden objective consideration. Remember your obligation!"

"My obligation?" Alexi growled. "What else have I ever thought of? Has there been a door?"

"No, not yet. But—"

"Then I'm not concerned. I believe what I believe." A sudden frown furrowed his brow. "Rebecca, why are you so set on this woman when I'm so certain it is Miss Parker?"

His friend's eyes flashed. "Because, Alexi, as I've said more times than I wish to recall, Prophecy has nothing to do with you *caring* for our seventh, and—"

He gave her a cold look and interrupted: "Yet I've always known it would."

Rebecca glanced down at her desk, blinked and swallowed a few times before looking back up at him. "Alexi, why are you looking for love elsewhere? It has been staring you in the face since that day, forever ago, on Westminster Bridge."

There was a horrible, embarrassing silence. Alexi stared deeply into the eyes of his dearest friend, his confidante . . . but not his lover. Never that.

"Aye," he sighed. "There's the rub. I'm sorry, Rebecca."

"Don't tell me you didn't know," she said with a sorrowful laugh.

"I care for you, Rebecca. I always have. Perhaps if we had lived other lives, I could have made you my wife."

Her face contorted. "Oh, thank you," she said. "Thank you very much for that declaration of pity. Dear God—"

"Certainly not *pity*, Rebecca."

"Do you love Miss Parker then?" she said, almost inaudibly, staring at her desk.

Alexi paused. "Rebecca," he finally sighed. "I am doing my best. This is not easy for any of us. I need your help."

"You had best make sure she stays quiet about whatever you have . . . done to her."

"I've not ruined her, if that's what you're—"

His friend held up a hand, wincing. "I don't want to hear it. Prophecy aside, we'll lose everything here if there's a scandal. I'll not hesitate to send either of you packing if this becomes a problem."

"Stop threatening me," Alexi barked. "I've insisted on secrecy. The dear girl will do anything I ask." His expression softened. "I know you're in a difficult position, Rebecca. In many ways. Trying times befall every mortal given our destiny. We are no different than any before us."

"We know nothing of those that came before us," she grumbled. "I wish they'd have left notes and a guidebook. But I suppose you are right, trying times is our lot."

Alexi's lips curved. "I would have hoped, after two decades, you might have learned I'm *always* right."

Rebecca groaned.

"Well, I'm off!" He rose quickly, exhibiting a youthful energy she'd not seen from him for years. At the door, he looked back at her. "Caution. I know, I know," he promised gently. Then he disappeared into the hall.

Rebecca sat quietly, staring at the closed door. Finally, ignoring the pain searing her heart, she filed the documents she'd been handling and again cursed her life.

THE CRACK BEGAN AS A HAIRLINE FISSURE THAT GREW AND THEN split. The windowpane burst, and a shard of glass fell and struck Josephine's hand where she was stacking dessert plates. *"Merde!"* she spat.

Walking to the front of La Belle, Josephine stared down the alley to see a glowing woman in rags who was tearing at her transparent hair and throwing her head back in silent rage; she floated several inches off the ground. Josephine returned and found Elijah, and pointedly drew him away from his conversation with Miss Lucille Linden. "Lord Withersby—a word with you?"

"Yes, my dove?" he murmured, leaning across the counter.

"We've got a Shrieker heading due south."

Elijah glanced at the window. "I suppose you'll make me replace that glass?"

"Tell Jane and Michael. What shall we do with Miss Linden?"

"I'll wipe her."

"Do you think she'll take to it?"

"Almost everyone does. It was said Prophecy won't have *exactly* our powers, so it should take. She didn't come running when the dog was on the loose, remember? Or when I abandoned her at the gala, either! Although, to tell the truth . . . would it be so harmful for her to see what we do? We have to address Prophecy with her, and soon. Let's just show her—"

"*Non.*" Josephine shook her head. "Only with Alexi's blessing, Elijah. You know that."

"But he's never here anymore. I think something's wrong with him. We may have to take matters into our own hands. Let's bring her along."

"Elijah, do *you* want to explain to Alexi why you broke our compact without his approval? And Rebecca isn't even here to ask."

The impetuous gentleman pouted but agreed. Jane, who had forsaken her usual solitude to spend a pleasant evening at the tavern with her friends, had sensed both the spirit and the blood on Josephine's hand.

"If ye'll be so kind as to excuse us, Miss Linden?" Jane said, eyeing the woman with caution. No matter her self-professed desperate circumstances and the other Guards' approval, from the moment they met, Jane found Miss Linden a bit too nice and certainly too beautiful. But there was an unmistakable *something* about her, something to be learned, so she could not be dismissed outright.

"Of course," the dark-haired woman replied sweetly.

Carrying her teacup to the counter, Jane grasped Josephine's injured hand. Dragging a finger over the cut, she concentrated until the Frenchwoman's skin closed over.

Elijah approached Miss Linden. "We'll return in a moment, and you won't even know we were gone," he said quietly, staring deep into her eyes and waving a hand before her face. The beautiful woman stared blankly ahead, and the assembled company evaluated her.

"Is she out?" Josephine asked.

"Looks snuffed to me," Michael chortled, rising from the table and bounding out the door.

They tore down the alley toward the tortured specter in rags. In her wake, glass windows had cracked or burst. Running past, the group blocked the spirit's path. As they lifted clasped hands, sparks of thin blue lightning coursed between their bodies. The ghost stopped and stared at them, agape.

Random passersby approached, but Elijah sent them wandering off with a flutter of a hand and a sardonic smile. They wouldn't remember a thing.

The four opened their mouths and a sweet, simple lullaby rose into the air. The spirit clawed at her hollow face and her form flickered. One by one the Guard moved their hands toward the spirit, and Michael let loose a jovial laugh. The spirit blinked. She opened a sagging jaw as if to recommence wailing, but the four placed their fingers to their lips and a soft "shhhh" echoed down the alley. The old woman's jaw closed and she hung her head. Her form slowly sank into the cobblestone street.

Lucille Linden watched all of this from the front door of the café with a wide smile. As the four made to return, she was quick to resume her seat at the table and play along for one last moment.

Laughing, the group walked to the bar, and Josephine began to pour glasses of wine. Elijah approached and snapped his fingers in front of Lucille's face. She looked up at him with a knowing smirk.

"Why is it," she murmured, her eyes alight, "that spirits are always hanging about you and your friends, and you feel the need to go and play with them? I simply *must* speak with that professor of yours."

Elijah Withersby stared at her, glanced at the others, and squirmed.

"WHY ARE YOU SO QUIET?" MARIANNA SCOLDED PERCY. THE TWO were sitting at the courtyard fountain.

"Because I've nothing to say. Do you still think I wandered off with someone the night of the ball? Just because you and Edward were chatting until dawn and had to resort to all manner of trickery to sneak into your respective halls doesn't mean I was so inclined."

The German girl giggled uncontrollably. Percy hadn't seen much of her friend since the night of the ball, but she did not take offense; there was plenty to occupy her. While she dared not even hint, she was dying to rhapsodize about the joy of being so near Alexi, of being kissed by Alexi . . . but she couldn't say a word and could only wonder if she'd ever be kissed again. She spent a great deal of time wondering that.

"Something is different about you. You seem less timid."

Percy smiled, her tinted glasses obscuring what naked eyes might have betrayed.

Miss Jennings startled them. "There you are, Miss Parker! I've been looking for you. This was tacked to your door," the woman blurted as she handed Percy a folded sheet of paper. Message delivered, she turned back toward the residence hall.

Percy and Marianna glanced at each other and laughed. "Poor old dear," Marianna said.

Recognizing Alexi's precise script, Percy took care to shield the missive from her friend.

To the pale nymph whom it concerns:
    Our meetings must now commence more regularly. Tonight,
wear something fine.

                                                    Yours,
                                                    —A

Percy lost her breath, staring.

"Well?"

"Oh . . . nothing at all. Reverend Mother wishing me well on an up-coming exam."

"Truly? I saw a spot of color rise to your cheek, right there." Marianna poked her friend in the jaw.

"No."

"Let me see the note."

"Marianna, please," Percy begged, an edge to her voice.

The German girl frowned and said, "You are hiding from me. Perhaps you must. But I do hope, soon, you will trust me enough that no matter how strange or forbidden—"

"Of course I trust you, dear heart," Percy interrupted. "Just allow me my silence. There are certain things I am not at liberty to discuss. Not at present. Please forgive me."

Percy looked up, past Promethe Hall, and her blood chilled. The sky had a sparkling, prismatic quality. Silhouetted horsemen rode the clouds, galloping between earth and sky. She almost felt the distant beat of the horses' hooves as if they were the pounding of her heart. The only meaning she could ascribe to the shadows was that of a set of apocalyptic harbingers. Stranger still, she was sure she heard dogs barking, deep growls and roars. A whimper escaped her.

"What is it, Percy?"

Casting aside her weighty dread, she glanced at her friend and then again at the sky. The vaporous horsemen were gone. "Must have been a vision—something I thought I saw past those walls."

Still, she heard yelping in the distance, growing nearer. Something was closing in.

As the clock chimed quarter of six, Percy looked at herself in the mirror to find delirious panic upon her face. She'd done the best she could: swept up her hair with filigree barrettes, applied a bit of color to her lips and cheeks, donned a midnight blue dress—a bit of finery sent by Reverend Mother. She clasped her pendant higher up on her neck so that it covered the fateful burn. With bell cuffs of lace, a scooped neck, and a doubled skirt, Percy hoped she was "fine" enough for whatever adventure lay ahead.

A sudden thought made her quake. Did he plan to take her *out* somewhere? Was he prepared for how people would stare? She fought back a fit of worried tears and tucked a thin scarf and glasses into her reticule.

Throwing a dark hooded cloak about her shoulders, she sneaked out the back door of her hall and kept to the courtyard shadows, avoiding any exterior doors where guards would be posted. She scurried to the professor's office and knocked.

Rather than bidding her enter, Alexi opened the door and drew her in. His hand on hers caused frissons through her body. "Good evening, Percy."

"Good evening, Profess—ah, Alexi," Percy said with a nervous chuckle.

His sharp features were inscrutable but his eyes sparkled. With what Percy hoped was reluctance, he released her hand and moved to take her cloak.

The fire and the candelabras were blazing. Alexi placed her cloak on the coat tree where his professorial robe was draped. He wore a blousy gray silk shirt beneath a thick black velvet vest cut perfectly to fit his broad torso. Music crackled from the phonograph. Bach.

He did not seem to mind how she stared at him as he returned to her side. "Thank you for coming, Percy. You look ravishing—perfect, in fact, for I intend to whisk you off to the opera tonight."

"The opera?" Percy exclaimed. "What a grand surprise!" Her eyes clouded in a mercurial panic. "Oh, Alexi, tell me this is not some game to you, some fleeting fancy that dares scandal and cruelty. I'm too fragile for such sport."

"I dare much, Percy, but not cruelty," he replied. "I wish to do nothing but what is meant to be."

"So cryptic, Alexi!" she murmured.

"Forgive me, my dear, but I can speak no other way," he replied.

Percy felt feverish. He kissed her gently on the cheek, his lips lingering too long to be polite; when he broke away, Percy nearly stumbled forward, having melted against him.

"I'm sorry, Miss Parker," he whispered.

"For what?" she asked, fisting her hands at her sides to keep from reaching for him.

"For being unable to keep from touching you." He spoke through clenched teeth and gripped his great marble desk as if to maintain stability.

"Don't apologize for what you've done to—*for* me." She blushed. "I didn't know life could be so thrilling until you walked into my classroom."

His expression remained inscrutable. He shook his head and remarked, "I hardly believe that my walking into a room could have such an effect."

"Oh, but it did," she assured him, laughing nervously. "You terrified me."

"And do I still terrify you?"

"Always," she whispered, but a smile twitched at her lips.

Alexi smiled suddenly, broadly. Delighted, Percy returned it. "Why, Professor, to see such an expression on your face! I thought you too cool a character."

"Now is not the appropriate time to test my temperature, Miss Parker," he murmured, unstopping a crystal decanter on his desk and pouring white wine for them both. "To the number seven," he said as he handed her one glass and lifted the other.

"Whatever that may mean," Percy countered, clinking glasses delicately, leveling a gaze at him as she carefully sipped, unused to tasting wine in any place save for Holy Communion. "Were it not for the strange things that have happened all my life, I might think you suggest something wicked."

"You think me wicked?" Alexi asked, a small smirk curving his mouth.

"Captivating, cunning, and, I fear, wholly above my grasp . . ." Percy stopped short, biting her lip. Perhaps there should be no discussion of grasps. She took a breath, leaned forward and continued, "You're not the only one sensing fate, Alexi. I'm seeing new and terrifying things.

Beyond your window, silhouetted horsemen ride the sky. I hear the dull pounding of their horses' hooves and the terrible barking of dogs! Something is about to happen, Alexi. I feel it in my bones, and I must tell you that, as delighted as I am to be here in your presence, I'm also frighten—"

There was a loud knock at the door. Percy jumped. She and Alexi looked at each other and Percy went to the desk without a word, plucking up her scarf and throwing it around her head, taking a book into her hands and placing the wine out of sight.

"Yes?" Alexi called.

Headmistress Thompson entered the room. "Ah," she began, giving Alexi a wary glare. "Have I stumbled upon a tutorial . . . on a weekend?" Percy's heart pounded, knowing she was not dressed for a lesson. They were surely found out, and she would be expelled!

"Miss Parker requires my assistance—as you know," Alexi stated. "How might I assist *you?*"

"You have a visitor who wishes a word with you, Professor—Miss Lucille Linden," the headmistress stated sharply.

Percy could glimpse the beautiful woman she had first seen at the ball, partially hidden behind Miss Thompson. A rebellious part of her wished to proclaim that she and Alexi weren't in the midst of a tutorial at all, but rather discussing the correct manner in which to commence a scandalous affair—and could they please be left to it?

Alexi, seeming similarly at a loss, hesitated. "Miss Thompson, would you allow us one further moment? I am advising Miss Parker on a personal matter in regard to a return to the convent. As she has no family to answer her questions, I consider it my duty to finish my appraisal. Would Miss Linden be so kind as to wait upon the bench outside? Miss Parker will send her in as she departs."

"Well, then," the headmistress bristled. "Good evening to you both."

The door shut behind the two uninvited women. Percy turned again to Alexi, and words tumbled forth before she could stop them. "Thank you for giving me a moment. I know that that woman outside is far more beautiful than I could ever hope to be, Alexi, and so I beg you not to trifle with my heart. If there should be something between you—"

"Percy, truly!"

She could not help herself. "So much is secret about you, Alexi. I'm wary of your silence. Whatever may happen here between you and her, remember, there are witnesses." She gestured to a floating figure near the phonograph. The spectral boy smiled and waved. "And remember, *I* can speak with them."

"Why, Miss Parker!"

"I now realize that there are times when timidity must be abandoned, Alexi, and that there are things worth a fight. I'm tired of spending my life afraid of what I do not know." Percy sighed, weary beyond her years, and rose to her feet. "I wish we could've gone to the opera tonight, but then again, I never thought I could. Good evening, and I'll await your next instruction." She gave the window a glance and added, "Make it soon, Professor, as I've no idea how quickly those horsemen will advance."

She curtseyed lightly and glided to the door, where she turned. "Lastly, yes—in my opinion, you are worth a fight." Then she exited, leaving him staring after her, slack-jawed.

As she proceeded down the hall, Percy thought about the scarf around her head. Steeling her courage, she whipped it off and strode down to the dimly lit rotunda at the center of the second floor. There she found Miss Linden on a small marble bench, sweeping skirts a sea of emerald around an irritatingly beautiful physique. When their eyes met, Miss Linden gasped and a look of threatened fascination appeared on her beautiful, creamy-skinned face. Percy felt a jolt of satisfaction.

She held her head high. If this was indeed a rivalry, she would stake a strong claim. "Good evening, Miss Linden, I am Percy Parker. Professor Rychman will see you now. The professor is very kind to me and spends a great deal of time concerned with my welfare, as would any truly gifted . . . tutor."

"Of course. I'm certain he's very talented," the beauty replied.

"Yes. I owe him much," Percy stated, flashing a smile and politely inclining her head. "Have a pleasant evening, Miss Linden."

The woman's eyes suddenly clouded. "Forgive me, Miss Parker, but . . . are you human? The professor seems to keep strange company."

The words cut to the quick, but Percy mastered herself. "I assure you: While I look like a ghost, I'm no spirit or demon. I'm nothing but a girl struggling to make her way in an intolerant world. I bleed, I love, and someday, I'll die. And you?"

Miss Linden smiled. "Much the same."

"Indeed. Good night." And with that, Percy swept off. But she could not help but turn her thoughts again to Alexi. *Strange company?* What would this woman know about it, or about him? To feel so close to someone and yet have no idea about his soul or his thoughts . . . Percy clenched her jaw and fled to her room.

ALEXI SHOOK THE LINGERING EFFECTS OF PERCY'S PRESENCE FROM his mind and opened the door to reveal the exquisite Miss Linden. "A pleasure to see you again, mademoiselle," he stated with a polite bow, gesturing her inside. "Do have a seat."

His visitor took her time evaluating his office and finally sat, turning to offer him a winning smile. "It is wonderful to see *you* again, Professor."

He nodded. "You're looking lovely as ever."

"Thank you, Professor." Her eyes sparked as she smiled. "Appearances are so important, are they not?"

"Perhaps," Alexi replied, uncertain if she referenced his being closeted with a student. "I trust you are well since last I saw you at the ball? I regret that work prevented me from bidding you a proper good evening. I hope you'll not find me hopelessly rude."

Miss Linden's smile remained flawless, but she spoke with crisp efficiency. "Professor, I have no doubt we could continue charming pleasantries for quite some time, but might I propose that we set such delights aside and press right to the point?"

Alexi raised an eyebrow. "I did not know you and I had business."

"As a matter of fact," the woman promised, "we do."

"Well, then, Miss Linden, please be so kind as to enlighten me."

The beauty leaned forward, her green eyes both inviting and mesmerizing. "It would appear, Professor, that you need me."

CHAPTER
TWENTY-TWO

THE DOOR OF THE CAFÉ BURST OPEN AND AN IMPRESSIVE WHIRLWIND of black fabric and wild dark hair made a direct line toward an unsuspecting Elijah Withersby. Lifting him from his seat by one thin arm, Alexi dragged the startled Elijah to a corner of the café and transfixed him with an arctic gaze. The few patrons remaining at such a late hour who did not belong to the Guard looked on in titillated interest, while Alexi's friends looked on in alarm.

"Hullo, Alexi, fancy seeing you here—"

"What did you tell Miss Linden?" Alexi growled, inches from Elijah's nose.

"Oh, her." Elijah smiled nervously. "Well, the wipe failed, Alexi—"

"She watched your entire little dance with that Shrieker—a few moments ago she told me all about it. She wants to help. Apparently you let on we were looking for an addition."

Elijah squirmed. "Alexi, let go of me, and let's not make a scene, shall we? Sit down and I'll tell you what was said."

Alexi reluctantly released his grip and Elijah rubbed his arm. The two joined Michael and Rebecca at the table and Alexi glowered at them all.

"Alexi, listen," Elijah began. "Miss Linden has been so intrigued— particularly by you. She's taken *refuge* here from God knows what, and feels connected to us . . . and, Alexi, we all feel it, too." He looked at the others, who nodded. "When I found out that she could see everything we did, I drew her aside and inquired more of her. She confessed that disturbing things have always happened to her. She wanted to know if we could shed light on her condition. I said my friends and I enjoyed a good haunting—"

"And that you were looking for someone like her! You had no right to impart our secrets!" Alexi snarled.

Rebecca's eyes widened. "Did you tell her that, Elijah? Without consulting us first?"

"I was terribly vague! I didn't share any secrets!" Elijah hissed. "I believe in nothing more than the subtle nature of our work, but she *saw*. Alexi, open your damn eyes. She's who we're looking for!" Elijah snapped. "The strength of my conviction is the reason I spoke of things I'd never, under any other circumstance, dare to reveal."

Michael and Rebecca stared anxiously at Alexi, who took a measured breath. He was careful to make his next declaration a calm one. "I would not be so sure."

"You just wait. I would bet the Withersby estate that we'll see a portal door any day now."

Alexi set his jaw. It would not do to discredit Elijah's beliefs, for Alexi understood his friend's reasoning. Yet he himself had a different notion, needed Prophecy to be otherwise. He glanced at Rebecca, who simply stared at him in silence.

"Why are you so hesitant, Alexi?" Josephine asked, taking a seat.

"There is . . . something else," he replied. "For now, say nothing outside of this group. Until you see a door as Prophecy decreed, keep Miss Linden at bay and in the dark. We cannot know whom to trust."

The Guard nodded, though it was clear they were all on edge.

Alexi offered to accompany Rebecca back to the academy. A carriage awaited them at the corner, so he helped her into the cab and took the seat across from her. He felt Rebecca's eyes bore into him, and he waited for her to speak.

"So you remain fixed. You stand by her as your choice?"

"Hmm?" Alexi kept his eyes on the passing alleyways of the dark city.

"Miss Parker. She remains your choice. I mean, you had her in your office after hours and on a weekend! For God's sake, did I not tell you to be cautious? I'll ask you again. Not that it has anything to do with Prophecy, but will make things more complicated: Do you *love* her, Alexi?"

He heard the words and could only turn to stare at his friend for a long moment. Finally he admitted, "I'm not sure I would know it if I were."

Rebecca's eyes narrowed with weary skepticism. "You would know, Alexi."

"No, I don't know that I would," he insisted, his broad shoulders tight with worry. "I forbade myself the very thought for so long, thinking only of that ethereal goddess we saw once in our youths . . . I forbade myself all sentiment until the time was right."

"And now the time is right." Rebecca sighed. "Is *she*?"

Alexi closed his eyes and leaned back into the leather of his seat. "In so many ways."

Rebecca's mouth contorted into an ugly grimace, but she kept silent.

The driver stopped in front of Promethe Hall. Alexi descended from the carriage and helped Rebecca out. Uncertain moments passed. Finally, she moved to embrace him and he returned it hesitantly. Ominous clouds began to tumble in on the whole of London, covering the moon with their dark mass. The salt taste of unsettled forces was potent in the air.

As she drew back, there was a moment where Rebecca lingered and watched his face, but she could see his mind laboring with conflict. She pulled away completely and murmured, "Bring her to us. Nothing else can be done until you bring her to us. We must see what you see, otherwise there shall be no happy end to Prophecy at all."

He nodded slowly. "Good night, my dear."

As Alexi turned and walked away, Rebecca felt something sharp drive deeper into her bosom. His footsteps echoed back from the broken stones of the narrow, pillared alley to the side of the great Athens portico, on toward Apollo Hall. She listened to those footfalls and waited for them to stop, to perhaps turn around, for him to come back and admit he was a fool for denying her all these years. Of course they did not.

She cursed herself for not taking advantage of his moment of hesitancy. She might have simply pressed her lips to his, to know what it would feel like, to know what she might have enjoyed were they not fated to such damnably odd lives. But a woman did not simply kiss a man, however long she'd known him and however much she cared for him; it would not do. These damnable standards of propriety kept her a gentlewoman but made her feel as hollow as the ghosts she saw.

While she was cursing things, she spared a moment for her morals. The damned Work kept her always on guard, never appreciated. If she wasn't sure that people would die without her contribution, she would have walked away from her fate long ago. Pressing her hand to the creases of her aging flesh, she wished a fleeting wish she would never dare utter: that her skin were younger and deathly white.

Heaving open the great front doors of the academy, she nodded curtly to the guard inside. Then, heedless of the hour, she went to her desk, listened in isolation to the coming storm.

The spirit who often floated near the chandelier in the main hall drifted through her door and bobbed up and down. Rebecca looked up and barked, "What do you want?"

The spirit frowned, and it appeared as though he was about to cry.

"Oh, for God's sake," Rebecca muttered. Exaggeratedly, she winked. Ghosts were creatures of routine, she had learned. It was always her custom to look up and wink at the young spirit, but she'd stormed past tonight and ignored him. Appeased, he remained staring at her with helpless sadness, as if he wanted to help but knew he couldn't. He mouthed something that looked like it could have been the word "Mother" before he vanished back through the door, but she couldn't be sure.

At one point in her life, she would have found the scene emotionally powerful, beautiful, and endearing; it would have renewed her faith in her work and herself, in that she mattered to those around her. But tonight she found no comfort even in the storm that broke overhead, and saw other clouds that would darken all her remaining days. She could think only of Alexi, realize he did not and could not return her feelings, that he was captivated instead by snow-white tresses and eyes shaded by glass, captivated perhaps to the point of catastrophe.

She wondered how to stop him. After a long moment of contemplation, she wrote a letter to the reverend mother of Miss Parker's convent. She could, with these few simple sentences, send the girl packing. But . . . Alexi would not forgive her.

Her pen stilled on the page as another thought occurred: Was this about Prophecy at all, or did she, without warrant, hate that ghost of a girl for purely personal reasons? Was she, Rebecca Thompson, one of those fated, as Prophecy warned, to be a betrayer?

Her sadness hardened inside as she put her face in her hands to cry. When all was said and done, there would be no heart of hers left to love or to betray.

* * *

PERCY HAD BEEN PACING HER ROOM FOR HOURS, BROODING AND REFUS-
ing to take down her hair or remove her lovely dress. A sharp rap
sounded at the door, startling her. Flying to attend, she found nothing
outside save a note tacked beneath the fading room number:

> *Come to the office. Presently.*
>
> *—A*

Making an eager bolt for Apollo Hall via out-of-the-way passages, she
found dread gnawing at her nerves. The distant barking seemed nearer,
and Percy could have sworn dark shapes were scurrying in the shadows.
All manner of strangeness frolicked with unusual menace this night.

Before she ducked into the hall, the night sky made her pause. There
was something new and alarming about the closeness of that sparkling
canopy of stars. It was as if, for the first time ever, she was aware of the
heavens as a finite layer, and this was because a small line was being
drawn above, a thin line like lightning, fractured and splitting further.
The sky was *cracking*.

Percy ran up the few flights of stairs to Alexi's office, darted in
without knocking and closed the door, her heart in her throat. He
was there waiting, standing pensively at his mantel, drinking a glass
of wine—perhaps the same one he'd poured earlier. Hers remained
untouched.

Her churning heart was elated to see him, yet she was fearful of any
new knowledge that this meeting might provide. Deciding to keep the
madness of her latest sight to herself, she focused on trying to control
her breath and on enjoying the wonders of the man before her—if indeed she had any opportunity.

"Are you all right, Persephone?" he asked.

She set her jaw. "Never mind me. You?"

"Thank you for returning."

"Of course."

The two fell into a long silence, staring at each other.

Finally, overwhelmed by emotion, Percy could no longer maintain
his stare and broke from it. Eternity lay within his eyes, and all she
wanted was to collapse in his hold and feel safe and loved. "What did

she want with you, Alexi?" she blurted, unable to keep jealousy from her tone. "Beautiful as she was."

"She wanted to join my club," was his reply. He took to his chair.

"You have a club?" Percy turned, raising an eyebrow. "Let me guess—a club of six, looking for someone new. To make seven."

"Yes," he replied, gesturing for her to sit opposite him in her familiar place; the air between them remained unbearably charged.

"And what, may I ask," Percy said carefully, "is the purpose of this club?"

"Public service, Percy, nothing more," Alexi remarked. "Now, I still owe you an opera, dear girl, but for now I need you to tell me—do you still see foreboding shapes on the horizon?" He directed her gaze out the window.

Percy looked. Nodding, she gulped, for the sky resembled an eggshell waiting to split. "Yes, the silhouettes are still there. I hear whispers, too, and strange noises. And I see . . . other frightening things. But I cannot make out what the whispers are telling me. Every now and then I hear the ticking of a clock, though there be none near me. And that barking! Please don't think me mad, Alexi—"

"I never did," he interrupted.

"The air is full of dread. I'm tired of seeing doors and shadowy figures and flames when there's so much beauty in the world," she murmured, staring longingly at Alexi's face for a moment.

"The visions are coming to me nightly now," she admitted, rising from her chair and crossing behind the desk, desperate to be closer to Alexi. Expecting to be rebuffed, she was instead surprised when he reached out, took one of her cool white hands, and pressed it to his lips.

Percy gasped at the sensation of his mouth against her hand. A shiver worked up her spine; her other hand was instantly required to steady herself upon the marble.

Alexi released her and Percy felt her head spin with a glimpse of a vision: The city raced by. She held on to a strong form as their horse pounded onward, away from something terrible—

Percy blinked, returning from the blur of the vision to see that her hands were clenched into trembling fists and she'd somehow found her chair once again. Dread of the vision lingered like acrid smoke in her nostrils.

Alexi was watching her. "Where did you just go, Percy?"

"I was on horseback, speeding away from London as if pursued. Something is . . ." She shivered violently. The distant barking had reached a crescendo and then fallen silent; it had not been silent in days. The temperature in the room dropped a drastic number of degrees. The hairs on the back of her neck rose. There was a far-off, echoing sound, like glass shattering. "Pursued," she repeated, suddenly terrified.

A SHADOWY FORM ROSE SLOWLY FROM BEHIND PERCY'S CHAIR, A pulsating black silhouette with the head of a huge, crimson-eyed, bloody-fanged dog. The form flickered and became a collection of canine bodies fused together, one head shifting into three, into ten, into forty.

"Alexi, is it just my imagination, or did the room just turn very cold?" she asked, and if her flesh could have gone a shade paler, it would have.

Alexi's mind spun at great speeds. "Percy, listen carefully. Close your eyes. Don't question me, just do as I say."

"Why? What—"

"Do as I say!"

Percy closed her eyes and trembled.

Alexi stood with silent ferocity, staring down the vaporous animal opposite him. Blue fire appeared along his hands as he locked the creature in a battle of wills. It sniffed Percy and she whimpered.

"Alexi, what in God's name is behind me?"

"Quiet! Rise slowly and keep your eyes closed. Swing widely to your right and run to the door. Run down to the stables, and get a boy to ready my horse and bring him to the portico, where I shall meet you. Percy, you *must* do as I say." They would trust in her vision, if she had the courage to obey him.

Unsteadily, she rose to her feet, her eyes still closed as he'd instructed. The monster growled. Percy cried, "Alexi!"

"Do as I say!"

She ran to the door and disappeared into the hall, shouting, "I'll wait for you. Come quickly!"

The beast swiped angrily at the air where Percy had been, its gruesome maw shifting from flickering cloud into a single, horrific hound's head. It snarled, preparing to strike.

Alexi called upon the inner forces that made him more than mortal.

Facing this beast, he felt an ancient rage not entirely his own; here was an old wound, an old score yet to be settled.

From his lips thundered a powerful command. For a moment the canine nightmare seemed frozen. Gritting his teeth, Alexi felt lightning course through his veins. A wind swept the room, scattering papers and whipping his black hair across his forehead. Halos of fire surrounded Alexi's outstretched hands, crackling to be released.

The abomination leaned back on pulsing haunches and tilted a vague head. Fire burst from Alexi's fingertips, and it yelped and retreated. Then, in a burst of frantic barking, the form shifted into a hundred doglike forms that disappeared like roaches from light, snorting as they vanished through the walls. Only barking lingered in the air.

Alexi bolted out the door as howls rang across the sky like inclement weather. The beast was not destroyed but merely regrouping, as it had done many times before.

THE JOURNEY TO THE STABLES TUCKED BEHIND ATHENE HALL WAS A blur. Percy flung open the doors to find a boy asleep on a chair. Nearly hysterical, she shook him. "Please, sir," she begged. "A horse. I need Professor Rychman's horse. It's an emergency!"

The boy woke terrified, thinking Percy a spirit. He fell out of his chair and scrambled backward.

"Please, sir, there is danger. I need help. Oh! No! I am not a ghost, I promise you, see?" Percy reached for his hand and squeezed it. The stablehand cried out. "Please, forgive my appearance, but I am flesh and blood! Professor Rychman is in danger and must get away! You must help me ready his horse!"

Seeing the tears in her eyes, the young man groggily acquiesced. He began to ready a beautiful black stallion whose huge, dark eyes were fiercely alert and intelligent. Of course such an impressive, elegant, onyx creature would be Alexi's horse, Percy thought.

Percy anxiously waited at the portico, where the stable boy had been all too happy to leave her, reins of Alexi's dark steed in her ghost-white hands. Assuming telling the guard at the door that there was a demon on the second floor would get her sent to the histrionic ward, she invented a medical emergency to dissuade the man from sending her to her room. The rest of the night watch seemed too spooked by her to care one way or the other, and they left Percy well enough alone.

A billowing storm of black fabric rounded the corner at top speed, and her heart leaped. "Alexi! Thank God you're not harmed!" Percy cried.

The barking began again above them. Without a word, Alexi mounted the horse and swept her up in front of him.

"Dearest Alexi, what was— Oh, dear God!" Percy looked over his shoulder and saw, just above the gargoyles that guarded the front entrance of the academy, a huge fanged dog with eyes like burning coals. Its head flickered into three heads, then ten, then more; it opened countless salivating jaws in a roar. The beast perched above their only escape route.

Percy screamed and tucked her head into Alexi's bosom. He loosed a powerful shout and spurred the horse forward. A paw swiped down toward their heads, but a shield of blue flame burst forth to protect them. Alexi's horse leaped past, racing down a narrow alley.

Percy could not get her bearings. A dark mist enfolded her brain, a dread filled her body, and damnations were murmured in her ears. She screamed as her sleeve was torn by something she could not see.

Alexi roared a word, a command to desist in a tongue Percy had never heard yet still understood. There was a crackling of blue lightning and a cloud lifted from around them as the mass of whirling, bestial forms rose into the night sky, snarling still and gnashing hundreds of teeth. Then there was only London: The nightmare vanished and the barking quieted.

"Are you all right, dear girl?" Alexi asked above the din of his horse's hooves upon the cobblestones.

Percy's shaking arms desperately clutched his chest. "I . . . believe so. What in God's name was that?"

Alexi sighed. "That, in *hell's* name, was something I never saw until recently. Running rampant through London, it is, and I can't help but think it's looking for something."

Percy shrank, catching his meaning. "Not . . . me?"

"What you just saw was the terror of Whitechapel. I don't know for sure why it came here, but . . ."

"Oh, God have mercy!" Percy cried. "You're certain that is the Ripper?"

"I only wish I wasn't."

Percy thought about her splintered heavens and wondered if, before this night, something had been in place to protect her. She looked up, afraid of what she might see, but low, thick clouds blocked the celestial view. "Am I in great danger, then?"

"Fear not, dear heart," Alexi declared.

"I was terrified to leave you!"

"Indeed," he replied. "I was hardly overjoyed to be left. But there are times when expert direction must be followed, no matter the fear."

Percy dared look up into his resolute face. "Oh, Alexi. Whatever that was, whatever is happening . . . I need you."

He smiled and met her gaze. "Good."

Their faces were so close, the heat of their cheeks and the parting of their mouths so inviting . . . Alexi looked away, but Percy could see the battle in his eyes.

Held captive by the moment, by the kiss that should have been, Percy put a hand to her forehead to quell the dizzying effects of desire. "What did you do, just then?" she asked, avoiding the magnetism of his eyes. "Did that fire erupt from the beast . . . or from you?"

"Many things will surprise you in the days to come," was Alexi's cryptic reply.

"I have no doubt of that. But—"

Alexi chuckled grimly. "The fire? That was mine."

"Goodness!" Percy breathed, clutching him tightly. "I would do anything for you, Alexi."

He cleared his throat. "Careful with your words, Miss Parker. You belie your pride—and your modesty."

She pressed fully against him. "We cannot unclasp our hearts in the least?"

He shuddered beneath her, clearly tempted. "It would hardly be proper."

"Then tell me something of what you do, Alexi, or what we are running from. Else I shall go mad!" she cried. That she had been ignorant for so long seemed a travesty in itself.

Alexi sighed. "To tell you a mere 'something' may be even more maddening. All I can say is this: The living need protection from supernatural forces they cannot comprehend. There is a group charged with maintaining the relative peace of day-to-day mortality, protecting it from the dead by a mix of their own mortal talents and a few . . . special forces."

Percy pursed her lips. "That could not be more vague, Alexi."

"Sometimes *vague* is all one has to go on; toward the undiscovered country, my dear."

"Ah," Percy muttered. "Well, I'm not any less maddened, my melancholy professor of Denmark. Quite illuminating indeed."

"Ride with me then, into the mouth of madness."

"Do I have any choice?"

"Of course. But shall I leave you at the roadside until that creature returns? That, of course, is your alternative. My dear Miss Parker, you're riding upon Prospero, the finest horse in all of England, and you're in the arms of a most accomplished professor. What more could a young lady hope for? It's almost like an opera itself."

Percy couldn't help but chuckle and relax against his powerful frame. Alexi gave her a flickering smirk, clasping her hand in his.

"Where are we going?" she asked, later.

"Out of the city limits. We must put distance between you and that thing. I would take you to my home but . . . my estate has not always been safe from spectral disturbance," he remarked. She thought she heard pain in his voice. "Also, trouble often follows The Guard, so I cannot take you to our collective command. Not yet."

"'The Guard'? That's your little club?"

Alexi smiled briefly. "I can only hope I'm not leaving them to another fight on their own . . ."

Storefronts and darkened flats of North London sped past Percy's watering eyes. The spirits of the city parted hastily, some bowing, some darting into walls but keeping one protruding eye on the mortals' hasty flight. These ghosts seemed as nervous as she, who was terrified that every gust of wind might be the breath of that ghastly canine presence.

Outside the city, north of his estate and the surrounding expanse of spirit-ridden heath, Alexi took in the open air and sensed its quality. "Safe. For now," he said.

Percy felt Prospero slow, and she broke from silence again, hungry for knowledge. "Tell me *something* of yourself. I know so little of you outside your classroom."

"If I tell you, will you remain rapt in my presence? Dare I break the enigma, the mystery of my person?"

Percy laughed nervously. "Has my fascination been so obvious?"

Alexi's eyes clouded as he glanced over his shoulder. "Father moved the family from Berlin to London when I was very young, in pursuit of a great medical career. When I was sixteen, my parents returned to Berlin, leaving me in charge of the property . . . and of my sister." He drew a harsh breath. "They were terrified of me."

Percy could not help but shudder. So much sorrow and fear in her dear professor's life.

Alexi continued, cool and casual. "I was apprenticed to a brilliant alchemist, a friend of my father's who, noticing my penchant for mixing powders and devouring old texts, took me under his tutelage. His secret passion was alchemy, though it was increasingly considered arcane. Thankfully, Athens still held interest in its basic principles—provided I coupled those with mathematics."

"How did you come to teach there?"

"My dear friend Rebecca."

"Headmistress Thompson?"

"Yes."

"I always thought the two of you were—"

"Friends, Percy, and have been for ages. We've worked closely together under incredibly trying circumstances. She, like I, has been groomed for an academic setting since childhood. I can't say I recall exactly how she came to run the school. I suppose I was so caught up in my research at the time . . ." He trailed off, as if trying to access a memory he could not locate. "At any rate, the academy was founded in the Quaker model, so Rebecca could, as a woman, serve as administrator." He eyed her. "We continued thus until, one day, a ghostly young woman who was barely competent in my class unsettled my life."

Percy made a face. "You lie, sir. I, unsettle the inimitable Professor Rychman?"

"Always," he replied, echoing her earlier sentiment.

Percy hid her flushed face in his chest, unable to hold back a giggle or stop her lips from pressing against his cloak in a phantom kiss. "But, Professor, did nothing happened between the start of your teaching career and my arrival?"

"Oh, quite a lot."

"Well?"

"The academic life is gratifying, noble work, but it does not constitute what you would call a 'thrill.' The excitement in a professor's life often comes from what he does *away* from his profession—but for me to answer that, my dear, would be rather personal," he intoned deliciously. He looked her over then added, "All in due time, my dear. I've told you what I do, Percy. I'm a bit of a police officer, nothing more."

"Did you have . . . lady friends?" Percy blurted, having no idea how else to continue, and wanting desperately to know.

"Why, Miss Parker, how bold of you! I have had thousands of lovers." When Percy gasped, he added nonchalantly, "We all have, at one time or another, from one life to the next. For each spirit, a thousand lives."

Percy narrowed her eyes. "You believe in reincarnation, then?"

"Of course. Don't you?"

She took a long moment of consideration, enough to stop bristling from her sudden jealous reaction to the thought of the many possible lovers Alexi had enjoyed, and then answered. "I've always been conflicted. Everything I was taught at the abbey denounced such a theory, yet surely it could happen; otherwise—"

"How could you see the things you've seen, or fall upon your knees in my office, spouting a foreign language while trapped in a painting? Or be so offended by the smell of a pomegranate?"

"But if this is so, my former life must have been wretched, for I see dreadful things." Percy fought back a sob.

"Tell me more of what you see."

"All in due time, Professor," she retorted.

Alexi pursed his lips. "Answer me this. You once mentioned there were certain aspects of your particular faith that fascinated you. May I ask what?"

"I don't suppose it will be of any use to you, but I have always been enthralled with the Immaculate Conception."

"Indeed?"

"Yes. The idea of something holy and godlike taking residence inside a mortal, to me, is a most beautiful thought. For something greater than humanity to inhabit a simple body, forsaking divinity for simple mortal flesh . . ." She sighed. "It seems so incredible."

Alexi was struck. "So, do you remember being queen of the under-world?"

"What?"

"Do you remember being a goddess?"

"I . . . No. Why would I?"

"You're Persephone."

"Hardly!" She laughed. "A name does not a goddess make. Though I clearly identify with that story—"

"Then why is Cerberus hunting you?"

Percy gasped. "You think *that's* what that thing was?"

"Perhaps. Do any of your visions give you a sense of your history?"

Percy searched her mind. Soaring angels, horsemen, cracking skies and fire . . . a nonsensical patchwork. She shook her head. "No. Surely, all my visions were to lead me to you. I think I'm just a strange girl with a strange fate who happens to have a coincidental name."

"Hmm." Alexi looked lost in thought. A few small homes became visible in the moonlight. "Ah, we have arrived."

Alexi tethered Prospero to the garden gate of a quaint cottage, dismounted, and lifted Percy down. The appealing edifice of stately gray stone was surrounded by flowers of all kinds. Lace curtains rustled behind open windows. Prospero nudged his master, stamping as if expecting remuneration for his fine work. Alexi smiled and fondly stroked the horse's muzzle. Percy followed suit, quelling the urge to slide her other arm around Alexi's waist.

Imagination got the better of her as she gazed at the cottage. She dreamed she was to be mistress of the place, and that the man who had taken her by the hand was her newlywed husband, ready to whisk his young wife inside.

Alexi stopped to examine her. "What now, wandering one?" he asked.

She turned to face him, and the thought struck her that all she wanted in the world was to proclaim three simple words of her heart—words he might accept and return. But staring into his stoic face, she could not go against his wishes. She instead turned to the flowers, shaking her head.

A maid rushed out the front door. "Professor! What brings you and— Oh, goodness! Milady!" The mousy young woman bobbed a quick curtsey.

"Isabel, would you rouse my sister and apologize for my late and un-announced arrival?"

"Certainly! But I need not rouse the mistress, she keeps such terrible hours. Come in! Come in!" the maid exclaimed, holding open the door. Percy smiled sweetly at her, but Isabel just stared back in shock.

A woman in a wheelchair, dressed in folds of black taffeta and slightly older than Alexi, rounded the corner of the entrance hall. "Brother, darling!" she cried in a deep, female voice. At that moment, the maid remembered her place and took their cloaks.

Grinning, Alexi darted forward and lifted the woman into his arms. He squeezed her tightly before gently lowering her back into her chair. "Hello, Alexandra—and before you chide me, yes, I know, it has been too long. Please forgive this strange visit; we simply had to es-cape the city.

"Alexandra, Miss Persephone Parker, whom I mentioned in my last letter. Percy, this is my sister, Miss Alexandra Rychman."

Percy, thrilled to know Alexi had written about her, smiled nervously at Alexandra. The woman's wide, watery eyes and chiseled features were similar but more feminine than her brother's; her dark, gray-streaked hair was swept atop her head in a severe coif. Her pale lips curved into a welcoming smile and she extended her hand.

"It is a pleasure to meet you, Miss Rychman," Percy said as they clasped hands.

"And you, dear. My, my, Alexi certainly has a way with acquain-tances. Never a dull moment or an ordinary soul. Though I must say, it is unlike him to take such care of a *pupil*."

"This one is rather special," Alexi stated. Percy turned a mottled pink.

"So it would seem. Come, my dears. I'll have Isabel put on some spiced tea."

Alexandra led them into the parlor, where she gestured for her brother and Percy to sit upon a divan accented with embroidered pillows. The room was decorated with paintings that Percy recognized as those of Miss Belledoux. Moonlight spilled through the lace curtains of the French doors and mixed with the light of several stained-glass lamps.

"Alexandra, where is that large wooden trunk I brought here years ago?" Alexi asked.

"Upstairs in the guest room, where you left it. And yes, it remains locked!" his sister teased, before turning to Percy. "He can be so maddeningly secretive."

"Indeed," Percy agreed.

Alexi seemed to delight in the pointed glance she gave him; he appeared lost for a moment. Then, jumping up, he said, "Excuse me a moment, please."

The ladies watched him go in a swirl of dark fabric as he darted out of the room and up the stairs. Alexandra sighed. "I learned at an early age that it's best not to ask too many questions about my brother and his work. But whatever it is," she said, "it—*he*—is good. Despite his secrecy and strange friends, he's never faltered from a noble path in life. Never."

Percy nodded. A long silence followed in which she felt excruciatingly examined, but she sat and calmly sipped the tea Isabel brought.

"When did you come to this lovely place, Miss Rychman?" she asked politely, admiring a bronze statue, a graceful couple dancing a stationary waltz across the mantel.

"Alexi bought the cottage nearly fifteen years ago, when it was clear that my state would make it difficult for me to be married off," the woman said.

"Ah." Percy nodded. "You have made it a lovely home."

"Thank you. I do my best. Fate dealt me a harsh blow," Alexandra stated.

"I take that to mean you were not always as you are?"

"I was eighteen. Alexi was fourteen, I believe. That day—it was the strangest thing, as if some sort of demon swept through our house—our parents' estate, where Alexi now lives alone. I fell from the top of the stairs; my parents always claimed the wind had crashed through the place suddenly, opening doors and cracking windows and startling me. But I felt something shove me. . . .

"My grandmother was there, and the shock of the accident stopped her heart," Alexandra's gaze looked inward, perhaps at a memory. "Alexi found us just after. He didn't think it was the wind, either. Our family was never the same, and one day our parents simply left. They did not like it when Alexi and I spoke of demons." Alexandra stared at Percy for a long moment. "You believe in such things, don't you? I can see it on your face."

"I do with all my heart."

"You, Miss Parker . . . you have led a hard life, I can imagine."

"I have led a *strange* life, Miss Rychman, and at times it has seemed hard. You understand. But I have been provided for. I'm grateful for Athens. I often wondered if I would ever be able to leave the abbey where I grew up. The sisters there were afraid that someone might whisk me off to some terrible sideshow"—Percy grimaced—"and there are moments when I still fear such an abduction. But your brother has taught me much, rallied me from self-pity, and helped me to find confidence. So, I am blessed—at the very least by his presence in my life."

"Indeed, my brother has taken an unusual interest in you and your welfare. He told me a young lady was in his care, and that he was sure that I would see you both soon." Alexandra smiled. "Alexi and his many secrets. Ah well, it is good to have company. And it is excellent to see my brother in company. He's kept himself so bitter and lonely all his life, I feared he'd keep on with his odd friends and never take a wife. And so I welcome you as his lady, and as a sister to me."

Percy's jaw dropped. "His wi—his *lady*? Oh! I . . . Why, no—"

"You needn't explain yourself, dear girl. Isabel has put on a hot bath for you upstairs if you care for one. I am sure you have had a harrowing night."

"Oh! That would be grand!" Percy's grateful smile held many kinds of thanks.

CHAPTER
TWENTY-THREE

MICHAEL SAT WITH A MUG OF CIDER, STARING AT THE FIRE IN HIS modest hearth. He kept a rustic little nook, priding himself on simple pleasures; he'd always saved the gilt and pomp for the church. In this room that boasted only a few threadbare chairs and a mantel topped with trinkets from various ancestors, Michael was content with his fire and cider. His abode lay near Athens Academy . . . but Rebecca and Alexi tended to forget he was so near, pairing up and darting off together. He had gotten used to that, but every now and then he would confess to himself and to God that he was a bit lonely.

He had attempted to sleep tonight but couldn't. Even his impervious humor had been rattled by the events of the past few days. During their work, he had smiled regardless, giving his friends the benefit of his warmth and light, but now, in the privacy of his home, he allowed his face to fall. He tried to reconcile his melancholy, naming it as penance to an Almighty power, and was relieved to believe in something larger than himself and his companions. Yet he knew that faith was not an infallible salve. Especially not when he thought of Rebecca Thompson.

The woman in question suddenly burst breathless through his front door in a rustle of thick linen skirts, her eyes wide and searching. "Michael, have you seen Alexi?" she blurted.

Always Alexi, Michael thought, and his usual touch of sadness and tinge of jealousy struck more acutely than ever.

"No, my dear, I haven't," he replied. "Why, is something wrong?"

"You feel the air, don't you?"

"Of course," Michael replied. "But it has been this way for some weeks—or building to this. Alexi should be found round one of his usual haunts."

"I fear he's left without notice. I cannot sense the slightest trace of him."

Michael frowned. "And you received no note?"

"Nothing. I am at a loss! Come with me, Michael, we must all meet; I feel it in my blood."

He rose and worriedly accompanied her into the night.

THE BRIGHT MOON GLARED DOWN FROM ABOVE AS FOUR CARRIAGES sped through separate streets to the wide expanse of Trafalgar Square. The horses seemed to converge at the same instant, as if some great hand guided them to this confluence. Hopping down from their respective cabs, the Guard milled about, speaking in hushed whispers.

"Where is Alexi?" Elijah asked.

"It would appear he has left town," Rebecca replied.

"What?"

"He is not currently in London."

"Well, where in the holy name of the saints is he?" Jane demanded, adding a few Gaelic curses under her breath.

"I can't say, but evidently he felt his business pressing enough to keep it from us." Rebecca shook her head and snorted. She was still burning with resentment, though she tried to shake it off.

"What do we do?" Josephine asked. "Something is about to descend. Surely Alexi has reason for his actions, but really, his timing is horrible!" She was taking note of how the clouds were making beautiful yet foreboding patterns, a nightmare scene she might be compelled to paint.

"It's Prophecy, isn't it?" Elijah asked.

"I'm sure he believes it has something to do with that," Rebecca replied with a sigh. "He thinks he has found her. He doesn't believe it's Miss Linden."

They could all feel the approach of something terrible. Wind whipped through Trafalgar Square and the temperature dropped drastically. The ladies pulled their cloaks tighter around them; the men buttoned their greatcoats. They all looked to the sky, worried.

"Let us not speak ill of him before we know the circumstances," Rebecca suggested, but her irritated tone betrayed her generous words. She was tired of making excuses for him. She owed him nothing. She was simply his *friend*.

"Shall we wait for a while together?" Jane asked, feeling an instinct to maintain close proximity to her comrades. Eerily, the whole of Trafalgar Square was empty. Where were London's finest? Her helpless?

"Why not," Elijah grumbled. "It doesn't appear we'll be getting much sleep this evening."

As if to prove Elijah's assessment, a gruesome form suddenly slithered, ran, galloped, and skittered all at once above their heads. Terror breathed down upon them, a terror that had become sadly familiar.

"The hellhound hath returned!" Michael proclaimed. The barking, frothing creature glared down at them with one pair of eyes and a hundred. It hovered, growling, snorting, snarling.

"Bind!" Rebecca cried. The Guard took hands; a glorious hum began to emanate from their circle, a light hanging on each of them like a halo.

The abomination was not impressed. It reached down vaporous paws in assault. The five stood fast against the constricting pain that tore at their lungs, and Michael breathed loudly, purposefully, reminding them that they had control of their own organs. The pain eased.

"Benediction!" Rebecca commanded. A verse lifted from their lips and into the air.

The ungodly creature spat and lashed. Though strained, the Guard held their ground, wondering if they could withstand the beast long enough for it to lose interest. Tears rolled silently down several cheeks. Even Michael's determined smile was belabored.

Josephine coughed suddenly, faltering; the circle was broken. The creature turned a ghastly set of heads in her direction and pounced. The people were knocked to the ground by chimerical claws. Wounded, their clothing torn and their skin scraped and bruised, damage never seen in all their years of the Grand Work, the friends cried out in alarm and cursed Alexi for his abandonment. If he were here, they had a fair fight; without him, they were doomed.

Suddenly there was a door.

ALEXI STARED AT THE WELL-WORN, BLACK, LEATHER-BOUND BOOK IN his hands, open to an entry written two years to the day after his young life changed forever:

Today is my anniversary. It is the anniversary of the day I became something new in that chapel, the day I—we—began patrolling the dead. Today I awoke from restless sleep with a keen sensation. Something additionally cataclysmic has occurred. I'm filled with longing, as if touched by a long-lost love upon waking. I yearn for that sensation again; the voice of that goddess is calling my name . . .

I heard a newborn's cry in my sleep. When I woke, a feather lay at the foot of my bed. The specimen is unlike any I have ever seen. Translucent, iridescent, and twice the length of my palm, the feather is luminous as I hold it. Life seems to hum within—and a strange blue light. It seems a talisman.

I am unsettled by a torrent of emotions I cannot place nor discern, but something is indeed coming to find me. I long for it . . . for her, that voice. My destiny was born today . . .

He shut the book with a triumphant exclamation. October 16, as he'd thought! Percy's birthday—it was the anniversary of the Guard's turning.

"Percy!" he cried, bounding into the hall.

"What is it, Alexi?" she called. Alexi strode toward the sound of Percy's voice and flung the door open without thinking.

Percy squealed, hastily covering her body with her white limbs. Alexi, seeing the bright blur of that slender, alabaster body, closed the door to the washroom with a similar exclamation. A flood of heat sent him reeling. "Oh! Percy! Terribly sorry! I found something you should see, and . . . sorry!"

"What *is* it?" Percy called, still breathless from shock.

"Never mind. Take your time, Perc—Miss Parker. I'll tell you . . . later."

Inside, Percy stifled a giggle. While she was scandalized that he'd seen a flash of her naked body, she was flattered that it had affected him. She'd never before seen him blush, and the look on his face seemed one of rapture . . . at least, it had been before his horror at the impropriety of the situation.

Percy bit her lip, smiling as she began to lather her body with scented soap and contemplate how perfectly magical it was to be even *considered* by a man like Alexi. Just to be in his private sphere was a blessing, especially as it dared scandal and expulsion for them both. She decided that even if he never revealed one thing more about his mysterious ways or her possible part in it, she didn't care, so long as she could be near him. To perhaps steal illicit kisses . . .

As she caressed herself with a small washcloth, she closed her eyes, leaned back into the water and couldn't help imagining his hand dragging the lathered linen across her, lingering lovingly on her bare white skin. Ashamed yet invigorated, her body tingled. But surely no one could see the entirety of her queer skin and still be attracted to her . . . Percy was suddenly certain that Alexi had withdrawn in shock and horror. His arousal had been her imagination. A frown replaced her girlish, giddy smile.

Percy dried and powdered herself. She appreciated the sensation of the thick satin nightdress she'd been given as it slid around her chilled body. The long braid of her hair damp against her neck, she slipped into the hall . . . and heard crackling music from a phonograph downstairs. A waltz?

Curious, Percy peeked between the rails of the staircase to behold Alexandra sitting in her wheelchair at the center of the living room and Alexi bowing slightly toward her. His sister chuckled as Alexi approached.

Carefully he lifted her out of her chair, holding her firmly around the waist; her legs dangled limply beneath. She laughed a tired yet happy laugh and laid her head upon his shoulder while placing her hand in his. Alexi effortlessly carried her around the floor in slow circles, as if he were dancing with a child.

"I remember when I taught you this dance. You were twelve," Alexandra said softly. "What an irony now, eh? I'm so lonely, Alexi. I don't know how much longer I can carry on."

He pressed his cheek to his sister's hair and replied softly, "I know, dear. I understand. I always have."

"Not now, dear, you don't. Not now that you have her," Alexandra countered, smiling, tears in her eyes. "She is gentle and strange, Alexi . . . but charming. How those unbelievable eyes glitter for you!"

"I do not *have* her, Alexandra. You must not make such assumptions. And I shall forever understand loneliness," Alexi replied.

"Let's not speak of it. Simply dance with me."

As they silently moved around the floor, Alexi felt, as he often did, that Alexandra's paralysis and their grandmother's passing were both somehow his fault. It was as if some evil from the spirit world had swung a warning paw that day, reminding him that no one close to him could ever truly be safe. No one but Prophecy.

Had he cursed sweet, gentle Percy Parker by bringing her into all this? Would she grow frightened of him as his parents had? No, surely. She was fated to be involved. She'd have to be fearless. She was Prophecy. She *had* to be.

The cylinder bumped, the waltz complete. Alexi and his sister continued moving, unaware and unconcerned. Then, as gently as he had lifted her, Alexi returned Alexandra to her seat with a rustle of taffeta skirts and a squeak from the wooden wheelchair.

Sensing another's gaze, Alexi looked over and found Percy watching him, her face aglow and her cheeks glistening with tears. The moment she was spied, however, she ducked out of sight. Alexi smirked. "Good night, Alexandra." He kissed his sister upon the cheek, then climbed the stairs, tingling with anticipation.

Percy was standing wide-eyed in the hall, dressed in a flattering satin nightdress. Alexi gently wiped away her tears. "My dear, what's this?" he asked, ignoring how utterly unheard of it was for him to see her in such a state of dishabille.

"You are so beautiful, Alexi!" she sobbed.

With a warm laugh, he opened his arms and Percy fell into them. His embrace closed around her and wrapped tight. They slid closer and closer, their arms entwining and their palms pressing tight until there was no space left and they were helplessly and indecorously locked. Keenly aware that she was only wearing a nightdress, Alexi became quite sure no amount of layers of clothing could conceal his body's reaction.

It would be so easy to whisk her into one of the rooms, part her robe and gaze upon that snow-white flesh again, to worship it as the light of the moon itself, to unleash years of pent-up passion upon that marble body, to take, to claim, to seize and devour Prophecy as his own. It was his right—

Perhaps she sensed his burning thoughts, for she pulled back. "Alexi," she began. "I lo—"

* * *

H<small>E SUDDENLY REELED BACKWARD AS IF STRUCK; HIS HANDS FLEW TO</small> his head as if he was in great pain.

"Alexi!" Percy cried, frightened.

"Something's wrong," he muttered, sinking to the floor and rubbing his temples. Percy recalled the night of the ball and how he had been called away. He looked up at her sadly. "My dear Percy. I hope soon you and I may . . . indulge," he said carefully, his jaw clenching, his eyes flickering with desire. "But I fear for my friends. I must return to London. You must stay here in safety."

"But—"

Alexi reached out and clasped her hands in his. "I don't dare return you to the eye of the storm, Percy; it isn't safe. I'll come for you in the morning."

He rose shakily to his feet, his face pinched with pain and anxiety. He raced down the stairs and Percy followed, stopping halfway to eavesdrop.

"I must be off to London again, Alexandra. I'm sorry, but there is something, perhaps something dangerous. . . ."

"Yes, yes, you and your mad work. I ought to be used to it," Alexandra replied; Percy could hear the smile in her voice.

"You must do me a favor. Keep Percy here tonight. I fear it isn't safe for her where I'm going. I'll come for her again in the morning."

"There's always a room prepared, Alexi. Don't worry."

Alexi gathered his cloak, hat, and a small black book Percy didn't recognize, then darted up the stairs to sweep her into his arms and bury his mouth against her neck, searing her skin with kisses. "I know I shouldn't, but I cannot help myself," he murmured against her throat as she gasped in pleasure. "Await me here and stay safe. I won't be long."

As he pulled back, Percy was struck by a terrifying thought. "Alexi . . . I'm not bringing this danger on you, am I?"

He smiled wearily. "Oh no, dear girl. It was brought on centuries ago. An old vendetta, between two antique creatures, that's playing out in our dreary little lives. Mortals made pawns by immortals—isn't it terrible? But soon, my dear, we'll settle the score. You and I."

Percy tried to smile through her confusion, but it came out more a worried grimace. Alexi groaned and winced, pulling away from her.

"Go, Alexi," Percy said softly, kissing him on the cheek and ushering him to the landing below. "And know that I—"

"I know, Percy," he said. Then he was out the door and mounting Prospero. There was work to be done.

THE SIGN THEY HAD BEEN WAITING NINETEEN YEARS TO SEE WAS floating over the western lane of Trafalgar Square. *The* sign. It was a dark rectangle with a dim interior, much like the portal that opened when their meetings commenced in the chapel. But this one had not been made by the Guard.

The canine abomination turned, ignoring his supine prey and staring instead at the portal. There was a sound—an unfamiliar, halting tune bellowed from a female throat. The monster's ears perked up and it bowed its head in subordination. Miss Linden strode into the square, her arms outstretched, power radiating from her, and her beautiful face terrible in its ferocity. The beast broke into a thousand clouds and vanished in a yelping flurry through the door. The portal crumbled into nothingness an instant later.

Miss Linden shuddered and stumbled forward with a cry of pain. When she recovered herself, her face was once more noble. She stared at the others and offered them an exhausted yet winning smile.

"I fancy a drink. How about all of you?"

REELING FROM THE EVENING'S EVENTS, PERCY WASTED NO TIME IN falling into the bed Isabel had shown her. As she was drifting off, a spirit floated through the wall and drifted close. The entrance of spirits into her rooms never startled her, though she didn't always converse with them.

The elegant old woman, dressed in fine clothing made of dark, heavy fabrics, with high collars and puffed sleeves, stared fiercely at Percy.

"*Zdravstvuyte,*" the old woman said, greeting her in Russian.

"*Zdravstvuyte,*" Percy replied. "*Ochen priyatno.*"

"Lovely to meet you, too, dear girl, but listen close, I've only a moment," the woman continued, still in Russian. "The firebird has come for you and you alone, child. I've been watching. Tell my grandson that he mustn't be fooled by the tricks of snakes. Tell him he needs to use fire to banish the darkness. His fire. It is the only way."

Her grandson—that must be Alexi, Percy thought. She didn't understand what the old woman meant, but she nodded and memorized the message. Alexi's grandmother returned the nod and vanished.

With a sigh, Percy once again tried drifting off to sleep, but barking rang distantly in her ears. At last she attempted a prayer: "Dear Lord, please help me solve a few riddles before receiving new ones. And bring my beloved safely back to me." She pressed her phoenix pendant—her *firebird*—to her breast. She now believed the symbol meant Alexi. If so, then he was here with her, even in his absence. In fact, he always had been. She had to find a way to make sure he always would be, no matter the dangers ahead.

CHAPTER TWENTY-FOUR

Teacups rattled on saucers at La Belle et La Bête, which was closed to everyone but an exhausted, nervous group of six, their jaws set and expressions stern. Jane had first healed everyone's wounds, then taken out needle and thread and mended her torn sleeve; she was now tending to her female companions' bustles and skirts. Elijah and Michael left their shirtsleeves in tatters.

"You must think me mad for having burst upon you like that," Miss Linden laughed, finally breaking the silence.

"After the events of this evening, which of us would dare?" Elijah replied.

"How did you find us, and then, how did you do what you did?" Rebecca asked.

Miss Linden paused, taking care with her words. "An unmistakable taste in my mouth occurs when something is . . . I could taste something amiss. And it's not yet right."

"Ye made that *thing* retreat. We must know how," Jane demanded.

Miss Linden shrugged. "All my life I've been plagued with strange company. Ghastly, nightmarish creatures, such as that one, are familiar. I've encountered all manner of the inexplicable."

Jane gaped. "A beast such as that? Here in England?"

"Your group must be a magnet for troubled souls," Miss Linden proposed. "But this was no mere troubled soul. No, when I speak of encountering other such nightmares, I speak of my time abroad, where there are many such creatures—forces of nature, really, things you've only heard of in myth." She paused as the group nodded in amazement. "Forgive me, but where *is* that unmistakable professor of yours? Shouldn't he be here?"

"We've been pondering that all evening," Rebecca replied. "We were in need of him."

Miss Linden looked troubled. "Indeed, how surprising! Elijah told me you were inseparable." She paused, absently grazing thumb and forefinger together as if spinning thread. "I confess that I hoped to see him. He intrigues me."

Placing the glass of wine she held tightly in her hand upon the table, Rebecca leveled her gaze once again upon their savior. "Professor Rychman is currently . . . preoccupied with other business."

Miss Linden's green eyes flashed. "He's with that ghost of a girl, isn't he?"

Jane and Michael looked confused, but Elijah and Josephine exchanged speculative glances. Rebecca gritted her teeth. The two Restoration wraiths in the corner ducked their heads together to gossip.

"Perhaps," Rebecca finally replied. "He thinks her of great importance."

"I met her," Miss Linden murmured.

"Yes, I imagine. Your impression?"

"I would not be so bold as to conjecture about someone whom I know so little—"

"I ask only for your *impression*, Miss Linden."

"Well," the woman began hesitantly, "I'm not sure she is as unassuming as she pretends. She seemed to wish to challenge me. I tell you, something is—"

"Rotten in the state of Denmark," Michael muttered.

"Yes," was Miss Linden's reply.

Glances and nods were exchanged among the Guard. The wraiths in the corner seemed to hold their breath.

"Perhaps we can make it right, my dear Miss Linden," Elijah declared, rising from the table.

"Please, call me Lucille."

"I suppose the saving of lives does indeed invite familiarity," he replied. "Do you trust us, Lucille?"

"Implicitly. Though I cannot claim any intimacy by right, I . . . I feel I belong here," she said eagerly. "We must stick together, our kind."

"Our kind? Have you met others like us?" Josephine asked.

"Never," Miss Linden responded in earnest. "I've been looking all my life for people like you. I feel as though my soul has seen centuries, and all for this purpose."

The Guard looked around at one another. There was a door, and here was the reason for it.

Rebecca cleared her throat. "Do you believe in prophecies, Lucille?"

"Why do you ask? Have you had one?"

"Yes, one heralded the coming of a friend to join our ranks."

"This friend, then . . . You feel it is I?" Lucille asked, breathless. As the Guard rustled in their chairs, she laughed suddenly, joyfully. "It's all I've ever wanted. To *matter*. To finally be a part of something important. Surrounded by strange forces all my life, overshadowed by them at every turn—to now have you as my own, and that ineffable Rychman, is my dream come true!"

"Have you spoken such impassioned sentiments to him?" Rebecca asked.

Lucille shook her head. "While I sense he is fascinated by me, he's been unwilling to reveal anything. A careful, guarded man, he keeps his secrets well. A capable leader."

"Save for abandoning us tonight," Elijah muttered.

"An inscrutable man with many reasons for his actions, I've no doubt," was Lucille's reply.

Jane piped up, her infamous disinterest melting. "Ye take his side, Miss Linden. It's nice to see he has a supporter."

"Or an admirer," Josephine corrected. Lucille colored and stared at the table.

"And the door," Jane continued softly. "Have ye ever opened a portal to the spirit world before?"

Lucille blinked.

"It's what our prophecy hinges upon," Rebecca clarified.

"Oh. Well, doors between this world and the next have always sort of . . . followed me," Lucille replied. "I wish I knew why. Perhaps this is my answer."

Rebecca rose and grabbed her by the elbow. "May I have a private word with you, Miss Linden?"

"Secrets, Rebecca?" Michael chided.

"Hush." Rebecca batted a hand in the air and drew Lucille into the alcove by the door. "Please forgive the strange manner in which we speak here."

"I assure you, I've dealt in odder exchanges."

"Indeed? Then, if I may be so bold, allow me ask you something delicate," Rebecca said.

"Anything."

"Do you feel that Alexi Rychman may have a very . . . personal place in your destiny?"

The woman stared into her eyes, and Rebecca felt the calming power of those emerald irises; Miss Linden's presence was an odd yet exciting balm. "I am certain, Miss Thompson, that my destiny involves him. I believe he *is* my destiny—even if he, at this point, does not share my conviction. He is a careful man, as you know, and very wise, for a mortal."

Rebecca's lips thinned, and for a moment she was taken aback. "Why, Miss Linden, are you not mortal?"

Lucille's eyes flashed. "Sadly, I am. Yet I feel like so much more."

Rebecca nodded and the two shared a smile of understanding. "Indeed, I know that feeling well."

Lucille's eyes narrowed. "Since we are displaying the fullest candor, Miss Thompson . . . Why did you ask me that question about my feelings?"

Rebecca sighed. "Alexi believes that our prophecy has an . . . intimate element, though it was never directly said to be so. But he's so damn stubborn. In his mind, the woman who fulfills Prophecy will be . . ."

Lucille drew in a long breath. *"His?"*

Rebecca nodded, grimacing.

"Oh, my," Lucille murmured. "How exciting." Then her powerful gaze clouded. "But he thinks the answer lies in that ghost girl!"

"I am afraid so," Rebecca said.

"How can I convince him to love me instead?" Lucille asked.

Rebecca blinked. "Well . . . that's just it; you don't have to. Alexi is misled on that point, making all of this more complicated—"

"But I'd *like* him to. All I've ever wanted is to be loved."

The headmistress pursed her lips. "Indeed."

"And I must tell you," Lucille continued, "that I fear for you if you keep that girl near."

Rebecca scoffed. "Come now. She's a timid thing, hardly a threat—"

Lucille shook her head. "I have seen what you do to spirits. She's much of one herself, I fear. Too much to be trusted." Leaning in, she whispered, "Could she not have been sent from the realm of your enemies? Her timidity, her awkward isolation—these things cause her to *appear* harmless. But if something else has taken hold in that body, causing that odd pallor . . . she could do a deal of harm. Forgive me, I prattle on! How presumptuous—"

"Your apprehensions are valid, Lucille. I will share them with the others," Rebecca promised, and with that they returned to the group.

"You do realize, my friends," Rebecca said bitterly, "that this will not be easy news for Alexi. He is sure he's found Prophecy in that student of his. He—"

As if on cue, Alexi Rychman burst through the door in an explosion of black fabric, clutching a book, his eyes bright. "Good morning, dear friends!" he began. "I felt you were in trouble so I came running, but the storm seems to have subsided. Good work, then! And I have . . . such news!" After taking a good look at his companions, he continued. "You all look dreadful. What in the hell has happened to your clothes?"

"We haven't slept," Elijah countered bitterly. "And we're in tatters because we were nearly *ripped*."

"Sit, Alexi," Michael commanded.

"I'd rather stand, thank you," Alexi replied.

Rebecca whirled upon him. With unease, Alexi noted that the beautiful Miss Linden stood behind her.

"What in the name of our Grand Work did you think you were doing," his friend murmured hotly, "abandoning us on an evening when the Balance was at its most precarious? We were crippled by your unexplained absence. How could you do such a thing?"

Michael recognized the need for privacy and waved, gesturing Miss Linden upstairs with an apologetic smile. Nodding, Miss Linden politely glided away.

Once she was out of sight, Alexi felt he had sufficient leave to retort, "You question me as if I were suspect? I acted for the very sake of Prophecy! Did you think I'd go on sudden holiday for the fun of it?"

"And since when does an illicit escape with your lover—oh, forgive me, your *student*—constitute aid to Prophecy?" Elijah demanded, his pale face flushed.

Alexi's jaw dropped. "Slanderous fools, what right have you to say this? That hellhound came to my office, came for Miss Parker. I could not fight it alone, so I moved her to safety."

"It came for *us*," Jane said. "Since when has the fate of a student come before us?"

"Because Miss Parker *is* Prophecy!" Alexi cried.

"The prophecy wasn't just given to you; it's not your toy or alchemical formula to keep and meddle with," Elijah stated. "It's *ours*. We are all in this together."

Alexi's gaze pierced him. "I know you think Prophecy points to Miss Linden. I realize that she is indeed incredible, with a presence unlike any other, with a beauty unmatched, and with the power to see spirits and know the unknowable. But *Persephone* Parker, named for my goddess, also sees spirits. She can speak with them in any language.

"Did Rebecca not declare our need for just such a translator when we worked in Fleet Street? Miss Parker has transporting visions, too. She was even granted a vision of our liturgy, the sacred text known only to us, which came to her in a dream!"

"Is that all?" Jane asked.

"No, it isn't. She has worn a phoenix pendant around her neck since she was a child. She was scalded by that very pendant the night we demanded Prophecy be shown!"

"Alexi, none of that matters now. Prophecy has shown herself—to *us*," Josephine countered. "We would have died tonight, Alexi. Do you understand that? We would have died if Miss Linden had not lent us aid. We owe Miss Linden our lives, and in her, Prophecy was fulfilled. *She opened a door.*"

Alexi stilled. "What?"

"A portal," Rebecca reiterated. "As was foretold."

There was a long, tense silence. Alexi shook his head, his body visibly taut. "No. This must be a trap. It isn't her."

Rebecca threw her hands in the air. "Oh, yes, it must be a trap! How foolish the rest of us are for believing we might have a part in this! You, who sacrificed everything to your fate, unlike we five . . . It could only be you to whom Prophecy would be revealed."

Alexi kept shaking his head. "No, my friends, I know. I know it isn't her."

Elijah's nostrils flared. "And that's your answer, *Professor*? You deny the one hard fact of Prophecy just because you 'know' things to be otherwise?"

Rebecca held up a hand and attempted to explain. "Alexi, I've never seen you like this. You're trying to pin Prophecy on a young girl when our seventh is supposed to be a peer. You're tearing around, refashioning facts so that it can be her. You're changed by her, as if by some spell. Where is our stoic, unfaltering cornerstone, willing to see only hard truth? There was a door to the spirit world, Alexi, through which the hellhound vanished. How much more plainly do we need the prophecy fulfilled?"

Alexi shook his head. "A trap. I . . . I don't trust her."

"Tell me, Alexi." Elijah leaned in. "Has your dear little Miss Parker *opened a door* for you?"

Rychman ignored any double entendre his rakish compatriot might intend. "She sees them in visions, she draws them. And that painting, Josephine—it was like a door that she went through, as if she were from that very age and time."

Jane made a face. "Her visions and mythical past won't help us when we're being attacked, as we were tonight. Alexi, what're we supposed to make of this? Ye may think this girl of yours is Prophecy all ye like— we've yet to get a glimpse of her."

"I've seen her," chorused Elijah, Josephine, and Rebecca.

Jane and Michael exchanged surprised glances.

"And?" Michael pressed.

Josephine said noncommittally, "I met her briefly. She's deathly pale and clearly enamored of Alexi. There's something about her, certainly— but nothing like what we've experienced in the presence of Miss Linden."

Elijah nodded in agreement.

"But Elijah," Alexi protested. "You saw a burning image when you touched her—an image that matched how the goddess spoke of the phoenix! And Josie, she was your inspiration for the very painting that sent her into a vision—"

"Alexi, none of those details connect to what we do or what we fight,"

Elijah interrupted. "I have seen many terrible sights after a casual touch. Josephine is inspired by many things. Tonight, our work included Miss Linden, and one particular of our prophecy revealed itself just as we were running out of time! Can that really mean nothing?"

Alexi shook his head, unwilling to be convinced. "But Persephone Parker is the one. A phoenix charm burning her flesh just as we demand a sign? How could that be, if she's not linked to us? How could she know our invocation?" He brandished the book—his diary. "I made an entry on the day she was born. I awoke that morning, knowing there had been a great alteration in the Balance—and that was two years to the day from when we learned of our own fates! We never saw my goddess again because she was born as Miss Parker!"

"Alexi, calm yourself, you're raving," Josephine said.

"And her pallor!" Alexi continued. "She appears as if she could be a spirit—and she can communicate with them! Does this not make her useful to us? She is not possessed as we are; she is truly reborn." He whirled to face his friend. "Josie, we've never dared ask . . . but please tell me when those white streaks first appeared in your hair."

Josephine faltered. "Since the moment of my possession," she replied quietly.

"As I thought. And I believe that something has been with Percy all her life—within her, from the womb—to make her whole body luminous. It is the shock of an outside power—a divine possession."

Everyone stared at him sadly, as if he were to be pitied. This riled him further. "I will bring her to you," he vowed. "You will know. But damn it all, there's no reason why you should fight me on this—you should simply trust me!"

"Alexi, facing death without you revoked your privilege of unconditional trust," Elijah snapped. "Oh, and did we mention there was a goddamned *door*?"

Alexi's fists rose and sparkles of blue fire trickled out.

Rebecca flew forward. "Haven't you considered that there may be more than one kind of trap, Alexi? You must consider them all. How many times have I prepared you for this moment? We were warned of betrayals and false prophets, of the 'mistakes of mortal hearts.'"

"Just because you *care* for Miss Parker does not make her our seventh. However innocent and guileless she may appear, she may in fact be sent from the ungodly realm, possessed by something harmful who looks to betray us. Appearing as no ordinary mortal, as you mention, with the ability to communicate with spirits—these very facts you present might be used to damn as easily as elevate."

Alexi shook his head. "Nonsense!"

"Alexi, she may not even be human."

"She's human, I assure you."

"What sort of experiments did you conduct upon her to reach *that* confident conclusion?" Elijah asked with a lecherous smirk.

Alexi pounded his fist violently upon a table. The gas lamps on the walls roared suddenly out of control, threatened to burn the place down.

"Alexi, please!" Josephine squealed. "Do you mean to kill us all?"

He raised one finger and the lamps dimmed; then he pointed at Elijah, who turned pale. "Never impugn her honor, Withersby," he warned, his voice deceptively calm. "And who are you to criticize me—you, who nearly caused a riot ten years ago by running off on a whim?"

"I was wrong, Alexi. I was very wrong," Elijah murmured, truly contrite. "And I've spent years repaying that debt. Don't make the same mistake."

Alexi held Elijah in a vicious stare for another unbearable moment; the lamps again burned high and the walls began to smolder. Finally, he made a casual gesture and the danger vanished—though the group coughed from the resulting smoke, waving their hands before their eyes. Elijah loosened his collar, sweat beading on his forehead.

"Alexi," Rebecca said. She moved slowly toward him. "Alexi, look what this is doing to you. You've withdrawn from us, nearly becoming a stranger. Alexi, however innocent the girl may seem . . . something may be working within her. Working to undo you. To undo all of us. Prophecy told us to listen to our instincts and stay together!"

Alexi's hands clenched and unclenched. "It is *my* life! Am I to disobey my heart, my instincts—?"

"Mortal hearts make mistakes, Alexi." Rebecca was shaking her head. "For the thousandth time, love has nothing to do with Prophecy; it's only confused and endangered us. You'd risk the whole of our work for this wisp of a girl, this timid curiosity—"

Josephine and Elijah looked at each other in surprise, then at Alexi. "Love? Love isn't a factor here, is it?"

"Alexi, listen to yourself," Rebecca continued. "We were warned of this. She is a trick, a pawn meant to test you. Clear your mind, stop and think of duty! You've never been swayed by passion. You have always been our anchor of reason."

Alexi smoldered. "How dare you. I've sacrificed everything, denied myself every scrap of companionship, pleasure, or comfort in my life. Now that Prophecy has come, my duty is to protect her. And you five, turned against me by Miss Linden—"

"We're not turning against you, Alexi," Rebecca insisted, tears in her eyes. "You're biased. Evidently, you must see the door yourself to be convinced. I'm sorry it's come to this."

Alexi stood nose to nose with her. She remained strong beneath his withering stare and added, "This isn't easy for any of us, Alexi. Hearts may be broken. I know all about that."

"You want Prophecy to be Miss Linden because it's obvious that I don't care about her, beautiful as she may be. Your jealousy is such that you'd rather push me toward someone I care nothing for, hoping that I might at last choose you instead—"

Rebecca slapped him across the face, rage in her eyes. "How dare you say such a thing, Alexi Rychman? You've fabricated Prophecy to be your lover when that was never so! How dare you blame me for trying to save you from yourself?"

Alexi's hand rose to his cheek. Tears spilled down Rebecca's flushed, defiant face. Everyone else stared on in horror, waiting for the walls to ignite.

"Has it come to this?" he growled. "You, of all people, Headmistress? Years of friendship and trust turned to petty violence?"

"Alexi," Jane interrupted, "don't blame Rebecca. We are all in agreement."

"All my years of leading you fools, and in the end they mean nothing. Fate has turned you against me. Well, I damn this fate!" Alexi fumed, turning to exit. "I shall make my own."

Michael jumped up suddenly and blocked him. In their nineteen years together, no one had ever seen the vicar angry. Until now. "You dare to alter Prophecy to suit your whim? You ignore the signs we are all given?"

"No." Alexi shook his head, trying to press past, but Michael would not budge.

"Alexi, don't think this isn't hard for us as well," the vicar stated.

"No, I see. Kiss me on both cheeks, my friends, and send me to the cross."

Elijah scoffed. "Oh, don't be dramatic—"

"Don't be cruel, Elijah," Alexi countered.

Rebecca was weeping. "Don't be utterly stupid and blind. Listen to us, for once. You're not omnipotent."

Alexi stared at his friends, searching for any ally, any hint of understanding, but there was none. Weariness broke through Alexi's anger. If there truly was a door, could he deny it? Could he walk away from the group he led? He would fail everyone and everything if he did. The truth of the sign, and the unreliability of emotion, something he'd forsworn long ago, made him strongly question his trust in himself.

"I hate this," he stated sadly, and felt something begin to die inside him. He needed space. Time. To clear his head from the muddy depths of passion. To be rid of everything and everyone, and in that quiet, lonely silence, discern. Lucille Linden had crept down the stairs and stood silently in a corner of the room. Alexi gazed upon her and a bitter taste rose to his lips. Could they possibly be right? Somehow, could it be possible that the innocent Miss Parker had blinded him? He had made a mistake before—one that had cost his sister her legs and his family their love. Could he afford to stand alone again? No. He could not afford to be stubborn, to be too righteous. His pride could not cost them all a fall, even if it meant he had to shatter hearts . . .

"May I speak?" Lucille asked. Her voice was like soothing warm music, though not in Alexi's preferred key; not the voice he longed to hear. Could he learn to tune his preference?

"Yes," Elijah replied. Alexi set his jaw.

"Please, my friends, I don't presume to know anything about how your esteemed faction operates. I can't say exactly how the doors operate. I've only seen them in times of stress and I cannot guarantee them even then. But let me spend a bit of time with you and let us see," she suggested gently.

The Guard turned to Alexi, staring expectantly. They were still his to command, if he would do so.

His shoulders fell. "I curse the day I received the burden that is this life," he stated, taking in his comrades. "I don't recognize any of you."

He turned to Miss Linden. "Very well, we'll have a meeting. Perhaps our chapel will return all of you to your senses." His voice was hollow, his shoulders stooped. Drawing his cloak about him, he turned slowly and moved to the door.

"I'll make arrangements for Miss Parker to be returned to her convent. The safest thing would be to keep her out of the way," Rebecca suggested quietly.

Alexi whirled on her. "Don't say one word to Percy. I will handle it," he said, and stormed out the door.

The Guard stood silent, staring helplessly.

Lucille glowed with soft warmth. She said softly, her eyes watering, "I feel for the first time in ages that I—and all of us—may at last be safe."

CHAPTER
TWENTY-FIVE

ISABEL ROUSED HER WITH A SHARP RAP ON THE DOOR AND PERCY rose and dressed alone, assuming, as she always did, that she was too frightening to receive help. When she finally made her way downstairs, Alexandra was awaiting her with scones and tea. Percy did not have the heart to admit she didn't have an appetite.

"I'm sure you're anxious to get back to your campus and to Alexi," the woman said, "so I won't hold you with pleasantries, but you simply must eat something; you'll waste away."

"Thank you, Miss Rychman, for your generosity and kindness," Percy replied, taking a scone out of politeness.

"Now, Alexi hasn't come, but he sent a driver for you." Percy was certain she appeared as crestfallen as she felt, for Alexandra was quick to add, "He must simply be busy, don't you worry. I'm sure you and I both worry too much when so much of his mystery we would never understand."

"Are you sure he's all right?"

"I'm sure he'll be at the school when you get there." Alexandra took Percy's soft white hands in hers. "Take care of him, dear girl. You've such a gentle heart—I see it in every part of you. He needs that desperately," she confided.

Percy smiled nervously. "But, Miss Rychman—"

"Break past his cold walls, Miss Parker! You must. You're the only one who can; he's never let anyone else near. He's so frozen without, but there's a fire within."

Percy nodded, thinking of their grandmother's message. She considered mentioning that she'd seen Alexandra's grandmother but thought better of it; she didn't want to add more madness to the mixture.

She couldn't stay any longer; her nerves would brook no further delay. She rose. "Thank you, Miss Rychman, for everything."

"Anyone that Alexi has taken the time to care about, which is hardly anyone, is always welcome here."

Percy stared out the carriage windows all the way back to London, wringing her hands and wondering why Alexi hadn't come for her in person. Surely it was because they couldn't take the risk of being seen creeping back onto the grounds together. Still, she found it odd he had not sent a note indicating her best course of action once she returned. She'd simply have to seek him out under the guise of academic pursuit.

City bells tolled nine. Percy thought guiltily about missing religious services, especially when her arms had been so recently locked around a man not her husband. She attempted to assuage her sin through fervent prayer. Yet the strange events that were bringing her and Alexi together had to be the work of God's hand. Or so she hoped.

When the driver pulled up to Athens's portico, Percy flew from the cab and scurried across the courtyard. She glanced up at the sky, but the clouds remained thick, keeping the heavenly canopy—cracked or whole—hidden.

She sped to Alexi's office and almost forgot to seek permission to enter. Recovering herself, she took a deep breath and knocked.

"Who is it?" barked a voice from within. Percy shrank back from the tone.

"Perc—It's Miss Parker, Professor Rychman," she called.

No answer. His door was unlocked, and she dared to open it. Alexi was staring blankly out the stained-glass window, its colors cast across his expressionless face. Percy crept into the room and closed the door behind her.

"Alexi, what is the matter?" she asked. He didn't reply, so she added sweetly, "I was worried when you did not come. Are you all right? Are your friends all right?" She approached slowly and reached out to touch his shoulder.

He gave her a brief, stony glance that caused her heart to freeze, then turned to evade her touch. "You came in unannounced and uninvited, Miss Parker," he began coldly.

Her heart stumbled. "My apologies, Alexi. I was presumptuous. Do forgive me; I didn't mean to intrude. May I visit you later this evening?

We've much to discuss," she added gently, hoping he'd turn with a weary smile, take her hand, and unburden himself.

"No. You may not," he declared. "Never again. I have realized your web of witchcraft, and I must distance myself from you."

Percy suddenly felt nauseated. "What do you mean?"

"I broke from your spell."

"Spell? What do you mean?" Percy asked, her breath failing. "I grant you, I do not look ordinary, but I'm no witch! I speak no incantations. I wield no charms. Your protection and concern were a gift you gave me of your free and dominant will—the greatest gift I've ever been given. And, if I'm not mistaken, you care—"

"I cannot explain to you any more than I could before. I simply cannot see you."

"Alexi, please—"

"No more. I can see you no more. That is all," he declared.

"But—"

"I should never have so blindly indulged in your company, Miss Parker."

Percy stumbled toward his desk and supported herself by leaning back against it, fearing that her knees would otherwise give way. "Alexi, not even a day has passed since you shielded me from that horrid beast. What about my safety? Even if you do not wish to . . . follow through on the promise of your embrace, you pledged to keep me safe! Why this change of heart?"

"I . . . I cannot care for you; it is ruining me."

"Ruining *you*? Tell me, what could have been ruined but my own honor?" She felt as if she had been slapped.

Alexi remained silent. Percy prayed for something, anything to counteract the horror of this unwarranted change of sentiment. "Have I been made such a fool that you'll not even look at me?" Her hand flew to her mouth. "Oh. Of course. You are ashamed of me. I'm not Beauty, not Snow White, but the Beast after all—"

Alexi still did not move or look at her as he spoke icily. "Miss Parker, you're a very intelligent girl. Don't indulge this senseless romanticism. Since the established rules of conduct in this place have been thoroughly and egregiously broken, I've arranged for a carriage to return you to the convent tomorrow. It is for the best."

Percy choked. "What?" She was barely able to whisper as her fingers fumbled at her throat, clutching her phoenix pendant. "You send me away; you punish me with no explanation, after all you did to me? You owe me something, not this cold, sudden banishment!" She approached him. "Look at me, Alexi. Will you not see my pain? Don't you know how terrified I am of the dogs, the horses, the blinking visions of fire? If you abandon me . . . might it not mean my death?"

Despite her proximity, his expression remained impenetrable. Perhaps he cringed; she could not be sure. "Don't be foolish. You'll live," he stated.

"Live with what—fond touches turned suddenly to lies while unnatural events and creatures drive me to madness?"

"I told you no lies. I promised you nothing," he growled.

"You promised me information and safety! I thought you might need me as much as I need you, and for some greater purpose, it seemed! Why play with my heart if you were only going to break it? I begged you not to toy with me and now you've ruined my life. My chances and opportunities here—"

"It is not your place to fight me, Miss Parker. Stand down," he said, without looking in her direction. "Silly girl, you shouldn't have been foolish enough to give me your heart. You overstep your bounds—"

"I'm not the one who did so, Professor!" Percy insisted, finding a surprising, righteous fury within her. "You broke the rules when you pressed your lips to mine. *You* kissed *me.*" She had to gasp so as not to sob, tasting that delightful yet devastating memory one final time. "There's a purpose for me. Don't leave me so ignorant. Is this merely because I am your student, and so now I, the one who has no power here, shall be punished? Does the headmistress demand that?"

Alexi clenched his fists. "She does, actually. You must be removed from my life, Miss Parker, no matter what we have shared. New aspects of my calling have come to light, and the matters do not, unfortunately, concern you. I can say no more—"

"You can say no more . . ." A crazed laugh tickled the back of her throat. "How convenient! And now you leave your pupil to the wolves. The very *sky* is breaking open, Alexi. I'd like to hear what the headmistress has to say about that—about Prophecy, about your little club, about how you touched me . . ."

Suddenly, she remembered the night prior. "Oh, I should tell you that your grandmother came to visit me at your sister's house. She warned me of snakes and told me to tell you to light the darkness with your fire, firebird. But perhaps that's useless information to you now, as I am useless to you now."

He whirled upon her, madness in his eyes, a desperation she'd never seen. He advanced upon her like an animal stalking prey. "A door, Percy. Please. Try. "

"What . . . Alexi, I don't understand what you want me to do—"

"It is foretold, Percy, that you will open a portal!"

"Alexi—"

"You must! From this world to the next! It is foretold and the goddess would not have lied to me!" he shouted, seizing Percy by the arms and shaking her. She cried out and shrank back.

"I would do anything for you, Alexi, but how can I do what I cannot comprehend?" Percy said wretchedly, frightened tears coursing down her cheeks. There was a horrid, miserable silence. For a brief moment, she thought she glimpsed utter devastation in the murky depths of his eyes. But as with all emotion, it was a flicker, and then gone.

"Then you are not what I thought you were and our paths must never cross again," Alexi stated simply. His face now showed no glimmer of pity. Percy sank to her knees on the office floor.

"A-Alexi . . . How can you—"

"Would it were otherwise," he murmured slowly. "But you are not Prophecy. You are a trap. And so you must go. I cannot have you here."

Percy was too stunned to move. Above her was a captivating yet suddenly foreign demon dressed in black robes and quivering with unfounded contempt. The pain in her breast was sharp as a rapier point, and she thought she might lose consciousness. Through the window behind Alexi, she saw the shadows of the horsemen in the sky, larger than before. Her fear intensified.

Alexi pointed to the door.

She stood, holding his gaze.

"Sending me away won't change how I much I love you, Alexi." She spoke the weighty words as if they were proclamations from heaven. She loved him dearly; there was no shame in that. What had begun as fascination had grown into true love, nurtured by his unfaltering acceptance of everything about her. She could not credit it had vanished entirely.

Alexi's eyes closed. His conflict was betrayed by the shaking hand he raked through his wild black locks. Percy rallied for a moment at this crack in his façade. Perhaps he would break down, confess the undying passion that he surely couldn't have crafted so disingenuously . . .

"Get out!" he cried, sweeping forward to drive her away.

She could bear no more. Percy ran into the hall; the door slammed behind her, its booming echo drowning the unearthly gasp of grief that tore from her throat. On the other side of the door, Alexi Rychman dropped to his knees and put his head in his hands, holding back an angry, pitiful wail.

PERCY WATCHED THE SUNSET TRACK ACROSS HER WALL.

There came a knock upon her door. She did not respond. After a long silence, the knock repeated.

"Percy, it is I, are you there?" Marianna asked.

"Yes, Marianna," Percy replied weakly.

"May I come in?"

"I . . . am not feeling well, Marianna. I think it best not to see me this evening. I fear I'd make you ill in turn." Percy found it difficult to think or speak in complete sentences.

"You are not well? May I get you anything?"

"No, Marianna. There is no medicine to cure this ailment."

"Oh."

"I will see you soon, my friend," Percy added, attempting to sound valiant.

"All right. Tomorrow then. Good night!" Marianna called, and Percy heard her slow, hesitant footsteps move off down the hall.

Percy sat perfectly still, knowing the truth. She would never see Marianna again. She would be whisked back to the convent in shame, there to live out an unfortunate life in silence. Perhaps she would cut that mercifully short with a sharp blade and hope God would understand. Unless that canine abomination found her first. She desperately hoped its fangs were quick.

* * *

In the drawing room of Lord Elijah Withersby's grand estate, Miss Linden and the Guard fell silent as Josephine ushered a swirl of black fabric and brooding shadow into the room.

"By all means, don't let me interrupt," Alexi said, his expression cold as he gestured for them to return to their conversations. He drifted to sit in a Queen Anne chair and stared into space, detached and silent. His compatriots watched him with caution. Finally Jane spoke softly to Miss Linden, who nodded and left the room.

Michael cleared his throat. "My dear Alexi," he began, somewhat sheepishly, "what on earth are we to do?"

Resting his elbows upon the arms of his chair, Alexi joined his fingertips at his chin. "Now you seek my guidance."

"We're lost without it, Alexi. You know that."

A long moment passed before he chose to reply. "I told Miss Persephone Parker that our acquaintance could no longer continue. She'll be sent away," he declared, every word tasting like poison. As his companions took a relieved breath, he added, "However, I do not condone my own actions."

"Alexi, we are grateful for your compliance. But you must believe in Miss Linden, otherwise—"

"Otherwise Prophecy is a fallacy?" He snorted.

"Please, Alexi," Michael begged. "This is new for all of us. We are concerned both for our mission and your welfare. We're at a loss."

"Your sentiments baffle me. If you cared, you'd have respected my heart. I forsook Miss Parker and I don't know what will become of her. Well, what does it matter? I wish you'd leave me to my fate rather than demand this charade of niceties. I'll do my damned duty. I trust you'll do the same."

"This bitter cold of yours is suffocating. We cannot do our duty with this strain," Josephine pleaded.

"Ah, *you* are strained! Perhaps if you saw the utter devastation of a sweet young lady searching desperately for answers—an innocent who did nothing wrong, whom I've abandoned to a strange, harsh fate—you might understand true strain!" Alexi jumped to his feet. "If you will believe it, I am actually struggling to retain some semblance of a professional manner."

From across the room, Rebecca stared at Alexi; his merciless gaze focused sharply on her. "After so many years together, I can't bear this!" she whispered, her fist clenched upon the mantel.

"It pains me as well. More than you know. And if you'd like to speak further about pain and suffering, Miss Thompson, you may seek me out in private, where I'm sure even more painful rumination awaits."

Rebecca's throat visibly constricted.

Alexi turned curtly to the assembled company, sardonic bitterness dripping from his words. "So. After denying my instincts, you ask for my edicts. Well, let's take Miss Linden's advice and have a meeting. Perhaps she'll open up the spirit world and it will be perfectly clear we're . . . meant to be. I expect she awaits us in the next room?"

Josephine nodded.

In the adjacent chamber, a small Turkish suite, Miss Linden had lit a perfumed candle and made herself comfortable. Bent over a notebook, she looked up as Alexi burst in. He coolly evaluated both her and the rich dressings of the room.

"Good evening, Professor," she said. "Will you sit with me a moment?"

He swept his robe aside and sat upon the small table, eyeing the small book in which she had been writing. "Your memoirs, Miss Linden?"

She laughed softly. "Exactly!" Her emerald eyes reflected the diffuse light, and her red lips were soft and plump. Her creamy skin, set against her impeccable black curls and the dark green of her garb and eyes, was flawless. Miss Linden was, Alexi had to acknowledge, with her beauty and regal carriage, everything that he and his compatriots had originally expected of a goddess.

"You will come with us to our hall tonight," he commanded.

"I shall do whatever you bid me do," she agreed, green eyes sparkling. "My dear professor, all of this is very sudden, very overwhelming. I'm sure you feel the same. However, I trust you and know that you'll guide me." She blushed and looked away. "I was drawn to you from the first, though I know you cannot say the same."

Her eyelids fluttered, and Alexi thought he glimpsed the glitter of tears. "Miss Linden—"

"No, Professor," she interrupted. "There is no need for you to make excuses. I feel for you and abhor the duty which forces you to forsake your heart. You and I are thrust into a most strange situation."

"Indeed," he replied.

"Miss Thompson told me that the prophecy, as you see it, would call for us . . ." She sighed.

"To be lovers," he concluded.

Lucille visibly shivered, causing her back to arch, pressing her voluptuous body against the table and toward him. "Yes. Lovers. But your heart lies with a paler face, doesn't it?" she whispered. "Such a strange girl—so timid and yet so passionate. What a poor, unfortunate creature!"

Alexi swallowed hard. "Please, do not speak of her."

"Very well, then. What can I do to make you . . ."

"To make me fall in love with you?"

Lucille gave a shrill, nervous laugh. "How this turns my world inside out. I find myself struggling for a man's notice, despite the fact that it has been preordained," she mourned. Alexi found he had no wish to comfort her. "Though I wield no sword, I'd gladly fight my rival."

"This is very difficult for me, Miss Linden."

"Call me Lucy, won't you?"

"Lucy, then. It is very difficult for many reasons."

"Tell me."

Alexi snorted. "Though my social graces have before been impugned, I'd rather not try the patience of a beautiful woman with the scattered thoughts of a dour and tedious man."

"Please, Professor, you're nothing of the sort. Let's put simple courtesies aside. If you and I must care for each other without the benefit of courtship—though I've betrayed my sense, modesty, and pride in admitting that I care for you already—it might help if you . . . 'unfold to me . . . why you are heavy,'" she pleaded with a small smile. "I hear you like Shakespeare."

There was a long silence as Alexi processed her words. He found it ironic that Lucy should quote Portia's plea to Brutus—Brutus, who was noble and yet a murderer, a betrayer. Alexi himself was no less. Brutus came to a dire and undignified end upon his own sword; Alexi wondered grimly if he'd someday do the same on some spectral threshold.

Chasms within him opened wider, but he forced himself to speak. "I prepared all my life for my coming fate, was obligated to lock my heart for countless years. Recently I saw the opportunity for my loneliness to end."

"Miss Parker?" Lucille prompted.

"I believed so . . ." Alexi faltered. "But that could not be proven on all counts. I, unused to such feelings, am at a loss. I've known duty, diligence, omens, spirits, and loneliness. But nothing like this." Having unclasped far more than was his custom, he felt ill and resentful.

"Dear Professor," Lucy said gently. "If you allow me, I can abate that loneliness of yours." Moving around the small table, in a gesture that somehow did not seem out of place given the circumstances, she knelt and looked up at him in earnest.

It was Percy's pale, stricken face that Alexi saw, and the memory of her similar earnestness as she sank to her knees on his office floor. Her sweet voice accosted him, a voice he'd grown eager to hear, begging for kindness and the answers rightly due her. He relived the wretched sound of her sobs as she fled his office, inexplicably cast aside.

He leaped to his feet, breaking out in a cold sweat, and was uncomfortably pinned by Lucille's gaze. As thunder roared outside the window, he turned away and said, "I'm sorry, Miss Linden, but I cannot continue this conversation at present."

Swiftly he returned to his compatriots, who looked expectant.

"My fellows, we cannot have a meeting tonight; I've grown distracted and that will only create weakness in our sacred space. We shall reconvene soon, but I beg you, not tonight." And with that, he ran out the door.

He had no desire to return to his empty estate—he would likely set it on fire and let it burn to the ground this time—and he did not believe he could face his sister and the questions she would doubtless pose. Instead, he escaped into academic paperwork, his usual solace, while the tempest broke viciously outside his office window.

When the clock down the hall chimed a late hour, he was certain it tolled the doom of all happiness he'd ever hoped to have.

CHAPTER

TWENTY-SIX

A THUNDERSTORM RAGED OUTSIDE PERCY'S WINDOW, UNLEASHING atmospheric fury upon the whole of London but Percy barely noticed. She lay in pain upon her floor, limbs twisted in the lacy folds of her nightdress. Something sharp had begun to heave within her; a strange, inhuman sort of pain, far beyond the seething ache one might expect from a broken heart. This was unnatural. Something deep inside was waking in rebellion. Something inside was eating her alive.

There were whispers in her mind, sounds that pelted her brain like the raindrops against her window. The lightning illuminated her writhing, white body. She felt a close presence but could see nothing. She feared she had turned demon and longed for a priest to exorcise her. She tried to call out to the spirits of Athens, to ask what might be happening to her, but could not form words.

She gagged on the sensation of something palpable and sour in her mouth, and, not having eaten that day, she found the pulpy kernels that suddenly burgeoned from her throat an additional terror. There was the same sickening smell of fruit as had nauseated her in her vision, and she coughed seeds onto the floor. She knew just what mythic sort of seeds they were, mysteriously and disgustingly expelled, and it did nothing for her sanity. When the goddess Persephone, kidnapped by Hades, king of the underworld, ate the fruit of the pomegranate, she'd been bound there and to him.

Percy did not remember being the bride of a god, nor did she ever wish to be. She heaved again, desperate to void the pulp she herself had never ingested.

The clock down the hall chimed a late hour. A bolt of lightning flashed so near her window that she cowered, thunder reverberating in her bones. She needed, now more than ever before, to be wrapped securely in Alexi's arms. She was sure she was meant nowhere else. An invisible force was urging her on, demanding at all costs that she run to him despite his betrayal, despite the fact that he was sending her away in the morning.

Something sharp twisted again within Percy's body and she began to shake as more pulp burst into her mouth. Her pendant burned; she felt something press toward her, intending to snuff the candle of her soul. She realized it sought to destroy Alexi, too.

She had to warn him. Beyond their hearts, something larger was at stake. A balance was sliding from light to dark.

As if to force Percy out into the storm, with a sharp crack her window shattered and the gale poured in. With a cry, she scrabbled backward. Blood seeped into her white gown from many tiny wounds made by glass, matching the ruby stains of vomited, half-digested pomegranate.

Percy screamed. She flung open her door and flew into the corridor, knowing only that she had to get to Alexi.

The tempest roaring outside fit Alexi's mood. *Love.* The word made him ill. It was foreign, unfair, and he'd done fine without it. What good was such a feeling if he could not have the one he wanted? What of those who could choose whom they loved? Jealousy scorched his heart, jealousy of normal men, faced with no other requirements than their personal desires.

Restless, he moved to the phonograph and sent an evocative aria into the room. An intense lightning strike drew him back to the window, where he contemplated throwing himself into the torrent.

A few girls, frightened by the storm, had gathered in the hall. They shrieked with fear as Percy's door flew open with a cry, revealing her mad-eyed and tousle-haired, patches of crimson spattered across her spectral whiteness. Percy didn't care. She raced past a gasping Miss Jennings and rushed headlong into the thunderstorm.

She was the only one daring the outdoors; even the school guards had taken shelter. In moments her snowy locks became sodden strings; her ruffled gown was plastered against her chilly, slender form. Nonetheless, she welcomed the stinging downpour, sobbing as she ran across the courtyard. Cold rain and hot saltwater mixed in her mouth.

Apollo Hall loomed ahead. Lightning blazed. Thunder screamed. Percy froze, staring up at a stained-glass window—*his*—where a shadowy form appeared.

The figure above was unmistakable, her only chance for safety and salvation. He was the answer; he could make the horsemen vanish and the dogs silent, and he could close up the broken heavens.

Frozen to the bone, her wounds throbbing, her stomach churning once more, shaking in misery, Percy dropped to her knees. She could fight no longer. Her meager knowledge—that she and Alexi were meant to be together, that if they were not, the balance between light and dark would be shattered—was insufficient to ward off whatever power had shattered her window and sought her end.

All faded to black.

A SHADE—A FRAIL, BEAUTEOUS NIGHTMARE—STOOD BENEATH HIS window. White hair whipped in all directions, her head thrown back, mouth wide open, white dress soaked and blotted with red . . . his dear Percy was there, torn by the storm's fury. The lament of the soprano keening from the bell of the phonograph could just as well have come from the mouth of the specter below, who suddenly collapsed onto the sopping flagstones.

Alexi bolted down the stairs and into the rain. In an instant he had scooped Percy into his arms. She was light as a feather, unconscious yet shuddering. Alexi gazed down at that marble visage which, even in this half-drowned state, he could not help but find beautiful.

"Persephone, you godforsaken romantic, what drove you to this?" he moaned, sickened by the sight of the blood on her gown as he whisked her off toward the infirmary. "Please, not me. Please let this not be my fault," he cried, knowing full well it was.

Alexi was a sight indeed when he swept into the infirmary, a veritable angel of death holding an apparition more fairy than human in his arms.

"Professor!" a nurse exclaimed, rushing to him. Alexi charged past her and laid Percy upon the nearest bed. An entourage of nurses clustered around.

"Professor Rychman, what on earth—"

"Take care of her," he commanded, raking a hand through sopping hair. "She collapsed outside my window. Make sure she goes nowhere until she is well."

"Yes, sir," they all agreed.

The medical staff dispersed to gather supplies, and he was given a moment alone to hover over her wet, bloodstained body. He knelt beside her, imagining her an angel that had plummeted from the heavens and into the sea, there perhaps to be drowned.

"Poor Ariel, my sweet cipher. Don't let the tempest claim you. I only wish I could," he murmured, kissing her moist forehead.

His lips lingered upon her a moment too long; he was desperate to place his aching lips upon her lifeless ones, rouse her like the prince did Sleeping Beauty. Finally he drew back, fighting a wealth of emotion he could not indulge, and fled. He must kill his heart once and for all, for it was a useless mortal contrivance that he abhorred.

Soaking, he stormed back to his office, stoked the fire in his hearth, and sat at his desk. Stricken, he buried his face on his crossed arms and remained frozen there in grief until sleep overtook him.

REBECCA HAD WANDERED HER APARTMENTS AT THE TOP OF PRO-methe Hall all night, wringing her hands, thinking she heard screaming.

Wracked by nerves, once the vicious storm had at last broken, she flitted across the courtyard, disquieted by the reaction of the restless specters of the academy who, one by one, turned to stare at her with odd mistrust.

The headmistress knocked, but there was no response. She tried the door and found it open, to her dismay. Entering, she saw Alexi slumped over the desk. Rebecca's blood ran cold.

"Alexi . . . ?" she asked tentatively.

His breathing was labored, his brow furrowed in a painful dream. Rebecca brushed a lock of hair from his moist forehead. With a start he bolted upright, dark eyes blurred and unfocused.

"Alexi, it's me," Rebecca fumbled. "I didn't mean to startle you."

He growled and rubbed his face in his hands, raking back tousled hair with quivering fingers. "What do you want?"

Rebecca took the chair opposite him. "This anguish in your heart, I cannot bear it. I must apologize. The night I struck you . . . something within me died."

"You killed something inside of me as well," he countered. "I never thought you and I would commit such childish acts."

"Forgive me, please, Alexi, I beg you." She reached a shaking hand across the table. He withdrew his hand from her reach, pinning her with a furious gaze. "Alexi, I never wished for this."

"Nor did I. But don't you dare speak words of contrition to me now, traitor."

Rebecca's mouth went slack. She had nothing to counter that terrible blow.

Something snapped in Alexi's eyes and his shoulders convulsed. His head fell suddenly into his hands. "She may be dying!" he cried.

"What?"

"My Percy—my dear, sweet girl . . . She wandered into the tempest. There was blood on her gown; she was feverish, shaking. She collapsed outside my window, crying up to me. I was watching the storm . . ."

"My God."

"Rebecca, I feel her slipping away. Terrible forces are at work upon her, and I feel her passionate, innocent soul draining from me. I promised to keep her safe and I don't know that I can!" He wailed, tears springing to his eyes. "Damn my heart! Cut it out! Cut it from me, Rebecca, please . . . !"

In an unprecedented act, Alexi Rychman began to sob.

"Oh, Alexi!" Rebecca's hand went to her mouth and she rushed to him, clasping him in an embrace.

"I promised I'd explain everything. I told her I'd protect her, but instead I may have killed her! What if she dies, Rebecca, without ever knowing? This damned prophecy aside, I *love* the girl!"

He fell helpless into her arms, weeping like a little boy. Rebecca cried with him. She reeled with a mixture of sympathy, the sting of his confession of love, and the bittersweet feel of her arms around him.

"Dear God, Alexi. What are we asking of you?"

PERCY LAY LIKE THE DEAD, SNOW WHITE WITHOUT A GLASS COFFIN. Only pale, bluish shadows distinguished her body from the pristine white sheets.

"Oh, Percy!" Marianna rushed to her friend's side, knelt, and took Percy's colorless hand. "What horrid distraction drove you to this?" she asked, seeing that the pale girl's arms were covered with small bandages.

A sheen of perspiration covered Percy's pearlescent skin. Her eyes roved beneath fluttering white lids, lost in dream-filled unconsciousness.

A wide-eyed nurse paused at the foot of Percy's bed. The German girl asked, "Miss, may I ask how long she has been here?"

"Since late last night."

Marianna's eyes filled with tears. "I've been inquiring of her everywhere. The girls in my corridor said they heard she went mad and rushed out into the storm. Who brought her here?"

"I did not see, miss, but I was told Professor Rychman found her. Oh, my, miss, how she's been murmuring!" The nurse spoke with noticeable discomfort. "Desperate pleas, but all in foreign tongues. I can't catch a word."

As the nurse hurried off, Marianna picked up a small towel at the bedside to blot the moisture pooling on Percy's forehead. "Percy, my sweet, you know what myth we learned about yesterday? I now know your namesake. We learned of poor Persephone, kidnapped and dragged below the earth. Please don't let the underworld take you, Percy, I could not bear it!"

The stricken girl's eyes suddenly shot open; Marianna gasped as her arm was clenched tightly by white hands. With a weak chuckle, Percy released her grip. "Hello, darling. Sorry—thought you were a demon come for me."

"Who has done this to you?" Marianna asked.

Percy shook her head gravely and replied with a bit of verse. "'Nobody, I myself'!"

Marianna shook her head. "No, no, my Desdemona, I'll not take Shakespeare for an answer. What Othello brought you to this?"

"From the moment he sent me away, everything has been falling apart!"

"Who, who sent you—?"

"I am mad, dear Marianna! Can one suffer a personal apocalypse, meant only for them? My world is coming to an end, and I see it all . . ."

"You are not coming to an end, Percy," her friend argued. "What is it that you see?"

"Dogs—horses and dogs, growing closer, snapping their hundreds of jaws, closer, closer, my fever burns, here a feather, there a portal, a burning bird, snakes . . . hounds . . . one or hundreds . . ."

"What drove you into the storm, Percy? And how were you injured?"

"Wounds of a shattered heart."

Marianna shuddered at the sound of her friend's rattling lungs. "Shattered by whom?"

Percy set her lips.

Marianna shook her head. "You leave me to guess?"

"It does not matter," Percy murmured.

"Oh, no, of course not! You are bloodied, driven to madness, half drowned in a maelstrom, but it does not matter," Marianna replied. She leaned close. "If that professor of yours—"

Reacting as if stabbed, Percy clapped a hand over her mouth. "Please!"

"I see." Marianna gritted her teeth. "You would shelter and defend the man to your very death."

Percy collapsed again on the bed. "I am on fire." Marianna dipped the towel in the washbasin and placed it upon her forehead. Percy's head lolled to the side and she murmured, "Sick with the scent of scorched feathers—"

"Feathers?"

"Something terrible from another time," Percy breathed, unable to focus. "Something's after me, and none of it's what we think . . ."

"What isn't? Percy, stay—*look* at me."

"Hell is not down. It's sideways," Percy murmured. Her eyelids closed.

"Percy?" There was no answer. Marianna felt for her friend's pulse, terrified, and found it racing. "Dear God, Persephone Parker, what is happening to you?"

CHAPTER
TWENTY-SEVEN

PERCY'S EYES SHOT OPEN. HER MIND'S EYE HAD BEEN STARING AT THE charred face of a once-beautiful man. Things were crawling on her. Flinging the covers aside, she jumped out of bed with a cry . . . but there was nothing there, just her own body.

"Miss Parker, you've just had another dream. Back to bed with you," a nurse commanded, rushing over and putting a hand on her forehead. "My God, your fever burns yet."

"I need a breath of air," Percy said, trotting awkwardly to the terrace doors. The nurse opened her mouth to reprimand such sudden exertion, but the sparkling madness burning in Percy's eyes stemmed all protest.

A heavy breeze cooled Percy's enflamed body, whipping through her thin hospital gown. She closed her eyes to relish the sensation and avoid staring at the sky, which remained broken into two separate layers. Her momentary peace was disturbed by the sound of familiar footsteps in the courtyard below: None other than her black-clad heartbreaker walked there. Percy shook violently.

In her heightened state, she could sense an energy about Alexi that was as dire as her own. On his arm was the beautiful Lucille Linden, in an immaculately tailored silver dress of a bright sheen. The threads of the sterling taffeta glinted even in the gray daylight, too glaring a companion to the professor's stoic comportment. The pair neared the fountain, almost directly beneath the balcony where Percy stood frozen. Spirits passing through the courtyard scoffed at the couple, behind Miss Linden's and Alexi's backs.

Watching them, Percy was overwhelmed by a wave of new horror. When she'd first glimpsed the woman at the gala ball, Percy had imagined Miss Linden's coiled black locks as serpents. This time, it was no trick of her imagination. Writhing and slithering over the woman's head, asps leered up at Percy with menace; their red eyes were made of fire, their forked tongues hissed flames.

Alexi halted as if he sensed something, but he did not look up.

Percy wailed aloud. Clapping a hand over her mouth, she curled into a huddled mess against the wall. Hot tears coursed down her cheeks as her body convulsed with dry heaves.

"Miss Parker?" The nurse rushed over and lifted her in strong arms. "Poor dear," the nurse sighed as she settled Percy under a sheet. "Your friend said she would return to sit with you soon. Until then, you must calm your nerves."

Percy's eyes rolled as her breath hitched, and she felt the darkness of unconsciousness claiming her once again. "All the creatures of the Old World, and nothing to protect me! The spirits are crying 'Beware,' but for what? He can't hear their warning! Oh, the snakes . . . what his grandmother warned—"

Percy fainted.

ALEXI HEARD A WRETCHED CRY ABOVE HIM, AND HE TURNED TO SEE A white figure flicker out of view on the infirmary level. His heart burned in his chest, and he looked at Miss Linden curiously as a shudder ascended his spine.

"What is it?" she asked gently. Not a hair, bead, or dainty bit of lace was out of place on her immaculate figure.

"I . . . thought I saw something," he choked out.

In the air around him, he could not help but note how the spirits of Athens, men and women of various ages and periods, stared at Miss Linden. Their transparent faces were inscrutable, yet each ghostly mouth moved. Alexi longed for Percy by his side so that he would know if the spirits were offering benediction or warning.

"So," Miss Linden began gently. "Tell me about tonight."

Alexi nodded. "I'm not entirely sure what to expect, but we've a secret place, the location and entrance of which came to us upon our possession, like an old, dormant memory resurfacing after many years.

"We were quite young," he continued, attempting to explain what he had always considered inexplicable, "when something slid through our bodies—a soul entering into our veins, claiming us for our Grand Work.

We were led to a sacred place where we received our prophecy from a goddess, the divine creature who told us what we are. We have a vague mythology." Alexi felt again uncomfortable. "I beg your patience, Miss Linden. I cannot tell you the whole of our history, in one brief turn about the courtyard."

"For my part, I was born strangely," Lucille volunteered haltingly. "As if I was born specifically *for* someone. I knew I had a magnetism, something that caused people . . . and spirits . . . to stare at me, be drawn to me. I knew I was meant to see and be seen by all manner of incredible things." She paused and tilted her head. "Professor, what else shall I expect from you and your peers?"

Alexi took a breath. "We will form a circle and sing incantations, I'll ask the Great Force for a benediction and see what, if anything, happens. I wish this were a science but it is not. Of course, we'll also be looking for that door of yours."

"Ah, yes, the sign."

"Miss Linden, I must attend to business. May I escort you to your carriage, and leave you until later this evening?"

"By all means, dear professor. And again—do call me Lucy, won't you?"

Alexi felt her watching his every move as he led her out onto the path to the waiting carriage, and opened its door.

"Thank you for the company, Professor," she stated warmly. Cocking her head to the side, she closed the distance between them, and waited, her wide green eyes searching his. She lightly placed her mouth to his cheek and kissed him. He stood rigid and allowed it. She drew back and ducked into the carriage.

"It will become easier," she said as he closed the door, his expression blank. She poked her head out the window and said gamesomely, "Soon you'll want to kiss me back! Until this evening, then."

Waving daintily as the carriage rolled off, Lucille kept her eyes upon him to the last, just as the sky again opened with rain.

His robes sodden, Alexi walked slowly, with dragging steps, up the stairs of Promethe Hall until he reached a cavernous white room that smelled sharply of medicinal fluids. A blond girl at her side, Percy lay as if entombed.

Marianna turned, sensing movement. She stared blankly at Percy's professor, taking in his tall form draped in damp black fabric, the crimson cravat around his disheveled collar like an open wound.

"What did you do?" she demanded.

The professor grimaced and said nothing. His dark eyes seemed focused on something above Percy's supine body; it seemed to rattle him. Marianna looked up but saw nothing. The professor turned and exited, trailing black fabric and raindrops, leaving a keen emptiness where his piercing presence had just seethed. Marianna sighed and turned once again to her friend, only to gasp in surprise.

Percy was staring in abject horror at the ceiling. Marianna felt the air around her grow unnaturally cold. Percy shuddered.

"Percy, what is it?"

"They're all watching."

"Who?"

"The haunts. They are all above me, staring down. Waiting for me to die."

"There is nothing there, Percy," Marianna said reassuringly.

"No, they are there, waiting for me to join them. I wonder how long they've been watching." She coughed, turning to Marianna with eyes full of tears. "I am in such pain, my friend. I don't know what is inside me. Or outside me."

One of the spirits hovering above Percy's bed moved closer. Marianna shivered as he passed. Percy recognized the spirit as the young boy who hovered around the chandelier near Athens's front door. His soft brogue murmured just over her head. "Miss, are you goin' to do somethin' about the mess you're in, or are you goin' to join us?"

Before Percy could begin to think of a reply, Marianna spoke again. "I do not know if I should tell you this," the German girl began, "considering I know not the role he may have played in this . . . but he came by. Your professor."

"Oh!" Percy's body flooded with both joy and fear. "A-and?"

"I asked him what he had done. Forgive me, Percy, but I had to."

Percy's hands fluttered at her sides. "What was his response?"

"He said nothing. He stared at you—sadly, I think—looked above you and left as abruptly as he came." The German girl halted as Percy burst into tears. "Oh, dear. Percy . . ."

Percy wept, her strength draining away while Marianna sat sentry next to her, begging her softly to hold on. A violent cough sent a bloody, pulpy substance dribbling out the corner of Percy's parched mouth. Marianna gasped at the garish crimson marring Percy's snowy cheek and dabbed at the gore with a cloth.

"You see, my friend," Percy rasped. "Whatever has awakened in me may kill me yet. . . ."

ALEXI PACED ABOUT HIS ESTATE. NEARNESS TO THE EXQUISITE MISS Linden had not cleared Percy from his thoughts, and he feared those reflections would influence the course of the coming ceremony. He tried to shove the image of her snowy face from his mind, but it was no use. He saw Percy's eyes through his bedroom window, heard her voice in the corners of his mind, felt her vibrant heart in every shadow; her lips rested upon his in a phantom kiss. A sinking realization came to him: Persephone Parker would haunt him forever.

With great effort, he imagined bringing Miss Linden to his estate, imagined her, lovely and poised, sitting with him in his drawing room. He picture her lounging in the arched alcoves of his parlor, dancing on the veranda, caressing his flesh behind the thick curtains of his four-post bed . . .

These things brought no such fire, no matter how exquisite Lucille's face and form. Percy, with her singular pallor, had shaken his steeled, embattled foundations and shone a curious light inside just when he had begun to lose faith; nothing else had ever brought such warmth to his existence.

Would it be for naught, the power and experience he had accrued through the years? So long he had toiled, leading the Guard, maintaining the Balance. Now was the moment of truth. If he chose incorrectly, if he pined for a marble angel when he was supposed to love a raven-haired temptress, would that be betraying his goddess, his friends, and his destiny?

Or was Rebecca right after all? Was love indeed *not* part of Prophecy? Was he free to love Percy no matter her relation to the Grand Work, or would fate always keep them apart?

The clock struck eleven. Kneeling, Alexi began to pray. He had never been one for heavenly supplication, but he supposed if there was ever a time for it, that time was now. He prayed for presence of mind, to know what to say and do in the coming hours. He begged for Percy's life and strength, for her to be kept safe at all costs. And he prayed that, even though he was certain that Prophecy was meant to be his lover, he might be able to love Percy anyway . . .

At length he donned cloak and top hat, readied the faithful Prospero, and set off for the intimate chapel that housed their divine mystery.

THE AIR WAS SICK. A VIRULENT FORCE WAS TEARING THROUGH THE streets toward a specific destination, ready for a reckoning. It growled and roiled and cut a path like a whirl of ancient blades. Its casualty would be an unspeakable shame. Neither Alexi nor his cohorts had any inkling that there would be another mutilated corpse in the morning, nor that this would be the worst. There would be nothing, when all was said and done, to ever suggest that this woman, torn utterly to pieces, had once been a human being. After fetching something of his mistress, the Ripper had struck again, swiping ferocious, merciless, unthinkable paws down Dorset Street, en route to the evening's festivities.

CHAPTER
TWENTY-EIGHT

LIGHT WAS THE MOST WELCOME SIGHT, AFTER DARKNESS. RUNNING into the field, Percy laughed. The sound brought spring, and her love would be waiting: beautiful, winged, safe. Not cold and lonely like he who was her husband in name but not in her heart. She had heard Love's rich voice, deep within her breast, his feathers murmuring upon her ear in her most shadowy hours. She knew he would come.

The call of a great bird sounded, and a warm wind surrounded her. Strong arms swept her into a cradle hold. Laughter greened the trees. The Muses rushed into the field, delighted by the reunion of their dearest friends.

"Darling!" murmured a rich voice. She beheld the speaker, winged and magnificent, chiseled, stoic and true; Balance, Truth and Light, he was. Her heart swelled.

"Love . . ." she breathed, as his dark eyes stared deeply into her own prismatic irises. "You waited for me!"

"Did you doubt 'forever,' we who created the word? We shall create so much, you and I, shall we not?" He smiled, irresistible, and placed a powerful hand upon her stomach. Her insides grew warm with fertile desire, and she knew she would take him in and then bear a god of Balance. This would make the world right again.

The noble face of her love grew grave. "Has he harmed you?"

She shook her head. "Other than stealing me? No. Speak not of him." She took in the scent of her lover: fresh air, foreign spices. He pursed perfect lips in a delighted smirk. She felt the weight of Darkness fall away like heavy linens, revealing her free and naked body for her beloved's appreciation, so different from her husband's cloying prison where she was meant to keep the dead at bay.

Her love kissed her deeply, his dark hair entwining with hers in the spring breeze. Tracing the lines of her body with his fingertips, he pressed against her, aching, desperate. In centuries to come, she would curse the day she had been so careless. She would forever curse the day she failed to look behind to the cave opening where burning eyes watched. She did not hear the growl from distant shadows.

He, winged and supposedly eternal, the Keeper of Peace, the Balance, drew back and stared at her, a woman who should never have become another god's bride . . . and burst into flame. She heard an unforgettable, ungodly shriek of agony as her lover's form exploded, his feathers scorched and smoldering. She screamed a scream that shook the heavens. Her terror made the rain come, but too late. Hysterical, she cradled the charred, reeking, unrecognizable body of her true love in her arms. The Muses watched, frozen in horror.

The wind lifted a huge feather into its gentle hands; the consoling wind, murmuring sweet sympathies, blew the feather upon the breeze. It began to float away of its own volition, stirring to life. Five Muses ran after it, while four others ran away in terror.

She watched her true love's corpse crumble to dust, then backed slowly away as madness began to overtake her. Wailing, she beat her fists into the ground until her hands bled. "This is far from the end!" she shrieked into the crimson mud. "The world will not release you! I cannot release you! It will not end this way. We shall return—!"

With a retching cry, Percy came to consciousness, found herself pounding her fists violently against her bed. Realizing she was not in a distant, ancient land but rather a London sickbed, she moaned, fell back, and drew the sheets over her head, seeking unsuccessfully to muffle the horrendous, never-ending growling. There came a new sound. Percy removed the sheets and opened her eyes.

A humming, translucent feather made of blue fire floated before her eyes. This feather of cerulean flame was strangely comforting, and it eased Percy's boiling blood. The feather floated closer and then retreated, away from her bed, beckoning.

She stared at the feather and asked a silent question: *Am I to follow?*
The feather burned brighter; its blue fire sparkled.
Yes, Percy realized. *I must follow, though this be the end of me.*

* * *

Six candles burst into spontaneous flame as Alexi threw wide the chapel door and strode down the aisle. The Guard, clumped near the altar inside, looked to him, full of anxious hope. His eyes were dead, his face unreadable. From his lips burst a decree, and his powerful arm shot forward, emitting a burst of lightning that spun toward the altar. A black door rent the air.

The chapel door opened to admit Lucille Linden, who threw her cloak aside to reveal an immense black satin gown. Everything about her was the picture of beauty. The Guard were transfixed by the sight.

Lucille approached Alexi with an outstretched hand. He nodded and she slid her arm into his.

"Lead on, Alexi," she said. He nodded slowly, as if trapped in a dream.

The feather bobbed and pulsed, impatient.

Are you leading me to my death? Percy wondered. The feather suddenly changed shape, its wispy blue barbs transforming into a burning Sacred Heart. The symbol evoked such yearning that Percy couldn't refuse to follow, no matter if it led to the undiscovered country.

She attempted to stand, but nausea sent her sprawling back upon the bed, sweat pouring off her brow. The image again became a feather. Beautiful music sounded and Percy felt suddenly lifted by a great, tingling hand. Her thin hospital gown clinging to her body, she stumbled forward. The feather receded toward the door of the infirmary, pulsing, waiting for her.

Neither of the nurses seemed to notice her. It was as if she were already a ghost. Perhaps she was.

Fumbling with the knob of the infirmary door, she was almost free when one of the nurses turned toward her. Percy was sure she was trapped. And yet, the nurse didn't see her; the woman's eyes lost focus and her mouth went slack, as if she had been dazed by a brilliant, hypnotic light. Percy looked down at her hands to find them glowing.

With Miss Linden in tow, the Guard descended into their sacred space. That Miss Linden, ostensibly an outsider, was able to set foot upon the stone stairs that had materialized from their inexplicable, private altar entrance, they felt, was not to be dismissed.

Lucy Linden gazed about with eager wonder. Alexi stood nearby. His stern face was ashen, hers flushed; he a statue, she a flower. Moving liquidly into their ritual circle, Alexi led Lucy to the center. Her smile was as dazzling as the crystalline bird above her head.

Alexi left her there and returned to the perimeter. A breeze and an ancient harmony filled the air, the first chord struck in a symphony tuned by angels. The circle of blue fire leaped to life, licking their ankles with harmless affection.

Alexi closed his eyes. "Great guiding force, hold fast within us now, each to the other," he said carefully. "As myth would have it: from the Flame of Phoenix, Feather did fall and Muse did follow. If we are birthed from that flame, then our fire needs a new candle. I submit the humility of my mortal judgment to your higher wisdom. We know no other way than to humbly present our choice. Is this she?" He opened his eyes.

A breeze coursed around the circle, becoming a whirlpool, urging them to draw close. Lucy held out a hand. Alexi moved forward, breaking from the circle of fellowship that closed again behind him, and the pair stared at each other, faces mere inches apart.

"Alexi Rychman," Lucille Linden said softly. "You are mine."

Alexi slid his arm around her black satin–clad waist, drew her against him and kissed her ruby lips.

PERCY SPAT BLOOD, CRIMSON FLUID WELLING UP SUDDENLY IN HER mouth. Her bare feet pattered against the smooth wooden floor. The halls were quiet. It was late. Only she and the ghosts were awake, she realized, as she moved down the corridor. They turned to her, eyes wide, and bowed as she passed.

The halls should have been dim, for it was night, but Percy could see as if it were day. Passing the glass windows of darkened office doors, she saw her reflection and could not recognize it for the nimbus around her body. She stopped and stared, her hand before her eyes.

The feather floated close and brushed her cheek with a warm kiss before slipping down the corridor, coaxing, urging Percy to keep moving, no matter if she was shocked by how much she appeared the angel. No matter if she still tasted blood.

* * *

"*MINE,* ALEXI . . ." LUCY REPEATED AS SHE DREW BACK FROM THE KISS, caressing his cheeks with both hands.

Kissing her had done nothing to thrill him and her touch left him cold. Her eyes shifted colors, emerald to ruby to black. Part of him shivered in dismayed recognition. His goddess had cycled through hues just the same.

Lucille said, "Now then, let's begin." She moved her arms in a grand gesture, as if drawing an invisible arrow back against a bow. In response, a circular tile on the wall shuddered and shifted, twisting out of place the way a screw would pull from a stud, spiraling out. The cylinder lengthened, parallel to the floor, as it invaded the room, glistening with crystal and metal grooves, silt and debris falling from its edges as it extended farther. With a final belching sound, the extraction fell at an angle, leaving a gaping hole beyond. A dim, hazy shaft of light emanated from behind the seal: an opening.

Another portal, as Prophecy had decreed! Their sacred space had proven responsive to Miss Linden's commands, and murmurs of excitement flew among the Guard. Rebecca and Alexi stared at each other and at the transformed wall. Lucille's beautiful face grew lovelier still.

"I've always wanted to come find you, to play with you. This time, when everything is at stake, I've caught up with you and I'll never let go. He will be so proud!"

Rebecca's eyes narrowed. *"Who?"*

Lucy's smile tightened. "You fools. Once upon a time, if you recall, there was a vicious score to settle. Once upon a time there was jealousy, betrayal, and justice dealt by fire. But let us forgive and forget, shall we? We could join, could reign in both realms as they become one! The sepulcher is pried open at last!" she cried, and flung out her arms.

"What the devil do you mean?" Alexi demanded. His very soul felt frozen.

"The division between worlds, held fast by the seals— *Wait.* Don't you know what you're keepers of?" Lucille asked, incredulous. She laughed. "You truly are useless mortal fools, if you don't even know your own purpose."

"We police spirits," Rebecca scoffed. "Of course we know—"

"Yes, yes, but when you run about and perform your little tricks, don't you realize you're holding the seals fast? The more spiritual havoc you allow up there on your mortal streets, the more this seal loosens." She gestured to the pin upon the floor.

"It seems that our teacher left that part out of our tutorial," Alexi muttered.

"For centuries the latch between life and death has been held safely closed by your little chapels. But now that you've let me *in*, we can fling wide the door right here and now! 'London Bridge is falling down, falling down . . .'" Lucille grinned.

The hearts of the Guard froze. Their fearful gazes snapped to the crevice in the wall, where a familiar growl sounded. The tumultuous mass of combined spirit mongrels leaped from the abyss and loped around the circle of blue flame with its one or one hundred heads snarling and snapping. Fresh blood and bits of flesh dripped from its ungodly fangs. One set of jaws held the compelling silver chain and ruby pendant Lucille had presented to Josephine as payment. Snatching the chain from the jowls of her pet, Lucille held the gem to her bosom. Its charm faded and it became its base matter; blood and soot, a wretched illusion that crumbled in her fingers. A laugh that sounded full of sand erupted from Lucille.

"What *are* you?" Alexi demanded.

"My fable has changed so much over the years! Careful! Don't stare too close—you'll turn to stone!" Lucy sniggered. Serpents shot from her skull, the black locks slithering outward, hissing, wrapping around the necks of the Guard. Forked, flaming tongues licked their faces as they struggled. Michael attempted to rally them with a moment of hope, or even half a chuckle to warm their hearts, but he could not speak or breathe. Alexi's neck, so close to Lucille's, was wrapped double by a serpent, the choking pressure driving him to his knees.

"Such passion!" Lucy cried, eyes becoming feline. "Let me taste it— suck it from you!" Reptilian jaws opened their mouths and spat. "Master, receive my gift—the scales of the Balance will tip in our favor as the division of worlds is destroyed! At last you see how much I am worth!" She glanced at the broken seal. "The door! The prophesied door!" she mocked with glee.

"Oh, dear God, what have we done . . . ?" Rebecca sobbed.

"Phoenix help us. And Percy, forgive me—" Alexi gasped, staring into the gaping hole where a dank dungeon of souls awaited command.

Lucy turned to the ghastly host. "Come, come! Come back to your beloved world and be as loud as you like!" she called before whirling back to the Guard, licking her lips. "And imagine just such a release happening all over the world—it occurs as we speak!"

Vile spirits began to pour from the wall, as if a gurgling sewer pipe of eternity had been unclogged and refuse now flowed free. Alexi pictured the horror of other orifices vomiting such phantasmagoria around the world, with no one there to stop the spillage. He felt a wave of defeat, worse even than the snakes that suffocated him.

"Oh, Alexi," Lucy said, staring down at him, her eyes once again emerald. More snakes slithered around her head, caressed her cheeks, and slid down her body. "Forget that weakling girl. You and I were meant to traverse the ages together. Come. Taste of me. I've been so lonely and neglected. Just like you. Do you remember what you used to be? So magnificent! Wisdom and Light, the very Balance itself! But ever since you were foolish enough to fall in love, you've understood nothing but loneliness and pathetic human pain. What a humiliating fall."

She crouched so that her face was level with his. "I will cure it all, Balance be damned," she murmured.

GASPING PAST THE CONSTRICTION IN HER THROAT, PERCY STUMBLED down to the ground floor and rounded the corner to see the open chapel door at the end of the hallway. A new sensation swelled within her, a heat beyond her high temperature, a seething power that obliterated her weakness and infused her with unknown strength, buoying her on a sea of singing, wind, and peace. Percy suddenly knew she could command any force before her, through her light, through her revived power.

"What am I?" she murmured. "And what am I sent to do here?"

Ancient words of a tongue she had never spoken yet always knew erupted from her lips, a stream of blessings and curses all at once. She stumbled as if pushed into the white, empty chapel of Athens, where everything seemed as it always did: The plain altar was draped in white cloth, the stained-glass angels stood silent sentry. But a sound grew in the silence, originating at the altar—a tearing sound—and her blood chilled.

The dark, gaping maw of a door began as a small square and grew before her, obliterating the sight of the altar. Its dense blackness and wisps of dancing blue flame were so much like the vision she'd drawn in Alexi's classroom that she was stunned. Terrible sounds emanated from beyond the portal. The feather bobbed between Percy and the door, then swelled and burst, leaving only smoke. There was a cry from the darkness.

"Alexi!" Percy realized. She ran forward, heedless of what might await her below, and threw herself into the void.

THE GUARD TRIED TO MURMUR CURSES, BENEDICTIONS, AND PRAYERS, but they couldn't connect to wield their collective power. Through their mortal weakness, that chink in the armor of their every incarnation, a wound birthed anarchy. Malevolent spirits poured through the seal, wailing and cackling, eager to terrorize the populace of the world's fulcrum city, to tip the balance from sanity to chaos and shatter divisions between journeys of the human spirit. All the while, an ancient foe, that chimerical hellhound, shifted his canine forms and waited, stoking his ravenous appetite.

"Why resist?" Lucille cried. "We don't have to fight anymore. All debts will clear and we'll begin anew. This was, at first, supposed to be about *her*, since Master lost his damnable bride again. Sending his faithful dog, I encouraged the beast to search out whores, expecting to find his errant girl in good company. Pity there were so many to choose from."

"Demon, what on earth—?" Alexi broke free of the serpent around his neck and leaped to his feet, diving forward to clamp his hands around Lucille's delicate throat.

Unhurried, she placed a finger on his forehead and he was again on his knees, as if his blood were suddenly turned to lead. "None of that old news matters. Now that we're together and there's something more than an ancient, pitiful love affair at stake, now that you'll join me—"

"Never!" Alexi cried.

"Truly?" Lucy pouted softly, her snakes undulating. "You're such a lovely man. I'd hate to lose a mind like yours."

"I knew you were never one of us, demon witch," Alexi spat.

Lucy sighed. Insects poured suddenly from every crack in the walls of the sacred space. Arachnids, roaches, and beetles crawled indiscriminately over marble floor, petticoats and frock coats, arms and legs. The Guard struggled to breathe, to scream.

"Tell whomever you serve that we do the Grand Work, not that of the devil!" Alexi cried.

"Don't you remember *anything*?" Lucy bellowed in a harpy's shriek. "There is no 'devil.' There is no 'hell.' There is only Unrest. There is no down, only sideways; the transparent beside the opaque, and a thin wall to separate them. I'm so damn sick of fallacies!"

Josephine and Jane, unconscious, were held up solely by their serpentine tethers; the rest were fading.

"Whatever suffices for hell—wherever there be suffering and horror—go there, where you belong!" Alexi lashed out with his last bit of strength.

"And I was trying to be so kind," Lucy murmured as insects scurried up her skirts.

The entire room around them burst into flame, not the blue fire of their Work but an inferno that would consume them. Michael and Rebecca tried to clasp hands, to wake the others into prayer and power, but all effort was futile. Spirits bent on harassing the living kept entering their world, floating through the fire, jaws wide with insatiable hunger. The world would be overrun; there would never again be peace.

Lucy's snakes were poised to strike, mouths wide and ready, fangs dripping.

"What a pity your lover never did find you this life around!" She giggled. "Maybe it *was* that unfortunate Miss Parker, after all. I wish she were here; I'd have liked to show her this final scene, this end to your nauseating drama. I did think once I brought you to your knees, she'd come running. Ah, well, she's a coward, I suppose."

She took a moment to stare around at the foundering companions, shook her head and shrugged. "Mortal arbiters between life and death, foolish romantics—sorry, remnants of a charred, dead god and his friends—your ends have come! It's time for *you* to cross the river!"

"*NO.*"

A female voice boomed behind them, and an amazing, blinding white form burst into view at the threshold of the altar door. After her bare white feet stepped into the space, the portal snapped shut with a thunderclap.

Eyes blazing like stars, hair wild and raging, snowy arms outstretched and glistening with light as her thin gown whipped in the wind of her own power, Persephone Parker descended through fire and entered the circle where Lucy stood staring. The spiders scattered and the dog squealed, tucking incorporeal tails between its legs. The inferno vanished.

Lifting a hand, every muscle in her compact form taut with energy, Percy spoke, and her words cast a marvelous echo. "Demon, you'll not destroy my world!"

The serpents retracted and the Guard fell to the floor, free. Lucille scowled.

Alexi stared up in desperate wonder as his beloved stood before him, the answer to his prayers, radiant from within. Rousing, his friends stared on in awe.

Percy looked at the spirits madly careening about the space. She frowned, then admonished them, "Go home." Her upraised hand closed into a fist. The pin between worlds roared, stone on stone, shifting against the floor. Commanded, it lifted, shuddering and shedding debris as it began to twist back into place.

The spirits shrieked, their disquieting noises audible only to Percy, who winced yet remained stalwart. As if pulled backward by strings, the horde was drawn back into the black hole. Clawing and screaming, angry specters were sucked into the netherworld, unable to shake London loose. Once the errant spirits were reclaimed, the tunnel closed with a resounding *shhhh*; the fulcrum upon which the entire Balance hung slid back into place with a stony and metallic crunch. The earth shuddered and settled, once again sealed.

A strange sound erupted from Percy's throat, an ancient, beautiful command that surprised her as she sang it. Obeying, a new door swung into place directly behind Lucille Linden, opening on a dark and indeterminate realm where dim figures waited in vast shadows, rank upon rank.

"Oh," Elijah murmured sheepishly, "*that* door!"

Skeletal hands began clawing at the edges of this threshold, scrabbling and clicking upon one another as they sought purchase.

Lucy turned and pursed her lips. "How dare you? Who do you think you are?"

"*Who do you say that I am?*" Percy asked.

Michael stirred. "You are the one whose coming was foretold," he murmured. Percy turned to him, her face shining with love.

Lucy crossed her arms. "So it is you after all. A fine mess you've gotten us all into. What the hell do you expect to do now?" she demanded, her crown of snakes slithering and hissing.

Percy laughed, her inner light brightening like a fresh ray of sun. "To settle the score!" she cried confidently.

Percy's body arched. Her mouth fell open and a painful, feminine gasp flew from her pale lips as a shaft of blinding blue-white light impaled her. The column of incandescence, floor to ceiling, pierced Percy's body at the sternum and held her just above the floor, arced in agony and radiance; an illuminated butterfly transfixed by a pin.

Her stillness lasted but an instant. Throwing a vanquishing arm out, Percy cried a brief command in that ancient tongue she was speaking for the first time, her voice containing an echo older than itself.

Lucy pouted. "I was hoping it wouldn't come to—"

A wave of light and power exploded from Percy's form in a deafening gust of blue flame and angelic chords, sending Lucy sprawling back toward the portal, which pulled her like a magnet. The insects and arachnids Lucy had summoned were sucked in as well, carried like tiny leaves in a gale. The hellhound followed, its many heads howling in defeat and punishment.

At the threshold, the thing known as Miss Lucille Linden began to harden. Her skin grayed and froze into stone. Fissures appeared. Her face cracked and split. An arm broke away. Her body disintegrated, falling in a heap of hissing dust that was drawn ash by ash into the deep nothing. The skeletal fingers around the sides of the portal clutched at her particles, rattling, until each speck was contained by their scrabbling hands. Everything disappeared inside, and only the open portal remained.

Percy floated toward the door, where she glimpsed figures reaching for her. Light hummed within her. Eyes fixed on this entryway to a foreign world, in a body not entirely her own, she drifted nearer the portal's edge, unsure where she was meant to go.

"Alexi," she whispered, pleading, "take me away from this unbeliev-able scene. I want to be with you."

"Percy," he choked out, scrambling to his feet, tears streaming down his face. He whirled to face his companions. "Now, do you see?

"Persephone, you mustn't enter! None of our kind have ever been able to cross such a threshold and return with their wits! Please, come away—"

"Alexi, help me," she cried, reaching out a shaking hand as she drifted closer to the opening.

He rushed forward, knowing through and through that his future was *her*. The moment their fingers touched he was immediately drawn up, into the light. He cried out in shock. Floating in close proximity, Alexi and Percy put their arms around each other with a sigh from their souls. Their arms could not hold each other close enough.

The moment they sealed their embrace, the portal shut. A tether of light began winding like ivy from Percy's pounding heart into Alexi's.

"Darling . . ." He pressed his head against her bosom, directly into the shaft of brightest light. Percy's arms slid around his neck and she pressed her trembling lips to his head.

The others scrambled to their feet. Taking hands hastily, still cough-ing and shaking, the Guard began to murmur a gentle incantation of praise and thanksgiving. The wind that whipped around the room turned sweet, a musical caress.

Percy whimpered as fever gripped her once more, pouring forth in light. She wanted to close her eyes and sleep for years. The flashing visions were gone, and all the demons. But Percy's mortal weakness was giving way beneath the strain. More than mere humanity coursed through her veins, but in the end, her veins were human and had limits. She and Alexi began to sink again to the ground.

"Alexi, accept me," Percy begged, her plea a strange counterpoint to her aura of power. Their eyes were locked, dark and light.

"Accept you as *what*, my love—what are you?" he asked.

"A mortal girl who needs you . . . and, I pray, whom you need, too," she choked out.

"Percy—"

"I've no strength, Alexi. I've used it all. Whatever is inside me is tearing me apart," Percy gasped. "I was drawn here, wherever this is, for a purpose you surely know far better than I. Thus, I give what remains of me to you, Alexi, whom I love with my whole heart. Whatever you need of my soul, it is entirely yours and always has been— Ah!"

Pain claimed her body in a brief seizure. The shaft of light collapsed suddenly, as did Percy, crumpling into Alexi's arms, a limp heap of white limbs and fabric.

"Oh, God," Alexi cried as he collapsed, still holding her.

Suddenly there was commotion. Jane attempted to focus her rattled heart enough to manifest a healing aura. Michael closed his eyes and with recovering cheer, attempted to quiet the frenetic nerves of his fellows. Josephine placed her locket, which contained a tiny portrait of their magical icon, around Percy's moist neck.

Elijah crept forward. "We were looking for *her* door. How terribly confusing! Well, I suppose we've found her now, haven't we? I daresay I liked her door a good deal more than that first one . . ." He would, per-haps, have continued to ramble had Jane not rapped him soundly on the skull.

"Thank heavens she found us," Rebecca murmured, placing a hand upon Alexi's shoulder.

Alexi shrank away from her hand, cradling his beloved. His fore-head against Percy's, he murmured, gently rocking her, "Don't leave me. After all this, you mustn't leave me."

"Alexi," Rebecca said gently. When he looked up, she glimpsed a mad light in his eyes.

"If she dies there will be no one to save us; we'll have failed Prophecy twice! That Gorgon will have won in the end, the sepulcher will be thrown open entirely and our world will be overtaken!"

Rebecca retreated fearfully into the shadows.

Shaking Percy, Alexi began to cry out something in the beautiful tongue bequeathed only to the Guard, and the rest began to chant furi-ously with him, invoking ancient prayers of healing and rebirth, but Percy remained lifeless and unaffected in Alexi's arms.

"Forgive me, Persephone, I do love you! My love never faltered, though I failed you . . ." He madly clutched her to him.

The warm wind of their prayers turned a bitter cold, and the ground began to tremble. Dread filled the room like water into a sinking ship. The group began to scream as the stone that had revealed itself as a guardian pin in their chapel began to wrest again from its moorings, the stained-glass window above them cracking.

Alexi could only whisper to his lifeless beloved, cradling her, murmuring praise and desperate regrets into her ear. "This is the end after all," he said. "You tried, but my failure doomed us all."

"Save us, Percy," he whispered. "It's your fate. My love, please be strong for me against this terrible darkness . . ."

Suddenly he remembered what his grandmother had said to him and to Percy. If there was ever a darkness that needed his fire . . .

In a burst of furious desperation, Alexi closed his eyes, using the last of his energies to turn the whole chapel into a small sun of cerulean flame. It danced in sapphire waves over her alabaster body, entwining her limbs and licking at her cool skin as if kissing her toward consciousness.

Enormous wings of feather and flame shot from Alexi's back, unfurling with a surge of blinding illumination. The rest of the Guard stumbled back. His black robes whipped about him. The same wings had burst forth as an omen in the academy above; they were now a proclamation of power, demanding that his lover come home to his arms.

Helpless tears of wonder poured down the cheeks of the Guard as their leader's glorious phantom wings wrapped his beloved in a cocoon of resurrection.

"From the Flame of the Phoenix, a Feather fell and Muses followed," Rebecca murmured, huddled beyond the circle, her face ashen and her throat bruised purple.

"My God, the old tale indeed," Michael cried, rushing to her side, lifting her to her feet and grasping her hands.

Limbs the color of moonlight shuddered. A strong will and gentle heart stirred back toward the mortal life Percy wanted more than anything. Invincible love prodded her to consciousness. She'd fought too hard to allow this mere mortal body to abandon fate. She'd not permit the wheel of the world's fate to turn to darkness, but would rouse to the lover who woke her with fire. She became aware of the musical wind and dancing auroras around and within her.

As a new peal of thunder shook the Guard's bones and apocalyptic horsemen threatened to bear down upon them, from Percy's dry lips came a sound, a soft feminine rasp: *"Shhh . . ."* The rumbling cavalcade dulled to a whisper. The ceiling held, and their sanctuary remained intact. The stones of the chapel settled back into place, the pin sealing the sepulcher once more.

Alexi's fire and his wings faded until wisps of smoke, like trails of frankincense from a censer, were all that remained. Percy's eyes shot open to pierce him with a crystalline stare.

"My love," he choked.

She evaluated him for a long moment. "You have some explaining to do."

Dark eyes pouring with tears, Alexi laughed; an echoing sound of pure joy.

Percy placed a finger to his lips, a chuckle turning into a sickly cough. Her head swiveled as she listened to the silence. There was no more barking, pounding, or murmuring in her mind. Only relief. Taking in her surroundings as best she could, she glanced at the six pairs of eyes that hovered over her, comforting in a distantly familiar way.

"What *was* all that . . . ?" Elijah asked, dumbly breaking the silence. Rebecca elbowed him.

"I was hoping you could tell me," Percy murmured, her eyes focusing. "Oh, it's you, with the touch. And— Oh! Headmistress! Why are *you* here?" She stared up at Alexi in confusion, her body wracked by shivers. He held her closer, but she clawed at him. "Please don't send me away tomorrow . . ."

Cupping her face in his hands, Alexi kissed her passionately. She gave in to the press of his lips, then pulled back, blushing. "Alexi. Goodness, does that mean—?"

Bringing her blushing face up again, he was sure to make this covenant eye to eye. "I failed you, Percy, but never again. Everything will be made clear to you."

"You made that promise previously," she reminded him.

"Yes. I was lost, my duty unclear, though my heart was not. I beg you, forgive me."

"You will see me again, then?" she murmured, aching. "You'll not send me back to the convent?"

"*See* you? I'll not allow you out of my sight from this moment on! Say you'll forgive me."

"Forgive you?" Percy coughed again. "Well, I am rather angry."

"You should be angry—with all of us." Rebecca stepped forward. "Your rejection had everything to do with us and nothing to do with Alexi; he is not the one to blame," she admitted shakily, glancing humbly at her friend and colleague.

"Bless me, for I have sinned!" Elijah cried, prostrating himself at Percy's feet.

"Get up, silly man." She laughed weakly. "You don't need a blessing; we all need a good night's rest. However . . . what in the name of Holy God just happened?"

"You're a goddess," Elijah whimpered.

"No, I'm a mortal woman with a horrid headache and a confused identity."

"No mere mortal girl could open a gate to the other side!" Elijah assured her.

Percy shrugged and winced. "Well, it would seem that serpentine friend of yours could, too, and I'd like to think I'm nothing like her . . ."

"No, no, you're clearly the greater power here. What incredible proof! Your business with those doors was *very* well done, if I may say. You've certainly proved us the consummate fools!" he exclaimed, his foppish sleeves flapping as he gesticulated absurdly. Rebecca made a move to elbow him again, but then realized it was no use and only shook her head and sighed.

"Well, it would've been nice to know my power, whatever it is, long ago. It might have saved us all a lot of trouble." Percy smirked half-heartedly.

Josephine asked, "Do you remember coming to us, years ago? Giving us a prophecy?"

"Oh, why . . . it's you, too—the painter. *Bonjour.* Well, mademoiselle, I don't know whether I've had such dreams or memories, but I've never before been capable of magic or divine acts." She turned to Alexi, giving in to the warmth of his embrace. "And I don't remember ever seeing *you,* my dear." She bit her lip. "I assure you, I'd never forget if I'd seen you before."

He drew his covetous embrace tighter, and pressed a finger to the soft skin over her racing heart. "Herein lies the magic," he declared softly, and Percy's face lit with a rapturous smile, unwittingly proving his point. "Inside this incredible, radiant heart is all the divinity we need. 'Tis the whole of my salvation."

Rebecca bent carefully over them. "Rest is what is best for you now, Miss Parker. Let answers come later. You're in good hands with your professor."

Staring up at Rebecca, that word struck Percy with sudden horror. "You won't . . . expel me for this, will you, Headmistress?"

The group laughed, some a bit guiltily.

"No, dear heart—since you rescued the world, we may have to make you faculty."

Rebecca gave Alexi an anemic smile; Percy, even in her weakened state, could see many complex things cross between them. Alexi nodded slowly, as if all might eventually pass.

"Give us a moment, please," he instructed his friends. "Regroup at the Withersby estate, where Percy and I will soon join you. Don't worry, there will be time enough for repentance." Flashing each and every one a caustic smirk, he waved them away.

Without protest, they quietly filed out. As they turned toward the stairway, the door to Athens and their normal world materialized with the sound of a small rip. Only Jane lingered, shifting for a moment on her feet and wringing her hands.

"I am so sorry, Alexi," she murmured. "There was a time when I did not trust that vile woman. I ought to have fought for Miss Percy. I failed you."

Alexi shook his head. "Every one of us failed. But all has been made right."

Jane wiped her eyes, crossed herself, and was the last to leave the sanctuary. The portal closed behind her, leaving Percy and Alexi alone.

Attempting to sit upright, Percy found she couldn't and collapsed once more into Alexi's clutch. Never had she been so exhausted, yet her heart pounded in his embrace and her body thrilled. "I've no idea what has happened to me. Where are we?" she murmured.

"A special place reserved for us alone, within the academy walls and yet far from them, neither here nor there. If not for you, this delicate place would have been destroyed—along with much more."

Percy shuddered. "If I'm meant to be here now, why were you so cruel?"

"I fear it was all a horrid test. I was in agony—"

"Good." Percy's eyes flashed. "You deserved to suffer, you were awful . . ."

Alexi's expression grew pained. "The Guard feared I was too taken with you to allow Prophecy to be fulfilled. More than our desires were at stake—"

"You thought it might be that Gorgon," Percy accused.

"*They* thought it was, but your power, the truth of your destiny proved everything." Alexi gasped, pressing her to him.

Her expression suddenly grew grave. "Alexi, promise you'll not abandon me this night. I can't bear it. Promise you'll not toy with me."

Dark eyes burned with desire and adoration. "Percy, the sanctity of our love is tied to the balance of our world and"—he drew a shaking breath—"my very life depends on it." Loosening the cravat around his abused throat, he pulled at a thin metal chain. A small silver ring was revealed.

"Strange that we've both worn symbols of our fate against our skin," Percy murmured, staring as he slipped the ring from the chain and held it before her. Delicately crafted, a single silver feather was wrapped into a slender circle. It took her a moment to realize what his presenting a ring to her meant, but when she did, she nearly shrieked in delight.

"I waited for ages to give this to my destined love, growing older and bitter, losing all hope. Then you waltzed in, Persephone Parker. You lifted me from the ashes. I love you. Your nearness is the cure to my cold, lonely world." Alexi pressed the ring into her palm, his hands trembling helplessly. "Heal me by becoming my wife."

The joyous cry from Percy's lips could have made flowers bloom. Perhaps it did, somewhere in window boxes above.

"Oh, my dear professor!" She laughed. "I've been yours from the very first." Her pale eyes burned with the blue flame that bound them all, that fire triumphant over darkness at last. "My God, your *wife!*" she squealed as he slipped the ring upon her finger. "I could only dream someone would have me so. For it to be you—"

"It must be me," Alexi interrupted. "My goddess may live on in you, but even if she doesn't . . . I need *you,* Percy."

He fondled her arms and nuzzled her neck as tears of joy and relief from the night's unearthly terrors spilled down her cheeks. "You will stay at my side tonight," he commanded, arms locking around her waist. When Percy drew back, blushing, eyes widening with excited uncertainty, he added, "I'll respect your modesty until we are wed, sweet girl, but you and I have much to discuss."

She nodded, shifting in his hold, and he gave a hiss. "Michael may have to wed us immediately," he groaned, no longer able to deny the contours of her body, so evident beneath the thin fabric of her gown.

The betrothed were permitted such passion . . .

All inhibition cast aside, Alexi slid an arm around Percy's neck and his lips fell to devour her throat, her shoulders. She gasped as she felt his palm graze her breast. Her skin thrilled, flushed, and tingled in places she blushed to acknowledge.

Responding to her sounds of pleasure, Alexi caressed his beloved with increasing hunger, his hands roaming and questing. A symphonic movement of touch and response, the light in the sacred chamber grew brighter. The mosaic bird above them glowed as if the heat of their pressing bodies had ignited a divine hearth.

Percy wept softly, joyously. Her hands seized and fluttered over him alternately. "You delight in this body, then? It arouses, not repulses?" she whispered with thinly veiled fear, while every trace of his fingertips caused entirely new delights.

"Is this not proof?" he panted. "Pale as you are, your features and body are singularly, beautifully perfect—flawless sculpture come to life, warming to my touch. I warrant, dear girl, that respecting your modesty shall be a—I'd best take my hands from you else I be unable to help myself! Oh, forgive me! You shiver with cold. Have my cloak," he begged.

"I don't shiver from the cold, Alexi!" Percy laughed. "How I rejoice that my strange skin could receive such a loving treatment! I imagined you, imagined this . . . but the *truth* of it!"

He descended upon her again, ravaging her lips, his hands began to once more wander.

There was a tearing sound. At first Percy assumed it was some part of her clothing, but then the corner of her eye saw that the altar door again gaped. "Ah. The door," she stated.

Alexi turned and groaned. "Perhaps the heavens know, as I do, that I'm about to lose all hope of control and make these stones our marriage bed," he muttered, reluctantly drawing back. "Come, love, our friends await." He unclasped his cloak. "Though we should let them. Lord knows I've waited for you forever! Yet . . . you do deserve an actual bed."

He wrapped his cloak around her with great care, as she quaked with nervous anticipation of the prospect. A sudden dreadful thought clouded her gaze. "Alexi?"

"Yes?"

"Am I still being sought, sniffed out by that Cerberus we fled, holding a grudge from a mythic past? Are we to be hunted, you and I, by . . . do we dare say Hades himself? Pursued by other strange minions like that Gorgon revealed herself to be?"

"I cannot say, Percy. I know only of Phoenix and the Muses."

"I had a vision you—what was surely you—died in flames, in my arms," Percy wailed, recalling the horror.

"Whatever we were, or we are, we've returned to each other. We certainly have foes yet to face; there was too much talk of settling scores for it to be over. But for now, darling . . . ?"

"For now I, Persephone Parker, am content with you, Professor Alexi Rychman, here in Queen Victoria's England, enamored with anything you do and anywhere we go!"

Alexi swept her into his arms and she squealed in delight, clinging to him as he carried her through the portal and past the altar. The sacred chamber closed dutifully behind them. He bore her down the church aisle and out of the silent, empty chapel, then through Promethe Hall's front doors and into a now-peaceful evening.

At the threshold of the academy, Alexi placed her on her feet and they gasped in unison at the sight before them. Dozens of peaceful spirits had gathered, the sorts of spirits that the Guard allowed to roam without censure, souls who couldn't quite let go or were tethered by living loved ones who couldn't let go. Patiently floating on either side of the portico, an incorporeal receiving line had formed. These spirits' expressions were filled with warm anticipation, and Percy smiled at each in turn.

Turning to Alexi, she kissed him reverently, a shaft of moonlight falling on both of their faces like a spotlight. The spirits applauded—and many remarked that it was about damn time.

"No matter future foes, Alexi, look what a life we will lead," Percy cried. "Look at our entourage!" Clutching his hand, she could hear murmuring tongues in all manner of accents and languages, and all were offering their regards and congratulations. "Oh," she breathed, blushing, flattered.

Percy stared at each spirit with respect. Each ghostly countenance took on an expression of peace before its glowing form dimmed. Many specters waved or blew kisses before they departed to their final rest, passage granted in return for their felicitations. The air felt at peace, never so balanced.

Venturing to look at the sky, Percy was relieved to see it no longer torn. The heavens, and her heart, were now whole. The scales were level.

"What do all these spirits tell you, my translator and my love?" Alexi asked softly.

Percy turned to him. Pale and powerful, she was a beaming, heavenly sight on the academy steps, bathed in and reflecting moonlight.

"They tell us, love, that eternity awaits."

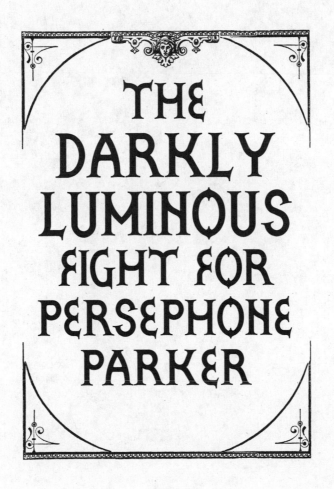

THE
DARKLY
LUMINOUS
FIGHT FOR
PERSEPHONE
PARKER

PROLOGUE

A most critical evening in the Year of Our Lord 1888

BEATRICE TIPTON KNEW A FEW THINGS AS SHE STOOD WITH HER EYES closed at the edge of the undiscovered country: She knew that her life had been sacrificed to what she hoped would indeed prove to be a greater good. She knew her corset was laced too tightly beneath the sensible layers of her dress—she should've thought to bring a traveling cloak, for the Whisper-world was colder than she'd expected. And she knew she had become a being like those she'd fought as the leader of the Guard. When she opened her eyes, she expected to see other ghosts; what she hadn't expected was to hear the scream of her husband.

They had gone into the Whisper-world side by side, hand in hand, to face the next grim adventure. They couldn't be separated so soon, not again . . . Beatrice's eyes shot open. She stood at one end of a long gray corridor of stone. The ceiling—if there was one—was masked by heavy charcoal clouds like trembling chandeliers of mist, roiling with unsettling shapes, hissing with soft sighs and eternal regrets. Water lapped at the toe of her sturdy boot; an impossibly black liquid as unwelcoming and seemingly alive as the mist.

At the other end of the dripping corridor was Ibrahim, wearing the fine tunic in which he had died. Once lush with the rich, honey-brown hues of his native Cairo, he was now fitted with the grayscale palette of a ghost, yet even in death Beatrice was struck by his handsome, distinguished figure. She glanced down to find that the gathered folds of her linen dress and its cloth-covered buttons, previously beige, were also gray; her skin had become sickly white. Death replaced bright colors with a wash of grim hues that darkened as the corridor drove toward the bosom of the Whisper-world.

"Bea," Ibrahim murmured. The water between their ghostly forms began to spread and deepen, transforming from a wide puddle into an ocean. An absurd fear gurgled in Beatrice's ghostly veins, a fear reflected on Ibrahim's face.

"Come back across, love," Beatrice said brightly, swallowing sudden terror, gesturing to her side of the water. "Our Lady said the doors are to be knit here from the periphery and I'll need your help. I cannot do without my Intuition—my second," she said with a rallying smile. "Come take my hand, it's only a bit of water."

Ibrahim had no time to agree or to move to join her. The Whisper-world was bent on separating, on isolating, and it would do its job. The water rose unnaturally and beat him back: horrific horse heads capping waves, fanged and red-eyed. Beatrice would close the distance, but the water whispered in soul-chilling misery. Rejecting what it wished to impart, she darted forward and flung out her hand. A trickle of blue flame, the only spot of color in this gray purgatory, leaped forth, then died quickly. She might once have been the leader of the Guard, but her power had long since gone to another.

She cursed herself. The Guard had been warned they might be attacked entering the Whisper-world and made captive to Darkness; she should have been prepared. Powerless, they would likely be imprisoned someplace beyond imagining. Prophecy's war was yet to be waged. Had the goddess left them entirely helpless?

"Ibra—" she started to cry out before a hand clamped over her mouth and an arm about her waist. She was pressed into the shadows, against a wall, where insidious moisture seeped through her lace collar and past her pinned-up locks to kiss her neck. A strong man held her fast, and while Beatrice prided herself on being a spirited fighter, she struggled against him in vain.

Ibrahim was driven into darkening depths. As frightened as he seemed, perhaps he intended to keep her safe by not alerting the agents of Darkness to her presence, for he did not call her name again.

The cresting waves of horses' heads gnashed around him, nipping bits of his death-gray flesh. He ducked beneath his arms and blurted out a familiar stanza, in Arabic: " 'To us a different language has been given, and a place besides heaven and hell. Those whose hearts are free have a different soul, a pure jewel excavated from a different mine.'" Oft used by him, her Guard's Intuition, the ancient Sufi words ever confounded misery's minions. The monstrous forms hesitated.

"I'll see you again, my love," Ibrahim called. "I choose to trust in you, Our Lady, and Prophecy!" He turned and fled farther into the labyrinth, leading the terrors on a desperate chase.

Beatrice sobbed against the palm of her unseen captor, her lover's words ringing in her ears. How odd for Ibrahim to have found faith in this terrible transition. Or perhaps he said those words—once her Guard's favorite verse—only for her, as a reminder to keep faith in the tasks to come.

"Let him go, leader, we cannot help him here alone," her captor said. His voice was gruff and heavily accented. Beatrice dimly recognized it as old Irish or Scots. Gaelic. "Help London's Guard and they can help him. You know what to do."

The man kept her pinned in his grasp but moved away from the wall and immediately she could breathe more easily. Whisper-world moisture, it would seem, was a potent poison. Beatrice stared into the gray eyes of a rugged spirit once as handsome as a warrior god, fabric draped over his firm, bare chest, metal bands and leather thongs encircling his arms. His hair was a gray mane down his back. He took his hand from her mouth.

"Who are you and what do you know about the Guard?" Beatrice murmured.

The man held up a pendant. It was a plain locket that sparked a familiar blue at the edges. His palm glowed with warm, pale light before fading, an echo of his power lingering in faint traces.

Beatrice gritted her teeth. "So you were a Healer. One of us. What does that mean to me now? I gave up the Grand Work years ago—to the very London set you mention. Can't you just leave me to aid my comrade?" She made to follow Ibrahim.

The man held her fast. "Hardly. My name is Aodhan, and Our Lady said to watch for you, Beatrice Tipton. Your work is far from done."

Beatrice scowled. "Yes, the doors and all that. Don't you think I knew she had come of age, don't you think, even without powers, we sensed it was time? Ibrahim can help—"

"He'll be corralled with the others. For now, you must go and make sure of Prophecy. Otherwise none of us will ever be free. Take this. Our Lady saved it for you. It holds power you'll need."

The man clasped the plain locket around her neck. The hazy blue nimbus about it identified its contents: ash of the Phoenix, held aside from his burial chamber. A sparkling, dancing tendril of fire snaked out from the pendant and kissed her throat. She opened her palm. An orb of cerulean flame appeared, steady, hers again to command. It was a comfort.

Beatrice furrowed her brow and looked again at Aodhan. "How is it you weren't imprisoned like the others?"

"Impossible love opens doors and frees souls," Aodhan murmured, and gestured behind him.

She turned and her heart seized at the sight of an open portal to England. Beatrice could recognize her native country anywhere, the patchwork sounds of London's cluttered brick lanes, the gritty smell of industry hanging thick in the gray air. She loved and hated it all at once, but it was colorful, scented, and alive, and she'd had no idea how much she could yearn for it in death.

"I've long been tied to the current Guard and their world," Aodhan continued. "By love and duty. And so must you be tied to their world, and to Our Lady, until the vendetta ends."

Beatrice held up a hand. She hated being reminded of duty. "I know I've no choice in this, so I'll not fight you. I'll fight for Ibrahim, and for the hope that Our Lady of Perpetual Trouble has found her destined love." She took a step toward London, then turned back, her hard face softening. "But how is she? Our Lady? Is she with the good professor, well and happy, as they both should be?"

Aodhan's chiseled face darkened. "You've not seen her?"

"Foundations in place, our Guard returned to Cairo, retired until in death our services would be once more called upon. Our Lady didn't want us to interfere once the course was set; we were to leave them to it. Isn't the girl at the academy?"

"I don't know. I don't think the Guard has found her. All I see is a darkening sky, and if they fail"—he gestured behind him, toward the terrible labyrinth of darkness—"misery will bleed with no suture to stop it. The pins loosened, the veil thin . . . we're about to split open. Not just

London, but everywhere. And you know we can't part the veil until *we're* ready, when the doors belong to Light and—"

Beatrice sighed. "Indeed. It seems Our Lady left me all the responsibility. Keep an eye on Ibrahim, will you?" She choked, her emotions getting the better of her. "We fought too hard for too long to be separated again."

Aodhan interjected with sincere empathy, "The Grand Work has never been easy for anyone."

Beatrice nodded a curt good-bye and turned toward England. She closed her eyes and the shadows receded. The incessant murmurings of misery shifted into a cacophony of clattering city sounds; a whiff of roasted chestnuts from a vendor down a bustling lane was followed by a passing factory-borne mist that tasted slightly sulfuric. The air was warmer. Late fall was turning cold in London, but anything felt warmer than the world of the dead. Opening her eyes, she saw the formidable red sandstone edifice that was her destination.

She looked down and frowned. Her feet floated above the cobblestones. Mundane particulars she'd taken for granted: the firm, solid press and the sound of her boots against stone. Still grayscale, she was also, now, transparent—invisible to most.

Floating up the sandstone stairs, Beatrice wafted through the hefty front door of Athens Academy. She stared back at the door she'd just floated through and then at the interior of the stately, Romanesque building. "Hello, old friend. It seems we've got work to do."

CHAPTER
ONE

"He's nearing," Headmistress Rebecca Thompson said quietly, carefully setting down her teacup lest her trembling hands overturn it and the saucer. A flurry of action began around her.

The lights were trimmed to their highest, to banish the evening's terrors. The best guest room, readied for their important charge, was again inspected. Clean clothing and fresh toiletries were set in place. A clatter from the kitchen below signaled that the maid rushed to prepare a fresh pot of tea.

Rebecca remained still and stiff in a high-backed chair, her trembling hand stilled on the knee of a gray wool dress that was quite the worse for wear. Absently she reached up to touch the bruise around her throat where a snake from the head of a Gorgon had nearly choked her to death. In the sumptuous drawing room of the grand Withersby estate, where Lord Elijah held more sway than a second son of the marquess should, such a thing as a Gorgon seemed impossible. But those called the Guard knew better.

"He's here," announced the beauteous Josephine Belledoux, anxiety heightening her French accent. Her typically immaculate coiffure was anything but—a barometer of the night's difficulties. Olive skin flushed, dark eyes wide, she threw open the door. Lifting her torn, doubled skirts, she ran outside, leaving the entrance open in welcome behind her.

Beneath the sheltering stone arches of the portico, a striking figure descended from a carriage and gave Josephine a brief nod of greeting. He placed a finger to his lips. "Keep everyone quiet." Professor Alexi Rychman's rich, low murmur carried like thunder, preceding the storm of his presence. "She's fast asleep, and I dare not wake her."

The professor's usual ensemble was smeared with ash. His finely tailored black frock coat and vest showed stress at the seams; one cuff of his white shirtsleeves was in tatters, his crimson cravat open and lopsided around his neck, the purpling bruise of the Gorgon's embrace gruesomely offsetting his sharply elegant features. But his dark eyes were focused. He'd smoothed his hair into some semblance of order. His pale face, while weary, was relieved.

He reached carefully into the cab, lifting an unconscious woman into his arms. Her petite body wrapped tightly in the folds of his cloak, it was as if Alexi Rychman held the moon swaddled in black, and the warm affection with which he stared at the girl made Josephine gape before she recovered herself. "We're overeager and filled with questions, desperate to know Miss Parker is well . . . and desperate for your forgiveness."

Alexi pursed his lips. "What, must I bless you all with oil and take you into a confessional?"

"Perhaps," Josephine murmured, preceding him up the walk. "I assume, since you're not driven to utter distraction, that she's resting?" He nodded. "And you've . . . made up?"

"As much as a few moments allowed."

"I can only imagine how weary she must be."

"God, yes—think of it," Alexi muttered in awe. "The poor girl woke from fever to find the man who shunned her half strangled while the bowels of hell poured out, then rescued us with entirely foreign powers. A possibly trying evening for a heretofore meek young lady."

"Bless her sweet, brave young heart," Josephine said as Alexi edged through the open door, careful not to knock his burden against the wood. "Speaking of which . . . how old is she, Alexi?"

"Nineteen," he replied. "Older than the other students at Athens by far," he added, trying to cast in a favorable light the fact that he had been her teacher.

"Nineteen," Josephine murmured, peering at the crease on Alexi's oft-furrowed brow and the lines near his eyes that placed him at nearly twice that number. "Won't you just be the envy of all?"

A smirk pulled the corner of his chiseled lips even as he hesitated in the foyer, wishing to bypass ceremony, yet knowing that his colleagues waited beyond the interior door.

"I'll hold them back," Josephine promised. "The best guest room has been made up; you may take her there directly. One moment."

She opened the door only far enough to slip into the main hall; even so, Alexi heard the Guard murmuring inquiries about Miss Parker's health and his own state of mind. In a moment Josephine returned, saying that she had convinced them to wait in the withdrawing room. Passing her without another word, Alexi glanced at the pallid face of their prophecy fulfilled, the seventh member of their exclusive Guard and the long-missing piece of his lonely heart.

With only the creak of his boots on the stairs, the slow breathing of his beloved, and the pounding of his own heart to accompany him, Alexi allowed his mind to wander to the sensual delights that would await him in the coming days.

A vague uncertainty damped his desire. What incredible power his dear Percy had shown, throwing herself into harm's way to save him and his fellows. But had she, inadvertently, escalated the dangers of the Whisper-world? He knew that she didn't understand the magic that had burst from within her and hoped that this evening didn't presage a further call to arms. There was much of vagary about his calling; it frustrated him to be so oft cast into the gray areas of divine mystery.

The guest room door was open, the lamps trimmed low, giving the gilt bedposts, fine tapestries, and paneled mahogany wood a resonant warmth. The bed was turned down, and Alexi slid Percy, cloak and all, under the covers. She stirred only slightly: a small pout when released. Alexi nearly climbed in beside her to indulge her with a continuing embrace . . . But Percy remained in sleep's hold and Alexi reminded himself he was a gentleman.

Tucking the covers to her bosom, he stepped back. A thousand sentiments were on his lips but he could only stare at her body, noting the minute difference between the color of her skin and the crisp white linens beneath her; noting anew the graceful lines of her face. How could she not think herself beautiful?

He sensed a presence and turned to see Vicar Michael Carroll just beyond the threshold. Bushy haired and ruddy cheeked, an affable man of the cloth, Michael had bright eyes and a smile Merlin would have coveted for its power; his capability for joy was the Guard's most potent balm throughout the years. But even Michael had seen unprecedented strain these past days, noticeable in the deepening circles beneath his eyes.

Alexi walked to the door and closed it quietly behind him, curtly addressing the vicar. "Mr. Carroll?"

"I know." Michael held up his hands in acquiescence. "I've been told to leave you alone, but I know you'll never sleep at this rate, and you need to rest. Your heart's been shut from my powers since our youth. Until now." He laid a gentle hand on Alexi's shoulder, a touch the professor would have shirked from any other. "You've broken open, my good man. I feel your anxiety and confusion, fear that she'll wake and want nothing to do with this destiny. She might even question whether she loves you."

Alexi opened his mouth to protest and found he couldn't.

"Love makes a man mad. So allow me to perform a little magic. It's the least I can do." Michael's eyes sparkled strangely.

Alexi stared at his friend, whose gift was knowing hearts, and a looming, burning question sprang to his lips. "What *is* she?"

Michael blinked. "Does it matter? She's Prophecy."

"But if she truly is her namesake, *Persephone*, then is she mortal at all? Will the Whisper-world keep coming to steal her away?" Tension turned Alexi's mouth into a grimace. "If she's a goddess, is she doomed to watch me age and die while she lives on—?"

"Alexi, whatever powers she may possess, I'm convinced Percy Parker is mortal, albeit a great channel for great deeds. Need I remind you she nearly died in your arms? If there's something of a goddess in her, divinity was forsaken to live a mortal life. It wouldn't be the first time in the history of mankind that—"

"Yes, thank you, Vicar, the comparison's not lost on me," Alexi muttered. His friend was staring at him with knowing amusement. Alexi found himself, to his chagrin, confessing. "I'm . . . addled. I feel quite odd."

"Welcome to *emotions*, Professor." Michael grinned.

"I couldn't . . . Before, I—"

"If you'll permit me?" Michael held his hand up over Alexi's heart, inhaled, exhaled, and bestowed his gift. Alexi felt his tension ease. His careening thoughts calmed to love's clarion focus: his desire to be by Percy's side, to be the strength that she needed, to let her passionate nature delight him and ease his weary soul. Indeed, nothing else mattered. For now.

"Thank you," Alexi said, furrowing his brow and puzzling over the complication that was Man.

"My pleasure."

"Now, for the sake of safety, I shall spend the night in this room. But if I hear one word of gossip against Miss Parker's honor—"

"You'll not be suspect, have no fear." Michael moved to the stairs. He stopped, a wistful smile on his lips. "One last thing, Professor. She *adores* you. Don't question that. The girl couldn't close her heart to me if she tried. It's too big, too radiant. A time may come for future worry, but for now, do enjoy true love. Not all of us can." A melancholy look crossed his face before he descended.

Alexi turned back to open the door. His eyes sought Percy's peaceful face, framed by its halo of shimmering spider-silk hair. She was as pale as the ghosts they both could see, yet more alive than anyone he'd known. And she made *him* feel alive. She was his. Not a god's, not destiny's, not the Guard's, not England's but *his*. He'd fight to death and beyond to keep it that way.

CHAPTER
TWO

The Whisper-world was in a state of unprecedented chaos. Not that Darkness didn't like a certain amount; he thrived in it, enjoyed creating it. He fancied chaos of his own making, carefully orchestrated and meticulously controlled, with crafted conflicts that built to climaxes, a well-made play that he, as director, could change at will. There was an art to his chaos. But this was not his, and it was not art.

The battle cries of his sworn enemies echoed down the endless halls; they had escaped their prison tower. Though it was surely *her* fault, he would round them all up again.

He glided through the careening forms of spirits too agitated to obey him or offer appropriate deference. His shadow reached out as he passed, black phantom limbs that shoved spirits out of his way while his body remained gracefully still and erect. Some he tossed toward the river to drown; others, he smashed against stone. His jaw ground with pleasure as he heard each satisfying crunch of bone and the gorgeous keening that was the last of a soul.

He glided toward a rectangular slate door with molten liquid bubbling around its edges. The haste and force with which the portal had been closed was evidenced by a few finger bones caught in the corners. Ash was everywhere, even filling what served as Darkness's nostrils as he touched the door that was still rumbling with residual tremors.

The Groundskeeper appeared, cursing the mess everyone was making of his riverbank, his gravestone gardens, his fountains of mist, and trellises of bones. At the mouth of the corridor, he paused, staring into the inscrutable shadow that rose tall and smothering: the lord of the land. The Groundskeeper bowed and scraped, his long coat brushing the wet ground.

"Ah, hello, Master," he sputtered. "The crash sent me runnin'.

Something dreadful's gone . . ." He bent to examine a heap of ash that hissed with vanquished heat. His eyes widened as he made out, just barely, the shape of a human figure in the grayness.

He cried out, voice cracking, and raked hands through his shock of calico hair. "Oh, no! My sweetie-snaky-lassie, my Gorgon-girl. What's this? What've you gone and done?" His voice shifted accents as he spoke.

Darkness stepped back, repulsed. This pile of ash was what remained of the Gorgon that had been his spy, his emissary, and best soldier. And where was the *dog*? If the dog were in pieces, this place had not yet seen his anger.

"I'll put you together again, my lovely," the Groundskeeper crowed. "You'll be as good as new, just let me just bottle you up! Indeed, Master?"

"Indeed," Darkness replied. "But you'll have to commence another Undoing. The seals must be opened. Pour the restless onto the earth until they drag her back!"

"But, Master." The Groundskeeper trembled. "The pins between worlds are sealed fast again." He held up fingers blackened with blood.

"Undo. Them. Again," Darkness growled. "As often as it takes."

"But, Master, my lovely needs me! The longer she's in pieces, the less of her I can—"

Darkness's shadow arms pounced, twisting the Groundskeeper's wrist and binding with his royal crimson cloak the creature congealed from a hundred spirits who'd once served human masters. Clutching his servant's bloody, sore hands with one preternatural grip, he held a razor-like nail to the Groundskeeper's throat with the other. The captive squealed like an animal as the nail cut deep, and the sound was caught up in the vast stone chambers and amplified, a warning that the master was not in a mood to be trifled with.

"Why do you punish those loyal to you?" the Groundskeeper gasped, pleading.

"Because I can't get my hands on who dearly deserves it," Darkness growled. He threw his servant to the floor and kicked his pathetic form for good measure. "Put my best soldier back together, then: Undo. The. Seals!"

"Yes, Master, of course," the Groundskeeper sniveled, crawling off to procure supplies. As he did, he began an awkward singsong rhyme: "Lucy-Ducy wore a nice dress, Lucy-Ducy made a great mess . . ."

Darkness stared at the sealed door. Anger stung his narrowed eyes and scarlet fire leaped from them. A sharp female voice scolded, "It won't do to light up the whole Whisper-world in one of your tantrums."

Growling, Darkness whirled to face a tall woman wearing the gray-scale of death. Her clothes were the sort of layered, stiff Western fashion that he knew his assistant had taken upon her mission to England.

"Who. Are. You?" he demanded, keeping himself cloaked in shadow so only the red light of his eyes could be seen. The woman set her jaw, and her eyes, perhaps once a magnificent blue, flashed with pride. If she was terrified, she did not look it, but he caught a whiff of fear off her freshly deceased flesh. The scent was tantalizing, delicious. He wanted more.

"My name is Beatrice Tipton, and I led the Guard until the post was ably taken up by my successor. It is my duty to tell you, sir, that all this nonsense between you and my lady *will* come to its inevitable, blessed end, and you will free the noble souls you've taken hostage—"

Darkness roared and the ghost winced. "You and that damned Guard! I will wage war for her, you know."

"Indeed," the woman breathed, trying to sound confident, but again he caught the intoxicating perfume of her fear. The ghost continued, narrowing her eyes: "Pity you can't cross over to the living realm to find her yourself. Perhaps a higher power indeed gave us that advantage. The doors have been blown wide, and your enemy aches for a fight," she warned, nodding to the corridor behind them.

A sudden racket prevented Darkness from questioning her further; a host of separate battle cries in every tongue and custom coalesced into a thunderous shout. He turned to behold a mob of gray spirit bodies in all manner of dress, a tumbling, angry sea of Guard. They invoked their sacred rites against him as they'd done for eons, disparate cultures made one with a binding language. Music rose in the air. There was enough magic left in them yet to try a fight. But the fact remained that they were trapped in *his* territory.

Darkness chuckled. He raised a fist. Water and shadows leaped to life in the form of dread horses, dark with gnashing teeth. The beasts charged, stampeding, eager for scraps of dead flesh. The Guards' battle song was drowned by thunderous hooves. Their advance halted, the spirits were driven mercilessly back. Squeezing his fists, Darkness pressed forward the suffocating shadows until voices cried out in agony.

A tapping drew his attention back to the nearby spirit. Desperately chanting something foreign, she rapped upon the heart of the seal between mortal and spirit world. A circle of blue fire flashed against the stone. Looking over her shoulder with enough smug triumph to infuriate him, she stepped nearly through to the other side. With only her head remaining, she said curtly, "If you'll excuse me, I've work to do. Have a lovely time cleaning up your mess." Then she vanished, along with the fire she'd created.

Darkness whipped shadows forward in a vicious blow, but these fell uselessly against the stone. Damn them! Damn *her*. War, indeed. He'd make it all come undone—every last mortal mind—and bring his rebellious prize home screaming. He'd break her divine body to his eternal will for *every* season.

BEATRICE TIPTON FORCED HER ESSENCE BACK INTO THE COLONNADED, circular room where everything had very nearly gone wrong just hours prior, and murmured thanks to the phoenix fire for facilitating such coming and going. Free of the oppressive terror that was Darkness, grateful he could not follow, she prayed that Ibrahim would be spared pain if he were again taken hostage. Darkness would not punish him further, as they'd not been seen together, and for that she was grateful. Aodhan had been more help to her than she'd known. To have a friend in the daunting tasks ahead was a comfort she dared not take for granted.

She beheld the sacred space and scowled. "Good God, all of you made a right mess of it in here, didn't you?" There were cracks in the walls and ash in the stones; the stained-glass ceiling of the burning-heart bird showed hairline fissures in its beautiful panes.

At the center of the floor, Beatrice bent over the great feather in the stone, blowing dust and grit aside. She touched her locket and opened her opposite hand. Blue fire leaped from her fingertips. Hurling it at the feather's tip, she saw a wisp of blue smoke curl up from a keyhole.

"The groundwork is laid. The first key ready to reveal its mysteries. Now, to knit the worlds. Ibrahim, don't worry. We'll free you as soon as we've the advantage." Then she flew from the floor, heaving a sigh. Blue fire coursed over her body, invigorating her, inside and out. "I hadn't thought it would feel so refreshing to be at Work again! Come now, my lady. To war!"

CHAPTER
THREE

Miss Persephone Parker lay deep in the honeyed thick of dreams, shifting between terrible vision and wonderful memory.

She was young and powerful, standing in an endless field of perfumed flowers. The sky was what she imagined of heaven. A beautiful black-haired man held her tightly in his arms and his great wings encircled their embrace, grazing her satin skin, which ached for his touch. Phoenix was more than man or angel; he was a god, a being of sense and light, reason and truth. He was the perfect complement to her life force of beauty and kindness, sensibility and love. Their mutual fellowship of light was blinding. Never had two beings been so suited. They loved each other not because it was destined but because it was right and mutually joyous. Their respective divine forces fit together as a puzzle, interlocked and stronger for it.

But jealousy set the god aflame—literally. Darkness set Phoenix on fire, and her lover died before her heavenly eyes. Screams shook the earth. Tears enough to drown the world flooded the ground. His great form crumbled to dust and the vendetta was born.

She turned to the cave from whence came murder. Red eyes burned from the shadows. Vengeance flared in her heretofore peaceful breast, fueling a hallowed blue fire forged from the remnants of her one true love—and somehow the girl who was now Miss Parker knew that what she viewed here was a score she would unfortunately have to settle herself.

The scene shifted from nightmare to memory. Here she recognized herself and remembered that friends called her Percy. A distinguished professor held her in his arms. Her body was corseted, swathed in satin, wreathed in heather. He wore a fine frock coat and waltzed with her by moonlight. His black hair lustrous in shafts of silver light, his dark eyes bright and compelling, this was her one true love. Acutely aware of the press of his hand and the curve of his lips, here was her destiny, the man who understood her, who unlocked her eerie visions and made everything strange about her beautiful.

The handsome, stoic face of Professor Alexi Rychman vanished, replaced by flashing, angry, red eyes and the all-too-familiar hissing of snakes. She launched herself toward consciousness before those eyes could find her.

Percy awoke in a large, unfamiliar room, upright in a strange bed with her thin nightgown askew upon her shoulders. She studied herself, seeing a black cloak cast back against the sheets and tiny flecks of ash lodged in the cuffs of her meager sleeves. She squinted, looking beyond the bed, her pale, sensitive eyes straining against bright light.

French doors covered by lace curtains led onto a terrace. Beyond, a few trees and chimneys were visible in the dense morning fog. The room was full of rich furnishings, fresh flowers, and finery. Percy had never set foot in a room so regal.

A tall clock near the bed chimed eight in echoing tones. Works of gilt-framed art on the walls seemed illuminated by their own paint and Percy recognized the distinct style of Miss Josephine Belledoux, a friend of her dear prof— Her heart seized. Where was he?

"Alexi!" Percy gasped.

"Percy," came the rich, beloved voice from close at hand and with a shock, Percy realized she was not alone in the bed. Her veins flooded with incapacitating heat.

With a rustle, the thick velvet duvet was tossed aside and Alexi groggily sat up beside her. His striking figure, as ever clad in black and gray, was in a state of uncommon disarray. A delectable sound escaped him as he reached for her hand and brought it to his lips, kissing the ring that had so recently betrothed her to him. It wasn't a dream. True, they'd just survived a nightmare, but she'd emerged from the other side victorious—and *his*.

The line of his sternum, the graceful curve of his collarbone, was a fresh sight glimpsed through the open neck of his clothing. This heretofore hidden treasure heightened Percy's feverish temperature. The hem of his signature scarlet cravat clung limply to his collar like a stream of stage blood. The purpling bruise around his neck reminded her of the night's horrific events. She'd never seen him so disheveled, and she'd never allowed herself such an intense flood of emotion at the sight of him.

Mere months ago, she could never have imagined this strange fairy tale: to have gone from an awkward student, trembling in this man's presence, to waking beside him as his intended. She found her awkwardness now layered with smoldering heat, making her feel all the more constrained and breathless; delicious torture.

"Do forgive the bold act of lying next to you, Percy," Alexi murmured. "But after last night I was too exhausted to keep watch and, dare I say, too covetous to be out of reach."

"If I'd awoken alone, Alexi, I'd have screamed for you something terrible." She glanced about the room. "Where are we?"

"The grand estate of Elijah Jay, Lord Withersby."

"Ah. Are the others here? Your . . . *Guard*?"

"Yes."

"Oh, goodness." Percy felt her face flush a mottled pink. "They don't suppose you and I have . . . ?"

"No, dear." Alexi could not hold back a smirk. "They do not imagine your modesty in jeopardy, if that's what concerns you."

"Ah. I . . . well, I wasn't sure if I ought to be embarrassed before your friends." She gave a nervous laugh.

"No, but . . . As the pleasures of holding you close are such a recent revelation, might your fiancé indulge his newfound heaven again?" What started as a polite request finished more as a demand.

Percy bit her lip, hard. "Please," she breathed, and collapsed against him clumsily. He wrapped his arms around her, breathing slowly as she relished his nearness. She dared to press her pale lips to the bared portion of his breast.

He shuddered in response, murmuring, "My love. As much as I'd like to forget recent terrible events, I must say it is the Guard who are embarrassed for having so courted danger. I did insist that Prophecy meant *you*. Please believe me. But they wanted none of it; instead, that horrid woman—"

Percy eased back to look up at him, stilling his mouth with her fingertips. "It's done, Alexi. While I barely survived the heartbreak, and *wouldn't* if it were to ever happen again"—Alexi started to make protest, but Percy continued—"we must move forward, you and I, and your Guard. Together." She grimaced and added, "You may apologize, however, for having been very cruel."

"I'm so sorry," he declared, cupping her white cheeks in his hands and staring unflinchingly into her eyes.

She was not inclined to doubt his sincerity. "Apology accepted," she murmured.

He drew her in, greedy. Her body thrilled everywhere at his touch, trembling deliciously in the throes of this foreign intimacy after so many years of thorough loneliness, an odd orphan hardly touched. Newfound heaven, indeed. But then her eyes clouded suddenly in the familiar onset of a vision: A large, black, open door. A long stone corridor shimmered in the dim beyond. Beckoning. Demanding. The sound of a river . . .

The vision blinked away. "Damn," Percy muttered, rousing from it. More doors.

Alexi brought her eyes up to meet his. "You curse at my embrace?"

Percy shook her head, laughing nervously. "No, a vision. I assure you, I'll never tire of your embrace."

"A vision? I was hoping you'd be done with those. Unless it was a vision of us entwined . . . ? For I assure you, that's in your future," he purred, dragging a finger down her cheek and tracing the hollow of her throat.

"Alas," she sighed after a momentary shiver of anticipation. "It was a door."

Alexi pursed his lips. "I was hoping you'd be done with those, too."

A dreadful, high-pitched shriek that only Percy could hear came through a painting as a ghost dressed in seventeenth-century foppery swept into the room and lurched, as if hoping to fright them. Alexi, who shared Percy's ability to see the spirit, evaluated her wincing reaction and grimaced.

"Shriekers," he muttered. "My least favorite spirits. Fitting, that a Withersby antecedent should be a noisemaker."

"Shh," Percy commanded. The spirit hung its head and, defeated, vanished through the closed terrace doors just as the bedroom door was flung wide and a boisterous French accent filled the room.

"Lord Withersby! You let them be!" Josephine stopped up short, realizing the spirit she chased was nowhere to be seen. Sheepishly, she turned to the couple who had tastefully disentangled themselves. "Forgive my intrusion, *mes amis*, I thought great uncle Withersby might have been after you. He likes to remove covers and do other unmentionable things, and I thought that might be a bit, well . . . Ah. Yes. Indeed. Hrm. Well, I'd better let you both dress for breakfast. All are assembled. Miss Parker, you'll find a change of clothes in the wardrobe. Alexi, you're far too tall for Elijah's clothes, so—"

"I'll continue to look like hell, Josie, thank you. We'll be down in a moment."

The woman nodded and disappeared.

"She seems awfully nervous," Percy noted, feeling her own unease.

"Our lives remain in your debt. If you hadn't come to the chapel, we would have died." Alexi looked away. "I'd have been the downfall of mortal civilization. Me, a *leader*," he spat.

Percy reached out and touched his cheek. "Whatever power lay dormant within me might never have woken without such cataclysm to bring it forth. And I'd have died if you hadn't been able to rouse me. Your light met mine and woke me from death's kiss. My God, though, Alexi . . . It was terrible in the making—all of it. It was as if something were eating me alive from the inside out."

"Your waking powers, surely, pressing against the limits of your mortality. Is that what drove you into the storm?" he asked.

"I tried to warn you," she murmured. "But I was burning up, maddened by whispers and fever, my body so weak."

Alexi glanced at her. "It wasn't just my . . . rejection that incapacitated you?"

Percy looked at him and raised an eyebrow. "Are you gauging the extent of your guilt or of my womanly weakness?"

Alexi appeared surprised by her directness. "Perhaps both."

Percy set her jaw. "While you devastated me, Alexi, my condition was compounded by having vomited pomegranate seeds that I never ingested."

Alexi's eyes widened. "Oh, my."

"Perhaps your guilt and my weakness are each given a bit of credit in the face of such inexplicable supernatural phenomena."

"Indeed," he murmured. "You've accepted my apology. But do you forgive me?"

A mere month ago, she might have blurted a silly schoolgirl's words. But harrowing circumstances had tempered Percy. He had been quite terrible while their destiny was misunderstood. But she stared at him now, at the love in his eyes, at the way his striking face was drawn with anxiety. She cherished the firm way he held her and knew that he was unequivocally hers and helplessly under her spell—which was all she needed to know, for she'd long ago been under his.

"Yes," she murmured. He released a kept breath and his body eased. "But I remain overwhelmed!" she continued. "I wake from fever only to find an entire other world accessible via the chapel of Athens Academy—a world from which such powers and terrors might come to hold court." She offered him a dazed smile. "I've much to learn."

"I've much to teach," Alexi murmured, his tone indicating not the Grand Work but instead something far more intimate. He seized her in an eager, questing kiss. Gasping with pleasure, she drew back. His eyes widened as her thin gown gaped open. The phoenix pendant around her neck dangled in the air between them, but the item of recent keen prophetic interest was overshadowed by bare skin.

His gaze might have set the room on fire—literally—had Percy not righted herself, her entire body flushing with rosy-patched color. "P-perhaps I'd best dress myself."

"Yes, yes." He turned away, clenching his fists in the bedclothes as she rose and moved to the side of the room. "But I've gone a lifetime waiting. I shan't wait much longer."

Percy turned to him, her hand on an ornate oriental dressing screen. She smiled, cultivating a never-before-used quality, the feminine wile. "I should hope it won't be long, *Professor,* else our tutorials in your office shall take an entirely distinct turn." His subsequent growl informed her he could well imagine it.

She dressed herself as Alexi attempted to straighten his appearance. The best he could do was retie his cravat, adjust his shirtsleeves, and smooth his waistcoat and hair. She glanced over the top of the dressing screen to find him, to her delight, straining to catch a glimpse of her, his attempt to be a gentleman failing.

Emerging in a layered, lace-trimmed muslin dress of her favorite light blue, she felt regal but unfinished. "Would you clasp the buttons up my back? I'm not used to elegant trappings that require aid," she admitted, breathless as he approached with smoldering eyes. Life with Alexi might make the mottled blush upon her cheeks a veritable tattoo.

He clasped each pearl button slowly. As his fingers fumbled over the last, at the nape of her neck, his hands trespassed up into her snowy hair. He pulled her against him and mused, "I wonder if Science is disappointed in me. Reason and moderation fly when my hand encounters you." Clearing his throat, he continued, affecting his instructor's voice surely as much for his sake as hers, "Miss Parker, now you must pull yourself together. My fellows expect much of you. And me. Hide your beguiling eyes, for if I show evidence of distraction, Lord Elijah Withersby for one will never let the matter alone. I'm sure they're all heartily gossiping as we speak."

And yet they dallied and perhaps would have again lost track of time, reason, and moderation, had Lord Withersby the Deceased not swept screaming again through the wall. Percy whirled to him with a firm look and a finger to her lips, shooing him off.

"To be insufferable, I see, runs in the Withersby bloodline," Alexi muttered, placing Percy's arm in his. "Shall we to breakfast, love?"

As they were about to leave the room, Percy noticed a colorful scarf upon a brass peg. She slid it through her fingers unconsciously, moving to wrap it around her head; such a habit it was to hide her pearlescent hair and pallor from full view.

Alexi caught her hands in his. "Miss Parker." His voice was stern, as though she were in one of his tutorials again. "I would not allow you your shields whilst in my office at Athens. What gives you the notion you would be permitted to hide now?" He sensuously slid the scarf from her neck, kissing her white throat. Percy's knees and breath gave way in a swoon and she steadied herself upon him. Smirking with a delighted haughtiness, Alexi recaptured her hand. "Come now. A mysterious group awaits us in the parlor below. You'll be privy to incredible secrets known only to six people within the whole of London, but that the whole of London depends on. Welcome to the Guard, Miss Parker."

As Alexi and Percy descended the mahogany staircase, the waiting company fell silent.

"Miss Parker," Alexi said, sweeping her proudly onto the parlor floor, "allow me to salvage some measure of civility after last night's . . . adventure. Some here you know." He indicated a severe, smartly dressed woman at the forefront of the room who regarded Percy with a detached air. How things had changed from the day she sat meekly in this woman's office! "The Intuition and second in command of the Guard, Headmistress Thompson."

The headmistress perched tensely on a cushioned bench, buttoned head to toe in gray wool. Percy bowed her head in greeting, and her voice sounded awkward in her ears, in striking contrast to the divine commands that had escaped her lips the night prior. "Good morning, Headmistress."

"Please," the headmistress said, her expression cool but her tone soft, "do call me Rebecca, Miss Parker. I believe we all owe you the utmost familiarity."

"Indeed, then, do call me Percy. All of you," Percy beseeched the group, offering a gentle smile that was eagerly returned. Yet, speaking to the headmistress in this capacity was uncomfortable. Percy shifted nervously on her feet.

"Miss Josephine Belledoux." Alexi gestured to the beautiful olive-skinned woman. "Our resident Artist."

"Yes, hello again, Josephine."

"*Bonjour*, Mademoiselle Percy. *Vous êtes très jolie,*" Josephine said, proud that her fine fashion had been put to good use. She herself was bedecked in a splendid gown that spoke more of a ball than breakfast, but her good cheer seemed celebratory enough to pull it off.

"*Merci beaucoup!*" Percy replied.

"And you and Lord Withersby met in Athens library if I'm not mistaken. The Memory."

Lord Withersby, a lean, flaxen-haired man in exceedingly fine clothes, was draped somewhat rakishly upon a spinet piano. He bounded to his feet and rushed over to kiss her hand. "Elijah, Miss Percy."

"Good morning, Elijah. Thank you for your generous hospitality. Your estate is breathtaking, and I hope you'll do me the honor of a tour. Oh!" Percy's hand fluttered to her mouth. "Please tell me my touch did not harm you. Nothing burning before your eyes like last time, I pray?"

"None at all, Miss Percy, but thank you for your consideration. I'll be delighted to show you around the estate. Auntie's away, allowing us the run of the place." He turned, his sharp face beaming. "Alexi, old boy, you've done well. She's infinitely more charming than you possibly deserve. At last you've found someone to make up for your deficiencies of geniality."

The company chuckled. Alexi's dark eyes gleamed as Percy affectionately squeezed his hand. "Might I remind you, Lord Withersby, that you're hardly in a position to poke fun," he cautioned.

"Oh, you needn't be worried, Alexi," Elijah replied. "If there was ever a doubt about your omnipotence, your Royal Eeriness, rest assured that we'll never again question the throne. We have been soundly beaten, and bow to our great leader."

"Bow, rather, to my darling Miss Parker," Alexi said, guiding her forward a step.

Elijah's eyes nearly leaped from his skull and his hands rose in dramatic flourish. "My God, Alexi, who are you? Either it's love or a severe blow to the head—though that's one and the same. Doth the great Professor Rychman defer to another? I'm feeling faint."

Percy glanced at Alexi, whose sculpted lips were pursed in a familiar expression of irritation. "You may call me Percy, too, Alexi," she murmured with a smile, steering clear of what was clearly an ongoing verbal battle.

Her beloved turned next to a tall, hearty woman in a simple dress, sporting dark blond hair flecked with a few strands of gray. "May I introduce Miss Lucretia Marie O'Shannon Connor, our Healer?"

The woman bounded forward. "Call me Jane, Miss Percy," she bubbled in an Irish brogue. "The rest is such a mouthful."

"None of us know whether that mouthful is her true name or, rather, a more romantic offering she dreamed up when we met." Rebecca smiled sardonically.

Jane's wide hazel eyes glittered. "The great mystery of our age."

"Last but certainly not least," Alexi stated, "Vicar Michael Carroll."

Michael came forward, his face amiable and ruddy cheeked, his bushy hair disheveled as if he'd been raking it in every direction all morning. Tears wet oceanic blue eyes. "My dear Miss Percy; radiant as moonlight, kind and gentle, with such a fierce, loyal heart. Oh, Alexi—if

I'd met her, I'd have known she was the one in the instant. I am so sorry. My God, to think we might have lost you, dear girl."

"Vicar Carroll here, our sentimentalist," Alexi said as Michael reached out and clasped Percy's hands, "is the Heart—a most valuable asset against the forces of Darkness."

Percy looked into the clergyman's sorrowful gaze, unsure what to do other than offer a smile, releasing his earnest soul from any further guilt. He excused himself to wipe his face with a handkerchief.

"That concludes our number, Percy," Alexi murmured. "If you will have us, my dear, your family awaits."

Percy looked around the room, feeling her orphan's heart swell in her chest, a giddy rush of grateful blessing. "I've always wanted a family," she replied, and even the sharp Elijah could not help but be visibly moved.

Alexi leaned close, his long, aquiline nose brushing Percy's ear, causing her to shiver in delight. "Shall I announce our marriage in the Athens chapel tomorrow?"

"Tomorrow?" Percy blurted, then blushed.

"Is it too soon?" Alexi raised an eyebrow.

"No," Percy gasped, still incredulous at the idea of any husband, let alone this one.

"Good."

A maid entered and curtseyed. Surprisingly, she did not start at the sight of Percy's deathly pallor. Either she had been informed or, perhaps just as likely, had grown accustomed to the unusual company Lord Withersby kept.

"Master, breakfast is ready." She barely concealed an Irish brogue.

"Indeed, Molly, thank you." Elijah rose.

The maid nodded, her red hair bobbing, and Jane winked and smiled. "Always good to see you, Molly m'lass." Hearing her accent, the girl let loose a broad smile and swept away with additional bounce.

The dining room, off the main foyer, was a white room whose carved ceiling rounded cavernously over a sumptuously set table upon a red silk runner. The very latest in gaslit chandeliers blazed above, making the room nearly as bright as the day outside, hazily visible through fine lace curtains and valances drawn and tied with golden cords. Percy, raised in the Spartan atmosphere of a convent, was unaccustomed to such domestic grandeur. Athens had been stately and impressive enough, but the Gothic halls were no substitute for the delicate, more intimate trappings of a fine home. When Elijah made an offhand comment about the estate being fitted within the year for the new electric light, she wondered if her simplicity was too evidenced by her subsequent gasp.

As Molly and a second housekeeper cleared the warming trays and the company was bade sit, Alexi, after placing Percy to his right, smugly took the head of the table. Elijah eyed him from the other end.

Alexi patiently waited for the staff to slide the carved wooden door closed behind them before plucking a luminescent white feather from his pocket and tapping it soundlessly against his crystal goblet. A sudden symphony filled the air. Percy started, looking around her with wide eyes. Alexi turned to her, schoolboy pride glistening in his eyes as he returned the feather to his breast pocket, and said, "A bit of atmospheric noise to discourage eavesdropping."

"How magical!"

"That's the *least* of our parlor tricks that may impress you." Alexi turned to his company. "Allow me to announce happy news. Miss Parker graciously agreed last night to become my wife. We shall return to Athens this evening, where we will be married on the morrow."

"Tomorrow? In a hurry, are we?" Elijah asked with smirk. He yelped when Josephine, seated nearby, tried to surreptitiously kick him under the table. "Why is it that, in the last few days, acts of actual physical violence directed toward my person have increased at an alarming rate?"

"Because," Rebecca was swift to clarify, "your capacity for the daft and the inappropriate has soared to such alarming heights as warrants a sound beating."

"In my own house, no less," Elijah pouted.

"In Auntie's house," Josephine reminded him sweetly.

Alexi turned to his betrothed and Percy grinned; meals at the convent had never been this lively. "You see, Percy, around the age of fourteen we were overtaken by the powers that would forever change our lives. The happening also, however, stunted certain persons' intellectual growth. I believe some of us never matured further."

"Those born insufferably haughty and miserable remained similarly unaltered," Elijah replied, meeting Alexi's gaze calmly as he took a sip of liqueur.

"But for reaping the benefits of an ever-expanding intellect," Alexi sallied. Elijah snorted. "And so my mind and my heart—the latter of which Miss Parker has taken upon herself to expand—shall be joined with hers in our chapel."

Percy, without the faintest idea of what to say, delicately sipped her glass of cordial, a blush burning her ears.

Jane smiled and gave a toast: "To the betrothed." It was eagerly met.

Percy, trembling, nodded thanks to all. She knew she ought to perhaps say something; they were all looking to her. She opened her mouth and wished her voice weren't so hard to find, but suddenly she didn't have to say a word. A black rectangle of a door popped to life behind Elijah, who whirled in alarm. A tall, middle-aged female spirit with intense features, tightly pinned hair, and a piercing gaze, clad in a snugly buttoned traveling dress of contemporary vintage, stepped to the threshold. Alexi jumped to his feet, blue fire immediately in his hand.

The woman opened her mouth, staring intently at Alexi, and said a word in a language Percy did not know and could not place, yet understood; uncanny facility with language was one of her many gifts. "Peace, friends."

Blue fire extended from Alexi's hands like water from a fountain. Headmistress Thompson rose, her head cocked to the side, her brow furrowed as if in recognition. Percy jumped also to her feet, realizing her ability as the Guard's new translator might never be more important.

"She says, 'Peace, friends,'" Percy repeated the words the others had not heard in the Guard's own particular tongue. The others started and Jane's cup clattered to her saucer.

"You can hear ghosts, Percy?" Jane squeaked.

"Yes," Percy said, unsure why that should alarm the Irishwoman or turn her a sudden bright red. The spirit at what Percy could only assume was the threshold of death smirked, as if knowing Jane's secret, before turning to address the company. She was lovely, in an Amazonian sort of way, her nose a hard, long line with nostrils that flared with strength.

"You likely do not recognize me, but I was one of you," she began. "My name is Mrs. Beatrice Tipton. Born in London, raised in Cairo, I was the leader of the Guard that came before you. The Guard that put the seeds of Prophecy into place."

Percy repeated this and cringed as Alexi pounded his fist against the table. "Really? Well, then, you could've left us some bloody clues, Mrs. Tipton," he barked.

Beatrice raised an eyebrow. "Destiny cannot hold your hand; you must find and make it for yourselves," she retorted. "Fate means nothing if you do nothing to embrace or honor it. You ended up here together. That's what matters." Percy translated, attempting to exchange the caustic tone for something more gentle, so as not to escalate Alexi's irritation. Her beloved sat, grumbling.

"But . . . I recognize you," Rebecca murmured, still standing.

Beatrice sized up the headmistress. "The vast mental catalogue that is your gift, Headmistress Intuition, serves you well. Indeed, you of all people must have seen me most. Though I tried to stay out of your way, I worked to make sure the sacred bricks of Athens Academy would fall under your capable auspices."

Rebecca's mouth opened at Percy's translation, and her body tensed as if a torrent of questions waited to spring forth. But Beatrice continued. "Do you recall your first charge, the day you received this fate?" She looked at each one of them, evaluating them, and they nodded. "You served my circle that day. That woman in the hospital was our Healer."

"But why did none of you say?" Josephine murmured. "We could have helped each other—"

Beatrice held up a hand. "Our tongues were literally shackled. Our powers gone. Our work done. When you arrived, we were again normal citizens. You see, two Guard are never in the same city. It has never happened like this, there has never been a Prophecy as such, the goddess, Our Lady, never took such a chance as this. It is an unprecedented time. An unprecedented future is before us. And the next phase of battle is at hand." Percy's heart sank as she translated.

"Haven't we fought enough?" Michael murmured.

"It's just begun," the spirit replied. "The Whisper-world is a hazardous place, and war must be brought into your mortal hands to settle the score once and for all." Here Beatrice looked at Percy, which did not go unnoticed.

"And this secondary score commences when?" Alexi asked coolly. "And how may we avoid it? I'll not put my bride anywhere near further danger."

Beatrice fixed him with a deep stare, profound sadness on her face.

"You know as well as I that there's no avoiding this. We were bound to serve vengeful gods." She turned with a look that was neither amenable nor even kind as Percy repeated her words, breathless, shrinking from that withering stare. "Tell me something, my lady." Beatrice leaned in, narrowing her eyes. "Do you remember anything of your former existence—the one you relinquished to become what you are now?"

"No," Percy answered, recalling that Alexi had once posited the same question. "I am no divinity. *Please,* I'm flesh and blood and don't understand what's happened to me or why, so please don't expect knowledge of a woman I never was, a woman I'm not," she blurted, visibly shaking as she clutched the tablecloth. Alexi stilled this by placing his hand atop hers.

Beatrice sighed, and her hard stare softened. "Then you, too, are nothing more than a pawn." Her piercing gaze found the rest of the Guard. "But we've a duty, friends, to free your fellows overtaken by Darkness's vengeance. You've a call to arms. The sooner you take to it, the sooner this damnable business will end. My part will begin past purgatory's walls. When it's time, you'll do yours."

Percy tried to mitigate Beatrice's tone. It was familiar, though, a quality she recognized in her betrothed. Perhaps leaders shared a certain profile.

"And shall we simply intuit our parts?" Alexi hissed. "Query destiny until she unfolds herself, or deign you to give us a bit of direction, Mrs. Tipton?"

"Do what I tell you, when I tell you," the spirit replied, folding her arms.

As Percy repeated this, Alexi straightened in his chair. "Indeed? Well, to my knowledge, I remain the leader." Blue sparks crackled around him, a spire of blue flame in his palm. "And I'm going on a honeymoon, and neither you nor the Whisper-world can change that. I'll fight if I must, but, good God, give us a *moment's* peace."

Beatrice eyed Percy bitterly, then Alexi, but her voice belied profound emotion. "Of course," she murmured. "Marry her. Celebrate love while you have the chance. Treasure it, please, for life is oft gone before it's even begun."

Percy blushed and turned to Alexi. "We're to marry and celebrate love. Treasure it, even."

Alexi's hand tightened over hers, and he addressed their visitor. "Mrs. Tipton, that's the first sensible thing you've said."

Beatrice smirked, and for a moment the two leaders' expressions were oddly similar. "I've work to do, regardless," she replied, "so consider yourself lucky to gain that time. I must work from the inside out. But you mustn't be gone long." The spirit retreated into the shadows, that damp gray darkness stretching out behind her into what seemed eternity. There came a sound of weeping and water. It was not a place Percy wished to visit.

The ghost came forward again, weary, conflicted. "Lady Percy, don't repeat this: I know the importance of trusting the family fate gave you, but as you've seen, no one, not even these fine people, are infallible. *Our* Heart, Ahmed, was a torrent of visions. None of us could keep up with him, not even you—what you were then—so nobody knew if he spoke truth or madness.

"But he warned of betrayals from people dearly close, so . . . do be careful. In the end, Miss Parker, you're the key to everything. It's your duty to protect yourself. No one here would intentionally harm you, but betrayals are always a part of great prophecies, aren't they?" She rallied a meek smile and murmured, "I'll see you soon. Try not to be afraid. Trust your heart. And don't refuse when called."

The ghost turned again to the darkness, lifted her shoulders as if steeling herself, took a deep breath and vanished. A lingering chill slid across the table as the portal shrank away.

Alexi was looking at Percy expectantly. "And?"

Percy stared at her companions, all of whom were looking at her with hope, warmth, and anxiety. Of all the times in her life, she had never felt safer than here with her beloved among these new friends. She could choose fear and to anticipate danger around every corner, or she could choose to boldly trust the bonds her heart had so long yearned for. The choice was easy.

"She said not to fear, to trust my heart. And I tell you, this morning, that my heart is with all of you—and I hope you will entrust yours to me in return."

Everyone smiled brightly, especially Michael. Alexi bent close to graze her temple with his lips and, as no one knew what else to say, the conversation turned to the more cheerful talk of a wedding.

"Mrs. Rychman and I shall take time also," Alexi said, "to adjust her to the estate of which she will be mistress. I trust you all to keep order. I expect no communication until a week has passed, after which Percy and I would ask you dine at our estate."

The intimate isolation of which he spoke, the word "wife," and the thought of sharing an estate with him, sounded incredible to Percy's ears, one of her hazy classroom daydreams. Only the sound of her tea-cup against its saucer and the thrilling press of Alexi's hand upon her knee convinced her otherwise. She belonged to a peculiar destiny, and to this man seated next to her. She'd always wished to belong.

The group quit the table for coffee. Rebecca and Alexi rose in uni-son. She touched his elbow, and he immediately drew her into an adjoin-ing, oak-paneled hallway. Percy stood frozen, blinking after the retreating figures, and she felt a sudden, surprising flare of jealousy. Would Alexi forever be at the bidding of Headmistress Thompson? Then she chided herself for being foolish. Alexi and the headmistress were her superiors, and she must respect stations established years before, regardless of the fact that Alexi was hers.

Her new friends were close at hand. Jane showed Percy into the with-drawing room and bade her sit on a sumptuously brocaded pouf. Jose-phine tossed a nonchalant nod toward Rebecca and Alexi and said, "You mustn't mind them. They're always sidling off into deep discussion, and have for years."

"Is that so?" Percy said.

"Without her and Alexi's strength," Jane assured, "we'd never outlast the spirits we battle."

"Of course." Percy nodded. "I have always admired the headmis-tress's obvious strength of character. In fact, I was always quite intimi-dated by her."

"We all have been," Josephine confided, taking up the role of hostess and passing out coffee from Molly's silver tray. "Between her and Alexi, we're never at a loss for intensity."

"Indeed," Percy murmured. "Oh! When I first met Alexi . . ."

"Terrify you, did he?" Jane smirked.

"Yes!"

Josephine laughed. "Don't tell him that, he'll take it as a compli-ment."

"Yes, he did." Percy grinned.

"When did it stop?" Josephine asked. "Your terror?"

Percy thought a moment. "I'd fled alone into a dark foyer at the academy ball, too nervous to be seen." Her voice dropped, and the women leaned closer. "But Alexi sought me out, waltzed with me in moonlight to an echo of music. I was lost to him forever." She blushed and looked at the floor. Jane sighed dreamily.

"Mon Dieu!" Josephine exclaimed. "We must procure you a wedding dress!"

"Oh!" Percy quaked. "What does one wear?"

"Leave that to me," Josephine assured her. "You'll have something fit for a goddess!"

Delight was reflected in Josephine's eyes, but Percy saw wistfulness, too. "Weddings," the Frenchwoman murmured. "They are beautiful things. Everyone should have one."

"You're very beautiful," Percy offered, when Jane reached out a hand and squeezed Josephine's, blushing. "I'm sure you'll have no trouble—"

"Oh, but Josephine likes trouble," Jane said, earning a sideways glance from the other woman. "Besides, this fate . . . limits our options."

Indeed, Percy thought, shifting awkwardly in her seat; none of these people were married. Because they were following the bidding of spirits and gods. And here she was, the young newcomer, up and marrying their leader, her professor. It was a lot to take in.

"Is there anyone we must not hesitate to invite?" Josephine asked, her melancholy gone.

Percy's hand flew to her mouth. "My God, my dearest Marianna! With no one to vouch for my whereabouts, heaven only knows what she'll think!"

"A matter for the headmistress." Josephine slipped into the hall and motioned for Rebecca to join them.

As he entered the room, Alexi's gaze went right to Percy, as if he'd known her exact location even through the wall. Jumping up, Percy offered him the seat by her side and darted to procure him coffee. He smiled broadly. She was unaccustomed to his smile, as he had always furrowed his brow at her before, scowling and brooding. So enthralling was the sight, she nearly spilled his cup. Alexi thanked her and bestowed a lingering kiss upon her cheek; Percy reddened, fell into her seat, and nearly dumped both their coffees.

The headmistress darted to a writing desk in the corner. "Of course, I should've thought to send word to Miss Farelei—my apologies, Miss Parker." Procuring a fountain pen and paper, she began scrawling. "I shall say you are well in health and shall return to the grounds this afternoon. Elijah," she called as she went to the window, "may I open the casement for a bit of business?"

"Yes, dear," the other drawled over his coffee, moving to lock the room's sliding doors to prevent intruders.

Rebecca opened the beveled glass panel and loosed a low whistle. An impressive black raven with something glittering on its breast fluttered onto the windowsill. "Frederic, Athene Hall, please," the headmistress said to the bird, who obediently opened its beak for the paper, emitted a muffled squawk, and flew off.

Elijah unlocked the doors again, to allow passage of the house staff, who were clearly not privy to the less-than-ordinary aspects of the lives of the Guard. Percy herself had never dreamed the headmistress made a pet of a raven, much less one who followed commands.

Jane leaned forward in her seat, grinning. "That's Frederic. I've a cat, Marlowe. They've been frightfully useful."

"I should say!"

Alexi patted her knee, enjoying her gaping astonishment.

It was then that the alarm sounded. Hands flew to temples and the company swayed on their feet. "Threadneedle Street. Luminous," Rebecca stated, often the first to know. The Guard rose obediently.

"Couldn't they give us a single day of respite?" Elijah muttered.

"Thank goodness, Percy," Jane exclaimed, taking her by the arm and leading her to the door. "I thought these niceties would never end. Now you get to see us as we truly are."

Josephine was clearly put out. "Could not they have waited until I was in less fine a dress?"

CHAPTER
FOUR

Percy allowed the whirlwind to happen around her and watched. She didn't dare posit questions; it was clear that the practices of their odd calling were well established, and she didn't want to seem the intrusive novice. Elijah fussed over Percy at the door, procuring blankets and a traveling cloak, thinking her still delicate and recovering from the previous evening's exertions. Percy was gracious and, indeed, once she drew the curtains of the carriage so that the bright light didn't hurt her eyes, quite comfortable.

The fine carriages of the Withersby estate ushered them expediently south. Alexi held Percy as their cab jostled into the city, which grew denser and darker with each passing street. He watched her squint out the window. "Are you ready for new wonders?"

Percy chuckled nervously, turning and looking up at him. "Truthfully, I'd rather talk about the wedding. What's happening at Threadneedle?"

He shrugged nonchalantly. "Not uncommon to find spiritual unrest in that general vicinity, center of the city and all. There was a plague pit nearby."

Percy shuddered then voiced a sudden worry. "Could I have done more harm than good? Perhaps it's that horrible woman coming for vengeance—"

"Hardly," Alexi scoffed. "You reduced her to ashes. You saved the day, my dear, and none of us shall forget it."

"You and the headmistress said 'Luminous.' What does that mean?"

"When something overtakes a human body—a possession with intent to harm—the bodies glow. When I first beheld you in my classroom, I thought as much of you."

"Ah," Percy said, recalling that first meeting. "But, Alexi . . . a possession requires exorcism."

He paused. "Admirable institution, the Catholic Church," he began, taking Percy's white hand in his. "And if for some reason we were entirely indisposed, I imagine the rite suffices. But the most permanent solution lies in what you shall soon see."

Percy shook her head. "And no one knows of you? Not the church? No one? How is this possible?"

"For that, you may in part thank Lord Withersby. He does have his uses. You'll see." Alexi pointed to a fine Tudor-style town house. "Here."

Percy turned her attention to the few random passersby. Some gazed around curiously, as if sensing something was wrong. All mortals had a certain capability to sense the unknowable, if few could actually see it. Six, it seemed, could truly affect it.

Once the Guard alighted from their respective carriages and the drivers were sent to wait at a safe distance, they linked hands on the street below and stared at the town house in question. Pale blue halos lit their bodies. When Alexi seized her hand, Percy felt a surge of energy blaze up her arm and into the core of her body. Elijah closed his eyes. He slipped a hand from Josephine's and snapped his fingers. All the lingering and curious citizens wandered off, as if they'd not seen a thing out of the ordinary.

A fresh wind whipped the edges of Percy's skirt and billowed Alexi's cloak. The same bluish flame that had roused her from the brink of death now surrounded them in a sapphire circle. A strange, ancient harmony rose, as if the breeze had tuned strings for them. Alexi's voice cut above it all, in a private command of peace. He turned calmly to Rebecca.

"Third-floor den, top of the stairs," the headmistress said. "Young male, catatonic. Luminous."

"Thank you," Alexi said, turning to Percy. "You, my dear, will remain directly behind me." His fellows he told, "The rest as per custom."

The company broke into formation, Alexi at the head, Michael directly on one side, Jane at the other. Percy furrowed her brow as the Irishwoman tied a leather apron around her waist that appeared stained with a dark substance of indiscernible origin. Alexi's steady hand guided Percy behind him, Rebecca close beside. Josephine had slung a rectangular canvas bag over her shoulder and brought up the rear with Elijah, who was scouting for further passersby.

"Once more into the breach, dear friends, once more," Alexi stated.

The house was charged. At the bidding of Michael's upraised hand, doors swung open. They passed through the entrance foyer and up two grand sets of stairs, passing befuddled, startled maids along the way. With calm waves, Elijah sent them lazing off with dumb expressions, lulling the tumult. The Guard tore into a fine room with carved cherry paneling from floor to ceiling. A long bar at one end, a wide hearth at the other, lush chairs and a few gaming tables sat sportingly in between. Ornate gaslight sconces burned low.

A pale young man lay crumpled and shuddering on the floor, in a disturbing state of disarray. Alexi directed a powerful gesture at him and a cord of blue lightning shot forth from his hand. The twitching heap of a man groaned, rolling onto his back, and Percy heard a hiss the rest of the group could not.

Jane rushed forward, crossing herself. She lifted a hand glowing with healing light, her palm a small star. She touched the victim's ashen face. His features were revealed as blood magically faded from his cheeks, unmatting from the place upon his crown where a gash mended beneath Jane's fingertips. "Aren't you a pretty one," she murmured, having taken his head onto her lap. Percy grimly realized the dark stains upon her apron were from similarly supernatural wounds.

Josephine strode the room, examining each wall as if measuring space. Rebecca took notes in a small book. Michael moved about, peering at his comrades as if determining symptoms. Elijah approached the subject upon the floor.

"What *is* that suit you're wearing?" He bent over the body. "These nouveau riche. I can't bear it. Excuse me, Miss Connor." Making a face, Elijah bent closer and touched a fingertip to the gentleman's nose. An odd shudder worked him back to his feet.

"Name?" Rebecca asked.

"Matthew Van Cortland. Dutch merchant. Textiles." Elijah's apparent disdain deepened. He stared down at the supine body. "Whatever are you doing in England, sir? You see, it hasn't been amenable to you, has it? Why don't you leave colonialism to us, thank y—"

"Nature of possession?" Rebecca curtly interrupted.

"I broke free," the possessing spirit cried. Percy winced, knowing she was the only one who could hear. "But there's a black dawn coming for you, just like the black plague—but for your mind! You'll ne'er be free. We'll turn the tables on you, just wait." Percy shuddered but said nothing.

Elijah slipped off one shoe and slid his foot beneath Van Cortland's knee.

"Lazy," Jane scoffed, batting at Elijah's foot.

Withersby's face twisted into something pale and helpless, and he wrested away with a growl. "Oh, and to waste such fine brandy!" He turned to face a long mahogany bar, where a decanter and tray of glasses lay broken on the floor in a pool of dark, pungent liquid.

"Well, our friend here seems to have escaped after last night's melee. Most of the offenders were driven back to their proper place, thanks to Miss Percy, but this one managed to indulge his fancy for Van Cortland's innards. He's right terrible, and took many a soul with him on his way to his mass black-death grave." Noticing Percy out of the corner of his eye, he said, "Why, my dear Miss Parker, are you all right?" Everyone turned to stare at her, sunk upon a nearby stool. She supposed she looked as ill as she felt.

"You just wait," the spirit gurgled, its voice wet from inside the mortal trappings of Van Cortland. "Wait and see what we'll do to you when you're dragged to the other side. Especially you who look just like us. I'm sure *special* treats await."

Percy flared with righteous indignation. She turned to Alexi and tried to speak calmly. "He's taunting, saying such things as would not befit a lady's repetition. Be thankful you have deaf ears tonight, friends." She waved a hand that they might not worry further over her.

Alexi turned. "In the presence of a lady? How dare you!" His hand issued a more powerful jolt, binding the victim in shackles of light. There was an immediate shift through Van Cortland's skin, the spirit within struggling to pull free.

The sight was revolting, but Percy watched. Alexi's sparking cords squeezed closer and closer, and she heard the spirit's tirade become struggling gasps. Josephine opened her bag to reveal its contents: a small, shimmering painting of an angel. Lifted out to hang upon the opposite wall, the image filled Percy with peace and joy all at once, and she felt the warmth of the phoenix pendant around her neck, flying upon the ruffled folds of her fine dress. Glancing down, she could see her pendant glowing with an empathetic light similar to that in the air here.

Josephine squinted, adjusted the corner of the frame and turned to kneel beside Jane. "Van Cortland, *mon chéri*," she murmured near the man's ear. "Do look at that image. It will soothe you, ease your troubled mind." She had to force open his lids, but once he caught sight of the painting, his eyes ceased their rolling dance of panic. "*Oui*, Matthew, focus. Your guardian angels are by your side, helping you fight. Now, you mustn't remove this painting. It's your guardian angel for life." Her hand was stroking mousy brown hair from his temples. Percy couldn't help noticing Elijah make another face.

With a small flutter of her fingertips, Jane countered the man's convulsions, some of which brought blood or bile trickling from his thin lips. His muscles unclenched and the fluids ceased, but the battle raged on within him. All the while, it was as if Alexi was drawing the slack from his illuminated threads of sapphire flame, binding the man's body partly like a weaver, partly like a conductor, constricting the terror with each deft movement, crushing the vehemence out of the terrible presence, light against the force of darkness.

Rebecca, secretarial duties sufficiently undertaken, returned pen and paper to her reticule. Her eyes closed then shot open, a pained breath escaping her. Michael was at once nearby, giving a soft, relaxing sigh. She gifted him with a genuine smile, all discomfort in her features vanishing.

"We must put it down as best we can, Alexi," she said, catching her breath. "There's nothing that it seeks in restlessness that it will not try to inflict by vengeance. It doesn't want peace and so we must dispel it."

"I couldn't agree more," Alexi replied, picking up the tempo of his conduction. The spirit shrieked in Percy's ears, and the fortitude of his vile proclamations was renewed.

"Bind," Alexi called. The group formed a circle, save Jane and Percy. Alexi transferred one cord of light into the palm opposite, as if they were luminous reins, and his swift hand caught Percy's arm and pulled her up and into the circle, where a bond of bluish flame connected each heart in light. A woven star that for years had known six now had seven points.

Percy felt the Guard's power, but there was another sensation here, something else pressing in: the unwelcome and stifling dread of death. Then there came a laugh—Michael's soft laugh—and she could breathe again.

The moment all hands clasped, Alexi shouted in their unknowable tongue, *"Hark."* Music burst tangibly into the air, magic that this union alone created, called sharply into service by their leader. It was lovely, coming partly from the air and partly from their throats, drawing now into a sweet *pianissimo.*

For a moment the spirit writhing in Van Cortland seemed to listen. The possessed man began to shake so violently that Jane could hardly control him. He flopped about, gasping for air in a hideous display. Jane swung her arm over him, now bending over his torso, her glowing, healing hand pressed directly to his heart. Maintaining life was a struggle, and she nearly had to pound upon his chest. He was hideous, his skin flickering from pale to bruised to rotting before their eyes. Each horrific shift, Jane countered with a renewed healing burst. But she was tiring.

There was a veritable explosion as Alexi, in his rich and masterful voice, issued a powerful, otherworldly chant that Percy could compare only to an Old Testament proclamation from God. The possessor hissed as if scalded and the nauseating metamorphoses of Van Cortland ceased.

The group heaved a huge communal breath and their circle drew closer. Rapt, Rebecca suddenly rattled off a philosophical admonishment that Percy believed was from Sophocles. The spirit growled and hurled unspeakable curses toward her, and Percy gasped until Alexi tossed a fireball down its throat, sufficiently garbling the sound.

"Thank you," Percy murmured.

"I wish you were as deaf as we tonight, dear," Alexi offered.

Van Cortland's body was now bound wholly by flame, and a peculiar chant Alexi named the Cantus of Disassembly flowed from the Guard, a music connected with wind, heartbeats, and eternity, bequeathed to their minds and hearts many years ago upon the Grand Work's birth within them. Yet it was somehow familiar to Percy.

There came one last gruesome gasp. Dark fluid was rustling beneath Van Cortland's nearly transparent flesh, in patterns as if he were full of liquid marble. Whether this was blood or the spirit's vile, vaguely tangible essence, it could not be determined, but whatever purity and magic the assembled company had brought to the air, it was being fouled by noxious gases from the usurped body, slipping out every orifice and leaking from beneath his fingernails.

Percy felt her stomach heave. Jane was rotating the star of her palm in slow curves over Van Cortland's body, leaving traces of light hovering in the misty shape of a Celtic knot. Her healing white light and Alexi's blue light of purification now bound together. A punctuation rose to each of their lips, Percy included, and their incredible benediction lulled into a final *"shhh."*

In a puff of sour-smelling smoke and with a final damning curse, the spirit at last departed the ravaged body of its victim. The group saw their foe for what it was, so rotted and disintegrated that it was but shreds of skin and muscle. This decomposed form lifted up to hover before them, swiveling its horrible head to stare from putrid sockets.

"You should have disassembled," Alexi said angrily. The horror dodged a blast of fire.

"You fools, you fools!" Its jaw flapped as it spoke for Percy's ears alone. "There's no end in sight. It is war, you know, now that the bride is gone. Hell has broken loose. You won't last. We'll win you yet! That fight on the borderland was only the begin—"

"Shut your unholy mouth!" Percy spat. Everyone whirled. She glanced down to see that her bosom had begun to glow white, just like the night prior. Alexi was at her side immediately, embracing, trying to move her behind him, to keep her away from the spirit. But she stood her ground.

"Well, well, so we meet again," the phantasm mocked. "I take it you'll try and banish me like you did at the school? You're such an odd little thing, aren't you? Are you even human? What are—?"

Percy's eyes flashed. A tearing sound thundered through the room, and suddenly a dark rectangular portal opened. Spread out behind was a long, dark corridor, and hazy forms floated there, seemingly unaware. Surely, the Whisper-world was at hand. Percy felt a churning power gather within her, but she remained unsure how to control it.

"Darling . . ." Alexi murmured warily, but her eyes stayed fixed on the doorway.

The spirit squealed. "You may banish me back, but I'll keep trying. We all will. Since the bitch fled, we're more resolved than ever."

It cried out as Percy threw her hand forward, thrusting the spirit toward the portal as if it were being dragged back by invisible hands. Beyond, Percy heard a slow singsong chant. "Lucy-Ducy wore a nice dress, Lucy-Ducy made a great mess." Her blood chilled. She dearly hoped the name was just a coincidence.

"Percy, what are you hearing?" Alexi murmured, a tinge of helplessness in his voice. "Tell me what you h—"

"It doesn't matter, love, just nonsense," she replied, forcing herself to remain calm. She took a step toward the portal, needing to clarify the eerie rhyme and yet sickened by it.

"Percy, no." Alexi took hold of her again.

A tall, glowing spirit appeared suddenly on the threshold, raising a firm hand in a command to halt. He was hard-featured and rugged, with fabric draped over a broad chest, metal bands and leather around strong arms, and a wild mane of hair. Jane gasped and clapped hands to her mouth. The spirit reached out a powerful hand, grabbed the pile of rot by the neck and tossed it to a heap at his feet where it smacked wetly with a grotesque cry.

Scanning them, the spirit found Jane. His eyes sparkled with fondness. "Oh, my dear Jane," he said in old Gaelic. "How I wish you could hear me and heed my warning."

"I can hear you," Percy replied in the same language. Jane whirled, shock and concern visible on her face.

"Oh!" the spirit declared. "Are you . . . ? Wait! Oh, pardon me, my lady, the power has awoken you." He fell to his knees.

"No." Percy blushed. "You needn't . . . Please, sir, do get up."

He beamed as he stood. "My name is Aodhan. I was a member of the Guard ages ago, and I guard still. There's a change comin', and I'll help be your guide, White Woman, but not now. This portal shouldn't be open long. It attracts the unwanted, and the Guard daren't enter." He tapped his temple with a transparent finger. "Isn't good for the minds."

Percy nodded.

"Do me one favor," Aodhan continued. "I know my dearest Jane cannot hear me. Would you please tell her, in private, that I love her?"

"It would be my honor," Percy replied.

"Now, I don't rightly know how this opened. I don't suppose you know how to close it?" Aodhan asked.

Percy whirled to Alexi, who was clearly perturbed by the one-sided conversation. "How did I close the portal last night?"

"I . . . believe you . . . cast your arm out," he replied, his hand a vise upon her.

Percy stretched out her arm, then closed her hand in a firm fist. With a popping sound, the door began to shrink. Aodhan waved good-bye as he receded from view and in an instant the door was no more. All eyes turned to Percy, who was staring at her hand. She shrugged, smiling nervously, no longer glowing. "Well . . . it seems I do have control over the portals, though I've no idea how I opened it in the first place."

"You were angry," Michael stated. "You were feeling threatened."

"Who was that man?" Rebecca barked. "Jane, he kept looking at you."

The Irishwoman's face was a mixture of confusion and fear, so Percy cut in swiftly. "His name is Aodhan, a member of the Guard long ago, and he pledges his help." Jane offered Percy a furtive, grateful glance. There would be a discussion sometime soon, but a moan from Van Cortland recalled them all to their task.

Briefly, Percy caught Alexi's attention. "It's all right, Alexi. For the moment, all is well."

"I certainly hope so," he said. Percy frowned as he released her, smoothing his dark clothes. He moved to examine the stains upon the floor left from the supernatural melee. Glancing up, he waved a hand and the dim room was suddenly well lit by a tall gas flame.

Thanks to Jane's aid, Van Cortland again resembled a human being, if not much of one. Josephine tried to keep his gaze on her visual benediction, but his eyes would not stay open. His pulse was faint. He would not rouse. His breaths were shallow. Elijah came over and examined him, and he and the two women shook their heads.

"It may take him a while to recover," Jane said sheepishly.

"If he shall," Rebecca remarked. "It's all right, Jane, it's not your fault. You did everything right. We all did."

Percy eyed Alexi in alarm. His stoic face betrayed almost nothing, yet Percy, who had spent so much time observing him, saw sadness there. He addressed her evident concern. "We cannot save them all. But we . . . usually do, Percy. We usually do." When she nodded and took his hand, the pinched look around his eyes eased slightly.

Michael went to each member of the group and placed a thumb upon the center of their backs, imparting a frisson of comfort, offering a smile to rally them from the hopelessness they felt. Elijah wandered off to soothe a few screaming maids who had somehow eluded his earlier spell.

Michael and Alexi lifted Van Cortland and carried him into the master bedroom. To his staff and family it would appear that he'd merely fallen ill with a mysterious ailment from which he would, hopefully, someday recover. Josephine followed, moving her work of art with them to hang at eye-line so it might be the first thing the victim would see: a ward and benediction.

Rebecca, having catalogued the particulars of the room the moment of their arrival, rearranged its contents to their exact prior placement, save the broken decanter and glasses, which she gathered into a small leather bag that she cinched and hung at her side. She caught Percy staring and explained, "The less evidence of destruction of his property, the better hope for recovery."

Alexi and Michael returned, and without another word the entire group made its way through the dark and now-slumbering house. "I'll gesture for a carriage to come round, Percy, wait here," Alexi commanded.

As he disappeared around the corner, Percy worried at his cool tone and the way he'd reacted to the portal. Things simply happened around her. It wasn't that she was trying to be trouble, but that spirit had been provoked by her, perhaps was more malevolent because of her. She heartily prayed for Van Cortland.

"Nicely done with the doors, Miss Parker, I think you're a quick study!" Michael exclaimed at her side.

She turned to him, grateful. "Thank you, Michael. I rather needed to hear that."

"Knowing hearts is my talent. Though I wish my words were always perfect." He glanced fleetingly at Rebecca, who was taking more notes outside the town house door.

The waiting carriages both rounded the corner. "Now that you've seen the Grand Work, what do you think?" Alexi asked as he approached Percy, collecting her firmly against him.

"You were incredible to behold, my love. Truly, Alexi, the Guard is a wonder." She thought a moment. "Music to fight the spirits. How odd and incredible. It's like it comes from the very air."

Alexi shrugged. "It wasn't we who determined our weaponry; our talents were set long ago by men and women now forgotten. Inspired by Muses, tuned by the heavens—I suppose they thought every restless spirit needed a lullaby. A Greek chorus, the holiest of holies." He smirked. "Would you rather we shout at them?"

"No, no, there's enough noise as is." Percy chuckled.

"Alexi, old chap," Elijah called, gesturing grandly. "You and your fiancée—good God, how odd to say that—should ride in the first, best carriage as guests of honor. Josie, you come, too. The rest of you follow."

Percy noted out of the corner of her eye that Rebecca's mouth thinned, masking a grimace. Perhaps, she thought, the headmistress was used to riding at Alexi's side; perhaps she had grown attached to little habits that Percy's presence would upset. As the Intuition began to walk away, Michael trotted after her with a tiny, "Wait, dear Rebecca. Wait for me."

Percy wondered if the headmistress didn't see, or refused to see.

CHAPTER
FIVE

"Alexi," Josephine began as the carriage jolted off toward the center of London, "I'll take charge of your lady's apparel."

"Ah, good. Specters and phantasms mustn't derail us, we've a wedding to prepare." He glanced at Percy, who gave him a joyous smile. "Bring the bill for what you buy her, Josie, and I shall remit."

The Frenchwoman turned to Percy, beaming. "There's a woman in Covent Garden—not the most reputable part of town, but her work's swift and exquisite. She tailors for the Royals all the time—"

"Josephine," Alexi interrupted, "do not have my bride looking like an act in a halfpenny theatrical."

"And why not?" Elijah cried, giving a sharp-toothed grin. "You stalk about all day in sweeping black robes. Isn't it fitting to have your bride trailing iridescent textiles like a votaress of Diana on her way to the . . . well, considering she's meeting you there, sacrificial altar? Oh, Miss Terry's Lady Macbeth at the Lyceum sports a gown of beetles' wings. Can you imagine? That would be quite fitting, your Royal Eeriness."

"You didn't want to treat me to a ride in your carriage," Alexi accused. "You wished to torture me." Percy giggled.

"The sweet lady has to know what she's getting into. You must have worked mighty magic indeed to have her so moony-eyed."

"You mustn't tease Alexi so about his manner, Lord Withersby," Percy said. "I'm far more the misfit. As for moony-eyed—well, I am . . . naturally." She blinked her opalescent eyes.

"I suppose you have a point," Elijah allowed. "Goodness. Your union—simply terrifying. Children living near your estate will tell such tales."

Alexi chuckled, pleased by the concept, but Percy let loose an audible gasp. "But I know nothing of estates! I've no dowry, nothing to bring to this marriage. I haven't the faintest idea how to run a household."

"Darling," Alexi said, "we shan't be entertaining or making a show of things like many of our station. Our destiny isn't for such luxuries. I believe your peculiar talents far outstrip domestic economy."

"Oh. All right then." But Percy was not convinced. The thought of making a home was as overwhelming as any supernatural task that lay ahead.

Josephine beamed. "Don't worry, Percy, the Guard will come calling. Besides, the Wentworths have been silently running the place for years. They'll run it just as smoothly with you as an addition."

"And more happily." Elijah snorted. "To have something sweet and dainty to look after, rather than his Royal Eeriness, Minister of the Constant Sneer . . ."

Percy glanced at her betrothed. "You don't sneer, do you?"

"See?" Alexi offered blandly to Elijah.

"Perhaps you've been spared, so far. But who knows what may happen now? My God. The bravery, my dear Miss Parker, the bravery of your young heart! Oh! Take note, Miss Parker—you see?" Elijah cried.

Percy turned. Alexi was indeed sneering. She laughed. "Why, I've never seen that look before, Lord Withersby. You must be its sole inspiration."

As Elijah folded his arms, Alexi changed topics. "Percy, we must discuss what's to become of you, as you cannot in good faith continue as a student. Athens is central to our work, and I want you near. We'll find a place."

"Thank you!" Percy exclaimed. Despite having only spent a quarter at Athens, she was quite fond of its stately Romanesque halls.

"So much change," Josephine breathed. "We've been waiting for our seventh for so long, and now that you're here, Percy, everything can change." She glanced hopefully at Elijah, who shifted a bit and turned to stare out the window. Though she tried to mask her disappointment, her expressive face hid nothing from Percy. Alexi seemed oblivious, lost in thought.

The carriage stopped, and Alexi helped Percy from it. Tucked quietly into the middle of London, a veritable castle of red sandstone rose before them. Percy shielded her eyes, gazing alternately at the familiar rough-hewn bricks, at her new friends, and at her new fiancé. Students milling about on the stairs stopped to stare. Percy had never before appeared without a scarf draped around her head. Her tinted glasses were some-where in her room, so her white-blue eyes strained against the light. Alexi waved all the youngsters away, gliding smoothly into his role as professor even if his battered attire did not match.

The second carriage pulled up. As the others disembarked, Alexi said, "Thank you for escorting us hence; we ask you to keep time until tomorrow morning's ceremony." He paused, then turned to address Michael. "Mr. Carroll, my good vicar, may I beg a favor?"

"Anything at all," Michael replied.

"Would you be so kind as to fetch my sister? She would be furious with me if she missed tomorrow."

"Oh, yes, Alexi. Alexandra *must* be present!" Percy exclaimed, think-ing of a recent harried evening at Miss Rychman's quaint cottage. The place had been a welcome respite from the spectral hound whose jaws seemed bent on searching out Percy. She prayed it had indeed been put to rest.

Alexi fished in a coat pocket. "These notes ought to suffice for the distance. Tell the driver nine Hampstead."

Percy, glancing at the assembled Guard, noticed Jane had departed. Josephine took her hand and whispered conspiratorially, "Percy, you must not forget to tell your friend your good news. Now, I'm off! You won't be disappointed." She strolled toward the theatre district, casting one final glance at Elijah.

"Rebecca, your office, in a moment," Alexi directed. The head-mistress nodded and disappeared through the main doors. "Percy, my dear"—Alexi steered her, opening the door and gesturing her inside—"I'll escort you to your hall, but then I must discuss how we inform the faculty of our new . . . status. I'll call on you this evening to bid you good night. You'd best not be seen to take my arm until we've properly informed the faculty."

"Of course."

Alexi leaned in as they traversed the entryway. "Although I wouldn't mind giving that dreary Mrs. Rathbine palpitations by seizing you in a kiss right here in the middle of the school."

Percy blushed and giggled and nearby students stopped to stare. "You can't, Professor," she murmured. "All think you inhumanly cold and without humor. A glimpse of affection would destroy your fearsome reputation."

"Right you are, Miss Parker," he replied. "Right you are. Now, Percy, speak nothing of the Guard or recent phenomena—not even to your dear friend."

"Alexi, if I told anyone of last night's particulars, I'd be deemed mad. However, Marianna will insist—"

"Say that as your fever worsened, I took your care upon myself. As for our marriage, it needs no explanation other than that you're madly in love with me. Wedlock was the only way to keep you from making a fool of yourself," he declared, a sporting light in his eye.

Percy giggled again, and side by side they opened the glass-paneled doors to the small cobblestone courtyard between the Athens clerestories. Blinking from the light, she lost her smile to a sudden thought. "But what of the institution at large? Privately the thought of scandal thrills me, but everyone will question a sudden marriage between professor and pup—"

Percy heard the squeal before she saw a figure fly at her. *"Mein Gott!"* cried a young German voice. Percy choked as arms flew around her neck. "Where in the whole"—Marianna fumbled for a choice English declamation—"*bloody* whole world have you been? I thought you were dead!" Her fair cheeks blazing and her wide green eyes filled with tears, she whirled upon Alexi. "And you! You! What on earth did you do?" she cried, brandishing her fists and offering a few German curses for emphasis.

"Marianna, please." Percy blushed and tried to grab the petite blonde by the arm, but her friend stood her ground. Two female students sitting on the angel fountain fell into immediate gossip, and a few male students, eyebrows raised, thought it best to disappear into their dormitory hall.

Alexi, a full two feet taller, eyed the furious German, who had taken to Percy on her first day and whom his betrothed simply adored. He smiled graciously but said nothing. Percy pulled Marianna back and attempted to smooth her friend's disheveled scarf and russet vest. "Marianna, my sweet, hush! Professor Rychman has meant me no harm, I am well again and everything is wond—"

"No! When I last saw you, you were nearly dead. What on earth happened between yesterday and this morning . . . ?" She turned again upon Alexi. "What spell have you cast over her? She was heartbroken just the day before, and you—why you look like you were in a brawl!"

"Marianna, there was no magic!" Percy insisted. "There was a great misunderstanding. Calm yourself. I have news, happy news."

Alexi spoke gently. "Miss Farelei, I understand your confusion. Please accept my apologies for any wrongs you feel I have done Miss Parker. I do not presume to know the confidences you may have shared, but rest assured I have only Percy's best interests in mind and would stake my life on her welfare."

Marianna blinked at him, scowling.

"Marianna." Percy took hold of her friend's hands. "We are to be married. Tomorrow morning. Here at the chapel. Alexi Rychman is to be my husband!"

The blond girl's jaw dropped, and it was a long moment before she could speak. "No. You jest."

Percy held up her ringed finger. Marianna turned to Alexi, gaping.

"It's true, Miss Farelei," he answered. "Please do us the honor of attending."

Marianna turned back to Percy, whose cheeks were scarlet, and screamed. She threw her arms around Percy and then, in turn, moved to throw her arms around the professor.

"There's no need to make a scene. Good God!" Alexi grimaced, awkwardly patting the girl's shoulder in an effort to extricate himself. Percy hid her face. Even she knew better than to embrace stern Professor Rychman in the middle of the academy courtyard.

"I would have never dreamed it!" Marianna cried, and Percy hushed her into a whisper. "I never thought I'd hear the end of her incessant pining over you."

"Marianna, honestly," Percy scolded. She noticed Alexi's mouth curve.

Her friend wore a wide grin. "How can you hush me? You cannot expect such exciting news to escape bold outbursts."

"Ladies, if you will excuse me, I will leave you to your blushes, giggles, and other absurdities. I've much to attend. But, please, as we've yet to inform the rest of the institution, try not to get everyone in an uproar." The twitch of a smile remained on his lips and Percy's blush persisted. Marianna giggled as he bowed slightly to Percy. "My dear, I shall come for you later this evening."

Marianna turned to Percy, who was drinking in the sight of her betrothed disappearing into Promethe Hall. In the next instant, the young women screamed and embraced each other, creating a bit of a scene. "Come, come." Percy dragged Marianna into the next hall. "We must tell Mina, the Apollo librarian. She'll be so shocked! But she's fond of me and the professor, and I'd hate for her not to be included."

Marianna couldn't stop giggling. "I daresay shocked faces will abound when you waltz through Athens in a wedding dress."

THE WHISPER-WORLD REMAINED RATHER A MESS. SOME OF THE spirits had torn themselves limb from limb; countless others had hurled themselves against Darkness. He'd grown weary of swatting them into pieces. Once he'd locked away his opposition once more, satisfied that they were appropriately wasting away, he glided in the form of shadows to the Groundskeeper's side. "Progress?"

"Slow," the Groundskeeper replied. He fussed with bottles and brooms along the corridor strewn with ash.

"Steady," Darkness said. "And keep undoing the seals. Be. Quick."

The Groundskeeper nodded, groveling. Once the telling shadows disappeared, his singsong voice, a mixture of every lower-class accent throughout the far-flung reaches of all empires, echoed out: "Lucy-Ducy wore a nice dress. Lucy-Ducy made a great mess." He carefully swept up the ashes, pausing at points to fill a number of glass jars using a garden trowel. He chanted at the piles of dust, "All the king's sweepers and all Ducy's ash, still will put Ducy together at last—"

A breeze swirled by, followed by a pack of wild spirits, and ashes tumbled away. The hollow-faced gentleman gave a pitiful howl and scrambled to catch the fleeing specks. The same spirits tore screaming down another corridor, inciting all those around them to lift up in banshee wails, and the Groundskeeper clapped his hands over his head in frustration, wiping his brow with his coat sleeve. "Why did this have to happen, my sweet Dussa-Do? Oh, look at you, you're all around me." He sighed and let loose a strange yearning sound. "Ashes, ashes, we all fall down!"

He fell to his knees, scattering the remains of his charge about him, picking up fistfuls of dust and massaging them with greedy hands. It was everything he could do to not roll about in the pieces. His breathing grew labored before his mottled eyes closed with shame and he released his hold. He hung his head and began to weep. Locks of black and gold hair spilled from his tattered seaman's cap over drawn features almost too dirty to be seen. "If I can put you together again, you'll tell me who did this to you. And you'll turn such eyes to them! But for now, I'll touch every piece of you. I'll track down every last speck. And when we put you together again, you'll turn such eyes, you will!"

He jumped up and tore off down a diagonal corridor. "West, east, north, south, another seal, another seal!" He sighed, putting his hand to his throat where the attack of his master still smarted. "So much work before war!"

HER OFFICE DOOR FLEW OPEN, SCATTERING PAPERS EVERYWHERE. "Alexi," Rebecca groused, "will you ever—?"

"Knock? You may yet teach me one day."

"A man about to be married ought to have better manners."

"Ah, but isn't there something devilishly charming about one who commands a room as he pleases? I do believe my betrothed is quite taken with the quality." Alexi smiled haughtily.

"Ask her after you've startled her in her boudoir once too often. It may grow tedious."

"Until then—"

"You shall remain a brute; yes, indeed. Now. What is to be done with your . . . fiancée?"

Alexi took the seat opposite. "We ought to have a linguistic department, considering Percy's uncanny ability with language. Athens could draw additional income from literary translation, fund a scholarship for women. She'd like that. She'll need an office. Perhaps eighty Apollo Hall."

"Alexi, language is a humanity. Her place would be in *this* hall, not yours. You mustn't make it entirely obvious how close at hand you'd like your young wife."

Alexi raised an eyebrow. "Right, then. Well, the Bay Room . . ."

Rebecca raised a hand. "It's haunted."

Alexi goggled. "And that should bother her?"

Pursing her lips, Rebecca moved to a cabinet of files. She withdrew a small folder and sat at her desk. "Some record should exist about shifting Miss Parker from student to faculty." Her brow furrowed as she opened Percy's file. "Oh. I forgot about this." She removed an envelope, the script upon which read: *Upon Miss P. Parker's completion of study or other emancipation.* It had been sent with the reverend mother's request for Percy's enrollment. Rebecca opened the letter and read aloud:

Dear Miss Thompson,

I trust you will understand the delicate nature of this missive and will share it with Miss Parker only when you deem it appropriate. Her mother died just after birth. I never mentioned a grave, but one does exist—in York. Miss Parker knows nothing of it, for it remains an unsettling sight.

I tremble as even I write this, but if there is any man who takes pity upon the poor girl, may he escort her hence to retrieve what was left there. This must sound nothing short of unholy, but I have prayed upon this matter so long I think it best to share it with you and have you appoint someone of upstanding mettle for the task.

I kept silent for fear of casting further pall over Miss Parker's already trying existence. She wants desperately to attend school; I couldn't overshadow her adventure thus. I hope you kept her at Athens as long as you were able. Convent walls were not meant for her spirit, one meant never to be contained, not even in praise of our Lord.

If you have concerns, please contact me. The location of the grave is known here at the convent, should you never speak with me directly. I apologize for the mysterious circumstances surrounding our dear girl, but they have always been the cloak about her white shoulders. It is not her fault she was born odd. I would it were otherwise.

Sincerely,
Reverend Mother Madeliena Theresa

Alexi examined the paper. "That answers the question of where to reserve a honeymoon cottage." He smiled and did not notice the fleeting flash of agony that passed over his friend's face. "I'll take her east. To the sea. Then inland to York." He rose. "May I leave the arrangements of the Bay Room to you, as I have countless other preparations to make? May I borrow Frederic to send missives?"

Rebecca nodded. After he gave thanks, the door closed behind him. She lifted hands to her forehead, wishing everything were otherwise.

ISABEL CAME BUSTLING INTO THE SITTING ROOM, A SILVER TRAY IN hand, and Alexandra Rychman looked up from her sewing to evaluate its contents: a small white card with rolling script. "Michael Carroll, ma'am. He apologizes for any inconvenience, but extends an invitation. He says it has to do with your brother."

"Show him in."

Alexandra, her features as striking as those of her younger brother, rolled her wheelchair from her sewing table and toward the threshold, smoothing the folds of her black taffeta dress. She loved visitors—few though she saw—and more so, any news of her brother.

Isabel led a broad-shouldered man with unruly pepper gray hair into the sitting room. He heralded sunshine, as if his very presence could cause a shift in seasons. No one could linger in winter near his cozy hearth.

"Miss Rychman!" He bounded toward her, taking her outstretched hand and kissing it. "Do you remember me? It's been years since."

"You're part of Alexi's little . . . clique."

"A founding member, yes, indeed." Michael chortled. "You're looking well, Miss Rychman, if I may say. And I hope you're feeling up for a bit of an adventure?"

Alexandra smiled. "Who *wouldn't*?"

Michael grinned and patted the nearby sofa in a gesture of triumph. "I ask myself that question daily!"

"Well, then?"

"Your brother has instructed me to bring you to London."

Alexandra's eyes sparkled. "Has he now? And what on earth is the occasion?"

Michael beamed. "Why—he's getting married!"

* * *

PERCY FABRICATED A CONVINCING ENOUGH STORY OF THE NIGHT PRIOR
and so distracted Marianna with titillating details of Alexi's first kiss
that possible gaps in the plot were entirely forgotten.

"You'll have an *estate*," Marianna murmured. "Is it far?"

"I shan't be closeted away. I'm to stay at Athens in some capacity. He
promised. Though his home isn't far, and I want you to visit."

"Oh. Good then." Marianna brightened. "I've been trying to be so
happy for you while ignoring how terribly sad I am at the thought of you
going away."

"You have Edward."

"While I love him desperately, he's no replacement for your company."

Percy was moved. "Those are the sweetest words anyone has ever—"

"I doubt that," Marianna interrupted, grinning. "Surely you've heard
sweeter things of late. From Professor Rychman, of all people. It does
amaze. He's so cold . . . until he looks at you."

"I know, it's very disconcerting. Isn't it wonderful?"

Footsteps sounded behind them. The dormitory chaperone, Miss
Jennings, a squat, unpleasant, mousy-haired woman, stood over them
looking terribly uncomfortable. "Miss Parker . . . a . . . gentleman is at
the door for you."

"A particular gentleman, Miss Jennings?" Percy asked.

"Er, yes. Professor Rychman, miss. But why a professor would be
calling on a student in the evening—"

"Ah, yes, my fiancé. Thank you kindly, I was expecting him."

The surprise turning to horror upon the woman's face was worth a
fortune, and Marianna masked a guffaw by sputtering into her teacup.
Percy threw her thick cloak about her shoulders, kissed Marianna's
forehead, and graciously swept past the chaperone, running to open the
door to her striking beloved.

He'd replaced his tattered clothes with a new, elegantly tailored
black frock coat and pressed trousers, as well as a fresh crimson cravat
and charcoal waistcoat. His mop of black hair was carefully combed
and his arms were clasped behind his back. "Good evening," he murmured, presenting a cluster of roses. He shot a disdainful glance at
Miss Jennings, who scowled from the doorway but quickly disappeared.

Percy gasped. "How beautiful," she murmured, taking them in her arms and allowing their perfume to wash over her. "Thank you."

"As we were not afforded a proper courtship, I thought there ought to be a few niceties somewhere in the midst of our mad affair. Come, take my arm, dear girl, there's something we must do."

"Of course." Percy slid her arm into his.

Roses on one arm, Alexi on the other, Percy felt like a princess as they entered Apollo Hall and ascended to his office. "A tutorial, at this hour, *Professor*?" she asked. He was, at times, an unpredictable man, a quality that had its delights.

Alexi gave her a scorching look. "Of sorts," he purred.

He swept her into his vast office teeming with books and fine furnishings and closed the door behind him. Percy raised her eyebrow at the sound of the clicking lock. He plucked the roses from her arms, tossed them on a nearby bookshelf, and waved his hand to set a fire roaring in the fireplace and his otherwise bare desk's candelabra ablaze. Then, scooping Percy into his arms, he carried her behind the desk and sat her upon it. She stared with wide eyes, her breath short and her body afire, though a corner of her mind wondered at the suspiciously clean marble surface.

He loomed, placing one hand on either side of her, and leaned in. "You see, my dear Miss Parker," he began in a businesslike tone edged with a growl. He pressed his forehead to hers. "Until I indulge one or two of the fantasies that began to accost me when you first came to call, I'll never again find this room the haven of academic productivity it once was. I'll be driven entirely to distraction unless I purge a few less-than-scholarly impulses from my blood."

All Percy could manage was an odd, gleeful sound that became a gasp when he descended upon her with a rain of kisses, his teeth fumbling at the lace around her throat, his hands pawing past layers of skirts to gain purchase against her flesh as he laid her back upon the desk's wide top. "At last," he murmured, "the insurmountable barrier between us lies in ruin."

"Indeed. And shall I, too, soon lie in ruin?" Percy asked, not bothering to choose between a nervous or lustful tone since she felt both so strongly.

Alexi pursed his lips, staring down at her in consternation. "No, darling, I'll give you the courtesy of a proper bed. I maintain you wed a gentleman. I did, after all, control myself during our lessons here. For the most part."

"There was that kiss." Percy giggled. "You threw me against the bookshelf."

"Ah, yes, there was that." He smirked. "How did that go, again?" He lifted and spun her. Her breath fled as he pressed her against the shelves for reenactment.

"Yes, that was it," she finally gasped, as he carried her again to the desk. "Alexi, were you really thinking such things during our tutorials? You seemed so cold!"

"I began to unhinge the moment I demanded you reveal yourself, the moment you removed your scarf, your gloves, your glasses, all your shrouds, and stood bravely before me, diamond blue eyes piercing my soul."

Percy frowned. "You looked at me in surprise then."

Alexi leaned closer. "You were a revelation."

Tears rimmed her eyes and she looked away, terrified that when he saw the whole of her on their wedding night—her whole, ghostly, naked flesh—he would be repulsed. She pulled him near, a hungry kiss to stave off her fear.

Alexi eventually pulled back, adjusting his clothes, his breathing ragged. "Do put yourself back together, darling. Seeing you all disheveled threatens to take the gentleman right out of me. Pull your cloak tight, dear, I see I've mauled your sleeve."

"Miss Jennings will call the police." Percy chuckled, rising to sit.

He helped her to her feet, cinching her cloak. "Tomorrow you shall be mine," he promised softly. Thrills worked up Percy's spine.

"Who will marry us?"

"Michael. He's clergy, after all. Church of England. Do you mind terribly that he's not Catholic?"

"Just don't tell Reverend Mother."

Leading her to the threshold, Alexi swept his lips against her ear. "Thank you for this indulgence." When Percy brought his hand to her lips and kissed the center of his palm, he growled, his fingertips dragging along her cheek. "You can't possibly know how I need you."

"Oh, I've some idea," she replied.

A tearing sound drew them from their clutch. They turned to the center of the room to find a large, open black rectangle before them, a door much like the portal Percy had opened at the Van Cortland residence. In an instant, blue fire leaped from Alexi's hands. Percy still marveled at the sight. He approached the portal. Nothing came out. There was no immediate sound, other than water, but as they inched closer, Percy heard it: distant screaming. And the chant that chilled Percy's blood.

"Lucy-Ducy wore a nice dress, Lucy-Ducy made a great mess . . ."

"Percy, stay back."

Percy moved behind Alexi but was unable to keep from poking her head around his arm to see. Deep in the darkness, a thick cluster of shadows moved. A flash of red eyes in the distance triggered instinctual panic within her. Percy clamped down on a scream and felt something sizzle upon her body. As her fists balled, the door snapped shut, and Percy's eyes were drawn to her chest, where the phoenix pendant flared red against her body's glowing white. Alexi turned, his eyes wide.

"Well . . ." Percy murmured, watching her light fade as the door closed. "It seems I've no control of when portals open, but Michael must be right: Whatever woke in me now reacts to danger. Did you see those eyes?"

"What?" he asked.

"The red eyes. You didn't see them?"

"No."

"Oh." Percy's stomach churned. She recognized those eyes from her vision of the cave, just before Phoenix burned. Oh, God, if something were to happen to Alexi . . . The very thought sent her into a furious, righteous rage, and it was only Alexi's surprise that alerted her she was radiant once again.

"Percy!"

"Oh." She looked down at her sternum, where a ball of white light again gathered. It dimmed. "See, it's defensive. I was just worrying about something happening to you, and it must have triggered my . . . light. Tell me you've some scientific term to offer, I sound utterly daft."

Alexi shook his head.

"It's comforting, I suppose," she said with a little smile, "that I have a defense."

Her beloved scowled. "Perhaps, but I don't like doors simply opening without warning or cause. Particularly not in our intimate moments. And whose were those red eyes?"

"I . . . couldn't be sure," Percy said, daring not to voice her supposition, shoving panic aside. She fully intended to revel in the throes of love, not anxiety. "Now, where were we?" She moved to kiss Alexi with such passion that he had to draw back lest her innocence truly be stripped.

Staring up at him, a random thought suddenly struck Percy, and she cocked her head. "If I'm indeed some part of the goddess Persephone, for I'm no *actual* deity, shouldn't I have warranted another name? Mine isn't very clever at all, then, is it? Rather obvious, really."

Alexi pursed his lips. "Perhaps to jog some ancient memory. None of us were clever about this to begin with."

"Yet we found each other in the end."

Alexi touched her cheek. "Thank heavens."

Escorting her back to Athene Hall, he murmured at her doorstep, "Until tomorrow, my darling. Try to rest."

"You do the same," she replied.

"I'll do my best," Alexi replied unconvincingly. They did not seem able to release hands, lingering until their reverie was broken by the front door being thrown wide.

"Now, I do not care if you two are engaged or not, Professor Rychman," Miss Jennings scoffed, her face flushed and pinched, "but I'll not have such an example set on my front steps. Oh, the shame! You'll have the whole faculty thinking they could have a wife of a student whenever they please."

"Calm yourself," Alexi began mildly. "Miss Parker was sent to me by Fate, you ungrateful commoner. I shall mate Prophecy, Miss Jennings. Miss Parker's a goddess of a girl, fit to make my wife, and I will do with her as I please."

Percy gasped, staring up at Alexi. His eyes, blazing with cerulean fire, mesmerized the chaperone before he turned to Percy and said, "I've always wanted to tell the truth. She won't remember a word and it felt lovely to say. Now, then." He indulged a languorous, wholly uncivil kiss, then ushered two dazed females back into the hall.

Left at last in her room, Percy stared out her window at passing spirits, their luminescent forms seemingly just as glad as she that talented workmen made damage done during the last horrible storm appear never to have happened. The ghosts bade her rest, but her eyes settled instead upon a hanging still life, a ripe pomegranate at its center. She'd turned the painting to the wall when she first arrived at Athens and didn't remember turning it back. Not wishing to destroy Athens's property but determined to rid her room of the piece, she carried the painting down the hall to a small, underutilized communal reading room. She placed the small canvas on a shelf and walked away, needing no reminder of that mythological fruit, which once bound a goddess to an underworld fate.

BEATRICE FOLLOWED THE GROUNDSKEEPER TO THE SEALS, KEEPING to the shadows, unnoticed. It was easy, considering the Whisper-world was a hissing, echoing, miserable labyrinth.

She watched as he turned each stone pin, heaving at them with great strain. This particular seal was a gritty, moist cylinder, hardly distinguishable from other rock but for the small trickle of blood that poured forth when the Groundskeeper shoved it. When opened, the fissure would leak the miasma of death into a fixed point in the mortal realm. After a pin was loosened, the Groundskeeper always ambled back to reconstruct his love. The work of opening the seals was coming along; Beatrice followed behind to reroute it.

Beatrice moved to the stone, keeping her boots clear of pooling crimson. She thought of the faltering goddess, her divinity rotting and withering under the fist of Darkness, how the form she bore had bled as she laid down the foundations for Beatrice to now finish, coupling hers and her lover's energy toward their goal. Perhaps this pool was her blood, refusing to dry. A relic.

She pressed the locket. Hallowed Phoenix fire sparkled in her hand, leaped onto and nestled in the wet stone, kissing the blood dry, creating a pulsing rectangle of possibility where before was only rough stone and the sour air of danger: The portal was rerouted to familiar, friendly bricks.

Beatrice took a deep breath. The current Guard . . . It wasn't that she didn't trust them, but when she'd broken into their breakfast and examined them, the table was rife with obstacles; she saw mortal frailty clouding each and every gaze. Every one of them ached for something, was unsettled by something, felt guilty, trapped, unappreciated, or unrequited. How keenly she felt their flaws.

Prophecy balanced on the edge of a knife and there was no divinity to ease her mind; that divinity died when the goddess gave herself to the world. The blue fire now held in her hand, this fractal remnant of Phoenix, was all that remained for Beatrice. It would take her someplace new, the next phase of her quest.

She missed Ibrahim, her Guard, sweet Iris Parker, the young mother who had been her charge, dead before she could appreciate her unique baby. And to Beatrice's surprise, she also missed that maddening goddess. Though she was a woman skeptical of prayer, Beatrice needed divinity, and she'd continue to do her best to make sure divinity needed them, too.

CHAPTER
SIX

THE STUNNING LIGHT OF MORNING WAS JOLTING. THE DAY WOULD eventually bring the night, and Percy thrilled with desire and trepidation. She knew nothing of intimacy, save the kisses and caresses Alexi had shared. A new education awaited.

She glided downstairs to the dining room, where an urn of hot water was kept for the restless or studious. Readying a cup of tea, she chose the spiced blend, for it reminded her of the scent of Alexi: clove and leather-bound books.

A rustle behind her proved to be Marianna, her eyes a bit groggy but her excitement palpable. "And how doth the bride-to-be?"

"Nervous."

"Of course. May Edward come?"

"Of course."

The girls sipped their tea, took hands and silently watched the sunrise. Only a hasty tread behind them eventually roused their comfortable quiet: the disdainful Miss Jennings, again with news. "Miss Parker. More company for you. Two French ladies." She grimaced. "Bearing a rather large box."

"Oh, do let them in." Percy turned to Marianna. "I believe it's my wedding dress!"

The two girls hurried to the door, where they found Josephine and a tiny woman whose black curls alone could be seen through the window. "Hello, Percy dear," Josephine called as they entered. "This is Madame Sue, a sorceress of the trade."

Percy made introductions to Marianna as the group moved upstairs and into her room. Madame Sue streaming fabrics dramatically from her own apparel.

"And how do you know Percy, Mademoiselle Belledoux?" Marianna asked, clearly admiring Josephine's gown.

"I'm a friend of the professor"—Josephine smiled—"and thus, of Miss Percy."

"And I am the hired help," Madame Sue volunteered, adjusting the corsage of pearl-tipped straight pins stuck to the lapel of her sweeping robe.

"The best seamstress on the isle, I tell you," Josephine said.

The box safely upon Percy's bed, Madame Sue did the honors. Everyone, save Madame, gasped. Inside the box lay the most beautiful assemblage of light-blue satin, lace, and sparkling silver thread that modern fashion could imagine. Percy lovingly scooped up the thickly corseted bodice. The plunging neckline was lined across the bosom with thin, starched lace and silver-and-seed-pearl-embroidered ivy. Out tumbled three-quarter sleeves from which lengthening layers of pale blue lace fell in bells. Full skirts were doubled and cinched with a pearl-strung cord. A curl of satin had been arranged at the small of the back, like a rose, which bustled the train before sweeping downward.

"Oh, madame," Percy breathed. Marianna's hand would not leave her mouth.

"Pleased?"

"More than I can possibly express. You are an exquisite talent."

"Thank you. Step in, let us make sure it fits. I adjust, then I sleep."

"I'm terribly sorry for the rush, madame," Percy said.

"No matter, people must marry when the fit seizes them, I suppose. You aren't expecting, are you?"

"No!" Percy cried, blushing as she was helped into the dress.

"Good." Madame yanked hard upon the corset strings, and Percy felt her ribs bend and her breath fly. "Ah. Fits well, this."

"Indeed," Percy squeaked, her already slender waist further tapered and her curves made voluptuous.

Madame disappeared somewhere behind the bustle and made a few adjustments. Reemerging with a small pair of scissors, she flitted about clipping threads, stood back and clapped her hands. *"Finis."*

"Madame!" Percy could not stop staring. "How can I thank you? Do stay for the wedding!"

"No. Weddings make me anxious. Promise me only that you will come by and let me experiment with your white face in other colors. And bring that eerie man of yours. I see him always in black. I make him a cloak of bright orange."

Everyone laughed before Josephine said, "Percy, I'll return for you at half past. I must go make sure Alexi's kept his head and the chapel is presentable. *Oui. Allons-y*, Madame." The two women then disappeared in rustles of fabric and French mutterings that Percy understood as Madame Sue's surprise that such a sweet, pleasant girl was to marry such a brooding man.

Percy and Marianna simply stared at each other.

"Marianna, I cannot believe this is happening."

"Nor can I. Most certainly not after your first quarter!"

They giggled. It was rather sudden, but Percy wasn't at liberty to explain.

Josephine entered Alexi's office to find him pacing. "Alexi."

"Hmm?"

"Has your suit arrived?"

"What? Suit? Oh, yes. Just now."

"May I see?"

Alexi pointed to the alcove where a long, exquisite suit coat hung beside a silk cravat of pale blue.

"Oh, Alexi, how lovely—and you even got the blue correct!"

"Give me a bit of credit."

"Constant black aside, you're always well appointed, yet I'm impressed. Now, you'd better—Alexi!"

"Yes?"

"Stop pacing, you're driving me mad."

Alexi moved to his desk and sat with unusual obedience that could only come from distraction. "What were you about to tell me?"

"Dress yourself. You never know what strange delays may occur. You had better tune the chapel, too. Heaven only knows what might erupt."

"Ah, yes. I suppose none of us has any idea." He tapped a quill incessantly upon the desk. Josephine had never seen him fidget.

"Alexi, I am sure this must be overwhelming for you."

"Yes." His low voice was slightly strained. "It is, a bit."

"You needn't be nervous. Besides that this has been foretold nearly all our lives, I daresay you can do no wrong. The girl's absolutely mad for you."

Alexi stared straight into Josephine's eyes, and then she saw the strangest of all sights, a foreign image to which they would all have to grow accustomed: his wide and genuine smile. "Yes. She is, isn't she?"

Josephine returned his smile and masked the ache within.

JANE WAS CLAD IN HER FINEST DRESS, STILL RELATIVELY PLAIN BUT IT would have to do. She found the headmistress staring out her office window, Frederic upon the inner sill, absently stroking his feathers. Wearing a bit more color than her usual custom, Rebecca was quite smartly dressed in a fitted purple jacket and mauve skirts. A cameo at her throat, lace cascading between the double-breasted folds of her jacket, it was clear she had taken great care.

"Good morning, m'dear," Jane said at the open office door. "You look stunning."

"Hello, Jane." Rebecca beckoned her in, her smile strained. "May I offer you tea?" She placed Frederic outside the window with a piece of bread and closed the casement.

Cup in hand, Jane asked, "Has he been by at all this morning?"

"No. That's best, isn't it?" Rebecca's gaze was particularly sharp.

"It will grow easier. We've had such a shock. We all must mend. But she's a sweet, dear presence—"

"Of course she is," Rebecca snapped. "And I will care for her, as we all must. I trust you to leave me to that; trust me in that."

"I didn't mean to suggest otherwise."

"I knew that none of this would be easy," Rebecca murmured, and a strained pause followed. "Only, I wish he wouldn't have—"

"What?"

"I shouldn't speak of it."

"To me, you may."

Rebecca looked up, surprised. Her friend wasn't one to speak volumes or make overtures; she had always been detached, and Rebecca loved her for it. This admission could be made to no one else: "When Alexi first admitted feelings for Miss Parker, I . . . pressed him on it, made my own confession, like a fool. He told me if we'd been born to another fate that he might have made me his wife." Bitterness drew down the corner of her lips.

Jane granted the statement a necessary, gracious few moments. "And I'm sure he meant it. He cares for you. You're close—"

"*Were* close," Rebecca muttered. "I cannot imagine the tenor of our acquaintance will continue."

"Of course it will; don't be absurd. There is no threat imposed upon the betrothed by your presence. You are Alexi's dearest friend."

"He has a new confidante."

"We all do. I have this strange feeling she'll take all our confessions before the year is through," Jane stated. "I'm sure she'll know my secrets soon."

"Your secrets, Jane?"

Her friend grinned. "Certainly. But, Rebecca, think of it: You've always been in Alexi's shadow, the both of you scowling away the hours. Now you must come into your own. You're too powerful to allow this to weaken you. You've had years to prepare."

Rebecca exhaled a long breath. "I'm glad you came this morning, Jane. Thank you. I suppose we'd better survey the chapel. Surely Josephine has thoughts on the arrangements."

"I must confess," Jane murmured, "I am looking forward to the few days Our Lord and Master will be out of town."

Rebecca raised an eyebrow, and saw a most mischievous light in her friend's green eyes. "Why do you say such a thing, Miss O'Shannon Connor?"

Jane escorted Rebecca out the door with a mysterious smile. "A bit of work to be done, Headmistress."

The chapel was a small white wonder of light and warmth, the stained-glass angels ablaze from within. Rebecca and Jane found Josephine in a flurry of movement, singing a French ballad and telling Elijah where to place several bouquets far larger than his head. Lord Withersby followed orders, grumbling and sneezing as she said a few pointed words about weddings.

"I don't suppose you'd like to do this madwoman's bidding, would you?" he asked pathetically at the door.

"No, watching you is far more entertaining," Jane replied.

Michael emerged from the sacristy in a white robe and a cleric's collar, a Bible in his hands. Rebecca moved down the aisle and declared, "Well, aren't you the picture of priestliness, Vicar Carroll."

He chuckled, flushing, opening his arms to gaze down at himself. "We ought to have some measure of formality and godliness, shouldn't we?" He flashed his winning smile.

"With Elijah Withersby present in a chapel?" Josephine called, having disappeared behind the altar. "We must take all precautions."

"A stroke of lightning might as easily smite you, my darling," Elijah called from behind an armful of lilies.

Josephine reemerged, candles in her hands. "Please elucidate, Lord Withersby. Do."

Elijah balked.

"Might we set discussion of sin aside for the moment, for Miss Percy's sake?" Michael begged wearily.

Every sill bore a candle and every pedestal a bouquet of lilies, the scent pervasive and welcoming. Once all was in place, as if on cue the chapel door was flung open and all candles burst immediately into flame. Alexi strode down the aisle, more compelling than ever, particularly elegant in his wedding attire. His hair was as neat as could be and his eyes were particularly stirring. When his companions remembered to breathe, they greeted him warmly.

"The man of the hour," Elijah said with good cheer and a sneeze.

"Hello, my friends." Alexi eyed the chapel. "Marvelous. Simply marvelous. Thank you." He offered Rebecca a lingering glance. She returned it with a smile. Jane squeezed her hand in silent encouragement.

"While you tune, Alexi, I'll be off to prepare your bride," Josephine said, and she darted down the aisle, shimmering in rustling golden taffeta. Elijah could not help but watch. When he saw Jane smirking at him from the pew across the aisle, he scowled.

Alexi drew a meaningful relic from his breast pocket—a thick, pale feather—and, with the powerful grace unique to him, moved to each window and tapped its stained-glass angel. Each glass seemed to vibrate, a soft hum rose, an invisible choir: The chapel would now allow no unwanted visitors.

Michael had disappeared but returned, opening wide the door for a woman in dark green. She advanced her wheelchair into the aisle, and

Alexi darted forward, sweeping his sister up in his arms and carrying her up the aisle to seat her in a front pew. "Alexandra, my dear!"

The woman observed the room with wonder, knowing there was something inexplicable, craning her neck as if to hear with better ears. "What news, and so sudden!" she exclaimed. "You made no hint of it a few days past, when the two of you visited. Surely this surprised Miss Percy as much as I!"

"Yes, indeed. But it couldn't be helped," Alexi replied, his eyes glittering. "I'm very glad you're here."

"I wouldn't miss it for the world."

Alexi kissed his sister upon the temple and took her hand, sitting to anxiously await his bride. He noticed his favorite librarian, Miss Mina Wilberforce, duck into the chapel; her amazed smile a bright white flash against dark brown skin. She'd long ago curried his favor by boldly having taken on the name of an emancipator rather than a master, and by proving she knew every book in the Athens catalogue. He hadn't thought to invite her, so he supposed Percy must have, of which he was frightfully glad. He had a host of friends here after all, to share in his sudden happiness.

Michael gestured to Jane, who fumbled beneath her pew for a fiddle and moved to sit with it in a chair at the altar.

"Ah, good. Music," Alexi stated.

MARIANNA OPENED THE DOOR TO JOSEPHINE, WHO FOUND PERCY sitting wide-eyed upon her bed as if she had not blinked in an hour. The German girl had swept up Percy's hair into artful spirals.

"Come, dear, it's nearly time." Josephine rustled in the garment box to reveal a pearl tiara, set with blue glass flowers, and a veil of pale blue. Percy gasped, as if it were the final touch of absolute reality. "Yes, my dear, he really is going to marry you," the Frenchwoman promised softly. "He really is." Marianna was quiet but smiled.

The train hooked and the crowning veil set, Percy stared in the mirror and her eyes watered. She had applied just the faintest hint of rouge to her cheeks and lips, and had lined her white eyelids with the thinnest gray, which caused the ice blue slivers of her irises to jump forth. Feeling beautiful, she plucked her phoenix pendant out to hang not against her skin but proudly in the open, a mark of the fate-forged bond of long ago.

The journey across the Athens courtyard was a spectacle of whispers and gaping mouths. Josephine and Marianna looked like proud family, escorting her. Percy could hear faint strains of a stringed instrument from inside the chapel, and fainter still, the ghostly trace of what she could only liken to an angelic choir.

If the Guard wondered why none of the harmless, gamesome spirits of Athens had wafted into the chapel, it was because they were all clustered at the outside door, awaiting the bride. A living gentleman stood among them, a handsome youth with wild, curly hair and a dimpled grin, blissfully unaware of the floating dead nearby.

"Oh, Percy, you are incredible!" said Edward Page, the young lad smitten with Marianna, who slid her arm onto his with unconscious ease. "Congratulations! As surprising as this is, congratulations on this most auspicious day!"

"Go on, you two." As Percy stepped away from view, Josephine ushered the young couple through the doors. Marianna turned to blow her friend a kiss, and they shared a familiar giggle—the last of their maidenhood.

There was a box at the door, and Josephine opened it to place a cluster of perfect white lilies wrapped in blue satin in Percy's trembling hands. Percy smiled at the bouquet, and at the misty-eyed Josephine, before returning her attention to the dead who'd come to see her wed.

"Leave this to us, Percy," said the boy with the soft brogue who usually kept to the main foyer chandelier. "We know you've no father to give you away, and so we wish to walk you down the aisle."

"Thank you all," Percy murmured, her eyes glimmering with tears. "That's very kind of you." She turned to Josephine. "You may go on, thank you. The spirits wish to present me." The Frenchwoman sighed in appreciation and slipped into the chapel.

The spirits encircled Percy. While she felt the air around her grow freezing, she was lost in the excitement on their faces. Their entire spectral strength amassed, they were just able to manipulate the door. Percy came into full view and those waiting inside were rendered breathless. A ghostly radiant goddess, she moved forward, floating in a loving and spectral procession to the haunting sound of Jane's strings.

Percy and Alexi were stunned by the sight of each other, overwhelmed by the magnetism that seized their hearts. He stood awaiting her at the base of the altar. Energy surged between them as they took hands. Percy took her place opposite him and, to her, the rest of the chapel disappeared.

They did not hear Michael's Bible verses; they heard only the beat of each other's hearts. They responded to the liturgy and made their vows, but it was as if their lips had not moved; they were each drowning deliriously in the sea of the other. They exchanged simple silver bands, and the gentle pressure of sliding rings onto each other's fingers was an inimitable delight.

When pronounced man and wife, Alexi lifted the veil to kiss her and she fell against him. Their kiss was of such fusion that they felt the ground tremble. The slight sound of angels grew into a bursting chorus. Rising from the candles and met by an aura of light from their bodies, white flame began to pool, merge, and expand into a hazy, egglike form that grew as their kiss sustained. As it ended, the form burst into a great, bird-shaped sun. The avian form threw open expansive wings, and a wave of heat and deafening music blew through the chapel.

The Guard cried out. A phoenix bathed in light, rising from the indomitable love within two mortal hearts—this was raw, divine power, their purpose and origin made manifest. Marianna and Edward squealed. Mina Wilberforce's hands went to her face. Alexandra gaped, tears streaming down her cheeks. Many of the attendant ghosts breathed sighs and vanished, at last sent to their rest.

Elijah turned to Marianna, Edward, and Mina. He pointed a finger toward each set of eyes. "As beautiful as this is," he began nonchalantly, "I'm terribly sorry, we'll have to pretend it never happened." Their gazes clouded, and soon only selective memories of a more mundane nature remained.

When Withersby turned toward Alexandra, Alexi stopped him. "No, Elijah. Let my sister keep this sight."

Alexandra eyed her brother with deepening wonder. "Thank you," she murmured.

"Are we married now?" Percy breathed, amazed by the blue-colored flame wreathing her beloved's eyes and her own. A thin line of the same traced the Guard's hearts, each to the other, a cord of light binding them fast. The phoenix pendant was a tiny sun around Percy's neck.

"By the gods themselves, it would seem," Alexi replied.

The couple walked down the aisle, arm in arm, unable to take their eyes from each other. Jane broke into a jig, and the assembled company bounced out of the chapel, Rebecca taking care to wheel Alexandra to safety as everyone embraced. Jane was lost to her music, a new spirit floating behind her. Aodhan's hard, deeply masculine features wore affection, and his ghostly hand hovered just above her shoulder. Beside him floated Beatrice Tipton.

Beatrice's expression was almost threatening. Her voice was kinder. "Go on, my lady," she said to Percy. "Enjoy what you've worked so very long to attain. Enjoy your mortal love and a bit of celebration. There's time soon enough for the rest. But please take care. Remember all I've said."

Percy swallowed and nodded. She turned to behold Alexi, who was ignorant of all but her. She delighted in his thirsty gaze before turning back to find Beatrice and Aodhan gone.

Michael, unable to contain his overflowing heart, swept Rebecca into the dance. She at first refused, but it was impossible to deny his joy for long and so she acquiesced with a chuckling sigh. It was Josephine's giggle that alerted them all to the host of gawking professors and students eyeing their dancing headmistress and their most mysterious, brooding professor, clearly wedded to and infatuated with their strangest student. Rebecca simply laughed; there was nothing else to be done. Jane continued to play, relocating beside Alexandra, who from her wheelchair watched as if the world had been made far more beautiful.

Alexi kissed Percy's hands and moved to kneel at his sister's side. "There is an ancient magic within us, Alexandra. I've never wished to keep secrets from you—"

She placed her hand on Alexi's shoulder and shook her head. "Thank you for what you allowed me to see. Oh, Percy. Goodness—Mrs. Rychman." Alexandra beamed as Percy knelt at her feet in rustling pool of blue satin. "You look incredible. The both of you . . . Alexi, what on earth made you finally allow someone close?"

Alexi tucked Percy's arm in his. "There was no way around this woman's radiance. Now, we must be off. You shall dine at our estate soon. Michael has instructions to escort you home."

"Good, then, brother. Thank you."

Percy jumped up to welcome Mina, who took her ivory hand in her own darker ones, murmuring, "Congratulations, Mrs. Rychman. I never doubted your husband's mind. What I doubted was that he could ever smile. How dear it is that you are the one to unearth such a miracle. Come find me after your honeymoon, I'll give you presents—books!"

Alexi bowed his head. "Hello, Miss Wilberforce, thank you for being a part of this special day."

"No—thank you, Professor, for proving love presses past barriers." The librarian lifted Percy's hand in hers, showcasing the contrast that had brought them together, triumphant. Both ladies were quietly overcome.

"I'm so glad to share this with you, Mina. It's been quite a quarter," Percy whispered.

"I should say."

Headmistress Thompson approached, and Mina stepped aside. Alexi stepped aside, too, watching with feigned disinterest as Rebecca said, "Allow me to congratulate you." She opened her arms, and Percy eagerly stepped into them.

"How can I thank you, Headmistress—?"

"Rebecca."

"Thank you for everything you've done in granting me a home here at Athens, before any of us knew this fate. You have been so kind to me from the first—"

Rebecca looked pained. "No, child, I—"

Percy gushed, undeterred, "I love Athens so deeply. I have a family now, a home, meaning, and suddenly life is glorious. You allowed these blessings to unfold. I am so grateful that you have granted me a place on the staff. Thank you for everything you have done, and will do, for Alexi and me."

The headmistress's face was unreadable, but when Percy took her hands to relinquish her wedding bouquet, Rebecca shook her head and refused. "Oh, no—" But Percy would not accept it back. "Ah, all right then." The woman chuckled, masking unease. "I believe your husband wishes to depart."

"Oh, Percy!" Elijah cried, as Alexi took her by the arm and the glowing couple walked off to cheers. "My dear, beware his Royal Eeriness! Heed my warnings! He has *terrible* designs on you! He'll take you to some desolate place, force you into black robes to recite mathematics!

You know not what you do! O, poor youth, sacrificed on the altar of the Constant Sneer!"

Percy laughed delightedly and turned to her love, who pursed his lips and arched an eyebrow at Elijah. She grinned. "Is that so, husband?"

"Oh, I've designs on you, my dear," he said, fixing her with a smoldering gaze. "Hardly terrible."

Percy shivered in anticipation.

A footman waited atop the front steps of Athens, holding a cloak for Percy; an ivy-bedecked carriage stood below. As the door of the cab closed her inside, Percy lifted the curtain to look back at the crowd. Rebecca's lips were thin, and her color wan; the bouquet hung limply from her hand. Michael was studying her. Elijah was still spouting dire warnings while Josephine pulled affectionately at his arm, begging him to desist. Alexandra was waving. In the portico shadow, Marianna and Edward were stealing a kiss. Aodhan again hovered over Jane. Beatrice seemed to be inspecting the foundations of Athens, tapping at the flagstones in an unsettling manner.

Percy chose to set all concern aside. "Thank you," she murmured to the heavens. "Let me live with this loving, mad family forever. I could never have dreamed such treasures mine."

She turned and reached a hand out the window, aching for her new husband, who was speaking to the driver and sliding tickets into his breast pocket. Alexi climbed in and relaxed across from her, and Percy gave one final wave out the window before the driver had them jostling off to the northeast. A questioning look crossed Percy's face.

"First, I shall take you to the sea. Then on to York, my love," Alexi responded before she could speak.

"How lovely! We'll see Reverend Mother, then?"

"I thought it might be nice to see where you spent your earliest years—but first I've some dreary, eerie nook where I intend to cloister you away and set upon you with black robes and endless theorems."

Percy laughed, her hands reaching for him. He shifted to sit beside her, and she burrowed close. She gasped with a sudden thought. "Are we to take a train, Alexi?"

"Certainly the most efficient way to travel."

"Oh! I've never been on a train!"

Alexi chuckled. "Even our simple adventures will be full of wonder.

You'll make my whole world new." He leaned close to brush her lips with his.

"Careful, Alexi, these hints of romance could ruin Elijah's image of you."

"You'll have tales, indeed. I promise."

The other train passengers stared, of course, at the white-skinned girl dressed like a princess. Percy, however, was so joyful and unaware, their looks grew more captivated than rude. Alexi found his defensive edge softening, for his bride remained wholly unruffled. The only eyes she noticed were his, which he kept fixed upon her. The day's light was so diffuse she was eventually able to stare out the window of their well-appointed car, eagerly watching the English countryside until she dozed on his shoulder.

They disembarked at York at twilight, the last of the sun fading in a final gasp of rich purple. Alexi helped Percy into the carriage procured at the station for the next leg of the journey. Drawing her into his arm, he noticed how the lace around her neck quaked. "Darling, are you cold?"

"No, my dear. Why do you ask?"

"You're shivering. Please tell me you're not frightened."

"What would I be frightened of?" she murmured with a smile. Alexi's awkwardness was not assuaged. "I know you will be gentle with me," she added.

"Of course I will be gentle."

"Though the breadth of our emotions may . . . tax our capacity for restraint."

"So I am not alone in feeling . . ."

"More than a mortal can contain?" Percy finished.

"Precisely." Alexi choked and turned away, hardly able to look at her until, after some time, the carriage pulled up outside a small cottage far from civilization, waves crashing in the distance. Looking like a thrilled schoolboy, he said, "You wait here a moment, I have to make sure everything is as I instructed."

He hopped out of the cab, unlashed a case, and darted up the walk, disappearing into a dark building where a single lamp burned in the window. In the several minutes that followed, Percy bit her lip and forgot to breathe.

She was startled by the carriage door swinging open. Alexi held out his hand for her, bidding the driver bring their remaining cases. The man did so, running ahead to place the bags inside and hurrying back to the carriage so as not to be an unwelcome presence. Percy and Alexi didn't notice him in the slightest; Alexi swept her up in his arms and strode away, carrying her to the cottage.

Her husband placed her just beyond the threshold, in the dark main room, removed her cloak, and made a small gesture with his hand. Countless candles on sills, end tables, mantel, all across the wide bay window that looked out upon the glittering sea burst into spontaneous flame at his command. Percy exclaimed in amazement. Alexi grinned.

Bundles of heather scattered about made the place smell like the rolling heath. Breathing deeply to take in the scent, Percy asked, "Alexi, did you arrange all this? Oh, wait until I tell Lord Withersby, he'll faint!" Alexi merely bowed his head in reply. She ran to the window, where the moon had risen to wash the sea with luminous silver. "Oh, the view!"

Waves crashed against the rocks. The water sparkled with moonlight and reflected flames danced in the windowpanes. A fire roared in the fireplace; the cool room was quickly becoming cozy. Behind Percy, Alexi opened the door to a bedroom and gestured again, igniting fires in a tall hearth and lighting candles all around the fine little room. Percy gasped again—Alexi's inexplicable power over fire a seduction of its own—and followed him into the smaller room.

A four-poster bed was hung with velvet curtains and trimmed with clusters of heather. "When you and I shared that moonlit dance at the academy ball, the floral crown woven into your hair—that scent would not leave my nostrils. I imagined you lying beside me, in a field of it. It was the first time I allowed myself to find you intoxicating. And the scent of it here, now, unlocks everything . . ."

Moving to open a narrow wooden door, he revealed a tiled washroom and a fresh array of candles that sprang to life with a wave of his hand. Steam poured from a copper tub. At the threshold of the bedroom, he gestured and the fires in the main room burned lower, making those in the bedroom all the brighter. He walked to the bed, mostly drawing the curtains, then sat in that opening, at the foot.

Percy was enthralled by the roaring fire reflected in his eyes.

He loosened his cravat, not blinking. "My dear," he purred, and the sound of his voice made her steady herself upon the door frame. "A scented bath awaits you, as does a bit of finery. I'll wait here."

Percy nodded, dazed. "Will you . . . unfasten me?" She turned her back to him and indicated her garment's clasps.

"Yes, love," he whispered.

She felt the lace around her shoulders release. His finger lingered there, tracing her nape and tugging gently on a lock of falling hair. He unclasped her necklace and drew the pendant aside. Bending over her shoulder, he stared at the scar where the pendant had once burned her, a mark of Prophecy, and traced it gently before his finger strayed to the swell of her bosom. Percy's breath hitched.

"That scar has beautiful memories," she murmured, smiling over her shoulder at him. "You kissed me for the first and most glorious time after seeing it. There is pain in this Great Work; I see that. But you are my reward . . ."

"My reward, indeed," he said, shuddering with pleasure to be so near her.

Unhooking an embroidered panel of her dress, his palm slid down the revealed laces of her corset. The ties loosened with his sharp tug, allowing Percy a deep breath. Then Alexi knelt, both hands at the small of her back. He fumbled with the layers of her bustle, opening a space where the thin muslin of her camisole was the only barrier between his fingertips and her flesh. She felt both his hands encircle her waist as he led her back a step.

He bent his head, lifted the bottom edge of her camisole and kissed the bare skin at the small of her back. A sharp breath and accompanying shiver worked up her spine. He unfastened the skirt along her side, one hook and eye after another. The satin hung down, the muslin against her skin fluttering as a small draft tickled the backs of her legs. Percy stood paralyzed, aching to know where his hands would travel next. But he simply took her hands, placed in them the bunched fabric of her skirt and patted her on the rear, sending her lurching forward.

"Oh. Thank you." Percy choked, turning to face him at the washroom, her loose dress starting to slip from her shoulders.

"Do you require further aid?" Alexi rasped, staring at the line of her collarbone.

"I won't be but a moment," she replied, biting her lip.

Shifting her skirts and closing the washroom door, she discovered a sumptuous lace gown hanging upon the back of the door, with ribbon closures from neck to toe. Percy blushed. It was nearly transparent, light blue lace without lining. A note attached to the first ribbon said, *Tie every bow. I have waited all my life for this night, and it must not go quickly.*

Mind hazy and heart pounding, she slipped her wedding dress from her body, hung the layers on a peg, then lifted her muslin undergarments over her head. She stared down at her white flesh and trembled as she stepped into the bathwater. It was lightly scented and perfectly warm, caressing her entire body, but its warmth could not stem her trembles. She drew soap along her arms and legs as everything inside her prickled. In mere moments, it was the right of powerful male hands to trespass every inch of her, and that would be her every pleasure.

She could not stay long in the water. Drying herself, she stared at her new gown. The lace felt incredible against her skin as she slid it on. Her shaking hands had trouble, but she tied each tie and unpinned her snow-white hair, glancing in the mirror to see that her blue-white irises had somehow grown as luminescent as those dark eyes awaiting her just outside. Never in her wildest dreams could she have imagined this scene. She longed to fling open the door and fly at him with passionate joy, but a fear lingered: What if the sight of her—the unmitigated, complete *whiteness* of her flesh—was too much?

There was no turning back. She opened the door.

Alexi gasped. There in the door frame, an angel appeared through misty clouds of steam. Her body was perfectly alabaster, its contours visible beneath the sheen of soft blue, and a waterfall of pearlescent hair tumbled over thin, delicate shoulders. Her eyes gleamed, tiny moons ringed in blue. Her cheeks had gained an even flush, and her pale lips were parted to allow quick, irregular intakes of breath. The shadows of her white skin were nearly the blue of the gown that clung to her thin body, every bow tied. She glided to him as if magnetized. The tips of each candle flame in the room rose, as if wishing a better view.

Alexi had replaced his wedding attire with a black silk robe that buttoned down the chest. He rose now as she moved to him. Their eyes locked, and their shaking hands found each other. Alexi cupped her face and slid an arm around her waist.

"I love you," Percy blurted.

He swept her into his arms, parted the bed curtains and laid her gently down. Her hair was a gleaming mass upon the pillow and blue lace spread about her like a pool of water. He stood there a moment as she gazed up at him, then, slowly, knelt. Billowing black silk slid over pale blue lace. He flicked the bed curtain shut behind him; now only the foot of the bed stood open, revealing the crackling fire.

"Percy," he whispered. "Before words fail us, as I know they will . . ." He lifted her so that she reclined upon his knees. "I need you to know that, Prophecy aside, no matter what divine remnants have taken up in us, I, as a mortal man, am desperate for you. I'd have loved you no matter my fate."

Grateful tears fell from her eyes. "How is it, Alexi, that you know what I crave to hear?"

Alexi smirked. "The benefits of marrying a man of genius. Now, Mrs. Rychman . . ." He slipped the first tie of her gown open at the neck while simultaneously undoing the first button of his robe, and she gasped. "I must kiss you and cease discussion"—another tie fell open—"as my senses flee." And another. Their subsequent kiss was nearly violent. He lowered himself to lie beside her, first pinning her down with a hand upon her shoulder, then scooping her tightly to him. When he at long last drew back, the phantom image of wispy blue wings folding in around Percy caught the corner of his eye, a spirit remnant, perhaps, of the force that guided their work and destiny.

He guided her hand to the buttons of his robe and was patient as her hands shook; he wanted her to do her part. One by one each tie was loosed, each button undone in slow, beautiful torture. A thin line of flesh could be traced down their bodies, but that was not enough. Alexi parted the lace of her gown and it fell to the bed. He took in the full sight of her blinding white, sculpted body. Her eerily breathtaking gaze filled with fearful tears. Those brought forth his own.

"Oh, Percy, don't be frightened," he murmured, a tear falling from his eye to her stomach, causing a tiny shiver.

"M-my love," she stammered. "I'm only frightened you may not like what you see."

Alexi moaned. "How I can convince you that I am *enslaved* by what I see?"

"I . . . suppose you shall show me," Percy replied with meek hope.

"My God, shall I. You are the epitome of beauty."

Slowly, reverently, he ran hands down the length of her colorless body. Percy arched upward with a soft cry. Alexi climbed above her and his robe parted. They stared at each other.

His tall body was well defined with such musculature as would befit a man of letters. Percy's eyes devoured each hard plane and angle. Everything about this man was impressive. Absolutely everything.

Alexi proceeded to prove to Percy that nothing about her unique flesh did anything but excite him, blessing every inch of her trembling skin with lingering, questing, exploratory kisses. In these delicate moments, if there were divine beings housed within them and drawing on ancient passion, Percy could not tell, for she was lost entirely within her own.

When Alexi could no longer bear delay, he joined their bodies with a frisson of pain and cries of pleasure. Their limbs wrapped tighter during the progressing stages of passion, and they only took their eyes from each other when kisses so required. Perhaps, Percy thought deliriously, they did see gods in each other's gazes.

They loved like music: Each touch garnered a soft sound, each shift of a body was underscored by an acute reaction, their breath kept time. The tempo of their connection progressed and relaxed, largo to allegro and again to largo, gasps spurring allegretto. Movements were repeated, a prolonged symphony with digressing interludes and desperate refrains, each with a gradual build. The orchestral duet at last grew too hot for their blood to contain, and the candles and hearth in the room erupted in an explosion of light, mirroring the indescribable ecstasy of the entwined couple before going suddenly out. Shuddering sighs mixed with deep kisses and tears. Percy heard her heart hammering in her ears, and Alexi's heart pounding where she laid her head on his chest, his ragged breath a rough breeze on her neck.

They remained locked together with wide, amazed eyes and clutching hands. Words would only diminish the power of what had just occurred, and so they sealed their good night with a languorous kiss. Alexi held Percy as close as he possibly could, and they drifted into blissful, well-earned sleep.

CHAPTER
SEVEN

BECAUSE OF THE WHISPER-WORLD'S ONGOING CHAOS, THE GROUNDS-keeper did not trust the pieces of his dear one not to be trampled upon, stolen, or digested. For safekeeping he moved her ashes and parts into a makeshift laboratory, a little gardening shed he'd long ago fashioned out of skeletons and gravestones. Upon a stone dais, right in the shed's center, lay a metal coffin. Glass jars, filled with meticulous care, lined a shelf just above his head, labeled for fingers, toes, elbows, breasts . . .

"Piece by piece, love," he murmured.

To his great pleasure, at times the ash would seem to scream and roar, proving there was fight in his lady yet. He was off to unfasten another seal, but he would return soon.

WITH THE GOOD PROFESSOR ABSENT FOR AN UNPRECEDENTED FEW days, the remaining Guard felt giddily unsupervised. This sense of wanton freedom manifested itself in each in very different ways.

Elijah Withersby made it very clear to Josephine Belledoux that she was to draw every shade and lock every door in Café La Belle et La Bête. He demanded she remove any potentially breakable object from the tables, floor, or bar, because he intended to utilize every possible surface to their amorous advantage. There would, subsequently, be discussion of marriage, and when that may or may not be appropriate . . . which would likely start a fight, which would likely end in lovemaking. They had their rituals, and fresh titillation came from the fact that their rites needn't be contained solely to the walls and surfaces found in the flat they secretly shared.

Jane studied plans of how to quietly break into a children's hospital.

She could only hope none of the rest of the Guard read the papers in the morning.

Headmistress Rebecca Thompson was experiencing a different, far less entertaining sort of abandon. From the moment Alexi left Athens, the fissure inside her had grown to cavernous proportions. She wandered to a nearby dim and empty pub for a less than savory meal. Returning to her office, she lit a gas lamp atop one of her file cabinets and kept it trimmed low. From her desk she pulled something she had never before used but had prepared for this day: a flask of potent liquor.

When she let Frederic in the window, the bird hopped about, inspecting his mistress from various angles. She removed her jacket, loosened the ties of her collar, and took a draught. The sensation that burned her throat was welcome; it would help numb what was breaking apart.

She leaned upon the desk and a strange growl emerged from her lips. Why couldn't she have a prophecy of her own? Was she not as swift, decisive, strong-willed, and suited for leadership? Why were she and the other four resigned to a lonely fate while Alexi alone might reap a life almost average? Could not all of the Guard be granted complementary companions as Percy was meant to augment Alexi?

But Rebecca didn't want just any companion. She wanted *him*—compelling, arrogant, difficult, honorable, inscrutable, magnetic, haughty, inimitable him. The man who was wed after the whirlwind course of a school quarter. The man who had never been and would never be hers.

The stinging draughts she took increased in both frequency and effect. Prickling numbness drifted down her limbs and blurred her unmatched mind. Her elbow brushed Percy's bridal bouquet. Scowling, she picked it up and began wresting the lily blossoms one from another. "He loves me not." She tossed a lily to the floor. "He loves me not." Another. "He loves me not." Soon all the blossoms lay mutilated upon the floor, the stalks cast aside as headless stumps.

Frederic noticed the change. She did not respond to his squawk nor his nibble upon her ear; made soft, strangled sounds of sorrow. The raven flew out the window.

There had been a time, long ago, when she contemplated how easy it would be to jump from Westminster Bridge, to fall lightly from that precipice, to sink heavily and leave the weight of her lonely heart at the bottom of the Thames. But her strong will—one that cherished the greater good of the Grand Work—hadn't allowed for serious consideration. When she turned away from that bridge at the age of twenty, a cluster of spirits had gathered at the crest, and one came close enough to mouth the words, "Thank you." The dead needed the Guard to keep order. They needed *her*. She had to keep order inside herself and out.

This had been enough to sustain Rebecca for a long while, but today the ache was too much to feel her life had any reward. Anger, too, was close at hand. She had never understood the burden of her heart, as she'd known from an early age that Alexi cared for her in friendship not passion. Her love was an inane trap, and not a day passed when she did not curse her womanly weakness.

"Cheers," she mumbled, raising her flask, her words thick and fumbling. She kicked a lily blossom. "Cheers to the newly wedded couple. May they find eternal bliss. May they tell me how in hell I might find just a *hint* of it. Just a bit of something." She felt the flask slip from her hand and tumble onto her desk, soaking a few scattered papers with a strong scent—a hazy realization as she collapsed onto her arms, weary and bitter, and slipped into unconsciousness.

She had no concept of the time when a soft knock at the door roused her. Sitting up with a jolt, she watched the room spin. "Who is it?" she called, her words slurred.

After a moment, a familiar voice replied. "Don't you know the soft rap of your friend?"

"Carroll? I'm busy. What do you want?"

"A not-so-little bird told me you were not well."

"I'm . . . fine."

"You do not sound so." There came the sound of him trying the knob. "Rebecca, open the door."

"Told you, I'm busy. I've . . . institution to run, you know."

"Of course you do. But it's well past the hours of business, even for a worker such as yourself. Rebecca, please unlock the door."

"I'm not in the mood for company," Rebecca replied.

"You leave me no choice, then, Headmistress." Rebecca heard an otherworldly sound familiar from their Work, and the door of her office swung open to reveal a well-dressed, cautious Michael Carroll, whose ever-untamed hair was in a state of relative calm. Barely able to lift her head, Rebecca had to take a moment before her eyes would focus.

The vicar's rosy cheeks flushed darker when he saw her. "Ho-ho," he breathed, entering and closing the door behind him. "What have we here, my dear headmistress?"

It took Rebecca a moment to realize that she was slumped in a puddle of alcohol which had soaked the sleeves of her blouse. The scent of it filled the room. An alarm sounded—she was not a woman to be seen like this—but she was too incapacitated and vulnerable to make any show of rectification.

And Michael knew her. When her eyes could focus, she recognized such a softness in him, such frightening concern and understanding, as if he could see right into her soul. She was furiously ashamed and knew he saw this, too.

"Michael, I . . ."

"You needn't explain." He walked around to her.

"But Michael, this isn't—"

"Like you? I know it isn't, dear." His arms were lifting her to her feet.

"What are you—?"

"I'm taking you upstairs."

"Oh, that isn't necessary. I'm just a bit . . . under the weather," Rebecca said curtly, taking a step and swaying. She sputtered, chuckling suddenly as he swept her into his arms. "I suppose I'm not well at all, actually." Frederic the raven had returned to perch upon the sill. Once he saw his mistress being attended, he flew off again into the darkness.

The vicar carried her out of her office and began to ascend the two flights of stairs to Rebecca's apartments. En route, a staff member came upon them and gasped. "Not to worry, not to worry," Michael was quick to respond. "The headmistress is under the weather, and I am a doctor as well as her friend, so she will be well managed." He wasn't a doctor but he forgave himself the lie. Anything to protect Rebecca's reputation.

Her apartments had a wide sitting room laid with Persian rugs and chairs covered in dark fabric, an adjoining bedroom, boudoir, and water closet. Michael sat Rebecca in her high-backed Queen Anne, and her head lolled to the side.

"Michael, what are you doing?" she mumbled as he left her to rummage in a pantry set apart from the sitting room by carved wooden doors.

"We must tidy you up a bit, my dear."

"I'm . . . fine. Come here. Come back."

"Yes, dear?" Michael had returned with water, handed her the glass, and bade her drink.

"Why did you come?" she asked slowly, her words almost an accusation.

"Because I felt the weight of your heart. I was already en route when Frederic found me. Such knowledge is my job, you know."

There was a long pause as Rebecca's face twisted. "But you didn't go to Alexi when his heart was heavy, did you? Not when we turned against him and made him forsake Miss Park—his bride."

"No, I didn't go to him then," Michael replied slowly. "And that was a mistake. I tried to gauge the damage, but I felt nothing. He kept it too well hid."

"Not from me," Rebecca said. "He didn't hide it from me. I saw him broken. We broke him. He loves her that much. *So much.*"

"Is that what this is about?"

"What?" Rebecca eyed him sharply before her eyes unfocused and she took a sip of water.

"About Alexi's love for his wife?"

Rebecca grimaced. "No. I just wonder why you're here. Save your talents for our work, not me. This has nothing to do with the Guard."

"Oh, but it does. All of us have hearts, my dear. And what goes on within them affects us—and those around us. *Deeply.* But come now. We must get you out of this soaked chemise." As if happy to change the subject, the vicar stalked off to rummage through her boudoir closets.

"Michael, what are you doing? I can certainly dress myself!"

"Here, then." He returned with a crimson quilted velvet robe and took Rebecca by the arm, leading her into the water closet and hanging the robe on the back of the door, which he then slid closed behind her. "I am standing right by this door until you dress in something that does not reek of whiskey."

"Don't be a pest."

"You are very welcome, my dear."

It was some time before the door slid back again, but when it did,

Michael smiled. Bleary-eyed and tousle-haired, with high, noble features—he wasn't sure he'd ever found her so lovely. The awkwardness of the moment caused them both to color slightly, before Rebecca again swayed on her feet.

Michael chuckled as she leaned against the door frame. "Come now, Headmistress, off to bed with you." He refilled her water glass, then led her by the shoulders into her bedroom. He placed the glass and two white tablets upon her bedside table, then turned to face her. In the light of the low-trimmed lamp, she appeared soft and youthfully frightened.

"Michael, please don't . . ."

"Speak of this? You know me well enough to know better."

"Thank you." She fell against him in a clumsy embrace.

Michael closed his eyes and slowly allowed his arms to encircle her. Gently he eased her down to the bed, pulled back the covers, and tucked her in, bending to gently brush from her drained face a waving lock of dark hair shot with silver. She looked up at him but could not hold his stare.

"Forgive this old spinster, Michael. I don't know what's gotten into me." Tears leaked from her downcast eyes.

Michael knelt by her bedside. "Don't apologize to me, Rebecca. I only wish I could heal your heart."

"I . . . I love him so," she murmured, her voice cracking.

Michael turned away. "I know. I know."

Rebecca, quietly crying, reached for his hand. After a long moment, Michael turned to face her. Dimly, through her tears, part of her realized there was something he wanted to say but was struggling against it. She could see it in his face: something sad and desperate, something lonely and furious, something startlingly familiar. But, she recalled, she was drunk. Nothing could be trusted, for she was a broken old woman.

He took a deep breath, and his usual smile returned to his face. "Shall I bring you breakfast tomorrow, dear Headmistress? Methinks you might not feel keen to wander down to the kitchens in the morning."

Rebecca gave a little moan and covered her face with her hands. "Oh, what you must think of me!"

"I think nothing but that I like eggs in the morning. You?"

Rebecca chuckled wearily. "Yes, yes."

"Good, then." Michael paused. "Shall . . . I leave you?"

"Yes, yes, you'd better," she hastily replied. The thought of company in her bedchamber, however innocent, was vaguely appealing yet entirely foreign and off-putting.

"Good night then, Rebecca."

When the vicar rose, she looked up, meeting his eyes. "Thank you, Michael. And . . . yes, company will be nice in the morning, indeed." Her still-incapacitated brain working slowly, she suddenly reached out. "Wait, I've a confession." Michael sat, ever attentive, and words tumbled clumsily forth: "I knew it was her. Somewhere within me, instinct told me Percy was our Prophecy from the start. I . . . I just didn't trust it. Whether that was because I was honestly concerned with her being a student, concerned about the traps of which we were warned, or if it was instead my own blind jealousy, I'll never know. I could have cost us everything."

Michael shook his head. "No, no, Rebecca. Nothing is up to just one of us. We have all been blinded differently. Alexi needed to be questioned. We hardly recognized him for his passion and vehemence. It was cause for discussion, then, as were the gifts we honestly noted in Miss Linden."

"Betrayal was a part of Prophecy, and I—"

"So it was," Michael interrupted. "But we've all scored little betrayals here and there, unwittingly, over the course of our work. We're mortal, and if the gods wanted something different, they shouldn't have sent us to do the job."

Rebecca nearly smiled. "You are so sensible."

"It's about time you thought so," he chided playfully. But he meant it. "Sweet dreams," he said, rising again. Rebecca sighed slightly as he slid her bedroom door closed behind him. On the other side, Michael sighed as well, aching keenly for all that remained unsaid.

CHAPTER
EIGHT

The black door hissed open again. Beyond, a shape. He did not often take form, but when he did, he wore that beautiful face. Tick . . . tock. Flesh . . . and bone. The beautiful face, looking about for something lost. Those terrible, burning red coals in the sockets of a skull. A burst of righteous fury. Those burning eyes blinked out, and soon afterward the hiss of the door closing. Peaceful darkness returned. For now. He couldn't know her. Not like this. It wasn't her anymore. But would he seek her nonetheless?

Percy stirred, her eyelids fluttering as she began to wake. She released the dream, refusing to give nightmares importance. Instead, she focused on the fact that her beloved lay naked against her. She heard the lull of the waves and opened her eyes enough to glimpse bright morning light play upon the curtains.

At the sound of her husband's breathing, she blushed, recalling each exotic moment of the night. How beautiful he looked while sleeping. . . . He stirred in turn, his eyes slowly opening. He emitted a soft, purring groan. The press of his warm, bare body sent a pulse of longing through hers.

"Good morning, love," he said.

"Good morning, indeed," Percy breathed, sighing and shivering as he kissed his way down her neck and back. The previous night hadn't merely whetted their appetite for each other, it had illuminated starvation.

As the next morning saw Michael arrive in the front hall of Athens Academy, he looked up into the transparent face of a young boy. The harmless haunt of the foyer chandelier, a particular favorite of Rebecca's, who had floated in the crystals for as long as Michael could remember, was gesturing worriedly up the stairs. It took a moment for Michael to realize the boy must have seen him carry Rebecca to her rooms.

He looked around to assure himself the foyer was entirely empty before he dared answer. "The headmistress is fine. Don't worry. She's simply tired."

The boy's brow furrowed in disbelief. He then pointed down the hall toward the headmistress's office, bobbing a bit for emphasis.

Michael walked under an arch into the hall beyond, his footsteps echoing across the polished marble. A few students ducked into doors here and there, late to classes, as normal. But . . . something wasn't quite right. And as he stood before the formidable door marked HEADMIS-TRESS, he recognized what it was: A narrow, unmarked door, subtle, and of the same wooden paneling as the walls, had appeared beside Rebecca's office, which Michael would swear was never there before.

Suddenly, a spirit burst through and nearly right through Michael, had she not floated back with an irritated bobbing, folding her arms over her chest. She was tall, and Michael recognized her from just before the wedding.

"Mrs. Tipton, isn't it? Hello. What are you doing?"

The ghost gave Michael a knowing, unsettling look. She opened her mouth and began speaking. He tried to follow the movements of her mouth, but it was no use; only Percy could hear the dead. The spirit batted her hand and, as she did, a bit of familiar blue fire leaped to life in her palm. Then she vanished.

The middle of the new doorway sizzled, and a flash of blue fire emblazoned upon it the number seven.

"CAN YOU FEEL THEM—YOUR FRIENDS?" PERCY ASKED SOFTLY, attempting to translate the expression on Alexi's face. They lounged side by side, sipping tea by the sitting-room hearth of their honeymoon cottage. "You have not often been away."

"True, duty requires us close. But there is no danger, if that concerns you. A few spectral rumblings, but nothing they can't handle."

"You would be able to sense if there was pressing danger?"

"Yes."

She wondered about mentioning Beatrice's hint of betrayal, wanting to know what her husband thought of it, but she was afraid it would sound like she was questioning the people he knew, loved, trusted, and led—or worse, questioning him. Until she had reason to doubt, she would stay alert, as advised.

"Can you sense other things? You cannot . . . read the mind, can you?" Percy asked, blushing, suddenly wondering if he'd known all the scandalous things she thought while sitting across from him at his office desk.

"Not exactly, no. Though I never had to read your mind, my sweet. Of your many talents, hiding your enraptured gaze was not one of them."

"Well, then"—Percy chuckled—"it's best that you married me. While my eyes may have been the first to betray my feelings, the rest of me surely would soon have followed."

"Oh?" he said, trailing a finger down her body. "Do demonstrate . . ."

Their day had been spent lazing about, sipping tea and a bit of champagne, kissing, caressing, and tumbling entwined onto a soft surface. Currently putting the divan to good use, they had not bothered to dress since they arrived, though Alexi had allowed Percy to replace her nearly transparent robe with a lined one. There were, after all, drafts. Not that this kept him from every now and then loosening her strings, at which Percy giggled but did not protest. Throughout her life she had been forced to hide her skin. With Alexi she—the whole of her—could exist without shame, in celebration.

He traced the line of her jaw, clearly still amazed by her. But Percy could see clouds covering his wonder and pulling darkly at his mood.

"What is it, love?" she asked.

"I cannot stop thinking about those red eyes. The ones you saw in the corridor."

Percy gulped. They'd been in her dream, too. "Yes?"

"Were they the eyes of that hellhound?"

"I . . . don't think so."

"Hades, then?"

Percy made a face. "Must we use these names? It's absurd. How can I treat them as anything more than myth?"

"What—the devil, then?" Alexi's eyes blazed with jealous fury. She'd never seen that look before, and it stole her breath with its oppressive intensity. "I don't care what that thing's name is, but no one will ever lay a hand on you. Is that clear? I don't care who or what might be seeking you out, but I have you now. You are mine."

"Yes, yes, love. There's no contest, Alexi. I want to be nowhere but with you. If something were to beckon me elsewhere . . . why, I wouldn't want to go. Tell me you don't question me!"

Alexi sighed. "I don't question your love. I just don't trust the forces that wish to tear everything apart, the ancient vendetta that began this in the first place. The goddess warned of a war when she lay the Grand Work at our feet. If it's true that we've only begun the fight . . . well, as Beatrice Tipton said, we are only pawns. But I don't want a war. And I don't want you to be anything other than mine."

Percy furrowed her brow. "What do you mean?"

Alexi looked away.

Percy moved to catch his eye. "Truly, Alexi. Do you not trust me? Do you not trust who or what I am?"

He stared out at the sea, his jaw clenched. "I just . . . I still don't know what you are."

Percy rose to her feet, agitated. "I was born flesh and blood. I am your wife. Don't tell me this has something to do with how I look—"

"Not in the slightest! It has to do with what comes out of you, where it comes from and who you may have been, the question of your status, whether goddess and immortal, or—"

"Alexi, I'm no goddess. I'm mortal."

"How do we know for sure?"

"I nearly died in your arms, Alexi. Shall we *further* test the theory of my mortality?" She shook her head. "I still have trouble accepting my own skin, all my queer qualities. I fell in love with you because you were the first man to ever make me think I could belong, that I was accept—"

"Percy, please don't upset yourself," Alexi demanded, rising and placing hands upon her arms. He guided her back to the sofa, held her covetously. "That's not what I wanted."

She sighed, turning to him with tears in her eyes. "I am too fragile to be questioned thus by someone so important to me. Please, accept me for anything I am and might be. I've no knowledge beyond your own. *Please.* The world does not accept me. I had hoped you . . ."

Alexi's jaw worked as she trailed off. He wiped the tears from her cheeks. "I do accept you, Percy. No matter if you have to watch me age and die before you, or I have to hold the Whisper-world off forever so it can't steal—"

"Is that what this is about?" Percy breathed.

"In part. Watching you sleep, a perfect angel at my side, I envisioned you twenty years from now, entirely unchanged, and me haggard—"

"We both shall age. And I am yours, forever, no matter what," she said.

"Yes," he murmured, accepting her words. "And I am yours."

They watched the sea as the sky grew dark.

Alexi finally waved a hand and all the candles in the sitting room burst into flame. He plucked a thin book from the console table and said, "I read something that made me think of you. A new poet, an Irishman named Yeats." He launched into a recitation, and Percy was rendered helpless by it:

> I bring you with reverent hands
> The books of my numberless dreams,
> White woman that passion has worn
> As the tide wears the dove-gray sands,
> And with heart more old than the horn
> That is brimmed from the pale fire of time:
> White woman with numberless dreams,
> I bring you my passionate rhyme.

He dropped the book. Percy had melted into his lap like a puddle of moonlight, drunk on his voice, staring up at him in adoration. "My white woman, indeed," he murmured. When there was such wonder, beauty, and passion in the world, what on earth could there possibly be to fear?

CHAPTER
NINE

THE GROUNDSKEEPER SCOWLED. "BE GONE, I'M HARD AT WORK!"

To his irritation, one particular wraith kept hanging about his makeshift laboratory on the riverbank. The chiseled-faced man had an intense look and was dressed in cloth and metal bands; at times, one of his hands glowed faintly. The Groundskeeper batted at him with his broom before focusing again on the rows of glass jars labeled with body parts. "I'll make you whole again, my sweetie-snaky-lassie. We'll sort out what happened, and what great punishments will be dealt! Lucy-Ducy had a nice dress, Lucy-Ducy made a great mess . . ."

Muttering, "Seal number twelve," he turned back to the coffin and gently patted the edge. "I'll be back, my lovely, but the Undoing continues without you. Soon you'll see your hard work come to fruition!"

As he ambled down a diagonal concourse of gray mist, mumbling and singing, a shape slipped out of the shadows behind him, following, concealing in a closed fist the blue fire that occasionally sparked from her palm and locket.

REBECCA THOMPSON'S FIRST NOTION OF DAYLIGHT CAME AS A POUNDING headache. Eyes still closed, she moaned. Why on earth was she in such a state? She threw off her covers, pried her lids open against the glare, and steadied herself with a hand on the bedside table. Something under her fingers drew her attention—a pair of tablets. She wondered how they'd gotten there but was thankful, and downed them with a similarly provided glass of water.

Her eyes widened when she stumbled into her washroom. The blouse she'd worn the night prior was soaking in a pail of water. She stared at it for some time before vaguely remembering having put it there. Then she gazed into the mirror and groaned. She looked as though she had awakened from death.

"Oh, no," she murmured, and her face fell into her hands. "Oh, Michael, I am so sorry."

But soon came a soft rap at the door and a voice calling, "Hallo! Eggs, as promised! Shall you welcome your breakfast, Headmistress?"

Rebecca straightened herself in the washroom mirror, ignoring the blush of shame that made her pale face seem actually more youthful for the color. She shuffled to open the door to her rooms. Michael Carroll entered in a rush of bluster, good cheer, and anarchic hair. He carried a steaming tray. Rebecca stared at the floor and gestured him farther into the room, closing the door behind him. "Morning, Michael, please forgive—"

"I told you, no apologies—and I'm starving," he said, breezing past her to place the tray upon a small table near the window overlooking the Athens courtyard. A newspaper sliding under the door spared her any more pleasantries; Michael, always eager for news, bounded to fetch it. "Well, what do we have here this fine morning? What news of common mortal—? Oh. Oh, dear."

Rebecca looked over to find him agape. A gurgling laugh began at the back of his throat. "What? What is it?"

"Could this be what I think?"

He brought the paper to Rebecca. She rubbed her eyes and focused on the blaring headline:

WARD OF TERMINALLY ILL CHILDREN CURED BY UNKNOWN MIRACLE!

A shining toddler was sketched mouthing a thank-you to a winged angel who looked awfully familiar. After reading a bit, Rebecca looked up at Michael, who only shrugged. Glancing back down at the paper, her face showed a mixture of awe and anger.

"Alexi is gone for a mere day, and look what happens."

"Shameful. Shameful! None of us can behave," Michael said. Rebecca looked up, flushing with guilt, only to see that he was laughing, his cheeks rosier than usual. "Hee-hee! Can you just imagine the nurses entering their ward to find their invalids throwing pillows and bouncing on mattresses?"

Michael's glee could not be contained, though Rebecca tried to fight its contagion. This would not please Alexi in the least; they were not supposed to make their work evident in any capacity, no matter how wonderful the consequences. She frowned. "How on earth did she do it?"

"I don't know, but we'll go and ask after we eat! Before we do, though, did you happen to notice there's a new door beside your door?"

"What?" Rebecca said.

"Beatrice Tipton is adding doors."

LUCRETIA MARIE O'SHANNON CONNOR, KNOWN SIMPLY AS JANE, SAT near the window of her flat with her embroidery, humming an old highland tune as a cool breeze trickled in from the slightly opened casement in her study. She'd had a glorious night, and Aodhan had been there. She wished he were with her now. She knew she had become too dependent upon his spectral company, but the older she grew, the more she pined for him. Regardless, it had been one of the very best nights of her life. And she knew his name, thanks to Miss Percy. A small but significant treasure when you could not hear or touch the man you loved.

A loud pounding upon the door made her prick her thumb. The plump white cat at her feet gave an annoyed growl before stalking downstairs and toward the door.

Michael Carroll bounded up the staircase, nearly trampling the beast. "Oh—careful there, Marlowe. My dear Lady Jane, how on earth did you do it?"

Jane blinked innocent eyes at him, but guilt heightened her Irish accent. "What in the name of Saint Hugh do y'mean?"

"The children's ward! Don't even think to deny it, you delightfully devilish gal. Oh—ha! Saint Hugh, patron to sick children, eh? Clever! Bloody brilliant!"

Jane noticed that Rebecca stood behind Michael, lacking his excitement. In fact, the headmistress looked peeved, even a bit ill. Jane's heart sank. She'd hoped no one would mind. They were sick children, for Mary and Joseph's sake! Alexi was the only one who should reprimand her. But then again, Rebecca might, too. She was, after all, second in command.

"I want to know everything!" Michael persisted.

"Michael, m'dear, there's nothing to tell. Rebecca, what is this raving all about?"

"Quite the sensation," Rebecca responded, pulling the paper from behind her back. "While I deeply respect the act, and though Elijah can daze anyone who pries . . . really, Jane, if Alexi were to hear—"

"Please don't tell him," Jane interrupted, urging Rebecca and Michael to sit. "You mustn't think I meant to create such a scene, but the light just spread. It was all around me and *in* me. It grew like sprouting flowers. Those sleeping bodies just radiated vines of that light that kept on growin'! One of the children stirred. She said the angels had come, just as she'd prayed. Oh, Rebecca, then the light spread to all of them. The whole room was thick with light, curing, wrapping, healing . . ." Her tears ran as freely, and Rebecca had to clear her throat and fight the onslaught.

Jane continued. "Once that glorious web started spinning, I couldn't stop it. It would have broken my heart. You don't know how much more I want to—"

When she choked, Rebecca leaned forward and placed a hand upon her knee. "Yes, love, I do. I cannot imagine having the depth of your gift and being so constrained. But you know why we must be judicious."

"I know. I do know. And I am sorry."

"Don't you dare apologize," Rebecca snapped. When Jane looked up, startled, she smiled. "I only wish I could have been there to see."

Michael spoke up. "How did you get in?"

"A handy bit of lock-picking," Jane replied, careful not to incriminate accessory forces. "I've gotten rather good at it," she added hastily.

Her friends knew better than to pry, but Rebecca rolled her eyes. "I'm sure."

"We're taking you to tea! Our treat!" Michael declared, grabbing Jane by the arm and marching her downstairs. Rebecca followed.

Jane grinned, feeling better than she ever had, save for one nagging worry: Before the miracle last night, Aodhan had somehow managed to trickle a bit of ash onto her hand and mouthed the word "Beware." She tried to ascertain more, but Aodhan was gone.

* * *

BEATRICE TIPTON WAS PREPARING ANOTHER NEW DOOR BETWEEN Athens Academy and the Whisper-world, following after the Grounds-keeper to undo his work with cerulean fire, when a putrid smell washed over her, heralding a powerful presence. The goddess had done well in hiding these portal thresholds deep in the murk, frightening and taxing as it must have been for a soul of such light to do so. From this location Beatrice watched a huge and hulking shadow—Darkness himself—hold out something raw and bloody.

"Come, come, we must put you back together," he said, a coaxing tone clear, though his voice sounded like the scrape of stone on stone. "Just as the Groundskeeper reassembles the Gorgon, you must become whole again, my pet."

"Good God," Beatrice murmured, watching the shadow of a hound whimper and slide into view.

She would have to quicken her pace. As much as she'd like to give the poor girl a rest, Persephone would be called out, whether she liked it or not. The "puppy" now knew whom it hunted, and when it became whole again, God help her. Beatrice wondered if there was a way to bury a part of that splintered creature to keep it from wholly reassembling.

The portion of Phoenix fire she controlled seemed to react to this thought. A tendril flared, a snaking trail of flame that dripped down from her locket, making a circle in the air and tightening it, sparkling as if in joy. Beatrice grinned. A leash? That might indeed do the trick. But for now her job remained the doors.

ALEXI WOULD HAVE SPENT WEEKS WITH HIS BELOVED BY THE SEA, BUT the tasks of the Guard could not go untended so long. One bit of marital business remained, however, at the Institute of the Blessed Virgin Mary, where Percy had been raised.

"I was expecting a dank, dark ruin," he said with slight disappoint-ment, staring at the Georgian edifice. The abbey's classic brick and woodwork façade was not wholly uninviting.

"Something more eerily romantic, perhaps?" Percy smiled, peering out the carriage window. "I lived here mere months ago, trapped like a ghost, beloved by Reverend Mother but desperately lonely. How life has changed!" She embraced him.

Drawn by the sound of their carriage, a novice poked her head out from a plain wooden door. Percy alighted and the novice nearly shrieked. "Miss Percy! I did not expect to see you again so soon!"

"I've a . . . break in term, Mary Caroline." When the sister stared at her companion, clearly baffled, Percy added. "And this is my husband, Professor Alexi Rychman."

The novice gasped before remembering herself. "Well, then. My regards! Surprises, indeed! Does the reverend mother know?"

Percy opened her mouth to reply, but Alexi spoke first. "I sent a telegram informing her of our arrival—and of our happy news."

"Good, then she'll be expecting you. I'll show you right in."

The novice escorted them through the front foyer and down a long, unadorned hall to a modest office, bobbed once and quickly disappeared into another wing. Outside the reverend mother's door, another sister, a willowy woman in a white dress, greeted the couple.

"Hello, Percy," she murmured. "Congratulations."

Percy nodded. "Thank you, Sister Mary Therese. This is my husband, Professor Alexi Rychman."

Alexi nodded. "A pleasure."

"The young Miss Percy never required my linguistic tutelage," the sister said with a strained smile.

"Indeed." Percy grinned. "I shan't forget the look on her face the day I was reading a book aloud in the courtyard in a language none of us had yet learned. What was it?"

"Greek," Sister Mary Therese answered immediately—and, Alexi noted, uncomfortably. She opened the door behind her, revealing a room lit by a great fire in a hearth, casting everything in yellow light. The reverend mother's voice boomed out.

"My dear Percy! Come embrace me before you introduce this husband of yours." She came around the desk, a wrinkled, round woman in a white habit. Wisps of mousy brown and gray hair poked insubordinately from her white coif. The reverend mother opened her arms and Percy ran her. "So quickly, Percy," the woman murmured with an amazed laugh. "This incredible news."

"Yes, Reverend Mother," Percy exclaimed joyfully. "I'm as shocked as you. May I present Professor Rychman."

Alexi approached and bowed in deference. "Reverend Mother, it is an honor to finally meet you. I owe you tremendous thanks, for I cannot imagine my life had you not sent Percy to Athens."

Percy blushed furiously, but while the reverend mother's smile was warm, the look in her eyes was far from trusting. "Indeed. Well, these convent walls could not contain such a woman as she, Professor, as I'm sure you understand. Mary Therese, do show Percy the new reliquary in the sacristy. I require a moment to consult with the professor on . . . *fiscal* matters."

With a wave and a tiny smile, Percy followed the reluctant sister into the hall.

"Professor," the reverend mother said as the door closed, "there are many reasons why I wish to speak with you alone."

Alexi pursed his lips. "I imagine finance ranks among the least important."

"Indeed."

"Well, if it is any concern at all, I am descended of a wealthy family and have many vested interests and a comfortable estate. Percy shall not lack."

"While I am pleased to hear that, I'm more concerned with your intentions."

Alexi raised an eyebrow. He had assumed he would be welcomed with relief, not questioned as a possible threat. "Why, my intention was to make Miss Parker my wife, which I have done."

"While Percy is admittedly unique, and older than the rest of your students, she was still your pupil. Is it not forbidden for there to be relations between—"

"Of course. And after Miss Parker and I confessed our mutual sentiments to each other, we were quick to withdraw her as a student and make our union complete. With all due respect, you surely know that— proud as I am of the academy—Percy was suited for Oxford, not Athens. The only class that gave her any trouble was mine, and I'd like to think that was due at least in part to distraction."

Levity infused his last comment, but there was none to be found on the reverend mother's face. "Professor, forgive my bold statements, but I am concerned that your interest in Percy may be of a fleeting, novel nature, and not one of lasting devotion. Perhaps you hastened into marriage due to . . . improprieties."

"I did not ruin the girl and marry her out of duty, if that is what you are insinuating, Reverend Mother," Alexi stated. "I maintain I am a gentleman."

"The girl is not an oddity, Professor, not something to be shown off at parlor séances. Her heart is vast with love but incredibly delicate. If you should ever abandon her to take up with another . . ." She shuddered. "The effect upon her would be cataclysmic. Irreparable."

Alexi sighed. "Reverend Mother. True, you know nothing about me, and one might fear a lover making some sort of curious trophy of Percy. This is hardly the case. You surely know the transformative power of my wife's radiant soul; I merely became the fortuitous recipient of her affections. I would have preferred not to marry a student, but the fact remained that Persephone was heaven-sent and I wished to do right by her as soon as possible. She will become a permanent member of our Athens staff; we plan to keep her busy with literary translation. Your strange, dear charge has become mistress of a fine estate, gained a husband and employment in a matter of months. She has not done poorly for herself, has she?"

"No." The reverend mother laughed. "It's far more than I could possibly have dreamed. Thank you, Professor, I am put at ease."

"The pleasure is mine, I assure you."

After a moment of pleased reflection, the old woman spoke. "There is yet another sobering matter."

"The grave of her mother," Alexi guessed. The woman nodded. "Percy has been strange business for you, hasn't she?"

"Yes. I always knew I had to take . . . special precautions. You're a man of science and will scoff at my reasoning, I'm sure."

"As I once told Percy, Reverend Mother, you'd be surprised how little I find strange. Percy was hesitant to tell me of her visions, of her interactions with the dead, yet I love her all the more for them. There's much about the universe that defies our explanation."

The old woman smiled. "Oh, my. A man of science with an open mind. What a treasure! I wish the rest of your kind were as forgiving to us clergy . . . In a dream, precisely nine months before the infant Percy arrived, the Holy Virgin proclaimed that unto us a strange child would come, but not to fear her, and whatever would be asked of her care, to do it. She proclaimed the girl would bring light and love to those lives she touched. How could I not obey? I sought to serve this prophesied child, and now . . . I rejoice that she has someone to love and protect her."

"That she has," Alexi said. "Now, you said 'whatever would be asked of her care' . . . ?"

"To attend to the burial of the mother as you will find. And then I was told of Athens. I made inquiries. Your school is not easy to find, you know."

Alexi smiled wryly. "Indeed, it is part of our . . . charm."

"Once examined, I saw the school was precisely suited for her. The Lord provided."

"Indeed," Alexi repeated. "Rest assured, my dear woman, I care for Percy more than I can express. I pledge my life for her safety."

The reverend mother moved to Alexi and embraced him. "I am grateful for you, Professor."

A knock came upon the door, and, grinning, the old woman called, "Come collect your husband, Percy."

Percy entered, moving as if she had to keep herself from running to him. "Business all attended?"

"Yes, love," Alexi replied. "It seems I've married a pale pauper. Not a penny to her name."

Percy looked mortified. "But—"

"And I don't mind a bit," Alexi stated, sliding his arm around her waist. It took Percy a moment to realize he'd been teasing. "Shall we take a turn round your old haunts?"

PERCY LED ALEXI ABOUT THE CLOISTER, FROM THE COURTYARD GAR-den where she had named every flower and staged her own faerie plays at age six, to the small gray confines of her old room with its one narrow window and within which she and her Elizabethan spirit friend Gregory had recited *Hamlet* in the dead of night. She explained the haunts of each of her spirit friends, only a few of whom still lingered against her uncanny knack for setting them to rest.

"Oh, Alexi," she exclaimed when the tour was finished. They sat on a courtyard bench. "Thank you for listening to tales of a weird childhood. I led a magical but desperately lonely life, knowing no one would ever understand or believe. How wondrous to have someone who understands, a lover who—" She bit her lip, shivering. The word "lover" was still such a deliciously fresh concept.

"Indeed," Alexi replied, kissing her blushing cheek. "You're a tonic of youth for an old man."

"Old man. Hardly," she scoffed. She drew near, looking furtively around to be sure they were alone. "You've proven otherwise," she murmured, brushing his lips with hers.

The sound he made, and the way his hands tightened upon her, were signs that his control was being tested. "My God, Mrs. Rychman, you lure a professor into marrying you, then drive him mad with desire inside convent walls? You were never meant for the sisterhood."

Percy blushed, giggling. "Is this where my melancholy prince tells me to 'get thee *from* a nunnery'?"

Alexi grinned. "Indeed. And we've turned tragedy into a happy ending. We are products of our fool romantic age in the end," he murmured, running a finger along her collarbone. "Now, what did Sister Mary ask of you?"

"If our hasty marriage was because you'd ruined me."

Alexi chuckled. "Your abbess wondered the same. Come then," he said, rising. "Onward."

They were escorted out the massive front doors by the reverend mother and a parade of the abbey's ghostly denizens, their numbers greatly diminished since Percy's birth. Percy waved one last time to those who remained while Alexi spoke with the carriage driver; then she settled in for yet another long journey.

Alexi took a deep breath. "Before we return to London, my love, we've one last appointment. We must pay our respects at the foot of your mother's grave."

Percy's brow furrowed. "My mother's grave? Why didn't I know about a grave?"

"I think we'll see soon enough," Alexi replied.

They traveled down a road thick with brush while the countryside around them grew wilder and increasingly unkempt. At last they reached an unmarked iron gate and fence that surrounded a narrow, deep patch of flat ground. White stones were scattered about inside the fence, jutting up from the earth.

Alexi helped Percy from the cab, then kept a tight grip on her arm as he opened the rusting gate on squealing hinges. Percy stared at the old, untended graves, the sandstone grave markers eroded beyond recognition, moss grown over the epitaphs. No spirits lingered here; either those interred had found peace or their lingering wraiths had managed to flee.

In a corner plot lined with thin-branched evergreens, two small stones lay apart from the rest. Alexi crossed directly toward them, and Percy felt her blood grow cooler with each step. Then she realized it wasn't just her blood; the air was drastically colder here, as if she were standing in the wake of a spirit. But she saw none.

The flat gray stone they sought was not nearly as worn as its neighbors. The moment Percy saw it she gasped and nearly fainted; Alexi's grip cinched about her waist, holding her firmly on her feet. The larger stone was inscribed: I. PARKER, MOTHER. The stone to its left: P. PARKER, INFANT.

"How cruel. To feel such a ghost already and then to see this?"

"You're flesh and blood, Percy," Alexi assured her. "There's another reason for this grim landmark. Be strong, love, and wait here a moment."

He strode toward a small equipment shed they had passed a few moments earlier, his black cloak billowing. He returned with a shovel in his hand.

"Oh God, Alexi," Percy said, her mind reeling, "what are you doing?"

He calmly drove the shovel into the earth beneath the smaller stone. Percy cried out. "Alexi!"

"Your infant body is not within this grave, Percy. So what is?"

The question could not stay unanswered. It did not take long to unearth a small, rotting wooden box the size of an infant's coffin. Alexi pried open the lid, revealing a metal container. That, opened, proved to contain an odd silver key and a clump of folded paper bound by twine. Alexi lifted both, brushed away a few specks of dirt, and handed them to his wife.

Percy accepted the items gingerly, her gloved hands shaking. She was scared to open the twine, and she hadn't the slightest idea about the key. She had lived her entire life without any knowledge of her mother and had become accustomed to that mystery. But looking into Alexi's eyes, she found strength.

He picked up the shovel and began refilling the grave. Replacing the patches of grass, he stepped on the ground to make it level so the disturbance of the earth would not be readily apparent.

"Allow me a moment, if you would," Percy said as he turned to look at her. Alexi nodded and obeyed, walking away without question.

Percy stared down at the larger tombstone. This lonely grave was all that remained of a true family. "Mother, so much has happened to me in such a short time, yet I never expected to see this. All I can think to do is offer thanks and pray for your peace. I'm sure I owe you more than my life.

"I've a husband! I wish we both could have known you. I only hope heaven grants you such comforts as he has given me." Her hand closed around her phoenix pendant. Out of the corner of her eye she saw Alexi standing just beyond the iron gate, patient, his arms folded in his cloak. He was her family now. As were the Guard.

Prayers finished, Percy crossed the cemetery toward him and was welcomed with a warm embrace. She lingered there, breathing in his subtle spices for a long moment before drawing back. "Well," she murmured, "shall we journey on?"

"Yes, my dear, I can hardly wait to bring you home."

This roused an eager smile, and in that moment all surprises and sorrows were forgotten.

In the carriage, Alexi shifted to allow her to claim her specific place in the crook of his arm. When she looked up, he nodded at the folded paper. "I'll not look, if you would rather—"

"No, Alexi, I wish to hide nothing from you. What do you suppose this key might be?"

Alexi examined it. "There is a tiny keyhole at the center of the floor of our sacred space below the chapel, and I have always wondered of it. Perhaps we shall try it there, though I hesitate to guess what we may unlock."

Frowning, Percy ran her finger across the peculiar knots and grooves of the key. Unclasping her necklace, she slid the key onto the chain, where it fell to rest beside the silver phoenix. Inspecting the bird, she asked, "Why would mother have given me this and withheld the rest?"

The open patch at her breast revealed the perfect imprint of the silver bird, the scar that had alarmed and excited Alexi and led to their first kiss. His gaze fell upon the mark and when he ran his thumb over the scar, her body responded with a tremor.

"This sign branded you, brought you to us, but apparently the prophecy required you shouldn't have that key until we were united."

Percy nodded. "I am so glad of your presence with me now," she said and took a deep breath before opening the accompanying letter. She read aloud: "'My dear child, while I'll never know you, I know about you. Much like the Lord, your coming was foretold. Do not be afraid. I am not. I was delivered from death to deliver you. I wish I were clever enough to devise a more delicate beginning, but there is only the strange wonder of your birth these words stand witness to.'"

Folding the paper with slightly trembling fingertips, Percy placed the note inside the breast pocket of her cloak, leaned into Alexi with her full weight and shut her eyes. "I . . . I'm too overwhelmed," she murmured as sleep claimed her.

So, again, beloved, I'm left to wonder, Alexi thought as the coach headed back to London, and Athens, where further secrets might be revealed, *what, exactly, are you?*

CHAPTER
TEN

IF THE BALANCE BETWEEN THE MORTAL AND THE SPIRIT WORLDS WAS
a tapestry, now and then a thread of that tapestry would begin to snarl,
perhaps tear. In response to such disruptions the Guard acted, smoothing each snag in the fabric. Rebecca's awareness of the flaws in the
pattern was unmatched; it was as if the whole of London were a map
written in her blood. The Pull at this moment was a rustle of leaves under
Rebecca's skin. Two familiar problems were brewing due east: one on
Rosebury, the other down Fleet. Perhaps the occupation would do her
good, assuage the lingering guilt that hung over her like the blade of a
guillotine.

As she had a horse brought to the Athens portico, a broad-shouldered
silhouette trotted up the alley. "Hallo, my dear. Feel the Pull, do you?"

"Yes, Michael," she replied, having hoisted herself sidesaddle onto the
mare. "And while I appreciate your diligence, I believe I can disassemble
these fools alone." She grimaced. "Seems to be the night for severed
heads."

Michael chuckled. "Ah, Goldsmith and Grimaldi. Of course you
can handle them. Still, I thought I would offer."

Rebecca shrugged. "I'm only fit for my own company."

"While I don't agree, I do believe you must prove to yourself why we
turn to you as well as Alexi. Now that he has his . . . preoccupations,
you'll need to step fully forward."

She stared down at him a moment before her expression softened.
"You are right."

Michael grinned. "I could smugly say 'I know,' but that sounds too
much like Alexi and we can't have that. I'll just thank you for agreeing."

"No. Thank *you,* my dear. I need someone to tell me sensible things,"

Rebecca murmured. Then she rode off, before he could add anything else.

In transit, her horse moving at a slow plod, Rebecca heard a familiar voice call her name. The Pull gave the Guard a sense of one another as well as of the task at hand.

"Elijah Withersby," Rebecca replied, halting her horse. "I can handle these heads perfectly w—"

"I d-didn't want you to have a go of tonight's work all alone because you thought none of us was available," Elijah stammered.

Rebecca looked down from the saddle, offering a look of irritation that rivaled Alexi's. She took a moment to evaluate her friend's disheveled appearance and with mild disgust noted his half-tucked shirttails and badly buttoned breeches.

"Why, thank you, Elijah," Rebecca began. "How thoughtful to be available in our moment of need."

"What can I say? I am a veritable icon of responsibility."

"So it would seem."

Elijah cursed as he caught the direction of Rebecca's eyes. He had rushed out of Josephine's amorous clutches and toward his higher calling, only to be betrayed by his pants. Josephine, at least, would remain without implication. Nor would the gaffe further tarnish his reputation, as he was erroneously assumed a libertine. Though—especially with Josephine's pointed behavior of late—did any of them truly believe the charade anymore? Surely the Guard had long since guessed they two knew each other in ways more intimate than friendship.

Not that he could admit it. What on earth would Alexi say, after all the ribbing, upon discovering Elijah's loyal, loving nature? The revelation would be a disaster. When he honored his promise to marry Josephine, everything would fall to pieces. Not just Alexi, either. His peers. His family. *Everything.* And yet he'd promised upon the prophesied addition of the Guard's seventh member . . .

"Shall I press on to business and leave you standing there staring?" Rebecca asked, interrupting his thoughts and shooing her hand at a young spirit taking the time to levitate apples from a nearby cart, to the owner's great dismay. Then she reconsidered.

"I suppose you might as well make yourself useful, since you're here," she allowed.

"As you wish!" Elijah said cheerfully, and promptly wiped the minds of all who'd seen the flying fruit. Passersby dispersed, oblivious. Disappointed, the spirit gave up and sank through the cobblestones, but not before offering the headmistress an impertinent gesture.

"Busy night," Rebecca stated conversationally. "I was just on my way to Ye Olde Cock Tavern. Then to Sadler's Wells."

Elijah made a face. "Oliver Goldsmith's head? Again? And that *clown*? They must have a cranial rivalry; they're always out in tandem."

"Each won't take but a minute, especially if we work together. We'll begin up Fleet Street."

Rebecca kicked her horse into a slow walk; Elijah strolled along beside her. "Damn writers," he opined, "loath to leave anything, frightened of fading into obscurity; it isn't Goldsmith's body haunting Fleet Street, it's merely his pride. Damn them all. There isn't a single noble profession in the world."

"Nobility comes only through *lack* of work, then?"

"My class is constituted entirely of sniveling idiots," he replied.

"What, then?" Rebecca laughed. "There must be some worthwhile task—"

"Yes," Elijah said firmly. "Ours. We're the world's only nobility, Rebecca. Though our rewards seem paltry." He eyed her. "How are you faring these days?"

Rebecca snorted. "What's come over you?"

"I was asking the questions, my dear." He grinned. "I was just wondering how it feels to be free of His Highness, if only for a bit."

Rebecca thought a moment. "Not bad, I suppose. Not bad."

"Good, then. Our leader Alexi may be, but you of all people oughtn't be kept at heel."

"He did not put me at heel." Her voice was cold.

"No, he didn't." Elijah's gaze was uncomfortably direct. "You did. He respects you the most of all of us. But you've never done yourself that honor, have you?"

A discomfited clearing of her throat was Rebecca's only response, and they walked in silence to the tavern.

"Hold on to your head, Oliver!" Elijah cried upon their arrival. "We come for it again, you witless sot! I never did like a single one of your tired phrases!"

He threw open the tavern door and burst inside with a raucous yell, drawing a pretend sword and crossing the entire first floor in a few bounds. Rebecca couldn't hold back a laugh. The burly man behind the bar moved to tackle him, but Elijah raised his arms in a swift, grand gesture, like a conductor halting a symphony orchestra. All was immediately quiet, the tavern's assemblage frozen in place, staring off into space. Unable to help himself, Elijah waved his arms about a bit, enjoying seeing the entire company nod and turn their heads in response like marionettes on strings. This caused him limitless glee, and Rebecca had to take his arms and gently lower them, lest he play giggling puppeteer all night.

"You allow me no fun," he pouted, a stray finger still making one slovenly drunkard's gaze turn loops.

Rebecca confiscated both his hands in hers and nearly pressed her nose to his. "Fun? What about Jane's recent lark? We cannot all be allowed to misbehave."

"I thought I saw something about a children's ward . . ." he began.

"And?"

"Brilliant." Elijah grinned.

"You picked the locks, didn't you?"

"Michael lets her into the parish wards all the time. I decided it was my turn."

The two of them walked onto the tavern's back stoop. Sure enough, Oliver Goldsmith's disembodied head bobbed at eye level in the back courtyard, his transparent features looking entirely offended.

"Stop scaring the barmaids with your corpse, Goldsmith . . . let your prose do it for you!" Elijah's magic pinned the writer by his century-dead eyes while Rebecca's incantations of banishment settled into a hush. The spirit was soon dispatched and they crossed back through the quiet pub. Elijah relinquished his control of the inhabitants with a flick of his wrist as the front door clicked shut behind them. He admitted, "I don't sense Grimaldi anymore, do you?"

Rebecca thought a moment and shook her head. The Pull was gone. "He must know that his colleague has been dispatched. Performers hate taking direction, especially from us."

"Fancy a drink?" Elijah offered.

Rebecca's stomach roiled, thinking of the night before. "Tea."

"Tea it is," he agreed. "To headquarters! La Belle et La Bête!"

The pair made their way to the small café and found all five of the remaining Guard gathered there. Rebecca's raven fluttered in and Jane's cat was entwined at her feet. The company partook of beverages, tall tales, and laughter. Much playful derision was directed at the absent Alexi. When Percy was spoken of, which was infrequent, it was with apprehensive reverence. Shop talk, as it were, was avoided completely. Rebecca debated mentioning the strange new doors at Athens, then decided to ignore them for the moment. Lifting her tea to her lips, she enjoyed its warmth and cherished her scrap of contentment.

The hour growing late, Michael was gentleman enough to see her safely back to the academy. He was always looking after her. She wasn't sure she'd ever acknowledged it, and only when he vanished back into the shadows did it occur to her that she ought to have thanked him more heartily.

She went to her office. Despite the late hour, there was paperwork to attend to, for which she was grateful. There was a budget to be balanced, a staff to compensate, a board to please, sponsors to court, supplies to order. The work was solid, dependable; there was a science to running an institution and Rebecca was master of it, grateful that some part of her life made sense.

Her occupation was like running a household, only magnified exponentially. This partly filled the ache of not having an estate of her own, partly made up for a lack of a husband and progeny. Partly. Her students were her children and the Guard her family. The Grand Work was her husband. Despite all this, an ache remained.

She was deep into the ledgers when a sensation hit her so sharply it knocked her forward, her fountain pen scratching out and bleeding darkly over the corner of the lined book and onto the blotter. Her breath was swiftly cut from her, as if by a knife. Her gift was sounding a raucous alarm. Miss Parker—*Mrs. Rychman,* she amended bitterly—would be compromised. Endangered. Before there was even a chance for Beatrice's predicted war, somehow she would be cut to the quick. And it would be by someone close to her.

Rebecca's blood chilled. Never before had the pique of her gift felt so violent or so raw. Opening her clenched fist to set her fountain pen to the side, she saw her hand was smeared black. She braced herself against her desk, hoping to still the trembles coursing up and down her spine. But no.

Rebecca shook her head. "No, none of us. It cannot be. We wouldn't." None of them wished ill upon the girl, and so—

She stared up at the ceiling of her office—a beautifully crafted, wooden-paneled affair, with its center scalloped fixture emitting soft gaslight—and needing, to Rebecca's chagrin, a bit of dusting—and prayed. "I don't know what it means," she said, wrestling with her gift, hoping that it would clarify itself once it heard her soft plea. "If I don't know how, or by whose hand harm will come to her, how am I to prevent it?"

The gift would not see reason. Only one thing remained clear: the dread certainty that Percy would be severely endangered by someone she knew. Rebecca steepled her ink-stained fingertips and slid her forehead down onto their point. Her throat tightened about her words, but at last they emerged, both strangled and defiant, half plea, half refusal:

"Not me. It shall not be me."

As the carriage slowed, Percy gasped. A great mansion of deep brown sandstone, with a gothic façade and arching windows latticed with wrought iron, the Rychman estate was nothing if not intimidating, a magical fortress. A thrill worked up her spine to call it home.

Alexi drank in her every expression. "I want to offer everything I can to please you," he murmured.

"Oh, how you do," she cried, fumbling to take his hands in hers.

The driver unloaded their trunks at the side portico, then drove his passengers to the front eaves, where a huge brass bird with outstretched wings held the ring of the door knocker in its talons. Alexi climbed out, swept Percy into his arms, and allowed the driver to open the front door. Percy's delicate fingers danced at the nape of his neck.

"Welcome home, Mrs. Rychman," he said, kissing her softly before carrying her into the house.

Everything was dark as he set her down inside, until he waved one hand and a chandelier above their heads glittered to life, illuminating an open foyer with vaulted ceilings. A winding banister rose to the second floor, where a balustrade jutted over the foyer. The wooden floor of the main hall led to glass doors at either end: Beyond one set of doors was the sitting room, beyond the other, the library. Both doorways were accented by sconces of dragons whose wings cradled glass cups of sparkling flame.

"Oh, Alexi."

Wide-eyed at the elegant splendor of the home, Percy dragged her husband by the hand as she toured the first floor. The windows at the front of the house belonged to an elegant dining room, separated from the sitting room by sliding doors. Steps in a corner of the dining room presumably descended to a kitchen. Several vases of towering roses were set upon the cream cloth covering the banquet table. Another chandelier, vast and circular, was the focal point of the room, draped with crystals that sparkled like diamonds.

Percy took in the open sitting room, which was replete with grand piano, divan, and impressive high-backed chairs near the hearth whose mantel bore the same rich gray marble that topped the end tables. Paintings of Josephine's particular style hung alongside classical, pastoral scenes; the paintings' deep color scheme lent richness to the cherry and mahogany wall panels. Spires of candelabra offered inviting, diffuse light.

Alexi smirked as she tugged him into his library, a room of dark green walls, cherry bookcases, and innumerable leather spines. Percy, lost in the sights and smells, recognized his scent—clove tea and leather-bound books—and leaned close to breathe him further.

Rococo writing desks and random laboratory equipment were arranged throughout the room, interspersed with worn chairs. A large phonograph took up one corner. The moment Percy's eyes fell upon the large, fluted bell, Alexi quickly stepped forward and turned the handle. With a sputtering hiss, out flowed a dark, tumbling Chopin etude. Percy found herself intoxicated anew by the way dim candlelight played on her husband's features.

Rejoicing at the music permeating the house, Percy pulled Alexi again into the foyer, then ran to the windows and unlatched the shutters, exposing the entire hall to a wash of moonlight. A wild, unkempt rose garden came into view, with a winding path to a grove of birch trees.

Alexi took in an awed breath. "My God, you become the very moonlight," he breathed. Percy looked down to see how bright her skin glowed. Her husband extinguished all other light with a wave of his hand. Her body and the moon itself were the only sources of illumination.

Alexi swept her into his arms and began to dance her around the foyer, pausing every now and then to steal a kiss. All through the house they spun, in and out of every room, a deeper kiss in each, finally waltzing up the stairs, swirling about the balcony and through each of the elegantly appointed bedrooms. Their laughing sighs whirled them into the master bedroom, which was furnished with a lavish four-poster bed thickly draped by burgundy curtains, an armoire, a wide hearth, and a leather-topped writing desk. A great arched window looked down onto the wild garden, and strands of ivy could be seen sneaking onto the panes of glass.

Arms around each other, they gazed down at their estate. Alexi softly kissed the crown of his wife's head. "Percy," he whispered. "I used to hate this lonely place, shuttered and collecting dust. The whole of it now brightens with your radiance. This is the first time it truly feels like home."

"How could I not shine, Alexi, with such blessings as these, as you—?" Her voice broke as she pressed her cheek to his breast.

The sentiment encouraged his covetous passion. She had assumed she would live her life entirely without such intimacies, but she'd been wrong. And Alexi held her afterward, all through the night. Percy, overwhelmed with the magnitude of her blessings, knew she'd never tire of their wonder.

JANE SAT ALONE IN HER STUDY, EYES CLOSED, ANTICIPATING. MARLOWE, her white cat, was curled around her leg. The clock chimed softly, marking the arrival of both the night and *him*. The air around her grew cold and she shuddered with delight. A chill pressed upon her lips like a feather made of ice. She opened her eyes at Aodhan's phantom kiss.

He drew back, the chill of his lips a lingering mist, and gestured for her to open her hand.

"You've brought me something?" she asked, a blush heating her cheeks until the look on his face stilled her pleasure. He trickled a stream of ash into her palm—ash that was real and substantial to the touch. Bewildered, Jane asked, "What? What is this you bring me?"

He grimaced and pointed to the clock, then tried gesticulating, but Jane could not fathom his meaning. The light of his shade flickered and he faded before he could offer further instruction.

THE NEXT MORNING, BEFORE BREAKFAST, ALEXI OFFERED PERCY A TOUR of the immediate grounds, and her excitement nearly had him skipping with her toward the rear garden. Braced by the brisk air, they strolled about the twisting, overgrown, cobbled path through thickets of what, to Alexi, was indiscernible foliage. Percy joyfully identified many of the plants, giving the names, blossoming seasons, and general particulars of each.

Returning, they found that the Wentworths, Alexi's household staff, had arrived. The couple did not live in the house, but rather in a nearby cottage, as Alexi wanted to keep his home clear of anyone not involved in the Grand Work. Warned by the detailed letter Alexi had sent, announcing his marriage and describing the new mistress of the house, they showed no surprise at Percy's singular pallor. A brief conversation made it clear that the Wentworths were not prone to gossip and that Percy's lack of domestic savvy would be no obstacle; Mrs. Wentworth would take care of everything. Their service was limited and modest, but thorough in regard.

The woman showed Percy to her boudoir, where the single trunk containing her meager possessions from Athens had been unpacked. To Percy's surprise, the entire wardrobe was full—Josephine had arranged for the creation and delivery of stylish dresses in various shades of blue and purple. The Frenchwoman had sent a note, writing that as she'd only seen Percy in these colors, she'd assumed they must be her favorites. At this, Percy burst into tears.

"Oh, madame, there's no need to cry," the round and rosy Mrs. Wentworth said with great concern. "The professor can send for a seamstress should these not be to your liking."

Percy laughed. "Oh, Mrs. Wentworth, I shed only grateful tears! I was raised an orphan, a pauper in a convent. My room at Athens was palace enough, but now the riches of this household . . . I don't possibly deserve such immense good fortune."

"And why on earth not, Mrs. Rychman? Dear creatures who, as you do, take nothing for granted, deserve every comfort, for you are of the mind to appreciate it. The master's a shrewd man who's kept his lamps trimmed low and his costs negligible. I believe he's only too happy to spend money on you, that it's a pleasure for you both."

"Why, Mrs. Wentworth, you are a domestic savant, indeed." Alexi's low, rich voice slid into the room with his person following close behind.

The woman colored. "Forgive me, Professor, I speak past my place, it's just that your wife—"

"I overheard her gracious tears, and I think, Mrs. Wentworth, that you spoke perfectly to the point."

The woman straightened proudly.

"Darling," Alexi said, pursing his lips, offering Percy his breast-pocket handkerchief. "Do grow accustomed to being provided for, will you?"

Percy stared up at him, fearing that his comment was a reproof, but his eyes sparkled with humor.

Though the dining room was large, they sat close and ate a leisurely breakfast. Percy's face was warmly lit beneath the magnificent, low-hanging chandelier, but her gaze clouded as she set down her silverware. "I ought not keep you waiting, Alexi," she said suddenly.

Her husband offered her a quizzical look.

"Mother's note," she clarified. "If you light a fire and sit beside me, I can face anything."

Alexi nodded and led her toward the study, pausing as Percy glided to the front wardrobe to procure the papers from the pocket of her cloak. They sat beside one another on a soft leather sofa. A flick of his hand provided light and warmth from the room's hearth. Percy beamed at this, nestled into Alexi's arm and opened her mother's letter for the second time.

"'My name is Iris Parker, and I was brought from sin to deliver you, whom divine mystery surrounds. I was born into a wicked life, but mother told me of the Lord, and the Holy Spirit was my only solace. Born with a heavy heart and wont to lapse into profound melancholy, I had clouds of darkness all about me.

"'The night my life changed, I'd been left for dead by a horde of drunken thieves after falling from a high balcony onto the courtyard stones of an inn. Here, I was sure, was my final stand. The fall seemed to have broken everything, and as I prayed to God to end my pain, there was a great light. I was shocked to wake, alive, in a stone room. A convent room. A bright star fell before me. In the light stood the Blessed Virgin. She was dressed in and full of light, bringing the music of angels. She kept shifting colors—'"

Alexi started, and Percy glanced at him. "Our goddess," he breathed, "who proclaimed Prophecy to us. Your reverend mother was granted a similar vision, surely by this same herald"—he stared at Percy, his expression complex—"assuring you would come to Athens. To me."

"And thank heavens for it," Percy murmured, turning again to the letter.

"'The Blessed Virgin proclaimed you like the Christ child, said that you would offer hearts peace and triumph despite all obstacles and iniquity. She said you were escaping a prison to reunite your soul, escaping an old vengeance, seeking to be reborn in love. She said you would do everything to make a life of pain into the life of love you were denied.

"'The heavenly creature wept as she spoke. Each tear was silver and sang with sorrow. She caught the droplets in her hand. She proclaimed I would henceforth be with child, and when she opened her hand the silver tears had formed the bird that you now wear around your neck. I wish I could leave you more than this talisman as inheritance, but this is no ordinary pendant. It is from the divine.'"

Percy plucked the phoenix pendant from her breast and brought it to her lips before continuing.

"'I do not know if you are a messiah, Persephone. That is the name I have been told to call you. Our Lady said so with such blushing fondness that I could not resist. The Virgin vanished, but a woman remained in the room. I started, but she told me not to be afraid, just like the shepherds in the field. Her name is Beatrice and she pens these words, as I never learned to write.'"

Percy and Alexi took a moment to stare at each other.

"'Beatrice, who understands pain and loss, is my sister in this journey. She confirmed my vision leads me on, unfailingly quiet and kind. We've descended the eastern English coast, always moving. We are en route inland to York, where the Institute of the Blessed Virgin shall surely take you. I shall leave these pages for you there and cover all traces of your birth from intrusive eyes.

"'Spirits are now visible to me, Persephone. I see them everywhere. Perhaps you will, too. Beatrice hushes them when they come too near, lest they kindle fires of madness in my mind. But . . . to have a purpose, Persephone, to become part of something greater than ourselves, to serve something lovely and mysteriously divine—this is the greatest validation of life itself.

"'I will make sure the sisters know to send you to find 'The Power and the Light' at a school in London. That was my instruction. The Power and the Light. Whatever that is, Persephone, it sounds stately and grand.'"

"It is our benediction," Alexi spoke up. "And the motto of Athens. It seems that the power of the Guard is tied to that building. But . . . I still don't understand. If all of this was carefully orchestrated, why wasn't I simply alerted to you from the first?"

Percy shrugged. "Beatrice said destiny could not hold our hands. I daresay falling in love with you of my own volition was far better than being told to do so."

They turned their eyes one last time to the scrawling script.

"'We've begun to fondly call you Percy. Forgive me your pet name, as I don't believe I shall know you long as a child. Still, let me indulge in such motherly contrivances. You're my last gift to give before I join the Lord. I'll cradle you, Percy my girl, and then be off. I sit without sadness as Beatrice writes this. I once begged for my constant darkness to end. You made my ending sweet and filled it with light.

"'There are dark forces that defy light. Some might search for you. I trust you'll see the light or the dark of them. I pray you find your way through.

"'If for some reason the sisters have failed in their duty and not sent you to London, you must go straightaway to the school, Athens. In London. You're awaited there, fated for a great love. But a storm comes. All the spirits are murmuring. The very air is filled with excitement. The clouds are swirling, and all the dogs are barking. You must be a very special girl, indeed, my miracle. God bless, my child. I'll hold you soon, and I'll speak to you in heaven.'"

Percy set the papers aside. Tears streamed down her face. Alexi lifted her chin and wiped her eyes before folding her close.

"I need you," she murmured, blurting the first thing she could think to say.

"And I love you," he replied, and kissed her cheek.

She exhaled slowly and felt comforting familiarity in the silence they kept together; two solitary creatures as they had always been. She had seen a brief moment of fear in his eyes, clearly as overwhelmed as she. Perhaps it was sometimes best to keep quiet, lest love's tempest lose its wondrous beauty for its dizzying effect.

CHAPTER

ELEVEN

IF ANYONE HAD BEEN WATCHING ON THE NIGHT OF THE RYCHMANS'
first estate dinner party, they would have seen that the guests appeared
to be an average group of middle- to upper-class English citizens, well
assembled and appointed.

Percy, excited, played hostess at the door. Alexi had retained no
house staff beyond those needed for dinner preparation so it was he who
took the coats and cloaks of the rest of the Guard to the wardrobe near
the door. He allowed his more congenial half to comment upon his
guests' formal attire and bid them enter the dining room.

Rebecca lingered at the entrance, pressing Percy's hand in hers. Holding it a bit too long, an odd light in her eyes, she spoke softly. "Welcome
back. I trust you had an enjoyable time. Now that you've returned, please
take care of yourself. You've wedded a dangerous fate. Please, *please* take
care and be alert."

Recalling Beatrice's words, Percy felt her blood chill at this warning.
Perhaps Rebecca's intuition sensed something her own visionary nature
could not anticipate.

Alexi's sharp ears picked up every word, and he fixed Rebecca with a
curious, concerned stare, but before anything further could be said,
Lord Withersby, who was bringing up the rear of the entourage,
nearly shoved Michael inside, then whisked Josephine hastily across
the threshold.

Stumbling into the foyer, he cried incredulously, "The light, Alexi!"
He flung his arms before his face as if blinded. "The sheer light of the
place!" Taking Percy's face in his hands, he kissed both of her cheeks.
"Why, I never knew this place was so grand! I've never seen it lit! This
husband of yours, madame, always prowled about here in the dark."

"So I've heard." Percy cast a smirk in Alexi's direction and Elijah gurgled in protest.

"You've got her smirking now, Alexi! Come, you oughtn't have affected such a change upon this sweet face. Soon, heaven forefend, you'll have her sneering. Who knows what disasters may yet befall her in this house, and you'll douse all the lamps again—"

"How was your time away?" Michael asked, deliberately changing the subject, and the tone of the conversation, with a warm chuckle. "The sea is lovely no matter the clime, I imagine."

"Indeed, Michael, indeed," Percy assured him.

She led the group toward the dining room, noticing that Elijah's mouth was pinched, his laugh pitched higher than usual. She resisted the urge to study the others, to determine if any of her new companions had had a particularly relaxing time in their absence or if all were more tightly wound than usual.

A hearty course sat ready on the guests' plates, though Mrs. Wentworth never did understand why Alexi didn't mind if the food went cold. The company took seats, leaving Percy and Alexi the ends of the table. Michael's fork poised over his dish.

"Percy, dear," Alexi began, "the flowers you provided are lovely, but would you mind moving them to the hutch?"

"Of course."

As she did so, Alexi waved a hand and a huge ball of fire flashed over the table, warming all plates and only slightly singeing napkin edges.

"I daresay I'll never tire of that!" Percy exclaimed. Alexi flickered a proud smile.

Michael and Jane were both immediately lost to the raptures of well-seasoned potatoes. The rest began to pick like birds at their meals.

"So, *mes amis,* did you sightsee along your journey?" Josephine asked.

Percy ducked behind her napkin, unfolding it slowly as her face had acquired mottled patches of rose. The only explorations they had undertaken were extremely personal.

"Our quaint cottage was quite relaxing," Alexi replied calmly. "Thankfully, no disturbances, ghostly or otherwise, befell us. I hope your time here was similarly quiet."

"A few admonishments here and there—" Rebecca began.

"Goldsmith's reprobate head again," Elijah interrupted.

Jane took a swift drink of wine.

"Model citizens, we were," Josephine declared. Elijah, seated beside her, threw an odd glance over his shoulder, making Percy wonder what adolescent behavior they had been up to.

"You'd best return to Athens as soon as possible, Alexi," Rebecca said hesitantly. "There have been . . . changes. I cannot explain it. Beatrice Tipton is doing something, creating doors. Actual, physical doors. It's odd."

Alexi furrowed his brow and was silent. Percy wasn't fond of the idea of doors, especially not portals to the beyond, and she was sure he agreed. "First thing in the morning," he declared.

"It was lovely to see Reverend Mother again," Percy offered, eager to restore normality to the table. "It was quite clear everyone was shocked by my marriage. While I enjoyed showing Alexi my old haunts, so to speak, I confess that Athens feels most like home these days."

"Reverend Mother," Alexi added, "quite approved of me."

"But I daresay, old chap, there must have been a bit of convincing the mum that you weren't some cad academic with a passing fancy for the young and studious."

Percy choked on her potatoes, but Alexi set his jaw. "My proper intentions and the advantages of my position were made quite clear, thank you."

"'Advantages of your position.' I'm sure."

Michael spoke up. "Elijah, wouldn't you like to introduce Mrs. Rychman more gradually to the insults and injury you routinely lob at her husband, or have you fully armed the battery this evening?"

"Perhaps it's best I learn to pick my offenses, as it appears I shall have many from which to choose," Percy replied, amused and a bit dazed, and everyone chuckled.

"To the wedded couple, their well-deserved holiday, and their safe and happy return to this fine estate," Michael said grandly, raising a glass. Everyone followed suit.

"Thank you, my friends," Alexi declared. "I think it hardly in need of announcement, but we would be well advised to hold a meeting tomorrow night in our chapel."

"Agreed," Rebecca seconded. "And you are aware of tomorrow's staff meeting at Athens, are you not?"

"Indeed. Percy and I shall both be in attendance," Alexi replied.

Percy shrank in her chair. She'd forgotten about her new role as a member of staff. She wondered if she was too shy for such an office, sure the faculty would regard her with curious disdain.

"Do come early," Rebecca said sharply. "To see the . . . changes. And take care." She stared at Percy a moment before picking up her drink.

Alexi nodded, then launched upon a surprising subject. "We were given a letter from my wife's late mother. It seems she knew Beatrice and was visited by our goddess. A prophecy this was, indeed, and she left items for future examination."

Percy busied herself with her tea, thankful Alexi did not go into details of the singular circumstance of her conception, lest Lord Withersby jokingly proclaim her the world's next messiah.

"I've much to ask Beatrice, but we ought not have her trying to speak to any of you directly," she said. "It seemed my mother went a bit mad from hearing spirits."

"Why, then, Mrs. Rychman, have you not?" Michael asked.

"I must be special," she replied, giving a small grin, knowing he meant no implication. "Or I'm completely mad already."

"You did marry Alexi," Elijah offered. When Josephine groaned, he added, "Come now, she nearly begged for that!"

"Whatever you might do to avoid baiting him, *ma chérie,* may aid in keeping this irredeemable predator at bay—for which we shall all be grateful," Josephine instructed tiredly. Percy simply nodded.

"We hoped he would give you a bit of respite, at least in your own home," Rebecca muttered. "Next time, you may have to accidentally forget to send his invitation."

"And the event would die a prompt and quiet death," Elijah assured her.

"Only peace and quiet—blessed peace and quiet—would survive," Rebecca replied, moving a cutlet from Elijah's plate to her own. "How splendid the thought."

After dinner and wine softened the jousts and eased all tensions, the gentlemen of the Guard retreated to the study for sherry and cigars, while the ladies sat in the parlor with coffee and a plate of small pastries that Josephine was loath to relinquish. After a long moment, Percy finally voiced her concern. "They won't be . . . talking about me over there, will they?" she asked meekly.

"Of course," Jane replied, shrugging. "I'm sorry, Percy, but it's the truth."

Josephine leaned in to add her opinion. "I have no doubt Elijah has by now made at least one inappropriate comment."

"If not five," Rebecca said.

Indeed, across the hall, in the suitably masculine den that had so delighted Percy earlier, Lord Withersby placed one thin hand upon Alexi's shoulder while the other jauntily swirled the liquor in his crystal snifter. "So, old chap, let's get right to the point. Tell me. Was your Persephone suitably divine?"

Michael, cigar in his mouth, gasped and sputtered smoke out his nostrils, wondering if Alexi would throw Elijah from the premises for his brazenness. Their leader turned very slowly to peer down his nose at Elijah; the expression on his face one that Lord Withersby had never seen. Relish glittering in his dark eyes; he exuded unmitigated triumph.

"Exquisite beyond words."

Elijah held up his hands in reverence, and in the silence that followed, only Michael could be heard, still forcing out his improperly inhaled smoke.

The ladies were engrossed in a pleasant discussion of what was to be done with the rear garden when Rebecca shot from her perch upon the divan and strode toward the closed glass doors, a hand at her forehead. In the room opposite, Alexi had done the same. They each flung wide the doors at the precise instant.

"Highgate," the two chorused.

"Again?" Josephine pouted. "Why always in my finest dresses?"

The Guard seated themselves in the conveyances in which they'd arrived, all courtesy of Elijah's estate. The drivers had spent the evening with the Wentworth family in Alexi's carriage house. Mr. Wentworth and his son, a painfully shy man who preferred horses to humans, didn't raise an eyebrow as Alexi helped them ready the teams to save time, but Percy was inspired to murmur to Josephine, "Heaven only knows what the servants must think."

Josephine smiled. "Elijah now and then tickles their minds so that they don't ask too many questions. They know we're out of the ordinary, and I secretly think they like us for it."

"What's Highgate?"

"The great graveyard, where London's most fashionable dead are interred. Quite a place to see," Josephine replied.

They set off, and soon tips of obelisks and angels in the distance heralded Highgate's approach. Alexi's hand was pressed firmly over Percy's, and he stared ahead with fastidious concentration. A congregation of ghosts glowed just inside the fast-approaching gate.

Alexi helped her down once the carriage pulled to a halt. Visiting hours had long since passed, but Michael held out his hand and the enormous locked gate swung wide. A ring of dead children coiled at the center and adult spirits lined the tall iron gates of Highgate, swaying.

And speaking. For Percy, there was no bugle call to arms, only a torrent of whispers. A dreadful singsong accosted her ears. "Lucy-Ducy wore a nice dress, Lucy-Ducy made a great mess . . ." The children's voices filled the air. Percy felt her stomach roil, and she wondered if the head of a cavalry charge felt the same.

"You hear something, don't you?" Alexi asked.

"They're all speaking, Alexi, the children, in some sickening rhyme, and the others . . . Well, the others think you have brought me as an offering. As one of them. But I don't know what they want."

"My attention. I've been away. These spectral delinquents require the firm hand of a master." And with that he gestured to the Guard, who darted forward among the grand monuments.

Surrounded by graceful angels, carved mausoleums, and fine crosses, a bright, full moon illuminating the scene, Percy couldn't help but be taken with the eerie light particular to a graveyard; the luminosity of an eternal crossroads.

Her husband lifted a hand toward the children, who suddenly seemed as curious as the adults to see Percy. Tendrils of blue flame snaked forth like ivy from his palm, and he became the great conductor. The transparent adult phantoms squealed and giggled or wailed like banshees, one by one realizing Percy was indeed living flesh. Before they could comment further, Alexi wrapped glowing cords of light around wrists, waists, and necks, attaching them in fiery shackles.

The cantus was begun, with Alexi insisting Percy join the circle. The Guard's voices lifted, focusing their power and whipping a wind around them, coalescing their ancient force. Alexi cried out a word in the ancient Guard tongue: the simple call to peace Percy had heard before. The specters reacted. Some drifted on, some simply faded, some sank into the ground, perhaps still too attached to their rotting coil to abandon it fully.

The hovering children watched the adult spirits around them fade and pouted, their fun cut short. They again took up their nursery rhyme. "Lucy-Ducy wore a nice dress, Lucy-Ducy made a great mess . . ."

The Guard's power rose again, the blue fire crackling forth from their circular conduit, reaching upward in tall flames that tickled the feet of the bobbing young spirits, who sobered, their small eyes angry. "Beware the wrath!" one little girl in a white nightgown called, wagging a finger at Alexi. "He'll lock you away, he will!" The other children picked up the new taunt. "He'll lock you all away!"

The girl in the nightgown floated close, getting louder. "She's coming. She's coming. She is coming!"

Long ago Percy had realized the calls of the dead often meant nothing at all. She hoped that was so now.

"What?" Alexi asked.

Percy winced. "'She is coming,' the girl screams."

Rebecca turned to Alexi. "Remember little Emily, the Luminous case months prior—?"

"I don't think this one means Prophecy," Alexi retorted. "Someone else."

Percy shuddered. The Guard turned back to the remaining ghosts.

"Children, I demand that you go to bed this instant!" Rebecca cried, using her best headmistress tone. Alexi followed the admonishment with a renewed swat of blue fire. The spirits screwed up their faces and descended, sinking again into the earth beneath the small gravestones marked with lambs and flowers, floating onward to where Percy did not know. The sight saddened her, but at least it was quiet.

Returning to their carriages, Rebecca asked, "Athens?"

Alexi raised an eyebrow. "Now?"

"I don't mean to alarm you, Alexi, but what's happening on the grounds is so . . . strange. Should you not come? There are matters—"

"Rebecca, dear, it's near midnight. Fresh phantasms can await the dawn."

"Indeed," said the headmistress, her mouth thinning. She straightened her shoulders and marched off.

Percy watched her retreat. A few paces behind her was Michael, attempting to be noticed. Rebecca deigned to allow him to help her into the carriage. A thought occurred. "You would have gone, wouldn't you? Before?" she asked Alexi.

"What do you mean?"

"Before our marriage. You would have gone to Athens. Rebecca seemed surprised. Disappointed. I'm all right, Alexi. If you should go, please don't hold back on my account."

"I'm taking you home, and that's final," he said. The look in his eyes made Percy's body flood with heat. "We must dole out your supernatural excitement in pieces. I'll not subject you to more, no matter what may lie in wait at Athens."

As the children foretold, she was nearly complete. The Groundskeeper hummed as he peered over the coffin lid. A female form lay in the coffin—his sweetie-snaky lass. Not much could be said for her condition, being that she was entirely ash, a headless body of congealed gray soot that registered tiny, hitching breaths from a quivering sternum. He had catalogued her requisite parts and mostly put them back. There were a few pieces missing, to his dismay, and he wasn't sure she'd come together exactly whole. Or what the effect would be. But something still lived and stirred in those ashes, angry.

Her head was the last of the large jars to be uncorked. He lifted it gently, ash inevitably flaking off for him to collect and return. The fragile head made rattling, hissing sounds, its mask of an open mouth frozen in a moment of rage and defeat. He attempted to soothe it. The body trembled as he poised the head above the crumbling neck. "That's it, my Dussa-do. Soon my pretty girl lives again."

He set the head atop the neck and massaged the ash together. The body hitched and seized, ash flaking off as a hideous growl sounded in the room like a growing storm. The ashen body sat up, slamming flaking hands on the side of the coffin. Its open mouth roared, and the entire Whisper-world shuddered with the echo.

"Where is she?!"

* * *

PERCY DRESSED FOR THE STAFF MEETING AT ATHENS IN DARK BLUE, in one of the dresses Josephine had provided. It was finer than that of any student and well suited for her new profession. She stared into her wardrobe mirror for a long moment, then dove into a drawer to pull a soft scarf of pale blue. She'd once wrapped herself in it daily and intended to keep it, and the familiar shield of her dark, tinted glasses, close at hand. She placed both items in her reticule.

Entering Alexi's study, she found him deep in a pile of notes, attempting to decipher which marks he had given to which student. A week of exams had been overtaken by grave prophecy, peril, and marriage.

"Alexi, will my old professors be in attendance at today's meeting?"

"Hmm? Yes, some of them will be there. Not everyone attends the meetings, however . . ." Alexi trailed off, raising his hand in triumph as he found what he sought. "Why?"

Percy drifted to a leather chair, staring out the window at the sky.

"Alexi, I disappeared. What will they think? What of my final tests? Will I not have to answer to them?"

"You fell ill. And then we were married," Alexi replied. "The staff has already been informed of our union. Our vows will appear sudden, perhaps even lecherous on my part, yet marriages have been made over less. There was every rumor about the headmistress and me, and I'm sure this outdoes anything they may have assumed of me prior. But there isn't a thing to be done for opinion," Alexi replied with a nonchalance Percy envied.

She grimaced, not wishing to recall her own assumptions of the closeness between him and the headmistress. "You're such a help." Then another thought made Percy gasp. "They'll think I'm with child."

"What?"

"They'll think that's why we had to marry so suddenly."

Alexi's brow furrowed a moment before he shrugged. "Perhaps."

"But, Alexi. What if I . . . what if we . . . ? I mean, could . . . ? *Can I?* Can we? Is that part of Prophecy? I . . ." Percy worked herself into breathless shock. "There's so much, Alexi, so much in this new life of ours, I'm . . . Forgive me . . ."

"My dear darling," Alexi said. He knelt before her and took her hands. "I don't care a whit what the staff may think, Percy, and I hope you'll soon feel the same. As to your question, my dear: Of course I've wondered. I don't know if we may conceive. There's no reason to assume it an impossibility, yet we mustn't expect it. We must take our lives one day at a time. Can you pledge to do so with me?"

When Alexi cupped her cheek, she stared into his dark eyes and could breathe again. "You calm me so," she murmured. But the thought was there, and she was not sure she could contain the raptures of her sudden sentiment.

"The idea of a little one does have its delights, though, does it not?" he murmured, making her wonder if he had the ability to read her mind. The two of them gazed quietly at each other before finally turning away from the powerful subject.

Mr. Wentworth drove them to London in the good professor's finest carriage. As Alexi settled opposite Percy, he watched her rustle in her reticule and withdraw her scarf. She pinned up her braid in ritualistic fashion, wrapped the scarf about her head, and slid her dark glasses upon her nose.

"I thought we discussed this," Alexi said, frowning. "Shall my wife hide herself?"

Percy bit her lip. He stared at her with that same unsentimental acceptance that had bolstered her from their first private meeting, the look that allowed her to believe she could escape the personal limitations of her ghostly appearance. She smiled. "I suppose if I was able to go without this in a ballroom, I might do so in a meeting. I derive such fortitude from you."

He almost smiled. "I've stubborn pride enough for us both."

CHAPTER
TWELVE

Entering under Athens's great Romanesque eaves once again, ever inspired by the stately red sandstone and the ornate tracery, Percy was glad they'd returned while the first period was in session, for the main foyer was rather empty. Considering she was no longer to hide beneath her trappings, she was glad to encounter fewer inevitable, discomfiting stares.

Outside her office, Rebecca showed Alexi and Percy the new, narrow door. A soft light emanated from beneath the wooden panel, which was marked with a seven.

Alexi folded his arms and peered close. "There's a draft. I don't suppose you've opened it?"

"Not while you were away, no. I thought it best to have our whole group present."

Alexi pursed his lips and turned the knob. Locked. He raised an eyebrow. "Skeletons in your closet?" When Rebecca scowled he suggested wryly, "I suppose haunts have keys and guest rooms now."

Percy pulled her phoenix pendant—and the new key that hung beside it—into view. "Perhaps this will open it."

Rebecca furrowed her brow, squinting. "And that came from . . . ?"

"My grave."

Rebecca looked in alarm at Alexi, who merely shook his head. "I believe your key is meant for our sacred space, Percy. We'll try it tonight."

"Speaking of meetings, ours is about to start," the headmistress stated, glancing at the watch on her waist-pocket chain. "I suppose we'll soon know if any of the faculty have noticed our little . . . renovations. Where do you think this leads, Alexi?"

"The spirit world—cold draft, eerie light and all," Alexi replied, and walked away toward the grand staircase. Rebecca and Percy hurried to catch up.

"But Alexi," the headmistress said. She leaned close and spoke softly, and Percy had to strain to hear as they walked. "Doors that open from the spirit world into ours—actual physical doors like we've never seen, and that are locked from this side? Don't we want to keep them shut?"

"I didn't say I was fond of the idea," he replied. He drew Percy forward so that they all three strode side by side. The act made Percy's heart swell: She would not be left out. She was privy to this madness, too, and her powerful, mysterious professor wanted her on his arm.

Rebecca moved ahead. Percy found herself wishing Michael were there; he always seemed ready to take the headmistress's arm. The first period was letting out and the murmur of students filled the arching halls with rustling noise.

As they ascended the stairs, Marianna rounded the corner, spied Percy, and ran to throw her arms around her friend's neck. Alexi moved out of the way as if dodging something dangerous.

"How was the honeymoon?" the blond girl crowed.

Percy blushed as a few staff turned with raised eyebrows. Alexi was staring at her expectantly, so she extricated herself from Marianna's grasp and said, "It was wondrous, darling, but I must go. I cannot be late to the staff meeting. I hope to see you soon!"

Her friend withdrew as if ashamed, for the first time staring at Percy as if she were something different. And it was true that she was, that things were altered. Yet Percy wanted to lose none of the warmth and delight of her friend, so she grasped Marianna's hands in hers. "We'll make time to talk, I promise. You simply must visit the estate."

Her friend nodded. "Of course, Mrs. Rychman," she replied.

Percy blushed. "While that title yet thrills me, you mustn't call me it. To you, of all people, I will always be Percy."

She kissed Marianna on the cheek and rushed to take her husband's outstretched hand. Glancing back, she saw the blonde smile, seemingly buoyant and unruffled, but glimpsed a slight melancholy in her lovely green eyes.

Athens staff meetings were held in a small lecture space on the second floor of Promethe Hall. The conversation stilled when Percy and

Alexi entered. Utterly unruffled, her beloved went about business with enough indifferent arrogance as to confound any possible critics. In fact, it became apparent that Alexi, while claiming no care for public opinion, was rather enjoying the idea of their scandal. A mischievous sparkle lurked in the corners of his sharp eyes as he boldly kept hold of her hand. She couldn't help but be amused despite all the eyes upon her.

Headmistress Thompson ran the meeting with brisk efficiency. When a teacher inquired about her recent health, Rebecca coughed and dismissed the notion with obvious embarrassment. Percy wondered what had happened.

Occasionally Alexi and the headmistress would glance at each other, perhaps wondering if the subject of architectural changes to Athens would arise.

But no one said anything, so it seemed the doors were only visible to the Guard.

Rebecca offered Percy a brief, formal welcome as the new linguistic appointment, and Percy was grateful for the utter lack of ceremony. Her former dormitory chaperone, Miss Jennings, kept a scowl on her face, stewing over the unexpected couple. If she had only done her job, her thickly knitted brows seemed to say, that haughty Rychman would never have been so bold.

Meeting adjourned, Percy released a breath and was the first to glide into the open foyer beyond. Alexi moved behind her. "Come, my dear, let me show you to your office."

"I've an office?"

At the end of a long hallway there was a paneled wooden door with freshly painted gold script that read: *Translation Services, Mrs. A. Rychman*. Alexi opened the heavy door, and the sight beyond caused Percy to gasp. The room was a fair size, with a bay window that took up nearly an entire wall and looked down onto the school courtyard. Light shone brilliantly through its Bavarian-style glass. Every furniture cushion was a royal purple. The walls held books, floor to ceiling. Percy was agape.

"Mrs. Rychman," her husband began grandly. "Our Athens translator and envy of all faculty as resident of the Bay Room."

"Oh, Alexi, I don't deserve this. How was this beautiful room not occupied?"

"Because it is most assuredly, and most constantly, haunted." He grinned. "I didn't think you'd mind."

A few books floated from a bookshelf and settled gently on the leather-topped desk, covers opening and pages turning. The temperature in the room dropped a number of degrees; a grayscale, square-jawed, professorial gentleman came through the bookcase and fixed Percy with a transparent stare. His hair was long and bound behind him. Percy glanced at the books on the desk: poetry in several languages.

The ghost held out his hand and a lovely woman with windswept hair slipped through the bookcase and into the room. Alexi nodded in greeting. "Professors, may I introduce your new tenant, our new linguistic administrator, my wife, Persephone? Percy, Professors Michael and Katherine Hart."

Percy smiled. She recognized them. Every year on their anniversary, these wraiths were known to waltz in the tiny graveyard behind Apollo Hall. She'd watched them, enraptured. The deceased academics eyed her appraisingly.

"Hello, Professors Hart." She made a small curtsey. "Pleasure to meet you. I see you have placed a book of sonnets on my desk. I do hope you'll do me the pleasure of reciting your favorites. I, unlike others, am able to hear your ghostly voices."

The floating forms turned to each other and smiled. Katherine said, in a sweet voice like the wind, "You'll do fine then. Perfect, in fact. Welcome." She took her husband's arm and remarked absently, "Lovely couple. Wonderful how those with gifts find each other." The two vanished back through the bookshelves.

"I remember them, you know," Percy said.

Alexi took a seat upon the bay window and gestured for her to join him. "The waltz in the graveyard?" He gave a slight smile. "I saw you from my office window that night, your arms open to them, starved for such a thing. I didn't know what else was to be done but teach you how."

"Our waltzes . . ." Percy breathed, remembering his lesson, then the academy ball, when the blooming flower of their affection could at last be denied no longer.

The sound of her breathless recollection compelled Alexi to kiss her. He drew back after a languorous moment to see Percy's eyes remained dreamily half open. "While I could easily busy myself with you in all manner of ways, I've a bit of business," he admitted. "As for your new position, I've a book for the Russian consulate. Your work will fund a scholarship for young girls in need of education. I had thought to bring the volume of English poetry with me but I confess, stealing a kiss from you in *your* office entirely derailed my more scholarly intentions. I'll fetch the volume now . . . lest I remove your clothing. I'm not sure the professors Hart would approve of *quite* so much . . . ardor in their midst." He smoothed and adjusted himself, stalking off before he could reconsider.

She watched him go and bit her lip, indulging a bit of a swoon against the bay window cushions.

"Oh, how you love him!" declared a strong female voice. "I admit it's a balm to my weary soul. I've worked so hard."

Having thought herself alone, Percy jumped to her feet and whirled to find a ghost floating near her desk. "Hello, Mrs. Tipton," she said.

The spirit straightened to greet Percy properly. Her presence in life must have been very potent, as intimidating as Alexi and the headmistress had been to Percy at first, as her shade lingered on in a form very nearly solid. "My lady!" She floated forward. "You look so much the spirit. I do wonder how you managed that particular trick."

"Excuse me?"

"Your color. I wondered how on earth you managed it."

Percy flushed. "No trick, madam. I certainly would not have chosen this coloration had it been within my power to affect."

"Well, it shall come in quite useful on the Whispering side."

Percy hoped Beatrice didn't mean what she assumed. "Would you . . . care to sit down?"

"No, no, you sit. I suppose you've questions for me."

"Indeed."

"Lovely wedding," Beatrice murmured. "Made me think of the rite Ibrahim and I had. Intimate. Powerful." Her eyes hardened. "But that was long ago. Where shall we begin?"

Percy sat again at her bay window, a sliver of sunlight falling across her lap. She wished she could busy her trembling hands with a cup of tea. "Please, tell me of my mother."

Beatrice stared at her a moment, impassive. "For the brief span I knew Iris, she was a good woman. Kind, generous." The ghost looked away. "Full of a faith I never understood, giving herself to her fate in a way that I admired. Because, damn it if I didn't fight my own fate." She turned again to Percy, her expression pained. "Remind me that you remember nothing of the old times, of the other side, of the life prior to your current flesh."

"All I know are the simple visions that led me to Alexi. Tiny flashes. Should I remember more?"

"No, it's just as well." Beatrice sighed. "You've begun again, a clean slate. I just have to remember not to lay any lingering resentments at your feet, my lady, for it isn't your fault."

"I'm Percy, please."

"Indeed. You're not my lady. You're Mrs. Alexi Rychman, and all is as it should be."

"Is it?" Percy asked.

Beatrice sighed. "I both loved and hated the Grand Work. In life I was a mortal pawn for an ancient vendetta, preparing for a prophecy of strangers, and I remain servile to it in death. I resented the powerful force that was Our Lady, and yet I loved her, for while she was not mortal she loved like one, wished to live as one, and loved the Guard like family. But she couldn't know the burdens she brought onto us by this calling. She had so many burdens of her own, her poor form faltering after so many years in that dark Whisper-world for which she was never meant. And so she never truly knew how it was for us."

Percy regarded Beatrice with open empathy. The spirit wafted closer, her edges softening. "But we must finish what we started. What began eons ago with a murder."

Percy shuddered in sudden recollection. "I relived a horrific death by fire, more vision than memory. There was a great, winged angel of a man, reminiscent of Alexi—"

"Yes. That was terrible history. Phoenix splintered under Darkness's fist, but he could not be quenched. He and his attendant Muses lived on in what became the Guard, using mortals to fight Darkness's viler whims. The goddess Persephone deteriorated without her true love, quite literally rotting in the Whisper-world. She awaited the day she could finally give over, could choose this side for good and be close to the pieces of that life she cherished. She brought remnants of Phoenix to this school. Eventually she was brave enough to choose this life. To become you, something immortal made flesh. Much like they say of Je—"

Percy's hands flew up. "No, you mustn't."

"Ah, yes, you're Catholic." Beatrice chuckled. "Theologically confusing, I'm sure. You could choose not to believe in anything, like me, and then be surprised by moments of supreme divinity. Tell me: Are you happy?"

Percy, reeling, took a moment, thought of Alexi and all that had changed. "Yes. I would say I am most blessed."

"Good." Beatrice nodded and stared out the window.

"Why the gift of language?" Percy asked suddenly. "Why can I hear, know, and speak each tongue I encounter?"

Beatrice stared at her. "Because death speaks every language." When Percy shuddered, Beatrice added, "The goddess spoke to all the dead. She was beloved for it. It seemed she passed on that gift to you. It taxed her immensely, but she tried to set as many to rest as she could. Sometimes it only takes one word of kindness, you know, to set a soul at ease."

Percy's eyes watered. "That's lovely," she murmured, feeling a sudden pride in her heritage, confident in her endeavor to carry on that noble work in this life.

Beatrice grinned a bit wickedly. "I wonder if your husband remembers you stealing to his bedside as a youth, making him a man . . ."

"I beg your pardon?!" Percy flushed.

The ghost batted her hand. "Don't be jealous. He only ever loved you. Divine, mortal, she who became you. As a divinity you—"

"*She*. I'm not—"

"She came to the Guard on their annunciation day. She proclaimed Prophecy. You may ask them about it."

Percy tried to calm herself. "Yes, Alexi mentioned her, and that some part of her might be guiding me—or inside me."

Beatrice nodded. "Desperate, she came to him in dreams. In Alexi she found the closest match to her beloved as ever was incarnate. She wiped his memory to make him fresh for what she would become, but not until afterward. She wanted to be with him as a bride, and was scared she would not find him in whatever she became. But here you sit."

Percy grimaced. While she had no right to be jealous, exactly, she was more confused than ever about her identity, and was suddenly afraid Alexi loved someone from his past.

A knock sounded at her door. "It is I, dear. Kindly open the door for me," called a low, rich, unmistakable voice.

"Such a striking boy. What a fierce and imperious man Rychman has grown to be. And how love transforms that stern face." Beatrice sat, hovering, on the desk while Percy scurried to the door.

Alexi swept in, carrying a double armful of books. "Your first assignment, my dear—a bit of Shelley's work to be translated into Russian as a gift to the czarina. A grand beginning, eh, a tale of two Percys, funding the education of the disadvantaged in a gift to royalty?" It was as he placed the stack through Beatrice that he noticed her on the desk. Jumping back, he straightened his robe and held his head high. "Ah. Percy, you didn't tell me you were receiving company."

She rushed forward. "My apologies, love, it was rather sudden."

"Hello, Mrs. Tipton." Alexi narrowed his eyes. "So, you arranged our lives, did you? Percy's mother—"

"Alexi," Percy admonished. A long moment passed as spirit and professor stared at each other.

"It's all right, Percy." Beatrice chuckled. "I knew he'd waste no time." She floated about the room as Percy repeated her every word. "What shall I tell you, and what must I leave to discovery? I, of all souls," Beatrice murmured evenly, "know the importance of being left to fend for oneself. It is the only way one learns. Survival in the face of uncertain terror makes one keen. You, Professor, are very keen."

Alexi was immediate in his reply. "Keen to know a few answers."

"I have no answers for you, Professor. I simply bear tidings of war."

Alexi set his jaw, focusing on the spirit even though it was Percy's voice that brought Beatrice's words to his ear. "You've relayed your message, then. Oughtn't you return to whatever sort of elysian fields lie beyond if you've nothing more to offer?"

Beatrice narrowed her eyes. Her transparent hands clenched. "We've no fields, Professor, they're burned and gone. An eternal prison fashioned by Darkness is all I've heard awaits our kind. We must yet earn the Great Beyond." The spirit turned to Percy and said, "I'm sorry, my dear, but you do realize what's ahead, don't you? Why all those portals open? You do realize that you'll have to go back."

"Go back?" Percy asked meekly.

"The hell she will," Alexi said, fury in his tone as he glared at Beatrice.

"You blend in with the spirits, my dear, it's brilliant. And it's the only way. You have to turn the keys to start the war. He won't know it's you. He won't have guessed what you've become."

Percy sat, reeling again. "Who . . . ?"

"Darkness."

"Darkness." Percy shuddered.

"What. What are you saying?" Alexi demanded, the last exchange not having been translated. He stood over her, mad with rage.

Beatrice floated beside them. "He isn't going to take this kindly, Percy, but it's the only way. Do not fear, you're not alone. Soon, I pray, we'll all finally be free from Darkness's shadow. But it will take a battle."

Percy related this last, attempting to strengthen her own voice, but it felt weak and young.

Alexi faced Beatrice, his eyes like fire. "I'm not letting her go there."

Percy seized his hand and brought it to her lips, not knowing what to say but yearning to touch him. His fingers twitched and he yanked them away.

"There's no other choice," Beatrice stated. "The doors have already begun linking the worlds for our vendetta's grand battle. If the doors open into *here,* into our territory, they won't open everywhere. This war must stay contained and corralled to our advantage."

"So that's what that's about," Percy said instead of translating.

"What?" Alexi barked.

"The doors," Percy explained, trying not to let his agitation panic her. "The new doors link the mortal and spirit worlds. Here. What you guessed is true."

"Athens shall be the epicenter of spiritual upheaval, then?" Alexi growled. "Isn't that what we've been trying to avoid all these years? Bringing spirits *to* us is antithetical to the very nature of our work!"

"It's precisely why we seized these stones, why Phoenix fire runs through them. Here is the only place that's safe. Our Lady and I made sure of it," Beatrice replied and Percy repeated.

"I'll not let the spirit world have this school, and certainly not my wife!" Alexi growled, pointing a threatening finger. Beatrice calmly returned his gaze. "If I have to keep her under lock and key, I shall. I nearly lost her once in this life, I won't make that same mistake twice." He clenched his fists and stormed out of the room, slamming the door behind him.

Percy and Beatrice stared after him for a long moment. "He does that sometimes," Percy murmured, "when he doesn't know what else to say, or when it seems he cannot control the situation. You mustn't mind—"

"Come now. Of course I don't mind, I've a hell of a temper. Alexi feels just as I did; used, angry, confused. I understand. But we're still part of a fate that will take us under if we don't fight back."

Percy sighed. She stared out the window down at the courtyard where a few students and staff milled. "I've no concept of a life other than this. I will fight for it alone, no matter that I cannot remember my past."

"I fight for love, too," Beatrice murmured. Percy looked up and met her intent gaze. "He's trapped inside the Whisper-world by the hand of Darkness. We died to make this right. Whether you remember your debt or not, it's your turn to help me. No matter what."

Percy's throat dried. "I've no wish to go against Alexi."

"You may have to, at first." Beatrice shrugged. "He'll come around."

"I won't lie—"

"I'm not asking you to," the spirit interrupted. "But when you're called, you'll come, and we'll finally settle the score. From what I've observed, there are powers within you when you need them."

Percy grimaced. "It would seem."

"Darkness will never stop looking for you. You might as well start learning the map."

Percy stared at her, confounded. "Map? What map?"

"In the Guard's private chambers. A key unlocks it. The one your mother and I planted."

Percy fumbled around her neck and brought up the key on her pendant. "This?"

"Yes, that. There's another key you'll have to find to make the merger complete. That one's a bit more difficult. You'll see soon enough. I have to go—more doors need knitting. The pins are loosening again, and when they're all nearly open, we'll be forced to make our move. Stay alert and be well, Percy."

"What about the betrayal of which you spoke? I've seen no hint of such, and I refuse to make my new family suspect for no cause."

Beatrice thought a moment. "That is likely best. I wish I could say, but the situation is no clearer to me. The Guard senses when one of their number is in danger. I can only hope that now extends to you, and that they'll rally to you when you need them." And with that, she vanished out the bay window.

Percy sighed heavily and supposed she ought to find and reassure her husband, but she found she didn't really want to speak to anyone. She just wanted some silence. Of course, when one heard the dead, peace and quiet was hard to come by. Her world would never be silent. Perhaps she would just sit with a cup of tea.

HAVING CLEANED AND ORGANIZED HER OFFICE WITH METICULOUS obsession, Rebecca sat stiffly in her chair, uneasy. The wool of her snug collar grazed her throat as she swallowed. How should she tell Alexi what her gift had proffered? While information should flow freely between leader and second, would Alexi not be maddened by a vague threat? Would she be granted enough foresight to keep everyone safe? Or was she stalling, out of fear or guilt . . . or out of some secret thought that if she just let things go Percy would simply end up out of the equation?

She shook her head, demanding better of herself. "No. I will fight for the girl. Not against her." But could she ever trust herself in matters concerning the woman Alexi Rychman loved? Worse: If she told him, wouldn't he secretly assume her to be the betrayer?

Just then, the man in question burst through her door and slammed it angrily behind him. "Beatrice says Percy will have to go back into the spirit world, where none of us dare go, to bring about the war to end it all."

Rebecca furrowed her brow. "Percy has to go back? But she just got here."

"Precisely my point. Why did we fight so hard for Prophecy if we're sending her right back into the abyss? I won't let her go."

"So the doors—"

"I don't know exactly," he growled. "The new doors in this building have something to do with the final battle. Athens will be the field of conflict between the mortal and spirit worlds."

"But we don't want the worlds joined—we've spent our lives trying to keep them separate!" Rebecca cried.

"I know," Alexi spat, having a friend in frustration fueling his ire. "Spirits tell Percy things I can't hear, the ramifications of which I don't understand, and I feel like a pawn in some farce."

"We've enough doors for one," Rebecca agreed. "I just noticed a new one down the humanities hall."

"We need a meeting. I'm not going to let one ghost determine our future, not after decades of work." He flung wide the door and nearly crashed into Percy, who was hesitating outside, her hand raised to knock.

She flinched as he glowered down at her, even as his gaze softened slightly in recognition and affection. "Have a nice tête-à-tête?" he asked.

Percy sighed, staring at him. "I've no more sense of what to think than you."

Alexi said nothing. Behind him, Percy glimpsed Rebecca watching impassively from her desk. She said, "I . . . thought maybe Miss Thompson would like a cup of tea. And you, of course. Would you like a cup of tea?"

"No thank you," her husband said, storming into the hallway and leaving the door open behind him. "But perhaps the headmistress will indulge you. We've early dinner plans. Do be ready when I call."

"Yes," Percy breathed. *"Professor,"* she added, her throat constricting as she watched him go.

The headmistress glanced out into the hall, then at Percy, her hard mouth and furrowed brow no more forgiving than Alexi's. Percy hesitated before turning away.

"Good God, girl, you look like a lost sheep." Rebecca grimaced. "Come and sit. I'll call for tea."

"Th-thank you, Headmistress."

"You may do away with that formality."

"Oh, I'm not sure that I can," Percy said.

Rebecca stared at her, scrutinizing her like she had the day Percy first sat in that chair, not terribly long ago. She shook her head. "You're just a girl," she muttered, turning away and pulling on the golden cord that signaled the servants in their hall, a flight below.

"And by that, should I be relieved or offended?" Percy asked.

Rebecca's lips twitched. "You know, you've a bit more spine now than you came here with."

"I had no choice." Percy shrugged. "I married Alexi."

"I wish I could tell you that your lot would be an easy one. But then again, surely even when a smitten schoolgirl, you foresaw a lifetime with a . . . difficult man."

Percy was exceedingly grateful for the knock at the door and the entrance of the plump and pleasant butler Percy had often seen bringing professors afternoon refreshments. He wheeled in a fine tray that held a hot silver pot and china teacups and made a bowing exit, giving Percy only one second glance.

Percy rose and prepared a cup of tea. "Sugar?"

"No. Thank you."

Percy passed the cup to Rebecca, then prepared her own drink, a little sugar softening the rich Darjeeling. They sat in awkward quiet made bearable by the business of tea.

"Do come to the estate for a visit," Percy blurted.

"I've a school to run, Mrs. Rychman," Rebecca said. "I've no time for such niceties, however generous the offer of . . . calling hours."

"Alexi said that women should have offices for those sorts of things. And so you and I do." Percy shrugged. "I remember being particularly heartened to hear you say you chose to run an institution rather than a household."

"And yet you ended up with a household," Rebecca replied, her lips thin.

"The greatest wonder of my weird life," Percy said, gazing into her tea.

There was a tapping at the window; Rebecca rose and let Frederic inside. The bird squawked and strutted about the headmistress's desk, shifting papers as he did. They both watched him, glad of the distraction while they sipped the remains of their tea.

"Thank you for the company, Headmistress," Percy murmured as she set down her empty cup. "You're always welcome in my office for the same."

Rebecca nodded curtly, once.

Feeling worse than before and just as friendless, Percy left. The Guard were more like business associates; the warmth of their initial welcome came from gratitude that she had unwittingly saved their lives and was not an indication that she would fit into their established social fabric.

Perhaps heaven was listening, as she was almost immediately provided for: Amid a rustle of skirts, a petite figure was suddenly in stride with her. "And how is the new lady of Athens?"

The familiar German accent made Percy sigh in relief. "Hallo, *meine liebe*. I'm exceedingly glad to see you. It's all been rather much, and I'm afraid I'm still reeling. They've even given me an office!"

Marianna made a mocking face, then grinned and dragged Percy to a bench by a window. She leaned in, her eyes bright. "Do tell, how is life with Herr Rychman?"

Percy blushed, sure Marianna was curious about their intimacy—which was the easiest and most glorious part of their union. Everything else was . . . "Complicated."

"Trouble so soon?" Marianna gasped.

"No," Percy assured her, glancing toward Rebecca's closed door.

Marianna saw and understood. "The headmistress's jealousy is driving you mad—" she blurted.

"No!" Percy batted her hand before her friend's mouth. "If I were to describe our situation you'd hardly believe it. It is the stuff of ghosts and visions."

"Ah. Your mysteries have something to do with him, after all? I'd have thought a man of science—"

"It isn't easy for him. Or me." Percy's mood clouded. How to speak of her heart without revealing more? "It's impossible to live solely for love when there are odd forces in our lives we don't entirely understand."

Marianna reflected. "He worries for you, then, which makes its own trouble."

"Quite wise. Yes, I do believe that's so."

"But strange forces aside, think of the miracles, Percy. Think how shocking that a man as cold as he could look so warmly at you. It's staggering."

"Truly?" Percy asked.

Marianna rolled her eyes. "You doubt it? After the rush of marrying him, do you still not see how he stares at you?"

Percy blushed, realizing how her confidence had been faltering, wilting slowly under Beatrice's vague threat, proclamations of future struggles and tasks, and Alexi's anger.

"Or . . . you had to marry him so quickly because he ruined you!" Marianna whispered. Percy's blush increased, and she shook her head. "He would have if you hadn't run immediately to that chapel!"

Percy leaned in, smiling. "That, perhaps, is true."

"So all of that smothering intensity of his, in the end, is worth something."

Percy bit her lip and stared at Marianna, the answer clear. They both blushed and sighed.

"Persephone, I've been looking for you," came a sharp voice. Percy looked up to find Alexi, her cloak on his arm, stern and stoic as if he were still her teacher.

"Hello, husband," she replied, choking off her giggles and rising to her feet.

"Hello, Professor," Marianna said.

Alexi glanced at the blond girl and bowed his head. "If you'll forgive me, Fräulein Farelei, I'm always taking your friend from your side."

"You've every right. Just so long as you give her back occasionally," came the reply, along with a wide smile.

Alexi held out his arm and Percy took it. When she glanced back, Marianna gestured toward Alexi's eyes, encouraging her to really see what her husband felt. Percy beamed and hoped her expression gave appropriate thanks.

"You've a guilty look of gossip about you," Alexi muttered.

Percy looked up at him and grinned. "Oh, *Professor*. I'm still your smitten, pining schoolgirl. These things cause blushes. And the occasional giggle. You mustn't take offense, as I can't promise it won't happen again."

A smile tugged at his mouth. He placed her cloak around her at the door. "I assumed you'd like a spot of dinner before our meeting. A restaurant. Unless a dormitory dining room pleases you more? Would I be allowed in?"

Percy giggled. "Hardly. Besides, I'm quite ignorant of London outside of Athens. Do educate me, husband."

Again, Alexi seemed pleased.

A few streets south sat a fine little establishment decorated with dark wood and sparkling glass. Two Athens staff at a corner table fell to murmuring the moment they arrived, but Alexi's haughty smirk bolstered Percy. She wished she cared as little as he, but they were both soon eating soup and speaking pleasantly of Athens trivialities. Percy was grateful for the distraction. Alexi's ire and talk of returning to a world and a life she did not remember would come soon enough.

Rebecca rose from the café table at La Belle et La Bête, coming to a realization. "I doubt Alexi will collect us here—he'll likely prefer private dining these days," she muttered, her lips thinning. "Come. Time for meeting."

"You're heavy laden," Josephine said quietly, taking her hand.

"I've been laden for years; you're only now noticing?"

Michael had procured her coat from the hooks at the door and was holding it out. "There's something you're not telling us," he said. Elijah and Jane glanced at each other, silently dressing for the chill outside.

"You mustn't get weary, darlings, the best is yet to come!" Rebecca declared with a hollow smile. "Poor Athens will bear the brunt of it. Come, let's hear it from Alexi. He's none too fond of the recent revelations."

"And dear Percy?" Jane spoke up.

Rebecca grimaced. "Poor girl doesn't understand a whit of what awaits. My instincts are unusually muddied, but they're clear on one thing."

"What?" Josephine asked.

"Doom."

Alexi and Percy sat in the Athens chapel. He'd hardly let go of her hand all evening, as if he dared not. Percy didn't mind; his desire to hold her, any part of her, made her feel secure.

The rest of the Guard arrived as one, suggesting they had all been together; Rebecca still wore the grim mask she'd taken since first mentioning that Athens was changing. Seeing them, Alexi sent a bolt of blue fire toward the plain altar, and a black dot grew into a two-dimensional door that somehow led to a world where their power reigned.

The Guard descended into the place. Alexi waited at the portal edge, his hand out. Percy remembered: This was the path she'd trod to save them. She went through, and Alexi descended behind her, the portal door closing after them.

Here in this colonnaded room at the edge of two worlds, he had pledged his love and revived Percy's flagging life. Hesitant, she stood outside the circle of the Guard until Alexi drew her next to him. A wind coursed the room. Percy heard the familiar song rise, the Guard's call to order, their affirmation of ancient power. A circle of blue flame leaped around their ankles, linking them.

"The Power and the Light!" Alexi cried. An enormous shaft of brilliant azure fire wreathed in white beams erupted from the center of the floor and connected with the great stained-glass firebird hanging above. The room hummed with power, recharging and fortifying them. They all blinked, the light too bright to stare into directly. "You are welcome here, Percy," Alexi murmured. "The light has never been so powerful." The rest nodded, impressed.

"I feel at home," Percy murmured, blushing. The light was like a drug, making the world wonderful and all her worries vanish, leaving only boundless love. She beamed at Alexi, who seemed dazzled by the sight.

"Are you going to stare moonbeams at each other all night, or is this a meeting?" Elijah drawled. Alexi pursed his lips as the rest giggled, Rebecca the only one clearly not amused.

Staring down his friends, Alexi donned his natural authority. "I assume Rebecca has alerted you to the curious changes to our center of operations." When the Guard nodded, he added, "Our battle has only just begun. Doors to the spirit world will continue to open and the spirit Beatrice, who claims she was one of us once, has boldly declared my wife will have to go into the spirit world."

The group began to murmur and to eye Percy in alarm.

"This cannot be," Alexi continued, quieting them. "There must be another way. I do not know if this spirit can be trusted."

"There's no reason she shouldn't be," Percy said softly.

Alexi's eyes flashed. "No reason? It would seem that, rather than separating the mortal and spirit worlds by the great walls we have tried to keep intact all these years, Beatrice is connecting them, creating new doors. The truth is, at any moment the Whisper-world might pour right in upon us."

Elijah asked, "If she was one of us and is now reversing our work, what has been our purpose all these years? Has our service in London been some sort of a joke?"

"Our future is unknown, our very purpose questioned by these suggestions," Alexi agreed. "Unfortunately, Prophecy has left us no map."

The last word jarred Percy. She hadn't thought to mention Beatrice's map reference to Alexi; it was too much all at once. Her mind was swimming with questions of divinity versus mortality, and with fear that Alexi loved a divine image more than her own flesh. Yet, perhaps she ought to offer up the key around her neck. Or would that disrupt the proceedings, bringing a new riot to the table? It was her key, found in her grave, so perhaps it was related more to her than to the current conflict. She would see to it on her own rather than distract her friends; she would study it as Beatrice suggested.

"We must watch as Athens changes," her husband was saying, "perhaps exorcise these doors back from whence they came. We must first assure ourselves these troubles do not affect our students, who are innocent of dealings with our Work."

"And we must, dear fellows, renew ourselves," Michael breathed, turning his face toward the fountain of light.

The Guard took time to do just that, breathing deeply, aware of each other soul in the circle and the preciousness of life. Their blood rushed refreshed in their veins.

"Until duty brings us next to your mercy," Alexi murmured to the sacred space.

The light faded but did not vanish. The bird above glittered as if subtly alive. Percy stared at it to the last, drinking in its replenishing warmth, as the Guard filed upward. Alexi lingered to collect her. For comfort as much as out of habit, she crossed herself and traversed the impossible threshold back into the more traditional church.

The hired carriage turned into their drive, and Alexi offered Percy a key to their darkened, empty home. With a kiss upon the cheek, he helped her down the step and onto the flagstone. "I'll be a moment," he explained, and was off behind the house, perhaps to take his beloved Prospero for a gallop.

Percy wandered into the shadows inside, turning gas lamps low and ascending to the second floor. In and out of rooms she glided, searching like a ghost in a haunt it could not quit, and arrived finally at a back chamber furnished only with a dusty harpsichord. Eager for the twinkling, antique sound to sort her mind, she rushed to the bench.

The instrument was out of tune and its notes had a dull, distant quality, as if the thick fog outside had suddenly infiltrated the room—or the fog of her own doubt, from which her rich Mozart etude, melancholy in its winding chords, could not untangle her. Alexi's embrace, she knew, might cure all, but she also respected their two solitary natures. Not every hardship could be met and resolved simply by touch.

After a bit of Beethoven, then Alexi's favorite, Chopin, Percy leaned against the top keyboard, causing a lingering, dissonant noise, when she heard, "My sentiments precisely."

Percy turned with a smile. Leaning against the frame, his cloak and frock coat removed, the sleeves of his charcoal shirt rolled up his forearms, his cravat open along the lines of his unbuttoned collar and a snifter of a dark liquid in hand, was her husband. Would she always be as struck by him as the day he first burst into her classroom and soul? It seemed so, especially with him in partial undress, in the comfort of his home. The sight of him now was a wish fulfilled. Her dear professor had come to her, to bid her relax and undress, to join and lie beside him.

"How you stare, Percy. Do I look that much a fright?" Alexi chuckled warily. His rakish look flushed her cheeks with longing.

"No! I . . ." Percy giggled. "To see you a bit undone utterly undoes me."

His chiseled lips curved and perfected the rakish picture. "You play beautifully, my dear. You must impress our guests when next we entertain." He held out a hand. "Come. Are you tired?"

Percy nodded and rose to meet him at the door. He offered her a sip from his snifter, sliding his other arm around her waist. One potent whiff, and the look on her face caused Alexi to withdraw it with an amused snort. The liquor, however, tasted sweet and heady in the clutch of his subsequent kiss. To the latter intoxicant they gave themselves eagerly, rather than ruminate upon the danger yet to come.

CHAPTER THIRTEEN

THE GRUESOME FACE OF ASH GROWLED, JAWS GRINDING IN ANGER, stony snakes on her cracked scalp slithering, hissing, flaking ash onto the ground. "I'm going to find her." The voice was coarse, wet gravestone. "She'll pay."

The Groundskeeper fussed. "You're hardly in a state—"

"Taking matters into my own hands. I'll prove to him I ought to have been queen all along!"

One by one, her fingers crumbled into heaps of ash. The rest of her body gracefully followed suit, like hourglass sands spilling uniformly down onto the cool stone floor. "Noooo!" the Groundskeeper howled as she again slipped away, particle by particle. "I've spent so much time puttin' you back, you can't come undone again!"

"Leave off, and leave me be," the ash hissed, congealing and trailing away in the shape of a long snake. "I've business on the other side. To see who is the greater power . . ."

THE ROUTINE OF BREAKFAST AND READYING FOR ATHENS, PERCY realized, would establish itself pleasantly. But there was an anxiety beneath her every move. The key against her bosom was growing warm, and she couldn't ignore it anymore.

After seeing Alexi to his classroom, weathering the stares of students who still were not used to the sight of her ghost-pale flesh or her new marital status, she murmured that she would be in her office, translating. This she did, for a bit, hoping Beatrice would breeze in to reassure her or tell her pleasant things about her mother. The ghostly professors Hart swept in to talk poetry, which was a delightful distraction, but she didn't feel she could allow herself the luxury for long.

Walking down and into the Athens chapel, she lifted her mother's key from her neck and held it tightly. Moving to the altar, she wondered how to get below. She sighed, shrugged, and threw her arm forward. A similar motion had vanquished an enemy once, and it did not disappoint now. A black spot appeared in midair, grew into a square, then lengthened into a door-size rectangle.

"Well . . . that was simple."

She wasn't fond of how simple it was. She didn't like the ability to do impossible things without knowing how she did them. But perhaps this wasn't down to her at all. Perhaps the very stones of Athens had been built to respond when she came calling.

Percy descended into the Guard's sanctuary. She glanced up at the bird, its prismatic beauty calming her. The fortifying pillar of power and light was absent, but she assumed only Alexi struck that particular fire.

Searching the edges of the feather carved into the dusty floor, she found what she sought on the tip, as Alexi had recalled. Her shaking hands fumbled with her necklace clasps, and the key slid to the floor with a clatter. A moment later, before she could think twice, she picked it up and jammed it into the hole. There was an enormous grating sound, and the room was suddenly awash in flame.

She screamed and threw up her arms, ducking, panicking of being burned alive. It took her a moment to see that the fire was blue and contained no heat, was harmful only to the dead. It was the now-familiar force and odd friend, Alexi's personal weapon: Phoenix fire.

Percy dropped her arms and perhaps in response, the flames lowered to a small height. They maintained a gently licking pattern on the floor: lines and angles opening into larger spaces. A floor plan. A map laid out in fire, forming the rectangles and squares that would seem to constitute floors, halls, and corridors of a building. It appeared to be Athens—yet not quite.

A circle of blue fire stood off to the side, separate. There was a tiny cerulean bulb of flame in its center. Percy moved closer. The pinprick of light moved, too.

"Me?" she murmured. As she retreated a step, the dot adjusted.

Two other blue spots showed in a small rectangle a few paces away on the great map, a room off a great open space. If that was the main foyer of Athens, the small offshoot would be in the approximate place of Headmistress Thompson's office. "Rebecca. And . . . Alexi?" Percy looked for other such spots.

At the top of the map, on a hazy outer perimeter, she saw a red ruby of flame, bright, like a glistening eye. Behind the mark was a swath of solid, sparkling blue.

The red spot was too familiar for Percy to ignore its possible meaning. It moved. Back and forth, as if pacing. A wispy shape floated above the red flame: a key. A second key in the hands of an ancient enemy . . . Beatrice had said there would be another.

Dread filled Percy's body and she yanked her key from the hole. The fiery map vanished into mist. The Guard's space was so quiet, her ragged breathing and heart roared in her ears. She ran up the stairs, out into Athens chapel and into the wing of Promethe Hall, about to run across to Alexi's office when she recalled his likely location on the map.

The map was correct. Alexi was in Rebecca's office, barking about how he could not find his wife. His voice carried into the hall. Grimacing, Percy knocked on the door.

Alexi threw it open. "There you are. Where have you—?"

"There's something you must see. In the chapel. Below."

"What were you doing there?" he asked, aghast.

"There's a map. My key went into the keyhole just like you said. It makes a map."

"You went there without me? A map of what?"

"I can't be sure," Percy replied, shrinking from his harshness.

Alexi sighed. "Show me. Now. Rebecca," he called over his shoulder, "call another meeting tonight."

"Yes, Alexi," Rebecca replied.

Alexi slammed the door, grabbed Percy by the arm, and began walking briskly down the hall. Percy couldn't help but ask, "Why are you angry with me?"

"You entered an unpredictable realm without aid or supervision! It isn't a place one goes alone—none of us do!"

"I never thought I was crossing you, Alexi. I was examining my mother's gift. How was I to know—?"

"What if portals open again and you're somewhere unbeknownst to me, unprotected?"

"I didn't want to trouble you—"

"I will *always* be troubled when you put yourself in harm's way."

"That isn't a harmful place—"

He snarled. "It can be. You've seen it so."

There was a strained, angry pause. Percy shook her head. "Alexi, you're acting like these new occurrences are somehow my fault. I want nothing but to be your loving wife. I want no portals, no war, no spirit world. I haven't come to you withholding knowledge. I'm at no advantage here," she pleaded against his seething silence. "It's my fate, too, you know!"

He continued to drag her forward, his gaze angry, his grip tight.

"Alexi?" she gasped.

"Yes?"

"You're hurting my arm."

He looked down to where his hand was a vise around her, then let go as if scalded and stared at her, his eyes wide. A flicker of shame crossed his face. "I'd never mean to hurt you," he whispered earnestly, his voice catching before his usual mask of stoicism returned.

"I know, love."

Brow furrowed in anxiety, Alexi stormed ahead. Percy let him go. He threw the chapel doors open roughly and Percy reached the threshold just as blue fire hurtled from his hand toward the altar. A dark doorway responded. Alexi waited, his hand held out. Percy took it. He met her gaze before they descended.

"It seems so long ago that I was here, shivering in your arms," she breathed.

"We were all shivering. Frightened, despairing, helpless without you," Alexi murmured, staring at the floor, at the carven feather symbol. His eyes narrowed, as if searching. "It feels like years ago, but it's hardly been a fortnight."

"Has it?"

"A great deal has happened," Alexi added with a partial smile. It faded. "And more will come."

Percy handed him her key. "The hole's where you said it would be."

Alexi bent, brushing grit from the grooves of the feather. "Let's hope Beatrice hasn't set a trap for us and it's indeed a map, not a door direct to hell."

"You may not like what she has to say, but we've no reason not to trust her," Percy repeated. "It's a map, I assure you."

Alexi set his jaw, slammed the key into its place, turned the lock, and rose as the room once again teemed with flame. Percy reflexively ducked, but Alexi remained still. "Do grow accustomed to this, Percy; fire is the one consistent measure of our power."

Percy lowered her arms and nodded. "It takes a bit of getting used to."

Alexi watched as the flames became a map.

"You see, it's very much like Athens," Percy pointed out.

"Not quite," Alexi said, gesturing to small areas. "These spots don't match our floor plan. Perhaps this is two places superimposed."

"The spirit world and Athens?" Percy breathed.

"Both." Alexi nodded. "What else could it be?"

"I believe this is our sacred space here." Percy pointed to the circle at the side. She walked him around, the fire licking at the hem of her skirts and his robes, harmless. "And the patches, us. Look here. Two spots in a circular room that move as we move. And one where the office of the headmistress might be."

"That bit of red, near the ocean of blue? It appears to be moving." Alexi squinted at the dot, the transparent, flickering icon of the key that hovered above. He moved closer.

Percy cringed, clutching the edge of his cloak. "It must be Darkness. Red. I've had visions of eyes that color, searching . . ."

Growling, Alexi swiftly bent and yanked the key from the lock. The fire vanished and the map was gone.

"Alexi!" She reached for him.

"I'll not have some constant reminder of a life you never remember living. Of a creature who has no claim over you." He paced, his boots echoing on the stone, his robe whipping about his ankles. "I'll not have any map lead the way to you. You are *my* wife, whose virgin body I claimed, free from whatever literal hell your powers may have—"

He finally saw past his rage and noticed her outstretched hands. He darted to her, scooped her into a smothering embrace, and she kissed him hungrily, hoping passion could shove aside her deepening dread.

"Alexi, I'm yours," she gasped. "This heart, soul, and body has never been anyone else's—nor will it!" She tore at her blouse and pointed to the mark of the phoenix. "That is the mark of our destiny, burned there when you prayed to find me. I've no other destiny but you."

He pressed his lips to her scar. His hands roved mercilessly, his clutch weakening her knees. She soon found herself on the cool stone floor, his dark robes engulfing her, his fingertips raking her body as he pinned her beneath him.

"You would wish for no other? You would forsake whatever divinity you may yet possess to remain with me? No matter what you learn, you are still mine?"

Percy's eyes widened as she stared up at him, wounded. "Truly, Alexi. Did my vow mean nothing? Don't you pledge the same?"

Her husband's eyes were fierce, and Percy couldn't tell if he was seething with passion or fear. Perhaps both.

"We're operating under uncommon circumstances," he hissed. "We have forces against us, pressuring, straining our vows so freshly made. Who knows what powers might break them—?"

Percy placed one of his hands on her scar and the other around her wedding band. "You're the only power that could break me, Alexi," she murmured in his ear. Craving a vow made tangible, she gratefully offered him acquiescence, hoping that intimacy in a place such as this sealed a further compact. "All of me rests wholly entrusted to your hands."

Concentric circles of blue fire erupted around their entwined bodies. Alexi cried out in the Guard tongue Percy had been born to understand, "My beloved is mine!"

They soon lay crumpled in a heap together upon the floor, dazed by a furious bout of passion. Stirring, Percy heard whispers dangerously close to her face and imagined red eyes burning down upon her.

Her eyes snapped open. The fiery gaze vanished and she saw only the luminous bird overhead. This image was so comforting, Percy wondered what sort of innate magic it possessed.

She turned to look at her husband. Alexi had drifted off to sleep, strings of black hair stuck to the moisture on his prominent cheekbones, his long nose pressed against the thick fabric of his cloak. She hadn't seen his face this peaceful since their honeymoon—which, she reminded herself, hadn't been very long ago. Would this mysterious fate of theirs make every week seem an eternity?

A terrible thought forced its way into her mind: When her husband slept, did he dream of a goddess? Perhaps the jealousy he felt was a remnant from another life, another love . . .

Without moving the arm slung possessively around her middle, she lifted her head, her neck stiff from the stone floor, to examine the state of her dress. Blushing, she wondered if their disheveled appearances would make their spontaneous activity entirely obvious. Thankfully, save for the collar she herself had dramatically ripped, the only real damage to her clothing was in the layers beneath her petticoats, evidence well hidden from view.

She turned to find Alexi staring at her. He snickered. "They'll think you've married a wild animal."

"I wonder." Percy grinned.

"There's a shop with fine and frivolous things just down Bloomsbury." He lifted her effortlessly to her feet. "Let me buy you something to mask our pastime."

"Otherwise Lord Withersby will never keep quiet."

"I daresay he'd flush with jealousy."

"Hardly. He only has eyes for Josephine. But answer me this," Percy blurted, suddenly set on learning the truth.

Alexi raised an eyebrow.

"Beatrice said that I . . . that your goddess came to you after your annunciation as the Guard, in dreams. Do you remember? Am I only something you love because . . . ?" She bit her lip and fought tears.

"Darling! First you worry I'll not love you for your skin. Now you worry I'll not love you if you're *not* that goddess?"

Percy blushed. "I don't know. I'm so confused."

"Well, we both have wondered who and what you are. But that doesn't change our vows. As for the past . . . I can say that the goddess, your predecessor, was my first love. I do recall hazy dreams, but I never imagined that she really—"

"But she did," Percy snapped, jealousy thundering in her heart.

"Those dreams stopped at sixteen. Around the time you were born. That cannot be coincidence." He smirked suddenly. "Do you remember me at sixteen?"

Percy blushed. "Of course not."

"I lived my whole life believing I'd marry whomever Prophecy directed. Love was never expressly stated and Rebecca vehemently denied it had anything to do with our task."

"Because she's in love with you!"

"I can't help that, or my instincts. When I met you I feared I might be doomed, for I loved you, regardless of Prophecy. If my words now can't reassure you, then I'm afraid nothing will."

Percy sighed. "It would seem we're both jealous of the intangible. Part of the burden of such strange lives."

He lifted her chin with a finger. "But a lifetime of jealousy will surely never do for either of us. Agreed?"

"Agreed."

Percy gazed into the darkness beyond the room's pillars. "What is out there, beyond the light? If I were to walk into that darkness, what would I find?"

Alexi held up his right hand and tilted it toward the light. Percy had never noticed the slight scar furrowing the skin. "I once walked to where the light fades. I reached out. I did not hold it there long. Afterward, I always made sure to keep to this side."

Percy shuddered. Perhaps he was right to be angry that she had come into this space alone.

THE WINDS OF THE WHISPER-WORLD WERE HOWLING. THE HELL-hounds were eating their own tails and whining, wishing to sharpen their teeth on real flesh again, but their canine forms remained partly scattered, unable to come together. To Darkness's ongoing chagrin, his amalgamous pet could not be recreated.

The winds blew across the river and battered a massive tower, wailing against its walls like a grieving widow. Inside, thousands of spirits floated silently imprisoned, awaiting a call they despaired they'd never hear.

A trickle of ash snaked around its base, hissing and mocking those inside. "I'm going to make her pay. And when I do, when I tear her stupid mortal body to pieces, all of you will rot here. Rot, rot, rot . . ."

"A NEW DILEMMA," ALEXI DECLARED ONCE EVERYONE WAS REASSEM-bled in their sacred space. Percy fiddled with the scarf draped strategically over the torn neck of her dress as he moved to insert her key. The blue fire again burst to great heights, then settled into lines. The red dot still paced in another space and time. The encircled Guard broke apart, examining and murmuring.

"What's this?" Josephine breathed, fascinated. She began walking the lines as if traveling the corridors herself.

"Looks like Athens, but . . ." Elijah traced the perimeters behind her.

"There we are, yes?" Michael pointed to the circle to the side. "Seven dots."

"And the red one?" Jane gulped. Alexi sighed.

"The enemy," Rebecca murmured.

Alexi nodded. "We can only guess. This map is very nearly Athens's floor plan, as you see, but not quite. The spirit and our Athens worlds, nearly identical. And they are likely merging closer every moment."

There was instant uproar among the Guard, a jumble of questions, frustrations, fears.

"What is that sea of blue?" Percy interrupted, pointing beyond the red dot.

"If it were simply a room, would it not look like an empty frame like the others? What fills this space?" Michael peered close.

Alexi's eyes widened. "We must have a host of comrades."

The Guard fell to nearly shouting. The idea that there was a space in which countless others of their kind existed was world shattering, them having spent their lives a meager, proud six; it was just as shocking as merging worlds they'd vowed to keep separate. Percy used the opportunity to reach down and pluck out the key, and no one seemed to notice. She fumbled beneath her scarf, returning the key to its former place.

"Silence!" Alexi cried. "I don't like this any more than you, to say the least. But another confrontation on a far larger scale than we have seen or imagined will surely make its way to us. Perhaps we may now take some consolation in the idea that we might not fight alone."

"That Gorgon was just the prologue," Rebecca stated.

There came a familiar tearing sound. The Guard circled at the ready, Alexi stepping in front of his wife as a shield. Percy illuminated, her power beginning to burn bright, preparing for battle. The Whisper-world through the portal roared in Percy's ears, its blackness total.

Aodhan popped into view, first bowing his head subtly to Jane, who blushed fiercely and looked away. He turned to Percy and said in Gaelic, "My lady."

Percy stepped forward. Alexi took her hand, held it tightly, limiting her movement.

"Careful," Aodhan warned. "She may have escaped. As soon as I saw her being reassembled, I stole a bit of her remains. I assumed then that she couldn't be re-formed . . . but I may have been wrong. I'm so sorry . . . I would have come to you sooner, but these portals aren't predictable."

Percy was baffled. "Who are you talking about?"

"The Gorgon."

The rest of the Guard looked on, unable to hear. Percy could hear Alexi's teeth grinding. She turned to him, begging patience. He looked away, glowering, but did not release her hand.

"Lucille Linden?" Percy clarified. Everyone shuddered.

"Be on the lookout."

Suddenly Beatrice appeared in the portal. "The troops eagerly await freedom," she stated.

"Troops?" Percy asked.

"Guards gone by. I told you it's your turn, they must be freed. Study that map, girl, you'll need it soon. But not yet. I've a last few doors to knit up behind these Whisper-world fools. You'll know when—you'll receive a sign. Go on, now, I'm sure your husband's had quite enough—"

"Percy, I've had enough of this," Alexi said, dragging her backward by the arm.

She turned to stare at her husband, and her white face flushed with frustration. "Alexi, let her speak to me! It concerns me and my fate, which then concerns all of you. Unless you'd like us to betray one another out of fear for the truth!"

The Guard raised eyebrows at a tone stronger than they'd ever heard her use. Alexi set his jaw and held her firm.

"Indeed. Let's get on with it, shall we?" Beatrice declared. "Leave you to it."

Percy stared at the spirit. "Leave me to what?"

"To study the map, and then at some point, when a portal opens before you and you are beckoned, you'll have to go through. Didn't I already tell you that? How many times must I tell you that you'll know when?"

"What is she saying?" Alexi hissed.

"At some point I'll have to go through, and I'll know when," Percy replied.

Her husband growled, turning to Beatrice. "I tell you, I'll not see her jeopardized."

"It isn't up to you, leader dear! Now, if you don't mind, I'm going to return to ensuring your survival when the battle comes—which I now see is a thankless job," the spirit growled in return. The portal narrowed.

"I'll be there for you—for all of you," Aodhan assured Percy softly. "All of us will. You'll not be alone." The portal snapped shut.

"Beatrice says they're both here to help, we'll not be alone," Percy repeated hollowly. "And that we ought to thank her." The grip on her arm tightened, which she hadn't thought possible. When she breathed his name, grimacing, he remembered himself, gave her a look of apology and eased his hold, but did not let go.

The group was silent.

"Well?" Elijah finally asked.

"Well, what?" Alexi spat. "If there is to be a war, we need not seek it out. It will come. When it comes, I'm sure we'll all know. Shall I send a telegram?"

"But don't we want to . . . prepare?"

"This isn't a cavalry exercise! We stand in our circle and use what magic we have, as we always do. Prophecy, fate, and destiny have given us no other weapons. We'll meet what comes when it comes. That's all there is."

No one said a word.

Percy yearned to ask Alexi to recall the Power and Light, to bask in that ceremonial surge of heaven that made all troubles small and insignificant. But the Guard was already filing out of the sanctuary and the opportunity was lost.

At the Athens portico, Alexi nearly tossed her into their carriage. She winced and rubbed her arm. He sat next to her in silence, his hand clenching upon the folds of her skirts.

"You might take a moment, Professor," Percy said quietly, a firm edge to her voice, "to think that your wife might be just as frustrated, confused, and frightened by these possibilities as you, and that she may be forced to interact with them all the more directly. I would appreciate support, not misdirected anger. Second-guessing almost had you failing Prophecy once. Let's not test it again."

Alexi's silence shifted from brooding to stunned. He stared at her, his expression shading from shame to terror. In this aching, naked, helpless moment when his stoic mask was let slip for her alone, when the Guard's mighty leader allowed her to glimpse the vulnerabilities of his soul, she was able to let her own hurt go.

Her clenching heart eased, love swelling like an overflowing cup. She kissed his lips softly, running a hand through his hair. His furrowed brow smoothed as he clutched her hands in his, his eyes speaking volumes his lips would have fumbled over. Silence still remained between them, but at last it was not strained.

At their estate, Alexi went directly to his study and Percy to her boudoir. Percy wasn't sure if he would join her in their bed or spend the whole night pacing. She wanted only to sit in silence and breathe. There were times in the convent when she had done that for hours, hearing only the occasional whisper of a passing ghost, the comforting low drone of a mass bell. She held her own service, privately, the murmur of the breeze her rosary, and knew that God was there.

"Our Lady," she muttered, glancing at her first confirmation rosary hung on her armoire, a string of pearls as white as she. "Leave divinity to someone else. If I must see ghosts, I must. Let me help put them to rest and then let me be. Must there be some grand finale? Can't something more powerful than I fight it?"

As she undressed, she was not ashamed to linger in the wicked thrill that unlacing her torn undergarments provided, for that fierce, mutual passion needed no apology. But looking up again, she paused at the mirror and could do nothing but stare at her arm. A nasty, burgeoning red and purple bruise marked the location of Alexi's firm grip. It needed apology. But now was not the time.

Slipping into the comfort of a luxurious white robe, she fancied that she was a votaress of the moon. Lighting and stoking a fire, she gathered her filmy white robes, perched on the window seat of their bedroom and pretended that she was part of the silver swath of light cutting boldly into the room.

A long while passed before she heard his foot on the stair. He paused at the doorway. She turned.

He was in that delicious disarray of undone buttons and shirtsleeves, a nearly empty snifter in hand. "Hello, my north star," he murmured. She moved to rise as he entered and set the snifter on the dresser and waved her to remain where she was. "No, no. Stay there in the moonlight. You're positively magical." He sat across from her on the window seat.

"Are you all right, love?" she asked.

"I will sometimes . . ."

"Need quiet. Yes, as will I."

He nodded, and his eyes flashed suddenly. "I'll fight to the death for you."

Percy's brow furrowed. "Let's hope it won't come to that."

He reached for her. Percy kept a hand on the ribbon that clasped her outer robe closed.

"Let me touch your skin," he murmured, taking her hands in his. "It calms me," he explained, sliding his fingertips under the robe and slipping it from her shoulders.

Percy grabbed, but she was too late. She'd hoped to keep the damning mark from his view, or at least spare it for another day, but his eyes widened and there was no distracting him. The mark was garish in the moonlight. His fingertips reached toward the bruise, trembling.

"How did this . . . ?" He looked at Percy in confusion.

"It doesn't hurt. Much," she said meekly.

Alexi's eyes were an emotional maelstrom. He jumped to his feet, unable to meet her gaze again.

"Alexi, please." Percy reached out.

He was out the door. His footsteps bounded down the grand staircase and the front door slammed. After some interminable moments, the pound of Prospero's hooves down the lane carried away into the night.

Percy was chilled by the utter silence of her house, blinking as the shaft of moonlight widened through the window. Rising, she went to her armoire and plucked free her string of rosary beads. Gliding to the bed, she slid back the velvet drapes and turned down the covers.

Yet another tempest. Storm and calm, then storm again. She sat against the headboard and tucked her knees up under her chin. The only sound was the click of her rosary beads, one by one, as she sought simply to breathe.

* * *

MICHAEL COULD FEEL A WEIGHT APPROACHING LIKE A SWINGING PEN-
dulum. Anticipating Alexi, he unlocked the door and brewed a hot cup
of mulled wine: one of their favorites to share, good for the darkest
nights of the year and the darkest hours of the soul. Alexi soon appeared
at the threshold—haunted, powerful, a strange creature that didn't quite
know himself anymore.

"Hullo, friend," Michael said. "Shall I take your cloak or do you plan
to pace about a bit and run away?"

Alexi furrowed his brow, stepping into Michael's tiny living room.
His small, simple quarters were bestowed upon him by the Anglican
Church in exchange for his modest services as parochial vicar to local
parishes. Alexi sat, then stood, removed his cloak, hung it on a wooden
peg, and sat again. Michael offered a mug; Alexi took it and sipped. He
set the tankard down unevenly, a drop spilling onto the rough wooden
table stained with years of hard use.

"There's a bruise on her arm," he said finally. "A large, ugly bruise."

Michael sipped his wine and said thoughtfully, "When we try to
protect those we love, we sometimes use unintentional force. I daresay
we've all been bruised by one another at some point."

"I was a man of measured control once. I prided myself on that
quality."

"Do you now wish to be violent?"

"Only against those forces who seek her out. But I dragged her away
from Rebecca's office and down to the chapel, and she . . . said I was
hurting her. And tonight I seized her just the same. I only saw the effect
when I tried to touch her, when I . . ." He trailed off, sure Michael understood.

"You don't recognize these things now inside you," the vicar stated.
"These baser urges of jealousy and lust, the ravages of fear and the com-
pulsion for control. Well . . ." Michael smiled wryly. "You understand
control, Alexi, but not in relation to someone you adore. Your courtship
was strange and harried, your lives hanging in the balance. You're both
practically children in terms of love, and children are often scared. We
react with improper force when we are scared."

Alexi took a long drink and was silent. Michael knew, from conversations past, mostly in their youth, before Alexi had fashioned the many

walls of his adulthood, that his own role was to clarify the maelstrom of the heart, not to expect an easy flow of conversation.

"While I believe Percy intuits all these things," he continued, "you cannot take it for granted. While I'm sure you apologized . . ." He halted as Alexi's eyes flashed with frustration. "While I'm sure you will apologize, and while I'm sure she knows you'd never mean to hurt her—"

"I told her that," Alexi snapped.

"Then why are you here?"

Alexi's knuckles were white. His breathing was slow and deep. "Because I'd let the spirit world take, seize, and rule this world if it meant she'd be left alone. This directly conflicts with my duty as mortal protector. In fulfilling Prophecy, have I lost my will to maintain it?"

"If that's the question, who should take your place as leader?"

Alexi's eyes widened and flashed with repugnance as he pounded the table with a fist.

Michael leaned in. "I thought so. Then you'd best get this under control. You'd best trust her, no matter what the fates may have her do. She's no one's pet. Not some mythical god's former bride, nor your toy—"

"Of course she's not a toy."

"Then let her approach the spirit world without making her feel she's betraying you. Let her do her job on the edge of danger. She isn't plotting, Alexi. She's not full of memories she'll not share or powers she's yet to reveal. She's a sweet girl overwhelmed by life, who only wants to love and be loved by you. Duty and fate will take their course. They must. But, 'Worry not for tomorrow. Sufficient for the day is its own trouble.' Don't make more."

"She . . . she has reassured me as well."

"Then why come to me? Don't you trust her words? Oh, Alexi, mend thy ways."

"I do! I don't trust *me*. I don't . . . know where to relegate this fear. My power is all that I've had, and my duty—and now *she* is all that I care about. And I seem to be hurting her. Where do I put all this instead . . . ?"

"Put your fire into your fire, your love into your wife, and your fear unto the Lord. Times like these are good for prayer."

Alexi rolled his eyes. "Dear One True God," he muttered, "please protect the mortal coil of a pagan goddess. Amen."

Michael chuckled and stroked his mustache. "'Persephone' is just a name for a spirit of beauty at a certain time in history. I'm sure we could argue a biblical place for her if it matters. Your wife has the name of that pagan goddess, but the fact remains that she's your mortal bride in the Year of Our Lord 1888—and she's Catholic, so pray for her, damn it. I don't care how confusing it is. And pray for us, to anyone. If the dead are about to flood Athens, divine goodwill couldn't hurt. Your prayers can be in Hindu, if you like. Now, go home. And apologize."

"Yes, Father," Alexi said wearily. Rising, he threw his cloak over his arm. "Thank you." Bowing, he saw himself out.

Michael hoped the Lord would grace Alexi with peace. He also allowed himself one moment to wonder if he himself would ever find it. Sipping his wine, he stared into the fire and simply breathed.

ALEXI FOUND PERCY TUCKED IN THEIR BED, ROSARY IN HAND. SHE gazed upon him calmly as he entered the room and removed his suit coat.

"Where did you go?" she asked quietly, not an accusation.

"To confess," he said. "Now I seek forgiveness."

Percy held out her arms, and he fell gladly into them.

AT AN HOUR TOO LATE FOR COMMON COMPANY AND YET TOO RATTLED to be alone, several of the Guard found themselves at La Belle et La Bête, a bottle of wine between them.

It was Elijah who broke the silence with classic inelegance. "He does push her about a great deal, doesn't he?"

"What did you expect?" Josephine asked honestly.

"Elijah, he *smiles*," Michael offered. "That's quite a change."

"I fear for them," Rebecca said softly and winced.

Josephine's heart went out to her. Surely everything Rebecca said would be tinged by her closeness to the matter. The slight flush on the headmistress's high cheekbones was a bloom of shame atop her cool and efficient exterior.

She continued, "While they are"—she swallowed—"*besotted* with each other, that does not erase character difficulties. She so timid, he so adamant. For us to succeed, I fear they must become the true partnership destiny demands. We all need to become one, else we court failure—betrayal, even."

The group looked at one another warily.

"There are forces keeping our hearts closed," Michael said. "I'm as guilty of it as any."

Jane turned away, her knee jostling the table and making brown-tinged flowers tremble in a vase. Josephine's bosom burned with a thousand things she wanted to say. Looking at the fading posies, she plucked the wilting stems free and moved to toss them in the basin behind the bar, ruing that she was behind on the most simple tasks of her café duties. That spoke to her own faltering heart, which was similarly tinged brown on the edges.

"Two people can love each other dearly," Josephine began, storming around to pluck fading bouquets from other tables. "But anxiety, fear, and silence can keep them apart. Percy and Alexi, of all people, cannot afford distance. None of us can." She dared glance at Elijah before looking away, feeling ill. This was not the time to speak of broken promises, but her patience waned. Elijah surely knew. He'd grown nearly as fidgety as Jane.

"We must support them," Michael rallied, "and stand up for Percy if she needs it. And ease the tempest that is our leader, if he needs it. We're all Alexi has; she's all he has, and he's constantly aware of that. Think how close he's come to losing her. Considering it's Alexi Rychman we're talking about—"

Elijah snorted. "Dear Percy's all the more of a saint."

"It isn't our business to discuss their marital dynamics," Rebecca commented tightly, absently dissecting a biscuit with her fork. "We must be sure we're no longer at odds like we once were in this very room. Our circle will never have faced such strain as I feel is to come. We need to be whole."

Josephine set her jaw. If the men they loved couldn't help their hearts be whole, what could be done? The women in the party couldn't just be whole on their own with a snap of their fingers. They were humans, with needs, and those needs were not without labor.

Her feelings must have shown, for Elijah's eyes widened with boyish helplessness. Squaring her shoulders, Josephine brought wine to the table for everyone but him. He could fend for himself.

With everyone on edge, it was no surprise that they soon dispersed. Elijah led the charge, darting out the door with such swiftness that it was a dagger into Josephine's heart.

Left alone with the café's frequent haunts, she wept freely as she rinsed wineglasses clean, fancying she was rinsing away the blood of a broken heart. When she turned back to the room, she started. She dropped the glass in her hand but the general, a ghost dressed in century-old military regalia, managed to settle it, tilted but unbroken, upon the bar.

Lord Elijah Withersby stood frozen in the doorway, an empty flower box on one arm, a corsage of fresh roses in an outstretched hand.

Josephine glanced around. While she'd been crying behind the bar, he'd quietly replaced all the faded posies she'd so angrily discarded. Red rosebuds elegantly filled each vase. She swallowed. Elijah had always performed small deeds of incredible beauty for her. Damn him, for those small acts kept her heart cloven to him.

He set down the box, his oft-harsh features gentle-seeming in the golden glow of the gaslight. She let him approach and pin the corsage upon the broad lapel of her blouse, but did not offer him a look of apology when, with a yelp, he pricked his finger and sucked upon it.

She folded her arms and stared at him. He began speaking, with his index finger still in his mouth. "Thith damned Work hath kept uth from leading anything rethembling a normal life," he said, then removed his finger and began to pace. "Josie. You know why I'm hesitating."

"*Dis-moi,*" she said.

He sighed. "I find most of my class disgusting, and I've said so numerous times. Still, I resent that I've never been able to . . . be a part of it. I've used my gifts to hide for the majority of my life. I am a stranger to my family, to my class—one that none of the rest of you would have been welcome in, but rightly mine. I float between, a ghost."

"There are worse things than to be a wealthy man with no responsibility."

Elijah's eyes flashed. "No responsibility? Do you and I lead such different lives?"

Josephine thought about saying that he was plain lazy, unable to handle the least responsibility. Indeed, he'd abandoned the Guard ten years prior—and had paid dearly for it. Only Josephine knew how dearly, and no matter her feelings of anger or betrayal, she could not pick at that particular scab.

"The name Withersby means nothing to me," Elijah continued in a pleading tone, "but for the rest of my family it means everything. Identity is a strange beast. I suppose I just want to know who and what I am before I make another sacrifice."

"Oh, *je suis un sacrifice,*" Josephine said through clenched teeth. "Years of exhausting farce keeping our tryst a secret and now I'm a sacrifice."

"Josie, we agreed long ago that to be the lone couple amid this damned group would be bloody awkward and more miserable than our exhausting farce."

"It was just an excuse."

"No, it wasn't! We truly acted for the sake of balance, considering our coterie's delicate dynamic. Josie, you always agreed with me. If you've been resenting it all these years, you needed to have told me."

"I assumed you'd keep your promise."

"And I . . . want to." He stopped pacing, his coat of many layers and frills stilling as his body did. "Josie. You know how much I love you. And I know I'm being selfish. But life isn't fair, and while I resent society for its impositions, I cannot change the fact that if I marry you, I'll be shunning it for good without ever truly having known it. That isn't fair."

"Staring at Rebecca, who has always loved the man who just married another, I'm yet reminded of what is and is not fair. You ought to consider yourself lucky." She fought back tears, her nostrils flared, her head tilted back, defiant. "Once you told me I could charm the royal family itself, that society would love me and forget my station in an instant.

"*Mon Dieu,* when did that sentiment vanish—with age? That's it. Not the flower of youth anymore, am I?" She wrested his corsage off her blouse, tearing the lace, and threw the small buds across the bar where they slid through the general's drooping, transparent head.

"Josie, good God! You're still our Helen of Troy—"

"Indeed? Well, if I've still the face that could launch a thousand ships, would you bloody set sail already? Haven't you heard a war's coming?

That's what people do: They marry the ones they love before they go off to maybe die. Your exclusive invitations to seasons, balls, and fetes be damned, you're a superficial coward and I'm a fool!"

She tossed her apron behind the bar and stormed upstairs, slamming the door behind her. Elijah sighed, rubbed his face with his hands, and locked the café door behind him. Then he went off to be an empty, unremarkable stranger in his vast estate, no closer to feeling at peace.

IF SOMEONE HAD BEEN PRAYING IN THE ATHENS CHAPEL AT MIDNIGHT, they might have noticed the thin trail of ash trickling from behind the white altar, a misty line snaking up and out through the chapel doors. The smoky particles slid inconspicuously out of Promethe Hall, gliding down the steps to the courtyard more like an unending insect than a snake, now, tumbling forward inch by inch on millipede legs, finding the shadows and lingering. It slithered on, across the cobbles, paying no heed or reverence to the angel fountain; it was sniffing something out.

Up to and under the door of Athene Hall, the ladies' quarters, and past the drowsy matron at the desk, silently the ashes sniffed one way and then the next, beginning an ascent up the wooden stairs. It stopped at door number seven, at a familiar scent. An enemy scent. She was here . . .

No, she *had been* here. Now, she was in their protection. But there was still a way. The ash trickled on, continuing its hunt.

CHAPTER
FOURTEEN

PERCY'S FIRST PERSONAL VISITOR AT THE RYCHMAN ESTATE—AN UN-
scheduled appearance as the constraints of her otherworldly profession
meant she could have no formal calling hours—was a man of the cloth.

"Hullo, Percy!" Michael said at the door, sweeping his cap off his
head.

"Hello, Vicar! Pleasure to see you! I assume you're here for Alexi? He's
just gone to Athens."

"Ah, but it's a vicar's duty to call upon the ladies of his congregation,
and while I know you're not a member of my Anglican parish, you're a
member of my far more exclusive assembly."

Percy smiled. "Do come in. I daresay Mrs. Wentworth cooked up
enough treats for an army."

"And I always have the appetite of one!"

Once settled in the sitting room and plied with the aforementioned
delights, the clergyman was quick to the point. "I don't suppose it's a
surprise your husband is fraught with worry. It isn't easy, you know, for
a man to deal honestly with the heart."

Percy eyed the vicar, daring to turn the tables. "Oh?"

Michael waggled his mustache. "You'll not get gossip out of me,
young lady."

"Fine," she retorted. "But I'm not used to talking about my own particulars. It's unsettling."

"You're the center of a maelstrom, bound to cause discussion."

"But . . . what if I really do have to go into the spirit world because
duty demands it? I don't want to go. Alexi doesn't want me to. But what
if I must go, and without his permission? He'll never forgive me, never
trust me . . ."

"If indeed you must go, we will be there to support you—and to support him when the time comes. But the both of you must not worry about tomorrow—"

"'Sufficient for the day is its own trouble,'" Percy murmured, finishing the Scripture. "Now, I rightly knew what I was getting into with him, Michael. I knew he was a brooding man. But I've never known him to be so mercurial."

Michael shrugged. "Love makes a man mad."

Percy narrowed her eyes, curious. "How have *you* managed to keep your wits?"

He raised an eyebrow but remained unruffled. "Secrets of the trade. Alchemy of the heart—most profound magic of all. But I'm not here for my sake." He leaned in. "I beg you realize Alexi's absolute adoration for you has turned everything on end, so have patience. If I know him, you'll need a lifetime supply."

Percy chuckled. After a moment, however, she was again bold: "When, Vicar, will you set patience aside and tell her?"

Michael made to act innocent.

"A war is coming," Percy continued. "We shall need all the love we have."

The vicar rose, giving her a dawning look. "Why, that's a most sensible thing to say, Mrs. Rychman. Most sensible." He kissed Percy on the cheek and allowed her to see him quietly out the door.

Percy had assumed she'd see Josephine before anyone, so it was a surprise that Jane was next. The Irishwoman seemed uneasy, so Percy donned her tinted glasses to protect her eyes and opened every shade; the full light seemed a more inviting environment for company.

"Aodhan," they chorused after a tense silence.

Jane sighed. "I suppose I'd best tell you about him."

"I don't mean to press you, but it may—"

"Help, yes. Thank you for telling me his name."

"My pleasure."

Jane took again to the tea she'd been brought, but could delay no longer. She entered an almost trancelike state as she related her past. "Our Work was a gift. I was a girl caught out of time, thrust into a world advancin' too quickly, growin' too broadly, and losin' all magic. I understood why I was chosen, but . . . there was somethin' more.

"Useless to my family, I was turned out at eighteen. Your husband found the Aldgate flat for me, but I was never so lonely. I know the Guard loves me, but I've not the beauty of Josephine, the efficiency of Rebecca, the confidence of Alexi, the wit of Elijah, or the joy of Michael. It didn't help that it took time for my talents to manifest. Initial victims suffered more than they should. I needed help, but no one knew how. Then, one night, there came a terrible sound on my doorstep.

"Outside lay a mass of white and red—a cat, terribly mauled. I can't bear to see a creature in pain. A cold draft came in as I took the creature to lie upon my table. The cat looked at something, fixed-like, and when I looked as well, I saw a man floating by my side, his hand upheld. Nameless to me, but beautiful. So beautiful. I pressed my palm to his cold mist and felt newfound strength. My hand glowed, and I suddenly understood why others' pain causes me such misery.

"I laid healing hands on the creature and the skin beneath the fur began to mend, the spilled blood rolling away. Aodhan . . . touched my face and took the tears from my cheeks. I gained both love and Marlowe that evening."

She stopped, and Percy took the cue to refill her tea, patient with the silence and not looking twice at Jane's fierce blush. Finally Percy said, "It's an incredible story. Thank you for sharing it with me."

Jane smiled, pleased. "Feels good to tell it. When we could spare it," she volunteered after another silence, "we went healing. I practiced with him, in alleys where the sick and dying lay untended, in sad, dim wards where the only light was our combined illumination."

"And the Guard never knew?"

"Elijah once touched me accidentally and saw what I'd been up to the night prior. He pledged to say nothing if I'd now and then take him along. We never said a word, only smiled at each other when all was said and done, enjoying our secret. Now and then Michael would let me into his parish children's ward, too."

"Brilliant." Percy grinned.

"Aodhan keeps me company, see. Now and then I'll play fiddle and we'll dance a reel—a piece of common heritage. I never told the group, for fear they'd think it 'fraternizing' with the opposition. Not a single word. Gentle spirits are no enemies, but are we to *love* them?" Jane asked, blushing. "And I do love him."

A popping noise resounded through the room and a black portal appeared over the tea table. Both ladies' hands went up and they jumped to their feet. Their visitor was the very spirit in question. His palms were outstretched in a gesture of peace and his broad shoulders took up the portal's full width. Jane went red, but Percy smiled.

"I cannot help it," Aodhan explained to Percy. "Now that she knows my name, I must try to come when she calls. Do tell her how much I love her, my lady, will you?"

Percy beamed at the ghost and then Jane. She relayed the man's message and watched tears flow down Jane's cheeks.

"And I you," the Irishwoman said. "Though you've heard me say it before. It's good to hear the same from you. Thank you," she added, turning to Percy.

"My honor."

Jane's tearstained face became thoughtful. "Loneliness has long been my burden. Before I ever saw a ghost I felt them—felt like one, myself. I'm sure you must understand."

Percy nodded but said nothing.

"I've never spoken about my names," Jane confessed. "The rest of the Guard assume it's some Catholic trapping. My Christian name is Jane. When I was very little, before we came to England, we lived beside a graveyard outside Dublin. I'd go there every day and visit two graves— two ill-kept graves separate from the others and on opposite sides, entirely isolated. Alone. Lucretia O'Shannon, Marie Connor . . . barely thirty years alive. The father of the parish must've given them a marker out of pity, a small comfort of little use in death . . ."

Jane shifted her gaze between Percy and Aodhan, who floated, rapt, at the portal. She went on. "I wondered if those young women had ever had a love. Surely they'd no family. Even in death they'd no one around them, even in the cold ground. My heart hurt for them, so separate, shunned, failures. I was terrified I'd turn out just the same—or worse, never have a marker, like so many families, perhaps even mine. I don't even know what happened to them," the Irishwoman murmured, her tearful eyes wide. Percy thought about her own mother's grave, similarly sorrowful, and took Jane's hand.

"My family disowned me, like what surely happened with these lonely women. But those lasses live on in me through their names, and I pray I share some of my blessings with them. Because I do feel blessed. If not for the Guard, I'd have turned out the same as them. Without Aodhan, I'd have gone into the ground never having loved. Even though my family is an inexplicable ragtag force against the restless dead, and my love is one that can never be requited, both things are a blessing. I fancy taking their names brought those two souls peace."

"Never requited?" Aodhan whispered. "We are two beings of one heart. A heart so big it can hold a grander family than she possibly knows, and all the great mysteries of the universe. What more is there?"

As Percy relayed his words, Beatrice suddenly popped into view behind him. "You could join him, you know," the ghost said to Jane. "End your fleshly existence, follow your lover into this undiscovered country . . ."

Aodhan turned in horror, but Percy nonetheless relayed what the female spirit said. Jane went red, flustered, her accent never so thick. "It's a sin to do so! To take yer life by yer own hand?" she cried. "Don'tcha think I've thought of it? I'd have done it already, to be with him, but . . . And there's work to do. I've the Guard, I've a duty—"

"And I'd never want such a thing!" Aodhan exclaimed.

Beatrice folded her arms, looking coldly furious. "A *sin*. The Grand Work sounded my death knell and I stepped forward to meet its chimes. If Ibrahim and I hadn't gone in when we did, none of you would likely be alive. Sacrifices are sometimes necessary." She vanished back into the darkness, the portal flickering as she did.

Aodhan sighed. "I'll see you soon, Jane, my love. I'll wait for you ever and always. Don't rush to be with me." He bowed, and just as Percy echoed his last word, the portal snapped shut. Jane stared, and her fingers absently caressed the air where the portal's edge had wavered.

"My first friend was a spirit. Who is to say whom we mustn't love?" Percy asked. "Why, for that matter, Alexi suspects I may not be human."

Jane wiped her eyes and stared. "Why would that matter?"

Lifting her teacup, Percy swirled her spoon around a few stray leaves. "What might it mean for our future? Am I really free to be here, to be Alexi's, or am I still bound elsewhere—in the spirit world? He's quite worried about fate."

"Then perhaps he should enjoy you while he has you. We're being too quiet, too careful—all of us." Jane straightened, her cheeks flushed. Her tone was suddenly righteous. "Josephine and Elijah should've married years ago. Michael, for the love of the Holy Saints, should bloody tell Rebecca how he feels. Rebecca needs to stop pining over your husband, and that worthy man shouldn't give your past a second thought. And I should be able to love my blessed Aodhan!" Her face was scarlet but proud. "There. I said everything, and I haven't even had a drink."

Percy grinned. "Cheers." She raised her teacup. "Thank you."

"The real task is up to you. Since you're new, sweet, and unassuming, you must convince us to stop worrying and love what we have. Otherwise we'll end up with nothing."

THE FOLLOWING DAY PERCY WAS DEEP IN TRANSLATION, HAPPILY BUSY in her office at Athens, when she heard a knock at her door. "Percy!" came a familiar call.

"Marianna, do come in!"

The door swung wide and her friend, blond hair slightly askew, came flouncing into the room. "Oooh, what a palace!" Percy rose from behind her desk to give the German girl a hearty hug, but Marianna pulled away with a pouting lip.

"Are you all right, my dear?" Percy asked, seeing that Marianna looked tired.

"Quite well, thank you. A bit fatigued, I confess. And you?" The girl drew back and whirled about the polished floor of the office, her eyes devouring every detail. "Life as Mrs. Rychman?"

Percy blushed. "Still incredible."

"How close does he look after you?"

Percy paused, surprised. She considered the bruise on her arm and told the truth. "He's very protective."

"And his estate . . . ?" Marianna offered a baiting grin.

"Not to be believed," Percy said. The two shared a familiar, girlish squeal. How many times had they shared fantastic dreams of marital bliss, dreams Percy never expected to come true? "Oh, Marianna, come tomorrow for a visit. Now that I'm staff . . . I'll excuse you from class." Percy grinned, sitting at her desk and scribbling a note. She tucked a bill in the paper. "There's fare for the driver. Alexi makes sure I always have money; just this morning he pressed it into my hand and said, 'I'll have you want for nothing.' And it's true—I want for nothing more than him." She was eager to share the happiness of her good fortune rather than dreadful portals and the warnings of ghosts.

"Just so long as he doesn't leave you alone," Marianna replied. When Percy furrowed her brow, her friend explained. "He broke your heart once, remember? That other woman in the courtyard?"

Percy blinked. She wasn't sure what she'd told Marianna in the haze of fever just before all hell broke loose. She must have mentioned seeing Alexi strolling with that monstrous woman, Lucille Linden. Shaking the memory from her mind, she said, "Yes, but that was all explained. There's nothing but confidence between us now." She handed Marianna the note.

Her friend's eyes, while sparkling with the usual mischief, held something else as well—an odd, detached distance. She said, "Of course. Now I'm off to torment Edward; your marriage has inspired me. Tomorrow, then! Your estate! I cannot wait to see where he keeps you!"

Percy frowned as Marianna gave a giggle and trotted out of the room, but before she could wonder if the tenor of their friendship had indeed changed forever, there came a shimmering dark portal in the center of the room. There was an odd silence within. Percy had prepared herself for the infernal nursery rhyme, but this silence was more frightening.

Beatrice stuck her head out. Percy started. "Dear God, Beatrice, this business is increasingly unnerving!"

"Only the beginning, princess. My. It's coming along nicely. Any day now, really."

"What?" Percy asked with dread.

Beatrice hopped out of the portal and it closed behind her. Shaking her head, she said with forced patience, as if addressing a child, "I've told you before: The worlds will become one and the real fight will begin. It's almost joined." She patted at the air where the portal had been. "I'm grateful for these paths the goddess created, otherwise I'd never be able to get around. He's got everything locked down now.

"Of course, to bring things to their inevitable head, there's still the key you'll have to get from Darkness. That's what we really ought to be training you for."

"But I . . ." Percy trailed off. Beatrice concentrated fiercely on the wall.

"Come on," the ghost encouraged the wooden panels. As if in response, suddenly there was a new wooden door, narrow and thin, next to the one that led into the hallway. A faint blue light pulsed around its slender width. Beatrice snorted in triumph.

"I don't understand, Beatrice. How do these new doors differ from the dark portals? Are we to open them?"

"Not yet. But when the time is right, they'll need to be flung wide so that reinforcements can fly directly to your aid. There will be a great swarm, like water through a tiny hole. We can't be congested, the floodgates must rise!"

"Reinforcements . . . ?"

"Darling, you put the key in the chapel lock. You saw the map. You know there's another key . . . in there," Beatrice gestured toward the Whisper-world. When Percy grimaced, noticing a few stray bones cluttering the corridor beyond, the ghost added, "Oh, don't mind those, he's dredging the river to make things exceedingly unpleasant."

Percy shuddered.

"When you bring the second key back to Athens and use it in the second lock, upstairs, the merger will begin. The chapel map will allow the Guard to watch you while you're in there." Beatrice pointed again behind her.

Percy shook her head. "Not only am I not sure what you mean, I'm terrified to go."

"Darling." The ghost clucked her tongue. "You'll find this will make sense once you trust your instincts. It was your plan, after all."

Percy balled her fists. "I'm not—!"

"The goddess. I know, I know. It's true, you're mortal flesh." The spirit looked at her gravely. "But you're also more. You'd do well to believe it." A moment later saw Beatrice's departure.

Percy sighed, baffled. Thankfully, Alexi's instincts hadn't been piqued by the portal's appearance and he hadn't come running. How she was to relay this latest exchange, she didn't know. Some time to determine a course of action was welcome.

She turned to her desk. In one last attempt at being a diligent professor, Alexi had left a book upon it with a note: *I ought to have tried this before. Indulge me, will you?* Percy opened the volume, which proved to be a Grecian tome on mathematics. Perusing it, a flood of disparate pieces fell into place in her mind, and she sat stunned as her barriers and blockades fell away amid the Greek characters and explanations. She chuckled. Thank goodness they hadn't tried this before, otherwise the private tutorials that brought them together might never have existed! Maybe her failures, too, had been somehow designed to bring them together. She had to tell him.

Traversing the familiar path to Apollo Hall, a familiar, titillating thrill worked through her body. She'd felt it on many a walk toward his classroom, that place she'd always both anticipated and dreaded. Strangely, Percy found her feelings unchanged; though her love had grown, so, too, had her fear of proving a fool.

Outside, she peered past those familiar gothic arches and into his classroom. He paced to and fro, in the midst of some maelstrom of algebraic explanations, and she grinned, watching his beautiful and fearsome presence rule the room. His emphatic points caused some of the younger students to jump. She was sure she'd jumped just the same.

A rustling noise made her turn. "Hello," Percy said to the flustered boy who approached, books for Alexi's class under his arm.

"Late. Again. I suppose he'll have my head for it."

"It's all right," Percy reassured him. "He's not always terrible."

The boy peered at her. "That's right. You married him, didn't you?"

Percy blushed. "Yes."

"Hmm." He stared at her a moment, and Percy braced herself for an insult. Instead: "Can he be kind, then?"

Percy smiled. "Quite."

"Proof," the boy said, raising a finger, "that no one is to be underestimated." And with that, he held his breath and entered the classroom.

Alexi whirled at the sound of the opening door. "Mr. Andrews, you are late again, making it four times within . . ." He trailed off, staring through the door.

Percy waved, allowing herself a rushing thrill that she'd derailed this fearsome academic's train of thought. She blew him a kiss, then withdrew, lest she prove a further distraction. A few students fell to gossip, and she could only imagine what they had to say.

Perhaps the moment alleviated Mr. Andrews's punishment. The class was abruptly silenced with a fearsome clap upon the podium that could be heard down the hall and Percy giggled again. She'd await him in his office and have time to practice how to both inform and reassure him of the tasks ahead. But how could she reassure him when she herself was terrified? She'd toss in the conversation with Beatrice amid a few correct geometric problems and hope he'd be too shocked and thrilled to care.

Ascending to his office, she noticed more strange panels that hadn't been present before, more new doors fit smoothly into the wood. The few students she saw wandering the halls seemed oblivious to their existence; but as only select people could see ghosts, she wondered if this was the same. Not many saw spirits. Of those, only a few became members of the Guard. What would her poor friends have to withstand? And Athens? What was the plan of her divine predecessor? There was more guesswork to Prophecy than seemed fair.

Having been given a key to Alexi's office along with her own, Percy let herself in. She stared fondly at the innumerable bookshelves, the open room with its vaulted ceiling and Gothic arched windows, the moody and intense gilt-framed canvasses on the wall, the fireplace behind the lavish marble desk topped with candelabra, and Alexi's huge leather chair. Memories washed over her: The time Mozart's *Requiem* beckoned all the ghosts of Athens to dance. The time he taught her to waltz. Their first kiss. Wonderful things had happened here, but frightening things, too. That spectral dog sniffing her out. The time Alexi cast her aside, thinking there'd been a mistake in destiny . . .

Ghosts wafted in and out through the walls of bookshelves. Moving to the chair opposite Alexi's desk, a desire struck her that she should send for tea, but it seemed this office, however fine, was not equipped with a bell pull. Yet, there was a service on a fine wheeled tray, near the lily-like bell of his phonograph. Tea sat at the ready, the diffusers full beside the saucers, water in the cups. But how would it be heated?

Percy laughed at her silliness. "Of course. My husband is magical!" Despite the unknown terrors that lay ahead, there were simple yet awesome comforts to their odd world.

Just as she was smiling over this, she heard Alexi's step on the threshold. She turned and ran to him, offering her husband a brief but adoring kiss. "Hello, love. I was about to ready tea." She moved to set the diffusers to steep.

"Step back, dear," he instructed. Waving his hand, he summoned a burst of fire above the kettle and cups.

As they settled in their chairs and Percy was about to launch into her news, there came a knock at the door. "Come in," Alexi called.

"Would you like me to—?"

"Just stay and sip your tea, Percy. We've nothing to hide. Not anymore."

The door opened and the Apollo Hall librarian, Mina Wilberforce, glided in, her beige frock a contrast to her dark skin. She nodded to them both. "Professor, Mrs. Rychman."

Alexi stood. "Hello, Miss Wilberforce."

Percy jumped up. "It's so good to see you, Mina! Would you like some tea?"

"Hello, Percy, and yes, thank you. I daresay I've never seen either of you with such a glow. This new life certainly agrees with you."

"Indeed." Alexi smiled, pulling another chair to the desk as Percy brought over a full teacup. Alexi bade them all sit. "To what do we owe the honor of your visit, Miss Wilberforce?"

Mina stared at the floor as if counting the boards. "I wish I came with nothing but friendship on my mind, but I've been noticing things."

Percy withheld a shudder. Alexi's face was blank.

"Heavens forgive me for saying so," the librarian continued awkwardly, "but, Professor, you're not the average gentleman. There's something special about you; I've always thought so. And, Percy, you're hardly ordinary yourself. I'll hope you'll not deem me mad when I say that the building and grounds of Athens are changing. Subtly, but I'm sure of it."

Alexi and Percy glanced at each other, then at Mina.

"For instance, the cobblestones," she continued. "They've always been laid in triplicate. Not in septuplet."

"The stones now sit in patterns of seven?" Alexi clarified.

"Yes, Professor. Athens has gone entirely to sevens. Wall panels and cut-glass windows—there were five diamond panes and now seven. The classroom numbers are different, as if we've suddenly more rooms. All in multiples of seven. I thought I saw a door, looking just like all of Athens's doors, but one that hadn't been there before. I looked again and it must have been some trick of the eye, for there was no sign of it upon closer examination. Is there something that confounds science at work here?" There was more consternation than concern in her expression, as if a supernatural answer would be an irritation rather than a fright.

Alexi set his jaw. "So it would seem, and I cannot offer explanation. Thank you, Miss Wilberforce, for bringing this to my attention. I shall look into it. Is there much gossip among the students?"

Percy wondered how much Elijah would have to clean up in the minds of students and staff.

Mina gave a small smile. "I doubt a soul loves this building more than I, save, perhaps, the headmistress. Athens is sacred to me, and I notice everything about it. I doubt the student body at large would catalogue such details. But thank you for confirming that I'm not mad."

"No, you're not mad," Alexi replied. "But if you'd mind not causing any uproar, the headmistress and I would greatly appreciate it."

Percy glanced at her husband, surprised he would be so forthcoming.

The librarian nodded and set her tea on the desk. "Tell me what's magical about the two of you," she said. "And about Athens. Please?"

Percy bit her lip, wondering what Alexi would do.

"I beg your pardon?" he said.

Mina sighed. "When I met you, Professor, and then you, Percy . . . I thought you might be persons with a sense beyond what is immediately knowable."

"Indeed," Alexi said, not a confirmation, not a denial.

"Is there some way I can help?"

Alexi's face remained blank, but his tone was earnest. "Pray, Miss Wilberforce."

"That I do." Mina wrung her hands. "Every day."

Alexi stared at her. Surely some mesmerism was employed, for Percy thought she glimpsed blue fire in his eyes, and Mina rose, calmed. "Thank you for tea. Do tell me if you determine the cause of transformation," she murmured. "I'd like to know if God—or the devil, for that matter—is a mathematician." She went out.

As the door closed behind their visitor, Percy stared at Alexi, who went to the window to gaze down at the cobblestones. He said, "Well, it seems we do have friends on that other side." Turning to Percy, the stained-glass window behind him giving him a halo, he added, "At least it's seven. That's *our* number. Not his. Beatrice did say something about troops, yes?"

"Yes. Troops we're to set free."

"Troops. That swath of blue on the map." His eyes lit, and he gave her a hopeful smile. "Thinking on it, that's the best news I've heard since you first said you love me."

Percy grinned. "And how about this news? That book you gave me?" She reached for a paper on his desk and scribbled out a few theorems she now knew to be correct, thanks to the Grecian text. She looked up at him and giggled, Shakespeare ever the best retort: "In the end it would seem it was 'all Greek to me.'"

Alexi laughed loudly and spun her about. "Come, let's have a meal, and then on to a drink with the others. I must toast to the fact I'm not a failed professor after all."

La Belle et La Bête was well worn with loving use, and Percy drank in every detail of the place Alexi had oft mentioned but that she had yet to visit. He led her through the front door, where the paint of some hundred years had chipped in ringed layers. She glimpsed several familiar faces of the Guard already inside.

Thinking of Jane, she paid special attention to the spirits. One at the bar wore an antiquated military uniform, toasting glory the empire had long forgotten. Two Restoration-clad ladies in the corner were murmuring brazen things about the mistress of the establishment and Lord Withersby—and while it was no terrible shock to Percy, given what she'd sensed between them, the language was more colorful than she appreciated. A former actor floated in from nearby Covent Garden, trailing a lavish costume and grayscale greasepaint, offering recreations of his finest theatrical moments to the windows and oblivious passersby. The Guard had long ignored these harmless haunts, but Percy couldn't help but take them in, her ability to hear their eternal and oft repetitive chatter adding to the café's colorful atmosphere.

The Guard gathered around a circular table, likely appearing loud and inappropriate to any outsider: fraternizing across class lines, myriad buttons undone, familiarity between unmarried men and women—all with a vicar presiding. But the few other patrons here didn't seem to notice, likely suspecting the seven of them to be a resident theatre troupe and thus excused. Empty bottles on tables, compliments of the gracious hostess, also might explain the relative obliviousness.

Alexi enjoyed watching Percy take in the scene. He leaned in and murmured richly in her ear. "This is a second home to me, Percy, and while it's hard to believe I've never brought you here, I've enjoyed bringing you home far better."

"*Bienvenue,* Percy!" Josephine rushed to kiss Percy on both blushing cheeks. "As you see, I keep the wine French, cheap, and flowing—a bit like my morals." She snorted and darted behind the bar to procure Alexi a spot of sherry.

Percy giggled. She had to remind herself that she was now a married adult and no longer a convent girl. Her skin might not have any color, but the world did, and she enjoyed it.

"What may I offer you?" the Frenchwoman asked, shoving the snifter into Alexi's hand.

"Well . . . a glass of red wine?"

Josephine pursed her lips. "Now, I'm no enemy of red wine, but I'm guessing that's the only drink a convent girl knows."

"Champagne then," Percy said.

"*Oui!*" Josephine clapped and darted off.

Alexi took Percy by the arm and sat her down beside Jane, who was insisting to Michael that Margaret Pole's incessant execution inside the tower of London was getting ridiculous. "The poor woman's not only runnin' round the scaffold, she's nearly acrobatic. I went to quiet her last night and she'd floated up the lancet windows, taunting her executioner to follow. It's been since 1541, and she was seventy-two— shouldn't she be tired by now? Vicar Carroll, go remind her martyrdom's no sport."

"I daresay watching would be sport." Michael grinned. "If more people saw ghosts, why, cricket would be supplanted in a heartbeat."

"Nil!" Elijah protested.

Jane waved a hand. "You're welcome to her. Charge admission." Everyone chortled at the thought.

Josephine set a bubbling glass of champagne before Percy and took a seat. Alexi launched right into business. "Athens is changing more than we thought," he stated, swirling his snifter.

"Back there with you then," Elijah said. "You're spoiling our fun."

Alexi continued, unperturbed. "All in multiples of seven. Windowpanes, floorboards, cobblestones—I daresay I've been so preoccupied I'd not noticed," he admitted, grazing Percy's hand with his own. "Our perceptive librarian did. This has, unfortunately, gone beyond our little coterie."

"The war. We can't ignore it," Rebecca said. "Truly, friends, it will be like nothing we've ever known."

"You said that about that hellhound. Jack the bloody Ripper," Elijah muttered.

Percy froze, suddenly stunned. It was because of her that those women in Whitechapel were dead. That dog, that *thing* had been looking for her. Tears sprang to her eyes.

"Yes, well, Prophecy continues, and each of its myriad parts is something we've never known," Alexi retorted. This didn't comfort Percy.

"Ah-ah, I feel where your mind is going, young lady, and it will do no good," Michael cautioned.

"It's my fault," she gasped, a huge and terrible pain seizing her.

Michael placed a thumb on her sternum and a jolt of light followed, chasing her sorrow and overtaking it with numbing calm. Percy eyed the vicar with renewed wonder.

"They will do you no good, Percy, those incapacitating thoughts. You need your heart, your energy, for the trials ahead." He turned to the others. "We all do. Hold on to joy. To happiness. To love." He made an effort not to let his eyes linger on Rebecca but failed; Percy noticed. "Hold to light, for darkness seeks to steal our breath."

The Guard all sat in uncomfortable silence. Josephine rose and brought back two more bottles of wine.

"But the number seven is *our* number, friends," Alexi rallied quietly. "There are indeed troops, spiritual friends who will fight on our side. I believe that now. No matter how strange it is to realize this . . . I feel a bit less left to the wolves."

This eased things enough for them to speak of trivialities for a bit, to tease Alexi, to act like all was as it should be. But while Percy didn't know the Guard perfectly well, she could tell it was a bit of a show. The underlying tension wouldn't go away so easily. Those doors had to open, and the mysteries to reveal themselves.

CHAPTER
FIFTEEN

THE NEXT DAY BEGAN IN PEACEFUL, SOLITARY QUIET ONCE ALEXI kissed her and left for Athens, this being her agreed-upon time for calling hours. While Alexi seemed ever reluctant to leave her, he made a point of her not being as tied to Athens as he had always been, allowing her to make more of a home of their estate.

Percy dressed in gauzy layers, indulging her habit of wandering like a resident ghost about her new home. She was still amazed by the estate's size, and that it was all, in part, hers.

For the lady of the house's pleasure, the Wentworths had stocked the small ground floor kitchen with treasures for afternoon tea. The family was thanked for their efforts before Percy sent them off to enjoy their day. To be perfectly honest, being waited upon made Percy uncomfortable and, considering the life of solitude she'd known, she loved having the whole manor to herself for a while.

She made light sandwiches on small breads experimenting with delicate ingredients she'd never dreamed of; at the convent, soup and gruel had been her constant fare. She couldn't wait to share the grounds with Marianna, to youthfully revel in these delights.

The knocker's loud clatter sent her running to usher in her beaming friend, whose eyes appeared glassy and gray, but whose smile was so welcome and familiar Percy overlooked for the moment whatever weariness plagued her.

"Oh, Percy!" Marianna had worn her finest dress, and she swept into the entrance foyer with appropriate appreciation.

"Wait until you see it all." Percy giggled, taking the blond girl's traveling cloak and stowing it.

In a tall hallway mirror, Marianna caught her reflection and paused to tuck a stubborn curl into the pile of locks that threatened to spill down her shoulders. She absently brushed her fingers on her bustle before turning to Percy with a girlish bounce. "So, a tour?"

Percy was only too happy to oblige. She swept Marianna about the estate, room by room, everywhere save the extremities, and her friend cooed in delight. Percy swelled with pride. When she opened the master bedroom and Marianna glimpsed the sumptuous furnishings and four-poster bed, a devilish grin was offered that made Percy blush fiercely.

"And does the master of the house show you every comfort in the privacy of these quarters?" the German girl asked huskily.

"Verily," Percy breathed, placing cool hands on her warm cheeks. "Oh, goodness—tea! I'm to offer you tea and confections as the lady of the estate," she added with theatrical grandeur, before giggling. "Alas, I'm a royal disaster at this. No one ever taught me fine manners at the convent, never thinking I'd have the good fortune to use them. I'm very out of my depth."

Marianna hummed, amused.

Percy led her friend into the parlor, where she'd drawn the curtains on one side to let light pour in, though the other side fell in shadow. Percy seated Marianna in the light and herself in the shade. "Enough about me and my absurdly grand house! How is your Edward?"

"Oh, he's fine. I've not seen much of him, though. He thinks I'm sad because I've lost you." Marianna cocked her head before righting it again. There was something almost marionette-like about the movement, and Percy found herself wondering if the other girl always had such quirks. Had her daydreams of Alexi kept her from seeing that her best friend was a bit odd? Or was something wrong?

"You've not lost me, dear. I'll be here and at Athens for you. You may visit anytime."

"Well, I have been dying to see more of you, darling, so he's not entirely wrong." Marianna abruptly rapped her hand on the round marble table, rattling the teacups on their saucers. She leaned forward. Her green eyes, tinged with gray, sparkled. "Tell me. How does it feel to be truly powerful?"

"What do you mean?" Percy asked. Her pulse quickened. Surely her friend meant the house, Alexi's wealth, her sudden station . . . "I'm not powerful, Marianna. Or, at least, if these trappings do improve one's station, I'm no different than I was before. Being deeply in love is the only change to my heart. The rest are simply blessings."

Marianna rose listlessly, squinting at the sculptures on the mantel. "Did you ever find out who you were? You were so preoccupied with visions, I was curious if that professor of yours told you who you are. Searching for answers, some powerless young lady who could be so much more . . ."

Percy laughed nervously. "I'm no one but myself. Percy Parker . . . Rychman." She moved to the tea tray, disturbed.

"Persephone," Marianna said.

"Yes."

"We're all wondering what our place is in this little farce, aren't we, and who will win in the end."

"Win what? What on earth are you—?" Percy, having busied herself with a plate of scones and clotted cream, turned to find herself alone in the parlor. "Marianna?" she asked. Silence.

She shook her head, assuming her friend had gone for the water closet. When minutes passed and Marianna did not return, Percy called out with a laugh, "What, are you off to procure some souvenir to take to school, some trinket of the fearsome Professor Rychman to dangle before his frightened students?" No answer.

Percy searched the first, second, then third floors of her home. Standing at the base of the attic stairs, she promised herself that, the first moment back at Athens, she would demand a doctor examine Marianna. Her friend looked a bit unwell, and her mind was clearly off, too. She'd have to ask Edward if he'd noticed anything.

"Marianna?" she called, her worry echoing up the stairs. Just that morning she had explored the attic, peeking under dusty cloths at lavish furniture for parties that had not been held for decades, gazing out the tiny dormer window onto the struggling garden far below. And it was there that Percy finally found Marianna, staring out that small window, her blond hair undone and spilling in a cascade down her back.

"Marianna." This time it was not a question but a demand. "What are you doing up here?"

"Indeed, a lovely house," the girl murmured. "A lovely life."

"Marianna . . . what's troubling you? You're not quite yourself." Percy approached her, boots creaking across the wooden boards.

Reaching a hand back, as if urging Percy forward, Marianna did not turn around. Percy approached, eager to discover the source of her friend's melancholy, her faraway gaze, her hollow voice . . .

Marianna seized her hand. Her grip was ice-cold. "Can you trust a man who leaves you all alone in a huge estate, far from all your precious friends? It's true that I'm not myself." The blond girl chuckled. "But I'm so very glad to see you again, Persephone."

Her body did not move, yet Marianna's head turned entirely backward—a sickening, unnatural swivel. A scream leaped to Percy's throat. Tears of gray ash poured from her friend's vacantly staring eyes.

It was certainly no longer Marianna who stood before her, broken and horrible, ash spilling from her mouth, soiling Marianna's fine taffeta garments and spattering Percy's face. Marianna's fallen hair now stirred to life, ashen snake skulls suddenly swarming over her scalp. It was the betrayal of which Beatrice warned and Percy felt a fool. But she'd never have dreamed . . . Perhaps a fatal oversight.

"Hello again!" A voice gurgled from deep inside Marianna's throat. It was the voice of Lucille Linden. The Gorgon who had once nearly killed the Guard had returned.

"Oh, God. Percy!"

Inside her Athens office, fear and despair overtook Rebecca like a bolt of lightning from above. The betrayal. It was happening. Her veins felt the pull of spectral activity, the pulsing pain a distinct sensation of something untoward coming upon one of the Guard. She gasped, jumped to her feet, and flew out the door.

Flinging open the Bay Room door, startling the professors Hart, who were silently reading to each other while floating above the window seat, she found Percy's office otherwise empty. Rebecca didn't take time to ponder the girl's whereabouts; she was out and across the courtyard in a rush, lifting her prim skirts and running toward Apollo Hall. She knew Alexi was in class.

She threw wide his door without a thought to caution, deference, or protocol. Seeing the look on her face, Alexi dropped the chalk he'd been using to scrawl equations on the board behind him.

"Your wife," Rebecca choked out.

Alexi ran up the aisle, had her by the elbow and out the door in an instant even as the students fell to chattering behind them.

"Where is she?" Rebecca breathed.

"What's wrong?" Alexi barked in the same instant. "Home," he answered. "Calling hours."

"Damn!" Rebecca cried. Home, not near. What if they were too late?

Alexi was beside himself as they ran to the rear stables. "What is it?" he demanded.

"A Pull. Pain, like I felt when the hellhound mauled Jane. I'm afraid something's got Percy," Rebecca panted.

Alexi shot ahead to the stalls, where Prospero anticipated his master, pawing the ground, wide black eyes fiercely alert and ready. A moment later, a blur of swirling black swept past Rebecca with a clatter of hooves and a deep cry for swift speed.

Rebecca procured one of the trusted mares kept at the school for emergency, used most often in service of the Guard. No amateur when it came to riding, she managed to keep Alexi in sight.

A mile from the school his hand flew to his head and his tall form shuddered and she knew he now felt the discord she had earlier. She prayed her warning had been in time.

Elijah rounded the corner, driving one of his carriages, heading for the academy. The vehicle wheeled round to follow Rebecca as she cried out and waved her hand, gesturing in a northerly direction. Rebecca glimpsed both Josephine and Jane, looking worried, through the windows. Michael, also on horseback, was close behind. The grim looks on everyone's faces made it clear they felt trouble as well.

Rebecca cursed herself. If she'd told Alexi the moment she'd had the first shudder of concern, the first fear of betrayal, perhaps he'd have kept Percy always close to hand. This delay could cost them everything, and it would be her fault. At least in part.

But if all the Guard were accounted for, who was responsible? Who was the betrayer?

* * *

PERCY SHRIEKED AGAIN. LUCILLE LAUGHED AND MARIANNA'S HAND seized Percy's throat. The blond girl's other arm struck the window, breaking the glass into dangerous shards and sending blood coursing down Marianna's delicate skin.

"You didn't really think I was so easily defeated, did you? Don't you realize that nothing is safe? No one is safe? You're a liability to all involved! Give up now before everyone you love suffers."

"No!" Percy choked. Her flesh started to burn with light.

"Yes, yes, you and that blasted magic of yours. I was unprepared for it before. But I'm invincible now."

"You don't even have your own body," Percy gasped. "You're hardly—"

"Shut up!"

"I always hated her," Lucille continued. "From the moment Darkness dragged her down there, mewling and weeping and retching fruit. I hated her light and colors and the noxious life sprouting in her sickening wake. I should have been a goddess, not a monster. Now she's mortal and I'm a goddess. How *stupid*." Lucille drew Percy's cheek close to the jagged glass. Percy struggled, but the supernatural strength flowing through her friend's body was besting her.

She tried to focus her light to strike a retaliating blow. But she still wasn't entirely sure how to use her power. She was, after all, just a mortal. Her heart begged Alexi to somehow hear her cry. Her face neared the jagged glass.

"Let's see. How did our puppy treat those victims? Just how did the Ripper cut their faces? Before I send you out this window, you'll look like all those girls who had to die before your daft Guard understood. Even then they were helpless! Pathetic, all of you. Pieces of dead gods. I'll take all your lives with me and *I* shall reign in shadow's seat—a place I adore, a beautiful place you wish to destroy. I'll turn your world Whisper instead!"

A surge of righteous anger bolstered Percy and her light expanded, edging Marianna's body back, loosening the grip on her neck. Lucille growled and Marianna's true voice cried out in pain.

"Marianna, darling, it's Percy," Percy choked, wedging her hand between her throat and the preternatural grip around it. "Fight the demon that has you. Fight her!"

Marianna whimpered, sounding like her friend again before her eyes clouded and she gagged, an ashen serpent crawling from her mouth.

Thunder sounded on the stairs, and friends' voices.

"Percy!" Alexi cried, bounding into the room and stunning Marianna's body with a dizzying jolt of blue fire. Lucille released Percy and she fell forward, one hand sliding down the broken glass. Scarlet blood poured garish from her white skin and Alexi dove to catch her. Snakes flaking gray ash slithered to lap Percy's blood from the sill.

The ashen serpent hanging from Marianna's mouth retracted into her throat and Lucille spoke with a gurgling hiss. "You again? Still failing your little sweetheart, Rychman?"

Another bolt aimed right for the mouth reeled Marianna's body backward, ash and spittle flying everywhere. Percy was woozy from pain and loss of blood, but Jane's lit hand was suddenly upon her, mending her deep gash with a tingling light.

"Our only failure is that we didn't cast your ashes to the four corners," Alexi roared, rushing forward and roughly grabbing the possessed body by the throat. Perhaps he couldn't see who it was through his rage.

"Alexi, please," Percy begged. "It's Marianna! She's taken over Marianna. Take care!"

Alexi stared at his quarry and scowled. "Damn it. *Bind!*"

The rest of the Guard hurried into their circle.

Bound by blue fire, Lucille Linden screamed within Marianna's body. The fact that she was now a possessing spirit gave Alexi's fire some advantage, but Lucille continued to spit hot ash to scald them, her snakes lashing out like fanged whips. Marianna's eyes, ears, nose, and mouth were fountains of clotted ash, a horrific sight Percy forced herself to watch because it was her fault.

"Cantus of Extinction!" Alexi cried. Notes of music rose beautiful and fearsome as the Guard encircled Marianna's body, Jane at her side. Wind whipped their clothes and the music of the Grand Work crested in the air.

Percy forced herself to stand and give them energy, trying to siphon off her light, which still felt unwieldy in her body, offering it into the torrent of blue fire that Alexi wreathed around Marianna's body, trying to suffocate the possessor. Michael breathed loudly, forcing them all to remember to do the same.

"Extinct? I'll never go extinct," Lucille shrieked, flapping Marianna's jaw like a grotesque puppet. The blond girl's eyes rolled back in her head, ashen tears still streaming.

Josephine stepped forward, holding an image on a locket before Marianna's shifting, gritty eyes. "Dear girl—"

Marianna's mouth twisted and Lucille gurgled from within. "Your pictures are meaningless to me. I'll kill this girl. Then your dear girl, finally, finally dead."

"Hush!" Alexi bellowed. A crackling bolt of fire sizzling Marianna's body, causing her to lurch violently and vomit more ash. It was good, perhaps, to see the offending substance purged, but Percy feared they were killing her friend in the process.

"We're losing her," Jane cried.

Percy panicked, her chest suddenly a white blaze.

A familiar ripping noise announced a portal. Aodhan came rushing out, either sensing danger from beyond or summoned by Percy's reactive light. "It's the Gorgon, Aodhan, taken over my friend!" Percy cried in his Gaelic tongue.

Jane eyed her beloved. "I don't know that I can do this all m'self," she admitted. "Please help if ye can."

Aodhan floated close, brushing a transparent hand over the Irishwoman's shoulder, staring grimly down at Marianna. He passed his other hand—glowing, healing—over Marianna's eyes, which fluttered. She moaned but remained unresponsive. To Percy he admitted, "Alas, spirits such as these will take revenge at all costs. The body will die."

"No!" Percy sobbed.

"Unless . . ." Aodhan's expression darkened.

"Unless what?"

"I take her in. Into the Whisper-world."

"Then she'll certainly die!"

"Not exactly. For a hapless mortal, not a Guard, there's time before damage is irreparable. Beatrice can help me. But you must come, my lady."

"I could rescue her from there once healed, and return her to the living here?" Percy asked, speaking still in Gaelic.

"Translate!" Alexi demanded.

One of his hands clamped upon Percy's shoulder, the other tightened around Marianna's blond-turned-serpentine curls. The Guard struggled to keep her possessed body still. It kept seizing up and going limp, ash snakes champing at whomever was closest.

Beatrice sidled into view at the threshold of the portal, gazing grimly down upon the situation. "So, it was her. I'm sorry, dear. We didn't know. But like Orpheus came for Eurydice, you may come, a god disguised. It's nearly all in place. They won't stop, things such as these," the ghost explained, gesturing disdainfully to Marianna's messy body. "Not until you settle it once and for all. Let the Healer and me deal with this. You and the Guard use the map and the doors. Knock, and the door will be opened.

"The time is upon you," Beatrice said, addressing them all, with Percy's echo a beat behind, allowing her friends to hear their predecessor's speech. "Your beloved Athens changes. There's no stopping it. If you want to blame someone, blame a goddess and her hapless Guard, but do not punish yourselves by doing nothing. Percy, you are the key. You must attend the destiny that awaits you."

When Alexi heard, he roared. "I told you, I'll not allow her in! Take me." A bolt of blue fire hurtled from his hand toward Beatrice, his intent unclear. But she held up a hand and the fire congealed, clearly hers to command.

The rest of the Guard gasped.

"It isn't your choice, leader! You can't go in or you'll fall to pieces! Accept the fact your wife is built for things you are not," Beatrice bellowed, Percy repeating her in choking murmurs. "Possessed as you are, a living Guard *cannot* step across—shall I regale you of ugly tales the goddess told me of those who tested this? It isn't a matter for discussion! Your stubbornness, however massive, cannot stop fate!"

Marianna's body convulsed, giving a horrific sound then a pathetic cry. The life was being choked out of her, the monster within desperate for someone to die. What was left of Percy's friend was begging for mercy, her eyes still spewing ash—and now a new horror: blood. Jane wiped her cheeks only to see them wetted again. Percy wept, clutching her fists at her breast as if she could grasp the light there and cast some spell of salvation.

"Cantus of Extinction," Alexi growled, showering blue fire upon the mane of snakes, which squealed and spat. "Resume it."

The Guard joined hands as Aodhan voiced caution. "Such a cantus may kill the girl. This is no ordinary possession."

"It may *kill* her, Alexi," Percy said on Aodhan's behalf, seizing her husband's hand. Blue fire tingled up her wrist.

"Well, then, what do the spirits advise?"

"Tell Jane to give me a lock of her hair," Aodhan stated, and floated back to the threshold of the Whisper-world, where his transparent body darkened to gray solidity. Percy furrowed her brow and repeated the request.

"This isn't the time for romance," Alexi growled.

"I'm not being romantic. I need a tether. Do as I say," Aodhan insisted. Percy translated.

Jane stared at her beloved. A practical woman who always thought to carry practical things, she pulled a penknife from her jacket pocket and without hesitation cut a long lock. She moved toward the portal, offering the hair in her open hand; Aodhan's hand grew transparent as it stretched across the threshold toward hers. A draft drew the hair across and in, to where he was solidly able to clutch and raise it. Both the lock and his hand glowed with healing light.

"We lost our gifts long ago, but they live on in Athens, and in you," he murmured, Percy maintaining his tone as she repeated his words. Jane was visibly moved as Aodhan kissed the lock of her hair and wound it about the leather band over his shoulder. The locket around Beatrice's throat pulsed with Phoenix fire.

"Now the girl," Beatrice murmured.

"Take good care of her," Percy said.

"Take good care of yourself," Beatrice countered. "And wear gray. We can't have mortal color giving you away. Don't forget."

As the Guard encircled and gingerly lifted Marianna's body, Alexi placed himself between his wife and her friend. "Percy, stay back."

They got the body unsteadily onto its feet, ashen snakes snapping at them, catching a strand of Josephine's hair and a corner of Elijah's fine suit. A burst of fire flew from Alexi's hands, flinging Marianna toward the portal. Aodhan and Beatrice caught her, their forms solid in the Whisper-world. Snakes flailing and sputtering, they dragged the body in. The portal closed.

Percy loosed a sob. The Guard's shoulders sagged in a group sigh, failure threatening to consume their hearts. Percy slid down the wall into a heap on the floor, shaking her head. "This is all my fault! I'm a disaster," she cried, tears flowing. "I'm a danger to all who come near, to all who are close to me, to all whom I lo—"

"I'll not hear another word," Michael barked, immediately on his knees at her side. "This is beyond any fault of yours, and you must accept that or we cannot move forward. Your fear is what our enemy wants!" He placed a firm hand on her collar and she felt a gust of calm.

"Friends, thank you," Alexi said quietly. "Give me leave to calm her. Don't go far. Make yourselves at home."

The Guard nodded and filed downstairs, Rebecca at the rear. Alexi grabbed her arm. "Bless you, Rebecca. If you hadn't felt the call when you did . . ." He faltered. Overcome with emotion neither of them did well expressing, she nodded curtly and exited.

Alexi eased Percy into his arms from the floor. Supporting her, he led her down into the parlor, where he swept a roaring fire into the hearth. He heated tea with another gesture, and forced a cup into his wife's shaking hands.

"I am a danger to those I love," Percy stated, guilt threatening to undo her sanity.

Alexi stared at her with both consternation and adoration. "This work means danger."

"But I—"

"What, shall you go and leave us? Try to lure the danger elsewhere? It follows us, Percy, and you were sent to us. This is our lot."

"I . . ." Percy's mouth moved to protest, but she had no words.

Her husband's expression was grim. "The day I was chosen to lead the Guard, an ill force swept through this house, paralyzing my sister and frightening my grandmother to death. It was, perhaps, an early taste of the trials that would come. My parents left me this house and a bit of money at the age of sixteen. They never said why, but I know it was because I frightened them. They thought I was ill luck. That I doomed the family name."

He eyed her, his expression as tortured as she'd ever seen. "This work will make you question everything, Percy, and make you despair. But you must persevere."

She nodded. They both had been dealt shares of pain, and she better understood his zealous protection. She'd chosen to take that doomed name, she was choosing him, this house, this life; and with her vow of marriage she'd promised never to abandon him.

He pressed her against him, stilling her shaking body with the embrace. "We must persevere," he insisted. "I am at your side."

"Thank God," Percy said. "Yet . . . don't be angry for what may be asked of me, what I cannot control. What must happen."

Alexi stared at the fire and held her tighter.

CHAPTER

SIXTEEN

INSIDE THE WHISPER-WORLD, AODHAN AND BEATRICE WERE HARD at work, trying to save the body and soul of an innocent victim.

They ferried Marianna away to a dim chamber where Beatrice mustered their hallowed fire, grateful her time at Athens had given her a store of power to augment her locket; otherwise she'd be useless, considering the enormity of this task.

At any other time, Beatrice admitted, brushing ash out of Marianna's curls with a comb, her actions would have caught the attention of this entire spectral world. The molten, ashen liquid seeping from the girl's facial orifices was a truly gruesome sight. But she and Aodhan went undisturbed, for the Whisper-world was a door hanging on one hinge. Beatrice didn't blame the current Guard for their hesitation. Their new task went against everything they'd all fought for, their whole thankless lives. She herself had fought destiny to only in the end acquiesce. Bleeding the Whisper-world onto Athens was dangerous, but it was the only way to regain balance.

Mortal and Whisper-world edges rubbed with freshly combustible friction. Long-sealed walls had cracked open, forgotten vaults now spewed fresh venom. Spirits that had never before mixed were now fighting and cursing along the river. All that remained a fortress unbroken was, unfortunately, the prison room where Darkness had corralled his sworn enemies. But that, too, was scheduled to soon crack open. So long as Mrs. Rychman kept her head.

Only a pile of restless ash evidenced their painstaking work, oozing grimly from Marianna's mouth with every healing burst Aodhan managed. He continually brushed the offending substance into a ceramic jar.

Other jars lined the edge of a yawning hole like the stacked skulls of an ancient crypt.

"What're you doing?" the Groundskeeper cried, shuffling into their grim workplace. "That's my Lucy in there. You let her go. You let her out. That host is alive! What are you doing? You're breaking every rule—"

"Be my guest and please extract your Lucy. We're just trying to return her," Beatrice offered graciously.

The Groundskeeper pointed. "You're the troublemaker."

"Why, so I am." Beatrice bowed. "Are you going to help your beloved or not? We could make sure she never leaves this body."

The Groundskeeper's face twisted, staring at the fire that sparked around Beatrice's neck and had leaped into her hand. He was clearly wary of her power. "No!"

"Then allow us to take care of this. Here are some of her parts—by all means, take them away." Beatrice gestured to the rows of jars.

"I'll expect more," he threatened, counting.

"Indeed." Beatrice nodded, standing aside as he rushed to scoop Lucille's remains into his arms. He soon scurried away, singing. "Lucy-Ducy wore a nice dress . . . Lucy-Ducy made a great mess!" His voice faded down the hall.

The two Guard went back to work. When the next jar was half full of ash, Beatrice lifted a rock, placed it inside and sealed the lid with twine and a burst of blue fire for good measure. She handed the hissing contents to Aodhan, who vanished, well aware of what to do with it.

From the moment the sun broke across the horizon, a heavy dread rose within those of the Guard who'd spent the night at the Rychman estate. Alexi was gentle, taking his wife into his arms, but the weight of failure was there between them as they woke, like a cold chill.

"All I can think of is Marianna," Percy murmured. She nestled into his shoulder, his nearness her only comfort. "Let the world pass us by, Alexi, just stay and hold me."

"Would it were that easy. I'd love nothing more. But the call is strong in my blood. There's work to be done at Athens; our safe house no longer safe. We put our students at risk if we tarry." He kissed her temple, then commanded, "Stay close to me today."

Percy nodded. But, what if there was a door? Would she take it at a run, to speed this inevitable dirge onward? Uncertainty would drive her mad. She had to trust Beatrice: She'd know when it was time.

Due to the abnormal and dangerous nature of what had occurred in the house, the Wentworths' leisure time was extended, Elijah wiping their minds a bit of any worry, and the Guard collectively took care of themselves.

Josephine had prepared cold breakfast and tea, and the others sat quietly in the parlor, eyeing Percy with funereal expressions. She graciously accepted the tea Jane hurried to offer as she entered.

Alexi broke the dreadful silence. "Friends, you feel the weight of Athens as I do, do you not?"

Everyone nodded.

"The storm gathers," Rebecca agreed. "We've a war to weather, friends. We must go and save those beloved bricks."

Michael lifted his hands. "May the congregation say amen."

In silence, Percy and Alexi packed a trunk of basic clothing, Percy thinking about Beatrice's advice and what might be expected and required of her. She placed her rosary in with some soft garments and did nothing to disturb Alexi's brooding quiet. There was nothing to say, but prayer filled her thoughts.

THEIR ANCHOR OF A BUILDING WAS ON A FAULT LINE READY FOR A fearsome quake, a shifting mystery. Athens was proving to have a character of its own, and none of the Guard could be sure whose side it was taking, its changes taking their sacred number or no. A luminosity grew about the stately bricks that gave students pause, as if they could not trust their own eyes. The sad truth was that they couldn't.

Staff and students were not sleeping, and many stated they were seeing ghosts. The Guard could not disagree: The Athens specters were plentiful and particularly active. Percy heard them babbling as if only recently dead, jarred into a new awareness of themselves.

Elijah was most taxed by it, adjusting the minds of the academy's residents, who understood only that neither they themselves nor the hairs on the backs of their necks could rest. Before long, all seven of the Guard had crowded into Rebecca's office. She handed Elijah her flask and no one even raised an eyebrow. "We can't run a school like this," she said.

Percy stared at the carpeting—a sensible and ordinary gray, like most of the headmistress's wardrobe—nightmares coursing her mind like a grim carousel. She'd stood silently at Alexi's side all morning, and they'd examined each new door Beatrice had erected about the grounds, each emblazoned with some variant of the number seven.

"We have no choice but to close the school," Alexi replied.

"I've done my best—a thorough wipe of every mind—but their fears will grow again. I can't be everywhere at once," Elijah said.

Rebecca shook her head. "I'll gather them into the auditorium. I'll tell them . . ."

"That you're giving them an extra bit of holiday," Michael said. "For being smashing students. I realize you never allow yourself holidays, Miss Thompson, but the world loves them. So do students. We're not too terribly far from Christmas. It's soon the season of love." He pounded his fist on a bookcase and smiled, and the others couldn't help but feel the stale air of the office seemed a bit easier to breathe.

Rebecca began to deliver sharp orders. "Alexi, have house wardens gather staff and students immediately into the auditorium. I'll need everyone's help to keep order. We must use whatever means necessary—all our usual tricks—to convince students and staff that Athens is granting them an enjoyable respite, nothing more. Then, my friends, we will shut ourselves within these walls for a siege."

Percy realized there was no specific task for her. She had no usual place in the Guard's work, had no established methodology to aid them. Yet, she had work of her own.

The others walked ahead, falling in behind Rebecca's brisk tread. Alexi led Percy to the side of the hallway and said, "Percy, I'll meet you in your office."

"No. Meet me in the sacred space. I must study that map."

"Percy, I'll not have you in there a—"

"Come for me when you've dispatched everyone," she interrupted and when he made another move to object, she continued: "Alexi, if the great maw of the Whisper-world is to open and bear down on us, I'd like to be prepared. That map is the only clue we have."

Alexi sighed. He lifted his hand to touch her face, but he was stopped by the passing students glancing at them out of the corners of their eyes. "My desperation in wanting to see you safe trumps all," he murmured. "Just . . . don't go in."

"We've time yet," she replied. It was a reassurance but no promise. Alexi clenched his jaw and his fists and stalked away.

Her tread was weary as she walked to the Athens chapel. She tried to think of how beautiful her wedding had been, of how much she loved Alexi and was lucky to have found him, and thoughts of how she had indeed been provided for brought some consolation. In a rear pew she found Mina Wilberforce, staring in consternation at the windows.

The librarian glanced up as she approached, and pointed down the line of amber-glass angels. "There are seven. There were six. How can one explain that? I pray it's God's work here, but I fear . . ." She trailed off, shaking her head.

"Have faith," Percy murmured. "Staff and students gather in the auditorium as we speak. Perhaps you'd like to join them."

"And you?"

Percy eyed the chapel. "If the devil's at work here, I think I'd best pray." She couldn't assure others of their sanity and have any remaining for herself.

"Indeed. Well, then. Bless you, dear girl."

"And you."

Left alone, Percy took a deep breath. Darting up the aisle, she threw her arm forward, opening the dark doorway and descending the stairs into the Guard's mysterious space. Pulling the key from her chain, she bent at the center of the floor and turned it in the feather. There came the usual grating sound and the rush of blue fire to which she was now accustomed. She almost pressed her face into the flames as the patterns formed on the floor; their tingling power was an intoxicant.

Instead, she rose and paced the perimeter of the map, determining the precise, rectangular lines of Athens; the courtyard in the middle, Promethe and Apollo halls, the girls' and boys' dormitories. Beyond that familiar floor plan, the flames were taller in some places, and she murmured, "Perhaps those are spaces of spirit world import? And surely this cannot be the whole of that realm. Surely there are parts to defy mortal sensibilities."

There were two faint blue glimmers nearer to the overlap with the academy, and Percy had to assume, and pray, that those represented Beatrice and Aodhan, keeping Marianna somewhere safe. But her eye followed the movement, and inevitably she was drawn back to the patch of red.

The red dot slowly traversed a circular space, the mark of a key still above it. Inside, the swath filled with blue.

Despite her better judgment, Percy moved closer. She bent to examine the circular area of blue—a space she hoped was filled with friends—and noticed that just outside its delineated lines of fire, there was moisture . . . and a murmur. A faint sound of rushing water. A river? Surely. Of course there would be a river. *The* river.

Alexi's footfall on the stair made her jump. "Well?" It was quite obvious he disapproved of her initiative.

"I've determined what is Athens and what may be what you call the Whisper-world. The flame has different heights there; the spaces are more circular. Of course, the more my eyes get used to the map, the more I believe that we only see the outline of those spaces of the Whisper-world that extend off from Athens, only those spaces that are meaningful to our fight. I cannot believe such a thing as the spirit realm would be an addition to an academy." She smiled wryly.

Alexi hummed. "The red mark circles that same sea of blue, perhaps patrolling our troops. And look. Did you notice these?" He pointed to places on the Athens perimeter that bled outward. At each juncture, a brighter horizontal line floated. On the scale of the map, each was about the height of a door.

"Beatrice's doors. We can see where they lead," Percy exclaimed.

"We've no idea where they'll lead," Alexi argued. "Or what's waiting on the other side."

"We should leave the map in place. We've no idea when any one of these doors might burst open. This map surely can't be seen from the other side, else Beatrice would have warned us, and who knows when the information will be helpful."

Alexi set his jaw but said nothing.

Percy didn't bother to ask if he heard the ticking of a clock. She assumed he didn't. But she did—ticking away the seconds of her life, or the seconds until battle? It was by far the most maddening development yet. She held out her hand, and Alexi took it, reluctantly leaving the key in the floor. They exited the sacred space, the flames licking low and steady behind them. As they stepped out into the chapel, the dark doorway snapped shut behind them.

Alexi secured his arm around her waist and they walked toward his office, nodding to passing students. The young people looked deliriously drugged as they carried their bags home for early holiday. Percy hoped these ghostly trials would be done by Christmas and that, as in Dickens's *Carol*, they'd all be granted their due blessings. The Guard could do nothing further until the building was safely and entirely cleared.

In his office, Alexi lit candelabra and a fire in the hearth with a wave of his hand. He turned the handle of his ornate phonograph, producing a bit of soothing Bach. Percy readied tea, which he warmed with a flick of his hand, and they sat, worlds away from the simple time when their biggest mystery was her visions—and the pleasant revelation that they *both* could see ghosts.

This office was a catalyst for visions. This time, Percy saw a portal. Beatrice stood within, indicating the time was nigh. A bright blue, transparent feather of flame floated before her face.

Alexi didn't notice Percy's distraction; he was busy adding alcohol to his tea from the flask Rebecca had given Elijah. "Were you always so fond of sherry?" she asked.

"Not nearly as much as I am of late."

Percy nodded. She couldn't blame him. "If we stay the night here, Alexi, where will we—"

Before she could finish, he gestured toward the far right side of his office, where a section of the room that didn't catch direct light from the windows was cloaked in darkness. Setting down his cup, he went to the trunk he'd left near the door and carefully slid it behind a bookshelf that jutted slightly from the wall. For the first time Percy realized that the floor-to-ceiling bookshelves there concealed an alcove. A bit of light bloomed from within, illuminating a narrow entrance.

Percy rose and examined the cozy alcove, discovering a small cot and a low table bearing a gas lamp, all surrounded by further bookshelves. Alexi placed the trunk by the bedside and edged past his wife, returning to his desk. Staring at the cot, which was strewn with two blankets and a rumpled pillow, Percy wondered how many nights he'd fallen wearily here rather than make the lonely journey to his dark estate.

Percy lifted the lid of the trunk they had packed. She had, as Beatrice directed, brought a slate-colored dress for her impending gray tasks. Instinctively she reached for her pearl rosary, thankful to have something with which to busy her fingers. Then she rejoined Alexi at his desk and sat upon his knee.

He perused a diary. "My first thoughts of you," he murmured, staring at the pages. "Clinical. I wrote clinical thoughts. I couldn't admit how much I loved you until you were nearly dead in my arms. And you hang on the precipice of danger now, Percy, making me realize it all the more. I . . ." He looked away, strangled by emotion. "I swear, if you take chances with your life, I'll never . . ."

Percy kissed his face.

He jumped up, setting her on her feet before him. "Let me go instead," he said desperately. "Let me set this in motion. I cannot simply let you go; it's against every principle I . . . I cannot bear to lose you."

"Alexi, my love. My dear champion." Percy put her hand on his lips. "You'll go mad if you so much as step across. None of us can take that risk. The Guard, London, and I—we all need you whole."

"And what ensures you *your* mind will fare better?"

She shrugged. "Because I am not like you. Because they tell me it was once home."

Alexi pounded his desk, tears in his eyes. "Your home is here with me!"

"I've never doubted that, and I never will, husband," she said. "When the Guard convinced you fate was not on our side, you parted ways with me and saw fit to make me suffer," she stated. The pain on Alexi's face worsened, and he opened his mouth to refute her. She put her hands lovingly to his cheeks. "We survived. Our love survived. And we shall again."

He stared at her in wonder. "How did my dear girl grow so brave?"

Percy grinned. "Didn't you hear? The meek shall inherit the earth." Alexi couldn't help but chuckle, a tear rolling down his cheek. She kissed him passionately and retreated. "But now I need Michael. I'd like him to pray with me."

As Percy suspected, she found the vicar not far from Rebecca's office. Around them, the school continued to empty, obedient and dazed students following the Guard's instruction. They could have rushed them out, but Elijah's gifts didn't work as well as a hurried demand. Far better to use a slow and sturdy suggestion. Elijah slumped near the main door, clearly exhausted. He wasn't used to "wiping" so many at a time, staff, students, and groundskeepers. Josephine stood beside her beau, shifting on her feet. Michael sat on a bench nearby, reading. Percy fiddled with the beads in her hand.

The vicar looked up and unleashed one of those winning smiles that could brighten any day. "Hullo, Mrs. Rychman. Shocked Alexi let you out of his sight, but glad we have the honor of your company."

Percy smiled wanly and sat beside him. She glanced at his book. "*The Castle of Otranto*?"

"It's positively dreadful." He nodded and laughed. "I adore it. But you're not here to discuss literature with me," he stated, waggling his mustache as she smirked. "I'd say you're looking pale, but that's a ridiculous redundancy."

She nodded, turning the beads in her fingertips, unable to find the words she needed. But Michael knew what she wanted without speaking. He clasped her hands in his, lowering his head.

"'In the beginning was the Word. And the Word was with God and the Word was God. He was in the beginning with God. All things were made through him, and without him was not anything made. That which has been made was life in him and the life was the light of mankind. The Light shines in the Darkness and the Darkness has not overcome it.'"

Percy's hands warmed and pulsed with power. Michael sent something soft and wonderful through their fingers, as if a dove of blessed assurance were cupped gently in her hands, as if hope now infused each pearl rosary bead. He said, softly, "Keep it close to you."

She nodded and tucked the rosary inside her corset, directly against her bosom. The beads seemed to pick up her heartbeat and magnify it. "Thank you, Vicar, for knowing just what I needed."

"Of course."

Percy rose and walked away, then bit her lip, realizing there was something else. She rushed back and fell to her knees before him, their hands again clasped. "There are times when we must make sure all things left unsaid are said. If something should happen to me, please impress my unfailing love upon Alexi, my greatest treasure, his love worth a thousand deaths. And you'd best make sure you leave nothing unsaid either. None of us should."

Michael stared up at her. "I should tell her," he murmured. The concept was clearly more terrifying to him than spiritual warfare.

"Yes." Percy smiled. "I think you should."

Michael nodded, blushed, and returned to his book.

The day had darkened swiftly.

A trickle of dazed students filed past, ignoring the assembled Guard per Elijah's bidding. Percy had never known the comfort of appearing so invisible.

Percy was heading for Alexi's office when he jumped out from behind a pillar and startled the very wits out of her. Gasping, she batted a hand at him as he scooped her up into his arms.

"W-why on earth?" she stammered.

"You've seen ghosts and gorgons. You're willing to stare down the whole of the Whisper-world. I thought nothing could frighten you." His tone was teasing, but a mournful truth lay beneath.

She laid her palm along his face. "Losing you. That is a terror from which I could never recover."

Alexi pursed his lips. Percy thought she saw a glimmer of a tear. He set her on her feet and swept her up the grand staircase.

"Alexi, what are you—?"

"Recalling my fondest memory," he murmured, taking her hand and spinning her across Promethe Hall's upper floor. The stately foyer was bathed in a soft purple dusk shifting toward moonlight—similar to the night of the academy ball, when Alexi had discovered Percy, feeling awkward and unloved, on this very floor.

That night he had waltzed her through starlight and shadows. That night, their feelings for each other had begun to overflow.

Percy heard a bow strike a string and a note of music rose like steam into the air. She turned to see Jane with her fiddle, winking. Another note came, then another, a lilting little waltz to recall them to that moment they first dared dream.

"May I have this dance, Persephone?"

Percy beamed. "Oh, please, Professor."

He lifted her gracefully into the dance he'd first taught her in his office. She seamlessly followed Alexi's lead, and they spun in and out of widening silver moonlit shafts, the sparkle in his dark eyes and the press of his hand giving her thrills that would keep her forever blushing for love of him.

She giggled as he spun her beneath his arm and snapped her back in an artful turn. "Ah, for more innocent times, Alexi."

He almost smiled. "I hate to ruin your reminiscence, but I abandoned you that night to deal with our canine friend who almost cleaved poor Jane in two. Hardly more innocent. And not long ago."

Percy winced. "How funny the mind, and memory. I feel ages older!"

"We all are, I suppose. Responsibilities weight wisdom."

"I was so eager for answers to my strange portents."

"After a longer life than yours, I'd say to be careful what you wish."

Percy chuckled. "Yes, yes, I should've never left the convent."

Alexi clutched her passionately, hands roaming free. "I daresay you can't go back." She squealed and laughed, feeling blessedly at ease.

They danced and Jane played.

Breaking every rule the Whisper-world sought to impose upon him, Aodhan appeared at Jane's side, his love its own portal. He didn't stay long. Nodding to Percy as he disappeared, his solemn gaze a promise that he didn't take his responsibility for granted, his raised hand was reassurance that her friend still lived.

The trio's mood grew lighter as the moon rose higher. More of the Guard appeared, and Percy was delighted as Elijah and Josephine joined them in their impromptu ball. Michael stood beaming, leaning against the balustrade and taking in his fellows, offering an occasional beautifully delivered verse.

For a little while the dread of death lifted from the halls of Athens.

DISTANT MUSIC LURED REBECCA FROM HER OFFICE. A KEENING FIDDLE, she assumed it was Jane's work.

She crept up the staircase, hearing murmurs and the occasional laugh. Hanging to the shadows a few steps from the landing, she took in the scene. Elijah and Josephine were arm in arm, swaying beside Jane as she played. Michael sang a soft and tender verse. Had she never realized the lovely timbre of his voice? They used their voices all the time. But that was the Work. This was their life. Their life was capable of simple, wondrous delights, perhaps, if she ever let herself enjoy them. He turned to look upon her at the words, "I'll be your paramour . . ."

Rebecca's throat closed and she turned away from Michael to stare at the couple before her. Alexi and Percy waltzed slowly through shafts of moonlight. They clearly delighted in their languorous steps, having lost all unmarried formality and strict upright carriage to press confidently close. A moonlit Percy was nothing short of an angel, graceful and blinding white, radiating love as pure as her skin was pale. Alexi, her stalwart protector, stared as if he couldn't bear to blink and lose sight of her for a moment. Rebecca silently retreated, letting tears come as they would.

She glided to the corner of the downstairs foyer, looking out over the courtyard awash with bright silver, the starkness of the moonlight matched the dawning realization in her soul: The pain of seeing them together would never lessen. Her little group faced more danger than they'd ever known, and all Rebecca could think about was how much she wished her life were otherwise, that all their lives were otherwise, that Alexi would finally realize she was the only woman for him. She had been with him all along, loving him from the very start, twenty years prior.

Shame on such thoughts. He and Percy were so stirringly beautiful, waltzing together. Only a villain would think otherwise. Pressing her forehead to the window, she welcomed the cool glass on her skin and felt the bright moon on her face, wondering how the creases of worry and loneliness must show like scars of battle.

"I know that certain things do not unfold according to our desires."

She hadn't heard the tread behind her, but the soft voice made Rebecca whirl. Michael stood partly in shadow, his bushy gray-peppered hair smoothed from its usual chaos. His entrancing blue eyes danced with an unusually bright light, and he continued. "I know we cannot always choose whom we love. And I know how it hurts to see the one we love looking adoringly at someone else. I *know*. I've been watching you watch Alexi for years."

Rebecca registered his words, gaped, flushed, and turned again to face the window, attempting to hide the transparency of her heart from Michael's unmatched scrutiny.

"I cannot replace him," Michael said, and waited patiently for her to turn. She did, and saw the same look on his face that she was sure she gave Alexi when he wasn't looking, the look that Alexi and Percy shared.

Rebecca had never thought to see someone turn such adoring warmth in her direction.

Michael continued with a bravery that surprised them both. "I do not fault you your emotions, though I must admit a certain jealousy as to their bent. I do not expect to change anything with these words. I know I am bold, and perhaps a fool. But I will remain silent no longer." His fortitude flickered, and he dropped his gaze. "I shall now return to a glass of wine. Or two. But as we're too old to play games, I felt it my duty to speak. At long last. At long, long last."

He offered her a smile that could warm the most inhuman of hearts, bowed slightly and retreated, leaving the thunderstruck Miss Thompson to stand alone once more, illuminated.

PERCY LAY TUCKED BENEATH THE ARM OF HER HUSBAND ON THE AL-cove cot in his office. She wished she could have lost herself forever in music and company, with friends, wine, and promises of tomorrow, bur-rowing finally at the end of the night into her husband's embrace so deeply that no mythic force could ever pry her free. Instead she found herself staring at Alexi's face, stern even in the deepest of sleep, shaking with nerves.

Surely Alexi only slumbered out of supreme force of will. Perhaps it was the sherry. She couldn't have slept if she'd drunk the whole bottle, though; the building was alive, as restless as she. Her blood and stom-ach churned. She thought she should go study the map to see if it had changed, to see if some miracle had made the red blazing mark fade blessedly away, but she feared the answer would be no.

She thought about the moment, so recent, when she had stared at her wedding dress and been so purely, incredulously happy. She recalled first glimpsing Alexi at the altar, awaiting her with those glowing jet eyes, pledging his love, the burst of heavenly light that exploded from their vows . . . Where had that simple happiness gone? Where was that burst of powerful light to ease the sting of darkness?

Silently, at her sleeping husband's side, Percy wept.

APPROPRIATING MATTRESSES FROM STUDENTS' ROOM, THE GUARD scattered themselves through Athens, choosing locations they deemed strategic.

Elijah stationed himself in the small foyer just outside Alexi's second-floor office, Josephine near the ground-floor entrance of Apollo Hall. Michael was to monitor the chapel. Rebecca wanted to be nowhere else but in the heart of her beloved Promethe Hall, and so she placed herself in the middle of that entrance foyer, staring up at the youthful ghost in the chandelier who kept tinkling the crystals in agitation. Jane was in the hall between Michael and Rebecca, very near to a few new Whisper-world doors that visibly unnerved her.

After fixing his mattress directly in the center of the chapel aisle, Michael made rounds. Leaving Alexi and Percy their privacy, he first went to Josephine, who had found paper and charcoal and was furiously sketching. He knelt at her side, kissed her temple and placed his hand over her heart, streaming a flood of relaxation and peace through her. "On this night, make sure you say everything best not left unsaid." Rising, he was surprised to see Elijah enter the room's low-trimmed gaslight. "Lord Withersby, I was just about to come and give you a bit of a benediction."

"One last plea for my mortal soul?" the man asked with a smirk. "No use, Vicar. But it's a night where certain things must not go without saying. And while I do love you, you weren't my intended recipient."

Michael grinned. "Why, Elijah Withersby, I *have* taught you a thing or two through the years. I'm impressed. Shocked, really."

Josephine smiled up from her pile of skirts and halo of charcoal dust; Elijah shooed the clergyman in the direction of the headmistress's office. "Go shock us in turn and take a bit of your own damned medicine."

Michael cleared his throat and straightened his ascot. "I'll have you know, I already did."

Elijah turned to Josephine with eyes she'd never seen so wide. He knelt beside her and said, "Well, Josie, that settles it—we're getting married."

She burst into happy tears and buried her face in his arm. And that's about the time they noticed the trickle of blue fire snaking about the floor and twining around their ankles, but Alexi was nowhere to be found and they didn't remember anything after the appearance of the ancient flame.

As if sleepwalking, the Guard shifted, moving where their unconscious minds led, all of them soon adrift in a sound sleep. The fire of the phoenix now took control.

CHAPTER
SEVENTEEN

IN THE MIDDLE OF THE NIGHT, AS PERCY LAY ATTEMPTING SLEEP, SHE was roused by a warm tickle on her cheek, like a feather's kiss. Her eyes opened to find that it was exactly that: A sparkling, floating feather made of blue fire hovered before her.

It was a familiar portent. She sat up, knowing she was meant to follow. It had been just such a talisman that once led her from a hospital bed to save the Guard from danger. Tears stung her eyes. She didn't want to go. But it was time. The school was empty and putting off the task only assured Marianna's death and delayed the inevitable.

The feather became a sacred heart—a strong, pounding heart aflame with power, the same image offered her the last time she was reticent— then sparkled and returned to the shape of a feather. Wafting toward her, it kissed her cheek again and caught one of her tears on its shimmering surface.

She turned to Alexi, whose powerful presence seemed terribly vulnerable in sleep. A luminous blue mist hung about his head; likely this kept him sleeping. An irony, this, that the fire he had been called to wield had such a mind of its own, even to the point of keeping its most powerful acolyte out of its way, a reminder to Percy that they only borrowed these powers, which were their own exterior forces of nature.

"I love you so. I love you so," she repeated, bending close to kiss him before thinking better of it as the feather shifted closer to her, then away, impatient. "Not even a kiss?" she murmured.

It bobbed again, then moved forward and pressed itself to her lips. She felt the heat of its touch.

"Thank you, I suppose," she muttered.

The blue fire that was a symbol of their work came from a mysterious source, the remnant of a splintered god. It had been a guide to her once before; she felt she had no choice but to trust it again. Rising, she slipped from its hanger what she prayed would not become her burial gown—gray, as instructed—and plucked her boots from the end of the bed. Last time she had dashed off in nothing more than an infirmary robe; this time, she would go properly attired.

Dressing, she took a last look around the office, a room full of unspoken promises and unfulfilled mysteries. Several ghosts hovered in the room, oddly silent, apparently as anxious as she to see what would happen next. Taking one last, wistful look around, she folded her cloak over her arm and slipped silently through the door. The feather bobbed ahead of her down the hall.

She was prepared to meet any number of the Guard along her path and was not disappointed. She found Elijah on the second floor, with Josephine in his arms, both of them sound asleep. A softly musical, blue-lit bit of cloud hovered about them. Percy smiled, tearful, wishing she could remain just as peacefully by Alexi's side, but the feather bounced, telling her not to linger.

Athens had always been a magical place for Percy, but she now had a feeling the grounds were an entity in themselves. The air had that particular quality that precedes a great storm, distantly rumbling, charged and ready for lightning to strike. The moonlight managed to cut wide, sweeping swaths in contradiction to the angles of windows.

Sliding her cloak around her shoulders, Percy carefully opened and shut the creaking front door of Apollo Hall as she exited, her breath clouding before her in the chill air of the courtyard. Academy ghosts glided about, each giving her a second glance, as they once again realized she wasn't actually one of them. If they spoke, it was in hushed murmurs to one another. Perhaps they were scared of her. More likely they were scared for her.

The angel of the courtyard stood at upright attention as always, a thin layer of ice crusting her fountain basin. But there was something different. Percy's blood chilled as she noticed that the book in those bronze fingers was now face out for all to see.

The feather halted in front of the statue, and Percy saw the book was inscribed. She almost didn't want to look, for fear her doom was writ there, but part caught her eye and she eased. The words were familiar:

In darkness, a door. In bound souls, a circle of fire.
Immortal force in mortal hearts.

It was the Guard's incantation, carved into their chapel, writ in their liturgy. Percy was fortified as she turned to the feather. It had wanted her to see this proclamation. It wanted her to know that she and the Guard were not alone, that a powerful magic surpassing their mortal bodies saturated even the mortar here, that the very stones she stood upon could cry out in support.

The feather sparkled, enlarging with pride, then moved on.

The main foyer of Promethe Hall was lit with its own growing light, an ethereal luminosity Percy had most often seen in the bodies of spirits or the particular glow of a graveyard, now a veritable mist hanging in the air. The fog seemed to cast a supernatural sheen on the newest doors. The feather let her look a moment before floating down to tickle her fingers, nudging her on.

She spotted Rebecca, asleep against the side of a huge wing-back chair in the center of the foyer, her hands clasped primly in her lap. Frederic perched upon a philosopher's bust nearby, his head tucked into his breast feathers, the dozing picture of Poe's eternal companion. Michael sat on a nearby bench, slouched against the window frame. A book of poetry lay on his lap. Perhaps he'd been reading to the headmistress.

The feather drew close and again kissed her as Percy's heart and tears once more swelled. A mist of luminous blue hung over each of the Guard, and she hoped their forced slumber was pleasant. Jane, farther down the hall, seemed peaceful, her white cat, Marlowe, curled against her shoulder, a bit of blue flame around his tail.

"Will no one wait awake with me?" Percy murmured.

The feather paused at the open door of the chapel, bobbing before the eerily glowing inner white walls. Percy suddenly wanted to run back across Athens and wake her husband, force him to stand at the door and wait for her, but she knew he'd be unable to simply bear witness while she broached the undiscovered country. She knew as well as this was a journey she had to make alone, little as she liked that thought.

"Beatrice, I need you," she begged. "Come tell me everything to expect."

The dark portal at the altar was already awaiting her. Percy reminded herself that Marianna was somewhere across a further threshold and that it was her fault that her friend was there. This was her task—this, and others yet unknown. For these reasons, she stepped through the portal and down the narrow stairs, the stones echoing softly as she entered the sacred space.

No second portal stood open in the Guard's private place, but as Percy stared into the impenetrable darkness beyond the stone columns that marked the circle's perimeter, she could have sworn the shadows moved and hissed. *Snakes.* Percy's blood roared with alarm.

There was a tearing sound, and a familiar form leaped from a fresh portal. "Ah, ah, careful with that light of yours," Beatrice scolded, her gray eyes feverish. "We can't give you away now that your disguise is so perfect." The spirit wafted to Percy's side, cooling her skin with a ghostly draft. Beatrice gestured to her gray skirts. "Good. You'll fit right in."

Percy noticed the reactive light burning at her bosom, and made to calm herself. The light receded. "I heard snakes, and that Gorgon—"

"It was just your imagination. That thing is still in pieces on the Whisper side."

"And Marianna?"

"Fading but alive. She can't stay much longer in our world before losing what color she has and becoming a shade." The portal to the Whisper-world, appropriate to its name, whispered in invitation.

"Ready?" Beatrice asked.

Percy envied the spirit's efficiency, her unwavering determination. She stepped forward, but what was she doing? Why was she always— all her life—moving blindly toward an unknown end? She hesitated at the portal, heart in her throat.

She turned to Beatrice. "No, it's too vague. I can no longer live with scraps of prophetic knowledge." She shook her head, retreating into the heart of the chapel, her feet firm on the stone feather in the flagstones. "Not until I understand more. Not until you prepare me."

Beatrice sighed. "We've no time—"

"Expediency won't help us if I'm utterly unprepared!" Percy hissed. "Darkness. I, unlike whatever chose to take this fleshly form, don't know or remember him."

The ghost eyed her, and her visible frustration softened. "Of course not. I expect too much of you, continue to consider you her. I am sorry."

Percy opened her arms, gesturing for Beatrice to go on.

"Our Lady," Beatrice began, "once explained Darkness as a sad, lonely, misguided force, neither man nor god, neither flesh nor air. The embodiment of disappointment, anger, terror, and bitterness, he presides over listless purgatory. While she pitied this creature made from the wastes of man, it was never her intent to keep him company. He had no right to steal her. Attempting to keep her pure, buoyant energy in such a cesspool has done more damage to the worlds than anything."

Percy took this in. Her Catholic sensibilities clung to the idea that there might be many different names and forms for divine spirits. "But he's not the devil, exactly . . . ?"

"I don't know your devil, child. I know that there are evil forces, and there are forces that are not evil. All forces cross into the Whisperworld. Not all of them stay."

"Where does Darkness fall on the spectrum?"

Beatrice shrugged. "He's Darkness. Unpleasant. I wouldn't trust him. Nor do I trust every mortal I meet. I don't know where evil comes from, and frankly it doesn't matter. Not right now. Histories and myths are renamed and reinvented eternally across the world. I can't speak to that. What I do *know*? This is your story. We must settle the old score between Persephone, her Phoenix, and their lineage of mortal friends— and the one that upset it all in the first place."

Percy stared at the portal, considering, and finally stepped toward it. This was her story. However improbable, it was hers. She knew the ending she wanted: for her husband and friends to live in peace. She sighed, closed her eyes, loosed a prayer, and lifted her foot.

The threshold was cold as she stepped across. Shivers coursed down her spine and her eyes snapped open to see spirits careening down a number of different corridors. Indeed, she blended right in. Here, a spirit's feet remained on the ground, and while white as shrouds, they were solid. It was good her white body wore gray, else the colors of her dress, however muted this world might make them, would make her like a painted daguerreotype, a shock against the monochrome.

The sights and sounds of purgatory were dulled, whispery, liquid. Soft grayscale. Nothing was sharp, everything seemed a bit delayed, slow, and blunted. The place smelled stale—not foul, like rotting flesh, but dusty, moldy, with an oddly sweet undercurrent like an exotic fruit. Percy forced herself not to linger over that scent, lest she once more retch phantom pomegranate.

The air hung weighty with moisture. The floor was wet. The river. She picked up her skirts, not wanting to drag the fine fabric through the muck of mortal misery.

A pervasive chill threatened to worm its way into her. When you finally felt that frost on your bone, Percy mused, you perhaps were here to stay. She wondered how cold poor Marianna felt, and where she was in this endless graystone labyrinth, and if any number of hearths would ever be able to reverse the damage.

Beatrice placed a solid hand on her shoulder. "Now, I won't be with you when you meet him—"

Percy whirled. "What? You said you'd be my constant guide!"

Beatrice stepped backward. "Darling, he knows me now, and I must be ready at the doors. Remember the path. Aodhan will be with you; he knows not to leave you unattended."

"Do other dangers await? What about the hellhound, guardian of these sideways shadows? If I fight it, as my light did once before, will I not give myself away?"

Beatrice nodded. "Aodhan and I have discussed this. We need to throw off your scent, to make you undetected to the beast. The abomination is still in pieces, but it might congeal at any time. Your nearly dead friend can help. Do what Aodhan tells you, even if it is unpleasant."

Percy groaned in sorrow. "Can I see her?"

"I'm taking you there now. You mustn't wake her, however, or she is lost. This way. Remember these turns. Think of the map. Have you studied it?"

"As best I can."

"These paths will help you when the worlds combine. Once her feet again touch the stones of your world, keeping your friend alive will be easier. However, you will need to remain focused on Darkness. He will go after Alexi and your living Guard first and foremost, I'm sure."

Percy felt inner forces growl.

"Do control yourself"—Beatrice scowled, glancing at Percy's growing luminescence—"or we'll not get far. Tell me you've got some Catholic trick that can calm you."

Percy murmured a few prayers so rote that it was like her muscles spoke them, the first words she'd learned in her convent youth, the first words taught her when ghosts and visions overwhelmed her young eyes. She breathed easier, and the telling light of her power eased to a faint glow.

"Indeed," Beatrice murmured, clearly lost in a memory. "The prayers of our youth, like rosaries in our blood."

This recalled Percy to her beads, and she felt Michael's calming gift against her skin, their infused mass tucked against her heart. She began moving again, stepping carefully.

Movement below caught her eye. As she stepped, there were tiny green sprouts that burst around her boots. Tiny spots of color amid the dreary gray: buds, blooms, red, pink and purple; color—spring and life. "Oh," she breathed, quite taken aback. "I'm making flowers."

Beatrice glanced down. "Ah. It seems this place is bringing out your predecessor's most charming qualities." Her face fell. "Pity they don't last."

Percy looked. Where there had been life an instant prior, now only dead husks remained. Gray curled petals and wilted black leaves.

"Not here," Beatrice added.

Percy frowned, terribly sad. She tugged on the laces of her skirts, and the fabric hung a bit lower. The fabric kissed the ground, hiding all traces of beautiful life created, then choked out by shadow.

They turned a corner and Beatrice tapped on an iron gate. Aodhan peered out, then beckoned them forward. Percy's hand went to her mouth. Under the jagged arch of a crypt, Marianna lay atop a stone tomb beneath a pale winding sheet that was the fading green of her dress. Her once-vibrant coloring was blanched, shifting to gray. Ash still trickled around her eyes and dribbled from the corners of her lips. Her hands lay outside the sheet, revealing crusted grit deep under her fingernails, faint crimson blood from gashes pooled in her cupped palms, and bruises shading the hollows of her fair skin. The damage looked all the more severe in the half-light.

Aodhan held the long lock of hair, Jane's gift, tightly, its touchstone of power allowing a healing glow to hover over Marianna. Ash rose to the surface below her skin and worked out her pores with a tiny hiss.

Percy felt bile churn in her stomach. "How is she?" she asked in Gaelic.

"Alive for now," Aodhan replied in kind. "She dreams heavily. Your mentalist will have to heal her. Come close, I've a gruesome task for you, but it's necessary to throw the dog off your scent." Aodhan repeated Beatrice's explanation, "It knows you too well."

Percy nodded and approached.

Aodhan dipped his fingertips in Marianna's pooled blood. The fluid seemed black as pitch and thick as tar. "Pull back your sleeves," he told Percy. When she did, grimacing, he rubbed blood and ash onto her wrists, up her arms.

"Forgive me," he said, and dabbed the viscous liquid—an unwelcome, horrid perfume—behind her lobes. Inhaling the coppery scent of her best friend's blood, Percy bit her lip to keep from crying out, hot tears cooling instantly upon her cheeks.

Aodhan wiped his sullied hands on the lace cuffs of Marianna's taffeta dress before ripping off the accents with a sound that grated in the close air. He handed Percy the soiled scraps. "Place these somewhere."

Percy closed her eyes and tucked the befouled fabric into her corset, forcing back seizures of revulsion. "I'm so sorry," she murmured to Marianna's sleeping form. She lowered her sleeves, grateful to keep the traces of gore hidden from her own eyes.

Aodhan was back at work, brushing what ash he could into a ceramic jar and adding that to a line of containers set along the edge of a nearby crevasse. "Don't worry." He gestured to the vessels. "I sent some to the bottom of the river. While there's unnatural life to this infernal grit, she won't come back remotely whole."

"Come, Percy," Beatrice whispered, taking her by the elbow. "Aodhan will lead you but must remain nearby in shadow for the sake of safety."

"Where are you going?"

"To Athens. Unless I'm there to stop him, I'm sure your stubborn husband will come in after you. Once you have that key, get out. Take it to the upstairs seal. Unlock those doors and open them!"

"Where exactly is the key?" Percy pleaded, her mind spinning.

"Oh, you'll see it. Off with you now. Darkness awaits," Beatrice said grimly. When Percy quaked, she added, "Remember, unless you act otherwise, he'll think you just another spirit."

"Just another spirit," Percy repeated, trying to rally, stepping farther into the cold shadows.

* * *

Alexi didn't dream often, but when he did, his dreams fell into distinct categories.

For a man who had seen so much of it, he never dreamed of the ghastly, of poltergeists or rotting shades. Rather, he dreamed of personal matters: of his paralyzed sister, forever damned to a cripple's half-life, in awe and fear of him. Of his parents vanishing in fright, his blood relatives hanging back as if he were contaminated by a disease that they never dared treat or bothered to comprehend.

Sometimes he dreamed of passionate matters—the "visitations" of his youth, vivid glimpses of an exquisite goddess. She'd vanished, presumably when Percy was born, at which point his dream lover no longer had a face. The other details remained, however, as an encouragement to keep waiting . . .

His dreams had been quiet of late, save for when he believed he woke to find Percy not at his side, but tonight he stood at the end of a stone corridor, breathing in both mold and sorrow. A stark gray light shone at the opposite end; sounds echoed against the dank stones. He recognized the impassioned female voice.

His stomach and fists clenched as he moved forward into the gray light, stepping onto a platform and looking down. Across a rushing river stood cracked columns and crumbling statues that stood silent sentry over a grand dais where an entwined couple writhed. Glimpses of ghost-white flesh maddened him.

"No," he choked. It wasn't her. Everyone was pale in this purgatory.

The man was a young and beautiful specimen, angelic like a pre-Raphaelite painting, nearly as pale as the woman he clutched, his mouth lean and cruel. The auburn tresses down his back looked more like streaming blood than hair. He was naked, his hands buried under immense folds of fabric.

The writhing woman's magnificent dress was a familiar light blue. Her face was hidden under masses of hair, but no other tresses were that pearlescent white, and he could have recognized anywhere those shocking white limbs and the sound of her gasps. And with the figure wearing Percy's wedding dress . . .

Alexi bellowed in fury as a roaring rush of fire leaped to his hands. His enemy turned to look at him with burning red eyes, flashing a lascivious smile. Alexi felt searing pain and looked down to find his hands enveloped in yellow-orange fire. The scent was nauseating, the agony unbearable. All he could do was stare at his wife, writhing in the grasp of the Whisper-world, property of Darkness at last.

With a wretched scream Alexi shot to his feet, throwing aside the covers of his office cot, making his office candelabra roar with tall flame before again going dark. "Percy!" he cried, resolved that he'd never again let her out of his sight. But she was gone.

Josephine's worried voice echoed in the hall outside: "Alexi?"

Head spinning, Alexi threw on his robes and flung wide the door, sending both Josephine and Elijah sprawling. He stormed out into the hall. "Where the bloody hell is she?"

He charged toward Promethe Hall with his friends hurrying in his wake. "Alexi, surely—"

"Were none of you standing guard?"

"I don't remember drifting off," Elijah admitted, shaking his head as if clearing it.

Alexi burst into the foyer of Promethe Hall to find Rebecca stirring in a chair. Michael was stretching against the wall. Their color drained upon sight of his expression.

"Why are none of you in place? Why do none of you realize she's gone?" he cried.

Jane came bounding from around the corner, Marlowe mewling at her feet. Frederic squawked from the chandelier above, the ghostly boy who floated there patting the bird's head.

"Gone?" Michael rushed forward. "I kept awake, reading to Rebecca, trying to pass the time, but sleep must have fallen so heavy—"

An explosion of helpless anger obliterated all else. Alexi raised his fist as if he was about to hit something or someone. Michael boldly held out his hand to counter him. The jolt of peaceful energy Michael delivered jarred away the unfounded violence. "Caution, Alexi," Michael said. "The Whisper-world presses in, affecting our minds and hearts. It wants to tear us all apart."

Alexi reeled back in shock, horrified by his clenched fist, which he instead used to rap against his own chest. "I was by her side!" he cried. "What a fool am I? How could I not have felt her go? How did I fail to feel her leave my arms?" His fury propelled him toward the chapel.

"Where the hell are you?" he bellowed. The images from his dream still seared his eyes.

The chapel doors were open. So was the black rectangle that led to their private, sacred space. Alexi growled and charged ahead, the Guard barely able to keep up. Frayed blue lightning crackled all around his body.

Racing down the stairs and into the chapel, he cursed to find the murmuring portal to the Whisper-world a wet, dark, open mouth floating at the center of the room, the fiery map licking at his feet. A small blue mark, with another at its side, moved inexorably toward the red dot in the distance.

"Alexi, no! You mustn't—" Rebecca cried from atop the stairs.

Charging the portal, he was just about to throw himself in when a ball of blue fire leaped out and struck him square in the chest. Thrown backward onto the stone floor, he saw Beatrice step into view, her eyes holding the same fiery determination as his. Her hands awash with blue flame, her stance wide, she eyed him sternly.

Her words floated from the edge of the Whisper-world, just strong enough to reach Alexi's ear. His proximity to that perilous barrier allowed for a barely audible admonishment magnified by fury to be the first time he heard directly from a spirit. "Oh, no you don't! This isn't the way to make yourself useful."

PERCY SQUINTED. THERE WAS A GUSTING WIND IN THE WHISPER-world, carrying dust and sour air, tangling her hair and invading her skirts. Spirits everywhere were squabbling, angry, and violent. The farther in she went, the more of a mess she found. Her slow steps made oddly dull sounds. Every hair of her neck was on end.

"Remember this path," Aodhan said softly, ducking a random blow by an eternally drunken sailor, deflecting him with a glowing hand that warned him not to try again. "You'll need to retrace it. We can't take the risk of you going out a wrong portal and ending up in some other level of this place. I've not dared to adventure the whole of it."

"I wouldn't want to," Percy replied, thinking of how her movement would be marked on the map. "We've been veering left."

She wondered how time passed here, and she prayed Alexi was still sleeping soundly, unaware of her absence. But she could have sworn she heard a distant roar that sounded distinctly familiar. She winced.

"You mustn't worry about him," Aodhan said, watching.

"Are you worried for Jane?"

Aodhan's lips thinned and he nodded, realizing such words were pointless. They would fear for those they loved.

"I'm scared to see this Darkness. I'm scared of what might happen inside me that I can't predict," Percy murmured. The sound of rushing water grew louder in her ears.

"Just remember, there are things about him that will make you wish to flee. Stay strong. Play his little games if you can, it may endear you to him, but stay strong."

"I don't want to be endeared," Percy said through clenched teeth.

"Well, you also don't want him to drag you across the river and imprison you with the rest of our sorry lot. You're not here for him, Persephone. You are here for *them*."

The careening spirits of the Whisper-world fell away as the corridor opened onto a huge gray space, the ceiling endless shadow, the path ahead a wide circle around a tall stone dais lined with crumbling stone pillars choked with dead ivy. Aodhan fell back. "I won't be far."

A vast stone tower sat behind the circular dais, its dark, deteriorating bricks reaching up to oblivion, and between Percy and that sweeping stone platform lay a rushing river that surrounded the steps up to the dais like a moat. Across the river, atop a wide and jagged stone throne, sat Darkness.

For the first time in the Whisper-world, Percy saw a bright color. Shimmering scarlet fabric floated around his naked torso, a corner hovering tastefully between his legs like a silken fig leaf. He was beautiful and sculpted like a classical masterpiece. Suddenly his form shifted and he was a mere skeleton.

Percy had to bite her lip. She stared at him, his face alternately breathtaking and a skull, blinking between the two as if the pendulum of a clock, ticking seconds, life spans, and eternity. It mesmerized her for a while, ticking her life away.

"H-hello," Percy finally managed to choke out, surprised a word came at all.

Darkness looked up. It was strange to think of this force of nature as a person, inhabiting a body, but it was, she supposed, just a form—something to relate to, something finite, a single illuminated point of a lightless infinity. She was grateful for this, and for her destined ability to tread these dread paths; otherwise she and her friends would be entirely outmatched. As it stood, things looked grim. She bit back the fear that threatened to consume her.

His red eyes burned at first, then cooled into sparkling rubies as fresh as the blush upon his youthful lips—when he had lips. He examined her a moment, swiveling his head to the side, his skull sockets taking her in from each angle.

Percy felt herself blush and inhaled, expanding her rib cage against her corset, which pressed her rosary beads into her flesh, calming her with the power Michael had placed in them.

"Why, hello indeed, miss. And welcome." He'd adopted her accent, her vernacular, perhaps to make her more comfortable. Perhaps to get information more easily out of her.

He rose and walked to the edge of the river, his scarlet drapes eddying in currents around his limbs, and beckoned her forward with a graceful hand that faded into reaching bone. "What cares shall you add?" he asked. His voice was youthful and attempted to be seductive. "Feed this river your sorrow." His hand, his bones, gestured languidly to the flowing black water. "Tell me something of yourself. What did loved ones call you?"

"Pearl," Percy replied, feeling her rosary beads chill on her skin, which was moist with sweat, nerves, and the river breeze.

"Pearl. Indeed. You appear quite the jewel. Did you live well?"

"I . . . lived life well. But I was young."

Darkness clucked a tongue that silenced as he became a skull. "Yes, yes, a tragedy. You, and your unborn child with you," he murmured, smiling. "Just the sort of sadness to make you linger here quite a while, if not forever."

Percy felt the world spin about her; she clutched at her skirts. Her *child*?

"You must be quite freshly dead, for you're luminous," Darkness continued casually.

Percy glanced down to see that her body had responded to his shocking revelation with a glowing inner light. A prayer for survival and the rush of Michael's power made tangible in her rosary beads allowed her the necessary breath of calm, else she'd surely give away her powers and

Darkness would trap her here, put her in that stone tower behind him. Her, and her child. She had to find the key and get out as soon as possible.

Her face gave her away. "Oh. You didn't know about the baby," Darkness breathed. "How delicious!" He clapped delighted skeletal hands that clicked, then resounded as flesh, then clicked again. "Cast it all to the river, dear, tell it your grief, add your sweet tears to the well from which we drink."

He seized a cup from his throne, bone against metal making a sickening scrape, and hopped down the many stairs to the water's edge, where he bent gracefully to dip the cup. "Come here, pretty girl. Drink with me." He reached for her as she took the final few steps to the bank. From beneath the water's surface, myriad human bones rose and formed a makeshift bridge.

Percy fought the terror threatening to overtake her. Crossing the river struck her as something to avoid, not to mention the horror of setting foot upon such a bridge.

"But what if I want to go back?" she said breathlessly. "If I'm freshly dead, perhaps there's still a place for me on earth. For me, my child . . ."

"Your husband, too, I suppose. Or are you a true unfortunate? Ruined?"

Percy stiffened at the insult. "My husband, too."

Those sculpted then scapular shoulders shrugged. "Very well, you may wait. I suppose there's a chance you might still live. Sometimes there come rare miracles." He cleared the river in a sudden gazelle's leap to stand beside her, sliding a bony hand around her waist. He bent his head close. "You know I'll have you in the end. I always have everyone in the end."

Suppressing her revulsion, Percy leaned away but managed not to jerk aside. She mustn't insult him, manipulation was key. "Not everyone stays here," she countered, her voice somehow calm. "This is not a final destination for all."

"True, but all pass through. And some I want to keep. I'm looking for a new wife, you know, as my old one's too much trouble. I'm looking for several, actually, in case I lose more of them."

"Oh?"

"Once my servant finally tells me where she's gone, I'll scatter her bits across the earth and end this silly drama for good. Drink up, pretty thing. Don't worry. This won't bind you. It'll make you wiser, sadder, perhaps, but it won't bind you."

Percy wasn't about to believe him; surely he had baited her predecessor with the same lie and pomegranate seeds. She turned horrified eyes into the golden cup, hoping to mask her shaking hands. Bringing it to her lips, she heard the liquid hiss within, murmur, beg, cry.

Darkness walked ahead of her to inspect something at the water's edge. Percy took the opportunity to set the cup upon a stone post before falling in again at his side. An upraised hand, begging for help, had caught his eye—or eye socket. He stepped upon the risen palm and pushed it back below the surface.

Percy's heart thundered anew. "But how is it you don't know where she is? Your wife, I mean. I'd have thought you omnipotent."

His pretty lips frowned before he had no expression but a row of teeth. "No, no, I leave omnipotence for another being who is strangely absent. You and I, my sweet, are pawns. I may be a knight or a castle, but we are both pieces in some elaborate game whose point none of us knows."

"Then, why find her?"

"Who, my wife? Because she's mine!"

In many ways, she sensed, Darkness was an angry child. Percy wondered if she could use that against him. "Oh, I see. Of course. One must fight for what is theirs." He appeared placated. He grinned, and his row of teeth gnashed in delight, and unable to help herself Percy added, "Unless it never was theirs to begin with."

Darkness glowered. His bones rattled. And that's when she saw it: The key she sought hung upon his sternum, when he was bone. It was encased in flesh when he was solid. If she could grab hold when he was bone, if she could grab and run . . . It was enough to make her nauseated with panic.

As if by the grace of a higher power, her mind's eye saw a vision: The key was in her hand. She was running toward Alexi, her bright light and fierce protector. If she pretended this was a dream, another of her visions, would it help?

Her eyes blinked back to the present moment and gazed upon empty eye sockets. Her heart surged with resolve. Darkness's head was cocked at a disturbing angle and he asked, "Do you toy with me, girl?"

Percy smiled demurely. "I wouldn't dream of it. Are you toying with me?"

"I toy with everyone."

Percy nodded. "Of course. Because you're very *potent*." Giving a coy smile, though fighting an inward shudder, she glanced at the tower behind his throne. "Why do you keep your seat of power here? It's hardly decorated, all this stone. I'd have thought you'd want something more lavish." She was risking much, pressing for information about that roomful of friendly blue fire, but she had to try. Her vision had just shown her victorious.

His cruel, beautiful mouth twisted. "Curious, aren't you?"

"I was born so. I suppose I died so."

"Well, then." Darkness held out a skeletal arm. "Shall I show you?"

Percy choked back disgust, smiled, and took his flesh then bone arm.

ONCE ALEXI HAD GOTTEN AGAIN TO HIS FEET, HE GLARED AT BEATRICE, who held another ball of flame in her hand, her expression intent. She pointed at the floor. Alexi followed her gaze. His eyes widened, and he watched two particular dots. He had to force himself not to cry out as the red flame sidled closer to the blue.

There was a sparkling line to the side of their demarked forms. A door. One of the new doors. Beatrice gestured and pointed below.

"I might see in, and watch for her safety?" he asked.

She gestured to the perimeters of the portal in which she stood, held out her hand and made a dramatic motion that seemed to speak to his head exploding.

"Yes, yes, I'll not go in."

She widened her eyes and held up her hand, emphatic.

"Yes, I promise. But thank you for showing me the way." Glancing at the map, he counted the corridors between and deduced where he should head. "Looks like the second floor. I'll not leave you to fend for yourself, Percy, beloved fool. I will do what I can."

He tore up the stairs and out toward Promethe Hall's grand staircase.

DARKNESS STROLLED WITH HER, BUT PERCY WAS CLEAR TO REMEMBER their path. She was encouraged by the fact that Aodhan stayed in view, far behind, visible to her only at the far corners of her eyes, stepping in and out of shadow.

When her guide's feet were skeletal, they echoed oddly against the stone. There was subtle movement around his heel and toe bones. Percy didn't stare. She truly didn't want to know what sprang from Darkness's step. She assumed it wasn't spring foliage.

It wasn't difficult for her to remember their route; they essentially moved in a wide circle. Their path curved around the dais, around the vast brick tower. The moatlike river rushed to their right and onward, its tributary path unknown, perhaps farther underground, and upon closer inspection Percy noticed that the items floating on its surface were not ordinary detritus; the occasional bone or odd remembrance, a flower, locket, portrait, or letter were this waterway's flotsam and jetsam.

Darkness watched her watching the items. "All the little things people think matter. None of it matters here. Trash, all of it. Human life."

"Do you hate humans?" she couldn't help but ask.

"They're the reason I'm here. Their sorrow made me at the dawn of time, their habitual discontent keeps me here, empowers me in the gray space of the freshly dead and those who live as if they were dead—and the dead who wish they lived." He giggled at his own awkward poetry. "Some dead enter here and refuse to leave. But eventually even they, who distrust the balm of eternal peace, give up their ghosts and fall into the river, their bones making it more and more shallow as they pile up, year after year."

Percy shuddered.

"I frighten you," Darkness murmured.

"No, it's interesting," Percy argued.

"It's all right. I frighten people." He leaned close. She could hear his bony jaw snap against her ear. "I like it."

Percy tried not to shrink away but couldn't help it, and the subsequent chuckle was unspeakably unpleasant.

"You'll grow accustomed to it. Even my enemies are now inured to life in the Whisper-world."

"Enemies?" Percy thrilled at the path of the conversation. "You've enemies?"

Darkness gnashed his teeth. "It started with my bride—the force I took rightfully for my own. She was made of feminine joy, loyalty, and youth. She was a creature of light. We were meant to be. We make the necessary pair, she, the light to my shadow!" he crowed. But then his beautiful face was pained, and his skull, too, grimaced. "She already had a lover, stupid girl, treating him like some angel, some paragon. I burned him to a crisp. But he lived on in human pawns, and her damnable heart would never surrender."

Percy didn't bother to hide her disturbed expression, for Darkness seemed to enjoy it. "What happened?"

"Muses followed what was left of him, seeing themselves as his votaries. They jumped into human flesh to form a rather troublesome cult."

"What do they do?"

"My sustenance is the sorrow and misery gathered unto me by restless minions I send to mortal earth. But the blasted Guard sends them back empty, starving me, while they live on! But in the end, all human flesh must come through here. Even they." He grinned. "They arrive in sets of six. Horrified to see me, of course."

Percy gulped. "And then?"

"I'm supposed to let any who wish move on to Peace." He waved his hand in disgust. "Not them. I've gathered them up, found them out, given them no peace. I've now collected them all into my woe." He giggled, and his jaw chattered.

They were now on the opposite side of the dais, where the rounded stone wall of the tower continued seamlessly. A lock dangled from a thick and rusty chain that hung from the endless shadow above. Out of the corner of Percy's eye, she saw Aodhan gesture for her to ply him further.

"Where are they? Your enemies?"

Darkness scowled. His skeletal jaw clenched. "Why?"

Percy affected embarrassment. "Forgive me. All of this is so fascinating."

"They're not more interesting than me. They're not more important than me," Darkness growled. "She always thought that. Always coddling and entertaining them, praising them for their work against me. But I found them, tore down their precious sanctuary, ruined their haven, and locked them all up! I enjoy punishing her and her hapless servants. They've become hollow, pitiful little wraiths, weak and useless. And she's gone, so they've no one now to help! They'll turn to me, they will, once they see she's abandoned them."

Percy leaned in. "I believe you. I believe in your power."

"Do you?"

"Show me."

Darkness looked wary. "Show you what?"

"I want to see what you've done to them," she said achingly. "I'm so curious, I just might ask to stay . . ." She waited until his scapula was a shoulder and dragged a finger down his arm.

He shuddered with an uncomfortably desirous sound and grinned at her, his ruby eyes sparkling. Growling hungrily, he dragged a skeletal finger down her cheek, returning the favor. Percy forced her shudder to appear one of desire.

Darkness plucked the key from his sternum and shoved it into the hanging lock. There was a rumbling and grating sound. "You'll see, Pearl, how pathetic they are—and how powerful I am. You'll. Want. To. Stay."

Percy's fingers itched to grab the key, but the moment had to be right. She inched surreptitiously closer to the lock.

Across the river, large bricks fell away to reveal a vast metal door, like the kind she imagined on ancient castles. The door swung open, and a bright but flickering light came from within: hundreds—thousands!—of ghosts, from every race and era of humankind. A few of them blinked, coming forward toward the opening, confused by the prospect of freedom from their cell. They were hollow forms, luminous only in flickering heartbeats. Separately their fires were all but burned out, but together they glowed. All the Guard that ever were.

Darkness made a sweeping gesture, and the river overflowed its banks toward the prisoners, lapping at the toes of those who dared come forward. The water hissed and nipped at them with predatory teeth. The Guard spirits whimpered like wounded animals, crying inhuman sounds and shuddering, staring at the water in horror, retreating as if scalded. Darkness giggled again.

Percy's heart broke for these poor mortal souls dragged innocently into a service they never wholly understood and left to rot, left off worse than dead, simply for trying to keep Darkness from harvesting his requisite horror. Her pity turned to anger. Her bosom burned with light, and several things converged at once.

A bent-shouldered man, once dark-skinned and handsome, stepped up onto a fallen rock and away from the oncoming tide of water. Staring at Percy, his dark eyes wide, he straightened, his tunic hanging less like rags and more like a priest's robe, and two words flew from his lips in what Percy recognized as Arabic: "Our Lady!"

The horde turned to stare across the water at Darkness, then at Percy. The assemblage of spirits fell reverently to their knees.

Darkness narrowed his eyes at her. His skull's eye sockets burned even blacker.

"She's here!" crowed a horrifically familiar voice. Percy whirled to behold an ash body with a head full of snakes, dragging and scraping into the chamber, a mere torso scrabbling toward them: Lucille Linden. Still the Gorgon lived, having half assembled while Beatrice and Aodhan were otherwise occupied. She squealed, her throat gurgling molten ash and her broken serpents rattling against the stones. "Right before your face, you damn fool! Mortal! Dash her brains against the rocks!"

Percy could feel her own light burning brighter, helplessly reactive.

Just as Darkness opened his mouth in rage, there was another sound—a roaring and tearing—and a portal opened high and distant in the air above and behind them. Percy looked up to see Alexi's silhouette and, beyond him, an upper Athens foyer and the Guard, chanting strengths and encouragement. Her world was not as far away as she had imagined.

Darkness whirled. "You? You *live*. And. You. Dare." His fury choked him as he shot a bony hand straight for her throat, toward her gathering light.

Percy dodged his initial clawing thrust but was unable to avoid the hard upswing of his fleshy fist, mashing her lip against her teeth, strands of her hair yanked away in bony fingertips. She reeled back in pain as red blood spurted onto her gray dress. Putting her hand to her lip, through the pain she nonetheless noticed how Darkness retracted his bones from her light.

"Damn you!" bellowed Alexi from above, from behind the portal. His booming voice carried, and it stunned all inhabitants of the Whisper-world over whom it washed. Out of the wave of fire bursting from him, a great and furious bird descended, made of roaring blue light. Its great wings and fearsome claws tore and beat against the alternately beautiful and skeletal body of its enemy. "She's not yours for the taking! She never has been!" the phoenix roared, Alexi's words reverberating from its mouth.

Darkness batted at its fiery blue wings and talons in rage and irritation, if not in defeat. Lucille's remains were kept at bay by other tendrils of blue fire, her writhing coils of hair hissing and snapping. In the distance there came barking, growing louder. Percy didn't want to wait for a third monster, so she seized her opportunity, snatched the key from the lock, and ran.

The Guard poured from their prison, clustered in sixes as they sought to cross the river. Their legions filled the vast gray landscape with increasing hope, freshening the mildewed air, and their arms stretched out toward where Alexi stood as an angelic sentinel, a conduit for a glorious rain of cerulean flame. The leaders of the ancient Guards drank in this energy, invigorated by the fire of the Grand Work that made them powerful once more. Percy felt as if she were witnessing a masterwork painting come to life, a heavenly host arming itself at the gates of hell.

It had to be a terrible strain on Alexi, to be the sole bearer of such power. Percy's heart seized with love and concern. She had to get out and pull him away.

"Angels have no sway here!" Darkness hissed. He cast aside Phoenix's blue fire as if it were a tattered cloak, his own red shroud flaring up around him like armor. The tick-tock of his skeleton to flesh now lingered more moments in bone. He growled, turning to Percy with his eyes bloody fire. The river growled and gurgled, and a surging wave rose that would surely rush to drag her under.

Something began in Percy's mind as soft music, and a voice not entirely her own flew from her lips—a voice that had once proclaimed great things, banished Gorgons, and saved the Guard's lives. "Perhaps not angels, but *I* once did," an elder power declared as her luminosity grew, unfettered.

An arc of light burst from Percy, landing a vicious slap upon Darkness's skull. Particles of bone flaked from his cheek. The light spread over the river and the black water became frosted glass; the Guard instantly poured across, swarming the opposite bank. Countless leader spirits added their power to the firebird form still harassing Darkness. Their shackles of firelight could not hold him in this realm, but they slowed him.

Darkness reeled, swatting at the blue fire all around. He stared down his empty breast, at the key that had been stolen. Flickering into the shape of a man, he gave a pathetic wail in Percy's retreating direction: "You'd tear my heart again?"

"This body doesn't know you," she cried over her shoulder as she darted away, her voice again her own. "And it seems you never had a heart to lose."

"You. Will. All. Pay." The voice of Darkness was amplified over the water, echoing, and he broke all remaining tendrils of flame with a blow. He flung an arm forward and the river gushed up, a wave of black water and morphing stone that crested toward her.

"Oh, I'm quite sure," Percy muttered. Standing firm, she gripped his key so tightly she thought its grooves might cut into her flesh.

There came a raucous yell, a countering battle cry, and Darkness's threat was defied. A wave of ghostly forms, brightening into blinding strength and purpose, made a wall before her, taking the brunt of the river's attack. This host of firelit Guard leaders held the line against the wave of stone, water, sentimental detritus, and bones; then they all turned to her and in many different tongues said, "Run."

Percy picked up her skirts and fled down the corridor through which she had come. Flowers continuously bloomed then died at her feet. Lucille's broken, burned body awaited her at the final intersection, shrieking and crawling and flinging herself forward, her snakes at full charge, molten dust spraying everywhere.

"Do you not learn?" Percy muttered as a crumbling hand grazed her bustle, snatching at the fabric. She seized her sturdy, doubled skirts and whipped them to the side in a blow, and Lucille's ashen head of snakes once again rolled off her body and down the corridor with renewed screaming. "Again, I prove the greater power," she stated, allowing herself a moment of pride.

But things weren't so simple. A molten snake head had affixed itself to her hem and was starting to set her garment afire.

"At your side, my lady." Aodhan appeared, his words a cool draft in her ear, his healing energy steadying her. He kicked the snake head from her skirt and crushed it under his boot. It gave a sickening hiss.

Percy ran as hard and fast as she could, a tidal wave of restless spirits and rage swelling up behind her. Aodhan and the Guard leaders stood between her and the gathering storm, but wind, dust, and bone bit at her flesh and chipped away at Aodhan's gray form.

"Place the key on Athens's soil, my lady, and we may finally have a chance," he called out through the tempest.

"And Marianna?"

"The worlds will merge and you can bring her safely home. But first you have to get back yourself! Keep running. I'll see to your friend!"

The light ahead was brightening. She could glimpse forms through the portal. Who was that on the other side? Alexi! Her hand shielded her eyes, his face all she wished to see. He had returned from the other portal and was standing guard here, fierce and furious.

"My love!" Percy cried.

Relief flooded his features when he first caught sight of her deep in the corridor, then his eyes widened at the chaos behind her. She was sure he cried her name, but the sound was drowned by Darkness's tumult.

A blaze of blue fire reached out and surrounded her, more powerful magic than she'd ever felt. The protective barrier lifted her off her feet and drew her through the portal, her own radiant white light mixing with Alexi's blue sorcery. She floated, a blindingly illuminated bundle, directly down into his waiting arms. He whisked her behind him as the Whisper-world portal slammed shut, the wave of Darkness's horror crashing impotently on the other side.

London's Guard encircled the couple, energy pouring forth, their arms outstretched and the wind of their magic whipping their clothes. They were ready for a fight. Jane touched her hand to Percy's split lip, healing it in the instant. Thunder roared across the sky. Percy wasn't sure from which world the sound originated.

Alexi whirled upon her, seizing her by the shoulders, desperate to keep hold of her. "Persephone, if you ever go in there again, I swear to you—"

"No, no, I've no need to go in there again," Percy said, laughing, almost hysterical. Was this relief, or terror? "It's coming to us. It's all coming here."

CHAPTER
EIGHTEEN

Alexi shooed the Guard out of the chapel before whirling on Percy. "What did he do to you?" he barked, raking hands through his hair, feeling his own choking desperation.

"You saw. Other than repulse and hit me, nothing."

"You were at his side—"

"Alexi, my dear husband, there'll be plenty of time for a chat about all this, but now you must protect me. My dear, you'll not only be protecting me, but the child I carry. Our child."

He felt as though he'd been struck. "Our child?"

"Yes, love. It would seem the Whisper-world can reveal some of life's mysteries."

Stunned, Alexi clasped his arms tightly around Percy. "And so you not only endangered yourself, but our child?"

Percy's lips thinned and her bright eyes flashed with anger. "I see the professor desires only to scold his student." She tried to pull away, to stare him down with balled fists, but he wouldn't let her go. "Whether you believe me or not, this was the only way. We both know that. You might praise me for my bravery." She wriggled an arm free to hold up the key before his face, anger leaving her tone. He could see her trying to shift toward kindness and celebration. He wanted to as well.

"Thank you for sending down your fire," she stated. "It gave me the moment I needed, and you empowered the Guard. Our troops, indeed! Well done. But now, if you'll excuse me, we've a war to commence."

Alexi's jaw twitched as he loosened his grip, but he sought her hands and clutched them in his. He was reeling. Their *child*? But she was right, he needed to praise her. "I am so proud of you, Percy. Of your extraordinary bravery. And you've no idea my relief, but I—"

"Hate it when I undertake risk without you. Yes, I'm *well* aware. Believe me, I certainly would have chosen to have my powerful protector by my side, but you need your wits, love, and those I couldn't guarantee past that threshold."

"I dreamed he was . . . ravaging you."

Percy made a face. "How utterly disgusting. Thank heavens it didn't happen." She turned away, prepared to run up the stairs.

"How can you be so nonchalant?" Alexi cried, whirling her back to face him.

Percy's eyes flashed again. "If I were to ruminate upon all that's just happened—indeed, upon what's about to happen—I would fall to pieces. Timidity was for my youth, Alexi. I'm a woman now. You helped make me so; now I beg you to be the leader I require." She placed her hand on her abdomen. "That *we* require."

Alexi's veil of madness parted. What Michael had said was true: This volatility was a disease of the merging worlds, was the master of the Whisper-world's dark ploy to sow the seeds of division. It was particularly potent poison against remnants of the Phoenix, but Alexi refused to further succumb.

He nodded, trying to shake the nearly druglike effect of fear from his body. "Of course, darling. The press of the worlds affects me . . ." He broke off, realizing apologies weren't enough. Not to her.

She seemed to harbor no ill will. Instead, she took his hand and led him up the stairs. "I should have foreseen that. Speak to me, love, and I'll separate myth from reality. You must trust me. I'd die for you, you realize. Love has given me strength my meek nature never imagined. I went in so that we might yet be free . . ."

Alexi's face contorted. "And I, an ungrateful, jealous wretch—"

"Your fire roused and saved me," Percy assured. "We desperately needed your intervention. But let your anger, fear, and jealousy now be fuel for a more productive fire. I need you to tell me where there's another lock." She dangled the key once more before him. "This was used to lock up the Guards, but now it will give them freedom from Darkness at last. Fitting."

"Will they fight for us?"

Percy stared at him as if he were daft. "Did you see what was happening in there? None of us has a choice but to fight, with no weapons but our thirst for this madness to end. That, I'm sure, is ammunition they've stored up in spades."

Their friends awaited them anxiously at the center of Promethe Hall. All of Athens was glowing a hazy sapphire color, the air becoming a readier medium to conduct their gifts.

"The school seal," Alexi declared, his eyes wide. "My friends, our brave Percy has the second key, direct from the heart of Darkness. Come." He gestured for them to follow him up the stairs to the stately open foyer where he and Percy had twice now shared impossibly beautiful waltzes.

"Alexi, remember the vision we saw here?" Rebecca said. "Your glorious wings?"

He nodded, bending over the seal so seemingly tied to their fate. His fingers searched out a keyhole, and there it was, in the motto, the dot over the *i* of the word "Light." Blue fire crackled around the mosaic edges.

Jamming the key into the lock caused a roar exponentially greater than the one generated by revealing the map below, as if a thousand stones rolled thunderously inside the walls of Athens. Azure fire streaked across every tile and floorboard and sizzled in the mortar. The noise became deafening, light pouring from underneath each of the new, hefty, unadorned wooden doors that were indistinguishable from Athens's other classrooms' entrances. Otherworldly light blazing from behind the barriers as they begged to open, convulsing against their hinges.

"Open the doors!" Alexi cried.

Michael and Rebecca scurried toward the first floor. As the doors shook yet harder, Elijah cried, "Josie, Jane, come—we've got to attend to Apollo Hall."

Jane's cat was nervously pacing, hackles up, a low whine in his throat, and Frederic hopped up and down on a nearby bench. The Irishwoman called out, "Marlowe, Frederic, to the headmistress's apartments! Take shelter!" The white cat did not need to be told twice and the black bird followed.

"Stay close to at least one other," Alexi called to his friends. "But open them quickly." He grabbed Percy by the hand to dart with her into the corridor off the foyer.

"Beware the water!" Percy added, crossing herself as her husband gripped the first doorknob to another world.

He flung open the door, and the two of them stumbled back against the wall, blinded. "The Power and the Light!" Alexi cried.

Percy heard an earthshaking reply in a hundred tongues, *"The Power and the Light!"*

A host of figures in bright blue light poured over them in a welcome deluge. Guard spirits flew one after another through the doorway. The moment they crossed into Athens and realized they could float, they careened up and away from the rushing tides of dark water that had threatened them on the Whisper side. The moisture leached toward Percy on the corridor floor, but as she backed away from it she noticed that here it seemed a harmless pool. She hoped it would stay that way.

Running to fling open the next door, Percy watched the entering Guards. Once they were within Athens's walls, the newcomers could sustain their powers. Some hands glowed with blue flame or soft white light; some of the visitors were reciting incantations. Some bore glyphs or runes on their palms, clothing, jewelry, or shields. Some were touching each other's hearts and laughing. All of these dear spirits of light and song would be needed, Percy knew, for the rest came pouring through the doors, too: the uninvited threat.

Jumbled among the beautiful goodness of the Guard of many eras were many dark and dangerous spirits. Rotting bodies and putrefying souls, ragged clothes and the stench of misery, they were loath to leave earth and unsuited for heaven. These spirits were the allies of Darkness, his army, and they shrieked through the halls of Athens, breaking glass and upending bricks. These were the foes of the released Guard. But Beatrice had been an able general, choosing their battleground wisely. Back at work again after wasting away behind Whisper-world walls, the forces of Light immediately joined battle.

Alexi led Percy along, his precise, scientific mind locating each iteration of seven. He called out their destinations as they hurtled forward, flinging doors open one after another, with yet more Guard and the ungodly pouring through. Alexi had the good sense to start shutting the doors once their allies were through, minimizing the standing river-water flood and limiting the number of their foes as much as possible.

Alexi's own Guard converged in the courtyard. Snow had begun to fall in strange patterns, either hanging suspended in the air or drifting at different speeds, as the air was awash with forces that muddied mortal minds. The voices had Percy's ears splitting. She envied the fact that the rest of her comrades experienced this haphazard battlefield in utter silence.

"All are open?" Alexi asked. Everyone nodded, breathless.

"Isn't it magnificent?" Jane cried, whirling around to behold the tumult. "Look at all of them. And here we thought we'd be alone!"

Percy had a hard time rejoicing. Where was Darkness? What rooms and vaults and hideous secrets were yet to open?

The ground beneath them gurgled and shook. The angel fountain, graceful throughout all elements, seemed suddenly frail. Her basin belched, black muck oozing from her spouts, and the drain at the center of the courtyard spewed foul water, its metal grate flying from its moorings.

The Guard sought higher ground, not wanting to test the perilous substance as bones began vomiting from the drain. Percy gave a small cry as foul muck landed on her skirt. She shook it off, following the others up an exterior staircase to the wide balcony of Promethe Hall. Gazing across the clerestory windows down into the alley outside the school grounds, she noticed the drains there too regurgitated bone and dark water.

Alexi set his jaw. "I'd held hope that Athens would take all of the wear, but perhaps a bit of collateral damage was inevitable," he murmured, holding her tightly to his side.

The muddied courtyard began to fill with individual combats. From an Asian Guard, Percy heard haiku directed toward a disemboweled spirit who kept throwing his intestines everywhere. She was thankful the absurd scene was in grayscale; otherwise she'd have retched. Another set of Guard, these six wearing thick robes and chanting in dulcet Russian tones, were trying to return the bones back to the depths from whence they came, though they made sure they themselves floated well above.

Percy gasped, hearing a dread sound. "Barking," she whispered. "That barking. It's back, the hell—"

As she spoke, an ink-black cloud snarled upward from the basin beneath the angel, a hundred bones gnashed in its one then countless salivating jaws. The hellhound responsible for the Ripper murders had returned, its teeth bared as it smelled its familiar prey. It showed one oozing dog's head, then three, then thirty; its constantly chimerical form gained mass and leaped up a full story to snap in Percy's face.

Alexi smacked its thirty snouts with blue fire. The Guard encircled Percy and began a cantus, the hymn blending in with those of the other Guards. All were of a relative pitch and in the common Guard language, developed for this sacred purpose, and they combined now to great effect. The Russian and Asian troupes turned their fiery songs upon the rear of the hound, which lashed out and tore edges of their cloaks and tunics, but yelped and plummeted back down onto the angel fountain to rock her on her basin.

Surprisingly, the angel retaliated. Sapphire lightning crackled around her graceful bronze body, her wings flapped, and her eyes blazed. She lashed out with her Guard-inscribed book, striking the hound squarely. It burst into a thousand acrid wisps of smoke. All the Guards froze for a moment in amazement and Percy took the opportunity to thank the Japanese and Russian Guards in their native tongues. More irreconcilable souls bounded into the courtyard and all returned to their work.

Luminous tendrils of blue flame poured from the angel's spouts, a life-giving fount of blessing from which the Guard alone could draw. "All of Athens comes to life to fight," Josephine breathed excitedly. "Reflecting and magnifying our powers!"

"So long as her foundations don't get turned against us," Rebecca cautioned. She gestured to the south side of the courtyard and the entrance to the ladies' dormitory. Dead ivy had begun to wind its way up the stairs. In its wake, the warm red sandstone of Athens's exterior bricks grew sooty, black water lapping at the base of the portico.

She glanced into the ballroom behind her and growled. All manner of pathetic creatures were hanging from chandeliers, overturning the furniture, and attempting lewd displays upon the busts of famous philosophers that lined the golden hall.

"Damn all of you. This is our ballroom, not a brothel!" Her tone was the one reserved for students found breaking the rules of no contact; in this mood, Rebecca could make a mother superior feel chastened. Flinging open the French doors, she charged onto the polished wooden floor with a stern recitation of common propriety taken from a contemporary ladies' handbook, making the offending phantasms screw up their faces in dismay.

An elegant African set of Guards appeared in the ballroom, leveling impressive proverbs to stun the wits of the rabble and confuse them away from destruction. Their mentalist and healer were attempting to keep several poltergeists from overturning fine divans. Their leader was an incredible woman whose hair was mostly covered in a light veil though trailing long locks. Her eyes held the fire, not her hands; without a sound between them, only a nod of proud recognition, she and Alexi began weaving and dodging in an intricate dance of shockingly efficient casting.

Their magic bound each and every offender to his spot, wailing and gnashing their teeth. One by one the disruptive spirits began to fade away, their bodies flickering or dissolving into wisps of smoke, or imploding with a small snap and a burst of light. It was either peace or nothingness for them, Percy assumed, for the power of Athens was creating Judgment Day for many and there were no second chances. The spirits seemed to realize it, too, for they offered Percy their last words, few of which were pleasant.

Seeing that the room was sufficiently secured, Alexi and the leader of the African Guard stared at each other and shared a smile.

"Thank you," Percy said in Swahili.

The black woman leader's smile grew. "Our pleasure," she replied in kind. Then she and her cohorts darted from the room, vanishing though the wall. Percy could hear dim sounds of a skirmish in the halls beyond.

Alexi nodded to his colleagues, who moved to open the ballroom's hefty doors. Beyond, their once-beautiful Athens looked monochromatic. Dust, ash, and grime coated formerly polished surfaces. The Romanesque arches were graying and the stones seemed rougher hewn.

Rebecca patted the walls. "Dear bricks, don't fail us now." Light sparked in the mortar, fighting the contagion.

As she passed beneath the arched ballroom doorway, Percy recalled having once been too terrified to pass through. That breathlessly exciting night of the academy ball, it had been the confidence given her by her best friend—

"Marianna!" she cried. Whirling to the others, who were rushing toward the main foyer, she called, "I don't know where Marianna is. Aodhan said he would bring her, but I haven't seen him since the Whisper-world."

"We can't have you go looking for her," Alexi replied.

Rebecca was kinder. Seeing that Percy was beginning to panic, she clamped a firm hand on the girl's shoulder, trying to snap her into focus. "Do you have any idea where they kept her? Can we access that place from Athens?"

"She was in a room off the threshold where I entered, and I entered from the sacred space below. The chapel. Is there a new door in the chapel?"

"I'll look," Rebecca stated. "We shouldn't all go, and you are most important."

Suddenly, a noise. While Percy heard it most clearly, they all felt it: The dog had regrouped.

"You'll need to go attend that." Rebecca shooed her compatriots toward the growing howls. "Let me seek out the girl."

"We shouldn't split," Alexi argued.

"Marianna Farelei is a student of Athens Academy. Our students are the only children I will ever have. Now, I am going to bring her home, and I'll not hear another word about it." So saying, Rebecca stormed off down the hallway. Michael stared at his companions for a moment before turning to dart after her.

Alexi set his jaw. "Well, friends . . ."

Percy clenched her fists, resolute. "I rebuked that dreadful canine once before. I'll do it again."

All of Athens darkened but for the light of their precious blue fire as they ran toward the chilling noises, which appeared to be coming from the auditorium. The sound rose to an unbearable crescendo as they crossed the threshold and stopped, taken aback by what they discovered. The auditorium was twice its former size, its ceiling having been replaced by a dark and stormy sky. There were no seats; instead the vast room sloped sharply down in narrow stone steps, like an ancient amphitheatre. Everything was Whisper-world gray.

The steps led to a black stone platform that crawled with movement. No, it wasn't a platform but the river of misery, water black and endless. Beyond that fluttered a thick, bloodred curtain.

Alexi muttered, "All the underworld's a stage . . ." Percy loosed a nervous snicker.

The barking peaked and then went silent, but this was its source. The

London Guard pressed into the top tiers of the amphitheatre and other Guards began to follow suit.

The silence did not bode well. Percy couldn't swallow for dread. Then, all of a sudden, the curtain was ripped asunder and the dispersed hellhounds came snapping forward, their heads numbering in the hundreds, leashes around their necks pulling something dreadful.

With a bloodcurdling scream, a pile of bones atop crimson fabric drenched in gore was pulled into view. The bones began to assemble in the air as the hounds snarled and drooled; toes built into feet, bones scrabbling upward to form legs and torso, arms and head. And then the blazing red eyes. Darkness's skull head shrieked, his red robes snapping up around him like enormous wings, liquid flying out from the unfurling mass to spatter them all. "I will drag *every last one* of you back to the depths!"

"Listen," Alexi cried in their communal tongue. Surely the first of their group had known this day would come, that their ageless forces would need common words. He wondered where in this assembly those souls were, or if they'd somehow managed sweet respite in some Beyond. He wished to thank them, and prayed they were correct in their calculations, if this moment had been their intent. "Our Sacred Lady, now mortal, remains in our ranks! We are unbeatable in concert! *Cantus!*"

A thousand voices rose, sending both Percy and Darkness reeling. The infernal dogs howled and lunged, causing shrieks from the front battalions of Guard as pieces of their gray ghost flesh were snagged in hellish teeth.

Darkness did not tick seconds in beauty anymore; in battle he was only bone. He lifted a forearm. The stones below him shuddered and a wave of dark water surged forward, a curling tide of hungry horror. Many of the gathered Guard screamed as some were dragged forward as if the water had hands, a violent undertow yanking them across the river, back to their prison. The sight broke Percy's heart.

The air had been souring for hours. The current atmosphere was one of pain and failure. The ceiling of hazy clouds roiled, descended, swept destructive breezes against cheeks and hands, between Guard members, whispering to each of their greatest fears, sapping strength and confidence. This wind was what kept spirits restless. They could all become so. It would be easier to give up . . . The Guards' hope plummeted.

"Hearts, we need you!" Alexi cried in the Guard tongue, giving the command for his absent Michael.

Hundreds of upraised fingers moved in fluid choreography. A warm gust of fresh air blew through the battlefield. The pitch of the clouds lightened. The gray walls flickered with shocks of blue lightning, and the cresting water receded. The Guard breathed deep; there were smiles and surges of hope, the occasional triumphant laugh.

"It's working," Percy whispered.

"Leaders, a dam against the tide!" Alexi called, and the other leaders cast forward a brilliant wall of azure fire, corralling the dark river with a barrier it could not surmount.

Percy noticed that from Alexi the Phoenix fire trailed off and away in sparkling rivulets, eddying toward the hearts and hands of the other leaders, he the great mouth of a glorious river. Jane's healing light was a thin and gauzy line that created an intricately woven web like a luminous Celtic knot to link her fellow healers. If she looked at the others, Percy knew she would see similar connections. Athens's bricks held and sustained Guard power, but so did the living Guard, acting as conduit. She prayed their strength would last beyond mortal limits.

Darkness's cry was a summons for his minions. The crimson robes flying around his skeleton became a flag, his bones the saber-rattling call for his specters to fight with everything they had, to show no mercy. He lifted a bony fist in the air and shrieked, the angry dead and the hellhounds doing the same. Percy clapped her hands over her ears, almost overcome.

"Darkness wants us for his own!" Alexi cried to the other Guard. "But we want Peace! Whatever peace there is to be had." The academy resounded with his army's affirmative response, and the great clash began.

Flickering with blue light, the auditorium was awash in battle. Alexi's command of the Guards was lost to separate instances of chaos. Guards were torn to pieces, but they gave as well as they got, including against the hellhound. The skull head of Darkness swiveled, his vertebrae clicking loudly, his digits razors. He was searching Percy out. Alexi stood before her, wondering how long he could hide her in the tumult.

REBECCA AND MICHAEL FOUGHT OFF COUNTLESS DEAD TO GET TO THE chapel, where they found that a stained-glass window of an angel was now a door. Blue light emanated from its sill. Climbing onto the ledge, Rebecca turned the latch that opened the window. The glass swung inward to reveal a small crypt. Marianna lay atop a stone tomb there, like a corpse, with Beatrice and Aodhan pacing to and fro before her.

The spectral pair turned in evident relief to see Rebecca and Michael. Hoisting Marianna up, ash still clinging to bits of her dress and hair, they practically threw her at the Londoners, then sped into Athens themselves, closing the window behind them with a gust of wind before flying off toward the fray.

"Well, then," Rebecca muttered, adjusting Marianna's position in Michael's hold. "Where on earth do we take her for safekeeping?"

"Do we bring her to the fight so we can keep an eye upon her? Where *is* the fight? I hear only barking but I assume poor Percy's hearing Armageddon itself."

Rebecca concentrated, using her senses to isolate the center of the storm. "The auditorium. But shouldn't we keep her outside all that mess?"

"Can we afford to stay separate?" Michael asked.

Rebecca grimly held the door as he carried Marianna into the hall beyond.

"COME OUT, COME OUT, LITTLE WHORE. I KNOW YOU'RE HERE," Darkness sang, his jaw flapping. His sledge of assembled bones was still pulled by hellhounds, his robes dripping a sickening precipitation of gore. The mixture oozed everywhere, the water sapping the will of the Guards, the blood inciting hunger in the unsatisfied dead.

Keeping to the rear of the auditorium, that wall of stone behind him, Alexi remained a steady conduit. But as Percy feared, the effort seemed to be taking a toll upon his body; she could see the tremors racking his powerful frame. But his gaze never left her, ready in an instant to transfer every ounce of his sorcery to protecting her.

Perhaps Darkness's senses were dulled by not having eyes; surely, he could tell living mortals were in the room. Or perhaps here, with the Whisper-world tied so close, his surroundings all seemed very much the same. A few of the spirit Guards nearest had formed a barrier in front of the living Guard, smashing back those enemies who dared venture too close.

* * *

How, Percy wondered, was one to kill a god? It was a problem. Whatever she'd once been, she'd gone and gotten herself mortal. That seemed a distinct disadvantage.

As if Darkness read her mind, he called out, "You'll curse the day you went mortal, pet. I know a few things about you that I'm sure you can't resist, no matter what form you take," he added with a giggle. His jaw fell open. Pulpy red liquid poured forth, a vomitous fountain, its sickly sweet smell distinctively rotten fruit.

Pomegranate. Percy heaved at the odor.

"There you are, Persephone, dear. Scent is the most potent of all memories, they say, especially with a mortal nose. It never ceased to turn your stomach—you always promised I sickened you." Darkness howled with laughter, suddenly rising up nearby, red robes flapping, foul juice dripping. As he advanced, insects and worms sprouted from beneath his bony feet, their scrabbling, writhing forms wriggling forward, desperate to help decompose the living Guard.

Alexi roared and summoned a coil of blue fire. Darkness dodged. His hellhounds lunged forward, but he restrained them and lifted a hand. "Ah, ah, ah!" A slash mark appeared on Percy's white face, and then Alexi's, and both stumbled back, their faces weeping blood. Jane was immediately at their side, reversing the damage.

Alexi's next blast of fire seared Darkness's shoulder, but the god just laughed. "You're a broken little human possessed by a feather. Some weaponry," he scoffed.

"Don't I have you to thank for it?" Alexi spat. He gathered a seething force that pressed forward in huge, gusting flames, an assault that knocked Darkness back several paces, singed and gouged. The hellhounds retreated, too, echoing their master's snarl.

Aodhan drifted into view, causing Jane to look up in relief. Percy looked over, too. The ghost anticipated her inquiry, saying, "The headmistress has your friend," and he added his efforts to transmitting the winding cord of Jane's light to others across the battlefield.

Percy's own protective light seared forth from her bosom, illuminating everything around her. Guards close by could partake of this bright warmth, absorbing strength and power against the onslaught.

Both Jane's and Aodhan's hands changed position, to maximize and reflect her radiance.

"This will never end," Darkness whispered terribly. "You can't kill me; mankind made me out of hate and sorrow. But you can avoid this. You can give up. Admit that all these centuries of fighting were senseless. Apologize to the legions of souls you've enslaved in this pettiness. Phoenix is broken! Admit it! Return to me and accept that the greater god wins!"

"Strike!" Alexi cried out, and many Guard who had been victorious in their individual skirmishes were now able to lend hands. Roaring bolts of blue fire came from all directions, encasing their foe.

Darkness screamed, still not beaten. "I will take something you love! You keep loving, so I must keep taking things away! I *will* break this pathetic habit of yours! I don't love, I take! And because I do not love, I must win!" He turned his fiery eyes upon a new morsel, ever targeting the vulnerable.

Rebecca and Michael had just arrived and were easing Marianna's body onto a shadowy ledge. As Darkness appraised her, the young woman shrieked in pain, her eyes opening for a brief, horrified moment. Elijah rushed over to wipe those nightmarish memories utterly away. Percy's anger widened her bright light.

The enemy's army was composed of predators seeking fresh, innocent blood; Marianna was now a pure, empty vessel, ripe once more for possession. Nauseating hunger burned in their eyes as they flew at her, ten then twenty, each trying to gain purchase and seize her. Percy cried out, trying to go to her, but Alexi kept her pinned within the protective circle of several Guards, her light maintaining a shield that seemed to keep the hounds of Darkness at bay.

"You're right," Michael cried to Rebecca. "We shouldn't have brought her here!" Lifting Marianna again, he and the headmistress fled, with both enemies and spectral friends giving chase.

"To my office," Rebecca commanded. The two of them rushed down several corridors, Michael carrying Marianna. In the office they found Frederic hopping up and down on a wooden file cabinet, distressed, having shed a few black feathers onto the floor.

"Frederic, you were supposed to take refuge with Marlowe!" Rebecca scolded. The bird squawked.

Michael dumped Marianna in a chair and spun to face their half-dozen pursuers. Three others had been almost immediately dispatched by a most obliging and efficient Aztec Guard. But keeping six devilish fiends from a vulnerable body was no small task. He and Rebecca started in with a fresh cantus, but were interrupted by a shriek. It was Percy's, and it made their blood chill. It was perhaps the most heartbreaking cry they'd ever heard. Alexi's anguished cry came swiftly after. Something was terribly wrong.

Michael and Rebecca stared at each other, ashen-faced. Thankfully, the Aztec Guard hadn't noticed, and went on pummeling the enemy spirits.

"Go, Michael," Rebecca commanded. "We're almost done. We can spare you."

"Rebecca, I—"

"Percy needs you. I feel it. I'll be all right."

Tears rimmed Michael's eyes. "Rebecca Thompson, don't you dare be a martyr for—"

She reached out, grabbed his neck, pulled him to her and pressed her lips briefly to his. "I may yet have something to live for. I'll be no martyr. Now go."

Michael nodded and ran out the door, heartened by the battle cry Rebecca unleashed, casting a spirit out into the hall with the gust, where it promptly disintegrated. She bellowed an impressive line of Blake, then a psalm for good measure.

DARKNESS IGNORED THE CERULEAN FIRE ALEXI CONTINUED TO throw; his red robes were ablaze, his eyes like burning coals. His skeletal jaw was a terrifying grin. He hovered a few yards away, barely held back by the forces arrayed against him. Out of the corner of her eye, Percy saw Michael race into the auditorium and wondered fleetingly about Marianna's fate.

"Oh, you sorry girl. You never should have chosen this path. It is fraught with misery. You've so much to lose. You may think you have power over me with your little army of friends, but you see, some part of your body still remembers."

"I'm not her," Percy hissed. "You do not own me."

"Your light is *hers*."

Percy shook her head. "She no longer exists. Accept that she's gone, has rejected your claim once and for all. You can't now have power over this flesh, for it was never yours."

"All flesh is mine," Darkness snarled. "You are what she became, and I will have power over her remains forever." He lunged, and his frosty aura made the Guards' breaths crystallize. "All that is and all that could be will be mine, too."

An eviscerating pain doubled Percy over to gasp for air and clutch at Alexi's arm, causing a jolt of blue fire to go astray. He caught her and cried for Jane, who turned back from where she'd been helping a Norse mentalist mauled by a hellhound. Jane's eyes widened in horror as she swiftly advanced.

Percy's lower body felt as though it were being ripped open. She clutched at her abdomen and her hands came away bloody. Red poured from between her legs and rolled down the sloping auditorium pitch. Insects birthed from the footsteps of Darkness frolicked in the crimson pool.

In a horrific sensation, Percy felt energy leaving her: her child, the child she'd not even had a chance to think about, to welcome, let alone cherish. Her heart and body cleaved in excruciating pain. Alexi must also have realized what was happening, for his cry was just as unbearable.

"No!" Percy screamed, tears choking her, her hands clawing at herself with rage, her face contorting in anguish. A great wind whipped her snowy hair, her eyes ferocious suns. "You'll not have me! Not my love and not my child! *Death will not have my child!*"

There were apparently lines, Beatrice noted with wonder, even Darkness could not cross. He had always wholly underestimated the power that was love. Blinding white light exploded from Percy's body in a thunderclap of brilliance that made everyone wince. The rays had some solidity; their dazzling shards pierced her foe and every vile spirit in range. The blast cracked the ribs around where Darkness ought to have had a heart and pulverized his torso, sending him hurtling into the lapping water at the bottom of the auditorium. His dogs splintered and dove into the water, howling and whining, the light too bright for their eyes. All insects and agents of decay were obliterated.

But the dual strains of the force she commanded and her loss of blood broke Percy's mortal body. She collapsed, caught by Alexi, who was barking orders for the leaders to continue striking Darkness without mercy even as he fell to his knees, sweat pouring off him, chest heaving. Remaining the sole living conduit for such a mass of eternal fire threatened to break him, too. But his fading wife needed him.

Beatrice rushed to bolster Alexi, taking aid from the handsome darker-skinned man who was at her side again at long last. Her work would be twice as strong for Ibrahim's presence. She closed her eyes and a surge of blue fire shot through her hands into Alexi, feeding him power to energize the gathered Guard who chanted for strength and to heal the mortal incarnation of their goddess. Alexi was a most powerful leader, but Beatrice had been one, too. She could feel Ibrahim's hand upon her shoulder, her support and comfort, her rock in all storms, allowing her to again take up the mantle of leader alongside the professor. Beatrice watched wondrous workings unfold around her.

Jane directed the healing, she and Aodhan deftly gathering and cleansing Percy's precious blood from the stones and surging it back toward her, replenishing what had been lost.

A small ball of light that did not seem directly connected to Percy hovered just above Percy's abdomen, hesitant, like a fading star about to fall from the sky.

"Ah, ah," Jane said, tears falling from her eyes. "Michael," she murmured, "help!"

With exceeding care, the light of Jane's hands guided the tiny star back. It hovered as if unsure, confused. Michael dropped to his knees beside it. "'The light shines in the darkness,'" he wept at the small, sparkling orb, "'and the darkness shall not overcome it.' *The darkness shall not overcome it!*" The star of wonder dove back into the safety of its mother and Percy's drooping eyes shot open. She gasped at the surge of pain that accompanied the flood of warmth.

Michael's tears getting the better of him, he stood and looked around, Beatrice assumed for the headmistress. His soul leaped to see her, ashen-faced, steadying herself against the door frame.

* * *

PERCY STIRRED. WHAT HAD BEEN AN UNIMAGINABLE AMOUNT OF blood lost was returned again to her veins, the horror reversed.

Leaders of all Guards pummeled Darkness with inexhaustible vengeance. His bones broke piece by piece; his miserable form disintegrated. The blue Phoenix fire living in the walls of Athens streamed in luminous waterfalls from the bricks, the balance having finally tipped in their favor, the gray pall reversed that had made this place the Whisperworld's domain.

Percy wanted to see. Healers of the Guards, in rows around her—with Jane at her right hand—urged her to sit back and lie still, but she struggled to stand, feeling her strength surge back into her with the force of righteousness.

Alexi's eyes were wolfish, his jaw clenched. One arm was back to protect Percy; his other hand continued casting fiery bolts into the shuddering pile of bones below, no matter that his magic was past spent; his fury sustained him. He would not stop until Darkness was dust.

Percy stared a moment at the distinguished, handsome Egyptian by Beatrice's side. It was the man who had first recognized Percy in the Whisper-world. This was surely the partner for whom Beatrice had fought so hard. Mr. Tipton bowed his head to Percy and she smiled that the lovers were reunited. But gladness soon faded as her eyes were drawn to her enemy's bones, encased in the neutralizing blue flame of Alexi and many other leaders.

Darkness yet stirred.

His bones jumped and something whistled through the air: A long shard of bone hurtled directly toward Percy, an unobstructed arrow seeking to pull her into death's arms after all. Time slowed, aching, terrible. Percy opened her mouth to cry out.

Jane stood just to Percy's right. In that fraction of a moment, something changed on her face.

She took a step to the left.

A sickening crunch sounded as the javelin of bone struck Jane in the back and burst through her. Blood bubbled up from her lips, a gory shard jutting out just below her brooch.

The wailing cry Percy heard from the Guard, living and dead, would haunt her forever. Jane's body slowly pitched forward. Aodhan was at her side, unable to catch her with his incorporeal hands. Alexi released

Percy and jumped forward, sweeping Jane gently to the floor, his eyes wide with shock.

The Guard healers swarmed. Jane was bathed in light, chants, words, cries. But the Irishwoman did not stir. They tried again. Stillness. The healers hung their heads and stepped back, stunned.

Rebecca, shrieking, sank to the ground on the threshold of the auditorium, shaking her head and refusing to believe. Michael ran to her and cradled her, unable to look at this final, unexpected loss. Josephine had reeled back until she was pressed against the stone wall, where she tore at her hair and ripped her sacred locket from her neck, hurling the pendant aside. Elijah stood frozen.

The blue-fire mortar of Athens, still working on bringing the room back to its normal state, erupted in reaction. Alexi's fury melded with it, fire leaping from every pore of his body, tumbling Percy aside. Every Guard leader gasped, for their bodies, too, gave up the borrowed ghost flame to create a roiling, gigantic fury of winged fire and talons.

The black river reversed to again become the lip of the Athens auditorium stage. Alexi's fiery bird swept down toward the pile of bones, raging, evaporating any lingering vile spirit and enveloping the shards of Darkness in an oblivion of blue.

To Percy's ears, all went quiet. All she could hear was her own breath and her heartbeat. And fainter still, she almost imagined another heartbeat. A tiny one. Her tears flowed as she stood deathly still, but the world kept wailing as they stared down at Jane's body.

A glimmering, shimmering transparent form—sexless, gorgeous, its hands lit with glowing light, a pearlescent spirit unlike any ghost the London Guard had ever seen—lifted from Jane's body. As it wafted in the air it made a sparkling noise, a symphony of stars, the exquisite orchestration of their Grand Work.

"Her possessor," Rebecca choked from the doorway, stumbling forward into the room. "A Muse." The healing spirit looked sadly down, bent to kiss Jane's body and took flight. It soared to the front of the stage, where it swept in and among the other Guards, administering music and glory, beauty and hope, though it had lost the bodily instrument it so adored.

It suddenly dawned on Percy that something not of this world had long had hold on Jane, and that perhaps she'd wanted to give over to that embrace, as Beatrice had even suggested. Percy forced herself to look at the body. Aodhan floated nearby, kneeling at Jane's side, stroking her cheek with phantom fingertips, murmuring odes of aching love, his gray face paler than she'd ever seen it.

Jane's grayscale spirit, lacking color but not vibrancy, lifted out of her body with a laugh. She floated several feet above the melee to look down at everyone. Aodhan leaped up with a cry, reaching to touch the hem of her garment and thrilling that he finally could. He did not bother to hide his joy.

Beatrice, who'd been watching with her hands clutched around Ibrahim, moved forward. "You see? It's all right."

The spirit of Jane smiled and moved to press Beatrice's outstretched hand before turning to her fellows. "What on earth are you all wailin' about?" she insisted, her brogue thick with delight. They stared at her dumbly, so Jane turned to Percy. "Oh, that's right, Percy. Would you tell them what I'm sayin'?"

"She . . ." Percy gulped. "She wonders what on earth you all are wailing about."

"We need you," Josephine cried.

Jane looked around and shook her head. "No, you don't. It's over."

"I . . . I didn't deserve that, Jane," Percy murmured, guilt overtaking her in a feverish rush. "I didn't want you to die so that I might live."

Jane batted her hand in the air. "You and your child are desperately needed in this world. In that moment, there was no other way. Just like Beatrice said. Some sensible sacrifices have merit." Percy translated, tears coursing down her cheeks. "Now I'm needed in *this* world," Jane declared, floating to Aodhan's side and caressing his cheek. "We needed to each follow our hearts to get to the appropriate end of this journey. I finally followed mine." She glanced at Michael. "And Darkness has not overcome me."

Aodhan took her hand. Jane closed her eyes in bliss, bringing his now-tactile hand to her lips, kissing it slowly, relishing contact after a lifetime separate. Giggling, she glanced at her friends. "Don't worry, you'll see me haunting about. And Percy, tell Alexi that if he blames himself for this—as I'm sure he will—that I will swap his sherry out for Irish whiskey until the end of his days."

Percy related this information, and the Guard, while they could not laugh, at least gave a few shaky smiles. The tears returned soon enough, especially once Jane's ghost jigged out of the room with Aodhan, Beatrice, and Ibrahim floating out alongside them, chatting gaily. The living Guard were left with the gruesome reality of Jane's body, which now lay in the aisle between auditorium seats, the last of the Whisper-world's dreadful amphitheatre having vanished.

Alexi bent and lifted the body. The bone that had pierced her had turned to sand, which cascaded away as Alexi moved. But they were not spared gore, as Jane's blood poured down his vest and dripped onto the floor in a thick trail. He laid her down upon a ledge at the back of the hall and unclasped his cloak to place it over her body, his face a mask of pain.

He charged suddenly back down the aisle, his torn robes flapping. Center stage, the sullied red fabric that reeked of dog urine and Darkness's inanimate bones were a blaze of blue light, burning merrily like a hearth fire, and some Guards lingered on to watch and warm themselves in vengeance's glow. With a warlike bellow, a terrible sound of grief, Alexi sent the last of his power, wave after wave of lightning, magic, energy, again and again into the remains, as if the more he pummeled it, the more he could ensure it could never hurt anyone again.

Percy ran to him; when she stumbled, Michael darted in to take her by the arm. The rest of Alexi's Guard hung back, knowing they didn't dare try to stop him.

He kept striking until he fell to his knees. Percy took him in her arms, which found new strength holding him. Her body muffled his heaving sobs. The blue bonfire of Darkness died down, its fuel gone, and the conflagration faded to flickering sapphire embers.

A wind picked up in the room, as did an ancient music, a heavenly balm. A murmur sounded, as the thick cerulean flames, entwined within every collected Guard, coalesced into enormous wings. Unlike Alexi's vengeful Phoenix, this time it formed an ephemeral, angelic form that was awesome in its beauty and possessed of fearsome masculine strength. "It is finished," the great angel whispered in all ears, hearts, and veins.

The vision floated out the door and Alexi somehow found the strength to pull out of Percy's grasp and follow it, breathing heavily and moving awkwardly. The remaining members of London's Guard were drawn along in his wake. Upstairs, to that sacred seal they ran, chasing

the divine bonfire to where it swirled over the motto of Athens, sparkling above the dictum of their Work before diving into the image, settling once more into the stone. With lingering licks of flame and then
stillness, Athens was again mere bricks of a normal mortal school, set
on a solid foundation.

The six survivors turned and beheld their mass of spectral fellows,
whose work was done. They had come to pay respects. They wafted forward, filing before Percy and Alexi, bowing or nodding.

Dimly Percy registered what words she was offered. She was told by
a few leaders and hearts that her child would prove important. While
Percy's instincts told her that this was most certainly true, all Percy
cared was that her husband and child were alive.

Beatrice floated forward from the crowd, her face troubled. "I would
have liked to have fought more at your side, my lady. But I needed to
find and fight with my Guard."

"I believe you've fought at my side often enough," Percy murmured.

"True." Beatrice smiled. Her quiet, stoic husband was beside her; she
took his hand and pressed it lovingly in both of hers. She gestured him
forward, attempting again to present him.

"Hello, my lady. Ibrahim Tipton at your service," he said in a rich
Arabian accent. "Raised by an Englishman, I learned to appreciate certain aspects of the country you've chosen as your own. I am glad to have
had a part in fighting for you here, then and now." She sensed he was
making peace with his past in this brief introduction.

"Hello, Mr. Tipton—and thank you," she murmured, sharing Beatrice's smile. "And where will all of you go? I pray you will go on toward
Peace!"

Beatrice's lips thinned. "Some didn't make it safely onward this day.
Some of us were overwhelmed, dragged back across the river. Some of
these Guard will take to that realm again, to rescue their friends who
fell. Some may choose to remain always vigilant. I cannot say. But most
of us will go to Peace. Long awaited, and far from here . . . Peace. I've
no idea what it will be like, but I've never anticipated anything so much
as this blessed day."

Behind Beatrice, another figure broke ranks. A thin man in dark
robes with skin that must have been darker in life and a face so engaging

it was hard to look away floated toward Percy. In Arabic he said, "While this war is at an end, keep your heart open to the world, my lady. You never know what battles your lineage may face, in the air, in the ground . . . Don't forget us. And don't close *every* door."

While the words themselves might have an ominous cast, the man, clearly the heart of his group, was so full of peace, assurance and love that Percy couldn't find any fear. He bowed and spun back to Ibrahim, clasping his friend's arm.

Beatrice spoke. "Don't mind Ahmed. He's always been full of tall, albeit brilliant, words. You, my lady, deserve a lifetime of peace. Please take it, for the worst is blessedly over. If Darkness is ever to manifest again, the good news is you're mortal and it won't be in your lifetime. And the cycle of the vendetta, at least, is at last broken. Good-bye, my friends. Good Work, and peace be ever with you."

"And also with you," Percy murmured. "Thank you for everything you did to bring me here. I'm sure it's been far more than I can fathom."

Beatrice paused. "Our Lady said before she took form that she hoped she'd have the good sense to thank me." She smiled. "She'd be pleased you're so sensible. And kind. She'd be most pleased by that. And by the man who adores you."

Percy turned to Alexi and took his hand. Only when he looked at Percy did the pain in her husband's eyes ease. She turned back, but Beatrice and her Guard were gone. The remaining Guards bowed and floated down the stairs.

The air of Athens was sweet; every hell-raising spirit was gone to oblivion or flung to the outer darkness. The press of dread was lifted from their veins, their minds clear in the stark dawn light. Only grief remained, and none of them was sure what to do.

Michael gestured toward the trail of pilgrim spirits leading down toward the chapel. "Come," he suggested. "Let us follow."

Alexi nodded. "I will bring Jane's body."

It felt like a funerary procession. The Guard directly ahead of them, some in buckskin and feathers, some in ballooning pants and curving hats, were consoling one another. Clearly one of their number had not made it to his peaceful moment. A grayish spirit that would have been a ruddy-skinned woman pressed her hands to her breast, raising high, keening notes into the air that only Percy heard. By the mourner's side, a man wearing an animal skin placed an arm around her shoulder, the feathers in his hair fluttering with the tiniest remainders of flickering blue flame. War, no matter how unusual, had its costs.

Soft pledges were made, vengeances were declared, and above all companionship was renewed, the one constant of their Work. Only Percy heard. Tears silently rolled down her cheeks; she was struck by the weight of her own mortality, far from the shifting and everlasting forms of divinity. Each moment was increasingly precious to her, and each moment urged her never to take even the slightest bit of life for granted. Her hand pressed to her abdomen, she closed her eyes and gave a thousand thanks, the rosary beads against her chest picking up the echo and flooding her soul with blessings.

As they passed Rebecca's office, en route to the chapel, the headmistress gestured Percy inside, where a grim, intense fifteenth-century Teutonic Guard, men and women in tunics and chain mail, floated in formation around Marianna, who lay unconscious in a chair. "This fine, fierce group insisted they would watch over their Germanic kin and gestured me out to join you in the last of the battle. I would not have left her unattended otherwise."

Relieved by the expression of tranquility on her friend's face, Percy rushed forward and kissed her softly on the forehead.

"We'll move her to the infirmary promptly," Rebecca promised, and held out her hand. "Now you should rejoin the others."

Percy took Rebecca's outstretched hand and brought it to her lips. "I cannot thank you enough. For everything."

Rebecca swallowed. "My duty and my pleasure."

Percy turned to the Teutonic Guard and bowed. They did the same. They moved in silence to the chapel.

Alexi set Jane's body atop the tomb of Athens's founder, careful to keep her covered with his cloak. He held out his hand for Percy, then kissed her forehead. She murmured her love and he kissed her again, a tear dripping onto her cheek.

The procession of spirit Guards filed down into the space sacred to them all, finally released to their private destinies. Michael reminded his companions to breathe by moving slowly past them, one by one, putting a hand to their constricted throats.

When the last of the Guard had vanished into the shadows of the sacred space, the Teutonic Guard being the last to go, Elijah, Josephine, Rebecca, and Michael were suddenly tugged forward as if something were being pulled from inside their bodies.

Wispy, shimmering forms more angel than human floated before them, nodded, blew kisses, sparkling with song and soulful splendor. The Muses who had inhabited them, whom they'd never faced, never known as individuals, only as incumbent powers, were now separate entities. Their indescribable faces full of pride, they moved close to their instruments and touched each cheek with adoration.

"With you we are greatly pleased. Now rest, beloveds," they said. "We're all due for a nice rest." Then, in unison, the divinities flew ahead.

Percy expected them to duck inside the portal, but instead the quartet held out their hands just before it. The portal snapped shut and the Muses sighed with weary relief. The four heavenly forms then flew back over the Guard's heads, following the same course the Phoenix fire had taken toward the center of the building. Percy assumed the divine friends intended to rest together, perhaps to settle into the stalwart bricks of Athens Academy.

The school chapel sat white and quiet. The amber stained-glass angels along the wall had lost their ethereal glow and looked now like ordinary windows. The silence was, to Percy, after all the raucous spiritual noise, deafening.

Alexi waved tiredly toward the altar. One candle sputtered to a low flame, but that was it. He stared at his hand.

Tensing, he cast that powerful arm forward again, expecting the portal to their sacred space to open as it always had under his command. The altar remained plain and bathed in white cloth, nothing supernatural about it.

"They're gone. Does that mean we are finished?" Michael breathed.

"I . . ." Rebecca searched her own mind. "I don't have my library. My mind doesn't have its resources."

"Damn," Elijah muttered. "It will be so much more difficult to get away with things."

Josephine smirked, then her eyes widened. "I wonder if the British Museum will take down my art. Will its protective charms have worn off?"

Alexi pursed his lips. "You spend your lives complaining about the Work, and now, when you're released—"

"Well, I complain about you to no end, Alexi. It doesn't mean I wouldn't miss the very hell out of you if you were gone. Such is the way of love," Elijah said, his brow furrowing.

Rebecca shook her head. "We're such mortals in the end. Never satisfied. But you have your café, Josie, and your art. Michael, the church. Elijah, your . . ."

"Wealth and ill manners," he was quick to offer. "Outlasting even the very face of death. Oh, and I have Josie. That's something, I suppose."

She swatted happily at his shoulder.

"Yes." Rebecca nodded. She turned to Alexi and looked him in the eye. "And you, Alexi, have Percy, this school, and . . . your child. Congratulations."

Alexi drew Percy close. Percy opened her mouth to offer Rebecca her blessings, but something in the headmistress's expression stilled her.

"I . . ." Rebecca said. Her hand moved unconsciously toward Michael. He blushed. While his gift might have vanished, his smile was still magic. Rebecca seemed to come to herself, as if she'd forgotten she was not alone. She cleared her throat. "I have the blessed bricks of Athens."

Her gazed flickered toward Jane's draped body and instead of taking Michael's hand she moved forward, her face betraying more emotion than she'd ever before let show.

"And Jane has . . ." Josephine tried, her voice breaking.

"The hand of her longtime love and the peace of eternal life," Michael spoke up from a few paces behind Rebecca.

They all stared at the black-draped body atop the tomb. Powers or no, spirits or no, that their living circle was incomplete was an irrevocable fact. Rebecca placed a hand on either side of Jane's covered head, and her tall spine bent and shuddered as silent tears poured down her face.

"Dear God," she gasped to the body, her shaking hand hovering over the Irishwoman's head as if wanting to touch but not wanting to feel the solidity of death beneath her fingertips. "Dear God, it should have been me."

There was a terrible silence. Michael clenched his fists, his hopeful face stricken. He stepped toward her. "Rebecca, you mustn't—"

She snapped jarringly into her usual stiff pose, clapped her hands together and swiftly wiped her eyes. "I think we ought to clean the auditorium," she said, her head high, crossing between them and toward the door. "And then I wouldn't mind a drink."

Her statement seemed to recall them to awareness of the physical. None of them had eaten in hours, all needed rest and sustenance both physical and spiritual. Needed time to mourn and time to heal.

DEEP BELOW LONDON, A FEW CLUSTERS OF BONES BOBBED ALONG IN sewer eddies. Amid small remembrances and other scraps of sentiment, a few sealed jars floated out along the Thames. Their contents hissed and rattled.

The river swept the jars into the estuary, where they were carried out into the North Sea and then bobbed onward toward the shores of France, gaining momentum.

EPILOGUE

Seven months later

PERCY SAT IN A TALL WICKER CHAIR AND LOOKED OUT AT HER LUSH and immaculate summer garden. She'd roused it from weeds to glory with uncanny skill, as if the plants sprouted from her very touch.

The birds in the bushes were nearly as raucous as the company. Alexi was fussing by her side, arranging pillows and setting still more food upon the tray beside her. Smiling up at him, her white-blue eyes blinked from beneath her wide hat. She tried to adjust forward, but her abdomen was round and huge beneath her flowing gown and she chuckled, for she couldn't truly move with any amount of grace.

"What do you need?" Alexi asked.

"Nothing, love, I'm just trying to get a better look at our friends."

He eased her forward, and they gazed at the assembled company, hand in hand. Josephine sat on the lap of Lord Withersby in a fine dress that nearly swallowed him with its absurd poufs, eagerly sharing the ways in which she was shocking high society, which remained obsessed with her. On the garden bench opposite, Michael was at Rebecca's side.

Alexandra Rychman's wheelchair sat beside the Withersbys, and she was placing bets on which members of Parliament or royalty would proposition Josephine first. Lord Withersby was adding handsomely to the pot, delighted by the game.

The Rychman estate had seen more activity in the past seven months than it had in Alexi's lifetime. The entire east wing had been opened up and refreshed and Alexandra had been moved into it; more staff had been hired to deal with the growing needs of a growing family, and there were weekly dinners with friends, teachers, and even students from Athens. Marianna and Edward, of course, hadn't been left out. Thankfully, Marianna did not recall anything of what happened during her first visit to the estate, or of the spectral war that had followed. Percy was only too happy to assure her that her nightmares were nothing more than mere dreams.

A sturdy woman stepped from the French doors and hovered over Percy anxiously.

"Yes, Mrs. Wentworth, what's troubling you now?" Percy looked up with a smile. "I swear, between you and Alexi, I've no chance to fuss over myself. You've anticipated me before I even think of a need."

"I just . . . I just don't know about all this activity," she said, refreshing Percy's tea. "It's too much for a woman in your condition. Generally women of your station go away and weather their months in fine country cottages, relaxed and quiet, unseen in this time—"

"But she's so beautiful, everyone should see her!" Alexi cried, kissing her slightly plumped cheeks, which blushed as his lips touched them.

Mrs. Wentworth folded her arms. "Now Mrs. Carroll there, that was quite the shock. I'd long given up hope for the headmistress. They're so sweet, Michael and she . . ."

"Yes, that," Percy said pointedly, staring at Rebecca and Michael with a smile. Marlowe, Jane's cat, lay curled at Rebecca's feet. "Those two are a story in and of themselves. Not without divine intervention. I'd say it was worthy of Dickens, wouldn't you, husband?" she asked, her eyes sparkling.

Alexi smirked. "'Twas a Christmas miracle, indeed."

"Be all of that as it may," Mrs. Wentworth continued, "Professor, don't you think your wife would best be safe, somewhere quiet and restful instead of weathering the howls of Lord Withersby and Mr. Carroll? Your dear sister Alexandra and I could give Percy good quiet company just an hour north. That way she wouldn't be excitable with all this entertaining—"

Percy chuckled. "My dear Mrs. Wentworth. I grew up a lonely orphan in a quiet convent. All I ever wanted in life was a family filling my home with life and noise. I never dreamed I'd have a husband, much less such a striking one, and I daresay I can't go without his company, or these howls of laughter, for even the length of a pregnancy." She gestured Mrs. Wentworth closer.

"You see," she murmured conspiratorially, "there was a very special and very secret duty that the lot of us had to keep. Dangerous. Elite. But we've done our service well, and have been rewarded with a . . . retirement. And so we're all making up for a deal of lost time. We deserve it."

She stared up with great gravity and Mrs. Wentworth's eyes widened, putting her hands to her lips. "Oh! Surely my lady means the Crown! You've been serving Her Majesty as spies, haven't you?"

"Something of the sort." Percy smiled.

"And if you tell anyone," Alexi said, "we'll have to dispatch you. So please keep running this estate as well as you do, and we'll live in it as we see fit."

Mrs. Wentworth straightened, her bosom puffed out with pride. "Indeed. Professor. My dear lady." She gave them both a salute and exited, head held high.

Percy put a hand over her mouth to keep from laughing. She turned to Alexi. "I'm sorry if I said something I oughtn't, but she would drive me mad."

Alexi grinned. "It's all right. We can say anything we like now that we're powerless. People saw bones pouring out of London's sewers, but what can we do? Children in hospital wards have been seeing an angel who looks suspiciously like Jane, but what can we do? Our little clan is finally living life. What else can we do?" He threw his hands jovially in the air.

She reached out to draw him into a kiss. He slid his chair closer, took one of her hands in his and placed his other hand on her womb. "You don't mind that I'm no longer filled with mysterious power?" he asked.

While his tone was disinterested, Percy knew he was desperate for reassurance. She also knew that though his life had lost its previous meaning, the life of a husband and father would resonate with a joy the Grand Work could never offer.

She snickered. "You don't mind that I'm not actually a goddess?"

Alexi shook his head. "I may still call you one, though."

"And I still think you're full of power."

His chiseled lips pursed in supreme satisfaction.

Percy leaned back in her chair, breathing deeply the scent of flowers, feeling the warmth of a small patch of sun on her white face, and knowing that she'd never been happier. She pressed their entwined fingers gently against her abdomen, and in response there was a movement from within, a tiny kick.

A soft gasp leaped from Alexi, and he dropped down before her. Sliding his hands around her, he laid his head upon her rounded womb and looked up at her in wonder; this fearsome, striking man brought to his knees by a tiny kick. That, Percy thought, was power enough.

"BLESS ME, FATHER, FOR I HAVE SINNED."

Percy felt the aged wooden scent of the confessional booth overwhelm her as she took a deep breath to calm herself. Safely confined within darkness that had undoubtedly given ear to hundreds of pleas and thousands of sins, her body eased. She had not confessed since her final convent days and her heart pounded with both guilt and giddy excitement.

"And of what sin are you guilty, my child?" The priest's voice was warm, yet the clarity in his every syllable made Percy feel unable to hide, even behind her shawl, even within the darkness behind the ornately carved wooden screen.

"I fancy someone."

Percy pressed her back against the cool mahogany wall as she closed her eyes. She focused on the acoustics, the tremulous, immediate sound two voices made in close and intimate revelation.

"I fancy someone I'd best not," Percy added softly.

"How would you describe your thoughts toward this person?"

Lids pressed shut, her mind's eye was locked on her professor. The moonlit foyer where they waltzed alone would not leave her mind. "Warm. All-consuming."

"Do you lust, child?"

"I would like to think mine is a sin of a more refined . . . perhaps unique nature."

"Are you intimate with this person?"

"N-no."

"And does this someone know of your affection?"

"Surely he . . . I . . . I don't know."

"Can you speak to him?"

"Of my sentiments? I dare not."

"Do you covet? Is this man bound to another—"

"No. He has no wife . . ."

"Chaste love, my child, itself is no sin, if performed under the watching eyes of the Lord. Loving, Godly courtship, leading to the sacred rite of marriage is encouraged—"

Percy felt sick to her stomach. "He is under the employ of an institution, Father. I am bound by more laws than those of the Lord. No matter, this schoolgirl fancy; even if he and I were acquainted under alternate circumstances, he'd hardly care for an oddity such as myself." Percy's fingers wove together in nervous melancholy.

"Children of God have no flaws once they have confessed their sins and have made themselves whole in the Lord."

"This child of God struggles with that truth, and does not feel whole."

"To bemoan your state and not give thanks to God for his gift of life, however wretched or different, is yet another sin. Turn your impossible affection inward; save some of it for your own heart."

Percy pressed harder against the wood at her back, squeezing her eyes closed as if she could force the image of Professor Rychman's striking face from her thoughts. A vision came instead.

Spirits hovered before her, smiling, in a formal processional line. Someone moved beside her. She turned to see who had taken her hand. Ah, her professor . . .

"Why so suddenly silent, my child?"

Percy was jarred from her vision and her eyes adjusted to the dim light beyond the screen of iron coils that cast an intricate pattern upon her ghostly-white hands.

"Oh, forgive me Father, I was . . . remembering a dream."

"Does the dream bear significance?"

"The prof—he was there beside me. Spirits too. I sense a powerful connection, a greater purpose to our acquaintance, which makes divesting emotion very difficult."

"Perhaps God has a specific plan for him in your life."

The word "perhaps" rang hollow in Percy's mind. She was weary of that word. "Something brews in the air, Father. I do not know whether to welcome it or to be frightened."

"Your sense of impending events, do they include the individual in question?"

"I find myself hoping that they do."

"Be careful of that hope. Pray for *purity* to come to you, my child. Pray for goodness, truth, and righteousness. Often prayers for our deepest wishes are not in God's plan. Trust God's will, and there will be a blessing in that brewing air. For the two of you."

"Perhaps."

Percy was beginning to truly despise that word. She didn't want *perhaps*. She wanted *yes*. For the two of them.

ELIJAH & JOSEPHINE, EXTRA SCENE

February 13, 1894, Café La Belle et La Bête, London

IT WAS LATE, AND THE REST OF WHAT WAS ONCE THE GUARD—THOUGH they were guardians no longer, they'd always think of themselves as such—had gone home. Josephine cleaned up behind her smooth wooden bar, offering a few choice admonishments in French to the ghosts who wished to readjust her glassware. She heard the key in the front door lock and smiled, sliding a heaping glass of wine across the bar for the richly dressed blond man in a foppish coat who entered and strode toward her, a grin transforming his sharp features.

"Ah, *mon cher*, and where have you been?" she asked, her French accent always heightened around him. Because he liked it.

"The rich have many errands," Elijah, Lord Withersby, said with a lofty chuckle.

Her lover of nearly twenty years, Elijah was now five years her husband. Silly as it now seemed, they'd long kept their affair hidden from they rest of their unlikely band of spectral police. Not because they cared about the opinions of their coterie, but because the Guard were dear friends and frankly the romantic dynamics among them had been wretchedly uncomfortable. A tangled mess of love triangles, with no one's yearnings requited save Josephine and Elijah.

Miss Percy Parker had changed all that in the fall of '88, had made their group of six into seven . . . among many other spectacular things. Her sweet and radiant presence had also changed the dynamics of the Guard, allowing love to take precedence for once, for all of them. Josephine would always cherish Percy most for that.

Elijah flopped down at the bar, making a face at the general, a resident ghost in a uniform of the late 1700s who had been drinking at that very spot for far longer than they'd owned the place.

"So, my sweet," he began at a drawl, absently tapping his bejeweled rings on the stem of his wineglass. "You've been making broad hints about tomorrow and I've learned I ought not ignore a lady's hints. Is there something I should be aware of, else I dash myself upon the treacherous rocks of feminine expectation?"

Josephine looked at her husband pointedly. "The *date*, tomorrow, Lord Withersby."

"Ah, yes, the fourteenth of February. Wretched month, February."

"This barkeep needs to know if she should mend and press her finery for an engagement or if she should keep her apron on instead to reluctantly serve the enamored coming through her doors."

"Saint Valentine. The man was beheaded, you know. That's romance for you. *Beheaded*, I say. There's hardly anything known about him, why he's all cherubim, hearts, and arrows is a mystery. Perhaps he was known for marrying Christians but as for love notes, flowers, and sweets; it's the fault of Chaucer and this fool romantic age. Would you have me go to absurd lengths for *Chaucer's* sake?"

Josephine shrugged. "For me."

He arched an eyebrow. "For absurd French sentimentalism?"

"I don't know about French sentimentalism any more than English." She curved her lips at him. "But we French are better at the ways of love . . ." Her expression made him shudder delightedly in his chair.

"That you are, my pet; that you are . . ."

"And it is a day marked to celebrate love, no matter how obscure or unrelated the traditions."

"And so I should put stock in a calendar mandate of romantic notions?"

"Well, you have before. We live in a society run by men, dear, and men need calendar dates to remind them to attend to basic niceties for their women. I recall many nice things you've done for me on certain appointments."

He leaned in over the bar. His cravat, woven with shimmering thread and tied with a too-large bow, bounced a bit as he spoke. "Since when am I predictable?"

Putting glasses on a shelf, she replied over her shoulder, "Never. Not even now, living with you, as your wife, do I dare make assumptions or take anything for granted. Why do you think, then, that I ask?"

As far as Josephine was concerned, this was their usual fond verbal volley. But Elijah's face darkened, and his voice was a terrible murmur. "Because you think I'll fail you."

There was a disquieting silence. Josephine reached out but he drew his hand away. "No, *cher*, of course not, you know—"

"Leave it." His tone gave her pause. She returned to her cleaning, watching him out of the corner of her eye and remembering.

Elijah had once—fifteen years ago now—done something terribly unpredictable indeed. After a terrible private argument with Josephine, he had abandoned the Guard. Being without their mentalist had put them in grave danger and cost a young life. . . . He had long ago repented, thrown himself at their feet and into Josie's arms. Still, everyone had spent no little time second-guessing Elijah then, and his desertion lingered, even so many years later, after so many proofs of his devotion.

She should have known better than to say anything that might raise that ghost of their shared past, Josephine thought, leaving Elijah to his glass of wine. She dabbed oil on a rag and began to polish the ornately carved bar shelves. She knew that his mistake pained him still, and the wretched event had indeed occurred in February, not too long from this date so marked by Victorian sentiment. The child that perished truly haunted him, especially near the anniversary of the youngster's death. That was Elijah's cross to bear, though Josie prayed he would someday find peace.

While she could not grant him serenity, perhaps she could distract him? The Grand Work had tied her to London all these years, and truly, she called herself a Londoner and loved the city and its people. But at her heart, Josephine was French, and she often pined for Paris. She'd been known, even during the long years of their Work, to take a few discreet days in that magical city, to breathe deeply and shed the spectral weight heaped on her soul.

As long as she was never gone for long and left enough paintings behind for her compatriots to hang before the eyes of the afflicted, her absence was not keenly felt. These days, thankfully, she was free to go on a whim.

Getting away from the city would also do Elijah good, Josephine decided. She would angle for a romantic excursion as much for his sake as her own. They two were dramatic, passionate souls, there was always a tension between them, but never enough to overturn the love they'd fought for since their youth. They'd never have lasted this long if they weren't made for each other.

Marshaling her arguments, she heard a step near the landing and whirled around. Was her husband simply going to walk out? Would they pass an unspeaking night at two separate ends of his fine estate? She opened her mouth to protest his departure but the bells on the door were already jingling.

She stamped her foot in frustration even as something white and rectangular caught her eye. He had left an envelope upon the bar.

The note read: "For partaking in absurd French sentimentalism. I do wish you'd trust me one day, Josie my love."

Inside were two ferry tickets and first-class train tickets to Paris. They'd leave in the morning. Josephine couldn't hold back her smile, or the tear that always came into her eye when he made these small, yet profound, gestures. Maybe this year, she thought, her husband would return to London just a bit less haunted by his past than when he left. She hoped.

Regardless, Josephine's heart was as buoyant as if Cupid had skewered it with arrows and was flying away with it. She did trust Elijah. With her soul and her life.

AUTHOR'S NOTE

WHY PERCY WAS BORN A PARKER—A PERSONAL TALE

In the fall of 2001, when the idea of the Strangely Beautiful series first occurred to me in a blaze of delirium one late night after play rehearsal, I took notes as Miss Percy took shape before me. She had a first name and a nickname but I was ambivalent about a last name. When I began my rough draft, I was working on more than five Shakespeare plays at once with the Cincinnati Shakespeare Company. We performed in southern Ohio schools during the day and returned to the theatre for rehearsals for mainstage plays.

One day, between tours, we had time to kill, and with seven actors in our van's close quarters, we headed out for some air. In southern Ohio's vast middle of nowhere, we drove aimlessly until, amidst the trees, a small graveyard was spotted. Spending fourteen hours a day with our cast meant we knew each other quite well. Jason, driving the van, turned and said, "Hey, Leanna, there's a graveyard, want out?" A graveyard connoisseur and long-time Goth girl, of course I cried "Yes!" and leaped out to explore.

Many of the graves were old and broken and only a few dated from the twentieth century, but all were clustered in the center of the graveyard. Except two. On the far end of the graveyard, just before a thin fence kept a wild forest from creeping in, were two small graves with a dead tree beside them. I walked to the graves as if magnetized; such a striking visual, these isolated graves, the dead tree . . . and then, I was struck by the markers. Plain gray granite read: I. PARKER, MOTHER. Smaller, beside it, the second marker: INFANT PARKER.

There were dates on the stones, of course, but I confess I don't remember them, because a scene and story began to unfold before me and I knew I had Percy's last name. I seem to recall the dates indicated mother and child hadn't died in childbirth. Inspiration overwhelmed me. Why these graves were separate and isolated could have been for many reasons but surely because she was a single mother; an unmarried woman having a child out of wedlock was enough to not be included in any cemetery, let alone alongside other "proper" families.

There were superstitions, prejudices, church policies, etc., regarding this, and the dead tree next to the graves only added to the chill of superstition and a lingering air of lonely neglect. I took the name Parker in honor of this striking scene, in tribute to all those unfairly isolated or disenfranchised (a theme I'd already established in my unusual heroine Percy), and even created a way to incorporate this real-life moment into *The Darkly Luminous Fight for Persephone Parker*. I hope you have enjoyed the story. And I hope the ghost of I. Parker is pleased with the way her name lives on. (More information and extras at www.leannareneehieber .com.)

ACKNOWLEDGMENTS

Special thanks: First and foremost, to the readers who have loved these books nearly as much as I have, and have kept the flame alive for this phoenix resurrection. To my agent, Nicholas Roman Lewis, for never ever giving up on any incarnation of Miss Percy. To my editor, Melissa Singer, my knight in shining armor, for saving these books and investing so much in me, along with the fine folk at Tor.

To C. Johnstone, whose beautifully unique artistic renditions of all my characters kept them alive and envisioned even when I couldn't see through the pain of losing them in their first publisher's collapse. In addition, to artists like Nancy Lee and Grace Whitley, whose visions of Percy and Alexi brought me pure joy, and to Hanna Ledford's clever shirts and unflagging support through the years.

To the readers who never stopped asking about Miss Violet, about the series, and about the musical (http://strangelybeautifulmusical .com), thank you for keeping every venture alive and in your hearts. To Marianne Mancusi and Chris Keeslar for Percy's first life; to my Diana Barry, Alethea Kontis, for brilliant words and countless supports; to Marcos for unflagging care; and to Marijo for still holding the brain cell. To Perseus and Draco, who understand Eternity Awaits better than anyone; to Paul Peterson, who remains the first audience; to Andy Waltzer (one of Percy's dearest friends); to my parents for being ceaselessly the world's best parents; and to the Fulbrights and their beautiful event horizons. Ex Astris.

About the Author

Author, actress, and playwright Leanna Renee Hieber grew up in rural Ohio, inventing ghost stories. She graduated with a BFA in theatre and a focus in the Victorian era from Miami University. She has adapted works of nineteenth-century literature for the stage, and her one-act plays have been produced around the United States.

The Strangely Beautiful Tale of Miss Percy Parker, her debut novel, won two Prism Awards (Best Fantasy, Best First Book) and was a Barnes & Noble bestseller. It is currently in development as a stage musical.

Darker Still: A Novel of Magic Most Foul, first in Hieber's young adult gothic historical paranormal saga, was an Indie Next selection and was a finalist for the Daphne du Maurier Award.

Hieber is an avid public speaker, having lectured and presented around the country at venerable institutions like the Guthrie Theater and New York University. She is a featured guest at many steampunk, sci-fi, and fantasy conventions and has taught workshops for writers' groups nationwide.

A member of the actors' unions AEA and SAG-AFTRA, Hieber lives in New York City, works in film and television on shows like *Boardwalk Empire*, gives ghost tours with Boroughs of the Dead, and crafts neo-Victorian and steampunk accessories for Torch & Arrow on Etsy (etsy.com/shop/torchandarrow). Visit her at www.leannareneehieber.com, on Twitter at @LeannaRenee, and on Facebook at www.facebook.com /lrhieber.

Battle is joined as British and American paranormal investigators clash over the Eterna Compound.

ETERNA
AND
OMEGA

LEANNA RENEE HIEBER

Clara Templeton fears the dangers of the Eterna Compound. And Harold Spire will pay any price to obtain it for Her Royal Majesty, Queen Victoria. Meanwhile, the hidden occult power that menaces both England and America continues to grow. Far from being dangerous, Eterna may hold the key to humanity's salvation.

★ **"A smart, boundlessly creative gas-lamp fantasy."**
—*RT Book Reviews* (4 stars) on *The Eterna Files*

"Rich in conceits as anything from Alan Moore."
—*Asimov's Science Fiction* on *The Eterna Files*

TOR

TOR-FORGE.COM